On the Wings of Music series
Book 1~ Ulutrita

I0586593

M.C. Schulman

On the Wings of Music- Ulutrita

Copyright © 2022 by: MC Schulman

Cover Art by Luuk Honey

Cover Art Formatting by How It Works

Library of Congress Cataloging-in-Publication Data has been applied for

ISBN 978-0-9974646-2-7

On the Wings of Music-Ulutrita

Chapter 1

"What the Myrnvar just happened?" Kryzyck let go a groan, cautiously brushed the dirt off his face, and opened his eyes. Clouds of dust swirled around. The spinning sensation he was experiencing began to subside.

"Okay. There's the blue sky up there so I'm laying on my back. Why is my other arm not moving? Am I paralyzed? And why am I hearing strange voices inside my head?" While he slowly regained his senses, the old, white haired miner tried to piece together what had happened.

"Last thing I remember is reaching out to grab the pointed end of cheap gold wire from the roll I was carrying. Dyth! I must have stepped off the trail and rolled down the hill. What an idiot I am! I've hiked up and down the side of this crater for years. Guess I should have paid more attention to my footing." He raised his head off the stoney ground and let go a laugh.

"Oh for Zym's sake! When I fell, the spool must have flown off my shoulder, and unraveled. I guess it wrapped around me as I rolled down the hillside. No wonder I can't move. How embarrassing! Nothing seems to be broken. I'm a little sore in a couple places, and the spot right behind my ear hurts, but other than that, I think I'm okay. But what is up with these weird voices I'm hearing?"

After struggling for a few moments to try and free himself, Kryzyck laid back down, took a deep breath, and shouted as loudly as possible. "Blrsynt! Blrsynt! I need some help up here!"

At the base of the crater, the strapping young lad was just loading up some tools when he heard his uncle's echoing cry. The two long necked creatures hitched to the wagon swung their heads up toward the slope. Their triangular ears twitched back and forth.

"Oh, blyrt!" The young man threw down the pick he was holding, and scanned the dry, brushy slope. "Don't worry Uncle! I'm coming! Where are you?"

Kryzyck cursed under his breath and tried once more to rise to a sitting position. "I'm up.......Gaaa!" The leather thong of the necklace he was wearing cinched tightly around his neck, forcing him to lie back down.

"Oh holy Zym! What an idiot I am! I need to loosen this necklace before it chokes me to death." With his free hand, he worked his fingers into the tightly wound leather thong, loosening it slightly.

"Okay, that's better, at least I can breathe now." His gnarled fingers slid across the smooth surface of the precious galena crystal that hung at the end of the necklace. "Wow, one end of the wire seems to have gotten jammed into the crack along the front of the crystal. Good thing it didn't stab me in the neck. Ah, there's Blrysnt's footsteps approaching. Over here!"

The young man came running up and stopped to access the situation. "Oh man, Uncle. Are you alright?"

Kryzyck managed to nod his head, which also caused entangled wire and leather thong to press harder on his throat. He gagged violently.

"Holy blyrt!" Blrsynt knelt down and began franticly tearing the wire off his uncle's torso. "This isn't working! I'm gonna have to roll you over!" The heavily muscled young man flipped his uncle over three times before Kryzyck's left arm became free from its bondage. Even though his legs were still wrapped tightly, the old man managed to hold up a hand to signal for his nephew to stop. Kryzyck pushed himself up to a sitting position and took a moment to assess his condition.

Blrsynt settled back on his haunches. "Looks like you had a bit of a fall. Are you alright?"

"Yeah, I think I'm fine. It's just these dyth voices in my head!"

The younger man bit his lip. His eyebrows crossed up with concern. "What're they saying?"

"I don't know. The language they're speaking isn't anything I understand." Kryzyck worked his fingers under the leather thong of the necklace to try and further loosen it. His movements caused the galena crystal to swing a couple inches to the left.

"Now all I hear is static." The old miner reached up and grasped the crystal between his thumb and index finger. He gave the shiny metallic cube a gentle twist. "Now they're back again. Whoa, that sounded like laughter! What the klynk is going on?"

"I have no idea, but I think we need to get you to a healer. Maybe you hit your head on a rock."

The wind blew Kryzyck's unruly white hair away from his ear long enough for Blrsynt to see a crimson stream of blood trickling down behind his uncle's ear. He carefully pushed a strand of hair away to reveal the end of the wire jammed into Kryzyck's head. In one quick move, the young man yanked it out.

"It's gone! The noise is gone! What did you just do?"

Blrsynt held the blood soaked wire end out in front of his uncle's face. Kryzyck grasped it with his left hand and continued rotating the crystal with his right. He sat fiddling with the apparatus while his nephew stood up and began coiling up the nearby wire. After unwrapping Kryzyck's legs, Blrsynt lifted his head to follow the ribbon of gold up the hillside. The grey-green leaves on dry desert bushes swayed in the breeze.

"Well Uncle, the styrk is going down, and I don't feel like climbing up the hill to retrieve the rest of the wire. I say we get you down to the wagon and go into town so we can have a heal...."

"I'm fine, just a little sore." Kryzyck stiffly rose to his feet and pounded a considerable amount of dust off his baggy, linen pants and shirt. The quickening breeze gladly carried it away.

"Honestly, I think you banged your head coming down..."

"I'm telling you, I'm fine. Something really amazing just happened. Let's go." The old miner pulled the end of the wire from the galena crystal and led the way down off the hill.

After a good night's sleep in their miner's shack, Kryzyck got up early and began loading up the wagon. He took a moment to stroke the wide, flat heads of the two styrns after sliding the yoke on them. The tawny animals stamped the ground with their knobby legs and made a low rumbling noise in response. Blrsynt came walking out of the shack.

"Are we going to work in the mine today?" he asked between bites of the piece of bread he was holding.

"No, we have to ride into Tyrl and show this to the Academy!" The old man heaved a wire spool into the wagon and jumped up onto the wooden seat. "Come on, get in. It's a long drive there."

Blrsynt shrugged and hauled his big frame up next to his uncle. They rambled along in silence for a while. The nephew watched the dry desert landscape roll by. His curiosity finally urged him to speak.

"So what exactly are we, or I guess, you, going to show them?"

"As you recall, yesterday, I was walking along daydreaming, and I fell down the hill. The loose end of the spool of wire I was carrying got jammed into my head, and after the rest of the spool payed out, the other end wound up stuck into a crack in the crystal on my necklace."

The young man looked over at his uncle's craggy face and wild, unkept white hair. He nodded in acknowledgment.

"When I stopped rolling, that's when I heard the voices."

"The voices," Blrsynt repeated.

"Yes, two distinctly different men's voices."

Kryzyck had been watching his nephew's reaction out of the corner of his eye. He recognized the expression of doubt on the young man's face.

"You don't believe me do you?"

"Well, I, uh, I think maybe you hit your head on a rock or something, and it.."

"You think I'm just a crazy old fool, don't you?"

Now the old man was stirred up. He let go of the reins and jumped to his feet. Blrsynt raised his big, rough hand.

"Calm down! I'm just saying that I don't see how a voice could come out of a spool of wire without being attached to a telemessage or something."

"I don't see how either! That's what we're going into Tyrl to find out. Here, let me show you."

He reached down and gave the reins a huge yank backwards. The long snakelike necks of the two styrns wrenched back toward the cart. Both animals reacted with a low, guttural growl. Kryzyck turned around and pulled the wire spool up onto the hard wooden seat.

"Okay, just hold still. This is going to hurt just a little."

The nephew watched Kryzyck slip the necklace over his head, and carefully insert one end of the wire into the cracked galena crystal. A gust of arid wind blew the old man's wild mane of white hair as he grabbed the other end of the wire and leaned toward his nephew.

"What're you going to do what that?" Blrsynt's eyes grew large with alarm.

"Well, I'm going to poke this into your head so you can hear the voices."

Blrsynt swallowed hard. The dry desert air and his nervous reaction to the proposition worked to close off his throat. Kryzyck jammed the wire just behind the young man's ear.

"Oww!"

"Hold still! I have to turn the crystal till you can hear it!"

Kryzyck slowly rotated the shiny crystal back and forth. He stared at the nephew's frightened face, hoping to see the spark of recognition. "Hear anything yet?"

The young man slowly shook his head. After several more seconds of turning the crystal, Kryzyck yanked the wire out, wiped the end off on his tattered shirt, and jammed it into his head just behind the ear.

"Let me see if I can get it to work. Here, hold this in place!" he instructed, motioning to the wire end.

Blrsynt reluctantly pinched the wire between his thick fingers and held it against his uncle's head. The old miner carefully rotated the crystal back and forth. After several minutes, he pulled his head away, and sat down with a thud.

"I can hear a buzzing, but no voices. I don't understand it."

"Maybe the voices are sleeping. What time of day was it that you heard them?"

"Well, the styrk was going down, so it was later in the day."

"Why don't we keep going, and when we stop for the night, you can try again."

The old man looked over at his youthful companion. A wide smile enhanced the deep lines on his face. "So you don't think I'm just a crazy old fool?"

Blrsynt hesitated for a moment, then burst out into a barrel chested laugh. "Yes, I think you are a crazy old fool, but I trust you. Come on, let's go."

The next day, they entered the gleaming city of Tyrl. No one paid any attention to them as they wound their way along the narrow streets. They looked like just another pair of miners coming into the city to sell their hard worked bounty. Blrsynt stared at the multi-story buildings and finely dressed citizens with a big smile on his face.

"You know, I could get used to living here."

"Not me, I like the simple miner's life. Get up early, work hard, go home. Way too much going on here. A young guy like you might enjoy all the activity. I'd hate to lose you as a worker though."

They pulled up to the shiny marble steps of the Academy, and both stared at the impressive façade.

"So we're going in there?" the nephew asked with more than a twinge of doubt.

"Yep." Kryzyck jumped down from the seat and led the styrns over to a rail positioned at the foot of the steps. He tied the reins up with just enough slack to let the thirsty animals stick their short muzzles down into the water trough.

The nephew eased his way down out of the seat and brushed two days of dirt off his rough miner's clothes. "Shouldn't we clean up first?"

Kryzyck shook his head. "Naw, they're going to think we're crazy anyway. If we were clean and crazy, I don't think it would matter. Come on, let's go."

The nephew reached into the back of the wagon and grabbed the wire spool. He ascended the stairs next to his uncle. A pair of men in gorgeous gold threaded robes came sweeping down past them. One of them held a shiny telescope under his arm. His companion held a rolled up piece of paper. Just as they passed the old man and his nephew, Kryzyck stopped and turned toward them.

"Excuse, me. I have something I'd like to show to the Academy. Who might I approach about that?"

Both men in their colorful, illustrious robes stopped, and scrutinized the ragged pair. The individual holding the paper crossed his arms which caused the rolled map to crinkle loudly.

"What do you want to show them?" he asked in an obviously skeptical tone. His sharp, angular features narrowed as he waited for an answer.

"It's a talking wire."

Both the robed men looked over at each other.

"You mean like a telemessager? Sorry, that's already been invented."

Unkind laughter echoed off the polished steps. Blrsynt blushed with embarrassment. After the chuckling died down, Kryzyck continued.

"No, this is different. You don't need a wire connected, I mean yes you do, but..."

"Look, later this morning in the lecture hall, one of the professors is going to demonstrate a talking wire box. Why don't you show it to him?" A compassionate smile on the dark face of the man holding the telescope softened the character of the discussion.

"Thanks. That's just what we'll do." Kryzyck ran up the remaining steps with his nephew close behind. They passed through the huge glass and copper doors and stood side by side in the high ceiling foyer. The sound of voices echoed from an open doorway on the opposite side of the space. The older man led the way into the great lecture hall. Blrsynt gasped as they entered the massive semi-circular room.

A wide stage was situated against the far wall. Rows and rows of benches radiated up from the stage. On the first few rows, men and women in dazzling multi-colored robes were seated. The two ragged miners walked down the sloping main aisle and took a seat several rows from the back. In front of them, a vast group of school children were fidgeting and generally acting up much to the consternation of their teachers.

Up on the stage, a short, balding man stood in front of several large, colorful drawings stretched over wooden frames. His small, taut features were pulled in a grin. After gazing out at the restless group of children for several moments, he walked to the edge of the stage, and held up his hands.

"My oh my! You all seem very excited to be here. I'm excited too. My name is Professor Grylt, and I teach science here at the Academy. Do any of you like science?" His narrow trimmed moustache quivered with every word he spoke.

The unruly group paid little attention to his question. Several of the teachers got up to deal with the most rowdy of their charges.

"I hate children," Kryzyck muttered out of the corner of his mouth.

"I'm just enjoying looking at the pretty teachers. Check out that one there with the wavy black hair. She's beautiful." Blrsynt gazed longingly at the harried woman standing up to scold a group of boys just several rows down.

"Yes, she is beautiful. You've been out in the desert too long. Tyrl is full of gorgeous women. Be careful or you might get snagged by one. I'd hate to lose you as a helper." A grin worked its way across Kryzyck's wrinkled, weather-beaten face. Back up on the stage, the professor resumed his presentation.

"Okay, well it seems like things are calming down, so I'm going to get started. Welcome to the Academy, and let me say we are very glad to have you all here." The professor rubbed his small hands together, then moved over toward the drawing on his far right.

"We're going to start with a short history lesson. Our planet experiences a catastrophic meteor strike every thousand or so years. As a result, Ulutrita is riddled with craters. Life has been challenged many times by these events. Our oceans harbor most of the life forms. Terrestrial animals and plants have been almost wiped out and forced to recover countless times. We don't have a huge variety of either, but we love what we have. The last significant strike was just over four hundred years ago.

The three-quarter mile wide meteor impacted right in the center of what we now call Yrl. Who knows where Yrl is?"

The professor searched the crowd for raised hands. He pointed to a small girl waving her arm in the air.

"Yes, you there by the aisle."

After rising up to stand, she wrung her hands together, and finally spoke in a high, squeaky voice. "Yrl is the big country west of here, across the sea. My grandparents are from there." She delivered her answer without breaking the serious expression on her dark brown face.

"Yes! Excellent, thank you. The dust thrown up by the impact plunged Ulutrita into a mini-frozen pluge age that is just beginning to end. For our own protection, lots of people here focus their energy and intellect on astronomy. Monitoring approaching asteroids and predicting where and when they might impact is a full time endeavor. On a positive note, the impacts also provide access to our planet's mineral wealth which I will cover in a bit. Any questions at this point?"

The professor scanned the noisy, active group for interested individuals, but perceiving none, he moved over to the next drawing.

"Okay, where was I? Oh yes, Ulutrita is situated right at the edge of a massive asteroid cloud. Comets and meteors have rained down for much of our ancient past." Grylt tapped the blueish ball of the planet right in the middle of the canvas, then swung the end of his pointer down by the smudge of the asteroid belt and over to the bright yellow sun.

"We have a relatively young stryrk that we orbit around which gives us our mostly warm, dry climate. Next, I'm going to talk a little about our mineral wealth and economy. We know that billions of years ago, when the universe was coalescing from the huge swirling clouds of gas and dust, the sphere that would become Ulutrita cooled extremely rapidly, thereby capturing all the soft metals from the primal elements.

As a result, gold is by far the most plentiful metal on our planet. It's mixed with all kinds of harder substances to produce a workable alloy. In its pure form, it covers the surfaces of the larger buildings in our bigger cities. The gleam of hammered gold at stryrkrise and stryrkset is immortalized over and over again in Ulutritan poetry.

The invention of the steam engine a hundred years ago has really advanced our civilization. In order to produce steam, we've had to manage and harvest the vast dry forests along this latitude. We also have a small amount of coal available, but it is usually only used in the most important industries. The recent ability of us to harness electricity has further advanced our civilization and promises to make our lives more comfortable. That's all I have for today. Um, do we have time for questions?"

From the first row of the school group, a tall, rangy man with a wire rim glasses got to his feet. "Thank you Professor, but unfortunately no. Students please thank the professor for his time." A collective "Thank you!" rose up all around him. "Teachers, if you will please lead your students out in an orderly manner."

Kryzyck and his nephew watched the group stream out while up on the stage, the large drawings were wheeled away. As soon as they were moved aside, a short, stout man with a tangled greying black beard walked out from behind the curtain. He carried a small wooden table that had a large metal horn resembling a flower sitting on it.

A thin bundle of wires was wrapped up beside the horn. A tall bespectacled man followed him with a similar apparatus which he set down on the opposite side of the stage. The wires were unrolled and screwed into a small wooden box at the base of the horn on the far device. Once they were secured the shorter man walked to center of the platform to address the crowd.

"My name is Professor Myrvst, head of the communications department. Please allow me to demonstrate the televocal transmitter."

The professor walked back over to his side of the stage, checked to make sure his assistant was ready, then bent over and spoke quietly into the horn. His assistant stuck his ear right into the matching horn on his end of the stage. The two men appeared to be having a conversation, although the audience couldn't hear what was being said. They both smiled, then straightened up to a standing position.

"And now, if any of you would like to try it out." Professor Myrvst offered, spreading his arms out wide. The hall was filled with the sound of people rising to their feet. In a matter of seconds, two lines formed, one at each end of the stage. They snaked all the way up the center aisle.

"Come on Blrsynt, let's give it a try. I want to get a closer look at the device." Kryzyck elbowed his nephew and headed off to the left. After about a half hour of waiting, his turn arrived.

"Mind if I examine the transmitter a little?" Kryzyck asked in a low voice.

"Not at all. Are you an inventor?" Professor Myrvst tried to smile, but he was getting tired.

Kryzyck cracked a sly grin and knelt down next to the table. "You might say that. How does the sound get transferred from the wires to the horn?"

"Ah, inside the small end of the horn is a thin membrane. The end of the wire is glued to it."

The old miner's brain ignited with ideas. From behind him, the next person in line began to impatiently tap his foot. Kryzyck looked up at the glaring individual, offered a quick apology, then shifted his gaze down to the far end of the stage where Blrsynt was waiting next to the other device. The old miner bent over and spoke directly into the horn.

"I just found out how the sound is transmitted. Can you hear me?"

"Yes! Yes! I heard every word. Isn't this amazing." a rough, scratchy voice replied.

"Just wait till I use this idea with my new discovery. Get ready for something really amazing!" The old miner stood to full height and stepped over next to the professor. "My name is Kryzyck Fourth Line."

"Myrvst Third Line."

"Pleased to meet you. Would you have time to take a look at this very interesting phenomenon that I recently discovered? It bears a lot of similarity to your televocal transmitter."

Professor Myrvst's baggy, sanguine face lit up. "Well, my presentation is just about over. Why don't you just wait till everyone clears out. Do you have it with you?"

Kryzyck gave an enthusiastic nod. "I'll go get it."

The old miner could hardly contain his excitement. He made his way down off the stage, and intercepted Blrsynt as he was heading back to the far end of the hall. "Hurry, grab the spool and come stand by the professor and I."

With that, Kryzyck turned and walked briskly back up to the stage. He stopped by the great burgundy curtain that hung behind the presenters. The old miner and his nephew waited patiently while the long line of finely dressed academicians tried out the televocal. The late afternoon sun was pouring through the high upper windows when the hall finally began to clear out. Professor Myrvst and his assistant accepted their last congratulations and began taking the devices apart.

"Professor Myrvst! Would it be alright if I demonstrated my invention now?" Kryzyck piped up.

The professor turned around slowly to address the miner. His eyes were red and bleary. Huge bags of loose skin hung under them.

"Oh, that's right. I did say that I would take a look. My, but I'm tired. If you don't mind, I'm going to take a seat." Myrvst plunked down hard on a nearby chair. "Ah, that's better. How long will it take to fire it up?"

"It's ready right now." Kryzyck knelt down and laid a hand on the spool. "So, you can see that I have one end of the wire stuck in this galena crystal, and the other end I'd like to attach to one of those membranes. Incidentally, when I discovered it, this end of the wire got jammed into my skull."

"Here, let me bring one of the horns over. We can connect it to the televocal lead." The assistant picked up the small wooden table and placed it next to the spool.

"My name's Lynflyn, by the way." Introductions were exchanged all around. Lynflyn took the other end of the miner's wire and screwed it down under the horn. "There, so what's next?"

The faint buzz of static crackled out of the horn. "Boy, I hope this works," Kryzyck muttered just under his breath. His heart beat rapidly as he slowly began rotating the crystal. The volume and tone of the static started to change. Just as the old miner's hope was fading, a garbled voice rang through the horn. Blrsynt jumped in place.

"Geez, that startled me!"

Kryzyck ever so slowly reversed the position of the crystal. Another short flurry of words came crackling out of the horn. Myrvst was snoring softly in his chair. The assistant quietly tip-toed over and gave the professor a gentle nudge.

"Huh? What? I just had my eyes closed." Myrvst rubbed his eyelids and broke into a sheepish grin. "Guess I dozed off. Did I miss anything?"

"Yes, Mister Kryzyck was demonstrating his invention."

"And?"

"It produced some sounds, maybe a voice speaking, but I for one couldn't understand what was being said."

Myrvst straightened up in his chair and moved his glasses back up the bridge of his nose. "Can you reproduce the sound?"

"I can certainly try." Kryzyck rotated the crystal this way and that, but all that came out of the horn was static. After several minutes, he looked up at the professor. "I guess it's not working."

"Tell you the truth, I'm so hungry, it's hard to concentrate. Do you and your nephew have plans for pyryst?"

The old miner shook his head. Professor Myrvst laboriously got to his feet. "Lynflyn, Mr. Kryzyck and his nephew will be our guests tonight!"

Blrsynt and his uncle grinned at each other. They quickly packed up the wire spool and assisted with the dismantling of the televocal.

"In a few short years, I will be able to pick up a televocal and call Sylstyn, my housekeeper, to tell her to prepare pyryst for four," Myrvst exclaimed.

The two miners followed the professor and his assistant out into the early evening air. A dusty, diffuse sunset was rapidly spreading to the west. Lynflyn set one of the small display tables down outside the huge copper doors and turned toward the professor.

"I'll go get the buggy."

Kryzyck and his nephew carried their device down the marble steps. The soft desert air blew the old miner's white hair up, then let it fall.

"What're you smiling about?" Blrysnt asked.

"There have been several times in my life where I made a decision that I just knew was right. This is one of them. I gotta feeling that big things are going to come from this. Who knows? Maybe we'll get rich! Forget about blasting rock and crushing up ore."

Chapter 2.

In the kitchen of Professor Myrvst's humble stone house, his young housekeeper was engrossed in the mildy pornographic novel a friend had lent her. When she heard the front door open, Sylstyn slammed the small black book shut, shoved it in a non-descript drawer, and hustled out of the kitchen. She heard the professor's familiar gruff voice, and two others.

"Oh great, he's probably brought some of his old, dried up friends from the Academy home again. I can't stand those lecherous fossils staring at me." She shot a glance in the mirror as she rounded the dining room. "Dyth, now I'm all flushed!"

Sylstyn burst into the entryway, a fake smile imprinted on her rosy cheeks. The professor and Lynflyn were carrying the low tables in. When the assistant stepped aside, Sylstyn caught her first full length view of Blrsynt. His wide shoulders, and pleasant, reasonably handsome face sent her to the point of ignition.

"Sylstyn, this is Mr. Kryzyck, and his nephew Blrsynt." Professor Myrvst set down the table he was carrying and walked over next to her.

Blrysnt took several steps forward and extended his hand. She grasped it lightly. Electricity shot up her arm.

"Pleased to meet you," he offered in his soft, kind voice.

"N-n-nice to meet you too."

Kryzyck was the last one in the door. He smiled at her and gave a quick bow.

"They will be staying for pyryst tonight. Do we have enough food for all of us?" the professor inquired.

"I, umm, was going to, I mean, I have a roast cooking. Yes," she managed to blurt out. Sweat was beginning to trickle down her neck. Sylstyn spun on her heels and retreated to the kitchen.

"Gentlemen, make yourselves at home. By the way, you aren't from Tyrl, are you?" Myrvst asked with a twist of his bushy eyebrows.

Kryzyck had been examining his grungy fingers. The question snapped him back to the moment. "No, uh, we have a mine out west of here. We rushed in to show someone our discovery."

"Well, if you'd like to stay here for a couple days, I do have a spare room."

Both Kryzyck and his nephew broke into beaming smiles. "That's very kind of you. Honestly, we hadn't really taken the time to even think about lodging."

"Very well then, Lynflyn, will you show them to the spare room?" Myrvst said graciously. "I'll go down into the cellar and get us something to drink."

Once back inside the safe and secure domain of the kitchen, Sylstyn splashed several handfuls of cold water over her heated face. In the process of leaning over the sink, her pelvis was pressed against the counter.

"Oh Zym! I feel like running out into the backyard, tearing off my clothes, and screaming at the top of my lungs. I hate being seventeen. This is going to be a long, agonizing meal!" Sylstyn took several deep breaths, straightened up, and began getting the dinner together.

When their meal was finished, Myrvst wiped his mouth with a napkin, and turned toward Kryzyck. "Shall we go experiment with your invention before it gets too late?"

The four men rose from the table and headed down the hall to the professor's work room.

"I left the spool in our room. I'll go get it," the nephew pipped up. While the other three entered the cluttered work room, he turned and walked briskly back down the hall. Upon entering the dining room, he paused to wait for Sylstyn to emerge from the kitchen.

She was placing the dishes in the sink and fantasizing about having sex with the young visitor over the dining room table. When she burst back into the dining room and saw him standing there, her nerve endings jumped. Sylstyn stood paralyzed.

"The pyryst was wonderful," Blrsynt offered in as smooth a tone as he could produce. The soothing effect of his words released her paralysis.

"Glad you liked it. Are you going to be staying here for a while?" The bright inviting smile that accompanied her question made him quiver.

"I hope so." Not wanting to seem too obvious, he turned, retrieved the spool, and joined the others in the workroom. Blrsynt set the spool on the worktable, as instructed. Myrvst was holding a long rectangular piece of dark metal. The professor slid the chunk of dark metal inside the spool and stepped back. Kryzyck ran his finger over the edge of the magnet, then turned toward his nephew.

"Professor Myrvst was just telling me how he was experimenting with wrapping a magnet with coils of wire. He thinks this might really improve the performance of our discovery. I guess there are advantages to being part of the Academy. Boy, I bet this chunk of metal was not cheap."

Lynflyn began screwing one end of the wire to a small wooden frame, while Kryzyck carefully poked the other end into his precious galena crystal. The professor was busy adjusting the thin diaphragm that would transmit the sound.

"Sometimes, these old fingers of mine just don't want to cooperate." Myrvst rose from his stooped position and held out the screwdriver. "Blrsynt, want to give it a try?"

The nephew had been standing around gazing at the piles of dirty dishes and tea cups with mold floating in them. Without saying a word, he took the tool from Myrvst, and quickly finished the task. Kryzyck let go a sigh of relief.

"Thanks Blrsynt. I don't know about the rest of you, but for some reason, I suddenly feel like we're on a race against time to get this hooked up."

Lynflyn wiped some sweat off his forehead. "Funny you should say that, I don't know why, but I too, am getting really anxious just watching."

Kryzyck gave a little shrug and began rotating the galena crystal ever so slowly. For several seconds the only sound to be heard coming from the lacquered horn was a low hiss. Everyone in the room jolted when the hiss was interrupted by a loud pop. Crackly static began to issue out of the horn. The static steadily grew louder as Kryzyck rotated the silvery crystal. With another marginal turn of the galena, a distinct human voice filled the room.

"Good evening, this is Reginald Fessenden broadcasting from Brant Rock, Massachusetts, December twenty-fourth, nineteen o'six. We will be playing a selection from Hayden's Largo, followed by a brief speech by my assistant Mr. Henry Stein, a live version of the popular Christmas hymn, Oh Holy Night, and conclude with a reading from Matthew."

Kryzyck's arthritic fingers were starting to seize up, but he held the crystal as still as possible. All those in the room stood motionless as more static poured out of the horn.

"Wish I knew what he just said. That was a man's voice, right?" Blrsynt commented from his place by the wall.

"I think so," the professor added. "It seems like we lost.....," Myrvst was cut off in mind sentence when the static was replaced by the rhythmic scratching of a Victrola needle just dropped onto a record. The scratching rapidly gave way to the stately, majestic strains of Handel's Largo.

Sylstyn was just putting the last of the dishes away when the sweeping melody found its way down to her. She put down the plate she was holding, and like a moth to the flame, let herself be led out of the kitchen and down the hall. She walked slowly and carefully down the creaky wooden floor, trying to make as little noise as possible.

Upon reaching the doorway, Sylstyn stuck her head around the opening, and took a quick scan of the people in the stuffy room. The tears streaming down Professor Myrvst's wrinkled cheeks, all the way into his beard, tugged at her heart strings. She fought the desire to rush over and embrace him.

When she directed her attention to Blrsynt, he gave a beckoning tilt of his head. Sylstyn shook her head in response. He stuck his lower lip out comically. His goofy expression was too much for her to ignore. With head slightly lowered, she tiptoed into the room, and stood next to him. After several more minutes, the divine, soothing music slowly trailed off.

"Oh, does it have to end!" Sylstyn whispered.

Myrvst wiped his long nose on his sleeve and ran a finger into the corner of his eye to clear the tears away. "My but that was beautiful."

"I've never heard anything like that in all my life," Blrsynt exclaimed.

"Amazing, truly amazing," Kryzyck added. His fingers were beginning to shake. He knelt down and rested his forearms on the edge of the table. The group waited expectantly, but all that issued out of the horn was static.

"Should I try and turn the crystal again?"

Myrvst shook his head. "Just wait."

At the point when the waiting had approached the unbearable state, the static was replaced by the first, tenuous notes of Reginald Fessenden's violin. Sylstyn's face glowed with happiness as the solo instrument's plaintive tone reached her ears. Her eyes grew big when he started singing.

"O, Holy Night! Most blessed Night!"

Without even thinking, she pressed her left side against Blrsynt. The warmth of her body and heady atmosphere of the room sent him into a state of euphoria. After the solitary instrument and accompanying voice slowly trailed off, the sound of static again filled the emotion charged space. Sylstyn sent another quick look over at Myrvst. Even behind his wire frame glasses, she could see his eyes were twinkling.

"Glory to God in the high-high-highest, and peace to, uh, on Ear-r-r-rth." The anxiety choked voice of Reginald Fassenden's wife Helen took the listeners completely by surprise.

Lynflyn's narrow face drew up in confusion. "That's someone different, right?"

Before any of the group could answer, the same deeper male voice rattled out of the horn. "This concludes our program for tonight. To all the listeners out there, we wish you all a very merry Christmas."

A noticeable click and the return of static signaled the end of the broadcast. Professor Myrvst rubbed his face.

"I believe that the way his voice was lowering indicated he was drawing things to a close."

"I'm going to have to stand up," Kryzyck groaned. "I'm getting too old to kneel like this."

Blrsynt reached over and pulled his uncle to his feet. The old miner set the crystal down, and all sound ceased.

"Amazing, truly amazing." Myrvst stroked his tangled beard while speaking.

"Professor, I'm at a total loss to try and explain that. Do you have any ideas?" Lynflyn asked with a tone of incredulousness.

Myrvst pondered his assistant's question, then moved toward the door. "Let's go into the parlor. I feel like we need to sit down and let this sink in."

Lynflyn followed the professor out, with Kryzyck close behind. Just before exiting the room, the nephew whispered into Sylstyn's ear.

"That sound was almost as beautiful as you are."

She turned to face him and stared right into his big brown eyes without blinking. Their lips were perilously close to touching.

"We should go into the parlor." Sylstyn flashed a delightful smile, then slipped out into the hall.

The two of them joined the older men in the well furnished parlor, taking seats opposite the professor.

"Should I make some zyd or something?" she asked quietly.

"No dear, I think we're all getting a little tired. It's been a busy day. I think we should go to bed and ponder what just happened. It might have been a miracle," Myrvst replied.

A huge yawn engulfed Kryzyck's face. "You had to mention going to bed, didn't you?"

"Tomorrow, we'll take the coil down to the Academy. We need to show this to the forum. This will cause quite a stir."

Lynflyn listened to the professor's words, then straightened up in his chair. "I looked at the forum schedule for tomorrow when we were there today. It's jam packed. Lycrk and that guy from over by Lake Cymryn are supposed to debate the presence of Zym, some astronomers are scheduled to talk about a comet that's headed this way. I don't see how we'll ever get in."

Kryzyck took a moment to analyze what had been said before speaking. "Tell you what, if we get more sounds like the ones we heard today to come out of that horn, everybody will stop and listen." The old miner looked over at his nephew. "I'm going to bed. I have a feeling that tomorrow is going to be a very momentous day."

Chapter 3.

Bright and earlier the next morning, Professor Myrvst, his assistant, and the two visiting miners got up, choked down a quick breakfast, and rushed out the door. While Blrsynt and Lynflyn readied the transportation, the two older men stood on the front steps enjoying the early morning sun. Professor Myrvst took another drink of his zyd and cleared his throat.

"Today is forum day. The street in front of the Academy is going to be a mad house. Lynflyn and I will pull around back to the area reserved for forum members. I'm not officially accepted into the forum, as you can tell by the lack of a vowel in my name, but word is that the televoice invention will probably change that." His face lit up at the notion.

Kryzyck and his nephew loaded up their device, then followed the professor over to the Academy. As he predicted, the street that ran in front of the large white marble building was bustling with activity. Styrn buggies were lined up wall to wall along the curb. A special detail had been assigned to clean up the manure from the large number of animals packed into the narrow space. Fights broke out between several of the male styrns.

After parking two blocks away, the old miner and his nephew scooped up the apparatus and joined the throng of finely robed characters heading into the Academy. They drew some interesting looks from all around. Blrsynt leaned over and whispered in his uncle's ear.

"Why are people staring at us?"

Kryzyck glanced around, frowned, and answered out of the corner of his thin mouth. "Because we're still wearing our ragged miner's clothes."

Up the wide steps they marched, occasionally having to make way for students carrying arm loads of textbooks and astronomers holding their shiny gold telescopes. Once inside the building, they began searching for Myrvst.

"The professor didn't say where to meet him, did he?" Kryzyck yelled over the din of hundreds of excited voices.

Blrsynt just shook his head and looked around at the huge crowd talking and milling about in the great high ceilinged foyer. There was a long line waiting outside the entrance to the lecture hall. Across the polished stone floor, another long line stretched out from the registration table. Blrsynt scanned the colorful, noisy crowd, and eventually spotted Myrvst in front of the table.

"There he is over there!" The nephew plowed through the crowd with his uncle in tow. He turned back to give Kryzyck a running commentary.

"The professor appears to be having a heated discussion with some guy taking names down. I can't hear what's being said, but the expression on both men's faces, and the way they're gesturing makes me think there's some disagreement between them. Oh! The professor just threw his hands up and is stomping off through the crowd. I just spotted Lynflyn over against that wall. I bet the professor is heading over there."

Blrsynt and his uncle changed course, and eventually arrived at the far wall. Myrvst was already seated on a stone bench. He was breathing heavily. His wrinkled face turned down in a scowl.

"So what's going on?" the nephew inquired.

"Well, Professor was trying to convince the officials to let you demonstrate your invention, but as I suspected, the agenda for today is overflowing. The registrar said that he could schedule you for two weeks from today," Lynflyn said with a sigh.

"Two weeks? We can't stay here that long," Kryzyck muttered.

A loud cheer from the crowd by the front door drew everyone's attention. The tightly packed throng parted to let a short, bald headed man in a striking gold and crimson robe enter the foyer.

"Who's that?" Blrsynt asked.

Lynflyn rose up from his seat slightly and craned his neck to get a look around the mass of people. "That would be Lycrk. His opponent in the debate should be arriving shortly."

"And did you say they were going to be debating the existence of Zym?" Lynflyn nodded in response. "What's your opinion on the matter?"

The assistant adjusted the glasses perched on his narrow nose before answering. "My opinion is that we are born, we live, we suffer, and we die. Just like that."

"Mmmm," the nephew hummed in acknowledgment.

The crowd parted again, and four finely dressed figures strode across the stone floor. Lynflyn anticipated the nephew's unspoken question.

"Those are the forum members. Head Regent Bokyl, Regents Krynut, Handynr, and Mihyn. The two walking together are married."

Myrvst jumped up from the bench and forced his way across the crowded foyer. Just before the forum members entered the hall, he reached out and grabbed the sleeve of Mihyn's gorgeous gold and purple robe.

"Regent! Sorry to bother you. You know me to be an honest and dedicated scholar. An invention was presented to me last night that needs very, very much to be evaluated by the forum today. It's as important, if not more important of an advancement than my televoice!"

The young, dignified woman stopped her forward progress, and turned to face her assailant. Mihyn studied the professor's flushed and sweaty face for a moment. The steely resolve of her pleasant, but hard features betrayed no indication of how she was going to react.

"You realize that what you are requesting is highly irregular. By the way, let go of my robe, please."

Myrvst released his grasp on her clothing and took a step back. Regent Mihyn glanced at the packed to overflowing hall, then returned her skeptical gaze to the professor.

"I don't have to remind you that today is about the worst day to request something like this. As soon as Drbyrl arrives, he and Lycrk are going to launch into their debate, and the whole place....."

"Regent Mihyn! Would you be so kind as to carry on your discussion during a break." Krynut paused to deliver the stern request just before leading the group into the hall. He was of average height, with a wiry build, and smooth, olive colored skin.

Mihyn gave a quick nod of her head, then swung back around. "We'll talk at the break." She sent a fleeting, emotionless smile back toward Myrvst, then continued forward.

The professor let go a sigh of relief and stepped out of the way. A gush of bodies followed the regents into the crowded hall. Myrvst bumped and jostled his way back to the waiting party. When he reached the far wall, the professor plunked back down onto the smooth stone bench and leaned his head of tangled hair against the wall.

"I'm getting too old for this. I managed to get a few words in with Regent Mihyn. She said she'll talk to us at the break."

Blrsynt and Lynflyn both gave each other a gentle punch on the shoulder. Kryzyck broke into a wide, wrinkled grin. Another titanic cheer rang out from the crowd standing by the front doors. The assistant stood on his tip toes to see what the commotion was.

"Oh boy, looks like Lycrk's opponent is here!"

"His name is Drbyrl," Myrvst said wearily.

The entire throng waiting by the front doors surged toward the hall. Chanting and shouts of encouragement rang out against the stone walls. Once the noisy group had passed by them, Myrvst reached over and tugged the old miner's tattered shirt.

"Let's get your invention set up. During the break, I'll get Regent Mihyn to come over here, and we'll give her a demonstration."

While the group began assembling Kryzyck's wire spool device, things inside the hall began to amp up. The regents were seated at their horseshoe shaped table at the foot of the stage. Lycrk had taken up a position on the far left side of the stage. His opponent, Drbyrl, stood at the other end. He was small and bony with a sweeping shock of gray hair. Even though the crowd was trying to whisper among itself, the cumulative noise was significant.

Head Regent Bokyl swung his large, barrel chested torso around in his chair and surveyed the packed house. A frown contorted his wide, ruddy face. He motioned for one of the hall bailiffs to approach. The bailiff walked over and leaned across the polished wood table.

"Yes, Head Regent?"

"I don't like the attitude of this crowd. This isn't a boxing match! It's a serious philosophical and theological discussion. I'm afraid that once things get under way, it's going to turn into a mob scene."

"What would you like my men and I to do?"

Regent Handynr, Mihyn's husband, had been listening to the exchange. He reached over and laid a hand on Bokyl's sleeve.

"My old friend, don't worry! It's going to get loud in here, no doubt about that. If things start to get out of hand, we'll just cut the debate short. Remember, we have a full schedule today. I say we give these two twenty minutes, then move on."

A nervous smile broke across Bokyl's rough face. "I can always count on you to assess and keep control of the situation. Great suggestion. Well, shall we get this wild event underway?"

Handynr smiled back, and leaned over to see what Krynut was doing. At his place on the far end of the table, the highly respected mathematician and astronomer was busy pouring over a sheath of papers. He was oblivious to the noisy, frenetic atmosphere.

"Off in his own world again," Handynr muttered to himself. "Regent Krynut, Regent Krynut!" His attempts at getting the bookish, stern faced regent's attention appeared to be unsuccessful. Handynr poked Bokyl in the shoulder.

"Will you ask Krynut if he is ready to begin?"

Bokyl tapped on the table surface next to the self-absorbed mathematician. Krynut jumped slightly in his seat.

"What? What's going on?"

"Are you ready to begin?"

Krynut glanced up at the stage with a look of bewilderment.

"Are you alright?" Bokyl asked.

The mathematician reshuffled his papers, scratched his short, well-clipped Van-Dyke beard, then turned toward the head regent.

"Yes, quite alright thank you. I didn't sleep much last night. The head of the astronomic society passed on some very interesting news late yesterday, and I spent most of the night verifying his calculations. If his observations are correct, in a few....."

"Never mind the dissertation! Are you ready to begin?"

Krynut gave as genuine a smile as his sanguine nature would allow and folded his fingers together in front of him. "Ready to begin."

Bokyl pushed back his chair, stood up, and turned to face the packed house. He took another quick scan of the restless, energized crowd, cleared his throat, and began speaking.

"All rise!"

The sound of four hundred bodies rising to their feet reverberated throughout the hall. In an attempt to get the head regent's attention, the bailiff standing to his right let go a purposeful cough. Bokyl craned his neck to the side, watched as the bailiff give a slight tilt of his head in the direction of the stage, then swung around to follow the motion.

On the right side of the stage, Drybyrl was sitting cross legged. A groan reverberated out of the head regent's wide chest. Staring directly at the seated speaker, he repeated in his loudest voice.

"All rise!"

Drybryl remained in lotus position. From the crowd behind him, Bokyl heard the rustle of clothing as the speaker's followers sat in unison. Angry murmurs began to filter out of the mostly standing crowd.

"Traitors!"

"Anarchists!"

"Shut up! We're freemen!"

The last audible outburst was followed by the sound of two men scuffling. The bailiffs rushed up into the center of the seating area and pulled the two combatants apart. They escorted the fighters out of the hall. Bokyl's lips were now trembling.

"As head regent of the Academy forum, I now declare this forum open!"

Cheers and a couple cat calls rang out in the hall. There was a collective thump as the crowd took its seats. Bokyl wiped sweat off his bulbous forehead and looked over at Handynr. The tall, well proportioned regent gave a silent thank you, then got to his feet.

"This debate is to proceed as follows, each participant will give a five minute opening statement, after which each will be allowed to ask a question of the other. It was determined before hand that whoever took the left side podium would go first."

Handynr turned toward the stage and gave Lycrk a nod. The stout, bald headed man in the brilliant gold and scarlet robe gripped the podium tight, bent his nicely domed head back, closed his eyes, and began.

"Oh Zym, give me the strength to carry out your will today. Infuse me with your wisdom, skill, and fire!"

His last words ignited the portion of the crowd that had come to support him. A roar shook the hall. Bokyl again rose to his feet and held both arms up.

"Audience will please refrain from making noise during the debate." His request was met by unhappy murmurs. Once the crowd had quieted down, the head regent turned back around and motioned toward Lycrk to continue.

"For as long as anyone can remember, or has record of, our world has been constantly struck with meteors and objects from the sky. Our race has endured hundreds, thousands of catastrophic events that have tested our will and perseverance. It is no secret that the intemperate, lascivious nature of man is the cause of these events!" Jeers of disagreement circled through the crowd.

"If we were to follow the strict laws laid down for us on the holy mountain so long ago, our wicked, fornicating race could be free of the burden of these calamities and rise up to the great potential that we are meant for!" A wave of subdued applause circled through the room.

Meanwhile out in the foyer, Myrvst and Kryzyck were trying to get the device to broadcast more of the mysterious voices when the volume of angry shouting coming from the hall dramatically rose. All four men hovering over the primitive crystal radio looked up.

"That doesn't sound good. I think a riot is going to break out!" Blrsynt commented.

"People arguing about religion and spirits. What a waste of time! That's why I stay out there in the crater," Kryzyck announced with no small measure of disgust. Another loud roar of dissent echoed from the hall. Professor Myrvst stood up from his kneeling position.

"I'm going to take a look and see what's going on. It sounds like things are getting heated in there."

At that same time, Sylstyn entered the building through the big copper front doors. She was loaded down with two large wicker baskets. Halfway across the foyer, she spotted Blrsynt and the group next to the side wall and hurried over. After setting the baskets down, she flashed a warm smile over at the nephew.

"So how are things going today?"

"Oh, it's been an interesting day. As you can hear, there's a lot of strong opinions being delivered during the first session. We haven't had a chance to demonstrate. Doesn't seem to be much coming out of the horn today."

"If you could make that same sound come out as you did last night, wow, that would be amazing. I felt like I was floating above the floor it was so beautiful."

"That was something, wasn't it?"

Lynflyn was standing up on the stone bench when Sylstyn arrived at the far wall. He jumped down and stared at the wicker baskets.

"Oh, hi. Looks like you brought myrf. Great, I'm starving."

He and Blrsynt wasted no time flinging open the baskets, and diving into the sumptuous lunch that Sylstyn has prepared. Kryzyck waited till the two had grabbed what they wanted, then walked over and peered into the basket nearest him.

"Hmm, looks like some pynfrs, zyts, and blynys. It smells great. Thank you for bringing this over."

"Well, Professor Myrvst asked me to bring some food down. He thought it was going to be a long day." While Kryzyck pulled one of the sandwiches out of the basket, Sylstyn bent over to examine the device. "So how do you work this thing?"

"Just hold the crystal with one hand, and make sure the wire doesn't slip out while you rotate it. When you hear something interesting, rotate it very slowly back. Not too complicated."

As if on cue, Professor Myrvst and Regent Mihyn came striding across the center of the high ceilinged foyer.

"Sylstyn! Glad you made it. And I see you brought myrf. How wonderful. I'm about to pass out from hunger." Myrvst stepped aside and held his arm out towards the regent. "Everyone, this is Regent Mihyn. She's a linguist and historian. Did I leave anything out?"

"You are too kind. Hello everyone, pleased to meet you," Mihyn responded in her best official tone. A smile graced her pleasant, but serious features.

Introductions were exchanged around the group, then the professor turned toward his housekeeper. "Well, let's give Regent Mihyn a demonstration." Sylstyn held the wire and crystal out to him, but the professor waved her off. "No, go ahead. I need to eat." Myrvst ducked behind the young woman and walked over to the stone bench.

When Sylstyn tried offering the objects to Kryzyck, he also declined. She drew in a quick breath, readjusted her grip on the shiny, cubic crystal, and with great concentration, began slowly turning it. A sizable crowd was now gathered around the device. Static crackled and popped out of the black lacquer horn. Sweat began to form above Sylstyn's lip. Her intense dislike of being the center of attention sent her into a mild panic.

Blrysnt recognized the look of displeasure on her face. Sensing his attention, she looked up. Her eyes pleaded with him to take over. The young man stepped around the edge of the low table and held out his hands.

"Want me to do it?"

She gave him the sweetest, "thanks for saving my life" smile he'd ever seen and handed over the wired crystal. With a sigh of relief, she hurried over, and stood next to the assistant. Blrsynt mimicked the method that she had used to hold the crystal. He rotated it as smoothly as possible. Static continued to roll out of the horn. The sound of people returning to the hall echoed from across the foyer. Regent Mihyn turned her head of wavy auburn hair toward the hall, then back to the demonstration.

"I'm going to have to go back in a minute," she whispered into Myrvst's ear.

After crunching through a bite of the cylindrical purple vegetable, he replied. "Hopefully, Blrsynt will find something. It seems……"

The professor's words were cut off by the loud issuance of a voice radiating from the horn. The voice began counting down from ten. Mihyn's highly arched eyebrows arched even higher.

"Oh! Most interesting. The language is not familiar at all."

At the edge of the now curious crowd gathered around the device, a tall man with a carefully trimmed moustache and beard stood with crossed arms. He leaned over to examine the simple collection of wires, spool, and horn.

"So is this some kind of trick?"

Kryzyck finished his meal, wiped his fingers on his ragged miner's pants, and straightened up before addressing the question. "No, it's not a trick, just an interesting discovery I made last week."

"Come on, there's somebody making these sounds off in a room here somewhere, right? I don't see any wires heading off, but they've got to be hidden, right?"

Kryzyck shook his head. "Honest, it's not a trick."

From inside the lecture hall, Head Regent Bokyl's gruff voice echoed out into the foyer. Mihyn spun around. "The next session is starting. I have to go!" In a whirl of carefully crafted purple and gold robe, she sped across the foyer toward the open hall door.

Chapter 4.

Mihyn made her way down the aisle, smoothed her dark hair, and tried to resume an air of dignity. She took her place next to Handynr. "What did I miss?" she whispered.

"The next presenter is going to be talking about salt intrusion into the ground pluge near Hylbs," her husband whispered back.

Mihyn nodded thoughtfully and settled into her chair. The presenter stood at the center of the stage, rigid as a pole. Shortly after he began his dry, uninspired talk, Mihyn's attention began to drift back to the minute or so of speech she had heard rumbling out of Kryzyck's invention. The desire to go back out and investigate further grew stronger by the minute.

"Are there any further questions?" Bokyl asked. His gravelly voice interrupted her thoughts. The head regent looked right at Mihyn. She shook her head. "Very well, I will let Regent Krynut introduce the next presenter."

The thin, wiry built mathematician rose to his feet, and turned to address the audience. "It is my honor and pleasure to introduce the head of our astronomy department, Professor Ymyl."

Applause echoed throughout the hall. Dressed in a superbly embroidered robe of deep blue and gold, the well known astronomer ascended the stage, and stood behind the podium. His long, sloping nose, and upturned sharp chin gave him a somewhat comical appearance.

"I've given so many presentations here, I zink I probably spend more time here zan at home." Polite laughter rippled through the crowd. "Last week, one of my colleagues made visual contact with Comet eleven twenty-three seventy-seven." He let the announcement sink in for effect. The sound of excited whispering drifted out from of the audience.

"For those of you of advanced age, like me, you may remember zis comet from last time it made an appearance forty-nine years ago. It's too early to tell whether it will put on an equally magnificent show as it deed last time, but our calculations indicate it will swing by Ulutrita with little or no chance of impact."

More applause rang out. Handynr leaned over and touched his wife's arm. "That's good news, wouldn't you say?"

Mihyn's dark brown eyes flickered. She turned to face her husband. "What did you say?"

"Never mind. You're obviously lost in thought about something."

She smiled and looked into his long, angular face. "I am lost in thought. Do you think there's intelligent life out there in space?"

"Wow, where did that question come from?"

She gave a half embarrassed smile. "Nowhere. I guess I'm just a little distracted today."

He returned the uncomfortable smile.

"When might we catch a glimpse of this comet?" Krynut asked.

"It vill circle round Domrysly in about six months, and swing by Ulutrita on its way out of our system," Professor Ymyl answered.

Mihyn forced herself to concentrate on the astronomer's factual description of the coming event. Try as she might, her focus was not on the speaker. A powerful sense of urgency swept over her. After several anxious moments, Mihyn quietly rose up out of her chair, slid it back as noiselessly as possible, and ducked around the end of the table.

A gush of relief swept through her as she exited the hall. Mihyn was so absorbed in her thoughts, she didn't even see Professor Myrvst standing in the doorway. Just as she passed, he gently laid a hand on her shoulder.

"Is anything wrong?"

It took Mihyn a moment to get over the surprise of his touch. She looked down at the polished floor, then back up at him. "Yes, something is wrong, but I don't know what it is."

Myrvst scrutinized her face as she spoke. Agitation and confusion drew lines in her soft skin. He looped his arm around hers. "Come on, let's go over and see what Kryzyck is up to."

The two of them walked across the now mostly empty foyer. Blrsynt, Sylstyn, and the old miner were taking turns tuning the device. When the two academics approached, Kryzyck set the crystal down, and flexed his cramped fingers.

"Regent, Professor, how goes it?"

"Have you been able to get it to produce any sounds?" Myrvst asked.

"On and off. Nothing for the last half hour."

The professor nodded, then looked over at Mihyn. She stood with the colorfully embroidered sleeves of her robe wrapped tightly across her chest. Her dark brown eyes tried to bore a hole into the apparatus.

"Regent, what's on your mind?"

"Are there any of those pynfyrs left?"

Sylstyn burst out laughing, then quickly stifled it. She held the basket out to Mihyn. The regent reached in and pulled a cluster of small red fruit out without looking up.

"Thanks." Everyone watched her carefully pluck the oblong fruit off the stem and slip them between her lips. After finishing the cluster, she turned toward Myrvst. "So, Professor, where do you think these voices are originating from?"

Myrvst pondered the question for a moment, scratched his tangled grey beard, then answered. "That's the question isn't it. We can transmit electrical signals across wires many hundreds of miles, but I'm at a loss to explain what is going on here. If we could understand what was being said, it would certainly make it easier to pinpoint the source."

"Right, I'm familiar with many of the languages spoken on our small planet. What I've heard come out of this is totally foreign to me."

"And what about that beautiful music we heard last night? I for one have never heard anything like that!" Sylstyn tossed out.

Mihyn snapped her head of wavy dark hair around to face the young woman. "Music? You heard music coming out of this?"

"Yes, incredible music. It made the Plykyn folk songs sound primitive," Myrvst added.

Mihyn stood without moving. She gave a huff of disbelief, shook her head a couple times, and let out a nervous laugh.

"I can really think of only two explanations. First and most probable, is that somehow you have managed to find some unknown language being spoken, even though my department has been cataloguing every one being spoken here for over a hundred years. The second, and I admit, wild possibility is that these transmissions did not originate on Ulutrita." The regent let her audacious statement sink in. "Can you try and find the voice again?"

Kryzyck repositioned his fingers around the precious crystal and began rotating it. Static surged and died several times. At three-quarters of a turn, a bit of garbled speech shot out of the horn. Mihyn took a step forward and grabbed his arm.

"Alright, here goes. Everyone, we're taking this into the hall. I'm going to get in big, big trouble for this, but ever since I heard that voice counting down, I've been unable to concentrate. We have to show this to the forum. Come on. Should we disconnect it?"

"Regent, are you sure about this? We've already had one altercation in there today. I'm guessing if we mention that these transmissions might be coming from somewhere out in space, we could have another fight on our hands." Myrvst sent a concerned glance toward the packed lecture hall.

"It doesn't matter. My intuition is screaming at me to do this. I can't ignore it. Come on, we better get in there." Mihyn's voice cracked slightly at the end of her request.

"I can walk and hold this. Blrsynt, can you carry the table?" Kryzyck asked.

"Sure."

The young man rose up off the bench, picked up the wooden table, and followed his uncle across the polished floor. Mihyn led the group up to the doorway into the hall. She stopped right at the threshold and turned to signal a halt.

Another presenter had just finished speaking. Applause rippled around the audience. Mihyn took a deep breath and strode into the hall.

At that same time, Bokyl stood up to introduce the next speaker. He caught sight of Mihyn coming down the main aisle. She made eye contact with him and walked right around the end of the horseshoe shaped table. Bokyl's round ruddy face contracted into a frown as she approached. Mihyn stopped right next to him. Her eyes blazed with a dark ferocity.

"Honorable Head Regent, I have a request."

"And that is?"

"Professor Myrvst was shown an invention yesterday that may have incredible significance to our culture. I would like to request he be given permission to give an immediate demonstration."

"Now?"

"Yes, now. Trust me Head Regent, this is something truly incredible."

Bokyl glanced out at the audience, over at Mihyn, down at the other two regents, then back at her. "I don't have to tell you that this is highly irregular. Highly irregular. I'll need to consult with the other two."

He walked down to where Krynut was sitting and leaned his considerable bulk forward. The mathematician was reading a stack of papers when the head regent appeared in front of him.

"What's the hold up?"

"Regent Mihyn has requested that we interrupt the regular schedule to let Professor Myrvst demonstrate some kind of new invention."

"Myrvst was here with his invention yesterday." Krynut laid his sheath of papers down and folded his hands over them.

Professor Myrvst had been watching the scene unfold from up at the foyer doorway. As soon as the head regent had approached Krynut, the professor began calmly walking down the center aisle and around the end of the horseshoe shaped table. He stopped right next to Mihyn. Bokyl looked over from his position in front of the mathematician.

"Professor Myrvst! What's this all about?" The head regent's gruff voice was now charged with emotion. His entire round frame appeared to be shaking slightly.

Murmurs of concern rose up from the crowd. Myrvst bit his lip. He could sense the rising tension in the room.

Regent Mihyn recognized the indecision on the professor's face. She laid a gentle hand on his arm. "Professor, it's okay. We can do this."

Her soothing words dropped the professor's anxiety just enough to allow him to speak. "Head Regent, as a special favor, I would like to request fifteen minutes of the forum's time."

Bokyl took in the request and pondered it for a moment. His face and bald head had begun to turn from pink to an alarming shade of scarlet. He directed his attention to the mathematician. "And what is your opinion on this highly irregular request?"

Krynut was his usual calm, unflappable self. He stroked his goatee several times before answering. "Seems to me that if the professor and Regent Mihyn think this demonstration is so important, it must be of some merit. I vote we allow them to proceed."

Bokyl turned his sweating, bright red face toward Handynr. "And you Regent?"

"I concur with Regent Krynut." Handynr shot a seething, scornful glance up at his wife. "Mihyn! What's going on here?" he whispered loudly. His voice was a mixture of confusion and anger.

Bokyl eased himself from a leaning to standing position and held his arms high. "Professor Myrvst has requested that we interrupt the normal proceedings to allow him to demonstrate some new invention. Bailiff! Please let me know when fifteen minutes is up!"

All eyes watched the two miners carry the device down the center aisle and follow Myrvst up onto the stage. Mihyn scooted around the end of the table, then plunked down next to her husband. Handynr scrutinized her face once she had settled.

Her skin was pale white, and she was sweating. Mihyn's intense dark eyes were beginning to glaze over. She stared at the stage without blinking. Her dry lips moved in silence. Handynr reached over and grasped her hand. It was shaking slightly.

"Dear, are you alright?"

"Actually, no. I feel terrible."

Just as Handynr was going to offer some sympathy, the professor's loud voice drew everyone's attention to the stage.

"Members of the forum and esteemed guests, thank you for giving us the opportunity to demonstrate this most incredible discovery." His opening words sent whispers of excitement through the crowd. "I'd like to introduce Mr. Kryzyck and his nephew, Mr. Blrsynt. Several days ago, they approached me with the simple device you see here."

Myrvst motioned toward the low table positioned near the front of the stage. Kryzyck held the galena crystal in his hand and looked out at the wall of faces staring in his direction. Panic began to well up inside him.

"Kryzyck! Start tuning." the professor said out of the corner of his mouth.

"What? Oh, okay." The old miner secured his grip on the crystal, and began rotating it, degree by degree. Static popped and hissed out of the horn. At one quarter of a turn, the hiss of static was broken by a loud blip. Kryzyck stopped turning the piece of galena and eased it back in the opposite direction.

The static lowered in intensity. It was replaced by the sound of a faint voice. With several more millimeters of tuning, the voice became surprisingly clear. What now issued out of the black lacquer horn was an experimental radio test from the University of Oslo.

From her seat at the table, Mihyn's anxiety level dropped. She squeezed her husband's hand and leaned toward him. "See, isn't it amazing?"

"Well, what exactly is it? I can't understand a word of what is being said."

"Neither can I. This seems to be a totally different language than what we've heard before."

The voice continued speaking in a slow methodical manner for several moments, then ended with the characteristic rise in tone that accompanied the delivery of a question. Myrvst gave the old miner a satisfied nod and turned back toward the audience.

Throughout the hall, whispers and low conversations about the meaning of the demonstration circulated. The professor looked down at the four regents sitting at the table. They all stared back at him with rapt attention.

"So, I'm sure many of you are now asking the question? What did I just hear?" Heads nodded all across the seated audience. "Anyone care to venture an answer?"

For several moments, there were no takers to his offer. Much discussion, and more than one short burst of laughter echoed off the stone walls. A hand shot up in the sixth row. Myrvst pointed to the wide-shouldered man, and he rose up out of his seat.

"It's obviously a human voice, speaking in some strange language."

"I think we all can agree with that. The next question is, where is this voice originating from?"

The individual standing bent over to confer with those seated beside him. After a moment of discussion and nodding of heads, he straightened back up, and looked directly at the professor. "I think that the speaker is somewhere in this building. Correct?"

Hands shot up all round the room. Myrvst pointed over at a dark skinned man dressed in a particularly brightly colored stripped robe. The man rose to his feet.

"I think the voice is being transferred by wires from somewhere in the city, or maybe another city."

A smile broke across Myrvst's wrinkled face. "A good guess, but look at the setup. Do you see any wires leading off the stage?"

More animated conversations circulated amongst the crowd. From his seat at the table, Bokyl turned toward the bailiff standing off to the side, and spoke in a loud, commanding voice. "Bailiff! How much time left?"

The official looked down at his pocket watch. "Seven minutes!"

"Professor, you have seven minutes to finish your demonstration. This game of questions is amusing, but time is running out."

The smile dropped off Myrvst's face. His countenance became determined and serious. "Thank you for helping to keep me on track. The voice you just heard is being transmitted wirelessly, that is obvious. Where it is originating is the big question. Regent Mihyn, will you give us your expert opinion on where this strange language is being spoken from? And let me remind the audience that the regent is one of the most respected linguists we have at the Academy."

Mihyn pushed her chair back and got to her feet. After turning to face the audience, she gripped the back of the chair for dear life.

"My name is Regent Mihyn. Many of know me, many don't. I am one of the directors of the linguistics branch here at the Academy. To the best of our knowledge, six hundred and eighty-three languages are actively spoken on our small, styrky planet. I'm fluent in seventeen of them. My personal opinion is that the voice you just heard, and one I heard earlier are not speaking in any tongue that originated here."

The hall erupted with excited discussions. From the far left side of the audience, a man with curly black hair and a long black beard jumped to his feet. "What are you suggesting? That the voices come from outer space? I'll tell you what they are! They are dark spirits that have invaded this hall! We need to....."

The man's angry harangue was drowned out by a chorus of boos and cat calls. Seated behind the curly haired man was Lycrk. He leaned over and shook the speaker's hand vigorously.

"Time's up!" the bailiff yelled.

"Thanks to Zym," Bokyl muttered. He got to his feet, and once again held his arms aloft. "Quiet! Everyone! Please restrain yourselves. I will not allow this forum to become a krydytr."

Gradually, all the heated discussions became subdued, then ended. When he was assured that the audience were all listening, Bokyl continued.

"Regent Mihyn, Professor Myrvst, I thank you for taking your time to present this most interesting demonstration. I'm an educator by trade and have little trained experience in the matters you are presenting. We have another several hours of presentations today, but I would like to recommend that the Academy investigate this phenomenon, eh, device, further. Next presenter please."

Chapter 5.

"Blrsynt, grab the table. Let's get out of here!" Kryzyck commanded while he began to coil up wire.

The two men carried the device off the stage, with Myrvst close behind. Mihyn watched them carefully pick their way down the stage steps, and up the aisle.

"I'll be right back," she whispered to her husband.

"Actually, I have to be over at the city administrative building in twenty minutes, so I guess I'll see you at home. Kym, my secretary said she was going to pick me up. She should be showing up any minute." Handynr flashed a quick smile at his wife before she turned and made her way out of the hall.

Halfway up the aisle, a young, somewhat thick bodied woman with pleasant roundish features stopped to greet Mihyn. "Hello Regent! I mean, Mrs. Third Line."

The exuberant greeting caused Mihyn to pause. "Nice to see you Kym."

"Do you know where Handynr, I mean Regent, I mean, oh! I need to slow down. My its stuffy in here!" The secretary fanned herself with a sheath of papers.

"Yes it is. He's right down there. Excuse me, but I need to...."

"Oh, I see him. Handynr! Come on, you're going to be late!"

Mihyn continued up the aisle. She let go a sigh of relief upon entering the cool, high ceilinged foyer. Against the wall, the two miners were securing the device for travel. Myrvst, his assistant, and his housekeeper were standing nearby. Sylstyn's face was shining with elation.

"Wow! That was the most lively forum session I've ever seen!"

Myrvst glanced back into the hall, then gently grabbed her arm. "We were lucky to get out of there in one piece. Let's pack this up, and head home."

Kryzyck finished wrapping up the wires and rose up from his crouch. "Anytime people start talking about dark spirits and such, it's time to leave. Blrsynt, let's carry this right out the front door."

Lynflyn hurried in front of them. When he opened one of the big copper doors, a gush of dry, dusty air blew in.

"I can't believe its late afternoon. What a day!" Kryzyck exclaimed as he left the building.

Back in the foyer, Mihyn and the professor had just arrived at the front doors. Before pushing on the latch, she turned to face him. "Can you bring the device to the afternoon linguistics department meeting tomorrow?"

"I don't see why not. You were brave to stand before the forum and make that claim about where the voices might be coming from. Together, we'll have to prove it. Right now, I want to go home, eat a nice pyryst, drink some mynth, and collapse into my chair. See you tomorrow."

Mihyn leaned forward and kissed his leathery cheek. A chorus of footsteps echoed off to their right.

"There they are! Blasphemers!"

Both the academicians turned to see what the source of the angry shouts was. A group of eight people, including Lycrk and the curly haired man from the hall came jogging toward them.

"Uh oh, this doesn't look good. Go, I'll try and stall them," Mihyn motioned toward the door.

Outside the building, Sylstyn and the old miner were gazing up at the dusty sunset just beginning to color the sky when the copper door behind them burst open.

"Where's Blrsynt and Lynflyn?" Myrvst asked.

"They went to get the styrns. Why?" Sylstyn sent a concerned glance over at him.

"There's a gang of Lycrk's followers coming this way. Come on, we have to go! You grab the wires. Kryzyck, can you carry the table?"

The old miner peered through the door glass and caught a glimpse of Mihyn standing defiantly on the other side. "Ya, sure." He bent down, grabbed the edges of the simple wooden table, and began to work his way down the marble steps.

Inside the foyer, Mihyn was trying to retain her composure. "I'm not here to engage in a theological discussion with you. As a scientist, my job is to observe natural phenomenon, and try to understand and explain it."

"And as a man of faith, my job is to identify evil, and eradicate it!" Lycrk boomed. His followers let out a resounding cheer. "Now if you'll excuse us, we'd like to continue outside and destroy that device before it corrupts all who listen to it!" Lycrk stood right in front of Mihyn. He waited for her to step out of the way, then with a huff of disgust, side stepped past her. "This way!"

As his followers passed by her, Mihyn caught snatches of whispered admonishments.

"Conjurer!"

"Corruptor!"

"You should stay at home!"

Lycrk burst out of the doors and scanned the sidewalk at the base of the steps. "Down there! They're getting away!" He hiked up the edges of his brilliantly colored robe and hopped down the steps. His supporters followed close behind.

On the street below, Kryzyck looked up when he heard the shout. "Oh great, here they come." He took his eyes off the rabid group descending toward him and searched the street for Blrsynt. A number of buggies passed back and forth. He finally spotted his nephew's big frame bobbing toward the Academy. "There he is! We're going to have to make a run for it."

Blrsynt rode along the rough cobblestone street whistling happily. "What a day! I sure didn't expect to have to stand up on that stage. And then the regent says she thinks the voices are coming from outer space! Could the day get any more weird?"

He directed the styrns into an empty spot about a block from the main building. His uncle's shout rang out just as he was pulling up to the curb. Blrsynt stood up on the floorboards of the wooden wagon, and tried to ascertain what was going on. He jumped down from the seat once he caught sight of his uncle and Sylstyn running down the sidewalk carrying the device. When the two of them arrived at the wagon, they were both heaving for breath.

"Those people.....Lycrk's followers.....we have to go!" Sylstyn sputtered.

"Why're they chasing you?" the nephew asked after reaching out to take the wooden table from his uncle.

Kryzyck bent over, took a couple deep breaths, then straightened up and put a hand on his nephew's solid shoulder. "They think the voices are coming from some kind of dark spirit. They want to destroy it."

Blrsynt's big wide face contorted into a frown. Without saying another word, he took the coil of wires from Sylstyn, and carried the device around to the back of the wagon. Just as he was placing it into the wagon bed, the first of Lycrk's incensed group arrived.

"Stop! Don't even try to get away. We're going to smash that horrible thing to bits!" a thin, wiry man with intense dark eyes screamed. He gave Sylstyn a hard shove.

She flew over the curb, and thankfully caught herself against the wooden slats of the wagon. "Blyrthole!" she hissed.

The man reached up and grabbed Blrsynt's right arm.

"Let go of me!" the nephew growled between gritted teeth.

"I'm sorry but I have......" A hard left hook silenced the man. He slid against the wagon and lay sprawled across the curb.

"Get in, let's make a run for it!" Blrsynt commanded.

Out in the middle of the street, Lynflyn came rolling up in the buggy. He spotted Myrvst standing red faced and winded. Lycrk's riled up mob streamed past the exhausted professor. The assistant pulled the buggy to a halt and yelled to his employer.

"Professor! Over here! Come on."

Myrvst wasted no time hobbling over the curb, and out to the waiting buggy. Once he had crawled inside, Lynflyn gave a crack of his whip. The two sandy brown styrns reared back slightly, then took off.

Blrsynt had just hopped up into the seat of the wagon. He reached down and pulled Sylstyn up beside him. Just as she was hauling herself up onto the seat, one of Lycrk's followers, a woman with narrow, pointed features, grabbed her ankle.

"Oh no you don't! You're not getting away this time!"

Sylstyn steadied herself with her free leg, tightened her grip on Blrsynt's hand, and planted her heel right in the woman's forehead. Her aggressor let go and toppled backward onto the sidewalk. Kryzyck has halfway up into the back of the wagon when Sylstyn unleashed the one-footed donkey kick. He grabbed the wooden slats and yelled up to his nephew.

"What're ya waitin' for boy? Let's get out of here! There's more of them coming."

"Okay Uncle. Hang on!"

Blrsynt gave the reins a hard slap. The styrns responded with their characteristic bawling honk. "Hee ya!" he called out to them.

Long, clawed toes dug into the cobblestones, and the wagon lurched out into the street. One of the rear wheels ran over the ankle of the man Blrsynt had decked. The pain of the impact brought him back to consciousness, and he let out a yell.

"Sorry," Kryzyck offered as they sped away.

Several of Lycrk's people chased them down the street, then gave up after a couple blocks. Upon reaching the main boulevard, Blrsynt ventured a glance over his shoulder, and seeing no one in pursuit, he pulled back slightly on the reins.

"You okay back there, Uncle?"

Kryzyck let go with one hand and shook some blood back into his fingers. "Ya, I'm fine. What a crazy bunch those people are! Turn up there."

He pointed toward the alley running next to Myrvst's modest house. Blrsynt guided the wagon along the thick hedge that ran along the alley. Lynflyn met them at the back of the house. He jogged out and grabbed the harness of the styrn closest to him.

"Is everybody alright? The professor is wiped out! He isn't used to running for his life."

Blrsynt pulled back hard on the reins, and the rangy animals came to a halt. He looked down at Sylstyn. She smiled up at him. "Yes, I think we're all fine. Whew! That was some get away!"

Kryzyck dropped down off the back of the wagon and walked around to side. "We better get the device back into the house. Who knows if those maniacs have followed us. Blrsynt, hand it down to me."

After stowing the device back in the workroom, the two miners joined the rest of the group in the dining room. Sylstyn and Lynflyn were busy filling glasses with an orange-colored liquid. Professor Myrvst sat at the head of the table. When his two guests entered the room, he motioned for them to sit.

"Gentlemen, glad to see we all made it back in one piece." The professor managed to smile despite being exhausted.

Kryzyck pulled a chair back and sat down hard. "Me too. I just wish we had been able to convince the forum of how important this discovery is. With all the chaos, it feels like it got overshadowed. Not sure what our next step is."

"That's already been decided for us," Myrvst replied. After taking a drink from the glass handed to him, he lowered his gaze and looked the miner square in the face. "We managed to impress Regent Mihyn enough that she wants us to bring the device into the weekly linguistics department meeting tomorrow."

Sylstyn let loose a squeal of joy. "That's great! They are just the people who need to hear it." She bent over and gave Myrvst a hug. "I hope you all are hungry, because I surely am."

The group devoured the quick dinner she put together. After finishing his plate, Blrsynt got up from his chair, and began clearing the table.

"You don't have to do that," Sylstyn said in a demure voice.

"I know I don't have to, but it's the least I can do. Uncle and I aren't used to having someone fix our meals for us."

By the time they finished putting the dishes away, Lynflyn had gone home, and Kryzyck was asleep in one of the parlor chairs. Myrvst came walking into the kitchen.

"Looks like you two have it under control." He continued past the young people and opened the back door. "What a lovely night." A powerful fragrance from the backyard blew into the kitchen.

"Wow, what is that wonderful smell?" Blrsynt exclaimed. He wedged himself next to the professor in the open door jamb and drew in a great breath of the delicate scent.

"Ah, that is the kymlyn tree you're smelling. It only blooms this time of year. That specimen is over forty years old."

"It certainly is nice," the young man commented. "Sylstyn, come over and smell this."

The housekeeper wiped her hands on a towel and walked over to the open door. Blrsynt stepped back to allow her full access to the outside. He watched expectantly as she closed her long-lashed eyelids and took a whiff.

"Mmmmm, oh, that is nice! It must be coming from those gorgeous purple and white nymfyrs. It's such a lovely night, such soft still air. We should go out and sit on the bench."

Myrvst yawned and gave a little wave before heading back toward the living room. "I'm exhausted. You two go ahead."

The young people bade him a goodnight and strolled out into the backyard. They settled onto the well-worn stone bench set up perpendicular to the house. Blrsynt stretched his arm out along the top of the granite bench. Sylstyn leaned back, letting her medium length auburn hair fall across his arm.

"What a gorgeous night!" she whispered.

Blrsynt nodded. He was thoroughly enjoying himself. Without thinking, she slid a couple inches closer to him, and leaned her shoulder into his chest. He gently stroked her hair. Sylstyn turned her head toward him, and their eyes met.

"It sure is nice having you and your uncle here."

"It's nice being here. I've worked out at the crater with Uncle for four years now. A little change of scenery is just what I needed."

Blrsynt took a long, leisurely scan of her big green eyes. He could hardly contain the emotion welling up inside his youthful heart. On impulse, he bent down to kiss her. Just before contact, she turned away.

"Please don't. I have a boyfriend, sort of."

The ambiguity of her last words, and doubtful emphasis of her voice brought Blrsynt back from the precipice of despair. "What do you mean, sort of?"

Sylstyn straightened up and turned to face him. "My boyfriend, we've been seeing each other for about two years, works as a mag driver. I only see him about four times a year. His name is Ryk. He's one of the best mag ropers there is. Last year, he won....."

"You're not talking about the Ryk? Are you? Ryk Sixth Line?" Sylstyn nodded her head. Blrsynt's heart sank. He didn't know much about mag driving, but everyone knew who Ryk Sixth Line was.

"Like I said, I only see him about four times a year. Every time he shows up, my bed always gets full of sand, it's really, oh, oops....."

Sylstyn cut herself off and blushed from forehead to chin. She saw the disappointment in Blrsynt's eyes. He quickly looked away. The intoxicating smell of the flowers and soft night air didn't seem so wonderful anymore. There were a couple agonizing moments of silence, then Sylstyn let out a prolonged sigh.

"The thing about Ryk is, being a mag rider, and being so famous, he has lots of girls. You know what they say about mag riders, a girl at every drive stop."

She watched his face out of the corner of her eye. There was still a look of pain spread across his broad features, then the smallest trace of a smile appeared. He tilted his head around to make eye contact. She folded her hands in her lap and tried to look apologetic. It worked. Blrsynt managed to rip off a short, ironic laugh. He reached over to give her a light slap on the knee.

"It must be tough having guys chasing after you all the time."

"I really wouldn't know about that. Ryk is the only boyfriend I've had lately, and he is only part time. What about you? There must be some girls in that town out there that you like."

Blrsynt crossed his legs and leaned back against the back of the bench. He stared up at the sky full of stars. "No actually, I don't have a girlfriend. Hey it's getting late. We better go in." He uncrossed his legs and eased himself forward. Sylstyn remained where she was.

"I suppose you're right. I really enjoyed sitting out here with you," she said quietly. In a flash of movement, she rose up, planted a warm, moist kiss on his cheek, then scampered across the lawn and into the house. Blrsynt sat there stunned and perplexed. After a moment, he rose slowly, and went inside also.

Chapter 6.

The next morning after a quick breakfast, Myrvst took the two miners clothes shopping. Sylstyn was washing windows up on a ladder when the crunch of buggy wheels on the street out front caused her to twist around. Kryzyck was the first to step out of the cab. The housekeeper let out a joyous squeal when she caught sight of the miner's crisp new striped shirt and snappy black vest. She scrambled dangerously fast down the ladder. Blrsynt hopped down from the driver seat and stretched his arms out in a modeling pose.

"Look at you two! What a transformation!" Sylstyn ran up and adjusted the collar of Blrsynt's green, button down shirt. He looked down at her pretty roundish face and long eyelashes. A quiver of excitement ran through him as her fingers slid around his neck. "There, that looks better."

Myrvst was the last one out of the cab. "Never mind the primping. We need to get the device loaded and head over to the Academy. I don't want to be late."

While the two miners went to retrieve the device, Sylstyn collected an arrangement of grooming aids. She returned to the front of the house carrying a stylish glass squirt bottle, a container of hair oil, and a large gold comb. When the uncle and nephew walked past her, she blasted both of them with a puff of cologne.

"Hey! Watch out! That almost hit me in the eyes." Blrsynt blinked several times.

"Sorry, stop moving for a minute."

Kryzyck stood in the middle of the sidewalk holding the horn and a loop of wire. Sylstyn set the perfume bottle down, shook some oil onto his unruly white hair, and combed furiously.

"Just, hold, on, one, minute." When she was done, the old miner's hair was styled into a high back flip above his forehead. "There you look great."

Myrvst drove the wagon around front, the device was loaded up, and off the trio went. At the main cross street, they could see lines of spectators on both sides of the wide avenue.

"Wonder what's going on?" Blrsynt pondered out loud.

"Oh that's right. This weekend is the mag roundup. Every year, they have a parade to celebrate the return of the mag drivers. There's a big party Dyrn day night. You and Syl might want to go," Myrvst said with a grin.

Moments later, they arrived at the Academy, unloaded the device, and hurried up to the third floor. While he led the way down the hallway, Myvst spoke over his shoulder.

"Looks like we'll make it with five minutes to spare. As soon as we get there, you two get the device set up." Once they reached the open doorway, he straightened the lapels of his well-used tweed suit coat, and swept in. His arrival drew the attention of the four women seated at the long table.

"Members of the linguistics board! Thank you so much for allowing us to demonstrate the, er, the device. We haven't named it yet. I would like to introduce Mr. Kryzyck, and his nephew, Mr. Blrsynt." The two miners filed in behind him and lined up against the wall. "Go ahead and put the table over there."

After the nephew set the device down, the professor continued with his introductions. "You two already know Regent Mihyn. This is Professor Rymnyr, Professor Nygnt, and Professor Hyntym."

As each linguist was introduced, the two miners dutifully nodded a greeting. Seated next to Mihyn was a somewhat portly woman with graying, piled up hair. Her middle aged features still reflected the beauty of her youth. Next to her was a dark skinned woman with a long, angular face. At the far end of the table, an older woman with big black glasses looked up from her notes when her name was mentioned, smiled briefly, then went back to her work.

It only took Myrvst and the two miners a couple minutes to get the device set up. Once the last wire was connected,

Kryzyck stood up, and held the galena crystal out toward Myrvst.

The professor shook his head. "Would you do the honors?"

Kryzyck wiped the sweat off his creased palms and pinched the metallic cube between his thumb and index finger. Myrvst turned to face the linguists.

"Very well, we're almost ready to begin. Before we start, I'd like Mr. Kryzyck to briefly describe how he discovered this amazing phenomenon."

"Well, uh, several weeks ago, I mean I think it was about a week ago, I uh, was carrying this spool of wire down the wall of the crater. I used to wear this galena crystal on a leather thong around my neck. I was kind of tired that day and fell off the trail. When I rolled down the hill, one end of the wire got jammed in the crack on this crystal, and the other end jammed into my skull, just behind my ear." Several of the women gasped. Kryzyck let out a quick laugh, then continued.

"It really wasn't that bad. Anyway, the leather thong was choking me, so as I unwound it, I heard voices inside my head. At first I thought I had just hit my head and was imagining it, but as I turned the crystal, the voices got louder, then drifted away. My nephew and I decided to come here to show Professor Myrvst what we had discovered."

All the women all nodded in approval. Professor Rymnyr raised her hand just as Kryzyck was about to continue. "You're not going to jam that wire into your skull today are you?"

"No. Professor Myrvst has used his considerable knowledge to improve on the accidental design."

Rymnyr smiled at him and nodded. Again, her hand went up. "One more question. What is it that you do for a living?"

"My nephew and I operate a metal mine in Crater one hundred forty-eight A."

"So you just work there?"

"No, I'm the owner."

Professor Nygnt turned her head of tight black curls toward her colleague. Her long, dark face was pulled down into a frown. "Can we get on with the demonstration?" she asked in a heavily accented voice.

"Yes of course. I was just trying to get some perspective on things," Rymnyr answered. She shot a sideways glance over at Nygnt. A forced smile briefly moved her red lips.

Kryzyck waited a moment to see if there were any further questions, and perceiving none, began to rotate the crystal. When all eyes had been drawn back to the old miner, Rymnyr leaned right next to Mihyn's ear, and whispered in the lowest volume possible.

"Black bitch!"

Mihyn lifted her pointed toed shoe under the table and gave her a light kick in the shin.

Loud static crackled out of the black lacquer horn. After the crystal had been turned approximately one quarter of the way round, a noticeable blip interrupted the annoying hiss of the static. Kryzyck let out the breath he had been holding, and ever so slowly, backed the shiny metallic crystal up. In a flash, a surprisingly clear voice issued from the horn.

"This is Ensign Thomas McFarlane, broadcasting from Bethesda, Maryland. Newport News, do you copy? Again, this is Ensign Thomas McFarlane, broadcasting from Bethesda, Maryland. Newport News, do you copy?"

Kryzyck held the crystal as motionless as his fingers were able. He glanced over at the women seated across the room. They were conversing in excited voices amongst themselves. Mihyn had risen up out of her chair.

"So far, I've heard two distinct languages being spoken by this thing, whatever it is. What you just heard is the most common. Anybody want to venture a guess as to the origin?"

Professor Hyntym pushed her chair back several inches, folded her long fingers together, and began to speak in her characteristic dead pan, emotionless voice. "Based on what little we heard, I would tend to lump this language in with the Plyntyn group. That is just a preliminary assessment." She turned away from the other women and directed her attention to Kryzyck. "Could you produce another example of that type of speech, please."

"I'll try." He carefully began rotating the crystal again.

"If I might jump in here. So far, the voices we've been able to generate have been largely random. Sometimes it's hours before we receive anything," Myrvst chimed in. The sound of someone clearing their throat from the direction of the open door to the hallway drew the attention of the group.

"Excuse me, but I just heard some very unusual voices a minute ago, and uh, who was speaking?" Professor Grylt, the diminutive biology professor searched the surprised faces of those present from his place in the doorway.

"Ah, Professor, come in!" Rymnyr held out her hand and motioned for Grylt to enter. He tip-toed over and stood back from the main table. "We were just listening to voices coming out of this amazing new invention, er discovery."

Professor Myrvst gave his colleague a welcoming nod, then turned back toward Kryzyck. "Proceed."

The old miner began to slowly rotate the crystal. Above the static, another loud blip rattled out of the horn. Kryzyck eased the cubic crystal back a few millimeters.

"This is Dover ferry station to Calais ferry station. Do you copy?" a Yorkshire-accented voice rang out.

"Calais ferry station here, oui, I copy, over."

"Right then, ferry just departing. Eighty-six passengers on board. Relatively high seas today, bloody strong wind blowing out of the south. Anticipate ferry will be between half hour and forty minutes late due to weather conditions, do you copy?"

"Dover ferry station, what was the last thing you said, over."

"Ferry will most probably be late by between thirty and forty minutes, do you copy?"

"Oui, ferry will be late, over."

Professor Rymnyr clapped her hands together. "That was marvelous! Two distinct voices conversing." She shifted in her seat and turned toward Myrvst. "So professor, where to start? First of all, congratulations on your new discovery. I'm not even going to ask you how it works. We'll save that for later. Most importantly, have you determined where these voices are originating from?"

In true professorial fashion, Myrvst stroked his tangled grey beard, folded his arms across his chest, and strode across the room. He stopped in front of the long table and looked up and down at the faces of the board.

"Professor Rymnyr and distinguished members of the board, I wish I could take credit for this amazing invention, but I really have to defer the honor to Mr. Kryzyck. If it were not for his fortunate accident last week, we might never have been able to witness this."

He turned at the waist and held out his arm toward the old miner. The board responded with a round of polite applause. Kryzyck bowed slightly. Myrvst returned his gaze to the four women seated before him.

"As to the geographic origin of these transmissions, I haven't a clue. My hope is that you will be able to identify the languages being spoken so I may organize an expedition to find the source and congratulate whoever it is that's producing them."

"Well, the last conversation appears to have been between two persons speaking the same language but with very different inflections," Professor Nygnt concluded. Her smooth, rich dark voice perfectly matched her smooth, dark skin.

Mihyn listened intently to her colleague's analysis. She could hardly contain her excitement. The short, painted fingernails of her left hand drummed nervously on the tabletop. Her great desire was for one of the board members to suggest that the voices were not from a Ulutritan source.

"It will certainly take some very careful examination of the syntax and word structure to even begin to decipher what is being said. Upon preliminary observation, I would say that I personally have never heard anything quite like this spoken here on Ulutrita. Would you all agree?" Rymnyr tossed out.

Professor Nygnt nodded her head. Seated next to her, Hyntym adjusted her thick black glasses before answering.

"As I said earlier, it bears some resemblance to the Plyntyn languages, particularly those spoken by the older members of that population."

Rymnyr took a moment to evaluate her colleague's comment. "With all due respect, I disagree. Having travelled extensively in the Krygyvyr region, I'm familiar with both classic and colloquial Plyntyn, and you are correct, the way this new kind of speech drops off tonally is similar, but I heard none of the tongue clicks that make Plyntyn so difficult to transcribe. In just the short amount of speech we heard, I jotted down several common words that I believe could be translated." She held up a sheet of paper covered with hastily scrawled notes.

Hyntym reached over and took the paper from her. The stoic professor silently mouthed the transcriptions her colleague had written down. Mihyn couldn't hold her opinion inside any longer.

"Yesterday, after hearing just a few phrases of this, and another language which I was unable to place, I came to a rather startling conclusion. I'm not known to jump to improbable explanations for things of which I have little understanding."

The pause in her statement gave Rymnyr a chance to jump in. "Well, out with it then! Right now you're talking in circles, and I for one am barely able to guess what comes next."

Mihyn looked over at her friend's gracefully aging face. She knew that Rymnyr could be savagely critical if presented with a theory that wasn't rock solid. She also knew what a long shot the explanation she was about to offer represented. Mihyn drew in a quick breath, then spoke in a rapid, anxious tone.

"Although I agree that it will take more studious analysis to determine exactly what is being said by these voices, I'm going to take a chance and venture that these transmissions as Professor Myrvst called them, are not originating on this planet."

Her audacious theory produced immediate reactions from the board. Nygnt made a hissing, clucking sound which among her people was indicative of disagreement. Rymnyr held a hand to her painted lips. She didn't want to laugh out loud. From her place at the end of the table, Professor Hyntym leaned forward, and stared at Mihyn.

"Did I hear you correctly. Not from this planet?"

Mihyn felt her face flush. Her lips quivered. All her confidence began to melt away.

"A most interesting theory," Myrvst pipped up. His words broke the tense silence. "That would certainly explain why the languages spoken, and the method of transmission are so unfamiliar."

"Well I for one am not willing to present such a preposterous idea to anyone till conclusive evidence can be produced!" Nygnt proclaimed. She straightened up, and sat in a most erect, defiant manner.

Professor Rymnyr shoved her chair back a couple inches and reclined in the space created. Her head tilted back over the top of the chair. She slid her feet slid forward till they almost touched Myrvst's polished shoes.

"Whooee! You are really stretching yourself out on a limb this time."

Rymnyr rolled her head over and stared at Mihyn. The younger regent struggled to regain her steely composure. She didn't know quite what to say. Mihyn swallowed hard and looked across the room at Kryzyck and his nephew.

"What do you two think?"

Kryzyck just shrugged. Blrsynt had been leaning against the wall, off in his own world through much of the discussion. When the pleasant but stern faced regent addressed him, he snapped to attention.

"I really don't know about the voices being from some other planet. What I do find interesting is that the voices seem much louder and clearer up here. What I'm wondering is, does being up on the third floor make all the difference?"

"That too is an interesting theory. There's one easy way to test it. We could go up on the roof." Myrvst answered before strolling back over to the table.

"I have a lecture to give in fifteen minutes. You'll have to excuse me," Professor Nygnt announced in a cold, businesslike voice.

"I have things I need to do also," Hyntym added.

The two women gathered up their things and rose up from their chairs together. They paused in front of the low table that Kryzyck stood guard over.

"Thank you for demonstrating your most curious invention for us. I'm sure there will be much discussion about in the future," Hyntym said graciously.

Kryzyck focused in on her serious face and nodded. The two women whisked out of the room. Their quiet conversation trailed off behind them. The sound of Professor Rynmyr's chair scraping across the tile floor drew the attention of those remaining. She dropped her elbows down onto the table and rested her cheeks in both hands.

"Well, deary, you certainly made an impression on them."

Mihyn looked down at her painted fingernails, then over at Rymnyr. She managed to produce a weak smile. "What kind of impression that is, we'll have to wait and see. I kind of regret making that outrageous suggestion, but in a way, I'm glad I did."

Professor Grylt had been quietly observing the proceedings. He slowly raised a hand. "If I might be so bold as to offer my own...."

"Professor! Yes, tell us what your opinion is, please," Rymnyr cut in.

An impish smile broke across Grylt's impish face. "Thank you Rymy, I mean Professor. I've been all over Ulutrita, and I have a good command of three of the many languages spoken here, but I've never heard anything like what came out of that horn earlier."

Rymnyr slammed her hands down hard on the table surface. Several of the people in the room jumped slightly at the concussion.

"Don't do that! You almost gave me a heart attack," Mihyn exclaimed.

"Sorry! It's just that the two logical explanations are now so clear. Either there are several cultures hiding somewhere here on Ulutrita that none of us have ever encountered, or this device has...." Rymnyr cut off her dissertation with a loud, cackling laugh. "I almost feel foolish saying it."

"It is an interesting proposition." Professor Grylt's face was now set with seriousness. "Somehow, it seems that these two gentlemen have tapped into communications from a source not widely recognized here. Oh, what time is it? Zym! I'm going to be late! Sorry, but I have to run. My roommate will be furious with me." Grylt blew a kiss to Rymnyr and waved while slipping out the door.

Myrvst watched the professor depart, then turned toward the miner and his nephew. "It's been a long day. Shall we head home?" At the suggestion, both men began disassembling the device.

"I suppose we should all go home and ponder this most momentous event. Gentlemen, thank you so much for taking time to demonstrate your device today. We'll be in touch." Rymnyr flashed a quick glimmering smile, swept up her stack of papers, and got to her feet.

"Yes, on behalf of our department, thank you," Mihyn added as she followed the professor out of the office.

The two women walked side by side down the hall. Once they were a sufficient distance from the open door, Rymnyr whispered into her friend's ear.

"Is the white haired gentleman married?"

A short while later, Myrvst and the two miners were again bouncing along the main road back to his house. A huge cloud of brown dust rose up before them. The professor squinted at the figures approaching from the right.

"Oh dyth! I completely forgot the mag drive is going on. We should have made a detour. Oh well, I guess we sit and wait for it to pass."

On the street in front of them, a large herd of brown colored, thick bodied, bawling animals swept by. The creatures had wide, bristly muzzles and stump-like legs. At the head of the herd, a pair of trail weary mag drivers rode back and forth keeping the animals moving forward. When they crossed the main street, the driver on the left side of the herd called out to his taller, well-built comrade.

"Hey Ryk, sure is nice to be back in Tyrl, ain't it?"

"Yep, can't wait to see Syl, Lylyn, and Jyn." Ryk spit a mouthful of saliva into the dusty air.

Chapter 7.

Bright and early the next morning, the sound of the kitchen door closing and someone humming woke Blrsynt. He lay there listening to the sounds of cupboards being opened, and packages rustling for a couple minutes before rolling out of bed. While still buttoning up his shirt, Blrysnt entered the kitchen. Sylstyn had her back to him. She swung around just as he came through the doorway.

"Oh! I didn't hear you come in. For such a big guy, you sure are quiet."

"Good morning to you too."

"I'm sorry. Good morning."

Sylstyn flashed a smile that lit up the sun drenched kitchen. She picked up a stack of plates from the counter, and swept past him, pigtails flying. With a clack of china and hum of her voice, she methodically set the table.

"Oh, there's some zyd in the kettle if you want some."

Blrsynt poured himself a cup and returned to the doorway. Just watching her busily go about her duties brought a smile to his face. "You're certainly extra cheery today."

"Ryk came home last night, and ….oops!" Her smooth round cheeks flushed red. She stopped setting the table and sent a quick apologetic glance his way. "Oh, and this weekend is the big Driver's Reunion party! Tonight they have the Driver's Dance, and tomorrow is the Phrynk Roundup."

"What's the Phrynk Roundup?"

"You've never heard of it?" Blrsynt shook his head. "Every year, when the drivers bring their mags into town, they have a competition to see who the best riders and ropers are. Ryk always takes first….." Sylstyn paused to contemplate for a moment. "You wanna go?"

Her abrupt invitation took him by surprise. He stood there in shock. "Sure."

"Great, the dance starts right after dark."

Later that day, Sylstyn prepared a sumptuous dinner, and began clearing the plates off the table. Professor Myrvst pushed back in his chair. He gave a satisfied burp.

"Excuse me, Syl that was another wonderful meal. Mr. Kryzyck, would you like to smoke a gynt?"

"That sounds like a great idea." The white haired miner handed his plate to Sylstyn just as his nephew jumped up from the table.

"Here, let me give you a hand. We should probably get going." Blrsynt flashed a quick smile, scooped up an arm load of dishes, and carried them into the kitchen. He began scrubbing the dishes while Sylstyn brought the remainder of the utensils in.

"For a young guy, you're pretty good at cleaning up."

"Yeah, I guess out at the crater, I'm sort of the housekeeper." He let go a quick laugh. "I'll take care of this, why don't you go ahead and get ready."

"Sure, be right back!"

Twenty minutes later, she reappeared wearing a well-tailored cotton dress, calf length with a saucy slit in the front. Her gorgeous chestnut colored hair was swept up and secured on top. The effect accentuated her roundish pleasant features. She stopped in the doorway leading to the kitchen, held out the edges of the skirt for emphasis, and struck a pose.

"How do I look?"

Blrsynt tossed the wet towel on the counter and gave her a good look up and down. "You want my honest opinion?"

"Of course!"

"You look delightful."

"Thanks! I love this dress. It's really nice for dancing cause it hangs really loose around my legs. Shall we go?"

"We shall!"

Blrsynt crooked his elbow, and waited till she hooked her arm around it. Together, they waltzed out into the dry evening air. Myrvst was seated on the bench facing the house. When the couple emerged from the house, he stuck the smoldering gynt between his lips, and applauded.

"Sylstyn, you look marvelous. Blrsynt, take care of her. These driver dances can get wild."

"Don't worry, I'll take good care of her." He let go of her arm and headed toward the gate. "Wait here, I'll go get the wagon."

"No, no, no. You can't take a pretty girl like her to the dance in a rambling old utility wagon. Take the buggy. Lynflyn got it rigged up earlier."

"Have a good time," Kryzyck offered from his chair.

Soon, the two young people were rolling down the avenue. The closer they got to the fairgrounds, the heavier the traffic became.

"Look at all these buggies. Guess we aren't the only ones going out tonight," Blrsynt observed.

"Just wait till you see how big the dance tent is." Sylstyn just happened to look up at the eastern sky. A huge streak of orange sliced across the reddish glow of twilight. She let out a gasp. "Oh no! I just saw an asteroid. Zym, I hope we don't have a strike."

"Hopefully it just burned up in the atmosphere."

They followed the stream of vehicles into the dusty fairgrounds and parked it over by a muddy little stream. Long strings of lanterns ran in a huge square grid across the grounds. Food stalls and merchant tents lined the near edge. The large dance tent stretched along the far side.

Right next to the lot where they parked, a corral held an enormous herd of baying, bawling mags. The noise of the animals and voices of the several hundred people already at the fairgrounds blended into a low roar. Blrsynt offered his arm to Sylstyn, and they followed the line of revelers toward the tent.

"Walk a little slower, okay. These lace up boots are hard to walk in on this soft ground," she commented while they made their way forward.

"Sure. Wow, that is a big tent!" Blrsynt took the opportunity to scan the brightly lit interior area beneath the canvas covering. "Looks like they have a band set up on that low stage right next to the dance floor."

"Oh yeah, mag drivers do like to dance. I can't remember the name of the lead singer. She's the woman with the long, curling locks and bright red lips standing next to the two guys tuning up the four string plydyrs." Sylstyn rose up on her tiptoes to get a better view. "I think that roundish thing on the stand in front of her is one of those new voice projectors, or whatever they're called."

"And of course just next to those round tables, that must be the bar. This is the first time I've seen power lights." As they moved along in line, Blrsynt pointed up at the ten-inch wide hand blown light bulbs strung from the central posts supporting the tent. Sylstyn squeezed his arm tightly.

"Oooh, this is exciting! I can't wait to dance. Oh, you *do* dance, right?"

"Yes, I'm not very good at it though."

"Don't worry, I can teach you some stuff."

Blrsynt cracked a wide grin and looked down at her twinkling green eyes. A jolt of excitement ran through both of them. Another move of the line, and they were under the tent.

"Shall we get something to drink. My throat is a little dusty," he suggested.

"Sounds good to me. I usually only drink ryl soda, but heck, this is a special night."

The bar was already packed with people. While they were waiting to get to the front, a loud voice from behind rang out.

"Hey Sly!"

Both the young people turned around to see who had called out her name. With one of the typical short crowned, tri-cornered mag driver hats pulled down tight across his curly black hair, Ryk muscled his way toward them. He was extremely handsome: brown, weather tanned skin, rough rugged features, and flashing dark eyes.

"Ryk!" Sylstyn opened her arms wide.

The mag driver pushed his way past the last person standing between them and swept her up in his arms. While giving her a powerful kiss, he swung Sylstyn's curvy body around in a circle. Everyone nearby, including Blrsynt had to step back. The kiss lasted much longer than the nephew had wished it would. Finally, the two broke off the smooch. Ryk still held her pressed against him. Her lovely round breasts rose up out of the low cut front of the dress.

"Ryk! Put me down!"

"Sure, Sly honey."

He relaxed his grip, then gave her firm, round bottom a playful squeeze as she slid off him. Sylstyn whacked his hand away. She smoothed out the wrinkles in her dress and took a step toward Blrsynt.

"Ryk, I'd like to intro......"

"Ryk? Ryk Six Line?" a well-dressed man standing at the bar in front of the nephew asked in an eager voice.

"The same!"

"Hey, let me buy you a drink! What'll you have?"

"I don't know. What are you drinking?"

"A klymr flip. Mixer! A klymr flip for the greatest mag driver alive."

Ryk smiled somewhat sheepishly, then turned back to Sylstyn. "Good to see you! By the way, you look gorgeous. You should wear your hair up like that more often."

She blushed. By this time, an interested crowd had pushed in. The well-dressed man at the bar wheeled around and held a short glass of a reddish liquid out toward Ryk.

"Here ya go!" After Ryk took the drink from him, the man retrieved his similar glass from the bar and lifted it high. "To Ryk Six Line. Ulutrita's greatest mag driver!"

A deafening roar spread across the crowded bar. Ryk clinked glasses with the man, said a quiet thanks, then downed the liquid. "Oh, that's good! Come on Sly, I got a table over there."

He gave the crowd a tip of his hat, grabbed Sylstyn's hand, and pulled her away from the bar. She looked over her shoulder and motioned with her head for Blrsynt to follow them. The nephew tried to wipe the indignant look off his face, but there was only so much he could do.

The tables that surrounded the dance floor were rapidly filling up. Ryk led them over to one in the far corner of the tent. Just before they reached the table, he let go of Sylstyn's hand, and took a moment to absorb the full majesty of her youthful beauty.

"I just can't get over how nice you look tonight! Guess I should have dressed up."

Sylstyn glanced down at his baggy linen pants, wide leather belt, big beaten up boots, and rough, long sleeved shirt. "You look like fine."

"Hey, let's grab a seat."

There were already six people seated at the table, four mag drivers, and two women. Three empty metal chairs lined the near side of the table. Ryk, Sylstyn, and Blrsynt stepped around the big wooden support pole, and stood behind the chairs.

"Hey everybody! This is my girl, Sylstyn."

Murmurs of hello rose up from the people seated at the table. Sylstyn smiled and gave a little wave of her hand. "Uh, this is my friend Blrsynt," she announced with a touch of awkwardness.

Ryk introduced himself, reached in front of Sylstyn's waist and offered his hand to Blrsynt. It took all the civility the young miner could summon to give it an honest shake. The three of them plunked down into the chairs at the same time.

"This table's a little far away from the bar, but at least we won't be bothered way over here. Speaking of bar, who needs a drink?" Ryk shouted.

Four hands went up. While Ryk took the orders, the sultry dark haired woman next to Blrsynt leaned over and tapped him on the arm.

"I think that seat is taken, but seeing as how there's nobody but you sitting in it, I guess it's yours."

She flashed a movie star smile and turned back the other way. Blrsynt fought the urge to just get up and leave. He quickly dismissed the idea and decided to at least wait till the music started.

Ryk tallied up the drink order and pulled a wad of bills out of his pocket. He shot a glance over at Blrsynt. "You want something, Bryn, er, what was your name again?"

"Blrsynt,"

"That's right, you want something?"

The young miner could feel his face burn. "Uh, I guess a physt."

Across the table, one of the mag drivers got to his feet. "Hey Ryk, if you're buyin' I'll go fetch the drinks."

"Thanks." Ryk reached over and let the salt and pepper haired driver take the wad of bills from him.

From the direction of the stage, a loud buzz, then tapping sound cut through the conversation. "Hello? Hello? Can you hear me? Good, welcome to the forty-third annual Phrynk Roundup!" the singer called out.

The entire tent erupted with hoots, whistles, and applause. Blrsynt turned around in his chair and looked out across the voluminous dance floor. Out of the corner of his eye, he noticed that Sylstyn was watching him. Their eyes met, and she gave him a warm, "everything is alright" smile. His anxiety dropped down a notch. From up on the stage, the singer again spoke into the primitive diaphragm microphone.

"We're going to start now, so we want everybody out on the dance floor! One, two, one, two, three, four."

The man playing the large, mag skin hoop drum beat a pulsing rhythm, and the rest of band kicked off a lively mag driver tune. Couples surged onto the dance floor. Without saying a word, Ryk grabbed Sylstyn's hand, pulled her gently up out of her chair, and the two of them threaded their way out into the dancing crowd.

From behind him, Blrsynt heard the crunch of boots on gravel. He turned to see a stocky mag driver with a long white moustache standing by the support pole. The man had his hands on his thick leather belt and was looking down at the seat Blrsynt was occupying.

"Ryf! Sit over here!" one of the other mag drivers called out from across the table. The white moustached driver muttered something and crunched around to the other side. Blrsynt couldn't help but smile. His attitude was improving.

"Watch out! Coming through!" The driver that had made the bar run set his load of glasses down. He grabbed his mug of foaming physt and raised it high. "To our old pal, Phrynk!"

Everyone at the table cheered and splashed down a drink. The band's first song ended with a thunderous stomping of boots on the dance floor. Ryk and Sylstyn came wandering back through the crowd of dancers. Stray strands of her hair floated about her head like wisps of smoke. Blrsynt could feel the heat of her body as she passed behind him.

"Whew! It is warm out there!" she gushed.

Ryk took off his tan, wide brimmed hat, and fanned her. "There, does that feel better?"

With his other hand, he reached out and grabbed a highball glass of amber liquid. The band struck up another bouncy dance tune. Ryk knocked back the drink and got to his feet.

"Come on Syl."

She fanned herself with her bare hand, let out a groan, and followed Ryk back out onto the dance floor. The strikingly beautiful, dark haired woman to Blrsynt's right leaned over next to him.

"So, are you a mag driver?"

"No, I'm a miner."

"Like an underground miner?"

"Not really, my uncle and I manage a precious metal mine in a crater."

"Sounds like hard work."

Blrsynt didn't quite know what to say in response so he just shrugged. For lack of anything better to do, he returned his attention to the dance floor.

"Ryk certainly is a good dancer."

"Ryk is good at everything," the woman added.

The song came to an end, and a few moments later, Sylstyn and Ryk returned to the table.

"Let's sit this next one out," she said after taking a long drink. Sylstyn billowed out the front of her dress several times, then looked over at Blrsynt. "Having fun?"

"Yeah, I'm having fun."

Her rosy face beamed in the electric light. Just below the edge of the tent, a bright yellow streak of light tore across the evening sky. Sylstyn let out a gasp.

"Oh Zym, I hate to see that!"

Along the same trajectory, a much bigger blazing ball of orange light appeared. A collective cry rose up from the people seated along the southwestern edge of the tent. The object flared briefly in the sky above the low buildings next to the fairgrounds. A boom echoed through the area as it exploded in a brilliant flash. The concussion rippled through the warm night air. All around the edge of the tent, people jumped to their feet. Behind the wood-railed paddock, the mags bawled even louder.

"Whoa, that was close!" Ryk sputtered.

Columns of smoke appeared in the direction of the blast. A fire bell rang out in the night.

"That looked like a bad one." Sylstyn lowered her voice to a whisper.

The crackle of the stage mike drew everyone's attention away from the crash. "Well, folks, don't know if you saw that or not, but we just missed a big old sky rock. Let's hope there aren't any more. We're gonna slow things down, and I'm going to sing one. This is an old favorite I'm sure you'll recognize."

Blrsynt drained half the contents of his mug and set it back down. The soft, soothing strains of the melody began to relax him. Above the crowd noise and music, the sound of angry voices reached his ears. He shifted around and focused his attention on the commotion at the far edge of the bar crowd.

A well proportioned woman with a big swoop of black hair was standing in front of a mag driver, gesturing in a threatening manner. When she jabbed a finger into his chest, the driver pointed over in Blrsynt's direction. The angry woman gave the driver a shove and pushed her way through the crowd. Blrsynt began casing out possible exit routes. He let out a gush of held breath when it became obvious that she was focused on Ryk.

The woman walked up behind him and knocked his hat forward. Ryk had been carrying on a lively conversation with the driver across the table. When the hat slid off his head, he turned around slowly. The happy expression on his rugged face vaporized in an instant.

"Hi Lylyn."

"We need to talk, now!"

Ryk leaned toward Sylstyn as he stood up. "Excuse me."

The woman sent a threatening glance down at Sylstyn, then led Ryk out from under the tent and across the sandy ground. The two of them stopped about a hundred yards from the tent. They stood facing each other. All of the people seated at the table turned to watch the encounter. Sylstyn scooted over into Ryk's empty chair and sided up next to Blrsynt.

"Oh boy! She is really letting him have it! Look at the way she's standing there with her hands on her hips, and Ryk's just standing there takin' a beating. Oh! Something she said must have struck a nerve. Now he just said something. Wow, look at the veins rising up on Ryk's neck. Uh oh, she just pointed toward the table. Now Ryk's letting her have it."

"Whew! I can feel the heat of the argument all the way over here!" the white moustached driver across the table exclaimed. His comment added a note of humor to the tension around the table. The two women next to Blrsynt began to talk in low voices.

In his place out beyond the tent, Ryk reached over and gently put his hand on Lylyn's abdomen. She smacked it away. He muttered a reply without really opening his mouth and walked off toward the bar. Lylyn called out something, then spun on her fancy boot heels, and stomped off in the opposite direction. The band finished their slow number to another thunderous peal of applause.

"I'll be right back." Sylstyn got to her feet and walked off in the direction of the latrines. The white moustached driver watched her leave, then shifted his attention to Blrsynt.

"Don't think we'll be seeing much more of Ryk tonight. Looks like you got your date back!"

The driver's observation brought a smile to Blrsynt's face. A few minutes later, Sylstyn came walking back from around the dance floor just as the band struck up.

"Will you dance with me?" she asked sweetly.

Blrsynt looked up at her irresistible, smiling face, and rose up from his chair. They spent the rest of the night on the dance floor. On the way home, she snuggled up next to him for warmth. The fires from the asteroid strike were still smoldering as they drove by the impact site. A small crowd of people were standing around the ruins of a house. Sylstyn shuddered when she saw the extent of the damage.

"I just hate it when those things fall out of the sky. So tomorrow is the big competition. Wanna go?"

"Wouldn't miss it."

"Great! It starts around ten, but the riding and roping events don't begin till later. Wanna pick me up around noon?"

"Noon it is."

She was silent for a minute, then straightened up in her seat. "Turn down that street there."

"I thought I'd be dropping you off at your little place over by Myrvst's."

"I don't work for the professor on the weekend, and my parents like it when I stay with them."

Blrsynt wheeled the buggy down a narrow street lined with large thorn trees.

"That one over there with the lamps lit out front."

The two of them sat looking up at the canopy of stars spreading as far as the eye could see. From one of the thorn trees next door, a night lykr trilled. Sylstyn pulled her hand out from around his waist to stifle a yawn.

"Oh, I must be more tired than I thought. I can't wait to get these boots off."

"Yeah, I'm tired too. It must be pretty late."

Blrsynt eased around in the seat so that he was facing her. Sylstyn moved forward, sliding her hands up his muscular back. For a brief moment, they just looked into each other's eyes. He bent down and kissed her. She returned the kiss. Her marvelously soft, warm lips sent waves of electricity through him. Sylstyn reached up and stroked his neck. After breaking off the kiss, they sat transfixed.

"Thank you for dancing with me tonight," she whispered.

"My pleasure."

One more quick kiss, and then she slid out of his arms, and down onto the sidewalk. "See you in the morning! Get a good night's sleep."

"I will."

He watched her sway up to the front door. Just before ducking in, she turned and waved at him. Blrsynt broke into a gigantic smile and nodded a goodbye. A shiver ran through his big, broad body.

"Man, I'm wired! I feel like racing this thing all the way back." He let out a yip of exhilaration and gave the reins a slap. The styrns bawled quietly, then moved him off into the night.

Chapter 8.

The next morning, Blrsynt washed the three shirts he owned. By noon, they were dry. The sun was already blazing away in the sky when he pulled up in front of Sylstyn's parents house. Blrsynt jumped down off the seat and walked up toward the house.

"Man, it feels like the top of my head is burning. I should have grabbed a hat."

Just before he made it to the small front porch, the front door opened. Sylstyn, and an older woman that was obviously her mother appeared in the doorway. Sylstyn stepped out onto sidewalk. Her bright floral calf length dress swung as she walked. She held a wide brimmed straw hat in her hands. Her long brown hair was again piled up on top of her head. After quick introductions, Sylstyn kissed her mother on the cheek, and followed Blrsynt down the sidewalk.

"You two have fun. We used to go to the Roundup every year, but the last couple times, the dust bothered your father," the mother called out from the open doorway.

"We will, bye bye." Sylstyn replied over her shoulder.

Blrsynt hopped up onto the seat first, and gently pulled her up next to him.

"What a nice day for the Roundup. Sometimes it's really windy this time of year," she said as the wagon bounced forward.

"It is a little hot."

They retraced the route back to the fairgrounds. Both of them looked over at the ruined stone house where a large piece of the asteroid had hit. A group of men were removing the damaged blocks from the side wall.

"I wonder if any one was hurt," Sylstyn said quietly.

"I don't see how they could have not been."

Both of their moods were somber till they reached the fairgrounds. Streams of buggies and riders on styrns funneled into the event. They parked on the far side of the grounds and followed the line of spectators toward the main arena.

Blrsynt scanned the crowd for any sign of Ryk. He sincerely hoped not to run into him. While he lagged behind keeping an eye out for his rival, Sylstyn plowed through the crowd, pulling him along. The brim of her floppy straw hat flapped like wings as she steered them forward.

"Come on! The bleachers are filling up fast. If we keep poking along we won't get a good seat!"

The sight of her rosy, vibrant smile helped to dissipate his anxiety. They managed to squeeze into the line going up the wooden stairs just as the announcer fired up this microphone.

"Ladies and gentlemen! Welcome to the forty-third annual Phrynk Roundup!" The crowd responded by stomping their boots and yelling back their approval. "Unfortunately, Mr. Phrynk himself can't be here to open the event, but I'm sure he is just as excited as everyone else to find out who the champions will be this year. Please remove your hats as we sing the Plyrm national anthem."

All heads turned toward the Plyrm flag hanging listlessly across the arena. After the song was finished, a massive cheer and round of applause rose up into the hot afternoon air. The crowd standing on the stairs slowly began to snake up into the stands.

Sylstyn spotted a couple empty seats in the middle of a row up above them. She dragged Blrsynt up, and plunked down just as another couple were approaching from the opposite side. Her light dress pulled up into her lap. Blrsynt glanced down at the smooth, white creaminess of her exposed thigh. He let out a sigh. The announcer's voice again echoed above the crowd noise.

"Alright, we will now begin the barrel racing part of our competition. The first rider is Lym Seven Line from the Cyrbyn Company!"

All through the afternoon's competition, Blrsynt kept an eye out for Ryk. Just as the sun was going down, his rival appeared.

"And now! The premier event of the day. The roping competition!" the announcer's voice echoed. From the far corner of the arena, the contestants came riding out. Hoots and whistles of approval rose up from the grandstand.

"There's Ryk!" Sylstyn yelled. "Wonder why he missed the riding competition?" She stood up, cupped her hands around her mouth, and shouted with all her might. "Hey Ryk! Good luck!"

Once the contestants were lined up on the dusty arena floor, the announcer resumed his commentary. "As most of you know, this is a progressive tournament. Only the top four finishers in each round will advance. The first competition is the simple mag throw."

To no one's surprise, Ryk had no trouble advancing through the preliminary brackets. Just as the stars were beginning to appear in the twilight sky, the final event took place.

A long cable was strung across the arena. The cable ran through a big metal ring with a four-foot length of chain attached. Dangling from the end of the chain was a basketball sized leather ball filled with sand. Two pieces of rope were tied to the ring and held by operators on opposite sides of the arena. By working together, the two operators could move the ball rapidly down along the cable and get it swinging high into the air.

All afternoon, Sylstyn had been chatting away, giving Blrsynt a running commentary on the various contestants, and their place in the standings. She continued her effort as the final roping competition began.

"Alright, so the first thing they're going to do is let all the contestants ride out, and take a practice run at it." Sylstyn leaned forward with her elbows on her knees. "I'm getting hungry, are you?"

"Yes, this is the last competition, right?"

"Yeah, they have to give out the awards though."

On poles ringing the arena, big electric bulbs had just been turned on. Their orange-yellow glow threw shadows across the sandy arena floor. Sylstyn turned to look back at the buzzing glass spheres.

"Wow, that's going to make it much harder. The contestants are going to be staring right into those bright lights."

The eight finalists came riding single file out of the side gate. Polite applause moved through the crowd. When Ryk entered on his jet black styrn, the politeness turned to whistles and rowdy cheers. Ryk took off his wide brimmed hat and waved at the crowd. All the finalists lined up right along the near side of the arena.

"You can tell who the favorite is!" Sylstyn commented.

Fifteen minutes later, the completion was whittled down to Ryk and one other contestant. A hush fell over the crowd as the mag driver dressed all in black spurred his styrn out toward the swinging leather ball. When his lariat went swinging just to the side of the target, the crowd gave a collective aaaww of sympathy.

"All right folks, if Ryk can snag it on this turn, he's the champ. If not, then both of them get another shot at it," the announcer boomed.

In a great whoosh of movement, the crowd got to their feet. All eyes watched Ryk cut left then right following the ball's traverse down the cable. With a characteristic flourish, he twisted in the saddle, and let fly a winning toss.

"Ladies and Gentlemen! Our winner this year is Ryk Six Line!" The announcer's jubilant voice echoed around the arena. A titanic roar rose up from the crowd.

Sylstyn and Blrsynt locked in an embrace. She let go and grabbed his hand. "Come on! They let people go down onto the arena floor to watch the winner get his trophy." Blrsynt allowed her to drag him down out of the bleachers.

"Would the four finalists please come up to the stage!" the announcer's voice rang out.

The entire arena was still buzzing with excited conversation and laughter. Gates along the perimeter of the arena were open, and a stream of mostly young people poured out of the stands. Sylstyn and Blrsynt ran across the sandy ground, and managed to pack into the group of spectators that were just below the stage. Off to the left, the top four contestants were being mobbed by well-wishers. All of them received hearty pats on the back, and a stream of compliments. The announcer let out a laugh. He grabbed the mike stand and walked over to the edge of the stage.

"Okay, let's get on with the awarding of the trophies. As soon as the finalists fight their way up here. Hopefully they'll all be in one piece."

The four finalists were at last able to squeeze through the happy crowd and ascend the rough wooden stage. After giving out the fourth, third, and second place trophy belts, the announcer took another look at the huge crowd assembled on the ground below him, then stepped back up to the mike.

"And this year's first place winner! Ryk Sixth Line!" The deafening roar that followed caused him to shrink away. Grinning like a fool, the announcer waited till the noise died down, then motioned toward the winner. "Ryk, step over here."

After a couple more handshakes and congratulations from the other finalists, Ryk walked over and stood next to the mike stand. The announcer put a hand on the driver's solid shoulder.

"Ryk, how many times have you won this competition?"

"This will be my seventh time."

The crowd let go another blasting cheer. From his place in front of the stage, Blrsynt looked around at the expectant faces, all staring with affection up at their hero. The wind blew the savory smell of things fried in mag fat from over on the midway. His stomach growled. For lack of anything better to do, he turned his attention to Sylstyn.

She stood with her face tilted slightly upward, chin jutting out with pride. Her starry eyed gaze and euphoric expression left little doubt in Blrsynt's mind that she was hopelessly in love with Ryk. He let go a sigh.

Sylstyn methodically rolled and unrolled the brim of her floppy straw hat while listening to every word the champion roper spoke. When Ryk's voice drop in pitch, Blrsynt forced himself to pay attention.

"........like to thank the Pylryt Mag Company for being such a good employer, and most of all, I'd like to thank my best girl..Lylyn... I love ya honey!"

Applause and hoots of approval filled the arena. Blrsynt snapped his head over to get a gauge of Sylstyn's reaction. What he saw made him wince. The delirious, euphoric glow on her face was gone. Her lips were pulled tight enough to force all blood out of them. Instead of rolling and unrolling the brim of her hat, she began to twist it to the point of breakage.

"Ryk, it is with pride that the Phrynk Roundup presents you with your eighth champion's buckle!" The announcer held up a massive shimmering silver belt buckle. He flashed it across the stage, then placed it into the mag driver's hands. "Ryk, I swear, if your styrn could fly, I bet you could rope the stryrks up in the sky!"

A final Ulutrita-shaking cheer rose up all around the arena. When the noise died down, the announcer continued. "Don't forget, tomorrow is the all comers race out by the stockyards. Contestants need to be there at ten o'clock. Thanks for showing up, and don't forget to stop by the midway! The food and physt tent are open till eleven."

Sylstyn wheeled on her boots and charged off through the milling crowd. Blrsynt slipped into the space she created. Once they were clear of the crowd, she stopped and turned back toward him.

"Hurry up, let's get the klynk out of here."

"Uh, want to get something to eat?" Blrsynt asked with just a touch of timidity.

"Later, I need some physt."

"Sounds good to me."

Sylstyn led him right over to the large rectangular tent smack in the center of the midway. She immediately pounded down two paper cups full of the fermented grain beverage and carried a third one out of the tent. Blrsynt took a quick scan of the stalls up and down the crowded lane.

"Ah, there's fried kymr over there. I think those blynys smell awful good."

"I want a big, greasy slyb."

Without speaking further, they headed back into the crowded midway. A loud gang of people came marching down from the opposite direction. Right in the middle, Ryk's handsome, dusky face appeared. Lylyn walked next to him. Her arms were wrapped tightly around his torso.

"Hey Sly, what about?...." Blrsynt stopped in front of the kymr stall. He turned to address his date, but she wasn't there. "Oh blyrt!"

It only took him a second to spot Ryk towering above most of the crowd. He also saw the back of Sylstyn's stylish, dark brown hairdo from her position planted directly in the path of the champion roper and his friends.

People began to move around the young woman standing defiantly smack in the center of the midway. Lylyn recognized the fury on Sylstyn's face. She pulled herself even closer to Ryk's side.

"Yep, I was a little worried, when Mynyr let loose, but......" Ryk stopped in mid-sentence when he caught sight of Sylstyn glaring at him. A hush fell over the joyous gang. Blrsynt eased up next to his date and whispered in her ear.

"Sly, let's go."

She didn't hear him. The mostly full cup of physt she had been carrying was resting at thigh level. Blrsynt looked down and saw her adjust her grip. When she pulled her arm back in preparation for the toss, Blrsynt reached down and grabbed her wrist.

"Hi Sly," Ryk offered in a decidedly cautious tone of voice.

"What are you kids up to?" Lylyn's mocking question made Blrsynt wince. He gently pulled Sylstyn to the side.

"Come on, its physt time!" the haggard looking driver at Ryk's side shouted. He led the raucous group into the physt tent. Ryk ventured a momentary, apologetic glance over at Sylstyn on his way past.

"You can let go of me!" Once Blrsynt released his grip on her wrist, she raised the cup to her lips, and half the liquid disappeared. "I hate that fyrg!"

Sylstyn stood staring at the rowdy group saddled up to the bar, then turned toward Blrsynt. The fire in her big green eyes had begun to die down. "Did you see a slyb stand?"

It took him a moment to compose himself. "Yeah, there's one over there. Let me get some of those blynys first." Blrsynt trotted down the midway and returned with a paper bowl full of fried dumplings. He then directed Sylstyn over to the sylb stall.

She ordered a huge sausage piled with grilled, aromatic vegetables. As they walked in no particular direction, she bit off savage hunks. Blrsynt quietly ate his blynys. He was at a loss for words. At the end of the midway, the enormous dance tent spread out before them. Music drifted over the midway sounds from the quartet playing on the stage.

"Do you feel like dancing?" he cautiously asked.

"No, I think we should leave."

Blrsynt gave a slight shrug and walked in the direction of the wagon. Every hundred yards or so, he glanced over at her profile. She no longer appeared to be fuming mad. Her eyes now had a faraway look to them.

"Do you like me?" she asked out of the blue.

"Uh, yes."

"I like you too."

While they walked along, Blrsynt struggled to make sense of what was happening. He was pretty sure that she wasn't angry with him. Most of her fury seemed to have been directed at Ryk.

Sylstyn stopped right at the edge of the parking area, turned, and looked him dead square in the eyes. "How much do you like me?"

"Uh, a lot?"

"A lot, or a whole lot?"

"A whole lot."

Blrsynt's sense of confusion was quickly replaced with joy as she leaned forward and planted a powerful, slyb-greased kiss on his lips. They broke off in time to breathe. He reached up and wiped the grease off his mouth. She tossed the remainder of the slyb into the dirt and looped her arm around his.

"I just can't believe him!" she commented mostly to herself.

"Forget him."

They climbed up onto the wagon and rolled along with the noise of the midway trailing off. When they came to the crossroad, he steered toward the right.

"No, go this way," she commanded.

"But your parent's house is over there."

"We're not going to my parent's house."

Blrsynt's eyebrows twitched as he directed the styrns back to the main road. After they had gone several blocks, she pointed down a narrow lane. "Turn here."

They rolled past thick thorn hedges. At the end of the long green wall, she again pointed. "Pull in here."

He tugged the reins over to the right and eased the wagon onto a patch of gravel. There was nowhere else to go, so he brought the vehicle to a stop.

"Where are we?"

"This is my place."

Sylstyn let go of his arm and hopped down to the ground. She strode across the gravel, extracted a key from her purse, and opened the back door. Before entering, she turned back toward him.

"Well, don't just sit there, come on in."

Blrsynt eased off the seat, tied up the styrns, and followed her in. She had already lit a lamp in the kitchen. Sylstyn led the way into the small, tidy living room.

"Sit down over there."

Blrsynt dutifully took a seat in the wide, overstuffed chair. She walked over, set the lamp on an end table, placed her hands on the arms of the chair, and gave him another powerful kiss.

"I'll be right back," she purred.

He watched her sway out of the room. Blrsynt was still not sure what exactly was transpiring, but the kiss she had just planted on his face was genuine. The soft flickering lamp light, and simple but cozy arrangement of the room helped him to relax.

A moment later, Sylstyn came strolling back into the room. Her beautiful youthful body was clothed in nothing but the black lingerie she had worn all day. She had undone her long brown hair. Sylstyn glided over and swiveled into his lap. She looked at his astonished face, and they kissed. He tentatively reached up and slid his hands over her shoulders. Her skin felt like fine, smooth porcelain. His fingers shook slightly at the touch.

"What's wrong?" she whispered.

"Uh, I don't......nothing's wrong."

Sylstyn leaned forward and laid her head on his shoulder. Her long silky hair spread out without a sound. Blrsynt wrapped his arms all the way across her back and sank into the cushion of the chair. He could feel her solid body begin to shake. Her tears wet the base of his neck.

Hours later, Blrsynt opened his eyes. The room was pitch black. Slowly, his vision began to adjust. He could make out the little end table, the bedroom door, and the extinguished lamp. The next thing he became aware of was the intense tingling in his left arm. He shook the sensation out, then slid the arm under her folded legs.

Steadily and silently, he carried her into the bedroom. There was barely enough room between the wall and mattress for him to squeeze by. With all the care that one uses to set down a precious vintage violin after inspecting it, he leaned over and laid her limp body onto the blanket. The weight of her not so dainty form pulled at his strong back and neck muscles. He let out a slight ooof once she was resting on the bed. Blrsynt slid his hands out from under her neck and legs. His fingers brushed over the incredible smoothness of her shoulder and back of her thighs.

She groaned slightly before rolling over onto her side. Blrsynt smiled in the darkness, and quietly pulled away. A sudden tugging on his left arm halted his progress.

"Where'dya think you're going?"

"Uh, home?"

"Not a chance!" She pulled him back down with considerable force.

"Can I at least take my boots off?"

"Sure."

Blrsynt sat on the edge of the bed and undid the laces on his beat up miner's boots. He could feel her move across the other side of the mattress. The quiet swoosh of lace sliding across smooth skin, and the warm smell of her body indicated that things were happening behind his back. There was a sudden heaviness of a body moving across the bed, then hands sliding around his waist.

"Here, let me help you."

While he worked on the leather laces and wool socks, she undid his belt, and started on the buttons of his long sleeve shirt. Blrsynt's heart began to thump in his chest. His breath came in quick bursts. She slid his shirt off while he rose up slightly and let his pants fall to the floor. Blrsynt swung his legs up onto the bed and rolled to his side.

Sylstyn was kneeling across from him. He took a leisurely gaze of her wonderfully full, round breasts, nicely curved tummy, and dark triangle. She slid forward and straddled him.

"Aren't you glad you didn't go home?"

Chapter 9.

The sound of metal banging in the other room woke Blrsynt from a deep sleep. Light filtered in from the shaded living room window. He lay there still trying to make sense of things.

"Boy, what in interesting evening. First she's hopping mad, then she gets romantic. I just don't get it. Well, I can hear her singing, so that's a good sign."

He slid off the bed and tiptoed naked out into the small, bright kitchen. She was standing in front of the window dressed in a short silk bathrobe. Her firm muscular calves shone in the morning light. The creak of floor boards caused her to turn her head around.

"Oh, good morning!"

He walked up beside her and slid his hands around the open front of the robe. She tilted her head back to let him kiss the side of her neck.

"Mmmm, maybe we should go back to bed."

"Yeah."

An hour later, they lay in each other's arms.

"Did I really eat a greasy, nasty slyb last night?"

"Yeah."

"And you kissed me?"

"Yeah."

"Ah! You must have really been feeling frisky. How much physt did I drink?"

"Oh, a couple, well about three big cups."

"That explains why my stomach is kind of unsteady. I hardly ever drink at all. I'm kind of hungry, how 'bout you?"

"I'm always hungry. I could use some zyd though."

"Stay here, I'll go put some pluge to boil."

"Actually, I think I'll get up too."

Right at noon, the two of them showed up at Myrvst's house. They walked hand in hand across the sunlit front yard. The door was unlocked so Sylstyn ventured in first.

Hello?"

"Sly? Is that you? We're back here in the workroom," Myrvst called from down the hall.

The two young people walked down the hallway and entered the stuffy workroom. "Honestly, I don't know why you don't open a window in here," she scolded.

Sylstyn let go of Blrsynt's hand and marched over to the wall of windows. When she pushed the heavy, thick pane open, the sound of lykrs chirping filled the room.

"Good morning, ah actually good afternoon!" Myrvst said brightly. A half-hearted smile spread across his face as he watched her walk back over and wrap her arms around Blrsynt's mid-section. Kryzyck just stood grinning.

"Did you have fun at the Roundup yesterday?" the professor continued.

"Yeah, Ryk won the competition as usual. What are you working on?"

Myrvst stepped forward and picked up the round metal dial he had been experimenting with. "Just about got this working." A loud, insistent rap on the front door drew everyone's attention. "Sly, will you......."

The housekeeper didn't need to wait for the professor to finish. She whisked out of the room and down the hall. Another hard knock vibrated the wooden door. "Alright, I'm coming."

Sylstyn swung the door open and looked up at the serious face of the messenger. He was dressed in an immaculate brown uniform with charcoal piping. He clicked his shiny, calf high boots together, and held out an envelope.

"An urgent message from Professor Rymnyr. If you would be so kind as to give this to Myrvst. Madame would like an immediate reply. I shall wait."

The messenger's overly formal demeanor made Sylstyn giggle. She held a hand to her mouth, accepted the envelope, and turned toward the hall.

"Oh, excuse me! Do come in."

"Thank you miss, but I prefer to wait out here."

Sylstyn shrugged, closed the door, and sped off to the workroom. The others were standing just where she had left them. All eyes were on her as she entered the room and handed the envelope to the professor.

"There's a very well dressed and formal messenger out there. He says this is an urgent message from Professor Rymnyr, and that she would like an immediate reply."

Myrvst took the fancy lavender envelope, tore it open with his index finger, pulled out the embossed letter, and began reading out loud.

"Dear Professor, I have been very busy reaching out to contacts about the invention. Last night I got inspired and went on a vision quest up on the hill." Myrvst temporarily dropped the letter down from in front of his face. He looked around at the other people in the room.

"When Professor Rymnyr says she has been on a vision quest, you can be assured that something really interesting is going to follow." He gave a grunt of disapproval and resumed reading.

"After dancing and chanting for six hours, I fell to the ground, and a marvelous vision swept through my exhausted, but exhilarated mind." Myrvst shot another cynical glance around the room. "Rest assured she was dancing and chanting stark naked I might add."

Sylstyn let out another giggle. The idea of round, buxom Professor Rymnyr out in the hills dancing naked was too funny for her to contain. "I'm sorry Professor. Please continue."

"Where was I? Oh yes....It is too elaborate to share in letters, so I would like to meet with you today. Could we get together with Mihyn and her husband at your house, say around three? My messenger will await your response. Yours dedicatedly, Rymnyr." Myrvst folded the letter and scratched his grey beard.

"Judging by the erratic handwriting, I'd say she is still, how shall I say? Under the influence of the vision quest." He turned toward the housekeeper. "Syl, would you be available to put together a pyryst for what, one, two, three, four, five, six, seven, maybe eight people this afternoon? Zym, what time is it anyway?" Myrvst pulled his ornate pocket watch out of his coat. "Good, its only one-thirty."

At precisely three o'clock, an open buggy pulled by a single burly styrn came rolling up out front. Handynr stopped under the shade of a big, hundred-year-old thorn tree, eased down off the seat, and tied the animal up to a post. After helping Mihyn down to the ground, they walked up toward the house.

"So any idea what this is all about?" he asked.

"With Professor Rymnyr, it's hard to say what she's got cooked up. The note she sent had a frantic kind of urgency to it. We'll find out soon."

At three-thirty, Myrvst flipped his watch open. "Hmm, Rymnyr is late. I hope she didn't fall asleep after her all night vision ordeal."

The sound of the front door banging open interrupted his observation. Several moments later, a disheveled, dirty, and somewhat frightening looking, Professor Rymnyr careened down the hall, and stood outside the work room, trying to catch her breath.

"Sorry...I'm...late.....Whew!...What a day! Night!" She let her tangled head of greying hair drop for a moment, then snapped it back up. "Say, do you suppose I could have a drink of that? It's frightfully hot out there."

Kryzyck poured a glass from the pitcher sitting on the workbench, walked over and handed it to her. Without even looking at him, she took the glass, upended and drained it.

"Ah, thank you. Mr. Kryzyck! How are you?"

"Very well. And how bout you? We hear that you had an eventful night." The old miner finished his greeting by sending soft, friendly smile her way.

"Oh, you wouldn't believe it! Get me a chair, and I'll tell you about it."

Kryzyck set one of the simple wooden chairs next to the door frame. Rymnyr sat down heavily, reached up and gave his arm a gentle squeeze, then began her tale.

"Where to begin? Oh yes, about this time yesterday, actually a little earlier, I was out pruning the dylplyr bushes when a tiny green and red nyr came buzzing right in front of my face. Now as you know, the Styrynts believed the nyrs were the messengers of Zym. The tiny nyr would not leave me alone. It lit on a branch next to my head and kept chittering.

After a few moments, it took to flight, did three enormous loops, and then flew off at great speed to the northeast. I took it as a sign that I should consult with my hoolum who is an expert on spiritual matters."

Myrvst held a hand beside his face and leaned toward Krycyzk. "Fortune teller."

"I raced down to her place on the northern edge of town, and found her sitting at her table, an array of small pyfyg bones laid out in a pattern. I was waiting for you to arrive, she told me. What is going on? I asked her. You *know*, she said. No, I really don't, I said. She laughed and spread her hand over the bones like this." Rymnyr mimicked the fortune teller's action by turning her hand palm up and swinging it in a smooth arc.

"This is you, she said, pointing to a little triangle of bones off to the side. And this, this is your task! In the center of the table was a sweep of bones, kind of like a comet's tail. What does it mean? I asked. She laughed again. That is your job! To find out what important task is waiting for you. Go! You know what to do!

On the way back home, I was puzzled. What was she talking about? The only really important thing that I could think of was the invention. That's when the idea of the vision quest sprang into my mind. As soon as I got home, I put on my special robe, gathered up the sacred herb and a tybr to beat on, and headed up the hill. The folks living along the aqueduct watched me from their stick dwellings. I'm sure they thought I was crazy."

A sarcastic smile pulled up the edges of Myrvst's moustache. When Rymnyr uttered the word "crazy", he let go a small, insincere cough. She flashed an irritated glance over at him, then continued.

"So anyway, I ingested the sacred herb, danced and chanted for hours, and right as it began to get dark, I could feel the spirit of the ancients take hold of me. I danced and chanted with all the fury I could muster. Sometime during the night, I fell from exhaustion.

While I lay there, I saw this marvelous vision! Long streams of light came winding all around Ulutrita from far in the distance. I started floating up in the air. Higher and higher I rose, right out into the blackness. From down below, I saw a sailing kyrft coming toward me. It had a huge billowing sail, and whooshed right past me, gliding along on the bands of light. Oh, the ecstasy of it!"

Rymnyr's darkly circled eyes were glinting with tears. Myrvst pulled a handkerchief out of his pocket and blotted the side of her face. A streak of dust stood out against the fine white fabric.

"Well my dear, that's a fine vision, but what does it mean?"

She yanked the handkerchief from his fingers and finished wiping away the moisture. "Sometimes Myrvst, you are so daft! What it means is that these voices we are hearing are coming to us from somewhere out among the stryrks. We are to build a kyrft and follow them to their point of origin."

The room fell deathly silent. Mihyn and her husband looked at each other. Their questioning gaze transmitted much uncertainty back and forth. Handynr put his hands in his pockets and leaned against the wall.

"So, Mihyn has filled me in on most of the details regarding this, uh invention, discovery, whatever it is. The part about voices from the stryks, I'm not so sure about." He scanned the faces of the other people in the room for signs of a favorable or unfavorable reaction to his statement. All he saw were blank expressions.

"Well, we'll see what happens tomorrow." Rymnyr replied hoarsely.

Mihyn looked over at her husband. He just shrugged. "Tell us professor, what's happening tomorrow?" she asked with a tone of annoyance.

"I've been busy. I talked the administrator of the forum into calling a special session tomorrow. The head of Phylr communications, the astronomy department, several finance ministers, oh and somebody from that company that's trying to build gliders big enough for people to actually fly are also going to be there. What time will pyryst be ready? All of a sudden, I'm starving."

"Yes, let's retire to the dining room." Myrvst slowly walked toward the door.

Mihyn sent another questioning glance over at her husband. She mouthed the words, "Did you know?" He shook his head of closely cut brown hair.

"Excuse me professor, but were you planning on telling my husband and I about the meeting?"

"I just did," Rymnyr replied. She laboriously got to her feet. Kryzyck had been standing against the wall, listening intently to her story. While the rest of the group filed out of the room, Rymnyr took a couple steps toward the miner.

"I'm feeling a bit faint. Would you mind escorting me back to my home after pyryst?"

At ten o'clock the next morning, Myrvst, Regents Mihyn and Handynr met in the high ceilinged foyer of the Academy.

"Good morning professor," Mihyn said dryly.

"Good morning to you both." Myrvst looked down over the top of his wire eyeglasses at the couple. His gaze settled on the wife's pale, tense face.

"Feeling alright today?"

Mihyn tried to reply, but the words stuck in her throat. She held up a slender hand and coughed twice. "Oh, I think I may be coming down with something. Yes, I'm fine, thank you."

Myrvst gave a slight twist of a smile. "A little nervous?"

"No, well actually yes. Aren't you?"

The professor took a moment to compose his reply. "You know, nervousness is not one of my traits. My parents died when I was quite young, and so all through my youth, I was exceedingly anxious. I guess I just grew out of it. Do you know where Professor Rymnyr is?"

Mihyn shook her head. The professor pulled his ornate pocket watch out and flipped the lid open.

"Hmm. I do hope she isn't late."

Across the marble floor, the big copper doors burst open. Kryzyck held one of them open while Rymnyr came sweeping in. She was attired in a brilliant orange flowing dress with red and black accents. Halfway across the foyer, she stepped on the hem and stumbled.

"Zym dyth it! I need to get this worked on. Everything is going to blyrt this morning!"

Rymnyr arrived at the spot where her colleagues were waiting and flashed an exasperated smile all around.

"You look stunning, my dear," Mihyn said out of politeness.

"To Zym I do! This gown used to fit perfectly. What a horrible morning I've had!"

"What was so horrible about it?"

"One of the servants has been sick, and they had to take her to the healer this morning. Also, we got up late," Kryzyck answered. A satisfied grin drifted across his face.

"I see. Look, people are starting to file into the lecture hall. We better get moving." Myrvst led the group over toward the hall door.

Rymnyr tripped twice on the front of her gown. She crossed the polished marble floor uttering expletives every few feet. Mihyn and her husband walked side by side. Handynr glanced over at his wife's tense features. He leaned into her mass of wavy hair.

"Try to smile. You look like you're going to receive a prison sentence."

"To tell you the truth, I'm really starting to doubt the sensibility of what we're about to present. I mean, what actual concrete evidence do we have? Almost nothing!" She whispered without looking over at him.

"I wish I could say something to refute your opinion, but it's just not there."

"I mean look at Rymnyr! She's assembled all these prestigious individuals that we have to try and convince of our highly implausible theory, and she appears to be in no shape to present. It looks like she and the miner were up all night klynking!"

Handynr suppressed the laugh that almost escaped from his lips. The two of them passed through lecture hall door and entered the noisy room. Extra tables had been placed in front of the stage. Left of the podium the head of Phyl Communications and several of his chief engineers were seated. Next to them, a table full of astronomers, mathematicians, and finance ministers sat talking excitedly among themselves.

The husband and wife regents look their usual spots directly in front of the podium. Mihyn began to hyperventilate. Her often uncooperative stomach churned. Rymnyr fussed non-stop with her uncomfortable dress as she and Kryzyck found their seats.

"Ah! I feel like ripping this stupid thing off and sitting here stark naked! As soon as I get home, this thing is getting burned."

Kryzyck reached over and squeezed her hand. "Try and relax. There's a lot riding on this meeting. Save your energy for the discussion. You seem very wound up today."

Rymnyr let go a long, exasperated sigh, and worked up enough energy for a droopy eyed smile. "Thanks, I'm glad you're here. You know what it is. I haven't used the hylyryskn powder for several years, and now I remember why. It makes me really anxious and annoyed the day after. Probably wasn't good planning on my part."

Now that all the dignitaries had taken their places in front of the stage, Head Regent Bokyl stood up at the center table, and turned to face the audience.

"May I have your attention please! First, let me say that I appreciate everyone making time for this most interesting special session that Professor Rynmyr has used her extensive influence to pull together today." He sent a stern, all business glance down at her. "Welcome to all our esteemed guests. At this point, I will turn this over to the professor."

Rymnyr rose up out of her chair, cleared her throat, and began speaking. "Yes, thank you all for attending this very important special session. A new invention was presented to Professor Myrvst and many of us here last week that we felt had the implications to change our society like never before. I would like to call Professor Myrvst up to explain just what these implications are. Professor?"

From his spot at the technical table, Myrvst got to his feet, and made his way to the space in front of the stage. "For those of you who have not witnessed this amazing invention, I will attempt to explain. Using nothing more than a spool of wire, a galena crystal for tuning, an electromagnet, and an amplification horn, we have been able to intercept some kind of wireless transmission of voices that speak in a variety of languages not recognized by our expert linguists here at the Academy. Regent Mihyn, would you be so kind as to elaborate on this?"

Mihyn's uncooperative stomach jolted at the sound of her name. She slid back her chair, swallowed the saliva pooling under her tongue, and joined Myrvst in front of the stage.

"What the professor outlined is quite accurate. On two occasions, I have listened to very clear examples of an individual speaking, and also, two individuals carrying on a conversation. The language and inflections used are not like anything the Academy has cataloged as current dialects being spoken here on Ulutrita."

The last sentence drew whispers and hushed reactions from the crowd. After gazing around at the now engaged audience, Mihyn took a deep breath, and continued.

"As a trained linguist, I have no conclusion other than that these intercepted voices are originating on some other planet."

The whispers and hushed conversations now were charged with energy. Several hands went up from the technical table. Mihyn pointed to the individual with the first hand up. A man dressed in a deep blue robe of shimmering fabric got to his feet, and turned sideways so the crowd could hear what he said.

"My name ees Professor Ymyl. I am the head of the astronomy department here at zee Academy. Your supposition zat these strange voices are originating on some other world ees very interesting. My department ees committed to studying zee other celestial bodies surrounding our own planet. Zee notion zat somewhere out there, another civilization has developed a method of transmitting messages to us ees intriguing, but pardon my candor, somewhat farfetched."

All through the crowd, heads nodded in agreement. Mihyn glanced nervously over at Rymnyr. The professor met her gaze, and mouthed the words, "Take another question."

"Thank you Professor Ymyl. Other questions?"

A broad shouldered man at the technical table raised his hand. Mihyn nodded to him, and the man rose up to a standing position.

"My name is Phylr Third Line. I am the president of Phylr Communications." Murmurs of awe circulated through the crowd. "We are at a fascinating time in the history of Ulutrita. With the help of our emerging communication technology, we can send messages through the wires to places all over the globe and receive a return in minutes. Professor Myrvst is working on a new device that will allow us to talk to others across the wires.

And now, Mr. Kryzyck who is sitting at the table next to me brings this new invention that may able to broadcast wireless voices. As to the origin of these strange, foreign speakers, that, I have no knowledge of. My company is interested in exploring the development of large scale application of this, if it proves to be a stable platform. Thank you."

While Phlyr bowed to the polite applause, Rymnyr left her seat to join Mihyn and Professor Myrvst in front of the stage. She stuck her head of highly piled greying hair close to both their faces.

"We seem to be going around aimlessly. We need to pull the argument together!" she whispered.

"Excuse me! Could I say something?" From his place at the far right table, a slender young man with unruly black hair spoke up. The three academicians broke their huddle and looked over in his direction. Mihyn motioned for him to stand.

"Hello, my name is Gyls Fourth Line. My father and I have been working on developing flying machines for several years now." The sound of interested conversation swelled within the crowd. "Our dream is to first of all develop the technology to allow people to break the bonds of Ulutritan travel, and one day, soar with the lykrs."

His last statement drew strong reactions from the audience, both in support, and in opposition. "Someday, we would like to be able to expand this technology to leave our home world and explore the stryrks."

As soon as the last word left his lips, the noise level in the room rose. Bokyl stood up and waved his hands in the air. "Quiet! Quiet please! It is imperative that you respect the right of those selected to speak without having to fight to be heard."

Mihyn looked over at the two people standing next to her. Myrvst peered out at the crowd over his wire-frame glasses. His wrinkled face betrayed not a trace of emotion. Professor Rymnyr, on the other hand, appeared to be on the edge of exploding. She bit her red lips, her round chin trembled. The professor's eyes darted all around the room. Mihyn reached over and grasped her sweaty hand.

"Rymy, do you want to say something?"

"Yes! Wish me luck." The professor let go of Mihyn's hand and turned to face the audience. "Today, we have heard some interesting opinions regarding Mr. Kryzyck's historic discovery. It will take some time for most of us to process all that has been presented. Over the last couple days, I have met with Professor Ymyl, and with Mr. Gyls and his father to gather information on what I consider the most monumental project we Tyrlians have ever undertaken!"

The restless, stirred up crowd suddenly became very still. Ever the dramatist, Rymnyr paused to let her statement sink in.

"On this day, the one hundredth-seventy eighth day of Flyglrm, I am proposing to the Academy that we create a special project for the said purpose of sending a group of brave explorers into space to find the source of these strange voices."

Chapter 10.

The force and volume of the crowd's reaction was impressive. A good number of those in attendance got to their feet. Angry voices and cat calls echoed off the white plaster walls. Bokyl plugged his ears at first, then stood up and raised his arms.

"Quiet! I demand quiet! Please. Everyone take your seats."

Little by little, the raging crowd complied. Several individuals still shouted from their chairs, but eventually order was restored. Once the noise level dropped, Bokyl strode around the end of the table, and stopped next to Rymnyr. She simply stood, proud as a peacock, relishing in the commotion she had stirred up.

"So Professor, you have created a huge stir once again. Now what?" Bokyl asked in a low, serious tone of voice.

She shifted her dreamy gaze from the animated crowd and looked deep into his eyes. "Head Regent, it should be obvious what comes now. We figure out what the first steps are."

Bokyl gave what could best be described as a truly animal-like snort. "Well, from my perspective, the first step is for you and your group to leave. Better yet, apologize to all these people for wasting their time. I have....."

"Look, we're almost done. Just a couple more details to this project that need to be outlined," Rymnyr snapped back at him.

Bokyl's bald head turned a bright reddish purple. He gritted his teeth hard and stormed off to his place at the center table. After plunking down hard, he folded his arms across his chest. Regent Handynr scooted over next to him. The heat from Bokyl's rage radiated out of his rotund body.

"I can't believe what I'm hearing," Handynr whispered.

"Your wife seems to be in on this preposterous proposal." Bokyl finished his statement by sending a scathing, joyless stare over at his colleague. While the two of them were conversing, Rynmyr directed her attention to the young inventor.

"Mr. Gyls, would you be so kind as to continue with the description of your part of the project?"

The tall gangly young man leaned over and said something to his father. Deep furrows formed on the older man's brow. He gave a hard shake of his head. Gyls flashed a nervous smile, patted his father's hand, and straightened back up.

"Um, where was I? Yesterday, Professor Rymnyr met with us and asked what we thought of the possibility of utilizing a comet that will be approaching Ulutrita in a year or so as a propulsion system for some kind of craft that could take people far out into space. I said I didn't know, but would be very interested in exploring the possibility."

Loud grumblings of disbelief rolled back and forth through the crowd. Bokyl unfolded his arms and not so quietly dropped his palms onto the tabletop.

"Professor Rymnyr, are you suggesting that we send some hapless explorers up into space chasing a comet?" He asked with more than a touch of incredulousness. Several individuals got to their feet and noisily left the lecture hall. Bokyl craned his neck around to watch them depart.

"As I recall, several years ago, a presentation was made to this forum concerning the possibility of using some kind of sail to power a craft out in space," Rymnyr replied.

"Oh yes, I do recall that presentation. That was given by the same person that suggested we tunnel straight through Ulutrita to save time travelling to the Wyr festival in Pylr." Sarcastic laughter circulated throughout the crowd. "Dear professor, thank Zym that this session is drawing to a close. I appreciate your willingness to discuss your wild fantasies here, but we have much more important issues to cover."

The head regent held up a sheet of paper. "I was just handed this before walking in. Seems that the conflict in Bosyra has flared up again." A collective groan rumbled the interior of the hall. "We have an archeological crew there that sent this message stating that they are pulling out because of the presence of armed troops. Regent Handynr, you might want to read this." Bokyl waited till the regent took the yellow telemessage sheet from him, then re-directed his attention to Rymnyr. "Anyway, would you like to make some closing statement?"

"Yes, by all means. Thank you all for allowing us to detail what we think the future holds for this new invention and to outline our albeit, ambitious plan to find the source of these mysterious voices. I had hoped that the discussion would have progressed further, but we shall continue our efforts to convince the Academy to officially endorse this project."

Rymnyr gave a quick bow and headed back to the table. A smattering of applause echoed in the hall, followed by the sound of people rising to their feet and exiting. Gyls rushed over to the table.

"Professor! I know the session didn't go quite as you planned, but I for one am really excited about your proposal." He shot a quick glance over at his father. The older man was just making his way around the far end of the table. Gyls lowered his voice and held up a hand to muffle his words.

"All I need to do is work on my father a little bit, and I think we can be of assistance."

Rymnyr's face lit up. "My dear young man, that is great news!"

The astronomers had also gotten up from the table and were heading toward the exit. Professor Ymyl walked up and put his hand on Rymnyr's shoulder.

"You are a very brave woman. The Academy ees much too constipated to take on an ambitious project like zees. I suggest vee make arrangements for you to talk to the Collria Society."

"That sounds like a great idea. Only problem is that the Collria is an exclusive men's only club, right?"

"Correct."

"Well, it seems like I would have……"

"I belong to the society."

"I am a member also," the head of Phylr Communications said from his position behind the astronomer.

Professor Ymyl's thin face burst into a grin. "See! It was meant to be. Let me confer with zee other members, and I'll get back to you. I must run along, but thank you for inviting us here. My staff and I have much to talk about." The professor bowed quickly, then whisked his way up the exit ramp with the communications executive close behind. At that same time, Gyls' father arrived at the table.

"We appreciate you and your son showing up today." Professor Rymnyr's sweet tone of voice failed to break the father's stoney expression. Gyls reached over and gently grasped his arm.

"Come on Father, let's go."

The older man shook it off. He stared hard into the professor's heavily painted eyes. "You think you're pretty special, don't you? All I really care about these days is making a living. This whole far-fetched plan sounds like some rich person's idle dream to me. It's going to take a lot of convincing to get me to spend any time on it, good day."

Gyls' narrow face flushed with embarrassment as he watched the older man stomp off up the ramp. "I apologize for my father's outburst. Right now, we're really struggling financially. I'll work on him. Thanks again."

He gave a quick wave, then hurried to catch up with his father. Rymnyr stood stunned for a moment as the rest of the crowd left the auditorium. She finally regained her composure and turned toward Kryzyck.

"Wow, I wasn't expecting that! Now I really need a drink. Oh zynk, I have a class in fifteen minutes."

Regent Krynut came walking up from where he had been sitting at the technical table. He stopped right in front of Rymnyr. His intense, tightly wound expression sent a jolt of panic through her.

"You look tired," Krynut said with a smirk.

"I'm spent."

"I think you're wasting the forum's time with this, but I'll be following your progress closely, if I have time. I have my own big project that I'll be unveiling."

With that, he turned and walked up the aisle. Mihyn had been observing the exchange between the two academics. Once Krynut left, she sided up next to her friend.

"Wonder what he meant by that?"

"Hard to say, he certainly creeps me out," Rymnyr replied.

Three days later, a large embossed envelope with gold strips along the border arrived at Professor's Rymnyr's mansion. Her man servant Frygr presented it to her at breakfast.

"Madame, this just arrived."

Rymnyr tore off another bite of sweet roll and took the fancy envelope from him. She mouthed the words "thank you". Using the butter knife, she ripped it open. Inside, an equally fancy sheet of paper, decorated with Styrynt themes, held the following message.

"The Benevolent Order of Collria requests the presence of Professor Rymnyr First Line at their meeting Spyr Day, 118, at 5:00 for the purpose of making a formal presentation to the Order of her proposed expedition to the stryks as outlined to the forum. She is encouraged to bring any materials deemed useful for the aid of communicating the important details of the expedition. A confirmation of this invitation is requested as soon as possible. Note: Styrynt attire is strongly suggested."

Rymnyr squealed with delight and leapt up from the table. Her small, furry pet flygrs were startled by the outburst and ran yipping out of the room.

"Oh my! I can't believe this. The Collrians actually want me to attend their meeting. I must tell Mihyn and Myrvst immediately. Fetch me a scrygy and samsyr."

The man servant complied with her request and placed a crisp sheet of paper on the table next to her. Rymnyr hastily scrawled out two messages, ripped the paper in half, gave each piece a quick fold, and held them out to him.

"Here! Have a messenger take these to them immediately. Oh, this is wonderful!"

A meeting was arranged at the mansion. Professor Ymyl, Gyls the inventor, Regent Mihyn, Professor Myrvst, and Kryzyck were all summoned. The guests began arriving at the specified hour and were ushered into the formal dining room. A wide slate chalkboard had been set up between two easels in front of the massive fireplace. Gyls was the last to show up.

"Wow, this is one fancy place!" he muttered to himself while a servant led him down the main hall. The rest of the guests all got to their feet when the servant led the tall, gangly inventor into the room.

"Welcome! Oh, I assumed your father would come too," Rymnyr said after grasping the young man's hand.

"I tried to talk him into it, but he hasn't really warmed to the idea yet."

"That's too bad. Please have a seat. Zyd?"

"Yes, thank you."

Rymnyr filled one of the beautiful floral design cups from the massive gold alloy zyd urn sitting against the far wall. She set it in front of Gyls, then walked back around to her place at the head of the table. She rested her hands on the back of the chair.

"Esteemed colleagues and friends. Thank you for attending this first of many important meetings concerning our proposed voyage to the stryrks." A shiver of excitement ran through her. "As you all know, Mr. Gyls and I have been invited to present our plan to the Collrians next week."

The inventor held up his hand. "Who are the Collrians, again?"

Rymnyr tilted her head back and let out a quick laugh. "Well, the Benevolent Order of Collria is one of the most prestigious men's organization in Tyrl. It's also highly secretive, and members are chosen from only the highest ranks of intellectia. I believe you are a member Professor Ymyl, correct?"

The wizened professor smiled and folded his fingers together. "Normally, vee don't divulge our membership, but since this meeting is being held in conjunction with a Collrian event, I am at liberty to confirm zat, yes I am a member. I believe Professor Myrvst has been nominated several times but has yet to complete zee initiation ceremony."

Myvst nodded. "I've been meaning to join. It's just that I'm so busy."

Professor Rymnyr smiled, then continued speaking. "At any rate, being asked to present the plan to them is a huge honor, and great opportunity to engage some of the wealthiest and most forward thinking men of our time. So, where shall we begin?"

The guests all looked around at each other. After a moment of silence, Myrvst adjusted his wire frame glasses, and leaned back in his richly carved high back chair.

"Seems to me that we should start with Ymyl explaining the details about the comet."

"I agree, Professor Ymyl, you have the floor," Rymnyr added.

The astronomer pushed back his chair, got to his feet, and walked over to the chalkboard. "Thank you. So, two years from now, Comet Vyryln vill be making another visit to Ulutrita." He drew a large circle on the board, and next to it, the swoosh of the comet. Myrvst held up his hand.

"How close will it pass to Ulutrita?"

Professor Ymyl gave a hesitant grin, then stood with his leathery hands folded in front of him. "Vell, that is a good question. Vee von't know exactly how close it vill come till it gets closer. All I can tell you at this point is it vill be close."

"Close," Myrvst echoed.

"Yes, close."

"Like perhaps, dangerously close?"

"Yes, eet's possible that it might come dangerously close. Like I said, vee von't know till it begins eet's approach next year."

"All the more reason to push ahead with this!" Rymnyr tossed out.

The other participants in the discussion looked at her quizzically. Mihyn had been sitting quietly. She turned toward the professor and slid her arm over the back of the chair.

"What exactly are you getting at?"

"If the comet crashes into Ulutrita and we manage to get some brave individuals safely off before the impact, then we've done a great service. Life is short."

Professor Myrvst gave a grunt of dissatisfaction. "I think we're getting off topic. Mr. Gyls did I recall from the forum presentation that you and the professor had discussed some specifics of the craft?"

The young inventor cleared his throat before answering. "Yes."

"Would you care to share those details with us?"

"Certainly." Gyls took another drink of zyd, picked up the roll of thick paper lying on the table in front of him, and walked over to the chalkboard. "Professor Ymyl, would you hold one end of the drawing?"

The astronomer reached over and grasped the edge of the thick yellow paper. When it was unrolled, the diagram of a cylindrical object with a long point at one end came into view.

"This is the first sketch for the craft," Gyls announced. He gazed around the room, and let the attendees get a good look before continuing. "As you can see by the drawing, toward the back are a pair of steering fins, one horizontal and one vertical. The fins are controlled by a gear mechanism. There is also a telescope mounted toward the back, and a single forward facing window above the cockpit. In the middle are very compact living quarters, a common area and waste removal mechanism mounted in the back wall."

"So how many people will this hold?" Myrvst asked.

"The professor and I discussed this briefly. We propose sending five up."

"And how long do you anticipate the voyage taking?" Mihyn inquired.

Gyls looked over at Rymnyr and shrugged. "That's kind of the big question. Since we really don't know where we're going, it could be a long time."

Myrvst let out a deep laugh. "Oh dear, excuse me. I didn't mean to sound rude! It's just that there are so many questions still unanswered here. How are you going to get this thing up into space? How are they going to breath? What are they going to eat? Oh, and pluge, how are they going to get pluge?"

He chuckled softly while settling back in his chair. "I fear that you are going to get laughed out of the Collrian Society. This isn't a bunch of school children you're going to meet with. They're the...."

"With all due respect, Professor. Yes, I agree, there are many questions to answer, that's why we're here," Rymnyr responded. She shot a fiery glance over his way. The smile disappeared from Myrvst's face. He straightened up in the chair.

"Very well, please continue."

Gyls reached over and took another drink of zyd. "I have considered your first question. In order to get the craft into space, I propose attaching it to a large balloon. I believe the record for the highest ascent at this time is around twenty thousand feet. Once we reach that height, I propose igniting a rocket that would boost us out beyond the planet."

"A rocket?" Ymyl inquired.

"Yes, like you see at big celebrations, only much bigger."

"I suppose it might work."

"So we have a potential means of propulsion," Myrvst commented. "What about air? From what I've heard, the current theory says there's no oxygen out there."

"Allow me to answer zat," Ymyl said with pride. "Vee know that Comet Vyrlyn is composed of mainly pluge ice. Vee also know zat by applying electricity to pluge, you get hydrogen and oxygen. If vee can capture the pluge coming off it, vee have breathable air."

"Alright, so assuming the voyagers can breathe. What moves them along once they are in space?" Myvst asked.

"Um, that's the part I'm not so sure about. I have also drawn up a design that uses a large sail. We know that at high altitudes, there are very strong winds that blow. I have heard theories that in space, these winds could be even more forceful," Gyls responded in a more or less confident manner.

"In the vision I had, the kyrft was under sail," Rymnyr added.

Myvst laughed again. "My dear professor, dreams are wonderful, but we can't depend on them for scientific direction, can we?"

The room fell silent. Kryzyck had been sitting at his place taking it all in. He took a drink of his zyd and swirled the brown liquid around in the cup. His eyebrows pulled close in thought. He wanted to say something, but was a bit intimidated by the highly educated meeting attendees. Myrvst looked across the table at him.

"Mr. Kryzyck, did you want to comment on that?"

"Who me?" The old miner scanned the faces of all in the room. Even though he knew they were all highly respected people in their fields, he also saw compassion and understanding in their faces. Kryzyck took a deep breath.

"How about if we rope the comet?"

His suggestion drew various responses. Rymnyr gave a loud gasp. She looked over at him with her mouth and eyes wide with surprise. Myrvst laughed so hard, tears flowed down the wrinkles beside his eyes. He wiped his damp face with a handkerchief.

"I'm sorry, please understand that I mean no disrespect. It's just that I can't help...." He broke down into laughter again. Once he had regained control, he directed his gaze over at the astronomer.

"No, surely you don't think that would work?" Ymyl's dark eyes didn't waver. Professor Myrvst glanced around at the other participants. "Are you serious?"

"Vee'd need a long rope." Ymyl answered in a dry, technical voice.

"A really long rope," Gyls chimed in.

"Mr. Kryzyck! I believe you have come up with a brilliant suggestion," Rymnyr gushed. She looked over at the old miner. Her grey-green eyes glittered with delight. "Oh, what a wonderful idea! This deserves a toast. Excuse me."

Rymnyr got up from her chair and hustled out into the hallway. Professor Myrvst watched her leave, then turned toward Mihyn.

"Regent, you've been kind of quiet tonight. What are your thoughts?"

"Oh, pardon me. I'm a little distracted tonight. Handynr just left for Bosyra this afternoon, and I guess I'm a bit worried about his safety."

Their host burst back into the room, followed by two servants carrying large gold platters laden with food, and several huge green glass bottles. "In the tradition of the ancient Styrynts, we've decided on a plan, so now, let's get drunk and think about it overnight!"

The rest of the night was spent eating and drinking considerable amounts. Mihyn excused herself after an hour. Rymnyr gave her a sloppy kiss on the cheek.

"Don't worry dear, Handynr will be fine. He knows how to take care of himself," she slurred.

Professors Myrvst and Ymyl stayed another hour and a half, then decided to leave.

"Thank you soooo much for coming," Rymnyr said to the two of them. She set her glass on the table and gripped each of them by the hand. "I feel soooo much more confident about the meeting with the Collrians."

"And remember, I'll be there when you make zee presentation, dressed in my finest senator's robe," Yyml replied.

Rymnyr let go a squeal and pulled both their hands to her ample breasts. She closed her violet shaded eyelids. "I feel soooo fortunate to be part of this historic venture. Thank you both again." She let their hands drop and looked at them with an expression of woozy happiness.

Gyls was the last guest to leave. He walked over to the hostess, his head lowered in thought. Tears were forming in Rymnyr's eyes when he looked up. She reached over and grabbed his hands.

"My dear young man! In two days, we will present this most exciting, ambitious plan before the Collrians. Oh, I can hardly contain myself!" She drew in a shuddering breath. Multicolored tears streaked down her face. "I feel that this may be the culmination of all my life work." She leaned forward and kissed the only bare skin on his bearded face. He blushed.

"Yes, I'm very excited too. So I'll see you on Pryn day, right?"

Gyls turned and headed out into the hall. Kryzyck pulled the big gilt door closed with a click. Rymnyr stood with eyes closed.

"Lock the door, darling."

Chapter 11.

On the day of the presentation, Rymnyr took special care to follow the required attire suggestion. Her extensive collection of Styrynt art offered plenty of examples to choose from. She selected a robe trimmed in deep purple and gold. A branch of wrought gold with leaves and berries was threaded through her period hairdo.

At precisely 5:00, she stepped out of her buggy in front of the address written on the letter. She looked around at the somewhat dilapidated store front. Her plucked eyebrows furrowed with concern. A dry dusty wind blew down the empty street.

"This can't be the place! The most prestigious men's society in Tyrl wouldn't meet on a lonely side street in the warehouse district! We must have read the directions wrong."

Her driver leaned forward and re-read the address. The wind died down for a minute, and from inside the boarded up building, the sound of raucous laughter drifted out.

"Ah, did you hear that?"

"Yes."

Rymnyr hiked up the hem of her robe, and walked across the sidewalk to the faded, sun blistered door. She gave it a hard rap. It opened a crack to reveal a pair of eyes that peered out. She held up the gold embossed envelope. Most of a hand reached through the crack to grab the envelope. The door shut with a crunch of sand.

Gyls and his father came rolling up from the end of the street. Both men squinted into the gusting wind. Their rough wagon pulled up facing Rymnyr. Gyls jumped down, and shielding his eyes from the flying sand, walked up next to the professor. Rymnyr looked over at him and forced herself not to laugh.

The young inventor had obviously tried his best to put a Styrynt costume together. A white tablecloth with a prominent red stain across the bottom had been hastily wrapped around his lanky frame. He wore the same black work boots as usual.

"Hello, professor."

"Hello, Gyls. Glad you could make it."

The beaten up door swung open. A tall very muscular man in an ornate gold helmet stood at attention. In his hand he held a spear. The man motioned with his head for the professor to enter. Gyls followed but was stopped by the diamond shaped point of the spear.

"Give him your invitation," Rymnyr whispered.

"Oh, yes of course."

Gyls fumbled with the armload of scrolled paper he was holding and managed to pull a gold embossed envelope from the bundle. The guard took the envelope from him and examined the letter within.

"Follow me," he commanded in an impossibly deep voice.

Rymnyr smiled in the dim light of the interior. "Isn't this exciting?"

"Yeah, sure. Where is he taking us?"

"Back to their meeting room, I guess?"

They followed the guard through the empty showroom, past a long vacated service counter and rows of bare shelves. The sound of laughter and loud conversation grew louder as they walked across the creaking wooden floor. They passed through a door, up a small flight of stairs, and onto a small landing.

At the far end of the landing, two more guards in similar attire stood in front of a set of double doors. As the group approached, both guards bowed, then opened the doors to reveal a large rectangular room with long tables running along the walls. A low stage was set up at the far end. Rymnyr walked through the opening doors and stopped just inside.

"Holy Zym! This is even more impressive than I imagined. Just look at the costumes of those members seated next to the stage!" She stepped aside and allowed Gyls to get a view of the smoky room. He let go a shallow cough.

"Most impressive. The gold work required to make those helmets is considerable. They seem to be patterned after lyrks of prey. Truly impressive. I like the way the point of the beaks extends right down to the end of their noses."

"I like the inverted nymfyr designs of the other two, the way the petals gracefully sweep out. Oh, this is all so marvelous!" She looped her arm in Gyl's and pulled him across the threshold. "Notice how everyone is dressed as Styrynt senators. The togas with fancy gold piping along the edges are exact replicas, as are the laurels of beaten gold perched on their heads."

Everyone in the room had a drink in their hand. Serving the loud, boisterous group was a team of young women dressed in short linen tunics tied snuggly around their waist. Rymnyr watched the servers bend over to fill the well-crafted drinking vessels being held up as they passed. She let go a little snort of a laugh.

"Oh my! They certainly are authentic. Nothing underneath those low cut tunics, that's for sure! Notice the variety of bejeweled gold hair combs, very detailed. Oh! And each server also has a dagger sheathed in their belt. I just love this!" She lifted a hand and waved it in front of her face. "Zym! How's a person supposed to breathe in here?"

"It is a little smoky," Gyls replied.

One of the flower helmeted officials finally noticed them and strode across the open space in the center of the room. He gave them a quick bow, then motioned for them to follow him. Just before they arrived at their seats, Gyls leaned over to whisper in Rymnyr's ear.

"The paintings and wall coverings seem like they are pretty accurate depictions of life during the Styrynt era."

"Indeed. Look at those statues behind the rows of chairs. I have several of the same ones at home," Rymnyr added with pride.

When the helmeted official spun around and held his arms out, the noise in the room dropped down a notch. Directly in front of the low stage, one of the guards made a deep bow, straightened back up, and gave the end of his spear a hard rap on the wooden floor. Most of the conversation ceased altogether.

The official picked up the long gilt staff that had been laying across the table in front of him and held it high. The red eyes of the expertly rendered serpent head at the end of the staff flashed in the hazy air.

"I have visitors that wish to address the Grand Order of Collria! Will you acknowledge them?"

A portly man seated perpendicular to the visitors got to his feet. "No! I do not recognize these visitors! Women are forbidden to address the Order." The room erupted in loud discussion. With a wave of the serpent headed staff, the official again brought the noise in the room down considerably.

"That is not specifically true," the official replied. It took another wave of his staff to quiet the reaction. "Women are forbidden to become members, but there is no rule about them addressing the Order. We checked." This last clarification was met with low grumblings. The official gazed out through the smoky interior, searching for signs of dissent on the faces of the members. His gold, inverted-flower helmet glinted as he moved right then left.

"Once again, does the Order recognize these visitors?"

Affirmative responses rose up from all around the room. The official broke into a smile, and again raised his staff high. "All rise for the pledge."

A great rustling of fabric and scraping of chair legs across floor filled the room. The official and everyone else in attendance turned to face the large marble statue positioned in the corner of the room. Once the pledge had been recited, the official again waved his staff in the air.

"Members may be seated." Another great rustling and thump of bodies on chairs followed. "As Grand Master of the Order, it's my pleasure to welcome Professor Rymnyr and Mr. Gyls. Sylr, show the guests to their seats."

The guard bowed, turned on his sandaled heels, and walked solemnly back across the floor. He led the visitors up to an empty spot near the left side of the stage. Several individuals offered a quick hello to Rymnyr as she passed. Gyls leaned over to whisper into her well-constructed hairdo.

"Looks like some of these people know you."

Her lips parted in a wide smile. "Oh yes, I know probably eighty percent of the men here. Most of them I get along with. There are a couple of them I can't stand. "

Once they were seated, one of the gorgeous servant women appeared behind them. "Can I get you something to drink?"

Gyls swung around in his seat and stared right into the woman's magnificent cleavage. His Adam's Apple bobbed up and down. He forced himself to look up at her smiling face.

"Just pluge, thanks."

"Oh come on, the Collrians have excellent taste. Order whatever you want!" Rymnyr commented from her seat.

"No really, pluge is fine. I don't drink."

"Hmm, suite yourself. I'd like a glass of whatever red mynth you have."

The servant woman nodded and turned to leave. Rymnyr watched her shapely form sway under the loose short tunic. "Like I said, the Collrians sure have good taste."

From his position next to the stage, the Grand Master again got to his feet, and waved the serpent headed staff in the air. "Alright, now that we are all seated, there is some quick business we need to attend to before our first presentation."

"First presentation? I thought it was just us!" Rymnyr commented. The servant girl returned and placed a goblet of rich dark mynth on the table. "Thank you dear." Rymnyr grasped the carefully crafted metal vessel, tilted it up, and promptly drained it.

"Oh! That is really good!" She leaned back in her chair and shouted at the servant. "Excuse me! Miss! Another please." The professor held out the empty goblet. Rymnyr watched the servant saunter back towards her. "What great dynts."

The professor's bawdy exclamation brought a bashful smile to Gyls' face. "Don't get too hammered. Remember this is our big chance," he offered in a halfway pleading tone.

Rymnyr reached over and patted his hand. "Don't you worry. I can drink with the best of them."

After several minutes of business being discussed, the Grand Master leaned forward, and made eye contact with Gyls. "Ready?"

"I have some diagrams I need to display. Can someone help me, uh put them up?"

One of the younger members was recruited to assist Gyls, and together the two young men tacked his canvases to a rafter above the stage. Once the diagrams were secured, Gyls took a moment to gaze out at the tables full of powerful, influential men dressed in togas. His confidence wavered slightly at presence of so many high-powered individuals. He sent a quick glance over at Rymnyr.

She had taken his chair and was conversing with a bald headed gentleman seated next to her. Both of them were laughing uproariously about something. Rymnyr took a sloppy drink of her mynth, laughed some more, then took another drink.

The young member that had helped with the diagrams was just folding up the ladder when Gyls walked over toward him and grabbed his sleeve. "Excuse me, will you tell Professor Rymnyr to come up here?"

"Absolutely."

Gyls watched the young man carefully negotiate the steep steps. After leaning the ladder against the wall, the helper stepped behind Rymnyr, and said something in her ear. The professor laid her hand on the bald gentleman's arm, grasped her goblet, and rather unsteadily made her way toward the stage.

Halfway up the stairs, she stepped on the hem of her robe, and plunged forward. Mynth sloshed out of her goblet, creating an arrow shaped stain on the white fabric. She cursed loudly. Gyls ran over to help her get to her feet.

"Professor! Are you alright?"

"Yes, I'm fine. Zym dyth it! I spilled my mynth! I'm not used to walking in this long robe."

He grasped her hand and led her up the remaining steps. She straightened the wrinkles out of her robe, then finished off the goblet.

"Ready?" she asked with mynth scented breath.

Gyls looked into her glassy grey-green eyes. He nodded with some hesitancy.

"I'll introduce us, then it's all yours." Rymnyr cleared her throat and turned toward the audience. "Esteemed members of the order. My associate and I are honored to be your guests tonight!" Applause, and some loud cheers circulated around the rectangular room. "Thank you for the excellent mynth!" She held up her empty goblet. "We are here to present the specifics of a project that will fire the imagination of all Ulutrita. We propose to send, how many voyagers?" Rymnyr turned back toward Gyls. He held up five fingers.

"Five brave voyagers on a trip to the stryrks." The sound of laughter and muffled conversation rose up from the crowd. "Mr. Gyls will give you the details."

The young inventor looked around at the confused faces of the attendees. "Professor. Tell them why we are going."

"Oh, yes. As most of you are aware, an acquaintance of mine and Professor Myrvst made an incredible discover a short time ago. He accidently invented a device that has picked up some kind of wireless transmission from a world not far away. Our goal is to find this world and make contact with its inhabitants."

Upon hearing the last proclamation, the smoky room was filled with the sound of animated conversations. The Grand Master picked up his staff and waved it in the air. "Quiet! Please let the professor finish her presentation, then we can entertain questions and discussions."

The room gradually quieted down. Rymnyr broke into a big, sloppy smile, and held her hand toward the inventor. "Very well, I now turn it over to Mr. Gyls."

"Hello everyone, my name is Gyls Third Line. My father and I have been working on plans for a device that will allow people to sail through the air like lykrs. Professor Rymnyr approached us several weeks ago about building a craft that will actually carry people beyond our planet and out into space. Needless to say, that is quite a request, but I have here a diagram of what that craft might look like."

Gyls swung around and pointed his arm up toward the canvas directly behind. After running through a quick description of the craft and its functions, he paused just a moment to let his words sink in.

"Any questions?" Hands went up all around the room. "You, sir." Gyls pointed to a tall, distinguished man with a closely cropped black beard near the back of the room.

The man got to his feet. He was indeed very tall. The way his coarse salt and pepper hair was cut around his forehead, and his goatee trimmed gave his face an amazing triangular appearance.

"I have lots of questions, but I'm sure everyone does. First, how are you going to get this craft up into the sky?"

"We propose attaching it to a series of high altitude phymlr balloons, like the ones that the Academy uses to monitor winds in the upper atmosphere, then igniting a large rocket to propel it the rest of the way."

The smile on Gyls' narrow face left little doubt about how much he was enjoying the opportunity to engage such a dignified group. More hands went up. Gyls pointed to a dark skinned individual at the far table. The man stood and spoke with a thickly accented voice.

"So once you are in space, then what? How do you propel it?"

Before Gyls could answer, one of the members at the front table got to his feet. Beneath the long glinting beak of his lykr head helmet, Gyls recognized Professor Ymyl's face. The inventor let out a sigh of relief. He bent over and called out to the astronomer.

"Professor, would you like to answer the question?"

"I'd be delighted." Ymyl pushed his chair back, walked over to the base of the stage, and began unfurling a long painted canvas. Another of the members got up from his seat at the opposite table and grasped the edge of the painting.

"This a diagram of the calculated path of Comet Vyrlyn, which vill pay Ulutrita another visit late next year. As you can see, vee calculate zat it vill pass very close. If our timing ees right, vee propose to launch this craft just before zee comet makes eets closest pass, zen using a loop of rope approximately three miles in diameter, snag zee nucleus, and ride it out into space."

The professor's plan drew an immediate and highly charged reaction from the order members. Laughter, shouts, and amazed exclamations rang out through the hazy room. Ymyl calmly gazed around at the mixture of smiling, frowning, and astounded faces.

A stocky, square headed man seated in the table opposite the officials got to his feet and stood glaring at the stage. His prominent chin, short efficient nose, and wide cheekbones projected an air of power. He appeared to be in his mid-thirties and was handsome in a blunt force kind of way. Ymyl pointed at him.

"You have a question?"

"Yes I do. Are you out of your mind?" The room erupted in laughter, then quickly quieted down. "My name is Lymdyr Nine Line, and I work in the steam train industry. We are just able to produce speeds of up to one hundred miles per hour with a train. I appreciate your ambition to develop this system, but really, there are so many untested variables to this. Who are you going to find that is foolish enough to get ferried up into the sky and blasted into space?"

Several places down from the man asking the questions, Regent Krynut slowly got to his feet. "I for one would offer to be part of this most ambitious project." The room buzzed with low volume reactions to his statement. "I too, am presenting a project tonight that although less revolutionary than this, has the potential to bring great changes to Ulutrita." The slight pause in Krynut's statement gave the Grand Master a chance to speak.

"It's a great honor to be present at a meeting of this magnitude. I believe our founder, Patimus of Collria...." He extended his arm out toward the large marble statue positioned in the corner of the room. "Would be flattered to know that his devotees are fortunate enough to be part of these discussions." He craned his neck around to address the presenters. "Professor, Mr. Gyls, please proceed."

Gyls looked around at the faces in the crowd. He struggled to regain his composure. "Professor Rymnyr! I seem to have lost my train of thought. What should we say now?"

The professor glanced back at him and smiled. "I've got it under control." She turned back toward the audience. "Professor Ymyl, will you kindly explain about air and pluge for the crew?"

Ymyl repeated his theory about collecting water from the comet trail. His explanation again drew audible responses from the seated members. While he fielded questions, the Grand Master rotated around in his chair, and spoke directly to Rymnyr.

"We're running over. Would you like to make a final statement?"

"I'd be delighted." She waited for two more questions to be answered, then stepped to the edge of the stage and waved at Professor Ymyl. "Professor, we need to wrap up." The astronomer nodded and returned to his chair. "There are many, many details that still need to be worked out with this voyage. We would like to give a hearty thanks to the Order for allowing us to present here and would like to invite any of you to help us make this dream a reality. Any ….."

"A dream? It's more like some kind of nightmare!" Lymdyr yelled from the table near the stage. All faces turned toward him. "I mean, really. This is the most preposterous idea I have ever heard! I for one…."

"When our ancestors built the first sailing kyrft and explored Ulutrita, they were met with the same doubtful reaction! We're just extending the hand of humanity a little farther out," Rymnyr shouted back. The normally pale white skin of her face was now deep red with anger.

"My dear professor, I suggest you go back to your students, and concentrate on teaching them language. Space travel is way beyond your capabilities. This is why women are not allowed in the Order!"

The last statement by Lymdyr brought a huge response from the members. It seemed that fights were on the verge of breaking out all around the smoky room. Gyls grabbed the professor by the arm and dragged her off the stage.

"Order! Order please, dyth it! I'll clear this hall out if I have to," the Grand Master yelled while waving his serpent staff vigorously in the air. The commotion slowly settled down. "There, that's better. Need I remind you all that considerate debate is one of the principal tenets of our order. Shouting and interrupting are not. Regent Krynut, are you ready?"

The mathematician rose from his spot next to the stage. "It will take me a moment to set up."

"Very well, let's all take a slight break, get something more to drink, and calm down a bit before this next presentation." The Grand Master plunked back down in his seat. Immediately, the room filled with the sound of eager voices.

Chapter 12.

Over beside the stage, Gyls and Rymnyr were still a bit stunned by the impact of their presentation.

"You can let go of my arm," she snarled. Her strong words shook Gyls back to the present. He released his grip, then pulled her chair back.

"Thank you." She slid down onto her seat and stared out across the room. Her grey-green eyes flashed with anger. "I can't believe the nerve of that square headed blyrthole!"

One of the servant women came walking out of the kitchen with a tray of drinks. The professor reached out and grabbed the hem of the woman's short tunic. The servant let out a yelp, almost spilling the tray. She turned around with a snap of her dark hair.

"Don't do that! Do you want something? I'll have one of the other girls stop by."

"You're dyth right I want something! Another goblet of that, oh Zym, I left mine up there on the stage."

"We'll get you another one." The servant swatted Rymnyr's hand away and hustled off down the row of chairs.

Gyls looked over at the professor. He rubbed hands together. "Well, now that our presentation is done, we should probably get out of here. I have....."

"Not on your life! This is the only chance I'll ever get to crash this party. We're staying till the end, that's final." Rymnyr flashed a triumphant grin. The inventor slumped down in his chair. A headache was beginning to pound in his temples.

"Really, professor, I think we should leave. I have things I..."

"Not a chance. Neither you or I will probably ever get invited here again. Relax, enjoy the experience while it lasts."

Gyls shot a quick glance over at Rymnyr's beaming face and eased up out of his chair. "I'm, going...to walk around."

Up on the stage, Krynut was busy assembling the wooden frame of his invention. Gyls watched for a few moments, then ascended the stairs, and kneeled beside the mathematician.

"Need a hand?"

Krynut looked up from his task. His olive skinned face was wound tight with concentration. "Actually, yes. If you can reach around and hold that nut, I'm having a Myrnvar of a time tightening these."

Gyls slid his arm around the back of the apparatus. "What exactly is this?"

"It's, a, hold on, one more turn, there. It's a calculating device. Grab one of those long rods over there, please."

Gyls withdrew his hand from the back of the device and picked up the lustrous grey metal piece from the pile lying on the stage. It was about as thick as a strand of linguine. As he turned to hand it to Krynut, the end of it struck the wooden frame. The narrow rod vibrated furiously in Gyl's hand.

"Oh no, did I damage it?"

"No, this stuff is incredibly strong. Hold the next nut, please." When the last of the graduated metal pieces was secured, Krynut pointed toward a cloth bag sitting over off to the side. "Bring that over here."

Gyls slid the bag over and handed it to him. Krynut opened the bag and placed one of the wooden balls it contained into each of the thirty-six wooden cups located above the upper end of the row of secured metal rods.

From his place at the foot of the stage, the Grand Master called out above the din of voices. "Are you about ready Regent? I think the members are getting rather tanked."

"Yes, we just finished." Krynut dusted off his toga and turned toward Gyls. "Thanks for your help. Might as well take your seat."

The Grand Master waved his serpent staff in the smoky air. "May I have your attention, Regent Krynut is now going to demonstrate for us a most interesting device he has invented. Regent, it's all yours."

"Thank you, to start off, let me give you some background information on this device. I'm sure most of you have been to Singing Rocks at the base of Plymtr Mountain. This strange, highly musical jumble of rocks has held a special fascination for me since I first visited the site as a child.

Two years ago, I got permission to remove some of them for analytical purposes. With the help of the Academy's geology and chemistry departments, we were able to determine that these rocks are actually a type of ore, from which a new and very hard metal can be smelted under extremely high temperatures. I have been able to work this metal into thin rods which vibrate powerfully when very specific sound waves hit them, particularly those generated by musical instruments." The buzz of low conversation swept around the room. "I will now demonstrate."

Krynut walked over to the edge of the stage, opened an instrument case, and withdrew a black lacquered metal horn. It was approximately three feet long, with holes drilled at intervals along the shaft. A large bell flared out at one end. The horn tapered down to a narrow mouthpiece at the other.

After walking back over to the device, Krynut positioned the bell directly in front of the wooden frame, took a breath, and blew a succession of notes at a moderately loud volume. Within their secured brackets, a number of the rods undulated into a shiny grey blur. The wooden balls sitting atop them rolled off the cups and fell into a track behind. Krynut dropped the horn from his lips and turned back to the audience.

"So, what does this all mean?" He stepped to the side of the device and pointed to one of the shiny metal pieces. "I have placed these rods at specific intervals along these four horizontal rails. Their placement represents logarithmic values. In the back of the rails, the rods are connected so that a pre-determined number vibrate together. When the balls get sent down the track, they wind up in these holes at the bottom which are marked with numeric values, as are the cups on top. By changing the connectors that allow specific rods to vibrate, I'm able to carry out amazingly complex, and accurate calculations very quickly."

He let the last statement sink in before continuing. While Krynut gazed around the room, he fought to keep the smile that wanted to explode across his otherwise sanguine features from developing. "I have this set for multiplication, would anyone care to throw out a complex set of numbers for verification?"

The smoky, rectangular room rumbled with the sound of men talking amongst themselves. From the table to the right of the stage, Lymdyr held his hand up. Krynut pointed at him from the stage.

"Yes."

The railroad man got to his feet. He took a moment to make sure all eyes were on him. His slicked back black hair glinted in the hazy light. "Earlier today, I was at a meeting of the board where we were discussing changes to the wage scale. It was not a very congenial meeting." Polite laughter rolled down the tables. "I happen to remember what the final figures presented were, if you'd like to use them."

"By all means."

Lymdyr rattled off a string of numbers. Krynut spun around, muttering the calculations to himself. He bent down, returned the wooden balls from the holders at the base of the device to the row of cups above, clicked some narrow levers that protruded from under each cup below the horizontal rail, and reached for his horn.

He gave his lips a quick lick, then blasted out a series of notes. The metal rods positioned vertically in the frame shuddered with the impact of the sound waves. Their movement sent the wooden balls rolling down the track in the back of the frame where they landed with a thunk in the numbered holes at the base. Krynut knelt down and called out the numbers.

"Two hundred thirty-seven thousand, eighty hundred and seventy-six."

Lymdyr let out a gruff sort of laugh. "Not bad. And I assume it can add, subtract, and divide?"

Krynut nodded his head. Many hands went up around the room. From his seat beside the stage, Gyls listened to some of the questions, then reached over, and laid a hand on Rymnyr's arm.

"Professor, I'd like to leave....."

"Gyls darling, this is Wybr," the professor blurted out. She leaned back and let the scrawny, bald headed man extend his hand. Gyls shook it as quickly as possible.

"Amazing plan you two are devising. I work in the accounting department at the council. If I can assist in drafting any kind of financial proposal, you let me know!"

Rymnyr bent forward and planted a sloppy kiss on the man's cheek. She miscalculated the force required which sent him reeling back slightly. Both of them exploded with laughter.

Gyls got up from his chair, walked to the back of the room, and leaned against the wall. Several of the servant women were gathered in the corner. They were talking amongst themselves and watching for signals that someone needed a drink. The one closest to Gyls ventured a glance over at him. She recognized the look of despair on his thin face.

The waitress stepped around her co-worker and stood next to him. Even though she was the oldest of the servants, her fine features still possessed a stunning beauty. Years of experience had blessed her with a strong maternal spirit.

"Are you alright, Love?"

The inventor turned and looked into her kind, middle-aged eyes. "Not really. I don't drink, and that seems to be the most popular activity here. The smoke gave me a headache as soon as we arrived."

"You're with the lady over near the stage, right?"

"Yes."

"She seems to be having a great time." Both Gyls and waitress looked over at Rymnyr and her new-found friend sitting very close to each other across the room. "Your presentation is done, right? Why don't you leave? We'll make sure she gets home."

Gyls straightened up from his slouch. An expression of hopefulness blossomed across his bearded face. "You really think so?"

"Sure, we send people home in buggies all the time. We've had to carry a few members out, but she looks like she could walk, maybe."

"Thanks, I think I'll do that." He flashed a quick smile her way, then hurried back to where Rymnyr and her new friend were still yucking it up. The booming voice of the Grand Master caused him to stop just behind them.

"Thank you Regent Krynut! My goodness, two astounding presentations in one night. I think this meeting will go down in the history of the order."

Thundering applause, whistles, and enthusiastic voices filled the room. From his spot at the far corner, Lymdyr got to his feet. His hard-chiseled facial features beamed happiness.

"Honorable Grand Master! I concur wholeheartedly with you. In honor of this momentous night, I propose we drink a toast!" His suggestion was met with a chorus of affirmations. "A bottle of Mintxeia, please, not the usual, but one of the fifty year-old!" The response from the crowd was deafening.

"Ooooh, I love Mintexia!" Professor Rymnyr squealed.

"Make that two bottles!" Regent Bokyl yelled from across the room.

The tall, salt and peppered haired man that had spoken earlier jumped to his feet. He towered above the table. "Make that three!"

As the servants scooted off to fill the order, many of the members began moving toward the big wooden doors. Those that remained broke into loud conversation. Gyls leaned over and whispered into Rymnyr's ear.

"Professor, I'm going. The servants will get you a buggy home. Is that alright?"

She reared her head back to look at him. "What? Did you say you're leaving?"

"Yes."

"Aw, well, goodnight. Come here." She reached under his wooly chin and drew his face toward her. "Thank you soooooo much for coming with me. We killed it tonight!" She planted a wet kiss on his cheek and slid her fingers down the side of his face. "Sure you don't want to stay?"

"I'm sure, see you soon."

Just as Gyls straightened back up, the young person that had helped him tack up his drawings walked up and held out the two rolled up canvases.

"Here ya go. That was quite the project that you and the professor presented. Not sure I believe it will ever fly, but I give you both credit for your ambition."

Gyls hefted the rolled up canvases with both arms. "Yeah, I think we convinced some of the members tonight. Anyway, thanks for your assistance. I gotta head home. I'm not usually up this late."

"I'll follow you out. These old guys will probably be here till styrkrise."

Rymnyr rose from her chair and took several unsteady steps toward the kitchen. "I need to use the ladies' room. Hah! I bet there isn't one." She moved off toward the hall, weaving back and forth. Wybr watched her ample bottom swing beneath her toga as she walked. Gyls and the younger member started toward the door. Wybr grabbed the inventor by the arm.

"Sure you don't want to stick around? I have a feeling it's going to be lots of fun!"

Gyls looked down at Wybr's leering features. "No thanks."

Once his arm was freed, the inventor continued working his way to the exit. Just on the other side of the big double doors, he joined the line of men filing out. The older servant walked by him carrying a bottle of brown liquid. She sent a quick departing smile at Gyls, then walked over to where Head Regent Bokyl was standing. He accepted the bottle from her and gave a little bow.

"Myrls, join us won't you? We're going to retire to the lounge. Much more comfortable there."

"I'd love to, are you sure?" she said with exaggerated humility.

"Of course! The Styrynt men always had beautiful women around when they celebrated."

Chapter 13.

Early the next morning, Sylstyn was up making breakfast in the sunlit kitchen. She hummed to herself while cutting up the bread. Blrsynt wandered in after just getting up. His short brown hair stuck up in several directions.

"Morning."

She turned around and sent a beaming smile his way. "Good morning!"

They kissed briefly, then she returned to her task. "There's zyd in the kettle over there. I have class this morning, so I'm going to put everything out, then run off. What are you and your uncle doing today?"

"Not sure. I know both he and Professor Myrvst are really anxious to see how the presentation went with, what's the name of that secret society?"

"The Collrians."

"Ah, yes."

Blrsynt poured some of the zyd into a cup and watched the vapor lazily float up. After taking a sip, he set the cup down, walked up behind Sylstyn, and slid his arms around her waist. When he pressed up against her, she let go a sigh and pressed back. The sound of footsteps on the creaking floorboards drifted in above the chirping of the lykrs outside.

"I think the professor is coming," Sylstyn whispered.

He gave her a final quick squeeze and eased his way over to the counter. Professor Myrvst tottered into the kitchen. He looked up at the two young people and smiled.

"Good morning,"

"Good morning, Professor. I have to run off to class, so I'm just going to put nymyr out, then leave." Sylstyn finished sawing several slices of bread and laid them on a plate.

While Myrvst was pouring himself a cup of zyd, Kryzyck entered the sun-lit dining room. He yawned and nodded to the other two. Professor Myrvst waited till the miner sat down, then leaned toward him.

"You didn't hear from Rymy last night did you?

"I did not."

Myrvst stroked his beard several times. "Hmmmm, I thought she would send a runner over last night with news of how the presentation went, but it must have gone later than expected. After we eat, I think we should head over to the Academy, and get a rundown."

An hour and a half later, Blrsynt pulled the buggy up in front of the wide Academy steps. His uncle and Myrvst hopped out. The younger man parked down the street and walked with a group of students hurrying along. Just ahead of him, two young men were conversing excitedly.

"Did you hear that war has broken out it Bosrya?"

"Yep, I guess the archeological team had to run for their lives."

Blrsynt caught up with the professor and his uncle at the top of big marble stairs. "I just heard that full on war has broken out in Bosyra."

"Yes, we were alerted about a week ago." Professor Myrvst commented without looking up.

They entered the high ceilinged foyer, and Myrvst led the way over to the information desk. "Can you tell me what Professor Rymnyr's schedule is today?"

A petite young woman with pulled back dark hair thumbed through some papers, then answered. "It looks like she has cancelled all her classes today."

"Hmm, thank you."

Myrvst's tangled grey eyebrows twitched. He walked back to where his companions were standing. "Professor Rymnyr cancelled her classes today. I hope she's not ill." The three of them shared a questioning look. "I know Head Regent Bokyl was there last night. Wait here, and I'll go up and ask him." Fifteen minutes later, Myrvst returned.

"Well, Bokyl said the presentation went well, and judging by his bedraggled appearance, I'd say the after presentation party went even better. We should probably go to up Phylgr and check on Rymy."

While the three of them headed back out the big copper doors, Myrvst chatted away. "Bokyl also said that the archaeologic team in Bosyra is safe, but Regent Handynr sent a telemessage saying that the situation is still very tense."

A short time later, they arrived at Rymnyr's opulent mansion. The costumed gatekeeper recognized them and swung the ornate gilded barrier open. Dazzling sunlight glinted off the dark green leaves of the thorn trees as they rolled down the long driveway.

The drive looped around a fountain directly in front of the dwelling. Blrsynt snickered when he noticed the expertly crafted figures locked in amorous union amid the flowing water. Kryzyck and the professor hopped out and walked up onto the porch. Myrvst swung the big metal knocker three times against the door. He waited patiently, then frowned.

"That's strange, usually someone is right there."

He gave it one more resounding bang. From the other side of the door, shuffling footsteps echoed. The door swung open, and Frygr's narrow face appeared.

"Madame is quite indisposed at the moment."

Myrvst looked over at the old miner, then turned back toward the open door. "Oh, I see. Is she ill?"

"Yes, deathly ill." The head servant flashed a huge grin at the visitors.

Kryzyck's brow wrinkled up with concern. "Might I slip in and talk to her?"

Frygr opened the door wide enough for the miner to enter.

"I'll wait out here," Myrvst offered.

The head servant and Kryzyck made their way down the main hall in silence. When they turned to head toward the living quarters, the miner spoke up.

"So when did she get sick?"

"She has only been home for about three hours. Let's just say that she had a touch too much fun last night."

Kryzyck opened the massive ornately carved bedroom door and quietly entered the room. Rymnyr lay motionless, face down on top of the bed. Her small feet stuck out over the end of the frame. The soft soles were dusted with dirt. Her elegant Styrynt sandals were nowhere to be found. Kryzyck eased his way around to the side of the bed and gently sat down.

Rymnyr groaned softly. Her elaborate hairdo was now just an unruly, greying mass of hair. Kryzyck reached out to stroke her hair, but decided against it. There was no smooth area to stroke. He bent down to whisper to her and ventured a glance at her expressionless face. Red lipstick was smeared in a rakish swoop across her chin and off to the right. Her entire being seemed to exude the smell of stale gynt smoke and alcohol.

"Rymy, are you alright?"

She groaned again, and her painted eyelids attempted to open. "Holy Zym! It's so bright in here. Close the curtains."

Kryzyck eased off the bed and complied with her request. Once the curtains were closed, she rolled over onto her side. He returned to her bedside and knelt on the rug. Her eyelids finally opened.

"It's nice to see you," she whispered. "Can you get me some pluge? I think there's a glass over on the dresser."

While Kryzyck retrieved the glass, she pulled her toga wrapped body to an upright position. After taking a long, shaky drink, the professor reached up and loosened the swatch of mostly white material wrapped around her neck.

"Why the dyth is my dress on backwards? Oh Zym, I have to lay back down. My head is pounding!" She collapsed back into a reclining position. "I am never, ever drinking Mintexia again."

Kryzyck reached over and patted her hand. "I think I better let you rest. I'll come back and check on you later."

She opened her eyes and gave him a weak smile. "Are you mad at me?"

The old miner frowned. "No, why would I be mad at you?"

"No reason. Just thought I'd ask."

He bent over, kissed her cheek, and walked quietly into the hall. Kryzyck let himself out the front door. Myrvst's buggy was parked beside the fountain, but his nephew and the professor were nowhere to be seen. He stepped off the cool shade of the porch, and into the hot sunlight of mid-morning.

From around the side of the house, he heard Blrsynt's deep laugh. The old miner crunched across the gravel driveway, down the sun dappled lawn, and around the massive wing of the house. His companions were standing outside the aviary watching a group of small primates cavorting behind the wire screen. Myrvst turned away from the action when he saw the miner approach.

"Oh, there you are. We were just watching to two male byngyrs fighting for the attention of the female. Zym, these creatures are fun to watch. How's Rymy?" Kryzyck waited a moment to answer. The professor's wrinkled smile faded slowly. "Is she alright?"

"Yes, yes, she's hugely hung over, and…., never mind, um, yes she's fine. We should come back later and get the full story."

Myrvst took a moment to scrutinize the miner's somber face. "I have classes all afternoon, but you two should come back. In the meantime, why don't you drop me off at the Academy and go talk to Gyls."

After their stop at the Academy, the two miners headed out toward the barrel factory that Gyls and his father owned. On the road leading north out of town, billows of dust swept over them. Blrsynt spit a gritty mouthful into the wind.

"Boy, this isn't much fun!" he grumbled. Eyes squinting against the wind, the young man ventured a glance over at his uncle. The older man sat upright on the seat. Although the wind and dust were pelting him just as relentlessly as his nephew, Kryzyck just stared straight ahead.

"Everything alright? You seem kind of quiet today."

"Yeah, everything's fine. Rymy said something kind of strange this morning, but considering her condition…." Kryzyck let his enigmatic response fly off in the wind. They rolled along and eventually a low collection of buildings appeared ahead.

"That must be it over there." Blrsynt guided the buggy off the road and around to the back of the nearest brick structure. Both styrns snorted heavily once he tied them up.

One of the workers directed the two miners to a single story structure with piles of wooden staves out front. Kryzyck walked over to the door, gave a knock, then gently pushed it open. Gyls and his father were bent over a table, examining some drawings. Both of them turned to see who had entered. The father had a scowl draped across his weathered face. Gyls was frowning too, but when he recognized the two visitors, his features softened into a smile.

"Blrsynt, Mr. Kryzyck, welcome, come on in."

The two men entered the room with a whoosh of sandy air. They walked over and stood before the table.

"Father, you remember Mr. Kryzyck from the meeting at the Academy, and this is his nephew, Blrsynt," Gyls said with a trifle of hesitation.

"Hyryl's the name," the father added. He held out his hand which both Blrsynt and the old miner shook.

"We were just discussing the project. I was telling Father what a great reception we had from some of the members last night. Now if they just agree to donate some dyrn to help with the construction, that will be great," Gyls ended his statement with a nervous laugh. "Would you like to see the shell?"

Blrsynt simply nodded a reply. He could sense the tension in the air. Gyls led them over to a long cylindrical object covered with a thick tan canvas in the back of the room. He tossed the edge of the covering up over the top of it, then stepped to the side.

"This is my prototype for the craft."

The visitors spent a few moments just taking a good look at the object before approaching it. Blrsynt leaned over and tapped the thick chevron shaped window on the nose of the craft.

"So, what's inside it?"

"Nothing yet. Would you like to see the plan for the actual one?"

"Sure."

"Excuse me gentlemen, but I have a business to run here. My son will be glad to show you his current flight of fantasy. Good day." The father shook his head and walked across the sandy floor toward the entrance. Once he had left, Gyls let out a resigned little sigh.

"As you can see, Father is still not one-hundred percent behind the project. He was fine with me working on flying machines, but this one is just a little beyond his grasp."

The inventor stepped over to a long table set perpendicular to the craft. With Blrsynt's help, he unrolled a wide piece of canvas. After spending a few minutes outlining the main features of the craft, Gyls stopped in mid-sentence to yawn.

"Ah, excuse me. I got home pretty late last night and had a hard time falling asleep."

"That's right. How did the presentation go?" Blrsynt asked.

"You know, I think it went well. I'd say half the members seemed genuinely interested, and the other half thought we were crazy. Professor Rymnyr made quite an impression on them."

Kryzyck was still leaning over the diagram. He lifted his head to make eye contact with Gyls. "What kind of impression?" A hint of suspicion colored the old miner's question.

"What I meant was, the professor is a very good speaker. She was able to inspire many of them with her vision for the project."

"I see." Kryzyck gave a short laugh and straightened up to full height. "So what's the next step after you get this prototype complete?"

"Well, I figure that's when the testing starts. The way I see it, we need to first determine if my idea of sending the craft up in balloons with a kykpowder rocket will work. I should be ready for that in a couple weeks."

"A couple weeks?" Kryzyck repeated. His voice was strung with excitement.

"Yeah, I mean, my aim is not to build a complete replica of the actual craft. We just need to make it the approximate weight and design."

"Wow, I don't have anything really important to do for the next couple weeks, would you like some help?" Blrsynt offered.

Gyls' thin, bearded face lit up. "I would love to have some help! As you saw, father is not too keen on the idea. He had a very tough childhood in Wyrtaz during the war. Making a living and having enough to eat are a big concern to him. I guess you and I are part of the new generation. We haven't suffered like our parents did."

"I grew up on a farm in the Klyrk delta. We were poor, but always had enough to eat. Heck, I got nothing really important to do either if you'd like some extra help," the old miner chimed in.

"Great! I can't believe how lucky I am. Yes, yes of course. I'd be more than happy to have the two of you help." Gyls' eyes were wide with elation. "When do you want to start?"

Blrsynt looked over at his uncle, then back at the inventor.

"How about now?"

Gyls clapped his hands together. A shudder of excitement ran through his rail thin frame.

"You're serious, aren't you? I can't believe that things are actually going to work out! Excuse me, I must be a little giddy from lack of sleep. Okay, calm down. I need to focus."

Chapter 14.

Over the next couple days, Kryzyck and his nephew diligently showed up and assisted Gyls with the work on the prototype. By the end of the week, it was ready for testing. Professor Rymnyr sent a messenger over to Myrvst's house requesting a meeting at her mansion. At noon on the Ulutritan equivalent of Saturday, Blrsynt, his uncle, and Professor Myrvst rode up together. Just as they turned off the boulevard and headed up the hill, the younger man directed his gaze up toward the sky.

"It sure feels like the hot part of the year has ended." Both the other passengers took in his observation without comment. "I like the way that low ceiling of clouds looks just like a soft, white comforter suspended above the ground."

Myrvst shifted in his seat and looked up as well. "This is my favorite time of year."

They followed three other buggies along the gravel driveway toward the gate. Blrsynt pulled gently on the reins to slow their progress. "Looks like the professor has invited several other people here."

"From what she said, there are four very prominent businessmen that are interested in the project," Kryzyck added.

Once they arrived at the large fountain, Blrsynt had to direct the buggy around to the far side of the circle to find an empty spot. The three of them got out and made their way up the stone steps. Frygr greeted them in the doorway.

"Welcome, the meeting will take place in the main dining room. I trust you know the way."

Kryzyck gave him a nod and led the group in. Along the south wall of the foyer, a huge floral arrangement sat. It had evidently been there for several days. The petals of the large white lilies were beginning to turn brown.

As the trio approached the dining room, the sound of loud, excited conversation echoed toward them. Two servants came rushing by them, arms laden with trays of food. The trio followed them into the brightly lit room. Rymnyr was engaged in a lively discussion with two of the Collria members; Symgyr, the very tall salt and peppered haired gentleman and Lymdyr, the square headed railroad man.

"Professor, you must come to the next meeting of the order. We haven't had that much fun in years, maybe ever!" Symgyr finished his invitation by breaking into a wide grin.

Lymdyr lifted a hand up beside his mouth and glanced back and forth in mock secrecy. "I'll probably be thrown out of the order for saying this, but I think we should nominate you as the first female member."

"Blasphemy!" the tall man yelled. All three of them burst out in laughter. At that same time, Kryzcyk's group entered the room. Rymnyr looked over at the new arrivals, excused herself, and walked over to meet them.

Myrvst spread his arms wide and gave her a hug. "Ah, professor. Nice to see you again."

She hugged him back. "Glad you could make it." After releasing him, she reached out and grasped Blrsynt's hand. "Welcome." She blew a quick kiss to Kryzyck and fluttered off to the next group. More guests filed in, and the din of conversation rose significantly. After several moments, Rymnyr held up a crystal glass, and tapped it lightly.

"It looks as though almost everyone is here, first of all, welcome. Thank you for taking the time to attend this first official meeting of what I would like to propose we deem, the Dymran Society." Applause echoed around the opulently decorated room. "As most of you know, Dymran was the messenger of the gods in the Styrynt pantheon. I feel it fitting that we dedicate this project to her. Please take a seat, and we can begin."

There was a great rustling of clothes and bouncing of chairs across the wooden floor. Rymnyr sat at the head of the table, with Bokyl next to her. Once the rotund head regent had dropped into his chair, he leaned over, placed his hand on her thigh, and whispered into her highly piled greying hair.

"Can't wait till we have the next all night celebration. Maybe tonight?"

She pulled back slightly, gently removed his hand from her thigh, and shot a perplexed glance at him. "Thank you for showing up Head Regent. This is strictly a business meeting."

He gave a low grunt and straightened up in his chair. "I'm still not convinced that this whole project isn't just a colossal waste of time, but I do congratulate you on getting such a high-powered group together."

Rymnyr responded with a tiny sarcastic smile, then shifted her attention back to the task at hand. She held up a piece of paper containing a list of the invitees. Her finger moved down the list as she scanned those seated.

"It looks like Gyls is the only one missing." From down the hall, the sound of hurried footsteps and low voices drifted into the room. "Ah, that must be him now."

Frygr poked his head around the carved door frame. "A Mr. Wybr is here. He insists that he is part of the group?" From behind the head servant, the small round head of the council accountant bobbed.

"Professor Rymnyr! Remember the night of the presentation? I offered to keep the financial records?"

Rymnyr shifted around in her chair to face the new arrival. The wrinkles on her forehead deepened as she tried to make sense of what Wybr was talking about. After several awkward moments, she made a beckoning motion with her hand.

"I certainly don't remember that, but come on in."

The head servant stepped aside, and the small, cricket like man rushed in. A cloth bag swung back and forth in his left hand. He made a beeline over to the professor. His face lit up with joy as he reached out and grasped her hand.

"Professor, I'm so glad to be in your presence again. I see you got the nymfyrs I sent. They are a token of my gratitude for the wonderful experience of the other night."

An uncomfortable silence fell over the table. Wybr stared into the professor's grey-green eyes. A euphoric smile was chiseled into his face.

"Um, yes, thank you. Please let go of my hand, and take a seat," Rymnyr offered in as kindly a voice as she could muster.

"Yes, whatever you say." All eyes watched Wybr turn and head around to an empty chair. Just before sitting down, he stopped and held the cloth bag high. "In honor of that momentous night of the Collria, I brought a bottle of fifty-year old Mintexia!"

Wybr's enthusiastic offer elicited a round of chuckling and whispers from the group. Rymnyr sent a suspicious little sideways glance at him, then got to her feet.

"Very well, I'll send a messenger out to see where Mr. Gyls is. Mr. Kryzyck, would you care to brief the group on the status of the prototype?"

The old miner slowly got up from his chair and looked around the table as he spoke. "Yes, of course. My nephew and I have been assisting Gyls in the construction of a replica of the craft. The plan is for us to test the propulsion system sometime next week. One of the issues we have run into is due to the outbreak of war in Bosyra, it may be difficult for us to obtain the amount of kykpowder needed to test the final rocket stage."

Lymdyr held up his arm. "We have stockpiles of kykpowder used for rail construction. How much do you need?"

"That's a good question. I think Gyls has…."

Kryzyck's answer was cut short by the sound of hurried footsteps in the hallway. The young inventor came jogging through the door and stopped just as he entered the room. He wiped a bead of sweat off his high bony forehead.

"Sorry I'm late. Our buggy axle broke just as I was coming up the hill. I've been meaning to fix…."

"Never mind Mr. Gyls, welcome. We're glad you made it. Please grab a seat. Oh, it looks like we are one short," Rymnyr observed.

From his place at the far side of the long, polished table, Wybr jumped to his feet. "Here, he can have my seat. I'll grab one of the chairs against the wall."

Before the professor could answer, the thin, stick of a man hustled over, picked up one of the richly upholstered arm chairs set against the wall, and carried it to the head of the table. He placed it right beside Rymnyr, and settled in. She took a quick look at the expectant puppy grin on his face, then switched her attention back to the young inventor.

"So, where were we? Oh yes, Mr. Gyls. How much kykpowder will you need for your test of the propulsion system?"

"My rough calculation is that somewhere between one and two hundred pounds should be sufficient to propel the craft from the upper limit of balloon height."

"Hmm, I'll have to have some kind of permit drawn up for that amount, but I don't see a problem," the railroad man replied.

"Very good. I'll put you two in touch. So, that covers propulsion, next is......."

From directly across the table, Symgyr raised his hand. Rymnyr looked into his piercing dark eyes and nodded for him to proceed.

"I'm a colleague of Mr. Lymdyr from the railroad. My company specializes in metallurgic development. I want to thank Professor Rymnyr for her most stimulating presentation at the order last week." A wicked smile formed an arc across the tall gentleman's face. "This project is of great interest to me, however, if I may digress, where exactly are these brave voyagers going?"

The buzz of multiple conversations filled the room. Rymnyr glanced over at Professor Ymyl, who was engaged in a discussion with Krynut. The first indications of panic and doubt appeared on her soft face. She scanned the table for help. Her furtive gaze settled on Professor Myrvst. He was leaning to the side while the head of Phylr Communications spoke into his ear. Myrvst looked back at the professor and smiled. His twinkling blue eyes radiated a message of reassurance. Rymnyr let out a sigh and fanned herself.

"I believe Professor Myrvst has something to say?" she called out above the collection of voices.

The sage, grey haired professor exchanged several more words with Phylr, then flashed a quick smile back toward Rymnyr. "My apologies professor. I just wanted to get our story straight. I always like to make sure I know what I'm talking about. Mr. Phylr has taken a keen interest in the device that Mr. Kryzyck invented, discovered, however you'd like to describe it. Over the last couple weeks, he and his company have used their extensive resources to try and determine a relative location from which these transmissions are originating. I will let him elaborate."

"Thank you for the introduction professor. With the help of Professor Ymyl's students at the Academy, we have set up three large replicas of Mr. Kryzyck's device on mountains tops all across Tymr. By measuring the signal strength from each of these, we have been able to mathematically triangulate where the signals are coming from. I could pass on the relative coordinates, but my point is, once out in space, I think it would be possible for the voyagers to follow the signal, using a technique similar to what we are doing."

"And where are these signals coming from?" Symgyr asked.

"Let's see. If my sense of direction is accurate, I'd say they are coming from, up there!" Phylr raised his arm and pointed toward the southwest corner of the ceiling.

The room erupted with laughter. Wybr took the opportunity to give Rymnyr's arm a squeeze. She reared back and stared at him with mild contempt.

"Quite a funny joke, don't you think?" he asked. His thin voice rattled with uncertainty.

"Yes, very funny. We're not here to make jokes however." She shook off his grasp and returned her attention to the dark skinned communication director. "Thank you for you update.

I'd like to keep us on track, so Mr. Gyls, when do you anticipate being ready to launch the prototype?"

"Once we have access to the kykpowder, and the balloons, we should be able to carry out a test in a week or so. Having Mr. Kryzyck and his nephew helping with the construction is a huge benefit."

Head Regent Bokyl had been quiet through the discussions. He leaned over and whispered in Rymnyr's ear, then addressed the group in a deep, booming voice.

"I hate to admit it, but hearing many of the most distinguished voices of learning and industry comment here is moving me closer to accepting this as a valid project. Anyway, the Academy has a supply of high altitude test balloons that I am willing to offer."

Applause rippled around the room. Rymnyr's face lit up with joy. "Oh, this is all so exciting! I think we have covered enough for tonight. I'd like to encourage you all to work together and share whatever updates you have by telemessage. Please include me, as I seem to have adopted the role of project coordinator."

"Project coordinator and party planner. Let's crack open that Mintexia!" Lymdyr said with a smile.

"Great idea!" Wybr responded. He jumped to his feet and pulled the bottle of amber colored liquid out of the cloth sack. Rymnyr looked over at it and gagged slightly.

"Dear, I don't know if I'm ready for any of that, but I'll get some glasses." She pushed her chair back and walked out toward the hall.

A few moments later, one of her servants appeared with a tray of faceted liquor glasses. Rymnyr took the tray and carried it back to the table. Wybr opened the bottle with a loud pop. The Mintexia was poured, and all but Gyls hefted a glass.

"To the project!" Lymdyr lifted his glass high.

"Here, here!" the group responded.

Rymnyr brought the glass up to her lips, then halted once the fumes hit her small, curved nose. The very smell of the licorice flavored libation made her shudder.

Wybr downed his and looked over at Rymnyr's unpleasant expression. "Go ahead dear, it's really quite good."

"Don't call me dear, professor will be fine. I fear my taste for Mintexia is gone." She gave him a polite smile, then turned to address the group. "Thank you all for attending. I'll send out invitations for the next meeting. Good night!"

Groans of displeasure rose up from several of the attendees. Slowly and grudgingly, they all bade each other goodnight, and filed out of the brightly lit room. Gyls, Myrvst, Kryzyck, his nephew and Wybr were the last to leave. The accountant filled the glasses again and held them up to the group.

"Another in celebration?"

Blrsynt was the only taker. Rymnyr held her nose and turned away. "I don't know if I'll ever be able to drink that again!"

Myrvst let go a dry laugh. "Well, I think we should head home. Mr. Gyls, do you need a ride?"

"What? I'm sorry, I was lost in thought. A ride? Yes, Father and I can fetch the broken buggy tomorrow. I tied the styrn up to a post. I hope it's still there."

All the invitees headed toward the door save for Wybr. With an ear to ear grin stretching his impish face, he watched the rest of the group depart. Rymnyr stood stock still for a moment, then turned toward him.

"Good night Mr. Wybr. I will let you know if we need your services."

"I thought we could spend a quiet night together."

"I appreciate your offer, but no, I have things to do. We will certainly need your services once the project gets rolling, so please understand that you will be notified of the next meeting."

Rymnyr stared right into his small, beady eyes. He rubbed his elbow, took a final scan of her stern face, then moved toward the door.

"Oh, keep the bottle of Mintexia, maybe the next big celebration we have….." His voice trailed off as he walked out of the room, shoulders dropped in defeat.

Chapter 15.

On the first clear day of the week, the project team assembled out on the dry lake bed west of town. Gyls, Lymdyr, and the demolition technician stood in the middle of the cracked, uneven ground. The railroad man pulled the fleece collar of his overcoat tight.

"I sure wish this incessant wind would quit." He turned toward Gyls. "Do you think it will effect the upward movement of the craft?" The young inventor stood shivering slightly, his hands shoved as deeply into the ripped pockets of his tweed jacket as they could go. He looked up at the brown, scrubby hillsides surrounding them.

"You know, I am a bit concerned about that. There are volunteer observers from the astronomical society with their telescopes setup and trained toward what they perceive to be the trajectory of the test craft. They may have a tough time following it unless this wind dies down."

Lymdyr gave a judicious nod of his head. "I have to tell you that a lot is riding on this test today." He let the seriousness of his statement sink in before continuing. "When the proposal was presented at the Collria meeting, I really thought it was a joke. After Regent Krynut demonstrated his calculating device, and you laid out your details at Rymnyr's place, I guess something snapped into place for me. Like I said, I hope this test goes well."

The technician had just finished carefully packing the one hundred and ten pounds of kykpowder into the four rockets affixed to the rear of the craft. He wiped his hands on the pants of his white jumpsuit and walked over to the group.

"Now see, the way I got these cylinders tapered, the powder is going to light, and she starts off slow. What I'm expecting to happen is the craft will gently nose up, then when these big mamas ignite, Wahoo! Off she goes! The flash of the powder should sever the balloon leads, and either she flies off into space, or she spirals around and crashes." The technician gave a slightly lopsided smile and looked around at the other observers. His jumpsuit flapped in the breeze.

"Boy, Mr. Lymdyr, it'd be a lot easier if this wind would quit. The minute we let go of those balloons, she's going to race off over town. Did you alert the authorities a hundred pounds of kykpowder might be dropping into the city?"

Lymdyr looked over at the slightly goofy face of the technician. "No, I didn't bother alerting the authorities. I assumed that by testing it out here away from town there wouldn't be any danger, but you're probably right, it's going to sail right over the city before it ignites." He pulled the stylish felt fedora down a little tighter over his head to keep it from flying away.

From their vantage point at the base of the low hills to the south, Kryzyck, Professor Rymnyr, and Mihyn stood comfortably out of the wind.

"Oh look, there come the balloons!" the professor called out.

A single wagon came rolling along the main road from town. Two students used all their weight to keep the four tethered rubber balloons under control. Two other students guided the styrns along the rutted path.

Rymnyr wrapped the edges of her heavy wool robe a bit tighter. "Glad I'm not standing out there in the open. Do you think Myrvst will make it in time?"

Regent Mihyn got up from the rock she was sitting on and looked off in the direction of the main road. "I don't see anybody coming up from town. If they do make it, it'll be close."

Almost one mile back toward town, Blrsynt was squinting into the wind. Sylsynt was sitting next to him, her face buried between his arm and chest. Professor Myrvst sat upright next to her. His glasses did a good job of blocking the flying dust.

"Do you think we'll miss the launch?" she asked. Her high voice was muffled by Blrsynt's thick wool shirt.

"I don't know. What time did they think the launch would be?"

"Ten o'clock. It took longer to fill the balloons than they anticipated. The compressor was not working that well, so the launch itself will be delayed," Myrvst answered.

Sylstyn snuggled a little closer to her boyfriend. "Well, I hope we don't miss it!"

"Ah, there look out between those straw bushes! I see the balloons," the professor shouted. He stood up slightly and pointed out across the flat plain. In the distance, the group could see the bright yellow balloons bouncing off each other beneath the thick net that had been secured to the wagon.

At the launch site, a slender student with a smartly trimmed black beard was overseeing the attachment of the balloons to the craft. "Okay, Hykmyr, make sure those ropes don't get tangled! Holy Zym! This wind is just blasting. Are you sure we can go forward with the launch?"

The technician was already securing the loose ends of the ropes to the thick cleat on the outside of the craft. He paused to yell back a response.

"I didn't bring four kegs of powder all the way out here to load 'em and then go home. Dyth right we're going to launch!"

"Whatever you say. Myrn! Klypky! When he gives the word, one of you undo the pegs holding the net, and then I'll help you yank it off." Despite the chaos of the moment, the bearded student had a brilliant smile on his face. "This is exciting isn't it?"

Gyls bent down and assisted the technician with the knots. "Okay, these look good. Do you have the fuse ready?"

"Yeah, I brought an altitude switch along, but since this may be our only test, I thought using the old reliable fuse would work best. As you can see, it's really long. This is the one we use for blasting deep down in the planet. It burns at approximately one foot per minute."

Gyls ran the calculation in his head. "So I predict we'll need about twenty feet."

"Ha! That's exactly how much I brought!" the technician slapped Gyls hard on the back. "Perfect! Are we good to go?"

Gyls looked over at the four students poised to release the large rubber balloons. He made eye contact with the bearded one.

"Ready?" the student yelled.

"Let me straighten these lines out and then I think we will be." Gyls turned back toward the technician. "Here we go. Start laying out the fuse. I'll give you the signal to light it. Got it?"

The technician nodded his head and began unrolling the coiled fuse. He stopped about twenty feet from the craft. Gyls walked along the ropes laid on the dry lakebed, arranging them as best he could. The wind seemed to calm slightly just as the inventor reached the group of students.

"When he lights the fuse, pull that net off as quickly and smoothly as possible." The four young students looked back at him with bright, expectant faces. "Okay, here we go!" Gyls held his hand up in the air, then dropped it. Sparks flew from the technician's striker. After several attempts, a wisp of white smoke trailed off with the wind. "Let 'em go!"

Two of the students pulled out the wooden pegs securing one side of the net, and the other two yanked it free. The balloons were carried off almost parallel to the ground before they began to gain altitude. Once the slack of the lines was taken up, the craft spun on the flat, dry ground then flew off into the air. A cheer rose up from the students.

Back on the road, Blrsynt was concentrating on keeping the wagon on the rutted trail. The joyous shouts of the students drew his attention just in time to see the cylindrical craft dragged up into the sky. Sylstyn gave him a powerful hug.

"Oh, there it goes!"

Myrvst tilted his head back and watched the object sweep out of sight. "It's up to the astronomers now."

Out on the windswept lake bed, Gyls held his big gold pocket watch out in front of him. The technician jogged over and stood next to him.

"So what time do the fireworks start?"

"At twenty-seven after. I doubt whether we'll see anything, that wind is really taking it to the east. Let's hope the people with the telescopes can follow it." Gyls kept his neck craned back and scanned the sky above him. "Some high clouds up north, but visibility is still good."

From their place by the low hill, Rymnyr shaded her eyes with an upraised hand. "Okay, well I lost sight of it. Shall we walk out and stand with Gyls? I brought a bottle of chinz to celebrate."

"Must you always be drinking?" Mihyn said with a sigh.

"Must you always be such a blyrt?"

The regent smiled at the comment. "It's just my nature. Sure, let's walk out there."

Kryzyck and the two women negotiated the scrubby bushes that clung to life at the edge of the lake bed. The high heels of Rymnyr's boots sunk into the coarse white sand once they left the vegetation zone.

"Perhaps you should have worn some flats," the old miner observed.

"I suppose you're right. Here, give me your arm."

Kryzyck reached out to steady her. She pulled him close and kissed his cheek. Mihyn strode out ahead of them. She arrived just as Gyls was counting down.

"5, 4, 3...."

A faint spark of yellow flashed far up above them, followed by a long swoosh of white smoke.

"There! I see the smoke trail," the technician shouted. He leaped into the air. The students huddled together on the back of the wagon jumped up and down, hugging each other.

Blrsynt pulled the wagon up next to the cheering students. Myrvst and his housekeeper stepped down off the wooden seat and walked over to join the group. Lymdyr had been staring up at the sky. When the two of them joined the group, he gave a quick tip of his hat.

"Nice to see you all again." He flashed the young woman a big, toothy grin which she ignored.

"So did the rockets fire?" Sylstyn asked.

"I think so. The smoke trail is heading straight up. We won't know for sure till the astronomers give us their information, but it looks good at this point," Gyls answered while still gazing up at the sky.

"Ooooh, a successful test! Kryzyck, be a dear and open this."

Rymnyr passed the thick glass bottle to the old miner which he deftly opened and handed back to her.

"A toast to a successful first test!" The professor took a healthy slug, and after wiping her red lips, she turned toward Gyls. "So, what's the next step?"

The inventor stood with his arms wrapped around his chest for warmth. When the bottle was handed to him, he just passed it along.

"Well, we'll need to check with Ymyl's team to see if the craft actually was propelled as high as we predicted. Assuming that it was, one of the next things I'd like to test out soon are the stabilization fins. I figure if we tow the craft behind a steam yacht or sailkyrft if it's windy, we should be able to approximate what it will be like plowing through the tail of the comet."

The others considered his statement in silence. Lymdyr took a drink from the bottle, then spoke up. "So you're suggesting testing it underpluge?"

"Yes."

"Oh. So you'll also be able to test the air storage."

"Correct."

"And you want to have the full crew aboard?" Kryzyck inquired.

"Not necessarily. We will need to have the approximate weight, but I figure two people should be able to man it."

"So, the next step is to build a working model?"

"Precisely. The fellow from the metallurgic company sent me a telemessage yesterday after you and Blrsynt had gone home. Here, I'll read it." Gyls reached into his jacket pocket and pulled a yellow sheet of paper out.

"Mr. Gyls, our research team just completed a project for the Plugians. They are working on a kyft that will travel underpluge with pressurized air. The team leader tells me that he doesn't think there will be any problem fabricating a similar system based on your design. When you have a shell built, bring it over, and the team will install the system." Gyls folded the paper back up and gave a satisfied smile.

Lymdyr was listening with rapt attention. He nodded several times while the inventor read the statement. "Well, two things. Phylr and I were out having drinks a couple days ago, and he told me that his company did so well last year that they bought a steam yacht and its located out at Lake Byrn. I'll ask him if they would be willing to volunteer it for the pluge test. Secondly, I've been talking with the men in our boiler workshop, and they are very interested in this project. I'd like to have some members of this group meet with them and go over exactly what the design is."

The bottle made it back to Rymnyr which she finished off. "Thank you Mr. Lymdyr. I'll contact the group to see what day would work for a visit to your facility. Oh, this is so exciting! I get chills thinking about the day of real launch!" She squeezed Kryzyck's arm. "Shall we go?" The old miner gave a nod. "Good day everyone, and again, congratulations on the successful test."

She and Kryzyck walked off toward the low hills. Mihyn offered a quiet goodbye and followed them. Halfway across the lake bed, Rymnyr swung her head around. "Mihyn dear, you sure are extra quiet today."

The regent walked with her slender hands jammed in the pockets of her coat. Her face was creased with worry lines. "I guess you're right. I have a lot on my mind these days. Handynr says he should be coming home in a month. I'm a little concerned for his safety."

"I'm sure he'll be alright."

Mihyn looked up at the gauzy high clouds. "I was also thinking about the reality of this project today. I mean, it's fine that we just launched a wooden tube full of nothing up into the sky, but there's a big difference between this, and sending five people up."

"Five extremely brave voyagers," Rymnyr added in a self-assured tone of voice.

"Hmmm, more like five crazy people with nothing to lose."

Chapter 16.

Gyls, Kryzyck, and his nephew worked many long hours to construct a second prototype craft. On the morning of the boiler factory tour, Blrsynt wrapped his jacket tightly as they rolled down the street to pick up Gyls and the craft.

"Boy, this must be the coldest day yet so far," the young man commented. He blew a jet of white vapor out between his pursed lips. "I can even see my breath."

"Yep, I had hoped to be back at the crater before fyngr set in, but looks like that's not going to happen," Kryzyck commented.

"Do you think we'll be back at work soon?"

The old miner looked over at his nephew's broad face. "Do you want to go back? Seems like you and Sylstyn are getting along well."

"No, I'm pretty happy here. It's just that I worry about Wylryn running the operation. How do you know he's not just sitting around doing nothing?"

"I have people checking up on him."

Both men looked over at each other and smiled. They pulled into the yard of the barrel factory and wheeled around the back of the main building. White smoke drifted up out of the brick chimney. Gyls and his father were just walking across the hard, rocky ground.

"Good morning!" Gyls said cheerfully. His father gave the two men in the wagon a nod of his head, then headed off toward the main building. "Pull up around the back door like you did last time."

The inventor rubbed his hands together as he walked. Blrsynt hopped down to help Gyls with the big wooden door. They slid it aside and stepped into the interior. Just inside the opening, Blrsynt gave the air a sniff.

"Wow, that myln smell is really strong!"

"Yeah, I was worried that it wouldn't be warm enough to dry completely last night. Guess we'll have to load it up anyway."

Using the big block and tackle pulley near the door, they hoisted the craft into the wagon, and rode off to the railroad yard. When they arrived, Lymdyr was waiting at the main gate. He was wrapped in an elegant grey trench coat with a collar of lustrous black fur. A fine black felt hat nicely accentuated the coat. In his hand, he held a large ceramic mug from which trails of steam rose.

"Good morning! I see you have the craft. The boiler workshop is that long building with the wide funnel sticking up at the end. Everyone else is sitting in my office trying to keep warm. Dyth chilly this morning, don't you think?"

"It certainly is," Kryzyck answered.

"Go ahead and drive over to the workshop. I'll bring the rest of the group in our company carriage."

Gyls and the two miners directed the wagon around the back side of the boiler workshop and halted in front of a huge open door. The sounds of metal being beaten and steam whooshing filled the chilly morning air. From the direction of the main brick office building, an open carriage quite a bit longer than the wagon came rolling up.

A burly man with rolled up sleeves and a cigar stuck out of the side of his mouth strode out of the workshop. He stopped next to the carriage.

"Morning Chief!"

"Good morning." Lymdyr turned back toward the group bundled up behind him. "Everyone, this is Mr. Symp. He's the boiler workshop foreman and will be showing us around today. Don't be deceived by his rough appearance. He's really a nice guy."

"These the really smart ones you said was going to pay us a visit?"

Lymdyr winced in reaction to the foreman's brash question. "Yes, Mr. Symp, this is the group that has approached us about fitting their craft with a system of pressure tanks and collection tubes."

"Collection tubes? What're they wanting to collect?"

"Well, they're going to need to collect pluge vapor, store some of it, and break the rest down into breathable air."

Symp's thick eyebrows scrunched down hard. His granite chin wrinkled up. "Breathable air? You mean some poor sap is going to get locked up in that thing?"

Lymdyr let go a subdued laugh. He ignored the foreman's question, stood up, and turned around to face his guests. "Let's head on into the workshop. It's nice and warm in there."

The passengers in the carriage disembarked and followed Lymdyr into the building. Symp walked over to the wagon, gave Gyls and the two miners a quick nod of welcome, and grabbed the harness of the styrn nearest to him.

"Morning Gents, I'll just lead you in."

The two beasts snorted and stared wide-eyed at the workers in the noisy boiler room. Symp muttered soothing words to the spooked animals while directing them to a wall of glass panes at the back of the room.

"Hang on while I open the door."

Kryzyck and his nephew waited for Symp and another man to slide the wall sized door to the side, then rolled inside. Long wooden tables with four-inch thick tops stretched along the walls. Equally thick posts held the sturdy tables in place. Workmen were hunched over the surfaces, filing, fitting, and measuring an assortment of alloy pieces. They looked up briefly at the visitors, then returned to their work.

With Symp's help, the craft was offloaded and set on wooden blocks in a corner of the room. The foreman dusted off his hands and stood next to Lymdyr. "What now Chief?"

"Let's have Mr. Kryzyck and his nephew take the wagon back outside, and the rest of us can go up to the design studio."

Symp strolled over to the wagon, ran his hand over the flat spot on the head of one of the styrns, then turned his attention to Kryzyck. "You fellas need a hand?"

"I think we got it," Blrsynt replied before climbing back up onto the seat.

The foreman returned to where the group was waiting. "Okay, everybody follow me." Symp led them around the tables and over to a stairway that was affixed to the wall. He stopped in front of a glass door at the top of the stairs. "Everybody here? Into the design studio we go." Without flourish, Symp opened the door and swept into the brightly lit room.

Large windows looked out on the dry hills to the east. The roof rafters were exposed along the outside wall, which created a space above the worker's heads. All manner of ornate gold work hung from hooks sunk into the massive beams.

Vines, leaves, tree branches, flowers, aquatic animals of all varieties; an astounding array of natural forms glittered up high. The visitors gasped in awe as they entered.

"Good morning! We have visitors," Symp announced once the last of the group filed past him.

A bent over old man with white Brillo brush hair looked up from his work. "Hey, we toll you, knock first! Look, look at this! I been working on this nymfyr petal since six. You come barging in here like a mag, I lible to break it. Sygalia!"

Symp sent a quick apologetic smile over at the old man, then headed toward the door. "Well, I'll leave Mr. Lymdyr to explain this part. Got to get back to work." After giving Professor Rymnyr an exaggerated wink, he waved to the rest of the guests, and bounced out of the room.

Lymdyr walked over to one of the work tables and sat down on the edge. A wide smile broke across his face when he looked up at the fantastic gold wrought shapes hanging above.

"Welcome to the design studio. Any of you that have ridden on the Gryn Belt rail system lately will recognize some of the expertly crafted decorations that you see around you. Iangly! Come over here please."

From behind a big desk on the west side of the room, a barrel chested man with the same white wiry hair as the others slowly walked over toward the group. Lymdyr put his arm around him.

"Folks, this is langly. He's in charge of this whole operation. Mr. Gyls, may I have your diagram please."

The inventor stepped around Professor Ymyl and handed over the rolled up canvas. Lymdyr laid the diagram out onto an open space on one of the tables in the center of the room. All the design staff crowded around to take a look. They chatted amongst themselves in their native dialect.

"May we keep thees?" langly asked.

"Yes, by all means." Gyls slid between langly and the man next to him. "This is a cutaway of course, but you see where I envision having collector openings up front, and tubing running back along this area. And over here, I thought we could have the storage tanks."

The design staff took a moment to examine the details of the diagram. Their lively banter filled the workroom. langly finished up discussing some key points with his staff, then broke into a sincere smile.

"You are geeefted draftsman and engineer. Eeees a good design. Walandro says that we could use pynfr leaf design for collection plate. Actually, pynfr vine motif might look good through whole thing. You like pynfr motif idea?"

While Gyls pondered the question, Professor Rymnyr leaned over the table to offer her opinion. "I think that is a superb idea! My it's warm in here. Hold that thought." She straightened back up and slid her heavy wool coat off. One of the design men took it from her. She was wearing a nicely tailored green and red pattern dress with a very low cut front. "I think a pynfr leaf design would be perfect! It reflects the Styrynt theme of the whole project."

One of the design men shoved a sheet of paper and a pencil across the table toward langly. He began furiously sketching out elaborate and detailed drawings. Professor Myrvst stood off to the side watching the proceedings.

"You know, we have the shell of the craft downstairs in the fabrication room if these gentlemen would like to get an idea of the scale."

Iangly's glittering blue-grey eyes flashed beneath the wrinkled lids. "Quen tangarle? I mean, what did he say? The craft is here?"

Lymdyr motioned toward the door. "Yes, let's go down to examine it."

The entire group trooped down the stairway and into the fabrication room. For the next twenty minutes, the designers swarmed around the craft, talking excitedly in their native language while scrawling down notes. Gyls stood next to them, offering whatever information he could. Symp and several of the boiler crew entered the room to see what all the fuss was about. A big, dark skinned man with shoulders like a mountain range ran his hand along the ribbed exterior.

"What zactly tis this?"

Gyls and one of the designers were taking measurements up near the nose. The inventor rose up from a squat to answer the boilerman's question. "It's a vehicle to transport voyagers into space."

The boiler worker let out a thunderous laugh. "What you mean, transport into space? Folks going to climb in dis and go up dere?" He pointed a finger toward the ceiling. Gyls nodded.

Another deep laugh exited the man's chest. "So you really goin' to send people up into de sky in dis?" He dusted off his palms and stuck his head into the interior of the craft.

"That's the plan. There's a lot of testing and calculating to do yet."

After pulling back out of the interior, the boiler worker sent a beaming grin over to Gyls. He made the characteristic circular motion around his heart, followed by a light jab with his index finger into his chest.

"I say a prayer to almighty Zym to watch over whoever get locked inside dis."

Symp walked up to the man and placed a hand on his shoulder. "Hey, Horym. I think a big, strong guy like you would be a good candidate for the trip!"

The boiler worker wagged an index finger at his boss. "No, no, no! Hursey would chain me up if I suggested dat!" He let go another deep, rumbling laugh, then turned to leave. Next to him, a shorter, but no less muscular boiler man stood eyeing the craft. Along his neck and forearms, crudely rendered blue tattoos snaked.

"These the people that hears voices from another world?" The man delivered the question with a noticeable amount of quiet aggression. His lips quivered while he spoke. "Seems like a bad idea to chase dark voices." With that, the boiler man narrowed his eyes in a disapproving manner and stomped off. He stopped next to a group of his co-workers and pointed back at the craft.

Over the next two months, work on the craft proceeded rapidly. By the first day of spring, it was ready for the in water test. Lymdyr had arranged for a special train that consisted of a small steam locomotive, a flat railcar for the craft, and three of the most plush passenger cars every constructed to haul it out to the lake. The members of the Dymran project, reporters from the local papers, and a host of dignitaries had been invited to the event.

A warm breeze blew up from the south as Rymnyr, Kryzyck, his nephew, and Sylstyn waited at the main Tyrl city siding for the special train to arrive. They had been instructed to assemble at the small cargo platform next to the regular passenger train dock. On the dock next to them, crowds of people loaded and unloaded. Shrill whistles blew every fifteen minutes. Through a scratchy speaker system, the arriving and departing train destination were announced. Sylstyn squeezed Blrsynt's arm and leaned over to look down the tracks.

"I don't see it yet. I wonder how come they're late?"

"It probably took longer for them to get it loaded than they expected," Kryzyck replied.

Rymnyr held up a small mirror and examined her middle aged face. "How do I look? I ran out of the blue eye shadow and had to mix in some green. I think it makes me look kind of like I have moss growing on my eyelids."

Kryzyck patted her soft arm. "You look marvelous dear. Ah, I think that might be them now."

All eyes followed the direction of the miner's outstretched arm. A train of unusually short length came rolling toward them. It blew three long whistle blasts, made two quick track switches, and pulled up in front of the group. Big blue and yellow banners were draped across the front of the engine.

The door to the first car swung open, and a very well dressed conductor flipped the wooden steps forward. He adjusted his black silk vest and descended to the platform. With practiced elegance, the conductor turned toward the four of them, bowed at the waist, and motioned for them to approach.

"Welcome aboard," he offered as the group passed him on the steps.

Rymnyr and the rest of the group entered the opulent passenger car. Fringed purple shades hung down above the windows. Rich burgundy velvet pattern wall paper covered the arched ceiling. Ornate oil lamps in the shape of cherubs holding wide braziers stuck out from the dark paneled walls at regular intervals.

In the middle of the aisle, Lymdyr stood conversing with one of the guests seated next to him. The arrival of the Dymran members caused him to straighten up. "Welcome aboard everyone." He reached over, and lightly pulled a short, but very curvy woman with a head of black, highly styled hair up from the seat. "This is my wife, Bynhyld." Introductions were exchanged all around.

"So, I think we're still waiting on some of the scientific team. We have large supply of mynth and chinz along. One of our waiters should be coming by shortly." Lymdyr bent down and scanned the crowded rail platform and adjacent area through the nearest window.

"Professor Ymyl won't be making it. He has a bad cold," Rymnyr commented.

"That's too bad." Lymdyr turned back around and gave the professor a good look up and down. "Might I say that you look magnificent today!"

Rymnyr blushed ever so slightly. "Thank you."

"Oh look, I think Regent Krynut just arrived."

All heads turned to watch the sharp faced mathematician climb out of the buggy that had just pulled up. Once on the ground, he held his hand up, and helped a woman in thin gauzy robes down. Her skin was as smooth and velvety as chocolate pudding. It glistened in the weak early spring sun. Her thick black hair was pulled tight in a ponytail. High cheekbones and a thin symmetrical nose highlighted her stunning features. She seemed to float down from the buggy. The conductor led them to the last car. They entered, and with a blast of the whistle, the train lurched forward.

In the end passenger car, Professor Rymnyr and Kryzyck had found seats right behind Mihyn and her husband. Head Regent Bokyl sat in the same row. He and Handynr were discussing the situation in Bosyra when Krynut and his date entered.

From the back row, a young, sandy haired man jumped up from his seat. He held a thick pad of paper and a pen in his hands. The reporter walked right up to Krynut and began firing off questions.

"Excuse me Regent, I'm from the Tyrl News. How did your speaking tour go?"

"Fine."

"Is it true that the government of Pynyr wants to use your invention as their computing standard?"

"Yes, would you back up and let us take a seat?" Krynut asked in a stoney voice.

"Oh yes, sorry. And this must be Princess Janela, the famous dancer from Bagul?" Janela offered a shy smile as a point of recognition. "So Regent, I understand that you are part of the Dymran project?"

"Yes."

"Does that mean that you believe the voices heard from the wireless audio device originate from another planet?" The man's youthful face couldn't hide his glee at presenting such a loaded question.

"I just finished visiting half the largest cities on Ulutrita which are also the ones most capable of producing some kind of wireless transmission. None of them have any idea where these voices are originating from. Does that answer your question?" Krynut's stern, biting response blew the grin off the reporter's face.

"Uh, yeah, thanks." The young man slunk back to his seat.

Gyls and his father were sitting up toward the front. The father watched a waiter enter the car carrying a tray of glasses. "You certainly have found a fancy bunch of people to hang around with."

"They're just dressed up for this occasion." Gyls answered in a quiet voice.

"They seem like a bunch of drunkards to me. You know your mother would not have approved of this."

Gyls looked over at the worry lines on his father's face, then out at the dry landscape rolling by. He let go a sigh.

A few minutes later, Rymnyr got up and worked her way down the aisle. She stopped next to the row where the inventor and his father were sitting.

"Mr. Gyls! I didn't notice you and your father were here. Are you enjoying the ride?"

"Oh, yes. This is certainly a very nice way to travel." Gyls sent a smile her way while his father looked up at the professor and scowled.

"I don't know if we've been introduced, but my name is Professor Rymnyr Third Line. I'm the unofficial head of the Dymran project." Rymnyr had to lean forward to extend her hand over the armrest. Gyl's father gently shook her hand twice, then let go.

"Nice to meet you," he said without emotion.

"Your son is a remarkable man. You should be proud of him."

"I am."

Rymnyr waited for him to say something else, but finally she straightened back up. "Do you need anything to drink?" Both men shook their heads. "Well, enjoy the rest of the ride. I think we should be at the lake in about thirty minutes." She flashed a quick smile and continued up the aisle.

Just as Rymnyr approached the door, Gyls leaped up out of the seat. "Professor! There is something I wanted to ask you."

She let go of the shiny door handle and walked back to their row. "Yes?"

"Who exactly is going to pilot the craft in the test today?"

"Oh, that's right. We hadn't decided for sure at the last meeting. Regent Krynut offered to steer, and we thought it would be a good idea for you to sit next to him since you designed the fin apparatus. There will also be a contingent of Plugians there to assist with any rescue."

"Rescue?" An expression of real concern swept across the father's face.

Behind the rouge layer, Rymnyr's cheeks flushed. She bit her lip before answering. "There is an element of.....dyth! I mean, anytime you experiment with a new procedure or technology, having a safety program set up is always advisable."

The professor stared down at the older man's serious expression. She was beginning to sweat. "I hope that answers your question." Using all her diplomatic skills, she forced herself to smile. "Excuse me. I'll be right back."

Gyls and his father watched her hustle off toward the door. The older man turned toward his son. "You can't even swim, can you?"

"No."

Chapter 17.

Twenty minutes later, the train and its elegant passengers pulled up to the siding. Lymdyr got to his feet and stood with his hands braced against the seat backs. "Esteemed guests! We have arrived. If you would all follow the main walk down to the harbor, we will gather in the wharf side pavilion for more drinks and refreshments."

Professor Rymnyr had finally worked her way through the long line at the only bathroom on the train just as they pulled up.

"Are we here?" she called out to him while easing her way down the aisle. The train shook slightly as it slowed to a stop. The unsteady nature of her high heel boots and her moderate level of intoxication caused her to lurch forward. Lymdyr reached out to steady her. "Oh my! Thank you. I wasn't prepared for that."

"My pleasure," he replied in a low, smooth voice.

She glanced into his leering face and returned a polite smile. "You can let go of me now."

He released his grip on her arm and stepped back along the row of seats. His wife waited till most of the car was empty, then got up from her seat and joined him.

"You know, women don't like it when you undress them with your eyes," she hissed into his ear.

"What are you talking about?" Lymdyr's question contained more than a hint of annoyance.

"You know what I'm talking about. Every time you look at that professor, you get this teenage boy look on your face. It's embarrassing!"

Lymdyr let out a huff of displeasure, then stomped off to the exit. A long line of passengers made their way down the hill to the harbor. Blrsynt and Sylstyn walked arm in arm along the concrete path. A stiff breeze blew off the lake. Out in the harbor, a huge collection of sailboats and yachts bobbed in the choppy water.

"Look at all the kyrfts!" Sylstyn commented. The breeze casually tossed some stray strands of her dark brown hair around her face. "I think today is the first day of kyrfting season."

Further down the promenade, Rymnyr and Kryzyck walked along with the group from the Academy.

"Oh, it's so nice to be out here again!" the professor gushed.

"You've been here before?" Mihyn asked. She and her husband kept pace beside them.

"Zym yes! When I was young, my father was the head of a large phynk. In the summer, the phynk would close for a week, and all the employees and their families would come out."

Mihyn turned her attention to the stately wooden structure spread out across a shoulder of land along the shore. "That certainly is an impressive building."

"Ah, yes. The resort has been here for almost one hundred years." Rymnyr giggled and leaned over toward the regent. "Right out there on the lake is where I lost my virginity," she whispered.

Mihyn smiled politely and squeezed her husband's arm. "It seems kind of rough out there. Do you think it will affect the test?"

Handynr scanned the glittering surface of the lake. His long, handsome face was dutifully tightened in official concern. "There does seem to be a chop. I'm sure everything will be fine. Oh look, there are the Plugians!" From down the hill, a group of young men in sharp olive-green uniforms marched.

Over at the end of the pier, Lymdyr stood tapping his well made patent leather shoe against the wooden pier while the tall, skinny assistant harbor master filled out his access form.

"Name of kyrft to be docked?"

"The Lady Lyln."

"Ah, the Lady. Doesn't she now have new owners?"

"Sorry, I wasn't listening." Lymdyr forced himself to pay attention to the unduly formal officer. "Oh, yes I think so."

"And the owner is now Phylr Communications?"

"Yes."

"Is Phylr here?"

"Yes. Look, this is a very important event. Can't we just forgo all this samsyrwork?"

"As you can see, the harbor is very busy today, being it's the opening...."

"I know it's busy, but we don't have all.... How about a drink?"

The young assistant harbor master looked at Lymdyr over his wire spectacles. His flaming red eyebrows scrunched together.

"Sir, I am not allowed to drink on duty."

"Oh, whatever!"

"Number of passengers embarking?"

"Zym! How should I know! Let's see, forty-five guests, nine Plugians. I don't know, somewhere around sixty?"

"The Lady is only licensed for forty-five plus crew."

Lymdyr whipped out his wallet, extracted a twenty dymyr note, crumpled it, and stuffed it into the space between the man's thumb and index finger that held his pencil.

"There! Finish the dyth form."

After making a quick glance around the immediate area, the young red haired man hastily tucked the bill into his pocket, made some quick scrawls on the form, and handed it to Lymdyr.

"A word of caution. The harbor master is in a foul mood today. He always is on the opening day of kyrfting season, but today is worse. He takes a nap from one to three each day. I suggest you wait till one to load. That way you'll decrease the chances of him coming aboard and fining you for being overloaded."

Lymdyr pulled his big gold watch out of his vest pocket. "That's an hour and a half from now!"

The young assistant harbor master shrugged, tipped his blue triangular hat, and sauntered off. Lymdyr cursed under his breath and headed into the high roofed pavilion. He spied

Krynut and his girlfriend over by the bar. After placing an order with the bartender, Lymdyr moved over to where the couple were standing. Krynut broke off his conversation with the princess when the railroad man arrived.

"What's up?"

"The boat is only rated for forty-five passengers. We have sixty."

Krynut's thin angular face became even more thin and angular. His arched eyebrows drew down severely. "So what exactly does that mean?"

"That means we have to wait till the cranky, old harbor master takes a nap before we can sail."

Outside the pavilion, a cheer rose up from those gathered on the pier when the wagon carrying the craft finally made its way down from the platform. Kryzyck and Gyls' father were seated up front. Gyls was standing in back next to the craft. He took a quick scan of the waterfront.

"Where's the kyrft? We're supposed to take off in twenty minutes."

Murmurs circulated through the crowd. The front doors of the pavilion swung open. Lymdyr came striding out. He held up his hand to shield his eyes against the spring sun. After working his way through the crowd, Lymdyr stood beside the wagon.

"Gentleman, there has been a slight change of plans. Due to uh, unforeseen events, we will have to wait till one to sail." A collective groan of dissatisfaction circled through the crowd. "I know, I know. I was looking forward to getting this underway also. The buffet is set up in the pavilion, so I invite you all to go in eat, have something to drink, and in about an hour, we'll set sail."

At precisely noon, a loud steam whistle rattled the windows of the pavilion. Outside on the pier, the big white painted bow of the Lady Lyln eased into view. Lymdyr spun around from his place in the line.

"May I have your attention! We'll start boarding in fifteen minutes! Fifteen minutes."

"Sometimes I can't believe how cheap you are," his wife grumbled.

"Cheap? You think this event is cheap? My dear, you have no idea how much dymr this cost."

"Well, I wouldn't serve this type of pyfg to anyone I know!" She gave a huff of disgust and walked over to a row of chairs.

Up in the wheelhouse of the Lady Lyln, Captain Phytorz steered the large ship up to the dock, and waited while his crew tied her off. He was an older gentleman with a wide chest and weathered, kindly face.

A high pitched steam whistle sounded from over to his right shoulder. He turned around, shielded his eyes from the sun, and peered out the side window. Alongside the Lady, a smaller ship almost identical in construction came chugging up.

"Oh, its Ryrgyn! Looks like they are having a parteee."

Phytorz twisted the knob on the wheelhouse door and stepped out on to the upper deck. On the smaller ship, a thick bodied man with a shock of white hair, and a big red nose poked his head out of the wheelhouse window.

"Hail Lady Lyln! Benna condia!"

"Benna condia to you Mr. Rygryn! A nice day for a cruise, no?"

Several beautiful women in sun dresses drifted about on the upper deck of the smaller vessel. Rygryn glanced over at them with a big smile, then looked back over at Captain Phytorz.

"Yes, a lovely day. We're entertaining some clients from Ryzrka. I think we'll head out to the island for a swim! See you out on the lake."

Rygryn pulled his head in and kissed a gorgeous, dark haired woman half his age who was standing next to him. Captain Phytorz scanned the deck of the smaller craft looking for the usual contingent of impeccably dressed sailors. He leaned over the rail and waved his arms. Rygryn put his hands on the woman's hips, moved her out of the way, and stuck his head of back out the window.

"Yes?"

"Rygryn! Where is your crew?"

The white haired man let go a laugh. "I fired them."

"You fired them? You can't pilot her by yourself!"

"Oh, can't I? Bytrm here is my new first mate. Get it! First mate?"

"Yes, I get it! Well, good luck."

Phytorz gave a quick wave, then returned to the wheelhouse. The captain stood still, stroking his well-trimmed wiry, white beard. He didn't flinch when the wheelhouse door opened, and his young first mate entered.

"Afternoon cap..." The serious, contemplative expression on the captain's face caused the first mate take notice. "Everything alright?"

Captain Phytorz drummed his hands on the highly polished wheel. "I was just talking with the captain of that smaller gryndla that just took off. He's trying to man the kryft without a crew."

The first mate's tight features lifted in surprise. "That doesn't sound good. Is he up for it?"

A smile broke across the captain's face. "Not really, especially if he starts drinking. What am I saying! He's probably already started. I should probably contact the harbor master about the it, but it's a little too late."

The first mate nodded and began jotting down figures from the gauges set into the wheelhouse wall. "Well, you've spent your whole life on kryfts, so I trust your judgement."

Guests had begun to board the Lady Lyn. Krynut and the princess walked arm in arm across the pier. Next to the gangplank, the Plugians were lined up in formation. Krynut stopped in front of the commander and held out his hand.

"Hello, my name is Regent Krynut, I'm going to be piloting the experimental craft today. I understand some of your men are going to accompany Gyls and myself?"

The commander's sun bronzed face lit up in a smile. "Yes sir! My men are ready to assist."

"Good, let's go run the plan by the captain. I want to make sure he knows exactly what to do." The regent turned and yelled over his shoulder. "Mr. Gyls! As soon as you are done, come up to the bridge. I want to brief the captain."

Gyls and two sailors were checking the lift straps from the lifeboat boom nearest the craft. Once they had finished the task, the inventor bounded up stairway leading to the upper deck and into the wheelhouse.

Krynut and three of the Plugians were positioned around the square map table. Captain Phytorz and his first mate were opposite them. A nautical map of the lake was unrolled on the table. With his index finger, Krynut traced their path.

"The plan is to head out toward this point. Right here, where it drops off, we launch. There'll be two aft lines that will connect to the nose of the craft. My guess is it'll float till we get under way, then the drag of the pluge will submerge us. Keep a steady speed. All we want to do is become fully submerged so we can test the steering. If you just stay in this deep channel, we should be fine. Keep out in the middle, avoid the island, of course. If we get into trouble, the Plugians brought along this emergency tagger."

Krynut held up a thick cylinder about two feet long and four inches wide. It had cardboard caps on each end and was wrapped with thick grey paper.

"If we get into trouble, and I hope we don't...." His comment brought a burst of nervous laughter from the group. "We'll jettison this out the waste tube. It's full of carbonate and this really, really bright blue dye. When it hits the pluge, you'll see bubbles and a bright blue slick. Any questions?" The group just stood in silence. "Alright, let's get going."

All the guests were ushered aboard, the gangplank was pulled up, and shortly after one o'clock, the Lady set sail. She chugged heavily out around the harbor. A sea of small and large sailboats glided alongside. Most of them veered off once they cleared the mouth of the harbor. The wind was dry and crisp out on the water. Many of the guests buttoned up their coats or pulled shawls tight.

Gyls' father stood near the stern. He looked out at the brown hills sweeping by. His son came down the stairs, spotted the older man's frizzy black hair, and walked over to him.

"Well, we're all set."

The father looked at his son's thin, bearded face. "You're nervous."

"Yes, I'm nervous. The first big test of any project makes me anxious."

Once the ship reached the mouth of the harbor, the captain swung the big two story ship in a wide arc out toward the center of the lake. When the water changed from dull sandy green to deep greenish blue, he threw the engine into neutral. The captain walked out on the upper deck and leaned over. Two sailors were standing next to the lifeboat boom from which the craft swung gently.

"Alright men, prepare to lower away!"

Krynut had changed into a full body swimsuit. He gave the princess a quick kiss and walked toward the port side. The three Plugians that would accompany him were already standing by. Another two of their platoon had joined them. Professor Rymnyr waited with them. She grasped Krynut's hand as he approached.

"Good luck."

Gyls rushed up from the stern of the boat. Krynut took a moment to look him up and down.

"Those clothes are going to be hard to swim in if we have to eject."

The inventor's face lost all expression. "Do you think we'll have to eject?"

"Let's hope not!" Krynut smacked Gyls on his narrow shoulder. "Too late to scrounge you up a swimsuit. Okay men, get ready to board."

Chapter 18.

Krynut, the Plugian commander, and two of his men made their way back to the stern. Two coils of the thick rope lay on the deck. Both had been secured to cleats on the port and starboard gunwales. Krynut reached down and picked up the free end of the rope at his feet. He looked at both the Plugians while speaking.

"Your job is to keep the ropes from getting tangled. Once we're in the pluge, go ahead and pay out the lines, nice and slow. If you see that tagger go off, you'll know something has happened. Commander, will you bring the other end up?"

After he and the Plugian secured the ropes to brackets on the nose of the craft, Krynut turned the big circular metal lock on the hatch. A moderate sized chain clunked tight, holding the hatch open in mid-air. He pulled himself up over the ribbed exterior, ducked around the left side of the cockpit, and eased down onto the seat.

The three Plugians followed him in. Two of them examined the bare framing of the crew cabins. Their mostly bald comrade stopped just behind the pilot seats. Light from the thick v-shaped window set in the roof of the craft illuminated the set of metal cranks mounted on the walls of the cockpit.

"Are those the controls?" the Plugian asked.

Without turning around, Krynut laid a hand on the left side crank. "Yes, these are for the vertical steering. Under the dash here, these foot pedals control the horizontal steering fins."

So, how does it propel itself out in space?"

"We're going to lasso a comet."

A short, abrupt laugh escaped from the Plugian's mouth. "You're joking, right?"

Krynut shook his head. "Not joking."

The Plugian eased back against the wooden framework of the quarters. "Ho man! I thought I'd heard everything!"

Outside the craft, Gyls stood staring into the open hatch. Rymnyr reached over and grasped his arm.

"Gyls, it will be fine. Go ahead," she offered in a low, soothing tone. With gentle pressure, she pushed him toward the opening.

The inventor took a deep breath and swung his leg up over the lip. After taking one last look at the bright afternoon sky, he pulled the hatch closed. He waited to hear the loud click of the locking mechanism, then spun the circular latch. With a slight squoosh of air, the hatch sealed.

Gyls ran a hand along his clammy face and eased over to the mass of pipes and gauges on the wall adjacent to the cockpit. It took a moment for his eyes to adjust to the dim light coming through the v-shaped window.

"Air tank full, that's good." After opening the valve a quarter turn, he shifted around to address the Plugian standing behind him. "What's your name?"

"Primary Hyln, sir!"

"Primary Hyln, I want you to watch those gauges over there. The big one on the left is the tank level. The smaller green one is the air pressure. Go ahead and crawl back there. See how the air pressure is sitting right at thirty millimeters? We want to keep it there. If it starts dropping, turn that valve below the air tank gauge. If it starts climbing, shut it down. Pay close attention to the tank level. If it starts dropping rapidly, that means we have a leak, and we'll need to evacuate. You got all that?"

"Yes, sir!"

Gyls tried to smile, but the urge to vomit overpowered all his emotions. He forced himself to breathe normally. Once the urge subsided, he wormed his way into the cockpit and took the seat next to Krynut. From outside the craft, the clanking of the steam winch vibrated through the ribbed wooden hull.

"I think we're going to start moving. Everybody brace yourself!" the regent shouted over his shoulder.

The other two Plugians were still exploring their surroundings. Krynut craned his neck back to see if they had heard his commands. "What's the guy behind us' name?"

"Hyln. Primary Hyln," Gyls whispered.

"Thanks." Krynut rose up out of the seat and leaned back toward the mass of pipes and gauges. "Primary Hyln."

The young Plugian stuffed in the crawl space shifted around to answer. "Yes, sir!"

"Tell your buddies in the back to brace themselves, please."

"Yes, sir!"

Hyln pulled himself out of the crawl space and stuck his head around the edge of the crew cabin frame. "Hey, blyrtholes! Come up here! The pilot is talking to you."

The other two men moved up the passageway toward the cockpit. Krynut turned around in the seat just as the craft was lifted off the deck. "I was going to tell you to hang on, but it's a little too late. What are your names?"

"Primary Zydk sir!" the olive skinned Plugian closest to the cockpit answered. His buzz cut haired comrade snapped rigid and saluted.

"Secondary Fyllr, sir!"

"Okay, my name is Regent Krynut, and this is Mr. Gyls. It's going to be really important that you listen to what we say. Got that?"

"Yes, sir!" both the Plugians answered.

"Who has the tagger?"

"I do, sir!" Fyllr answered.

"Okay, your only job right now is to hang onto that. Got it?"

"Yes, sir!"

"And if I give the order to evacuate, what are you going to do?"

"I'll eject the tagger, sir!"

"And do you know how to eject it?"

"No, sir!"

Krynut sighed in frustration. He turned toward Gyls. "When we get going, can you show him how to eject the tagger?"

The inventor was staring straight ahead. His lips moved slowly under his wiry moustache. Krynut waited for him to respond. He finally reached over and shook Gyls' arm.

"Are you alright?"

"Huh? Yeah, oh yeah. I'm alright. I was just praying."

Krynut's features pulled up into a scowl. He opened his mouth to speak, but the clanking of the steam winch and squealing of the rusty lifeboat pulley distracted him. The craft bucked slightly, then all became calm.

"When we get going, show him how to eject the tagger, okay?"

"Sure. I think we're floating." Gyls leaned back and looked out the v-shaped window. Nothing but blue sky and some water droplets were visible. "They should be paying out the lines right now. Hopefully, we'll feel an initial tug, then off we go."

The only sounds now were the lap of waves against the hull and the background chug of the Lady's steam engine. There was a brief increase in the chugging frequency as the ship motored away.

A small crowd was packed on both the Lady's upper and lower decks. Most of the Dymran group and their guests were huddled on the main deck, trying hard to stay out of the wind. All eyes were on the cylindrical object bobbing on the choppy lake surface forty yards behind. The lines gradually tightened, and with a cheer from the crowd, it began to skim across the water.

Back in the craft, Krynut bounced against the cockpit seat. "We're moving."

"Yep, I think we're still on the surface," Gyls added. "Seems like they're moving too fast."

On the stern of the Lady, the wind whipped Kryzyck's long white hair around behind him. "Myrvst, what do you think. Are we going too fast? The craft seems to be skimming across the surface."

"Yes, I would agree."

The old miner walked briskly across the deck, then ran up the short set of steps to the wheelhouse. He gave a quick knock and pushed on the metal handle.

"Tell the captain to back it down a little. We want the craft to glide just under the surface, not skim across the top."

The first mate passed the request on to the captain. Phytorz leaned down and yelled into the speaking tube that allowed him to communicate with the engine room. "Cut down to ahead half speed!"

Back in the craft, Krynut and Gyls continued to stare up at the window. The slap of waves hitting the nose became less noticeable.

"We're slowing," the regent commented.

"Yeah, look." Gyls pointed up to the green lake water swirling around the outside of the v-shaped window. With a graceful swoosh, the interior of the craft was plunged into dim, diffuse underwater lighting. A smile spread across Gyls' pale, thin face. "We're submerged!"

"That we are."

Gyls turned around in his seat. "Hyln, how's the air pressure?"

"No change, sir."

The inventor leaned back and stuck his face right next to the window. He squinted into the green, glowing light. "Boy, it's hard to tell how deep we are. I'd guess we're down maybe four, five feet. I can just see waves breaking above us."

"Shall we give the steering a try?" Krynut inquired.

"Absolutely. Here, let me install the single person control." Gyls reached down and pulled a long metal tube from under the dash. He inserted the ends into a notch in both wall-mounted crank handles and snapped it in place. Ever so gently, he pushed upward on the tube. Both cranks turned a few degrees. The Plugians adjusted their stance as the nose of the craft dropped down. Gyls gave the tube a downward push, and the nose rose. After leveling them off again, he lifted his hands off the tube.

"It's all yours."

Krynut repeated the actions and brought them back to neutral position. "Wow, it responds well with the vertical controls. Should we try the horizontal?"

"Yeah, might as well." Gyls eased his feet onto the floor pedals and very cautiously applied pressure to the left one. The nose swung left, and the whole craft began to rotate counterclockwise. The crew had to hang on as it shifted beneath them. Gyls hastily released the pressure on the pedal. "Whoa! I didn't expect it to do that."

"Perhaps it needs some stabilization."

Back on the surface, Captain Phytorz stood staring out through the big front window of the wheelhouse. "Kyr, we're coming up on the island, keep an extra watch for kyrfts cutting across the channel. On a day like this, everybody will be anchored on the lee side."

"Yes, sir," the first mate acknowledged. He lifted the shiny gold telescope from its rack and scanned the water around the island. "Sure are lots of kyrfts out today. I'm going out on the deck for a better look."

The mate opened the door and stepped out onto the windy upper deck. He pulled his gold braided white hat down tighter over his head. One of the deckhands walked up next to him.

"Nice day to be cruising, don't you think?"

"Lovely day. She's a little sluggish. I think we might be just a tad overloaded," the mate replied.

"Just a tad."

As they drew opposite the island, Rygryn's white sparkling ship came into view, nestled in a big circular cove.

"Oh, look, it's the Klybth!" The first mate swung his telescope over at the yacht. A smile spread across his clean shaven face. "Oh, man. Are they having fun or what?"

The deckhand stepped over to the rail and squinted into the mid-afternoon glare. "It's too far away to see anything. Let me borrow the glass."

"Okay, but just for a second." The mate handed the telescope over and watched the deckhand's face with anticipation.

After sighting in the large double deckered ship, the deckhand slid the focus tube out. To his surprise, the lens zoomed in on the gorgeous and quite naked, water-slicked backside of one of the guests. The woman was just climbing up out of the water. In the sheltered cove just off the ship's starboard side, many of the passengers were floating or swimming in the shallow water. None of them had a stitch of clothing on.

"I see what you mean. I'm going to apply for a position on that kyrft!"

On the anchored ship, Rygryn lay across a chaise lounge, sunning his lily white belly. He opened one eye as the sound of the Lady's steam engine grew louder. The flash of white plowing down the channel caused him to sit up.

"By Zym, there she is!" Rygryn secured the towel around his waist and yelled in his deep, booming voice. "Hey! Everybody out of the pluge! We're going to race the Lady!"

Squeals of delight echoed off the rocky cliffs of the island. A great thrashing and foaming broke the surface of the cove. One by one, the guests swam over and pulled their slick bodies up onto the deck. Rygryn waddled up to the bow. His first mate was lying on a lounge chair with her eyes closed. He poked her on the shoulder.

"Hey! I was resting!"

"Sorry, dear. I'm going to stoke the boiler, then head up to the wheelhouse. Make sure all the guests get back on board. Oh, and bring me up a double klymr and soda."

"Yes, Captain," the stunning, dark haired woman replied grudgingly.

Rygryn broke into a smile. "That's my mate!" He reached down, gave her long, shapely thigh a squeeze, then made his way off to the boiler room.

A short time later, he emerged from below decks, sweating profusely. He grabbed his captain's uniform from where it was heaped in a pile and buckled his pants while climbing the stairs to the wheelhouse.

"Now then, where is the Lady?" Rygryn stood next to Bytrm and squinted out into the glaring sunlight. Off in the distance, he could see the other ship's wide stern with a foamy wake trailing off into the green, churning water behind. What he didn't see was the pair of ropes cutting through the foam. "Dyth! She's got a good head start. Everyone on board?"

"Yes, Captain. Oh, and here's your drink."

Rygryn took the glass from her, downed half of it, and smacked his lips. "Ah, just like I like it. I'm going to need another of these!"

He reached down with his free hand and jammed the throttle forward. With a clunk, the big shaft under the deck engaged and began turning.

Up in the wheelhouse of the Lady, the first mate was just examining the nautical chart. He made a mental note of the important items and returned to the captain's side.

"Sir, see that long point jutting out? I suggest we swing out and head back up there. The channel ends about half a mile beyond. If we take the turn nice and slow, the craft should be able to swing around without snagging. What do we have, about three hundred feet of rope out?"

Captain Phytorz kept one hand on the wheel and turned around to look out the side window. "That sounds about right."

As the Lady approached the finger-like point of land, the captain gave the order to slow, and spun the wheel hard to the left. The big ship curved in a graceful arc across the glinting water. With the change in course, the late afternoon sun poured into the wheelhouse. A wide sheet of glare obscured everything to the port side in their path.

"Dyth, I thought the stryk would be up higher rather than right in our faces!" Phytorz grumbled. He pulled the visored cap down to shield his eyes. After a few minutes of struggling against the bright yellow light, he caught sight of a stark white object cruising toward them.

'Hey, a kyrft.... Oh, that's got to be Rygryn's floating party coming up. Give them a blast of the whistle."

The first mate reached up and pulled on the chain hanging from the ceiling. A hissing noise followed by a shrill echoing blast issued from the steam tube above them. In response, Rygryn sent a more high pitched whistle blast back across the water. On the observation decks of the Lady, heads turned to see what had produced the sound.

Lymdyr was discussing business with several local business tycoons. He leaned back out of the circle and squinted into the wind. "Here comes Rygryn! That crazy old bastard is probably wanting to race."

The head of Phlyr Communications let out a sarcastic laugh. "Even as loaded down as we are, this baby's got twice the styrn power as his does."

Chapter 19.

In the almost identical, but smaller wheelhouse of his ship, Rygryn saw the Lady make her turn. "Aha! Now's my chance! They're heading back out into the lake. I'll cut across her wake just as she passes, and we'll have our race. So Dear, some nautical rules. Never cut across the bow of an approaching kyrft unless you know you can make it. For some reason, we're dogging it a little. I think it's the wind. We have to wait till she passes and come up behind her. Since Phytorz is an acquaintance of mine, I'm going to cut it close. Really close "

"How close?" Bytrm asked with trepidation.

Rygryn started to laugh, but was seized by a coughing fit. When it subsided, he continued. "Let's just say that you'll be able to hand a drink to one of their passengers if you wanted to. By the way, where's my second one?"

Down under the waves, the olive skinned Plugian had just taken his turn steering. Krynut looked at the huge grin on the young man's face as they changed place. The Plugian let him pass by, then sat on a cross piece of the crew cabin framework. His buzz cut comrade slapped him on the knee.

"What'd ya think? Pretty fun?"

"Yeah, real fun. Hey, Mister, oh, I forgot your name. Anyway, thanks for letting me steer."

"I'm gonna build me one of these when I get out," the buzz cut Plugian commented.

At that moment, the craft pulled hard to the left, causing all aboard to brace themselves. Gyls stood up and peered out the window. "We're turning. I think we reached the end of the channel, and we're heading back."

"Good, I'm not really that keen on tight places like this. I'll be glad to see the stryrk again," the bald Plugian stuck back in the crawl space offered.

"How are we doing on the air tank?"

"Just fine. The gauge shows us still almost full."

Gyls eased back down in the seat. "We have plenty of air. I think we've tested about as much as we can. Unless...."

"Unless what?" Krynut sent a quick glance over at the young inventor's face.

"Unless we want to try taking her down for a dive."

"Ooh, that sounds fleet," the buzz cut Plugian replied.

His olive skinned comrade punched him in the arm. "Enough of that stupid jive. Talk like a regular person."

"Suppose it would be worth seeing how she handles pressure," Krynut thought out loud. "Everybody okay with a dive?"

Two "Yes" responses rang out in the dim interior. The Plugian tucked back in the crawl space just looked out at the pilots. His dark eyes flashed just a trace of panic. Krynut didn't catch that in the low light. More importantly, he really didn't care. They were going to dive.

At that same time up in the wheelhouse of the Lady, the first mate held up his hand to block the glaring sunlight. "Captain, Rygryn is steaming right at us. Should we be concerned?"

Phyrtorz was having a devil of a time dealing with the late afternoon sun blazing right into his face. He swung his gaze off to port and had to wait for the black dots in his vision to clear.

"The old fool's probably asleep at the wheel. Give him a blast."

"Yes, sir." The mate reached up and sent out two short warning whistles.

"They're ready for a race alright!" Rygryn shouted when the shrill steam whistle blasts reached his ears. "Here, take the wheel." Bytrm reluctantly stepped forward and took control of the ship. Rygryn opened the wheelhouse door, walked over to the rail, and waved frantically at the larger ship.

"Sir, now the other captain appears to be waving at us," the Lady's first mate reported.

"Wave back," Phytorz replied without taking his eyes off the course ahead.

Rygryn saw the flash of the first mate's crisp white sleeve waving. He danced a little jig in celebration. "There! That's the signal! The race is one. Whoopee!"

One hundred feet behind him, the anchor of Rygryn's ship broke free of the sandy bottom it had been plowing through and fell gracefully into the deep channel. The sudden lack of drag shot the boat ahead by a knot. The jolly old man had to grab the rail as his craft picked up speed. Shouts of surprise echoed from the startled guests below. Rygryn re-entered the wheelhouse and slid his arm around Bytrm's slender waist.

"She likes you," he crooned.

Bytrm turned her head of fabulous wavy hair toward him. "What are you talking about?"

"The kyrft. Didn't you feel the way she kicked 'er into high gear once you were in control?"

Bytrm frowned and swung the wheel to the left. "All I did was keep it on the same heading. Do you want to come around behind them like you talked about?"

"Yep. Hard to port." Rygryn gave the throttle an extra push forward. His ship was now heading at a right angle to the Lady.

On the larger vessel, the passengers crowded on the port side for a look at the bevy of beauties Rygryn had brought along for his foreign guests. With the weight of all forty-five passengers shifted to port, the Lady began listing several degrees. Up in the wheelhouse, the mate gripped the chart table to steady himself.

"Whoa! What just happened?"

On the lower deck, one of the crew looked over at the water rushing by only six inches from the gunwale. He yelled over to another crew member standing nearby.

"Hey, we're riding awfully low!"

Back in the submerged craft, Krynut was about to execute the dive when Gyls reached over and laid a hand on his arm. "Wait a second!"

"What is it?"

"Listen."

Both of them remained stock still, focusing on the sounds around them. They could hear the rhythmic chugging of the Lady droning on the surface above. The wooden hull of the craft gave an occasion creak. From over by Gyl's side of the craft, a fast paced, higher frequency chugging sound started out faint, and gradually grew louder.

"Sounds like another steam engine," Krynut whispered.

"Yeah, and it's headed this way."

Gyls stood up and looked out the window. He jammed his head of tangled black hair against the ceiling in a desperate attempt to get a visual on the source of the engine sound.

Up on the surface, Rygryn's ship plowed just seventy feet from the Lady's stern. As soon as it cut across the submerged lines trailing off the larger vessel, shouts of alarm rose up from some of the passengers.

The Plugian stationed on the starboard side yelled obscenities and waved both arms in the air. Mihyn and her husband were standing behind him. She squeezed Handynr's fingers to the breaking point. Kryzyck ran back to the transom and hung off one of the guy lines.

"Hey you stupid klynking idiot! Watch out for the lines!" He gritted his teeth as Rygryn's yacht sliced across the Lady's wake.

Back down under the surface, Gyls saw the foamy propeller wash streak overhead. He was too busy watching the bubbly track to notice the anchor line straight and tight as an arrow cutting through the deep just behind it. The sound of Rygryn's engine gradually trailed off.

"I don't know what that was all about. Go ahead and take 'er down." Gyls lowered himself back down into the cockpit seat.

"Diving." Krynut eased the metal connector tube up toward his chest. The light in the interior darkened slightly as the pointed nose swung down toward the depths.

Sailing through the deep water like a monstrous fisherman's hook, Rygryn's anchor searched for a likely prey. The diving craft was the only fish big enough for the lure. With sickening precision, the anchor swung along on its tight line, and smacked the forward window hard. The triple thick glass cracked in a spider web pattern. Water shot in a powerful stream from the center of the web. The anchor bounced off and caught the port side line, rotating the craft around with force.

None of the crew had time to react. They were tossed hard to the right. Krynut slid along the connector tube and wound up jammed against Gyls' bony legs. The Plugian watching the gauges hit the tubing hard, splitting his lip. The other two fell backward over the cabin framework.

The stream of water shooting out of the damaged window hit the port side interior wall at mid-ship. As luck would have it, the tagger had been stowed behind a support rail just below the point of impact. The water cascading down the ribs activated the carbonate. A loud fizzing, followed by an opaque, billowing cloud of violet erupted from the area.

"Uh oh!" Gyls whipped around in the seat and stared wide-eyed at the growing mass of color.

Once the port side line connected to the stern of the Lady tightened, the craft ceased its rotation. The olive skinned Plugian swore in his native language, then thrust himself forward out of the framework. He jammed his palm against the jet of water spurting through the broken window.

"Hey! Give me something to block this with. A shirt. A piece of cloth. Anything!"

Gyls ripped the front of his white button shirt open. He fought with one of the sleeves, but finally managed to shove it into the Plugian's outstretched hand. The shirt did little to slow the stream of water. Krynut pulled himself back to an upright position and pushed the control tube down. The nose slowly began to rise.

"Well, at least we're headed back up." He shot a quick glance back at the ever growing cloud of brilliant blue that was heading his way. The bald Plugian still crammed in the crawl space inhaled a lung full and began coughing spasmodically.

"Oh blyrt! Oh blyrt! This is bad," his comrade up by the damaged window shouted. He looked over at the swelling cloud of violet, then down at his comrade dragging himself out of the crawl space. "Holy klynk! Hyln. Are you alright?"

Both Gyls and Krynut turned around in time to catch a glimpse of the blood soaked Plugian just before a wave of opaque blue wafted over them.

"I gotta get outta here!" the bloodied Plugian screamed. He jumped forward and grabbed the circular metal hatch latch.

"No! No! Don't," the buzz cut Plugian called out from his place by the crew cabin framework.

Two spins were enough to send a spray of water hissing out the left side of the hatch. Krynut climbed up onto the seat as cold lake water swirled about his feet.

"Alright men! Get ready to evacuate."

"I can't swim!" Gyls shouted.

"Oh blessed klynking Zym!" Krynut yelled back. "Why didn't....never mind."

The force of water pressure tore the hatch open. In a supremely surreal moment, the gushing lake water fully activated the tagger. All the occupants were painted bright blue just before the interior flooded. Both the olive skinned Plugian and his bloodied companion were knocked back by the force of the water. Krynut absorbed the impact of the first man. The bloodied Plugian was washed right into Gyls' chest. He elbowed the young inventor in the throat, then submerged and fought his way through the open hatchway. Krynut and the olive skinned Plugian followed him out into lake.

Gyls jammed himself up into the toxic blue haze of the air pocket trapped near the ceiling. He tried to breath, but the swirling blue vapors burned his lungs. A head popped up next to him.

"Buddy! Come on! We gotta swim out." The buzz cut Plugian grabbed Gyls' arm and yanked him under. With the stark reality of the moment and panic of impending death clanging warning bells inside his head, Gyls allowed himself to be towed out the hatch and into the sunlight streaked, green depths. He looked around at the tangle of lines rising up from the craft as it continued to be pulled away.

The Plugian grabbed Gyl's hand and wrapped it around the starboard side line. He pointed up toward the surface, then gave several powerful kicks and dissolved into the green. Gyls began pulling himself along the line. His injured lungs threatened to give up and allow themselves to flood with lake water.

A large portion of the passengers had walked around to the stern to watch Rygryn's floating party power across the Lady's wake. On the upper deck, two finely dressed women were standing next to the back rail. With one hand on the rail, and the other holding her elaborate plumed hat tightly onto her head, the woman on the left happened to direct her gaze out to the choppy water fifty yards behind the stern. Her eyes zeroed in on the torrent of air bubbles from the unsealed craft that had just hit the surface.

"Yngrd, what do you suppose is going on out there?

"Where?"

The woman on the left pointed at the bubbles boiling up on the water behind them. Her companion squinted out in the indicated direction and let out a scream when the first three blue-stained crew members broke the surface. The other woman shrieked even louder.

On the main deck below, the Plugian manning the port side lines climbed up on the transom and craned his neck around to find the source of the screams. The two women on the upper deck were jumping up and down while pointing out over the rail. He followed the direction of their frantic movements.

"Oh holy Zym! We got men in the pluge. Go tell the commander!"

His comrade jumped over a hatch cover, and in a voice only a military person can summon, he yelled loud enough to be heard above the wind, engine noise, and murmur of the crowd gathered mid-ship. "Commander! Commander! We got men coming up out of the craft!"

The burly commander instantly recognized the serious tone of his charge's voice. He moved several well dressed passengers out of the way and hustled back to the stern. The rest of the crowd followed him. On the upper deck above, ten passengers also made their way toward the stern. The added weight dipped the back end of the Lady down into the water.

Both Plugians manning the lines jumped back as a plume of green slid over the painted rail. Screams of panic and outrage followed the wave as it swept over many pairs of expensive dress shoes and high heels. The crowd surged back in reaction.

Sylstyn and Professor Rymnyr had been sitting on the starboard gunwale thoroughly enjoying the later afternoon breeze when the first hideous screams rang out from the upper deck. They both watched the crowd of passengers drift back toward the stern. Sylstyn stood up, but couldn't see above the heads of the mob, so she grabbed the guy wires and climbed up onto the gunwale.

"I wonder what's going on?"

Rymnyr got to her feet and stepped up onto a support beam beneath the gunwale. At that moment, the crowd suddenly turned and raced back to mid-ship as the water surged over the stern. The forward movement of the passengers caused the deck to pitch violently. Sylstyn and Professor Rymnyr were knocked from their perch. An older gentleman tried to reach for the professor, but ended up getting tossed overboard with them.

Up in the wheelhouse, Captain Phytorz and the first mate felt the deck under them rock when the stern dropped.

"What the klynk is happening?" the captain yelled.

"I don't know! I don't know! I think we're sinking!"

The first mate steadied himself and worked his way across the angled upper deck. He opened the wheelhouse door just in time to hear the screams from down below and feel the deck shift back to normal. The passengers on the upper deck turned and stared at him with a look of pleading terror. Keeping a tight grip on the outer rail, he thrust his head over the side.

"Holy dyth!"

"What is going on?" Captain Phytorz shouted from the back of the wheelhouse.

"I don't know! We've got passengers overboard! Pluge is pouring off the deck! I think something's going on with the boiler. We got steam rising up from below."

"I can't get a response from the engine room. I just shut the engine down. Go down and get a status report!"

"Yes, sir!"

Just as the mate was turning to run down the stairs, a tall, balding gentleman in a finely tailored black suit grabbed him by the arm. The man's panicked wife stood at his side. "Hey, is the kyrft sinking?"

The mate looked up into the man's steely grey eyes. "I don't think so. I need to go down to the main deck and see."

The man released his grip, and the mate charged down the steps. When he arrived at the water soaked deck, one of the sailors struggling to manually release a lifeboat on the starboard side called out to him.

"Mr. Tyrn! We got people in the pluge!"

"I know, go ahead and launch the lifekyrft." At that same instant, two of the Plugians climbed up on the gunwale and leaped off the side. "What in Zym's name are they doing?" The first mate ran over and watched the Plugians swim out toward the three people drifting away. "Oh, holy klynking blyrt!"

The head of Phylr Communications was standing off to the side with a group of wet, influential guests. He heard the first mate's exclamation and ran toward him. "Mr. Tyrn! What exactly is going on?"

"I don't know sir! I just got down here. It appears we have people in the pluge..." Over Phylr's shoulder, he caught sight of the first bright blue crew of the craft being pulled up over the stern. "Oh Zym!" It took a moment for the initial shock of having blue people aboard the ship to wear off, but the mate was finally able to compose himself.

"Okay, I don't think the kyrft is sinking. It looks like what happened was everyone moved to the stern, and we took on pluge. I'm going to go down to the boiler room. I'll get a status and brief you."

Lymdyr and his wife stood nearby. She was watching the chaos with her arms tightly crossed. "Why don't you do something rather than just stand there looking proud."

He sent a sideways glance over at her scornful expression. "What would you like me to do?"

"I don't know! You're in charge of this fiasco, right?"

Lymdyr was just about to deliver a seething reply when he heard shouts from the stern ring out.

"Hey! You're dragging a line!" the Plugian on the port side bellowed. He stood up on the gunwale and pointed at Rygryn's anchor line slicing through the water.

In the wheelhouse of the smaller ship, Bytrm was just beginning to execute the wide arcing turn to pull them around in preparation for the race. The Plugian's loud voice caught her attention. She stuck her head out window and watched him repeatedly point toward the hull.

"Take over here please." Without saying anything further, Bytrm waited till Rygryn took the wheel from her, then hurried out onto the deck. When she leaned over the rail, her eyes fell on the taut anchor line cutting through the glassy water and disappearing into the depths. She let out a gasp.

"Rygryn! I mean Captain! Is there supposed to be a rope hanging off the front of the kyrft?"

The rotund captain stuck his head out of the open window. "What did you say?"

"I said, there's a rope leading from the front of the kyrft out into the pluge."

A look of instantaneous shock rippled across his ruddy face. "Get in here and take the wheel!"

They passed each with a swish. He rested his huge belly on the rail and squinted down at the gleaming water. "Oh klynk! Holy klynking mother of Zym! The anchor." Rygryn swung around and yelled through the open window. "I forgot to pull up the dyth anchor! No wonder we were bogged down. Why didn't you remind me? You're the first mate!"

Bytrm snapped her head in his direction. Her perfect, almond shaped eyes threw daggers at him. Her full luscious lips were pulled tight. "How dare you accuse me of causing this! You're a stupid drunken old fool!"

He recoiled at the barrage and turned back toward the rail. It was then that he noticed the two lines coming off the Lady's stern. Even from the distance he could tell by their sharp angle that they were hopelessly tangled in the anchor.

"Cut the engines," he muttered with a shake of his round, sunburnt head.

"You cut the klynking engines! I'm done dealing with you!" Bytrm exited the wheelhouse and stomped past Rygryn without looking at him.

Chapter 20.

Back on the Lady, two sailors were just pulling the lifeboat up next to the side of the ship. Rymnyr and the older gentleman that had gone overboard were laughing. Sylstyn sat with her arms tightly crossed. She looked forever like an angry, wet cat. Kryzyck reached out and helped the professor aboard.

"Oh, nothing like a refreshing swim!" she cackled.

Her beautiful bouffant had been reduced to a pile of tangled greying strands. Blrsynt pulled his girlfriend up over the gunwale and wrapped a blanket around her. Lymdyr came walking up with a glass of yellow liquid.

"Here professor, this'll warm you. I am so terribly sorry about this!"

Rymnyr accepted the glass from him and took a big drink. Right next to her, Sylstyn balled up the hem of her soaked dress to let the water drain out.

"Are you okay, dear?" the professor asked.

"Yes, I'm fine. Wet, but fine. I'm just zynked that the Plugian insisted on dragging me back to the kyrft. I'm a good swimmer! I didn't need his help." Sylstyn cursed under her breath.

"Here take this. I'm going to check on the crew." Rymnyr handed the glass over, and while wringing water out of her dress, made her way back to the stern. Kryzyck followed close behind.

The two of them found Gyls sitting on the deck with a blanket over his shoulders. His knobby knees were pulled up, head hanging down. Swatches of blue were shot across his tangled black hair. His father knelt next to him.

Krynut and his girlfriend were standing nearby. When Rymnyr arrived, he let go of Janela's hand, and allowed the professor to hug him.

"That was a close one, eh?" Rymnyr asked in a low voice.

"Yes, very close."

The professor released her grip and tilted her dripping pile of hair toward Gyls. "How's he doing?"

"Not so good. He took a big lung full of the dye. I think he's pretty traumatized. He can't swim, either."

"Oh, I didn't know that."

"Neither did I."

The professor bent down to lightly touch Gyl's blue shoulder. "It's me Professor Rymnyr. How are you?"

With some effort, the inventor lifted his head and looked up at her with a vacant, watery stare. "Actually, I'm not doing too badly, considering…." A violent coughing fit interrupted his statement. He hung his head back down. The father rubbed his son's back several times, then rose to a standing position.

"I need to get him off this kyrft and back home. He needs to rest."

Rymnyr nodded in agreement. "We will as soon as we can. I'm very sorry for the worry and anguish that today has brought."

The father looked at her makeup smeared face. He gave a hmmpf in response.

"How's the craft?" Gyls asked in a scratchy voice. His head remained lowered.

"Not sure. We won't know till we bring her up," Krynut answered.

No one spoke for several moments. Kryzyck had been observing the interactions from off to the side. After waiting another couple seconds, he cleared his throat and spoke in a quiet, solemn voice.

"What happened down there?"

"We ran into something." Krynut's enigmatic answer was followed by another vacant silence.

"What? Like a rock?"

"Not sure. We were executing a dive, and pow! Something hit and broke the front window."

"Maybe you hit the bottom?"

"No, Zym no. We were in very deep pluge. Maybe a submerged log or something."

"She sure did handle well," Gyls added without lifting his head.

"Well, guess we better untangle the lines, and haul 'er up." Krynut stared out at the glassy water.

"Not much untangling to do now," the Plugian on the right responded.

"What'd you mean?"

"Well, ever since that old fool cut the anchor line he was dragging, the lines have straightened out again. I will say this. I helped lift that thing out of the wagon, but now, it's full of pluge. Gonna be a dyth sight heavier."

Kryzyck reached over, grabbed the line, and gave it a good hard tug. "I think they have the boiler working, but I don't know how advisable it will be to try and winch it up. I'd hate to have one of these lines snap."

Krynut looked over at the two Plugians. "Go round up your buddies. Let's try pulling it in."

Rymnyr wrung out another handful of water from her dress. "I need another drink."

She and Kryzyck moved back toward mid-ship and stopped near the steps leading to the upper deck. Lymdyr and his wife, Mihyn and her husband, Head Regent Bokyl, and Professor Myrvst were all gathered in a group. After taking a swig from the bottle Lymdyr had produced, Handynr passed it over to Professor Rymnyr, and slid his arm around Mihyn.

"All this chaos is bringing back memories of that last awful day in Bosyra. I haven't thought about it since we got back."

"I haven't had time to read the official transcript. What exactly happened?" Bokyl inquired.

"Well, I don't know if you've been to the capital of Bosyra..."

"I have."

"Okay, then you know that it's ringed by low hills, and the only rail line comes through a deep notch in those hills." Handynr's Adam's Apple bobbed in his throat. "Uh, we managed to get the archaeologic crew out on styrn back while the rebels were shelling the city non-stop. That last night, Kym and I were huddled in this burnt out building waiting for word that it was safe to move out.

Around three in the morning, some Terrans holding lanterns arrived and loaded us into open wagons. We spent the next four hours bumping along covered in tarps. I remember hearing bullets whizz over us a couple times."

"Well, we're just glad you, your secretary, and the archaeologic crew made it back safe. Kym's family was very concerned. I didn't realize she was so young."

Professor Rymnyr gave a quick shudder. "A breeze is starting to kick up. I don't know about the rest of you, but I'm getting chilled. I think we should go find a place out of the wind."

While the group moved off toward the rows of benches along the main cabin, Krynut and the contingent of the Plugians assembled at the stern. The regent waited till the men took up positions along the rail, then spoke directly to their commander.

"What I think we should do is bring it up to the surface, leave about twenty feet of line out, and tow it back to the pier. It'll probably take us an hour to get it out of the pluge. While we work on that, the passengers can board the train. This crowd has had enough fun for one day."

"Okay men, half of you grab this side, half, the other. On the count of three, start pulling," the commander called out.

On both sides of the stern, the men lined up and gripped the wet, cold rope. While he heaved along with them, the commander carried on a conversation with Krynut.

"If I'm not mistaken, you have some military training, correct?"

A thin trace of a smile broke across the regent's face. "Why yes, I retired from the Terran Land Forces several years ago."

"I thought so," the rough faced commander smiled back. "What rank?"

"I made it all the way to fran."

"Most impressive, Fran Krynut."

"After twenty minutes of hauling, the long, pointed nose punctured the surface. A tired cheer rose up from the group. The Plugian commander rubbed his forearms.

"Good job, men. Go ahead and tie her off tight. I'll tell the captain we're ready to head back."

Once the lines were secured, the Plugians flopped wherever they could find a comfortable spot. The familiar chug chug of the steam engine, and a long blast of the whistle signaled the return to motion. White smoke again poured out of the stack. In the sky above, the long, wispy clouds were just beginning to show some color. The vivid crimson and orange reflected in the dark water, giving the appearance of flames.

Phylr waited till the light was just dim enough to make it difficult to see, then he walked around behind the back of the pillar by the engine room steps. He pulled the metal door of the small rectangular black box open, then flipped a switch. Strings of large electric lights sprang to life all along the underside of the deck. An oooh of appreciation rose up from the tired crowd.

The ship plowed its way back to the pier in relative silence. A fair number of the passengers fell asleep in their places on the row of benches under the upper deck. The Dymran group had all assembled on the port side of the ship. Lymdyr and his wife were seated at the far end of the bench. He eased out from under her grasp so as not to wake her.

Krynut and Janela were snuggled up tight right next to them. Lymdyr shot a quick glance over at the brightly lit resort, then positioned himself at the mid-point of the ship and squatted down.

"Hey everyone, I have a great idea. When we get back to the dock, I'm going to run up to the resort, and see if I can, uh, use my influence to grab us four, maybe five rooms for the night. I don't know about you all, but I could use a good meal, a couple strong drinks, and a nice quiet end to this day. What do you think about that?"

The hopefulness in his voice caught the attention of the somber group. Rymnyr and Sylstyn were folded up together, sandwiched between their boyfriends. The professor's mascara streaked face lit up at the offer.

"Mr. Lymdyr, I think that's a great suggestion. Sylstyn and I would love to take our sodden dresses off for a while. The thought of sitting on that train, soaking wet, was starting to make me sad."

Handnyr gave his narrow chin a stroke. "I'll have to send a telemessage to the office, but it's a possibility."

From down below the deck, the chug chug of the steam engines slowed. Heads lifted all up and down the long bench as the ship approached the dock. Lymdyr shot up to a standing position.

"Great, I'll disembark as soon as I can and make the arrangements."

Moments later, the ship eased up to the dock. The crew made themselves busy tying off the lanyards and preparing the gangplank. Krynut and Janela were in the middle of a very heated, private discussion when Captain Phytorz came strolling down the stairs.

"I can't just spend the night with you! We're not married!" The princess' whispered words carried a touch of venom.

Krynut held up a hand, then turned away from his girlfriend, and rushed over to speak with Phytorz. "Captain, I appreciate your efforts today. I have one last favor?"

"Yes?"

"We're going to haul the craft up out of the pluge and we need the sailors to help."

"Why not use the winch?"

Krynut stopped to contemplate the suggestion. His face broke into a smile. "You know, I hadn't even considered that."

Phytorz let go a deep, rumbling laugh. "That's why I'm the captain." He patted the regent on his blue-stained arm. "I'll go get my engineer working on it."

As soon as the ship was secured, Lymdyr hopped up on the gunwale, grabbed one of the guy wires, and shouted out to the passengers.

"May I have your attention please! Once we are clear to disembark, go ahead and make your way up to the train. Thanks for all your patience during this difficult day." With dramatic flair, Lymdyr finished his statement by swinging over the gunwale down onto the dock.

The groggy passengers began to line up next to the area of the deck where the gangplank would soon be placed. A mixture of quiet laughter and just under the breath complaints circled amongst them. At the stern, the Plugians, Krynut, and the ship's engineer, Mr. Swydr, were preparing to haul the craft up. The engineer squinted out over the inky black water, then turned to Krynut.

"So, I'm thinking that we pull 'er up close, haul it around to the side, then use the lifekryft pulleys to lift her out of the pluge."

"Yes, that seems like a plan," Krynut replied.

The gangplank was eventually lowered onto the dock, and with the winch creaking and whining in the background, the passengers disembarked. Some of them trudged drearily up the hill to the train while others stayed to watch the craft being pulled up out of the lake.

Lymdyr came jogging back from the resort. He caught sight of several members of the Dymran group lined up along the dock, hurried over to them, and squeezed in next to Professor Rymnyr and Kryzyck.

"So what's going on?"

The old miner answered without taking his eyes off the black silhouette of the craft bobbing off the side of the Lady. "They just secured the lifekryft straps, and now they're going to try and lift it out of the pluge."

Fifteen minutes later, the craft was lowered onto the dock. The remainder of the passengers, including the Plugians made their way up the hill. Lymdyr laid a hand on Professor Rymnyr's shoulder.

"Okay, everything is set. I have five rooms. All you need to do is go up to the front desk and say you are part of our group. I'm going to run up and check on the train. Go ahead and let the rest of the group know about the rooms, if you would."

"Absolutely. Oh, thank you so much. You don't know how badly I want to strip off this wet dress."

The railroad man flashed a quick smile and began walking up the hill. Mihyn had been standing off to the side, listening. Rymnyr sent a quick glance over at her friend's deeply furrowed, pale features.

"Where's Handynr?"

"He went up to check for telemessages. Evidently, there have been some updates on the situation in Bosyra. I'll have to check with him when he gets back," she said quietly.

While Lymdyr strode up toward the train, he made no attempt to suppress the satisfied grin from beaming across his face. "Well old boy, you managed to salvage something out of this disastrous day! A nice night at the resort and a big glass of klymr sound pretty good at this point."

He waited till the last of the passengers had entered the car, then swung up onto the steps, yanked the door open, and made his grand entrance. The Plugians were seated near the back of the car, laughing and joking in unusually loud voices. The group of journalists were right in front of them, furiously scrawling notes on their pads of paper.

Lymdyr apologized for the wait, thanked the crowd, then bade them good night. When he swung back down to the ground outside the car, Regent Mihyn and her husband were just approaching. Handynr reached out and extended his hand.

"Thank you for all you've done today. We'd love to stay, but I just got word that there's a Plugian blockade in the Bosyran port of Myol, so I'm meeting with our adviser tomorrow." After shaking hands with Lymdyr, he looked down at his wife.

"Are you sure you don't want to stay? It's not every day that you get an offer to spend the night at the Chief Polatsi resort."

Mihyn smiled politely. "No, it's alright. I have lots to do tomorrow anyway."

Handynr slid his arm around her shoulder. "Dear, I really think you should take Mr. Lymdyr's offer. I mean, tomorrow is going to be a long, strenuous day for me, so...."

The couple remained fixed in each other's gaze for a moment. Her husband's overly enthusiastic suggestion that she stay, combined with the fleeting smile that passed over his face struck Mihyn as highly unusual. She let go a sigh and returned her attention to Lymdyr.

"Thanks again, but I just don't think it will work."

"Well, sorry you can't join us. Hope everything works out with the situation on Bosyra. Zym knows we don't need to get dragged into another regional conflict," Lymdyr replied.

He patted Mihyn on the arm as she ascended the steps. After giving the engineer the signal to depart, Lymdyr began walking back down the hill.

"What a day!"

At that same time, his wife was making her way up the path. Once he had dropped down off the tracks, she recognized him, hiked up her long skirt, and quickened her pace.

Lymdyr let gravity pull him down the hill. He was worn out from the excitement of the day. The crunch of Bynhyld's stylish black boots on the gravel caused him to look up from his meditation. He could tell by the way she was charging up the hill that something was amiss. Lymdyr slowed his gait and prepared for the worst.

"Where have you been? Did the train just leave?" Bynhyld snapped.

Lymdyr held up his hands as if trying to deflect her anger. "Relax! It's all taken care of," he offered in as jolly a tone as his tired self could produce.

"What's all taken care of? You're not making much sense."

He took several steps forward. "We're staying here tonight."

"What? You could have asked me first!" She stared at him with the look of unbelief that only couples who have been together for long periods of time can produce. Her head of wavy black hair was cocked to the side. "Really, so we're staying here tonight?" He nodded in confirmation. "Well, I wish you had told me this morning. I would have packed another set of clothes."

"I didn't know we were going to stay till just a little while ago." Bynhyld made a tsk sound with her tongue, and without a word, stomped off toward the resort. "I'm going to go down and make sure the craft is secured. Meet me at the front desk," Lymdyr called out as her form gradually disappeared into the darkness. He let out a gushing breath of relief.

"Her reaction wasn't half as bad as I thought it would be. Someday, I'm going to have to get rid of her." Lymdyr whistled a happy little tune while strolling down to the dock.

Later that evening, the members of the Dymran group were seated in the dining room of the resort enjoying a sumptuous meal. Professor Rymnyr wiped her mouth with a napkin and settled back into her chair.

"Boy, I didn't realize how hungry I was! I think it's time to start the discussion about who is going to be part of the crew for the voyage."

Professor Myrvst finished his cup of zyd and poured himself another. "I've been thinking about that, too. If I recall Gyls' diagram, he included tiny living quarters for five people."

Krynut stopped eating the colorful pasta dish set before him. He silently inventoried the unfinished compartments in the craft. "Yes, I count five."

"And have we determined what exactly the qualifications for these five should be?" Myrvst asked.

Professor Rymnyr finished off her glass of pale green mynth. She leaned over and laid her hand on Kryzyck's arm. "Be a dear and pour me another glass please." While the old miner reached over and complied with her request, she answered.

"The list I have includes a pilot, a science officer, an engineer, a healer, and a translator."

Head Regent Bokyl let go a snorting laugh. He finished chewing through the piece of mag steak in his mouth before responding. "A translator? We're not even sure what language these transmissions are generated in!"

A smile broke across Rymnyr's face. "Ah, that's not entirely correct. My department has pieced together almost one hundred words from transcripts of recent communications."

"Well, I think the crew list needs to be edited," Bokyl added. "Which one of those academics listed is going to be able to rope a comet? Better question, who on Ulutrita is a good enough rope handler to lasso a comet?"

Sitting at her place across the table, Sylstyn nudged Blrsynt's shin with her foot. "We know who could lasso a comet, don't we!" she whispered.

Lymdyr finished picking the meat off the whole pyfg that lay eviscerated on his plate. He glanced around at the contented faces of his guests. "Seems like the next step will be to put together a list of candidates."

"I agree. Shall we meet next week?" Rymnyr tossed out. The group nodded in agreement. "Good, we can have it at my home. Once we get a list of likely candidates for the voyage, we can begin the screening process. It may take us a while to find some willing participants." The professor yawned deeply. "Oh, excuse me. I think it's time for me to turn in." She rotated in her chair and fixed her gaze on the railroad man. "Thank you again for hosting this incredible day."

"My pleasure."

On their way back to the room, Lymdyr and his wife walked in silence. He searched for something meaningful to say, but ended up thinking out loud instead.

"Well, at least we got some useful discussion taken care of."

Bynhyld offered a low grunt in response. She walked with her head slightly lowered. "I suppose you're planning on being part of the crew. It seems like something you'd want to do."

Lymdyr let out a sharp laugh and looked down at her all too serious face. "You've got to be kidding! What qualities do I have that would benefit the project?"

Chapter 21.

Over the next couple weeks, the damage to the craft was repaired and work continued to progress quickly. On a Pryn day afternoon, Head Regent Bokyl was busy writing responses to requests for project applications. Professor Ymyl came hobbling into his office and stood in front of the big wooden desk.

"Head Regent! I yust got a telemessage from zee observatory on Mount Clymr."

Bokyl stopped writing, shook out the cramp in his hand, and looked up at the astronomer. The older man's blue, grey eyes were wide and twinkling. His lips were held open and tense.

"And?"

"Here, read for yourself." Ymyl held out the yellow sheet which the head regent snatched away from him. His small rodent like eyes whirred back and forth down the text.

"Holy Zym. We better get the word out. I think Rymnyr is still here. Myrvst has gone home. Regent Krynut is in a meeting, as is Mihyn. I'll go ask them to come up here after they are done. You go find Rymnyr and have her meet us here. Dyth! And everything was going so well!" Bokyl's big, almost perfectly round head flushed a bright crimson.

After interrupting the meeting Krynut and Mihyn were in, he sent a messenger to Professor Myrvst's house, and to Gyls' barrel factory, then huffed and puffed his way back up to his office. When Bokyl returned to his office, Professors Ymyl and Rymnyr were waiting.

"So Ymyl just gave me the bad news. Is there any way we can make it work now?" Rymnyr's question was tinged with desperation.

The head regent plunked down in his chair, wiped some sweat off his bald head, and leaned back to answer. "I have no idea. When the others get here, hopefully they can help make the determination. Everything was going so well. I knew we'd run into a snag."

Voices and footsteps echoing down the hall drew the attention of the trio. Mihyn entered the office first, with Krynut close behind. They both looked around at the shocked faces of their colleagues.

"So what's going on?" Krynut asked.

Bokyl turned toward the old astronomer. "Tell them."

Ymyl folded his hands together, looked down at the floor, then back up at the new arrivals.

"Vee yust received zee latest observations from Mount Clymr as to the comet's current trajectory. Vee ran them through your calculating machine, and it indicated that zee comet would be at its closest pass to Ulutrita in six months."

Mihyn let out a short gasp. Krynut stood with his arms crossed tightly. "Did you try running the calculation several times?"

Ymyl nodded. "Yust for a test, vee entered zee observations for zee last several months that were calculated by hand and got zee same answers. I think zee predication is correct. Jym at zee observatory said they could see it without the aid of zee telescope last night."

A scowl of concern spread across Krynut's face. His high, arched eyebrows pulled down into an angry V. "Well, we need to get the project team together. Lymdyr is off inspecting the rail lines all the way out in Rynyl. I suppose we could try and get word to him. Dyth! Things were going so well."

"I think we better finalize who exactly is going on the voyage. We'll need to make sure they get whatever training is needed," Bokyl added.

Professor Rymnyr scooted around in her chair to face him. "I have a pretty good idea of who I think should go. Shall we make a list?"

"I don't see why not." Bokyl pulled a sheet of paper from his desk drawer and began to write. "So, the positions so far are pilot, science officer, linguist....engineer and healer. Is that correct?"

Rymnyr leaned back, crossed her legs, and spread her arms out across the back of the chair. "I've been thinking about the selections. Assuming they do make it to wherever these transmissions are coming from, seems like it would be a good idea to include someone to officially represent our culture."

"You mean like an ambassador?" Mihyn inquired.

"Exactly! Who knows what kind of reception they'll receive. Could be friendly, could be hostile. Imagine what would happen if some visitors dropped out of the sky right here in Tyrl."

"Ambassador," Boky repeated back. "So which position do we substitute for? I say we combine one of the others with healer. Lots of people have healer training of some kind or another."

Professor Myrvst came stumbling through the door. His frizzy grey hair was pushed over to the side, one shirt tail hung out. Bokyl let go a deep laugh.

"My Zym man! What did you do, just wake up?"

The professor adjusted his wire frame glasses and looked around the room. "Why yes, I did just get up. I had settled down for a nap, which I was enjoying quite thoroughly, when the messenger arrived. What's all the panic about?"

Professor Rymnyr patted the empty chair seat next to her. "Come here and have a seat. We'll fill you in."

Pattering footsteps and sounds of labored breathing floated into the room from outside in the hall. Gyls' lanky frame suddenly lurched into view. He paused inside the door frame to steady himself. His thin face was more pale than usual. His mouth hung open. Professor Rymnyr noticed the look of distress on his face, jumped to her feet, and hustled over to him.

"Oh, dear! Are you alright?"

Gyls gasped and wheezed several times before he was able to answer. He held a finger up, then finally managed to get his breath under control. "Yes.....yes.....It's.....just that .....I'm not used.....to exerting....myself. I ran all the way up from....the sidewalk."

Rymnyr scanned his dry, reddened eyes. "Here, let me help you to a chair."

"No, no thanks. I'm fine." He politely shook his way out of her grasp and walked over to an empty chair next to Krynut. Gyls dropped down, then tilted his head back against the wall. The other people seated in the room shared a worried glance. After a moment, he pulled himself into an upright position and looked around at the frowning faces.

"Really, I'm fine! No need to worry. So what's all the excitement about?"

Professor Ymyl had been on the verge of napping in the warm office. He seemed to have come back to life once Gyls arrived. The venerable old astronomer leaned out and addressed the two new arrivals.

"Based on some recent calculations from zee observations from Mount Clymr, and zee new level of accuracy we can achieve with Regent Krynut's device, it looks like zee comet will be at its closest approach two months earlier than expected."

Professor Myrvst sat slumped in his chair. His only reaction was the lifting of his bushy eyebrows. He did rotate his head slightly to make eye contact with the rest of the group. "Well, that certainly poses some problems, doesn't it?"

Gyls ran a hand over his scraggly black beard. "Hmmm, that is big news."

"Perhaps you could give us an update on the construction progress?" Rymnyr commented while returning to her seat.

Before answering, Gyls leaned forward, balanced an elbow on each knee, and clasped his hands together. "Construction is progressing well. It's really a big help to have Blrsynt out there. He's a fast learner." The inventor swung his head over to face Krynut. "That metal you discovered is a real challenge to work with. It's so brittle that we keep having to send large pieces back to the railroad shop. It simply doesn't want to bend. Oh, and by the way, Professor Ymyl, any time you want to send the telescope over, we're ready to install it."

"So in short, do you think you can have the work done in six months?" Professor Rymnyr asked.

Gyls straightened back up, gave a wheezing cough, and looked over at her. "Excuse me, Zym! I wish I could get rid of this cough! Six months will be cutting it close. I was hoping to run some additional tests on the steering. Actually, thank you for reminding me." He reached into his dusty black pants and pulled out a folded sheet of paper.

"I couldn't sleep last night because my mind was racing, so I got up and made this list. Here are the important things that I think still need to be done. Number one, we......"

Rymnyr held up a hand. "Head Regent! Write these down."

Bokyl let get one of his characteristic, low growls. "Didn't think I'd have to be the scribe also."

"Number one, I've been thinking about how the craft will re-enter the atmosphere of whatever planet they finally reach. I propose we send a huge folded sail up with them. I have some diagrams here." Gyls pulled another wrinkled, folded paper out, and showed it to the group.

"Secondly, what kind of food are we going send up with them? Obviously, weight is a factor for getting the craft out into space. Thirdly, we need to begin work on the rope, cable, whatever will be used to lasso the comet. Oh, and whoever is going to do the lassoing better start practicing."

After making his last recommendation, Gyls looked around at the solemn faces of the group. He let go a quiet laugh. "Gee, I didn't mean to ruin everyone's attitude by reading my list."

Regent Mihyn rubbed her hands together. "No, thank you for putting it together. I think we are all just feeling a little daunted by the amount of things left to do."

Gyls nodded and took a second look at the list. "I have something else written here, but I can't quite read it. Something about pillows. Oh, right. The carpenters from the railroad have completed the crew cabins, and now, somebody needs to do the finish work. Yesterday, I was working on the inside of the craft, and I laid down on one of the bunks, but there weren't any pillows."

Polite laughter followed his comments. Bokyl continued writing. He spoke without looking up. "I'm sure the railroad has a whole department of interior designers that can upholster the crew cabins. Comfy pillows are the last thing I'm worried about."

Professor Rymnyr leaned over and whispered something in Mihyn's ear. The pretty, but stern faced regent listened intently, nodding twice. Rymnyr patted her on the knee, then straightened up in her chair.

"Regent Mihyn and I would like to make some personnel recommendations right now." Bokyl motioned for her to continue. "We would like to nominate Regent Krynut for the position of pilot, and Mr. Gyls for the position of engineer."

The professor's statement drew a very different response from the two nominees. Krynut's narrow face threatened to break into a smile. He suppressed it. Gyls stared over at Professor Rymnyr. His features were frozen in disbelief. Bokyl let the nominations sink in for a moment before responding.

"And what do the candidates have to say?"

Krynut sat rigid as a board in his chair. He made eye contact with the group while answering. "I have to admit that this is really no surprise. I've been planning on being part of the crew from the beginning. I would be glad to accept the nomination with approval from the group."

"Thank you Regent," Rymnyr said graciously. "Any discussion from the group?" Heads shook all around the room. "Wonderful! Regent Krynut is the first confirmed member of the crew." The group let loose a round of applause. When it died down, Rymnyr directed her gaze toward Gyls.

"Any thoughts on your part, Mr. Gyls?"

The mention of his name seemed to shake the inventor from his mild catatonic state. He fidgeted in his chair and picked at his fingernails before answering. "Wow, I really hadn't considered the possibility of being selected as part of the crew. I have to say that I'm a bit torn. One the one hand, it would be a huge honor to take part in the mission. On the other hand, I really don't know if I could handle being sealed up in that small space for any length of time. Even working on it in the familiar shop, I get panicky thinking about what happened at the lake."

He dropped his gaze to the floor and swallowed hard. What he didn't tell the group was that he had been experiencing reoccurring nightmares about being trapped in the craft, and that the extremely vivid and terrifying dreams were causing him to wake sweat drenched and gasping for breath.

The inventor's less than enthusiastic response to the offer melted the broad smile off Rymnyr's face. "Well, Mr. Gyls, I think at this point we'd like you to consider the position, but would also like to give you some time to think it over."

"Thank you," he said quietly.

"Moving down the crew list, we have ambassador, linguist, and science officer."

"Well, we have two of the best linguists in the Academy right here in our midst," Bokyl replied with a big, shiny grin. He propped his elbows up on the desk and stared at the two women. "Oh, and if I'm not mistaken, one of them is married to an ambassador. How fortunate!"

A shudder ran through Mihyn's lithe body. The gravity of Bokyl's statement threatened to send her into a panic. Her lips began to tremble. She gripped the arms of the chair tightly. Rymnyr's soothing voice helped to lower her level of anxiety.

"I think it would be best for you to discuss the situation with Handynr before you make a commitment."

Mihyn turned her head of wavy dark brown hair toward the professor and nodded in agreement. She relaxed her death grip on the chair arms.

"The next position is science officer. Any suggestions?" Rymnyr asked.

Professor Ymyl rubbed his pointy chin. "I sink zee obvious choice there vould be Professor Grylt from zee biology department. Oh, excuse me. I'm not actually part of your group, but I thought I'd make a suggestion."

Rymnyr held up her hand. "No need to apologize. Everyone here greatly respects your opinion. I think Grylt is an excellent candidate."

"He's not exactly young," Bokyl commented from his place behind the desk. Krynut straightened up in his chair, and spoke in a smooth, authoritative voice.

"That's true, but have you ever tried to keep up with him on a field survey? Several years ago, he and I were working on the Porgin dam project, and I watched he and his crew working in the outflow. They were counting the numbers of some little, silver pyfg, and he scampered about like a teenager. I believe he also had some military training when he was young."

"I'm pretty sure he was a field healer during the Lamdyn war," Bokyl responded.

"Well then, seems like he is a good candidate. I'll make it a point of meeting with him soon," Professor Rymnyr replied before settling back in her chair. "So what position does that leave us with?"

Gyls looked down at the folded paper in his hands. "One thing we haven't addressed is, who is going to actually be responsible for roping the comet?"

Bokyl gave an angry growl. "That's the one part of the mission that I still have serious doubts about. Isn't there a better way to propel the craft?"

No one responded. Gyls continued staring down at the folded paper, then raised his head, leaned back, and closed his eyes. "I just don't know. There might be a better solution. Maybe we should consult with some of Lymdyr's engineers." His voice was brittle and weak.

"It's been a long day. I suggest we adjourn, think about these last couple points, then reconvene when Lymdyr comes back in town." Rymnyr concluded her statement by stacking up the papers she was holding.

The group all got up from their chairs and filed out of the office. Ymyl, Myrvst, and Krynut walked side by side down the hall in silence. When they were halfway to the stairs, the astronomer slowed his pace.

"Gentlemen, there ees something else I vas going to bring up, but I vas not sure how the non-scientific members would react." His enigmatic statement caused Krynut to shift his gaze from the floor up to Ymyl's stoic features. Myrvst just continued walking.

"Jym did not include another piece of very interesting, and I must say, confounding information in zee telemessage. One of his students that just returned from the observatory came into my office this morning. Several months ago, Jym mentioned that zee tail of zee comet seemed to have an aberration. I believe he called it a bulge. I didn't think much of it. What zee student told me this morning ees that Jym now thinks zee bulge is a separate and newly discovered celestial phenomenon."

"Newly discovered?" Krynut echoed.

"Yes, evidently it vas not there a year ago."

"Hmmmm, and did the student say what Jym thought this, uh, phenomenon was?"

Ymyl shook his head. "Not specifically, but he did say that eet was most peculiar. He called it zee Cloud."

Chapter 22.

Krynut, Myrvst and Ymyl descended the stairs together, and all headed off in different directions once they reached the foyer. Professor Rymnyr was talking with a colleague when Krynut approached her on his way out.

"Regent! Hang on a minute. I'll walk out with you." She ended the conversation, then hurried over to him. "Whew! I haven't seen the head regent that bugged about something for a while."

Krynut walked next to her, stroking his pointed, goateed chin. When they reached the front doors, Rymnyr shot a glance over at his very serious face.

"Got something on your mind?"

"You might say so. I'm just thinking about how I'm going to break the news to the princess that I've accepted a position on the crew."

Rymnyr pushed the door open and waited till Krynut stepped passed her. She laid a hand on his shoulder. "I'm sure everything will work out fine."

He tried to force a smile, but failed. "Thanks. I'm going to talk to her right now."

A short time later, Professor Myrvst returned home. He was greeted by the sound of Sylstyn singing away happily. The click of the door shutting caught her attention.

"Is that you, professor?"

"Yes, dear."

Myrvst plodded across the entryway and leaned against the door frame. His housekeeper's ebullient mood subsided when she caught sight of his droopy, fatigued appearance.

"Oh, you look tired!"

"I am. I was just settling down for a nap earlier, then a frantic messenger fairly beat the door down, so I figured I'd better get up. Bokyl called an emergency meeting of the Dymrans. Is Blrsynt here?"

"No, he should be coming back from Gyls' shop any minute. Do you want a drink?"

Myrvst pondered the question. He looked over Sylstyn's shoulder at the reddish-orange light flooding into the backyard. "You know, that sounds great. Will you bring it to me out at the bench? I feel like I need a little quiet time."

"Of course I will! Maybe I'll make one for Blrsynt too. He's been putting in some long hours lately."

On his way toward the back door, Myrvst leaned over and kissed Sylstyn on the cheek. "I don't know what I'd do without you."

She gave him a quick return kiss on his leathery cheek. The professor eased down the back steps and walked slowly across the dry crunchy grass. Stubborn green shoots were just beginning to poke up under his feet. Several minutes later, Blrsynt arrived home. He closed the gate, started toward the house, then stopped in mid-stride.

"Oh! Good afternoon professor. You startled me."

"Good afternoon to you. Come, sit."

Myrvst patted the warm, grey stone surface next to him. Blrsynt tossed his jacket over the barbeque pit, set his wooden lunch box down, and complied with the request.

The back door banged open, and Sylstyn came wheeling out. She skillfully descended the steps carrying a gold tray with three glasses on it. After distributing a drink to each of the men, she took one herself, set the tray on the firepit and dropped down next to Blrsynt.

"Glad you made one for yourself. It's such a lovely afternoon, almost evening. Pyrst can wait," Myrvst commented.

After giving her boyfriend a quick but powerful kiss, Sylstyn raised her glass high. "Life is short."

"Ah yes, life is short," the professor repeated. All three of them clinked glasses.

Blrsynt wiped his lips and turned toward Sylstyn. "How was your day?"

"Oh, it was okay. I had two classes, one of which is super boring. How was yours?"

"Well, Gyls and I were fighting with the metal covering again. I swear, that stuff is so hard to work with. It's extremely light, but very rigid. It just doesn't want to bend. Then about two o'clock, a messenger in a cab came and took him to some kind of meeting." Blrsynt switched his attention over to the professor. "I guess you were probably there too?"

Myrvst was scrutinizing the pink blossoms just starting to open on the thorn tree. He replied without taking his eyes off them. "Oh yes, Professor Ymyl informed the group that the comet is going to arrive two months ahead of schedule."

"What?" Blrsynt pulled his arm off Sylstyn's shoulder and sat upright. "You're kidding!"

"No, they recalculated the orbit with the help of Regent Krynut's device. They even redid some of their previous ones as a check."

"Wow, will that even give you enough time?" Sylstyn asked.

"That really changes things!" Blrsynt ran his fingers around the wet surface of the glass.

"Yes, it does. The meeting took on a whole different feeling once that was announced. We did select a couple of the crew members, though." Myrvst took another drink. The two young people waited with great anticipation for him to continue.

"Regent Krynut has agreed to pilot the craft. Professor Grylt, I don't think you know him, has been nominated for the science officer. Head Regent Bokyl mentioned sending Regents Mihyn and Handynr, but that remains to be seen. And, let's see, oh yes, they talked about Gyls taking the position as engineer."

Blrsynt gave a short yip of a laugh. "How interesting. To tell you the truth, ever since that accident out at the lake, he hasn't been doing so well."

"Yes, he didn't seem too perky today. My guess is, we'll have to find another healthier candidate. I think whoever it is will need to know that craft from top to bottom." Myrvst sat in contemplative silence for a moment. Out of the corner of his eye, he snuck a look at Blrsynt's reaction.

"We ended the meeting talking about who is going to ride along to rope the comet."

Sylstyn spit out the mouthful of thyn juice she was drinking. "Sorry, I didn't mean to spray! That's right, I forgot that the plan is to rope the comet." She wiped some liquid off her lips, then settled back against the bench. "Wow! Isn't there a better way to get the craft into space?"

"Well, we've spent some time trying to work out other options, but none have come to light."

Sylstyn tossed her medium length brown hair back and sat up straight. "I have my engineering class tomorrow. I'm going to propose that as a class project, we devise an alternate plan. Roping a comet! That sounds like something out of a cheap science fiction dyrft."

"Yes, it does." A dry laugh vibrated out of Myrvst's chest. "Anyway, I like your idea. Make sure you mention that we only have six months to design and test whatever you come up with."

All three of them sat quietly for a while. Blrsynt took a drink, slid his arm back over Sylstyn's shoulder, and looked over at her lovely, wide face. "You know, if they need someone to rope a comet, we could certainly recommend someone."

Sylstyn turned and looked at him quizzically. "Who? Oh, you're not thinking about? Hah! Can you imagine Ryk climbing into that craft and getting blasted into space? They'd have to stow a couple barrels of physt just to keep him under control!"

Across town, Regent Krynut pushed the tall glass and wooden door to the Arts Center open and made his way up to the viewing balcony above the performance stage. He took a seat far from the other spectators. Krynut rubbed his face with both hands, leaned forward in the chair, rested his elbows along the rail, and gazed down.

Watching the graceful, fluid movements of the dancers helped him relax just a bit. His eyes quickly settled on Janela. Being the only brown skinned dancer, it was easy for him to pick her out of the group. He unbuttoned his jacket. The air up by the ceiling was warm and humid, with an underlying scent of exertion.

Once the practice session was over, Krynut hurried down the stairs, and waited in the hall outside the locker room. After several moments, Princess Janela and several other dancers came out and said their goodbyes. When she caught sight of Krynut leaning against the wall, a smile swept across her glistening features.

"Hello. I didn't expect to see you."

"Hello. You looked very nice out there dancing."

Janela's lips twisted quizzically. "Thank you." She took a moment to scrutinize his joyless face. "Is everything alright?"

"Yes." He straightened up, and put all his energy into forcing the ominous, glowering mood that was consuming him into the background. "Would you like to go get some zyd?"

"Sure." Janela swung the satchel higher up on her shoulder and headed toward the door. Before pushing it open, she turned and shot another inquisitory glance back at him. They both exited out into the cool, dry evening air. After walking along the storefronts in silence for a while, she finally spoke.

"We have a performance on Pylsday. Will you be able to come?"

Without even thinking about his busy schedule, he answered. "Of course."

"Good. I think Madame Nylyt is going to give me one of the solos during the midpoint."

"That would be wonderful."

"Are you sure everything is alright?"

"Yes. I've just had a busy day."

Krynut held the door open for her, and they slid into the fragrant, inviting atmosphere of the zyd room. Laughter and conversation bounced off the well-decorated walls. Oil lamps of various sizes and designs flickered in the corners. They selected one of only several open tables right in the center of the small room.

"This is nice." Krynut spent just a moment looking around at the collection of paintings hung at random places on the wood paneled walls.

"Have you never been in here before?"

"Maybe once or twice."

A waitress took their order and for a moment, both of them were silent. Krynut had to force himself to ignore the conversations swirling around them. He felt supremely distracted. Janela's black velvet voice brought him back to the present.

"So was your day any busier than usual?"

Krynut pulled his chair as close to the square table as possible and leaned forward. "Not really. Just some big decisions to be made."

The waitress swung by and deposited two steaming china cups and a small ceramic pot on the table. Krynut felt his heart begin to beat fast. He was hoping to put off the inevitable, but knew that he had to get it over with.

"We had a meeting of the Dymran project today."

Janela looked up from her stirring. "Oh."

An explosion of laughter swept over them from the big table behind Janela. The princess smiled and turned around to see what was happening. Krynut ventured a sip of the fragrant zyd. It was scorching hot.

"We discussed who would be part of the crew today."

Janela absorbed the words without changing her expression. Her eyes searched his face for further information. Something in the seriousness of his immaculately groomed appearance gave it away. The smile evaporated from her lips.

"I was selected to be the pilot." Krynut's voice was low and devoid of expression.

She let the metal spoon fall from her grasp. It clanked against the saucer before hitting the tabletop. She brought her hands up and covered her face. A barely detectable cry of anguish escaped through the wall of her thin, dark fingers. She slowly lowered her hands and stared down at the table.

"That's why you seem so tense. You were agonizing about how to break the news to me." There was an electric moment of silence and stillness. Her head snapped up. Ferocity burned in her coal black eyes.

"And I'm sure there was no way the well-respected regent like yourself could say no. I mean, in addition to receiving the Pylrm medal, and being named one of Ulutrita's top mathematicians, you were the logical choice! Well, at least you have said it! I'm sure you feel much better." The cold, churning anger behind her words smacked him like an open handed slap.

"I don't feel any better. Please keep your voice down."

"Well, thank you for being honest. Ha!" Her sharp, twang of a laugh cut through the murmur of voices around them. She eased away from the table and draped a graceful arm over the back of the chair. Her chin quivered in despair. Tears flooded her eyes. Before they could spill out onto her cheeks, she whisked them away with her fingertip. Janela diverted her gaze out onto the evening darkened street, then back at his stony face.

"It's a good thing I didn't send the letter to my grandfather."

"What letter?" Krynut's voice was choked with dread.

"After our night at the resort, when you said......" Janela's surging emotions forced her to pause. She drew in a shuddering breath. "I composed a letter to my grandfather telling him about our plans for m-m-marriage. I guess that has now changed." She tilted her head to the side, and looked at him with a mocking, tortured smile. "I will tear it up as soon as I get home. Better yet, I'll burn it. We are finished." She angrily pushed her chair back and started to rise up.

Krynut shot his hand across the table in an attempt to grasp her hand. She recoiled like someone trying to avoid the bite of a poisonous snake. "Janela, this doesn't have to be the end."

"What? You want me to be your little zyngr for the next six months?" Her response was loud enough to draw attention from all in the immediate area. Time and conversation seemed to stop briefly. She glared at Krynut with a fury the temperature of which threatened to burn him alive.

In one darting move, she leapt up, spun out of the chair, and raced toward the door. The force with which she slammed it nearly broke the glass. Krynut sat frozen with shock. He pulled a bill out of his shirt pocket, dropped it on the table, and left the cozy tea room.

Krynut stuffed his hands into his pants pockets and made his way along the cracked sidewalk. He walked past dark, closed storefronts with his head lowered. Occasionally, another person or couple drifted by. He thought about getting a stiff drink somewhere, but decided that a long walk would be the best option. The gloom that draped over him was so profound that it dredged up his worst childhood memory. On his eleventh birthday, he accidentally killed his mother's pet long-tailed lykr with a slingshot. The supremely painful memory caused him to walk even faster.

Krynut covered the four miles back to his apartment in record time. He sat in the dark, tearing himself apart over his decision. Eventually, he fell asleep in the big, upholstered chair.

Chapter 23.

That same night, Regent Mihyn had gotten home before her husband, and sat up reading. Just before ten, she heard the front door open. Handynr tossed his long coat over the back of the couch, circled around it, and sat down with a thump. He leaned back and closed his eyes. Mihyn set her book on the coffee table.

"You're home late. Are you hungry?"

Handynr remained motionless for a while with his forearms draped across his leather work bag. "I am hungry. I just don't feel like eating. Think I'll just get a drink of pluge and go to sleep."

Thirty minutes later, Mihyn eased herself into bed. Her husband's deep measured breathing left little doubt about his state of consciousness. She stared at his profile in the darkness. Even though they had been married for almost fourteen years, his perfectly straight nose, the very appealing sharp curve at its end, and his hard, angular chin still sent a ripple of warmth through her. The idea of waking him made her frown. She drew in a breath and spoke as quietly as possible.

"Darling?"

"Yes?" Handynr replied with considerable effort.

"We had a meeting of the Dymran project today."

"Wonderful."

"It appears that the comet is going to be closest to Ulutrita two month's sooner than expected."

"Why are you telling me this?"

Mihyn's nerve and resolve began to wane. In the darkness, she gently bit her lip. "I know you're tired. I just have to ask you something." Mihyn again stared at his face, waiting for him to acknowledge. He lay there like a corpse. "Honey?"

"Yes?" His voice was gravelly and terse.

"There are two crew positions they mentioned today. A linguist and an ambassador."

"Wonderful. I hope you find someone to fill them. Goodnight."

Early the next morning, Mihyn woke to the sound of lykrs chirping out in the thorn trees. She pulled the covers back and slid her naked, lithe body out of bed. After grabbing her robe from the closet, Mihyn tiptoed out of the bedroom. Grey light filtered into the small house from the gauzy drapes covering the front window.

She noiselessly made her way into the kitchen, lit the oil stove, and placed a pan of water on the burner. When she pulled the chair back where her husband's work bag sat, the leather object quite gracefully tipped to the side and fell to the floor. It landed upside down, disgorging its contents of papers, and not a small number of mauve envelopes.

Mihyn knelt down to retrieve the spilled contents. She was extra careful scooping up the papers in an effort to keep them in order. While her fingers slid over the pile of envelopes, deep furrows formed on her forehead.

"This is weird. Why would he have all these fancy decorative envelopes in his bag? They certainly don't look official."

Without even thinking, she picked up one that was half open, slid her fingers in, and began to remove the mauve letter. She stopped just of removing it from the envelope.

"I should probably not do this. It might be some very important correspondence." With a satisfied sweep of her hand, she added the envelope to the pile, returned all the contents to the bag, and placed it back on the chair.

Later that day over at Professor Myrvt's house, Blrsynt wheeled the wagon up the gravel driveway like he did at the end of every workday. He ventured a glance over the low hedge that bordered the backyard. Sylstyn and the professor were standing side by side, gazing up into the sky. After putting the vehicle away, he pushed the gate open and joined them.

"Oh, hi Blrsynt! Come here." Sylstyn kissed him, then grabbed his shoulders and rotated his big, bulky frame to the proper position. Even though it was still an hour and a half till dark, the white smudge of the approaching comet was clearly visible.

"Isn't it wonderful!" she gushed.

"Yes, it is. I suppose it is just going to get bigger and bigger too."

"Much bigger by the time it reaches its closest approach. As usual, people are already starting to worry about it crashing into Ulutrita," Professor Myrvst added.

Sylstyn slid an arm around Blrsynt's waist and pulled herself up next to him. "I've got some big news." The joy in her voice prompted both men to pull their attention away from the comet.

Blrsynt looked down at her smirking face. "Well?"

"Professor Bynkr said that he met with the head regent this morning, and my advanced mechanical class is going to work on a test plan for the Dymran project propulsion system."

"That's great!" Blrsynt replied.

"We spent all afternoon drawing up plans for a test site. Tomorrow, we're going to go out to an old mine up somewhere along Hyrm road and do a site visit. Maybe you and Gyls can meet us there."

"We still have a ton of work to do, but I'll ask him in the morning. So what exactly did your class come up with?"

Sylstyn released him from her grip, tossed her long auburn hair, and stood a tad more upright. The tone of her voice changed from eager enthusiasm to an air of authority.

"Well, we thought that some sort of swinging mechanism would approximate the action needed to rope the comet. We drew up plans for a tall scaffolding that a mock-up of the comet nucleus could swing from. Atop the scaffolding will be a place for the roper to stand. There's an old mine site with a huge gully that runs straight down where we think we could set it up. Vyrny and I are in charge of designing the scale model of the nucleus."

Professor Myrvst looked over at her radiant, smiling face. "What an exciting project! I'm sure your class will learn a lot from this. Oh, by the way, I took your suggestion, and mentioned to Bokyl that that Ryk fellow would be a logical choice for training the crew at roping."

"Great! It'd be nice to see him……." Sylstyn stopped herself in mid-sentence and glanced up at Blrsynt. The young man's eyebrows pulled down in a scowl.

Interest in the approaching comet reached far and wide, very far, and very wide. It reached all the way across the soon to be explored void of space to our own planet. On December 26, Earth year 1913, at the corner of State Street and Tulane Ave in New Orleans, Louisiana, Sammy Greenfield and his sister stared longingly at the shelves full of food in a small grocery as they walked along the sidewalk.

"Man, I'm hungry," Sammy remarked.

When they approached an open air newspaper stand, Sister Tracy glanced down at the front page of one of the papers. "Well, will ya lookit that."

Sammy stopped next to her. Without even really being conscious of what he was doing, the eleven-year-old laid a hand on the solid object in his coat pocket, then took a step forward to see what she was pointing at.

On the upper right corner of the front page, a large drawing depicting the massive swoop of a comet very close to, and on a collision course with Earth stood out in stark detail. Sister Tracy bent down to inspect the associated article.

"Says here that a big comet's coming in a couple years might smack right into us." She looked over at her brother to try and gauge his reaction. He was transfixed by a row of huge sausages hanging in a butcher shop window two doors down.

"What're you looking at?"

"See them big old sausages over there," he replied in a slow, hushed voice.

"Yeah, I see 'em."

"Come on."

Against her better judgement, Tracy followed him over and the two of them stood directly in front of the window. Sammy spoke out of the corner of his mouth.

"Okay, listen up good. I'm going to walk in there nice and slow, like I admirin' them. Then real quick I'll cut one down, throw it out to you, and you high tail in down the street. They'll chase after me, but I kin out run 'em. You got that?"

Before Tracy had time to react to her brother's catastrophically bad idea, Sammy strolled into the shop. From behind the counter, the owner of the store sent an unfriendly glance over at the skinny Black child standing just inside the door, then turned back to the task at hand. Sammy clicked open the knife he had "borrowed" from his mother's boyfriend, grabbed the hefty, three-foot long sausage with his right hand, and began sawing away at the greasy twine holding it suspended. The knife was considerable duller than he had imagined.

"Hey, get yer hands off a that! Hey! What'dya think yer doing?"

Sammy's face jumped in panic as the large, and now angry butcher swung around the end of the counter. When the man was almost on him, Sammy let go of the sausage, and lifted both his hands in a gesture of surrender.

"Don't you wave that knife at me, you God damn little coon!"

Out on the sidewalk, Tracy covered her mouth with both hands, and burst into tears. As luck would have it, two policemen had just crossed the street, and were approaching the store. When they heard the butcher's deep booming shout, both of them jogged up to see what the commotion was. The first officer in caught sight of the knife in Sammy's hand and grabbed the boy's wrist.

"What the hell do you think you're doin', threatnin' a store owner?"

"Honest! I weren't threatnin' nobody! I was just trying to steal....." Before Sammy could finish his pitiful explanation, the officer hauled him out the door.

"Let's go! You're going down ta the precinct office."

Meanwhile back on Ulutrita, progress on the project accelerated. Sylstyn's class put in long hours supervising the construction of the test scaffold. Telemessages were sent out to the town nearest to Ryk's mag outfit in an effort to contact him.

On a windy spring day, Sylstyn and her class gathered on the side of the scrub covered desert hillside next to the three hundred-foot scaffolding. It was their first official test run. The mock up nucleus was a combination of two hundred pounds of rubber applied to a thick wire frame. The nucleus was roughly spherical in shape, and approximately twenty-five feet across.

A long wooden beam stuck out perpendicular to the platform atop the scaffolding. Sixty feet of chain hung down from the end of the beam to which the nucleus was attached. Two hundred feet of lanyard was tied halfway up the chain to allow the team to get the rubber ball swinging. Professor Bynkr, the head of the engineering department, stood up on a rock to address his students.

"Alright, let's see, Ryf, Byngy, you and I are going to climb up and be the lassoers. Kyrl, grab some of the stronger guys and man the pulling rope." He reached down and tossed a pile of mag skin work gloves onto the rocky ground. "Everybody, grab a pair. There should be enough to go around."

"What about us?" Sylstyn asked.

Professor Bynkr stared into her soulful green eyes. "You and Vyrny just stand there and look pretty."

Snickering laughter circled through the group of male students as they bent down and pulled the coarse leather gloves from the pile. The professor and his chosen crew ascended the tall wooden scaffolding. The other group of students grabbed the long, ivory colored lanyard tied twenty feet above the rubber nucleus and scrambled up the steep hillside.

"What a jerk!" Sylstyn muttered.

"Absolutely," the statuesque brown skinned young woman next to her added.

It took a few minutes for Professor Bynkr and the two students he had selected to ascend the scaffolding. Once they were on top, the professor let go a nervous peal of laughter, and leaned out over the rail.

"Zym! It sure is high up here. What a view! We can see the entire Tyrl valley up here. Come here and take a look." The two students grudgingly walked over and took up places on either side of him. Bynkr pointed toward the south.

"Over across the valley is where all the rich people live, right up next to the southern mountains. And out to the east, at the end of the valley, there's the road snaking out to the salt pluge."

A particularly strong gust of wind hit them. All three gripped the wooden rail. The scaffolding swayed ever so slightly.

"Ha! This is great up here, isn't it?" Bynkr yelled.

The smaller, slightly built student looked over at the professor's broad, mutton-chopped face. "Let's just get this done and get the Zym off of here."

"What? Are you scared?"

"Yeah, as a matter of fact I am, a little."

"Oh, come on! Think about the people that are going to be blasting up into space on this project. What'd you think they're going to feel like?" Bynkr leaned over the rail and yelled down at the ground crew.

"You guys ready down there?"

"Should we start it swinging?" one of the students on the ground yelled back.

"Swing away!"

The ground crew began yanking on the lanyard. Up along the ragged gash in the mountainside the heavy rubber nucleus drifted. Try as they might, Bynkr and the students up on the platform weren't able to make the lasso work.

After an hour and a half of observing their failed efforts, the ground crew lost interest. While Bynkr and the two students discussed new strategies, the rest of the class decided to hold a stone chucking contest. All the students standing around the scaffolding hurried to grab a rock.

From up on the platform, Professor Bynkr looked down at the activity. "What's going on down there? Oh klynk it! Let's call it a day." He coiled up the long lasso rope, then held it over the edge of the platform. "Look out below! We're coming down."

The class scattered once they saw the big coil of rope falling their way.

"Thank Zym! Looks like he's finally giving it up," Vyrny commented as she backed up across the rocky ground.

"Tell ya what. There's only one person I know that'd be able to lasso that," Sylstyn remarked.

The next day, Ryk and two other drivers made a rare appearance in the shabby railroad stop of Phyt Hill. They ambled into the one street town looking somewhat ragged. The temperature had dipped well below freezing the night before, consequently, none of the men had gotten much sleep. Their faces were red from the wind chill, and their hands were cold and stiff inside their leather gloves. They had hardly talked at all on the hour and a half ride.

"This sure ain't much of a town," the black moustached driver beside Ryk muttered as he looked over at the row of beaten up, unpainted buildings.

"No it ain't," was all Ryk had to say. "Let's go get the lantern wicks, that part for the wagon, and get the Zym outta here! I still can't believe Jyn forgot to order them. What kinda dyth fool goes out on a drive and forgets extra wicks?"

"Don't ya wanna stop in for a snort?" the driver with the long, stringy blonde hair and crooked nose tossed out.

Ryk swung his head up one side, then down the other of the bleak little outpost town. His wide-brimmed hat flapped in the breeze. "I dunno. Don't see nothing here that looks at all appealin'. And for me, that says alot. "

A trio of gruff faced men walked toward them, then stopped under a store awning. The wooden structure was leaning heavily to the side and appeared to be on the verge of collapse. Ryk looked over at the suspicious group, gave the smallest nod of his head as possible, then continued scanning the meager surroundings.

"Suppose we should ask them where the hardware store is?" the blonde driver inquired.

"Naw, if we can't find it in this pitiful little dump, it ain't worth finding. I bet it's that place up there with the smoking stovepipe."

Ryk motioned toward a building with sagging porch and dirt obscured windows on their left. The three drivers pulled their mounts up in front, jumped down, secured the animals, and stepped up on the wooden boardwalk. Ryk shoved the door with force, and it scraped open. Inside, a thick layer of dust covered the floor and most of the shelves. Directly in the center of the room, a round wood stove crackled. The three of them walked over next to it and held out their painfully cold hands.

"Kinna nippy out there ain't it?" the small, pointy chinned man behind the counter chirped.

"Yes 'tis," Ryk replied over his shoulder.

"You fellas come from far?"

"Jus' over by the Hok river," the black moustached driver chimed in.

"You mag drivers?"

"Yep," the blonde driver answered.

The man reached into a drawer, pulled out a folded yellow telemessage sheet, and held it at arm's length. "Wouldn't be one of you anamed Ryk Six Line, would they?"

Ryk turned his big wide frame stiffly around. "As a matter of fact, yes, that'd be me."

"Well, got some messages from Tyrl for ya."

The wooden floorboards creaked as Ryk walked over and carefully extracted the three yellow sheets from the man's claw-like fingers. His dark eyes darted back and forth across the typed lines. Deep furrows creased his brow.

"Well, what's they say?" the blonde driver called out.

Ryk let his arm drop down to the side. "I was worried they was from Lylyn, but it's some message about the Academy folks needin' me to come help them with some kinda project." He tossed the sheets onto the countertop.

"Ya gonna answer 'em?" the clerk asked.

"Naw. I got no reason to contact anybody at the Academy, 'cept maybe for one." Ryk turned back toward his fellow driver. "Let's get what we need and get outta here."

Chapter 24.

When Lymdyr returned to Tyrl from his travels, he was besieged by telemessages and requests for meetings. Toward the end of the day, some railroad executives showed up to discuss a bridge project. While they droned on about whether the city would pay for it or not, Lymdyr's mind wandered into visions of tall, cold glasses of physt.

"What are your thoughts?" the grey-haired executive sitting across the table asked. When Lymdyr didn't respond, the man leaned forward and banged on the table with his palm.

"Lymdyr! Are you listening?"

"What? Oh, yes! Actually no. I apologize. I've had so much thrown into my lap today, I'm having trouble processing it all. Can we take this up tomorrow?"

The executive stroked his long white moustache. "Very well, but we need to make a decision by the end of the week." With a creak of chairs and rustle of fine clothing, the four officials got up from their chairs, and filed out of the room. Lymdyr sat and watched them exit.

"My Zym! I'm gone for a couple weeks, and the whole place goes to blyrt!"

He was enjoying the new found silence in the boardroom when a gentle knock broke his meditation. The door eased open, and the small, pinched face of one of the secretaries appeared in the opening.

"Sorry to bother you Mr. Lymdyr. There are two people from the Academy here. A, uh, big round gentleman, and a fancy dressed middle-aged lady. They insist on meeting with you."

Lymdyr let out an exhausted laugh. He leaned back in the chair and folded his hands behind his head. "That would be Head Regent Bokyl and Professor Rymnyr I would guess. Send them in. Everybody else in Tyrl has managed to grab some of my time, they might as well too."

"Very well. I'll go get them."

"Oh, Mrs. Vyrtyl!"

"Yes?"

"Can you see if there's any hyryn in the building?"

The woman's thin red lips pursed and pulled off to the side. "Hmm. Kyrn has a bottle of mynth from last Plyn's Day. I'm sure she wouldn't mind if you want it."

"Yes, that will be fine. And a couple glasses, please."

A few moments later, the door opened again, and the small, slightly stooped secretary led Professor Rymnyr and Head Regent Bokyl in. She walked around the side of the big table and set the open bottle and three glasses in front of him.

"Thank you. It's been a long day," Lymdyr said graciously.

"You're welcome."

The secretary flashed a quick smile before ducking out of the room. The two visitors each pulled a chair back and sat opposite Lymdyr. He poured a glass full, then looked up at them.

"Would you like some?"

Bokyl held up his hands and waved him off. "No thanks."

Professor Rymnyr waited till his eyes met hers. The grin on her roughed cheeks was answer enough. Lymdyr filled a second glass, rose up out of his chair, and slid it across to her.

"This is my first day back, and it's been a doozy. Cheers." The two of them clinked glasses. After taking a good long drink, he settled back in his chair. "Ah, that's better. Might I say you look very nice today, professor."

Rymnyr took a sip, swirled it around in her mouth, then looked quizzically at the pink liquid. "Thank you. My, this is interesting."

Lymdyr let go a short laugh. "Interesting and cheap."

"I hate to break up your mynth tasting party, but there are things we need to discuss," Bokyl said gruffly.

Rymnyr took another drink. "Oh just ignore him. He's been in a foul mood for weeks."

"Well, I seem to be the only one involved in this project that is the least bit concerned about the short time frame we are under."

Lymdyr finished his glass and poured another. "I did receive your telemessages, but it wasn't really convenient for me to send back replies. Why don't you run down what the big issues are at present?"

Bokyl and Professor Rymnyr glanced over at each other. She gestured for him to him to start.

"The primary concern I have right now is the propulsion system. Our third year engineering students built a test platform up on Plyk mountain, and have been trying to work out how to lasso a small mockup of the comet nucleus."

The mynth was starting to relax Lymdyr. His ruddy cheeks became even ruddier. The worry lines on his forehead melted away.

"And how is that going?"

"At this point it's a miserable failure!" Bokyl snorted. "Several people have suggested enlisting the help of this Ryk fellow who is supposedly the champion mag roper, but I can't seem to get him to reply." Bokyl's round, shiny head began to change from pink to crimson.

"Okay, so that's one big problem. What else?"

"We still have not selected an engineer for the crew. Really, I think that is the main area of concern right now. Supposedly, the work on the craft is nearing completion," Rymnyr answered.

"If you two have time, we could go over to the shop and see it. From what I hear, they are just putting the finishing touches on it."

"That sounds like a great idea. Maybe getting a look at the final design will help boost my enthusiasm for this crazy project." Bokyl let out a whoosh of a sigh.

Lymdyr led the group to the outside door. He pushed it open with a powerful stiff arm action. "Man, am I glad to get out of there. People have been jumping all over me today!"

The three of them walked diagonally across the dirt path that ran in front of the administrative building. Bokyl strode forward, his wide torso pitched at an angle. Professor Rymnyr followed several steps behind.

"Would you guys slow down a bit? It's kind of hard to keep up with these heels."

"So, tell me about this Ryk fella," Lymdyr answered while slowing the pace of his travel. Bokyl caught up with him to answer.

"From what people tell me, Ryk Six Line is the champion mag roper, and has won the competition several years running. Right now, he's out driving a herd near some Zym forsaken town of Phyt Hill, or something like that."

"I see, go on."

"I've sent several telemessages out, but only got one back. Seems that Ryk was in town a couple days ago and did get the messages. The telemessage operator responded, Ryk himself did not."

"Well, seems like we need to send someone out there to talk to him in person. Does he work for Pylryt?"

"Yes."

"I figured as much. Let me contact them and see what I can do."

A powerful gust of wind swept between the maintenance shed and the big, glass windowed design shop. Professor Rymnyr's off white frilly dress billowed out. All three had to cover their eyes to keep the blowing dust from blinding them. Lymdyr yanked the side door open and ushered the other two in. The wind assisted in slamming the door shut behind them.

"My! That was a strong gust," Rymnyr commented as she tried to re-arrange her jostled self.

The workers in the fabrication room took a break from their tasks and looked up at the new arrivals. Lymdyr gave them a nod while leading the guests across the floor. He glanced around the spacious workroom, and his gaze fell on the dull grey metal skin of the craft. It was sitting up on blocks against the far wall.

"There she is!"

The thin metal skin had been expertly fabricated to fit around the lateral ribs of the frame. Just aft of where the pointed nose swept out from the main body, two rectangular bronze plates, one on either side of the hull were positioned. The plates followed the contour of the body. The smooth polished concave surfaces were crafted such that the plates funneled up to a half inch wide hole. Professor Rymnyr took a couple steps forward and ran her fingers around the shiny surface.

"Very nice workmanship. What are these for?"

"Those are the collectors," a low serious voice behind the group answered.

All three of them turned to see who had responded. The lead fabricator stood with his arms crossed. His black frame glasses were perched in front of his big, owl-like eyes.

Professor Rymnyr broke into a smile. She let her fingers drift across the intricate engraving on the plate's surface. "I love all the extra detail!"

For a fraction of a second, the lead fabricator's thin lips rose into a grin. "Yes, Iangly and his group kind of outdid themselves on this one." He walked forward, placed his hand on the polished bronze hatch lever, gave it a quick turn, and swung the cover open. The light from the big windows high up toward the ceiling illuminated the finished interior. After moving off to the side, he gestured toward the opening.

"Go ahead and climb in."

"Oh, this is soooo exciting." Rymnyr ascended the wooden step, braced herself on the edge of the hatch opening, and peered inside. "It is absolutely stunning!" Her head of highly piled greying hair swung left then right. "My oh my!" She eased back out of the opening and held out her hand. "Will you help me? I'm not as agile as I used to be."

The fabricator grasped her hand, and steadied her as she swung a leg over the opening, planted her foot on the wooden decking, and pulled herself in.

"Thank you." Rymnyr stood just inside the hatch, and let her eyes scan the well-crafted interior. Light from the chevron-shaped window above the cockpit helped to illuminate the details. "Amazing, absolutely amazing."

Bokyl walked over to the step and peered inside. "Yes, quite nice. If you would care to move your fat behind out of the way, the rest of us would like to inspect it, also."

"Watch it buster!" Rymnyr stepped over toward the cockpit after delivering her retort.

Lymdyr and the lead fabricator looked over at each other and chuckled. Bokyl bent down and crawled over the lip. His face flushed with the exertion. Once the head regent had cleared the opening, Lymdyr jaunted up onto the step, grasped the polished hand rail affixed above the inside of the craft, and swung himself in. The lead fabricator waited till the opening was clear, then followed him in.

Professor Rymnyr had moved off toward the rear of the interior. Bokyl remained in the widest space just in back of the cockpit. Lymdyr opened the door to one of the crew quarters and stood off to the side to let light from the hatch filter into the dark space. Everywhere they looked, the metal door levers, rod fixtures, and even hinge plates had been carefully crafted into animal heads, plant parts, and other natural forms.

"With the hatch closed, it will be kind of dark in here, don't you think?" Rymnyr asked.

"We noticed that early on," the fabricator replied. He leaned his lanky frame over, and tapped a grapefruit sized hand blown light bulb protruding from its porcelain fixture on the wall beside him. "These are brand new. We commissioned that company in Shylrn to make us these small models."

Bokyl carefully turned his girth around in the tight space and squinted at the bulb. "That's all well and good, but how are they powered?"

For the second time, the fabricator's tight thin, lips rose in a smile. "I'm glad you asked." The lead fabricator threaded his way into the space between the cockpit seats and the edge of the crew cabin. "I don't know if you can see back here or not, but this is where all the pressure and temperature gauges are." The fabricator carefully turned around in the cramped space to see if the others were listening. Satisfied that they were, he resumed his narrative.

"And then over here, this whole contraption is the power generator." He pointed toward a snail shell shaped object made out of brass. A pair of narrow tubes entered at the open part of the shell and then exited near the point of the whorl. At the actual terminus of the spiral, a crank jutted out perpendicular to the body of the shell. The shiny handle was shaped like the body of a dog-like animal in full stride. From the animal's head, a pivoting hand grip stuck out. The lead fabricator wrapped his fingers around the handle.

"Okay, throw the switch on whatever light you want lit."

Professor Rymnyr reached up and clicked the light switch in the passageway. The fabricator began rotating the crank. It made a laborious whizzing noise that increased in pitch as he cranked harder. The long filaments inside the bulb began to glow red, then white. A cool dry light illuminated the center of the craft. It flickered depending on how smoothly the man turned the crank.

"Very nice!" Rymnyr remarked. She gazed around at the now sufficiently lit exterior of the crew cabins. After pushing one of the doors open, she side-stepped in. "Pretty cramped, but nice, very nice."

Lymdyr stuck his head into the open doorway, then moved aside to keep from blocking the light. "There's the bed, a nice little desk over here, some shelves."

From his spot wedged in the corner of the cockpit, Bokyl leaned out toward the light. "So somebody is going to have to crank that all the time?"

"No, Zym no! See these lines coming in? Once they open the collectors, the wind from the comet will turn it. Whew! My arm's getting tired. At least they'll get some exercise."

Lymdyr slipped into the open cabin and whispered into Professor's Rymnyr's ear. "Maybe we should try out one of these beds?"

She turned just far enough to look into his expectant hazel eyes. "Out!"

He gave a snort of a laugh and backed into the passageway. Rymnyr followed him after taking one last look at the furnishings. The fabricator let go of the handle, and the light pulsed to a stop. He shook the tiredness out of his arm as he worked his way forward.

"I actually really like being in here. Got any vacancies on the crew list?"

"Well, we have a confirmation on the pilot and the science officer. Regents Mihyn and Handynr haven't officially accepted yet, and then there's the engineer position." Bokyl's gruff voice trailed off at the end of his list.

The fabricator cocked his head to the side in a questioning manner. Rymnyr recognized his confused look.

"What the head regent means is that the engineer position is not filled. We have several candidates, but until….."

"Until we can get that stupid mag driver in here to train someone to lasso the comet, we are pretty well klynked!" Bokyl rose up from his crouch and smacked his bald head on one of the wall supports. "Zym dyth it! This craft is not built for fat men!" He reached up and rubbed his shiny head. "Are we done?"

Lymdyr had wandered back to the space at the end of the crew cabins. He looked up at light shining down from a circular opening in the top of the craft. "What's this hole for?"

The fabricator stepped by Rymnyr and edged his way along the outer wall. "That's where the telescope is going. See the interlocking flanges? That's another special design that will allow the telescope to rotate while still being airtight."

The clanging of a bell out in the main shop reverberated through the craft.

"Wow, quitting time already?" Lymdyr remarked.

"I guess so. Anybody have any further questions?" the fabricator asked. Hearing no responses, he moved back along the wall and pulled himself out of the hatch. The other three followed.

"Thank you for showing us the craft," Rymnyr said graciously.

The head fabricator smiled once more and gave a quick bow. "My pleasure." He turned and followed his workers out the side door. Bokyl and Professor Rymnyr walked single file behind them. Lymdyr brought up the rear. Once outside, the three of them headed back to the administrative building.

"So what's the plan for getting the mag driver out here? What was his name?" Lymdyr asked.

"Ryk Six Line. At this point, short of sending someone out to get him, I don't know what to do," Bokyl replied in a voice twinged with resignation.

Large puffy clouds were blowing in from the north. They took turns obscuring the sun, then quickly allowing it to flare back. When the trio rounded the big assembly shop, the wind hit them.

"Ah!" Rymnyr gasped. She quickly reached down and secured the fluttering hem of her skirt.

"Where is he?" Lymdyr yelled above the gusting wind.

Bokyl squinted his already small eyes down into slits. "Some Zym forsaken place called Phyt Hill."

"I know where that is. There's a railroad stop there. Not much else. What say I go out there and try and convince him to work with us."

Bokyl's slitted eyes and the curve of his smiling mouth formed a perfect ruddy circle. "That would be most agreeable. When can you head out?"

Lymdyr raised his head and looked off toward the dry scrubby hills that ringed the railroad complex. "Oh, maybe day after tomorrow."

The head regent clapped his hands together. "That is the best news I've heard lately! Perhaps this crazy, improbably project is finally going to fly."

Chapter 25.

Three days later, Lymdyr stepped off the train at Phyt Hill. He gazed around at the sandblasted wooden buildings, all eleven of them.

"What a blyrt hole!"

One other person got off with him, an old dried up twig of a man with a beaten up wide-brimmed hat and patched trench coat. Lymdyr heaved his heavy shoulder bag up onto his arm and followed the unsteady man along the concrete platform.

"Excuse me! Are you from here?"

The man looked up at Lymdyr with dried up, red streaked eyes. "Are you kidding? Who would want to live in this place! No, thank Zym, I'm just here for a couple days, then I'm gone."

"I was just wondering if there is a place to stay here."

"Wouldn't know," the man replied. He shrugged and continued on his way.

Lymdyr stopped at the edge of the platform, and took another scan of the dull, bleached buildings. The closest one to him had most of the windows broken out. A good sized sand dune was forming at the door. The structure next to it had two rectangular windows set about six feet off the boardwalk.

Further down the line, his gaze fell on the assortment of tools, work clothes and barrels of hardware that sat behind a pair of tall, front windows. Lymdyr stepped across the rutted, uneven street and up onto the boardwalk. He listened for sounds of activity in the storefront with the two high windows. Some low murmuring was all he heard. He continued along the boardwalk, pushed the door to the hardware store open, and ducked in.

A couple scraggly looking men in what appeared to be miner's clothes eyed him as he entered. Their dirt streaked faces showed no emotion, and perhaps a little apprehension. Both of them stopped fingering the pickaxes they had been looking at and gave Lymdyr a good sizing up. The railroad man immediately was hit with a wave of self-consciousness.

He glanced down at his expensive brown leather riding pants, finely tailored corduroy shirt, matching brown vest with black piping, and full length duster. Lymdyr offered a polite smile, then looked around for the proprietor.

The small, birdlike clerk came bobbing up from the back of the store. His round head was lowered. He appeared to be talking to himself. The clerk walked up to the edge of the counter and looked up with a start.

"Oh! Hello! I didn't see you come in. May I help you?"

Lymdyr set his heavy leather duffel bag on the floor with a thud. "Yes, I'm looking for a man named Ryk Six Line."

The clerk's face snapped to attention. Behind the skewed glasses, his eyes betrayed a look of concern. "He's not here," the clerk replied with a slight break in his voice. There was a moment of dead silence. The crackle of the wood stove and sigh of the wind outside were the only sounds. "You a law officer?"

Lymdyr's broad, 30-something face broke into a smile. He pushed his spotless felt hat back and laughed. "No, no, not at all. I just need to talk to him."

The clerk let out a high pitched cackle and placed his hands on the counter. "Whew, the way you came sneaking in here, all official looking and such, I thought for sure you was the Law."

Lymdyr looked over at the miners. Both of them were smiling, too. They continued fingering the tools in the rack in front of them.

"Ryk's camped out down by the Hok River with his outfit. They were in town last week."

"Thanks. I need to find a room for a couple days, and a styrn to ride."

The clerk drummed his sharp fingernails on the counter. He glanced over at the miners, then back at Lymdyr. "Honestly sir, I can't recommend the boarding house. They've had some, er, problems, lately. And to tell you the truth, I don't know of anyone who can rent you out a styrn. You might go next door to the tavern and ask around. Sorry I'm not much help, but as you can see, things are pretty quiet around here lately."

"Thanks for your help."

Lymdyr readjusted his hat, shouldered his bag, and slipped back out onto the boardwalk. He paused to look up and down the deserted street.

"The sooner I talk to Ryk and get out of this dismal place, the better." He walked over to the battered door of the tavern, gave it a hard pull, and stepped in.

It took a moment for his eyes to adjust to the dark interior. Two oil lamps at either end of the bar were the only source of light, save for the small windows above him. Six round tables placed at random intervals on what appeared to be a dance floor were the only objects other than the long bar.

At one of the tables, a large, ragged woman and a small thin man with wispy hair that stuck out in several directions were the sole customers. Behind the bar, a short olive skinned man with a very wide waist leaned against the counter. No one spoke as Lymdyr walked toward him. Sand crunched under his boots.

He stopped in front of the bar and was going to set his bag on the floor, but the dirt and refuse littering the area made him think twice. After setting the bag on one of the stools lining the bar, Lymdyr placed the reinforced elbows of his duster on the edge of the bar and looked into the barkeep's face.

The man's puffy, blotched skin was peppered with small narrow scars. One eyebrow drooped down, evidence of a serious facial bone injury. He had thick lips with several discolored scars where they had been spilt. The bartender stared at Lymdyr without saying a word. For several awkward moments, the two men sized each up.

A feeling of revulsion rose up in Lymdyr. The notion of giving up and catching the next train back to Tyrl flashed through his mind, but his sense of duty convinced him not to. He forced himself to relax. The barkeep recognized the release of tension in the visitor.

"Something I can help you with?"

Lymdyr took a deep breath of the stale, rancid air, almost causing himself to choke. "Yeah, I'd like a glass of pyryn."

Just as the barkeep turned to fill the order, a raspy, hag-like voice called out. "Well, ain't you fancy!" Lymdyr glanced over his shoulder at the source of the noise. "Yeah! I'm talking to you, fancy britches." The woman seated at the table behind him finished off her statement by letting go an emphysemic laugh.

"Ah, stow it Myrnth," her emaciated companion said in a deadpan voice. "He ain't botherin' nobody."

The barkeep swung back around and placed a dusty glass half full of a clear liquid on the bar. Lymdyr picked up the glass and took a sip. It burned like fire going down. A thin layer of particles drifted across the oily surface of the liquid. He caught sight of the bartender's massive swollen knuckled hand before it dropped below the bar top

"Did you used to be a fighter?" Lymdyr asked, somewhat breathless.

"Yeah he used to be a fighter, fancy britches," the voice behind him ground out. "And a dyth good one too!"

"He's not talking to you, Myrnth." The barkeep's words rang with annoyance. "Leave him be."

The woman turned back toward her companion, grumbling to herself in response. She sneered and poked a strand of grey, stringy hair away from her face.

"Just ignore her. She's got nobody to talk to. Yes, I used to fight. Been a long time though. You need anything else?"

Lymdyr took another small drink and waited till the fire subsided. "I'm going to be in town for a couple days and need a place to stay. I also need to rent a styrn."

The barkeep took a moment to ponder the request. He laid his big, battered hands on the edge of the bar. "Well, ain't but one place to stay here, and I don't think a fella like you'd want anything to do with it. Did you bring a tent or anything with ya?" Lymdyr shook his head. "Hmm, I'd suggest goin' next door and buyin' a tarp. It's not so cold at night anymore." The barkeep paused to brush a bright green flying creature away from his face. "What ya need a styrn for?"

"I need to go talk to someone down by the Hok River."

The barkeep nodded his head and drew a figure on the dust of the counter with his finger. "I can't think of nobody rents styrns. Jyrn's got a wagon he'd probably haul you down there in." He leaned over and shouted at the table.

"Hey Jyrn! Wake up! This fella needs someone to take him down to the Hok. You interested?"

The skeletally thin man's face snapped back to life. He wiped some drool off his lips, rubbed his heavy lidded eyes, and looked over at the visitor.

"I suppose I could. When's he wantin' to go?"

Lymdyr turned around to answer. "Tomorrow morning would be fine. How about if we meet outside here at daylight?"

"Daylight? Dyth! I don't usually get up much before nine!" The man broke into a smile that revealed his crooked, stained teeth.

"How much you willin' to pay?" the woman rasped out.

Lymdyr swung his head back toward the barkeep. He gave his shoulders a quick shrug and waited for a response.

"Oh, I don't know, offer him ten dymyrs. That should be enough to keep him drunk for a couple days," the barkeep mumbled.

Lymdyr took another small drink and turned back toward the table. "Ten dymyrs round trip."

"Ha!" The woman reached over and slapped the stick thin man on the arm. She looked up at Lymdyr, and her heavily lined, hollow eyed face pulled up in a grin. "We'll take it! Hyrl! Bring us a bowl of them frynrs. We'll pay you when we get the dyrn."

Lymdyr finished his drink, set a coin on the bar, and headed toward the front door. He stopped beside the table. "So get down here as early as you can tomorrow, okay?"

The wisp of a man nodded in reply. Lymdyr continued out onto the street and entered the hardware store. The clerk was just turning down the oil lamps in the back of the store. His small, bird-like head popped out from around one of the shelves when he heard the door open.

"Oh, hello! I was just closing up. Do you need anything?"

Lymdyr let out a snorting laugh. "Yes, as a matter of fact, I need several things. I need a decent place to stay, although it seems like I'll be camping out. I need some food, and I'm Zym sure not going to eat anything that guy next door cooks."

"Oh no, no, no! You didn't eat or drink anything over there did you?"

"Well, I drank some pyryn, but I doubt even he could taint that."

A high pitched cackle burst out of the clerk's mouth. "Yes, I agree." He walked up toward the front, dusting his hands off as he went. "Now food-wise, there is a lady what lives down the road toward the Hok. She's got a couple kids, and at times, she'll fix a meal for folks. You could give her a try."

Lymdyr pondered the possibility and scratched his stubbly chin. "Hmm, doesn't sound bad. So you say she lives down that way?" He pointed in the direction opposite the rail station.

"Yes. A big ram shackle place. Actually, three buildings nailed together. Lots of stuff in the yard. The kids'll probably be running around fightin' and carry in on."

"I'll give it a try. I do need a tarp and a blanket."

A few moments later, he tucked the thick striped wool blanket and rolled up canvas tarp under his arm and headed toward the door.

"Good luck," the clerk called out.

"Thanks."

Lymdyr stepped out onto the broken boardwalk, glanced up and down the mostly deserted street, and began walking. A pair of scruffy looking young men walked on the opposite side of the street. They stared at him with contempt. He shot a quick glance over at them, then averted his eyes.

"The sooner I get out of here the better. Contact Ryk, convince him to come to Tyrl, and get the Zym out. Should take only two or three days. I sure didn't plan on sleeping outside."

The boardwalk ended, and he stepped down onto the dusty, hard ground. Beside him, a few dilapidated work sheds remained precariously upright amid piles of rusting equipment. Even those thinned out as he moved out of the main section of town. A side road wound up to a flat top hill off to his left. More discarded junk lined the road. After another couple minutes of walking, he spotted the top of a huge thorn tree rising above the low, scrubby desert landscape.

The outline of a group of buildings began to take shape behind the grey trunk of the tree. A blast of dry, cool wind blew up into his face. He had to squint to keep the sand out. A large rope hung down from one of the tree limbs.

"Looks like a place where some kids might live."

He could now see that the low flat building was actually three structures pushed against each other. The one facing the road appeared to have been built with some care. It had wood frame windows and vertical siding. The other two extensions were much less well constructed. They looked to have been cobbled together with odd pieces of plywood, discarded beams, and planks of varying sizes.

Two mangy looking fryrns rose up out of the dirt yard and charged. Their wide paws kicked up little poofs of dust with each stroke. They growled and circled around him. Their flexible tails curled and uncurled rhythmically. Lymdyr looked down at their thin yellow fur. He stopped to let them sniff his boots. They both skidded away as he resumed walking.

Once he entered the yard, the fyrns tilted their domed heads back and began howling. Lymdyr worked his way around rusting pieces of mining equipment and several small forts built with rotting plywood, and stepped up onto the small, covered porch. From behind the rough paneled exterior of the building, he could hear the loud voices of several children yelling. Lymdyr shifted his load, made a fist, and leaned forward.

Before he could knock, the sturdy weathered door opened just far enough for a small, dark face to appear.

"Wha'you want? Husband is not here."

Lymdyr stood there, somewhat stunned. His eyes moved between the woman's shiny, mahogany colored skin, and her large, soft brown eyes. The skin on her cheeks was stretched tight. A narrow nose that flared out at the end, and a prominent chin gave her an air of ferocity.

She stuck the rest of her bandana covered head out into the early evening air and took a quick scan of the yard. Upon seeing nothing unusual, the woman moved into the space of the open door and straightened up to her full height of just over five feet.

"You notta enforce man?" Before Lymdyr could answer, a loud child scream rended the air. The woman stepped back and pulled the door almost closed. Nothing but her small, rough fingers showed. A stream of angry commands in a language Lymdyr didn't recognize reverberated through the door. Some timid child responses drifted out to him. The door slowly swung back open, and the small but obviously fierce woman leaned against the jamb. She folded her arms across the patched house dress.

"What you want?"

The comic aspect of his entire experience so far that day was too much for Lymdyr to contain. He let go an exasperated laugh and readjusted the blanket and tarp he was holding.

"The clerk at the store said you prepare meals for travelers."

The woman's face jumped in surprise. "You wanna eat? Das all?"

Lymdyr nodded. Her full, rounded dark lips stretched into a radiant smile. The setting sun hit the two shiny gold teeth hiding behind them.

"Oh, man! I thought you a come a lookin' for my husband. Come! Come in! You jus' in time."

She swung the creaking door open and stepped aside. Lymdyr followed her in. The living room was bare save for several well-worn pieces of furniture. At the back of the room, a big table stood illuminated by a single hissing oil lamp. Around the table were three thin, dark children, and the two scruffy miners he had encountered earlier at the store.

"Jus put yo things ona de couch." The woman pointed to a beaten up overstuffed sofa against the wall. "Don't put em on de floor. It's kinda dirty." Lymdyr walked over and gladly dumped his load on the fraying fabric. He turned back toward her and almost ran into her outstretched hand.

"My name ees Gwydol."

"Lymdyr Nineth Line. Pleased to meet you."

They shook hands quickly, then Gwydol hurried into the kitchen area. An interesting variety of smells wafted through the closed in atmosphere of the house. A rich, spicy aroma from the large pot of stew bubbling away on the improvised metal stove was the dominant scent. Underneath that, the musky smell of humanity rose up with a touch of pipe gynt smoke underneath.

Lymdyr followed her into the room. Just before taking the empty seat next to the miners, he looked down at the children. Their big, dark eyes peered back at him suspiciously. Gwydol returned to the dining room with a large bowl of stew and placed it on the table in front of him.

"Der ya go." She took a step back and crossed her arms again. "Chilrun, dis is Mr. Limedar. Mr. Limedar, dis here is a Polo, Syrn, and Jak. Say hello chilrun."

In barely audible voices, the children mumbled a hello. Gwydol let go a cackling laugh. Her two gold front teeth flashed in the lamplight. "Ya gotta 'scuse dem, dey not a used to seein' no fancy dress man round here."

Lymdyr smiled, and without hesitation dove into the stew. The first bite was quite hot, but after blowing on the surface a couple times, it became palatable. Once his mouth adjusted to the temperature, he was able to appreciate the complex flavor.

"So, what a bring you out here?" she asked while strolling back into the kitchen.

After finishing the mouthful, he turned to answer. "I'm heading down to the Hok River tomorrow. I need to talk with one of the mag drivers."

"Lots of good pyfg in de Hok. Come zymyn, me an de chilrun go down der," Gwydol commented while methodically stirring the stew. "Where you stayin?"

"Well, that's a good question. The clerk advised that I not stay at the boarding house, so I guess I'll camp out."

Gwydol let out another burst of laughter. "Ya man. Dat some good advice. Fancy fella like you probably not get away without bein' robbed der. You got a tent?"

Lymdyr ate another mouthful, then shook his head. "All I got is a tarp and a blanket."

She nodded and walked over next to the miners. Both of them were quietly finishing up their meal.

"You fellas want mo?"

They both shook their heads and stood up at the same time. The white haired miner dropped some coins on the table.

"I thank ya agin. Me and Thyr ain't very good cooks. Comin inta town is 'bout our only chance to git some decent food."

He muttered a goodbye and led the way around the big round table. Gwydol scooped up the coins and followed the men out. When she returned, her children were sitting, staring silently at Lymdyr.

"Doan jes sit der staring. Clean up de dishes," she snapped. The children reluctantly got up from their places and began clearing the table. Gwydol watched them for a moment, then turned toward the last guest.

"You want some mo?"

"Yes, I believe I would."

She reached over, took the empty bowl from him, and carried it back to the makeshift stove. After re-filling it, she set it down in front of him.

"Ya know. I'm a thinkin' that if you wanna sleep on de couch, da'd be fine. Fancy fella like you don't needa be sleeping in de dust."

He stopped swirling his spoon in the steamy bowl and looked up at her. Lymdyr took a minute to examine the fine lines at the edge of her dark eyes, and the creases that framed her full lips. She appeared to be about his age. A bit of a smirk flashed across his face.

"So you'd be okay with me sleeping on the couch?"

She gave an exaggerated nod. "Thas what I said din't I?"

Lymdyr's tension and frustration from his difficult day melted away. He leaned back in the creaking wooden chair.

"You know? I think that sounds like a great idea!" He stared up at her, grinning like a fool. Her eyes moved all around his wide face, taking in the minute details. Lymdyr watched her eyes shift back and forth under the long eyelashes.

"I do have to get up early to meet, whatever that guy's name is tomorrow."

"Oh doan worry! I git up plenty early."

Chapter 26.

Just before daylight, Lymdyr was awakened by a metallic squeaking noise. He lay in the dark slowly coming back to consciousness. His not-quite awake sensory systems tried to register what they were perceiving; the sound of light footsteps moving across the wooden floor, a match being struck, the sharp smell of sulfur, glass scraping across metal, flickering lamplight, twigs snapping, more metallic squeaking, flavored gynt smoke? Lymdyr pulled the blanket aside and swung his feet down to the floor.

"Dat you Mr. Limedar?" Gwydol asked in a quiet voice.

"Yes, its me." The light from the kitchen spread across the dusty floor in a long rectangular. He could make out the outline of a clay pipe jutting out from her shadow.

"I gonna go out and fill de bucket. Be right back."

Lymdyr jumped to his feet. He hobbled over to the doorway, shielding his eyes from the light, and held out a hand.

"Give me the bucket. I'll go fill it up."

Gwydol let out a sharp crack of a laugh. "Days a pump over by de fasden shed. I'll go feed de fasdens while you fetch de pluge." She blew a narrow column of smoke his way and handed over the bucket. Lymdyr took it from her, then stepped back into the dark room to put his boots on.

After a quick breakfast, he hurried back to town, and stood outside the grimy tavern. Forty minutes later, he was still waiting. A total of six people passed him by that morning. Not one even appeared inclined to smile. A constant wind blew up from the river, scattering sand across his long, black leather duster. The sun was fully up, but a layer of gauzy high clouds gave everything a muted, dull appearance.

Just as he was getting ready to enter the tavern to inquire, the ambling form of the rail thin man and his ragged styrns appeared from the direction of the train station. Lymdyr crossed his arms tightly and stared at the man's sunken face.

The more-dead than alive styrns stopped right in front of the hardware store. Lymdyr gave the pitiful animals a good looking over. Both had large patches of fur missing, and narrow scars around the bases of their long necks. He pulled himself up into the seat next to the driver.

"'Morning," Jyrn offered.

"Good morning. Kind of late aren't you?"

Jyrn turned his head of wispy grey hair toward Lymdyr and broke into a crooked toothed smile. "Zym no, I ain't late! Sometimes I don't get up till after noon." He let go a foul breathed laugh and whipped the reins. The styrns laboriously pulled the wagon forward.

They had only travelled about fifty feet when the rear wheel behind Lymdyr began to vibrate. He turned around in the seat and watched it rotate sloppily on the axle.

"You know, that rear wheel's about to fall off."

"Naw, been like that for most of a year."

Lymdyr shifted forward, gave a huff of disgust, and stared out at the scrubby desert vegetation. They bumped and rattled down the rutted road for ninety minutes. The high clouds finally dissipated, and bright sunlight shone all around. On their left, a tall ridge of mountains gradually veered off to the south. On their right, the flat river bottomland extended to the north.

As they neared the river, the tops of some trees appeared. Their bright green spring foliage was a welcome change in comparison with the brown, grey desert shrubs. The dry air now had a softness of river moisture and smell of algae to it.

"Ya might wanna hold on. This last part's kindly steep," Jyrn cautioned.

Lymdyr glanced at the road ahead. They were just dropping down off the historic high water mark for the river. Forty feet ahead, the road took a steep dive. Lymdyr watched intently as they moved closer. He began to squirm in the seat. Closer and closer they moved toward what appeared to be the edge of a cliff. He could see the road heading off across the sandy bottom land below them.

Right at the edge of the drop, Jyrn pulled the reins hard to the left. The road switched back twice before leveling off. Sliding and grunting in the soft, dusty soil, the styrns struggled to keep the wagon from overtaking them. The one on Lymdyr's side bawled angrily.

"Isn't there an easier way down?"

Jyrn shook his head. "Nope, ain't but one way down and one way out. Them mags tear up this road every year. It's not bad today."

Lymdyr gripped the splintered edge of the seat to keep from getting tossed over the front of the wagon. By now, the styrns had hunched forward in an attempt to brace themselves. The wagon bucked and shook as they dropped off the last switchback onto the flat, sandy bottom land.

Lykrs chirped and wheeled overhead. Lush green grass sprang up along the small rivulets that flowed down from above. A thick tangle of willows followed each of the streams as they moved down toward the main channel. The road sank down into the wet areas and reappeared at regular intervals.

Smoke from a campfire drifted up ahead. Surrounded by the lushness of the bottomland, Lymdyr began to relax. He looked over his shoulder at the steep bank they had just dropped down from. Big, flat pieces of sandstone jutted up out of the eroding hillside. Along many of the smooth brown surfaces, white petroglyphs of animals and people were visible in the morning light.

Jyrn negotiated the web of two-track trails that intersected and split before them. Any semblance of a road finally disappeared into an expanse of sand. Down the by river's edge, tall trees hung together in clumps.

Beneath one of the larger clumps, a line of canvas tents was strung. Wooden equipment boxes lay in haphazard piles along with heaps of riding tack. From the branches of one of the trees, a good sized animal with antlers and long spindly legs hung. Small flying creatures buzzed in a thick cloud around its open belly. Twenty yards from the camp, Jyrn pulled the styrns to a halt.

"Can't go no farther. We'll git stuck."

The styrns bawled and sniffed the moist air. Their big nostrils sucked in the crisp, clean scent of the river. Jyrn climbed down off the wagon with great care. Lymdyr jumped down and landed with a thud into the soft sand.

From one of the tents, a head poked out, followed by the body of a medium-sized young man. He stood at the opening of the tent and observed in silence.

Jyrn fought with the styrn harnesses, but eventually freed the ragged animals. They plodded across the sand and down to the nearest pool of water.

From downstream of the camp, four sleek styrns came loping out. Two were the familiar tawny color. One of the others was jet black, and other, reddish brown. The four well cared for animals curled their lips up and barred their wide, well-worn teeth. In response, Jyrn's animals raised their heads from the water and repeated the gesture.

Lymdyr and his driver walked toward the camp. The young man standing by the tent pushed sand around nervously with his boot. As they got closer, Lymdyr could see details of the young man's face. He appeared to be about eighteen or twenty. The most striking feature was the long scar running from his forehead down beneath a grey fabric patch covering his left eye. The scar terminated just below his cheek. His thick black hair stuck up like a haystack. The young man took a couple limping steps forward, and one-eyed Lymdyr suspiciously.

"You from the mag company?"

"No."

The young man's look of concern melted into a wide, welcoming grin. "Oh! I thought for sure you was here to inspect the mags. There's some kinda illness going around with lots of the herds, and the guys been sayin' that sooner or later, one of the big shots from the company gonna show up. Heck! I was all worried. My name's Phyl, by the way." His mangled face glowed with happiness.

After some quick introductions, Lymdyr got down to business. "I'm here to see Ryk Six Line."

"Well, he ain't here just now." Rather than provide further information, Phyl just stood, swaying slowly back and forth.

"When will he be back?" Lymdyr tried to suppress his anger, but was only partially successful. The question came out sounding like a demand.

"Same time they usually is back." There was another annoying pause before the young man finished his response. "Just about stryrkset."

Lymdyr threw his hands up in the air and turned away. He bit his lip, cursed under his breath, then after regaining control of his emotions, slowly turned back around.

"How far away are they?"

"No tellin'. They left about two hours ago. My guess is they took the herd way down by the island. Most of the grass around here already been et. You boys like some myrf? I was jess about ready to cook up them two flyrms I caught earlier."

The young man pointed over at two big, flat amphibians that were laying in a patch of grass under one of the trees. Jyrn walked over and knelt down beside them. He grabbed the wet rope strung through their gills and lifted the top one up.

"Dyth. This one on the bottom is huge!"

"Ah, that's nothing. There's much bigger ones out there. Yesterday, I had one on that liked to pull me right into the river. Bring um over here, and I'll cut em up."

For the rest of the day, Phyl and Jyrn amused themselves by chasing the scaly crymrs that scuttled beneath the bushes, throwing rocks in the river, and wandering about the area. Lymdyr tried his best to keep occupied. He ended up sitting in the shade and whittling a piece of driftwood for lack of anything better to do.

A wind kicked up toward the late afternoon. It swept through the thick green foliage of the trees. The rustle of the leaves temporarily obscured the constant murmur of the river. Just as the sun was beginning to drop behind the ridge to the south, the four well cared for styrns got up from their resting places all at once. The long necked animals pawed the ground and bawled pitifully. All four of them turned their wide, flat heads towards the west. Their big, fuzzy nostrils flared in and out.

Jyrn was dozing against one of the tree trunks. Phyl had laid down for a nap in his tent. The whining, whistling of the styrns woke him up. "The boys must be back," he muttered while crawling to his feet.

Above the tinkle of the river washing over the smooth stones, a low rumble rose. It gradually grew louder. Several sharp barks cut through the late afternoon air. Phyl ran his dirty fingers through the forest of stiff black hair atop his head.

"Yep, they're back."

Lymdyr dropped the stick he was whittling and got to his feet. Phyl limped across camp and onto a narrow trail that paralleled the river. He stopped and beckoned to Lymdyr.

"Come on."

The railroad man followed him along the path, which gradually broke out of the trees onto a big sandy flat. Driftwood posts had been pounded into the sand at ten foot intervals, and cross members lashed to them. Into the makeshift corral, three riders were herding a collection of spotted mags. The bristly, wide bodied animals banged into each other, and let out low moaning growls as they were directed into the pen.

Two muscular and very shaggy fyrns circled back and forth at the perimeter of the herd. They snarled and snapped at the thick legs of the mags, occasionally charging one of the animals if it strayed from the herd. The bigger of the two had the characteristic mane of silky bluish hair which designated it as a male.

When the last of the mags had entered the corral, the rider with the long, stringy black hair jumped down off his mount, and swung the driftwood gate closed. Both of the shaggy, straw-colored fyrns loped over to him. He reached down and gave their domed heads a scratch.

It was just at that time the driver happened to glance over toward the edge of the trees. When he caught sight of Lymdyr, the driver stopped scratching the animal's heads and stiffened in alarm. The ever alert fyrns at his feet sensed his apprehension. Hackles instantly rose up along their bony backs, and both took off at a run around the edge of the corral. They snarled and let out their characteristic warbling howls. Their rounded paws threw up sand with each stride. Phyl saw them coming and held up his hands.

"It's okay! He's a friend!"

The two animals took up position on either side of Lymdyr. They crouched low, back legs braced for a leap. The bigger one fluffed up its mane of bluish hair in a show of dominance. With long sharp teeth barred and retractable claws at the ready, they presented a fearsome sight. Phyl tried his best to get them to back down.

"That's enough! I said it's okay."

The black haired rider had jumped back on his styrn, and trotted around to the edge of the trees. Ryk and the blonde, crooked nose rider followed him over. Through his widely spaced teeth, the black haired rider let out a shrill whistle. The two snarling animals relaxed slightly and looked up at him. He glared down at Lymdyr.

"Who the klynk are you?"

"This here's Mr. Lymdyr," Phyl offered in an apologetic tone.

The black haired driver sent another suspicious glance at the stranger, then spurred his styrn forward. Phyl and Lymdyr had to jump out of the way to avoid being trampled. The other two drivers swept by followed by the pair of fryns. Both of the tawny animals gave Lymdyr a final snarl as they trotted by.

"Kyrg ain't the most friendly guy. Come on," Phyl commented while limping back toward camp. He and Lymdyr walked along the trail in silence.

When the two of them entered the camp, the riders had already dismounted and were pulling the saddles off their styrns. They arrived just in time to see the fryns wake Jyrn from his nap. Both of the animals had given him a good sniffing over. The one on the right stuck its flat triangular nose against Jyrn's cheek. The older man's sagging, wrinkled eyelids fluttered, then sprang open.

"Holy Zym!"

His scrawny, pile of bones body recoiled against the tree trunk. Wide eyed with panic, he looked from one of the curious animals to the other. Their long serpentine tails coiled and uncoiled behind them.

"It's okay! They're just getting used to you," Phyl called out. "Persin! Zylr! Leave him alone!"

At the sound of their names, both the fryns turned their heads in Phyl's direction. Satisfied that they had examined the visitor, they padded across the sand, and climbed into a tree over by the tents. With a contented grunt, both of them stretched out along one of the thick, round branches. Phyl limped over to the tree, reached up and scratched them under their narrow chins.

Lymdyr stood at the edge of camp, evaluating the situation. His eyes shifted back and forth between the individuals. From his brief encounter with the black haired driver, Lymdyr knew to tread lightly. He guessed that the taller man was Ryk. The crooked nose and open, relaxed features of the blonde driver seemed to indicate that he was no threat.

After taking a deep breath, Lymdyr strode across the sandy ground. The black haired rider had pulled his short, front grip shotgun out of the neck holster on his styrn. When he saw the visitor walking purposefully in his general direction, his deeply lined face hardened. He raised the weapon and moved on an intercept course.

"Look buddy, whatever you're sellin', we don't want any of!"

Lymdyr glanced over at the intense black eyes fixed menacingly on him under the sweeping charcoal smudges of the driver's eyebrows. His gaze dropped down to the weapon clenched in the driver's hand. Lymdyr forced himself to smile. A nervous laugh escaped from his lips.

"Honestly, I'm just here to talk to Ryk." He motioned toward the tall, darker skinned driver without taking his eyes off the armed man. "I assume that's him."

Lymdyr waited till the gun was lowered toward the ground, then casually walked another ten feet forward. Ryk now had quit coiling up the reins of his harness and was staring at visitor.

"Hello! Are you Ryk Six Line?" Lymdyr asked in as confident a tone as he could muster.

"Yeah."

"My name is Lymdyr Nine Line. I'm a representative of the Dymran Society. Perhaps you've heard of us?"

The blank, suspicious look on Ryk's face made Lymdyr wince. Out of the corner of his eye he caught a flash of movement.

"Alright, I don't know what you want, but ya better....." the black haired driver snarled while advancing toward him.

"Kryg! Take it down a notch! Let the man finish," Ryk interrupted.

From his spot by the clump of trees, the blonde haired driver also chimed in. "Ya, let the man finish."

Lymdyr waited just a millisecond for any action to take place, then continued speaking in a smooth, low voice.

"The Dymran Society is heading up a very ambitious program to send some brave travelers out to the stryrks to try and contact, umm. We would like to invite you to be part of this historic project. We need you to train one of our crew."

Sweat began to run down Lymdyr's flank. He struggled to try and control his rapid breathing. The suspicious look on Ryk's face wasn't helping his anxiety. The mag driver's thin eyebrows were cocked in a questioning manner.

"What kind of training you thinking about?"

"We would like you to train one of our crew to lasso something. You are the champion roper, right?

"Yeah." Ryk's tense face relaxed. He continued coiling up the harness. "I ain't got time to train anybody."

Lymdyr could sense his opportunity slipping away. "Like I said, this is a historic venture. In the future...."

"The man said he doesn't have time!" Krygr barked. He flashed a final angry glance at Lymdyr, then turned toward Phyl. "Are you gonna stand there scratchin' them animals all night, or are you gonna get pyryst goin?"

Phyl's narrow face dropped for a moment. "Sorry, I's just listening to what Mr. Lymdyr was saying."

"I know what you was doin! Get you worthless little byz movin!"

"What is your klynkin' problem?" the blonde haired driver snapped.

"Don't you start with me!" Kyrg pointed a big, long nailed finger over at his comrade.

The tension within the camp all but dissolved Lymdyr's hope of accomplishing his task. He made eye contact with Jyrn and gave a little flip of his head back toward the road.

"Well, Ryk, I think you should consider being part of the project. Gentlemen, thanks for your time." With that, Lymdyr turned, and marched off across the sand.

Phyl had moved over to the wooden boxes and began pulling metal plates out. As the two guests passed by him, the young man stopped and looked up at them.

"Are ya sure you don't wanna stay for pyryst? You and Jyrn did help cut up...."

"They ain't stayin' for pyryst!" Kryg bellowed.

Chapter 27.

By the time Lymdyr and his guide rounded up the mangy styrns and got them harnessed, the sun had already set. A damp, chill from the river settled into the bottom land as they bumped their way back up the road. After two hours of silent travel, they pulled up in front of Gwydol's ram shackle compound. Lymdyr reached into his coat pocket, pulled out four big coins, then glanced over at Jyrn. The man's eyelids were mostly closed.

"Hey! Here you go."

Lymdyr dropped the coins onto the Jyrn's outstretched hand and jumped down into a poof of soft dust. A flicker of flame off to the side of the house caught his attention. He strained his eyes in the darkness. Against the black silhouette of the mountain to the south, he could just make out the outline of a human form. The glowing red coal of a pipe illuminated Gwydol's small, fine featured face.

Lymdyr walked across the junk strewn yard and stopped beside her. The two mangy fyrns were coiled up on the opposite side of fire. They lifted their heads, let go a low growl, then settled back down. Gwydol said something to them in her native language. She drew a long pull on the pipe. The night breeze drifted fragrant smoke into Lymdyr's face. Gwydol slid the stem out of her mouth and smiled at him.

"So, how it go today?"

Lymdyr gave a huff of frustration. He reached back and rubbed his stiff, aching neck.

"Oh, I guess you could say it was a failure. I spent all day down there at the river, listening to their one-eyed helper tell me all about life in a mag camp, and then bounced along for the last two hours in a busted up wagon."

Lymdyr realized he was rambling and ceased his monologue. Gwydol squatted down, stirred the last of the embers, then slowly rose back up. She locked him in a mesmerizing gaze. Even in the dim starlight, he could see a curious black fire burning deep in her eyes.

"Anyway, Ryk wasn't interested. I think I probably should have thought more carefully about what I was going to say." Desperately wanting to change the subject, he sighed and looked around at the outline of the desert shrubs that grew along the edge of the yard.

"So, what are you doing out here?"

Gwydol let go a rattling cackle of a laugh. "Lookin' up at de stryrks."

For lack of anything better to do, Lymdyr tilted his head back, and took in the sea of pinpoint lights spreading out above. "They sure are pretty."

"Pretty, and useful."

Lymdyr winced as he rotated his head back down to look at her. His neck muscles were spasming. "Useful?"

"Ya, de tell you a lot about what is happenin', and what is a gonna happen."

Gwydol's cryptic answer struck him as amusing. He broke into a wide grin. "Okay."

The doubting tone of his response drew an immediate reaction from her. Gwydol pushed her narrow shoulders back and stood as tall as possible. "Wha? You think I'm a kiddin?"

Lymdyr's negotiating skills had been taxed by his day at the river. He ran a hand over his chin and tried to suppress the smirk from forming on his face. She was not to be fooled.

"Ya, you don't believe me! What day you born?"

"Fifth of Nymr, four hundred seventy."

"Okay, I'm a not so good at figurin' in my head. Take dat day an subtract from today."

Lymdyr tapped his fingers together. "Two seventeen."

Gwydol stuck the pipe back into her mouth and turned sideways. She lifted her hand up toward the sky, oriented it with north, then swung it roughly two-hundred and seventeen degrees to the right. For several moments she just stared up at stars. After taking a pull from the pipe, she gave her assessment.

"Hmm, ya see dem three stryrks all together? They's pointing directly at de boatman. Dat means you gonna return here soon." She let go a mischievous giggle and looked back at him to gauge his reaction. Lymdyr just smiled. "Let me check somethin' else."

Gwydol held both her arms out and backed up several steps. Her firm bottom pushed up against his groin. Lymdyr stood staring down at her small, handkerchief covered head. He wasn't sure quite what was going on.

Just over her shoulder, he could see the curve of her lovely rounded breasts loosely supported by the worn, mid-length linen dress she was wearing. A flame of desire began to supplant his sense of failure. He remained still while Gwydol made some additional motions with her arms, then stopped to ponder.

"Oh, now dat's interestin! De ditch digger hard at work."

Lymdyr stooped down to follow the direction of her gaze. A nerve along his spine twinged between the taunt muscles.

"Ah!"

She swiveled around and looked up at his grimacing face. "You got sumpin' wrong with your neck?"

"Yes, the muscles are spasming."

Much to his surprise, Gwydol pressed herself against him, slid her hand up, and began massaging his neck. Lymdyr let out a delirious groan.

"That feels great."

She grabbed his hand and gently pulled him toward the house. "Come, I rub your tight muscles."

A suggestive comment flickered in Lymdyr's exhausted brain, but he was too tired to vocalize. The snicker that escaped from his lips was all he could manage.

Once inside the house, Gwydol set her pipe into a bowl on the dining table. "Go ahead, take your shirt off, and lie on your belly on de couch."

He dropped his shirt onto the floor, eased down onto the worn fabric, and closed his eyes. The weight of her sitting next to him gently rocked his tired body. Her hands slid over his shoulders and began massaging his taut muscles.

"Boy, you a not kidding," she whispered.

"Thanks," he said halfway into the cushion pressed against his face.

Her small, rough fingers moved up to his neck. She worked the stiff strand of muscle against each other.

"Whew, dis hard work. I need to take de handkerchief off. I'm beginin' to sweat!"

He felt her fingers drift off. There was a rustle of fabric. Her strong, non-perfumed scent drifted down to him. He lay blissfully relaxed. Her hands returned to the now warm, less tense shoulders. To his surprise, he also felt the soft cushion of her small breasts, and weight of her body against his back. Her dry, firm lips kissed their way along his neck.

Lymdyr's eyes shot open. He rolled ever so slowly to the side. She lifted slightly, then lowered herself back down. Her diminutive, grinning face filled his field of vision. He closed his eyes and kissed her. Her mouth tasted of fragrant gynt and exertion. He could feel her hands undoing his belt. Lymdyr slid his arm out from the back cushion and embraced her.

Several hours later, he was awakened by a small voice calling out in the darkness. One of Gwydol's children was standing in front of the couch. Lymdyr was jammed into the space where the back and seat cushions met. Gwydol was tightly tucked against him, her rough black hair buried in his chest. He gently laid his hand on her shoulder.

"Mamma, mamma. I dropped zynck in de bed again," the small boy repeated.

Gwydol grunted. Her long eyelashes fluttered. She craned her neck around toward the boy. "Whas' de matter, baby?"

The boy repeated his words for a third time. Gwydol eased off Lymdyr's chest and reached out to touch the boy's wet night shirt. "Ah baby. I toll you to git up if you need a go."

The boy looked down at the dusty floor. His lower lip stuck out. "I know."

Gwydol muttered a few words. She swung her thin, muscular legs out from under the blanket. "Come on, less go clean you up." She rose and took the boy by the hand. Lymdyr watched her taut, smooth bottom flex as she walked across the floor. He lay there smiling in the darkness.

Grey morning light from the kitchen window gradually brought the features of the sparse living room into view. Lymdyr reached down, found his thick canvas riding pants on the floor, and pulled his pocket watch out. He flipped it open, and after tilting it back and forth a few times, was able to discern the position of the hands. The soft voices of mother and child drifted in from the kitchen.

"You go sleep in my bed. Mama love you."

Lymdyr pulled himself upright and began sliding his pants on. A moment later, Gwydol appeared at the entrance to the living room. He looked over at the gorgeous outline of her small pointy breasts, rounded belly, and smooth thighs.

"Whas' up?"

Gwydol gracefully tiptoed over, sat next to him, and wrapped her arms around his bare torso. He leaned over and kissed the top of her head.

"If I make it down the station in the next twenty minutes, I can catch the early train. There's so much I have to do when I get back."

While he bent forward to retrieve the rest of his clothes, she remained pressed against him. Once he was fully dressed, Lymdyr reached down and ran his hand up and down her silky thigh. She purred in the dim light.

"You think you be comin' back?" she asked with a hint of playfulness. He let his hand drift across the rough space between her thighs.

"Pretty sure I will." He bent forward, kissed her dry lips, then rose to his feet.

"You don't wanna eat before you go?"

"I am hungry, but if I can catch the early train, that will be best."

She pulled the grey, scratchy blanket around her and watched him finish dressing. After sliding his duster on, he knelt down and gently placed his hands on her knees.

"Thanks. That was the perfect way to end a rough day."

In response, she offered a somewhat weak smile. "Hey, don't forget your tarp and blanket." Gwydol began to unwrap. He reached up and stopped her hand from moving.

"Keep them. The lighter I travel the better. Goodbye." He planted another kiss on her lips, which she only marginally returned, then stood up. In one swift motion, he snagged the strap on his bag and whooshed toward the front door.

At five that afternoon, the members of the Dymran Project began to filter into Bokyl's office. Professor Rymnyr's piercing laugh echoing down the hall signaled her arrival. She and Regent Mihyn walked in together.

"Good afternoon!" Rymnyr said cheerily.

Bokyl looked up from his work and gave a sneer of welcome. The two women took up places over on the left side of the room. Professor Myrvst came shuffling in next. His wrinkled face looked more haggard than ever. He eased into a chair on the opposite side of the room.

"You look tired," Rymnyr commented.

"I am tired."

She waited for further information, then turned toward Bokyl. "So what's the latest?"

The head regent set down the pen he had been writing furiously with and folded his thick arms across each other. "Two things, Lymdyr headed back from Phyt Hill this morning. I sent a buggy out to pick him up. He should be here shortly. The second bit of information is that Professor Grylt is back."

"Ooh! Now that's good news." Rymnyr's face lit up with joy.

As if on cue, Grylt came walking into the office. The small, mostly bald professor stopped, glanced around at the staring faces, then broke into a huge grin. The ends of his thin moustache curled high.

"Well, it looks like I've stumbled into the right place!" His high, reedy voice filled the room.

"Professor! So good to see you." Rymnyr called out.

Grylt swung his shoulders and arms in a comic manner while walking over to her. He gently shook the professor's hand. Rymnyr let go, then motioned toward the others.

"And I think you know the rest of our group."

Grylt gave a little wave to those present and plunked down next to Myrvst. "Head Regent, let me say what an honor it is to be offered a position with this program. You certainly have gathered a fine group together."

"Oh, spare the formalities please! We have some serious matters to discuss, but yes, welcome. We're glad you're back. I don't know how many of the telemessages I sent you received, so I'll just recap where we are. So, the craft is nearly complete. When Lymdyr returns, we'll arrange to have you go out to the yard and see it."

"You won't believe what a wonderful job the artisans did with it! I really view it as a work of art as opposed to a craft for travel," Professor Rymnyr gushed.

"Well, if we don't find a way to snag a ride on that comet, it will be a work of art floating above Ulutrita with five people on board," Bokyl replied. "The crew so far are Regent Krynut who is out of town, yourself, Regents Mihyn and Handynr, pending their final approval." Bokyl levelled his steely gaze at Mihyn.

"Have you talked any more with Handynr about the voyage?"

"He's out of town again," she replied with a twinge of apology.

"As always."

"As always," Mihyn echoed. "When he gets back, I plan on getting either a firm commitment or rejection. I did broach the issue last week."

"And?"

She fired off a clipped little laugh, unwound her fingers, and eased back in the chair. "He was too tired to formulate a reasonable answer."

"Well, I suggest you try again, soon. The last member of the crew will be an engineer. Gyls, who has done much of the design work is a candidate, although his health is somewhat in question. The main task we need to focus on is to get this candidate sufficiently well trained in roping that they will be able to lasso the comet and propel them through space."

Bokyl paused, and looked into Professor Grylt's thin, bony face. The professor had been listening with rapt attention until the last statement. When Bokyl mentioned the lassoing part, Grylt's wispy eyebrows rose in surprise.

"In case you didn't catch that hint of sarcasm, Head Regent Bokyl is still not convinced that lassoing the comet for propulsion is the best plan," Professor Myrvst chimed in. He was sprawled out in the chair. The loose buttons on his shirt revealed narrow glimpses of his bulging, hairy belly. Grylt straightened up slightly and folded his hands together.

"Well, I realize that I am the newest member here, but I have to be honest. The idea of capturing a comet and using it to pull oneself along does seem a little farfetched. I mean, not being an engineer, I'm speaking just from a practical standpoint. Did the group ever consider building a pair of giant wings and have the craft flap along to wherever it is we are going? Oh, yes, by the way, where exactly are we going?"

Professor Myrvst hauled himself to a more or less sitting position, rubbed his already red, dry eyes, and leaned toward Grylt.

"Phylr Communication has installed several large capacity devices based on the Mr. Kryzyck's invention up on the mountains around Tyrl. By running their triangulations of where they've picked up the signals, uh, voices from through Krynut's amazing calculating machine, we've discovered something very interesting." Myrvst paused for just a moment. The room became deathly quiet.

"Several months ago, one of the junior astronomers noticed a sort of bulge in the comet's tail. As the comet got closer, Ymyl and his department were able to ascertain that this bulge is actually a separate phenomenon. They refer to as the Cloud. I guess it's a big, well, not a galaxy, but a mass of.....I apologize for not being very articulate. Perhaps Ymyl can fill in the details. Anyway, the transmissions seem to be coming from the Cloud. One of Phylr's devices picked up what we think is a daily broadcast from the source. Every thirty-nine hours, this same voice comes up for exactly seventeen minutes, and we think we've discovered something about their numbering system. Their system is...."

"We're getting off track!" Bokyl roared. His outburst caused both of the women to jump slightly. "Sorry, it's just that I feel our time is so limited that we must really focus on getting the final pieces of this project wrapped up. What do we have, four months now?"

"Something like that," Myrvst said dryly.

The sound of rapid boot steps clicking down the otherwise silent hall drew the attention of the group. Lymdyr came swinging into the room, stopped to size up the seating situation, then dropped into a chair next to Myrvst. His slicked back hair had a shiny, opaque appearance due to the accumulation of dust it had attracted. His face was wind-blown and tanned.

"Glad you could make," Bokyl called out.

"Thanks. It was quite a trip. I did meet with Ryk, but he didn't seem at all interested in the project. You've got to understand, he's a mag driver. He probably has barely any concept of what space is all about. He herds big, noisy, smelly animals for a living!" Lymdyr let go a short, sharp laugh. "You'll have to excuse me, I just got off the train, and I need some pyryst, a whole line of drinks, a bath, and a good night's sleep."

"We were just filling Professor Grylt in on the details of the project." Rymnyr finished her comment with a courteous smile.

The railroad man leaned in front of Myrvst and held out his hand. "Lymdyr Nine Line. Pleased to meet you."

"Professor Grylt, pleased to meet you."

The two men shook quickly, then settled back in their chairs. Lymdyr bent forward and rested his elbows on his knees.

"So if any of you have any suggestions on ways to convince Ryk to come up here, or other people that might be able to train whoever we select, please let us know." He glanced around at the blank faces of all those present.

"What if we offer him dyrn?" Mihyn suggested.

Lymdyr rubbed his dirt streaked hands together. "You know, I don't think he'd go for it. He really seems like a simple kind of guy that likes riding around on styrns, camping out, and chasing mags."

"Well, it's been a long day. I challenge each of you to come up with a way to get Ryk up here, or our beloved project might never come to fruition." Bokyl lifted himself up out of his chair and stacked the papers on the desk in front of him into a neat pile. The others got up and slowly filed out of the office.

Chapter 28.

Several hours later, Professor Myrvst was sitting on the stone bench in the backyard. A flock of bright red lykrs flitted around the thorn tree by the back hedge. Their cheerful songs and the warm, dry air created an inviting atmosphere in the small, but cozy yard. Myrvst leaned back and looked up at the large white smear of the comet, suspended high above. His doubts about whether the project would ever materialize sent a stab of remorse through him. Before he could sink further into a funk, the crunch of buggy wheels in the alley snapped him back to the present. After putting the styrns away, Blrsynt came striding through the gate.

"Good evening, Professor."

"Good evening, Blrsynt."

The young man swung the gate shut and proceeded up toward the back of the house. The kitchen door opened with a bang. Sylstyn came running out, raced up to him, and wrapped her arms round him.

"Hi there!" After a longer than usual kiss, they broke off, and walked together back toward the professor. "Would you like a drink? Pyryst is just about ready. Professor wants to eat out here since it's so nice."

Blrsynt looked over at her beaming face. "Yeah, I'll take one. You're sure in a good mood tonight."

"Yes, I am. It's a beautiful kyrsht night. I had a final project due, which I got turned in on time. I'm just in a good mood. Go ahead and sit down by Professor, and I'll bring it out." She leaned over planted a powerful smooch on his cheek. "You know, I really love you!"

Blrsynt searched her face for any telltale signs of mischief. The overwhelming joy that it radiated masked anything secretive.

"I love you too," he whispered.

Sylstyn let go and sauntered into the house. Blrsynt waited for the professor to scoot over, then sat down next to him. His attention was captured by the activity in the thorn tree. After a moment of silence, Myrvst spoke up.

"How was work today?"

Blrsynt crossed his legs, slid his hands over a knee, and cantilevered himself against the bench. "Oh, it went okay. Gyls threw his back out, so I had to act as foreman for the stave crew."

"We had another meeting of the Dymran society this afternoon."

Blrsynt turned his head toward the professor. "How did that go?"

"There's still two details that need to be worked out. We still need to nail down the final crew member. What we're looking for is a strong, able bodied person to act as engineer." Myrvst let his words sink in. He snuck a quick look over at Blrsynt's reaction.

Sylstyn came swinging out of the kitchen door carrying a tray with three glasses. She waited till the two men had taken one, then grasped the third glass, and held it high.

"Life is short."

After the toast was completed, all three of them took a drink. Sylstyn bent down and gave Blrsynt a playful bump of her wide hip. He slid over as far as he could to let her sit. Once she had settled next to him, Blrsynt reached over and gently stroked her long, lustrous hair.

"Wow, your hair has gotten really thick."

"Yeah, it always does that in the kyrsht. I think it's the warm days." Sylstyn took a small drink, then jumped to her feet. "Blyr, will you help me bring pyryst out?"

Moments later, the couple returned from the house laden with plates, silverware and a steaming dish. A small collapsible wooden table was setup in front of the bench, and dinner was served. Sylstyn wolfed down two plates of the creamy, magyng dish.

"Man, Syl, I've never seen you eat so much," Blrsynt commented between mouthfuls.

"It must be all the exercise I'm getting out there on the testing hill."

Myrvst wiped a string of white magyng off his tangled beard. "So how is it going out there?"

Sylstyn's beaming expression momentarily dropped into a frown. "Not good. Ramos managed to get the rope around the practice nucleus once yesterday. We really need Ryk to come up and give us some lessons."

"Well, it doesn't look like that is going to happen anytime soon. Mr. Lymdyr went all the way out to Phyt Hill to try and convince him, but didn't succeed." Myrvst replied.

"Ryk is really a pretty simple guy. I think Mr. Lymdyr just didn't approach him with the right pitch."

"Maybe you ought to give him some pointers," Blrsynt added.

Sylstyn set down her fork and glared at him. Blrsynt stopped chewing. He could see the fire building in her big, green eyes. He averted his gaze and resumed eating.

"If you want to get to Ryk, you have to enter his world. All he cares about is riding around on styrns, partying, chasing women, and winning the roping competition." Sylstyn cleaned off her plate and set it down on the weathered wooden table. Blrsynt let go a short chuckle.

"What's so funny?" Sylstyn asked.

"I was just remembering the competition last mygrym. That guy next to us said something about the old mag driver the event is named after, and almost got punched out. For some reason, it just struck me as funny."

Sylstyn pushed a swatch of her glossy, auburn hair back away from her face. "Phrynk. The driver they named the competition after is named Phrynk. Ryk idolizes him."

Myrvst set his plate down and took a drink. His lips twisted back and forth under his wiry grey moustache. "Suppose we get that Phrynk fellow to go out and talk to Ryk."

Sylstyn took a moment to contemplate the suggestion. "That would probably work. Only problem is, Phrynk is so old, they'd have to wheel him down there." She brushed a small winged creature away from Blrsynt's face. "Well, I have some studying to do." She slid off the bench and began gathering up the plates. Blrsynt got to his feet and assisted in the cleanup. Myrvst sat pondering.

Late the next morning, the highly efficient Tyrl postal service delivered a letter to Lymdyr. He was reviewing a stack of invoices when his secretary whisked into his office and tossed the letter down. It landed right on top of the stack.

"Thanks!" Lymdyr yelled instinctively.

The secretary stopped and hung onto the door frame. "You're welcome. Don't work too hard."

She flashed a bright smile, then sashayed out into the main room. Lymdyr leaned back in his chair and scrutinized the letter. With a swipe of his finger, he tore the envelope open, and extracted the paper. It read:

"Mr. Lymdyr. Good news! My housekeeper had a great suggestion regarding ways to convince Ryk to help us. Evidently, he idolizes a certain venerable old mag driver named Phrynk, who the annual mag competition is named after. She suggested having Phrynk talk him into helping. I suggest we contact this person immediately and see if they are willing to work with us. As a side note, it occurred to me that Kryzyck's nephew, Blrsynt, might be a good candidate for the engineer crew position. I will contact the rest of the group.

Myrvst"

Lymdyr let out a whoop of triumph. He took a large drink from his over-sized cup of zyd, jumped up out of his chair, strode down pass several offices, and veered into the third one down the row. A thick bodied man was drafting a letter at his desk when Lymdyr called out from the doorway.

"Good morning Kryl!"

"Good morning. What's up?"

"You know a lot about mag drivers, right?"

"Yeah, I know a thing or two." The man behind the desk gestured toward the wall to his right. Several paintings of stylized mag drivers sitting nobly on their mounts, gathered around a campfire, and fording a river hung above a long credenza. On the surface of it a large mag skull shone perfectly white in the late morning light. Various pieces of mag driver paraphernalia stretched out on either side of it.

"What'dya need?"

"Do you know a guy named Phrynk?"

A big, sweaty smile blossomed on Kyrl's face. He relaxed his shoulders, set his elbows on the desk, and leaned into them.

"I should say so. He's just about the most famous driver of them all. See that old metal dynograph sitting in the middle of the shelf? That's him holding the lariat. I'm the skinny kid second from the left."

Lymdyr took a couple steps toward the wall and squinted. "What? The kid with the dark pants? That's you?"

"Uh huh."

"But he has a head of dark wavy hair!" Lymdyr turned his gaze back toward the desk. "All you got is white bristles!"

Kryl let out a low laugh. "Yeah, that was a while ago."

"Know how I can contact that Phyrnk fella?"

After sliding back in his leather chair, Kryl looked over at the fuzzy dynograph plate as he spoke. "He lives at an old folk's home over by Hyn Park. What do you want to contact him about?"

"I need to ask a favor of him. Think he'd be up for a trip to Phyt Hill?" Lymdyr tried hard to suppress the foolish grin on his face from expanding.

"Boy, I don't know. Phrynk is old, really old. He's still alive, barely. Up until a couple years ago, he used to preside at the mag competition they have after the big drive in mygrym. He just got too old and senile."

Lymdyr's surging confidence began to sag. He gave the door jamb a quick little slap. "Thanks for the information. Guess I need to go pay him a visit. See ya."

Late that afternoon, Lymdyr arrived at Happy Years retirement home. The one story ranch style facility sat adjacent to a park. A six-foot bronze alloy fence surrounded the building and delineated the property from the stand of large trees alongside and behind it. Across the front of the structure, a wide, covered porch lined with rocking chairs ran the entire length. Lymdyr looked back over his shoulder at the buggy driver.

"I'll be about a half hour."

He walked up the gravel path, undid the latch on the front gate, and entered the compound. Several attendants were pushing wheelchair bound residents down the concrete paths that snaked across the lush green lawn. Several more were assisting stooped over residents as they gently walked along.

"I hate places like this!"

Lymdyr's face curled in a sneer. He continued up onto the porch, pulled the screen door open, and entered. A nicely polished dark wooden counter jutted off perpendicular to the front wall of windows. Behind it, two middle-aged women sat. The one closest to Lymdyr flashed a warm smile.

"Hello. Can we help you?"

Lymdyr placed his hands on the counter and looked down at the receptionist. "Yes! I believe you can. Is there a Mr. Phrynk that lives here?" he asked in a condescendingly cheery tone.

"Oh yes, Mr. Phrynk has been here for some time."

"Excellent! My name is Lymdyr Nine Line, and I represent the Blue Line Railroad Company." He paused to see if the title had made an impression. The two women glanced over at each other and giggled.

"It is my pleasure to inform you that my esteemed company would like to offer a great opportunity to Mr. Phrynk. We would like to talk to him about being part of a project we are funding that has the potential to change the course of history." Again, he added a dramatic pause to his presentation. The women stared at him with rapt attention. "Would it be possible for me to have a few words with Mr. Phrynk?"

"That depends," the woman on his right replied. She had the hardened, but kindly face of a long time nurse. "He sleeps a lot in the afternoon. Plus, Mr. Phrynk is not all there. His mental functions are rapidly slipping away." She turned toward her coworker. "Byrty, do you want to take this gentleman to see Mr. Phrynk?"

"I'd be delighted." The grey-haired, pleasantly featured woman got up from her chair, and moved ponderously around the counter. "Follow me."

Lymdyr smiled down at the seated nursed, then walked behind his guide. As soon as entered the resident wing, the smells of old people hit his senses. The whole place had a stale biscuit aroma, punctuated by occasional bathroom smells. Lymdyr sent sideway glances into the rooms as he walked by. He could see old people sitting idly in chairs, folding clothes, being assisted by staff, or lying motionless in bed.

"Zym! I can't wait to get out of here," he thought to himself.

They walked down a short corridor, then turned toward the left, and arrived at a big sturdy wooden door. The nurse pulled a ring of keys out of her off white uniform, undid the lock, and held the door open for him.

"Mr. Phrynk is in our special care wing. We have to keep the doors locked."

Lymdyr nodded and walked through the doorway. The special care wing was much noisier than the previous area. Shouts and random babbling of confused old people echoed from several of the rooms. Lymdyr tried to keep from sneering, but was only partially successful. Halfway down the hall, the nurse stopped at an open door, then beckoned for him to enter.

The walls of the small room were covered with framed certificates. A nicely rendered bronze statue of a mag driver on his styrn stood on the long table opposite the door. In the big leather chair next to the bed, an old man sat. His hook nose and pointy chin arched toward each other. The man's extraordinarily wide, knobby hands rested on the arms of the chair.

He was dressed in a traditional mag driver outfit. A billowy linen shirt and coarse linen pants covered up his flabby body. Boots on his feet, and a vest over the shirt completed his attire. He appeared to be asleep. The nurse walked quietly over to him. She laid a hand on his shoulder.

"Mr. Phrynk. Mr. Phyrnk. Someone is here to see you!"

The old man's mouth spasmed several times. The lines in his face deepened, then relaxed. At last, the droopy eyelids rolled up. He let out a whoosh of breath, and stiffly rotated his mostly hairless, age spotted head toward her.

"Myrn! Myrn! What time is it? We've got to go over to Hyrk's house." His voice rattled unsteadily. His greenish brown eyes searched the nurse's face in a desperate attempt to identify her.

With a hand still on Phyrnk's shoulder, the nurse glanced over at Lymdyr, gave an apologetic shrug, then returned her attention to the old man. "Mr. Phrynk? This man is from the railroad. He wants to talk to you."

The old mag driver turned his bewildered gaze toward the visitor. Lymdyr put on his best proud face. Phrynk looked over at the nurse, then back at the visitor.

"Go ahead," the nurse whispered.

Lymdyr knelt down next to the chair. "Mr. Phrynk. My name is Lymdyr Nine Line. Pleased to meet you." He held out his hand. The old man just stared at him.

"Mr. Phyrnk. I'd like to have you talk to Ryk Six Line for me. I'm part....."

"Ryk!" the old man sputtered. His dull, greenish brown eyes suddenly flashed with life. His quivering lips drew up into a smile. "Ryk. It's good to see you. Wow, you've changed a lot." The old man reached out and grabbed Lymdyr's hand.

The nurse leaned down and whispered into his ear. "He thinks you're that Ryk fellow."

Lymdyr scanned the old man's baggy, leathery face. The look of joy on his aged features was unmistakable. "Mr. Phrynk. I'm not Ryk, but I'd like you to think about coming with me to see him. I have something I'd like you to ask him."

"Oh, you're not Ryk?"

"No."

"Well, where is he?"

"He's down at the Hok river, tending to a herd."

Phrynk nodded his head. He let go of Lymdyr's hand and braced himself on the arms of the chair. To the surprise of both the nurse and visitor, the old man pulled himself to his feet. He tottered over to the dresser against the wall, stared at it for a moment, then began slowly and methodically opening and closing the drawers. Phrynk opened the third drawer down, rummaged around, and finally pulled out a rolled up object.

With great difficulty, his arthritic, swollen hands managed to unroll the material and hold it out. It appeared to be a belt fashioned from some kind of grey, scaly skin. Along the edges, an intricate design made with multicolored beads added a splash of color.

"This was a present from a Kuran chief that used to live by the Hok. He was a great fellow. Got shot by some mag drivers when he refused to give up the land," Phrynk rasped out.

Both Lymdyr and the nurse looked down at the finely crafted belt. A gurgling sound, followed by a powerful odor, interrupted their appreciation of the object.

"Oh, I just blryt my pants," Phrynk said matter-of-factly.

Lymdyr gagged and walked out of the room. The nurse followed him. Once out in the hallway, she reached into a pocket of her uniform, extracted a small bell, and rang it several times. From the nursing station down the hall, two young men got up from their chairs and made their way toward her.

"Thank you for letting me talk to him. I .....(gag) must be going." Lymdyr tried to control his revulsion, but couldn't stop his eyes from watering. The nurse looked over at him and gave a compassionate smile.

"You're welcome. Hang on a minute. I'll have to let you out." When the two young men reached the spot, the nurse stepped to the side. "Mr. Phrynk has had an accident."

The first attendant walked past her and held his nose. "Oh, Mr. Phrynk! We got to clean you up."

Chapter 29.

The next day, Lymdyr sent out a telemessage to the clerk at the store in Phyt Hill. A reply came back that afternoon. It read.

"Mr. Lymdyr, have not seen Ryk for several weeks. Expect the group to show up any day. Will definitely pass on your request to have Ryk meet with Mr. Phrynk."

By the end of the week, Lymdyr had not received word from Ryk. He decided to call together a meeting of the project. They met in Bokyl's office. As usual, Professor Rymnyr and Regent Mihyn were seated along the west wall. Kryzyck and the professor sat next to each other, holding hands. On the opposite wall, Professors Grylt and Myrvst, and Lymdyr were lined up. Head Regent Bokyl drummed his fingers on the desktop. He glanced up at the big clock noisily ticking on the wall.

"Did someone contact Krynut about this meeting?"

"Yes, I saw him this morning," Myrvst answered.

As if on cue, Regent Krynut appeared in the doorway. His narrow, pointy features were pressed down tightly. He entered the room and sat down hard.

"I hear things are not going well." Krynut's voice was steely and firm.

The room became hushed. Head Regent Bokyl wove his fingers together and lowered his head slightly.

"What exactly have you heard? By the way, welcome back."

Bokyl's congeniality went unnoticed. Krynut shifted in his chair so that he was now facing the big desk.

"Well, I hear that the plan for attaching the craft to the comet is a miserable failure."

Bokyl gazed around the room, searching for someone to answer the allegation. All he saw were stunned faces. Myrvst stroked the end of his tangled grey beard. He leaned back against the wall.

"Maybe miserable failure is a bit strong. Lymdyr and I have been working to try and get the champion roper to come out and train, uh, whoever gets selected as the final crew member." The professor leaned forward and directed his gaze down the row. "Perhaps you'd like to fill in some details, Mr. Lymdyr?"

"Myrvst and I came up with a plan several weeks ago to have a gentleman named Phrynk Nine Line approach this champion roper about helping us. We are putting the final details together for getting the two of them to meet. The roper, his name is Ryk Six Line, is currently working out in Phyt Hill, while Phrynk lives, uh, at a facility here in Tyrl. I expect to be able to bring them together as early as this time next week." Lymdyr drew in a great, deep breath. A bead of sweat rolled down his cheek.

"And what if this Ryk character still says no?" Bokyl's deep voice boomed.

Lymdyr tried not to wince. That was the one question he feared would be proposed. A jolt of nervous electricity shot up from his stomach. He took a moment to calm himself.

"After speaking with Phrynk, I am totally convinced that Ryk will come around. They've known each other for years. Ryk idolizes the old man." Lymdyr suppressed the smirk that was trying to form after the delivery of his exaggerated statement.

The tension in the room began to thaw. Bokyl scooted back in his chair. "I hope to Zym that you are right." He swung his gaze from Lymdyr back to the serious, joyless features of Krynut. "Regent, were there any other issues that you have been made aware of?"

"We still need to select someone for the engineer position, correct? I thought Gyls would be here to address that."

Bokyl gave a low huff. "Gyls threw his back out last week. He's incapacitated."

"Lymdyr and I have also been discussing that. We think that Kryzyck's nephew, Blrsynt, would be a good candidate," Myrvst tossed out.

The reaction was instantaneous. Kryzyck looked like he had been struck in the face. His weathered, thin features jolted in surprise. Professor Rymnyr clapped her hands together.

"Oh, what a marvelous suggestion! He's such a nice, capable young man." She leaned over and looked at the old miner's stunned face. "What do you think?"

"Blrsynt hasn't had a great deal of formal education, but he is bright. He was very helpful in the final construction of the craft, so I would assume he has some intimate knowledge of how it was put together. I suppose he would be a good candidate. He's strong, resourceful….."

"I plan on approaching him with the formal request as soon as the group approves it." Myrvst's exuberant response stood in stark contrast to the old miner's hesitant reaction.

Krynut took a moment to analyze the suggestion, then offered his opinion. "I don't know the man, but it sounds like no one has any great objections. We should try and identify several candidates in case he declines. I'll ask the head of the engineering department if he has any suggestions. There is currently a shortage of kykpowder as a result of the conflict in Bosyra. Has anyone addressed that issue?"

Lymdyr's calm and confidence had returned. He sat up straight in his chair. "My company has a huge stockpile. I have that covered."

"What's the kykpowder for again" Professor Grylt asked from his place at the end of the row.

"After the craft is floated up into the atmosphere by balloons, a charge will be ignited that propels it out into space," Myrvst explained.

"Ah, somewhat like a giant firework," Grylt responded with an impish grin.

"I need to get home fairly soon. My wife and I are going to a performance tonight," Bokyl interjected. "Is there anything else we need to discuss?" None of the group responded, so he rose up from his chair. "Thank you all for coming this afternoon. Mr. Lymdyr, keep us in the loop as far as the situation with this Ryk fellow."

"Will do," the railroad man answered.

"Good day everyone," Bokyl said as he swept out of the room. The rest of the group got to their feet. Just as his big bulky frame passed through the door, the head regent stopped. He took a step back and looked over at Mihyn.

"Have you spoken with Regent Handynr yet?"

The hesitation in her response and startled expression on her pleasant yet severe features left little doubt about what Mihyn's answer would be. "He just got back several days ago, so I wanted to let him...."

"I'll take that as a no," Bokyl cut in.

Mihyn glared up at him. Her indecisiveness suddenly transformed to irritation. "I'll ask him and get the final word tonight."

"Good, I'll expect an answer in the morning." Bokyl flashed a cruel smile, then whisked out into the hallway.

After watching him watched disappear around the door frame, Professor Rymnyr directed her attention to Mihyn. "You haven't asked him yet?"

"I did ask him several weeks ago. I just haven't had a chance to get the final word." Her narrow chin trembled as she spoke.

Rymnyr reached over, squeezed Mihyn's hand, and whispered into her ear. "You might want to treat him extra nice if he agrees." She stepped back to gauge Mihyn's reaction. The regent's soft brown eyes still betrayed the fear deep within.

"It'll be alright." Rymnyr squeezed her friend's hand again, then walked off toward the door.

Mihyn made her way alone out of the office and down to street in front of the Academy. She ignored several greetings from passersby. After climbing up into one of the buggies for hire, Mihyn began methodically plotting out her plan for getting a final decision from Handynr.

She started by composing a shopping list. Her mood began to brighten as she looked out at the fully open blossoms on the thorn trees. They flashed a vivid pink in the afternoon sun. A small trace of a smile worked its way across her serious expression.

"It figures that Rymy would suggest that we klynk tonight. Would he suspect I had an ulterior motive? Nah, it's been a while. Funny how some people are so caught up in physical pleasures. I guess both Handynr and I are more inclined to put our energies into lofty goals rather than enjoy the base pleasures in life. I like making love. It's just not high on my list of things to do."

She bought a bottle of mynth at the store down the street, and prepared a nice, but simple meal of mag steaks with sautéed vegetables. Then she waited.

After another twenty minutes, her highly motivated self could sit and wait no longer. Mihyn walked around the small, bungalow type house looking for things that needed to be brought into order. She swept the floor. She washed the dishes. Just as she was undertaking the refolding of towels and sheets in the linen closet, the front door creaked open.

"Honey, is that you?" Mihyn called out.

"Yeah, what smells so good?"

She glided down the hallway to meet him. Handynr stood on one leg by the door, removing his shoe. Mihyn could tell by the redness of his eyes that it had been a long day. She walked up and kissed him.

"I hope you're hungry. I made something different tonight."

"Yes, I certainly am. What's the occasion?"

His question took her by surprise. Mihyn stood frozen for a moment. "Nothing really."

"Nothing," he echoed. Handynr pulled off his second shoe and stood looking at her. He waited for details. None came forth. He gave a small grunt and walked past her.

Mihyn watched the leather bag hung over his shoulder swinging with every step. The question of whether there were more fancy mauve envelopes inside it shot through her already excited state of mind. She bit her lower lip.

"Wow, a bottle of mynth." After examining the label, he set it back down, then turned toward her. "Alright, really now. What's up?"

Mihyn folded her arms tightly and walked into the kitchen. "A couple of the big issues with the Dymran project got resolved today, and I guess I felt like celebrating."

"Ah, I know that's been weighing heavily on you lately."

"You can say that again." She stared up at his handsome, thin face. "Go ahead and open the mynth. I'll set the table."

"I think I might just do that." Handynr set his leather work bag onto one of the chairs and began opening the bottle. The couple went about their respective tasks independently, like they always did. Mihyn carried two plates over to the table, placed one in the spot she always sat, then moved around the end of the table.

On her way past the leather bag, she slowed and sent an eagle-eyed glance into the shadowy interior. Her heart began to beat harder. Unfortunately, it was propped against the back of the chair in such a manner that no light shone in.

Handynr popped the cork, poured two glasses of the dark green liquid, and took a drink. "Good choice. You're sure this won't give you a headache?"

"No, as long as I eat something, plus you know I hardly drink anything anyway."

He carried a glass over and held it out. She slid her elegant fingers around the stem, gradually easing it from his grasp.

"Life is short," he offered as a toast.

"Life is short."

They had a pleasant supper, chatting about work. Handynr outlined the latest development in the Bosyra war. When he had finished eating, a huge yawn spread across his face.

"Oh, excuse me! It's been a long day. Shall we go relax on the couch?"

"Sure."

They both got up from the table and plunked down on the couch. Mihyn held up the wine bottle. "Would you like some more?"

"Sure, just a little."

She topped off his glass to half full. He lifted his stocking feet and set them on the low table. For a moment, they both just sat and stared at the large painting on the opposite wall. Mihyn snuggled up against him. He leaned over and kissed her wavy hair.

"Thanks for the great pyryst. And the mynth." Handynr set his glass down on the table and leaned back. After a moment, his eyes closed. His breathing began to slow.

"Honey? Don't you want to know what the decisions about the Dymran project were?"

He grunted and worked up the energy to nod his reclined head. She grasped his hand tightly in an effort to keep him from falling asleep.

"We've just about completed selecting the crew. That was a big step in nearing the final phase. We think that Kryzyck's nephew might take the engineer position." A vibrating snore escaped from Handynr's mouth. "Honey?"

His eyelids bounced open. He reached up and wiped a trace of drool off his lip. Handynr pulled himself to an upright sitting position.

"Wow, I think I just dozed off."

"Yes, you did. Did you hear what I just said?"

"Something about crew."

"I said that they still want you and I to be part of the crew."

Handynr tilted his head of short, light brown hair toward her. He looked deep into Mihyn's eyes, then eased back against the couch.

"That's right. You did mention that before." He drew in a great, chest filling breath, and let it slowly escape. "I don't know Honey. To just up and leave seems like a pretty serious decision. I mean, what would we do with the house?"

Mihyn burrowed into his shoulder. "Well, you said your sister was looking for a place to live right? She could watch the house for us."

Handynr pulled himself up to an erect sitting position. His voice became serious and decisive. "Watch the house till what? As I recall, there really isn't any provision for the crew coming back."

She winced slightly at the sternness of his reply. Mihyn lay cat-like, curled up against him, pondering the next move. Handynr leaned forward and placed an elbow on each knee. With both hands, he supported the weight of his head.

"I mean, it sounds like an amazing adventure, but we don't have a lot of time to decide. Didn't you say a couple days ago that the project was scheduled to launch in four months?"

"Fourteen weeks to be exact."

"I mean seriously. Are you willing to venture out on this mission, by Zym's grace arrive at some world we know nothing about, and quite possibly stay there for the rest of your life?"

Mihyn took a moment to respond. She slid her arms around his trim waist.

"It's not like we know nothing about where those signals are coming from. My department has identified about four hundred words. Any civilization that can send some kind of messages this far out across space has to be somewhat technologically advanced, wouldn't you say?"

"Can I just think about it for a couple days?" His voice now had a dry hoarseness to it.

"Sure. Why don't you go to bed, and after I get things cleaned up, I'll be right in."

She laid a hand on his arched back. Her fingers drifted across it as he lifted himself up off the couch. Once Handynr had disappeared down the hall, Mihyn swung her legs out, and headed into the kitchen. Her heart again began to beat fast. She forced herself not to look at his leather work bag.

Mihyn methodically piled the plates and utensils into the sink. Twice during her actions, she sent a quick, furtive glance into the dark interior of the work bag. Now that the table was cleared, Mihyn moved around the living room cranking the oil lamps off. When her fingers touched the valve of the last lamp, she paused.

"Zym dyth it! I'm going to obsess about this all night. I'll just take a look to ease my mind. Even if there are more envelopes, they're probably just invitations to some boring formal diplomatic event."

Noiselessly, she padded back over to the kitchen table, and very gently parted the leather opening. In the dim light, three of the mauve envelopes appeared neatly stacked within. Without making a sound Mihyn slid a chair back and sat down. Deep, deep creases folded up the skin of her forehead. She leaned far over, slid her hand into the bag, felt for one of the textured envelopes, and pulled it out. Mihyn brought the stationary up to her nose and sniffed it.

"Oh klynk!"

The powerful scent of perfume caused her stomach to retract into a tight ball. With shaking fingers, she opened the envelope, and pulled the neatly folded mauve paper out. Her eyes zeroed on the decidedly feminine, sweeping cursive letters. The words "Dearest", "Love", and "Can't live without", jumped out in the dim light. Fighting the urge to vomit, Mihyn carefully refolded the letter, slid it back into the envelope, and returned it to the bag.

She breathed in and out with quick, unhealthy bursts. For several minutes, she sat staring at the tabletop. With great effort, Mihyn shook off the depression that threatened to drown her, got to her feet, killed the remaining lamp, then felt her way down the hall. Standing in the darkness, she slid her clothes off, and climbed in next to Handynr. He was laying on his back. She pressed against him and stroked his prominent forehead. His lips rose slightly in a smile.

"That feels nice, but I really need to sleep."

Handynr rolled to the side with his slender back facing her. She opened her mouth to speak, but ended up letting out a sigh of resignation. After staring up at the ceiling for hours, she finally fell asleep.

When Mihyn woke up, the sun was already streaming through the curtains. While she lay there slowly coming back to consciousness, her mind began reviewing the events of the previous evening. She was equally proud that the question of joining the crew had finally been discussed, and deeply remorseful for having examined the letter. Mihyn thumped the mattress hard and dragged herself out of bed. In a sleep deprived fog, she grabbed her robe, and stumbled into the brightly lit kitchen.

Out the back window, she could see Handynr walking across the lawn with an armload of sticks. Mihyn steadied herself along the counter and watched him toss the sticks onto the small fire burning in the crumbling brick fire pit near the fence. A questioning frown spread across her features. Her already anxious stomach jumped. Mihyn pushed the back door open and yelled out to her husband.

"What are you doing out there?"

Handynr dusted off his hands and strode over toward the house. "Oh, just cleaning up the yard. It's been ages since I did any yardwork. And a good morning to you!" He flashed his best diplomatic smile, then returned to the side yard for more debris.

Mihyn let the door swing shut and leaned back against the counter. Confusion, irritation, and flashes of anger swept through her morning mood. She raised her head and sent a quick inquisitory glance over at the now empty chair where the leather bag should have been. A jolt of real concern pulled her away from the counter.

She rushed into the living room, whirled left, then right, and continued on into the hall. The flash of brown over by the coat closet caught her eye. Without even the slightest concern whether anyone was watching or not, she hurried over, expanded the opening of the work bag from where it hung on the doorknob, and looked inside.

"Son of a fyrg! They're gone!"

Chapter 30.

Across town, Blrsynt woke to the sound of hammering. It was gentle at first, then became house shaking. He tossed the covers aside, scratched his head, and wandered out of the bedroom. The sound appeared to be coming from the bathroom. Blrsynt stuck his head around the door. Sylstyn's long lustrous hair and her bare shoulder came into view.

"Syl! What are you doing?"

The hammering stopped. His girlfriend let out an anguished sigh. Blrsynt pushed the door all the way open. Sylstyn stood, hammer in hand, completely naked. Blrsynt twitched. It had been a while since he had seen her fully unclothed in the daylight. From the profile, her youthful breasts seemed more full than usual. Her cute belly stuck out just that much farther. Without looking over at him, she swung the door slowly back and forth. As it neared the closing position, the hinge produced a raw, scraping noise.

"Why are you beating on the bathroom door first thing in the morning with nothing on?" Blrsynt asked in a soft, serious voice.

"I got up to go zynk, and just got tired of this door not closing. I think the hinge is shot. There's so much around this cottage that needs to be fixed. It's driving me crazy!" She tossed the hammer across the floor, backed up against the wall, then slid down to a sitting position. Her wide, lovely face was torqued with frustration. Blrsynt smiled and eased down next to her.

"We can get a new hinge at the store. How come you're so agitated?"

Sylstyn titled her head back and rested it against the wall. After a moment, she rolled to the side so she could see his face.

"I don't know. I guess finals has got me a little exhausted." She reached over and stroked his chin. Blrsynt dropped his head down to kiss her fingers. They exchanged a blissful, loving glance. Her big green eyes glinted in the morning light.

"Blrsynt, I'm lying. Finals isn't the problem." A pause that both of them would remember for years to come froze time on that sunny morning. "I'm pregnant." The goofy grin on Blrsynt's face slid onto the floor and evaporated. "It's okay, really. I've already told my parents."

His shock and disbelief manifested itself in the form of a short laugh. "It's okay? That's a strange thing to say."

Sylstyn reached over and interlocked her fingers with his, gripping him tightly. It was almost like she was afraid he would run. She tried making eye contact with him, but he just stared at the floor, mouth hanging open, shoulders slumped.

"I thought you were taking the special zyd?"

"I am, I mean I was. I ran out last month, and I guess I was too busy to get more. I really didn't think not taking it for a week would make any difference. I guess we klynked more often than I thought."

She finished off her admonition with a little defeated sort of laugh. Sylstyn let her head rest back against the wall, and the tears began to flow.

"I'm sorry. I know it's all my fault. You don't need to hang around. I know you have other things you want to do!" The still morning air was filled by her spasmodic sobbing.

"What are you talking about?" Blrsynt's voice now resonated with more than a hint of agitation. He shifted around and pulled her heaving torso next to him. Her warm tears trickled down his chest. "I'm not going anywhere."

"Yes you are!" Sylstyn jerked her head back. Strands of long, dark hair were plastered against her cheeks. "I know that Professor has asked you to be part of the crew."

After the last words left her mouth, she again broke down and sobbed. Blrsynt lowered his head so that they were now nose to nose. He stared into her eyes, which now had the shiny, wide open look of a frightened child. Blrsynt reached up and stroked her cheek.

"So you're worried that I'm going to go off on the voyage?"

"Uh huh," she emphasized with a quick nod.

The tone of her voice, and simple nod struck him as also very childlike. "Ah, Syl. The professor did ask me, once. Especially now, there's no way I'm going." He again pulled her tight onto his chest.

"I've ruined everything.....everything." Her crying energy seemed to be waning. The sobs and sniffs gradually decreased in intensity.

"Stop. You haven't ruined a thing. We just need to get a plan together. I mean, wow! We're going to have a baby!"

Sylstyn wiped her dripping nose against the back of her hand. With difficulty, she extracted the mass of hair stuck to both her cheeks and raised her head to look at him. A new and different kind of smile graced his wide, strong features.

"A baby! We are going to have a baby!" he repeated. His voice contained elements of wonderment and joy.

Blrsynt turned to meet her gaze. Rather than sadness and regret, her tear dampened face had the look of stunned unbelief.

He leaned over and kissed her. She simply kissed back, then slid her hand around the back of his head, and fairly swallowed the front of his face. An unparalleled excitement rose up in both of them. They broke off long enough to breathe.

"Let's go back to bed," he whispered.

Later that morning, in the dusty nowhere town of Phyt Hill, Ryk and his comrades entered the general store. It was an unseasonably warm day. The air in the store was stuffy and uncomfortable. As soon as the clerk saw who had entered, he pulled three yellow telemessage sheets from the drawer.

"Mr. Ryk? I have some important correspondence for you. I was hopin' that you'd be showin' up soon!"

The clerk held the stiff yellow sheets up with his claw-like hand. Ryk walked over and tore the sheets out of his grip. He scanned them for a second, then ripped the bundle in two.

"You have my permission to respond to that rich, fake-byzr railroad flunky and tell him I ain't goin' nowhere!"

"Will do Mr. Ryk. Sorry to bother you."

The clerk's telemessage reply reached Lymdyr by mid-afternoon. His secretary was making her usual rounds after lunch. She walked by the telemessage station and noticed the yellow sheet sticking up out of Lymdyr's box. Without breaking her stride, Byrdyl snagged the message, and read it as she walked.

"Oh, dear! He's not going to like this."

The secretary stood in the doorway of Lymdyr's office for a moment, then gave a pretend cough to draw his attention.

"Byrdyl, what're you doing out there? Come on in. Sorry I didn't notice. I'm just responding to all these requests from the governor and his staff. What's up?"

The secretary sashayed toward the desk and let the telemessage slip from her fingers. It floated down and settled across his pile of letters.

"What have we here?" Lymdyr asked in his best dramatic voice. "Good news?"

Byrdyl shook her head. The railroad man frowned and picked up the sheet. She watched his wide set eyes move across the page.

"Dyth! I had a feeling that stupid mag driver wasn't going to cooperate!" He tossed the sheet over his shoulder, leaned forward in his chair, and pressed his head between his hands. "What am I going to do Byrdyl? Without his help, this whole thing may fall apart."

She looked down at his flushed, fatigued face. Byrdyl turned slightly, eased her small, round bottom on the edge of his desk, crossed her legs, and propped herself up with one arm.

"Well, Mr. Lymdyr. I'd say your options are pretty limited. You gotta get him up here. It's too late to go chasing anyone else to help. Didn't you go visit that old mag driver fellow that he supposedly adores?"

"Yes." The compression of Lymdyr's cheeks somewhat obscured his response.

"And what did he say?"

Lymdyr rocked back in his chair. His linen shirt was darkened with patches of sweat. "Phrynk is old. Old and more than a little senile. It would be tough to haul him down there to convince Ryk."

"Don't really see that you have that much choice."

"Zym! Why does this have to be so hard? My brain is mush. So what's my next move?"

Byrdyl held a finger up to her orange colored lips. "Here's the plan! The first thing we're going to have to do is get the mag company's approval for you to haul Ryk out of the drive and up here. I'll arrange a meeting with them. How about taking them out for a lavish pyryst?"

"Sounds great. Care to join me?"

The secretary sent a look of comic reproach down at him. "Watch yourself. I'm married, you know!"

"Just kidding. Go on. I like the plan so far."

Byrdyl readjusted her seat on the edge of the desk and continued. "It shouldn't be too hard for you to convince them. If this Mr. Phyrnk is as old and feeble as you say, it could be tough getting him down there to meet Ryk. Any chance that you could have them meet in that grimy little town?"

Lymdyr stared at her firm bottom planted on the edge of his desk, caught himself, and shifted his focus up to her face.

"You know what we could do? There's a railroad station there, not much else really. We could put him on the train, and at least get him that far. I may have to sweet talk the attendants at the old folk's home."

Byrdyl slid off the desk, smoothed the wrinkles off her tight fitting dress, and crossed her arms. "I'll draft an invitation to the mag company and send it out. He works for Pylrt's?"

"Yes. Guess I'll pay another visit to the old folk's home."

Two days later, Lymdyr wined and dined the mag company executives, and was able to convince them to let Ryk leave the drive for a month. When the ridiculously expensive dinner concluded, he grabbed a hired buggy, and directed the driver to the old folk's home.

Lymdyr burped loudly while the buggy bumped along down the boulevard. He swayed back and forth in the seat. The interior of the buggy was beginning to get stuffy, so he unsteadily reached over, and cranked the window open. It stuck mid-way. The force he exerted to open it fully caused the metal handle to break off.

"Oops!" He snickered, and tossed it out into the cool, night air. Lymdyr stuck his flushed face out into the opening. The air rushing by instantly evaporated the sweat from his skin. It sobered him up just a tad. He looked out at the darkened shops and deserted streets.

"I supposed I should have let Bynhyld know I would be home really late." A shade drifted down onto his celebratory spirit. "Our relationship has never been great. The last couple years it's really become hostile." For a moment, his blocky features softened in sadness. While he continued to stare out the window, the big, scrubby evergreen trees of the park came into view.

The buggy lurched to a stop in front of the silent old folk's home. Lymdyr popped the door open and jumped to the ground. From the pond at the park, noisy night amphibians croaked back and forth.

"I'll be back out in fifteen minutes," he called up to the driver.

Lymdyr walked with purpose up to the metal fence that enclosed the grounds. In the darkness, he failed to negotiate the concrete step, and tripped mid-stride. After regaining his balance, Lymdyr took a moment to look up at the darkened building. There was only one light visible all along the low front. He frowned, slid his fingers into his vest pocket, and extracted his pocket watch. With practiced skill, he popped the case open, and tilted the face away to get a read.

"Dyth! I didn't realize it was so late. Klynk! I didn't think pyryst would take that long. Should I just come back tomorrow?" Just as he was about to abandon his mission, the silhouette of a figure passed in front of the rectangular window.

Lymdyr fumbled with the gate, but finally managed to swing it open. He strolled up unto the porch and knocked as lightly as possible on the front door. Through the gauzy curtain on the inside, he could see a figure rise from behind the desk and move around the end of the counter. A hand pulled the curtain aside, and a face appeared behind the window.

"Who is it?" A raspy, female voice inquired.

"My name is Lymdyr Nine Line. I was here a couple weeks ago to talk with Mr. Phrynk. I apologize for....."

Before he could finish his statement, the face moved away from the window. The lock on the front door clunked, and swung open to reveal the short, pleasantly featured nurse that had escorted him to Phyrnk's room on the first visit.

"Good evening Mr. Lymdyr. Yes, I remember you. Please come in."

The nurse stepped out of the way. Lymdyr took a deep breath of the musty night air and entered. The nurse closed the door, clicked the lock shut, and returned to her place behind the desk. After settling back into her place, she rested her elbows on the desk, and looked up at him.

"So, what can I do for you?"

Lymdyr put on his best, happy-to-see-you smile, and laid his hands on the counter. He took a moment to let his well-trained executive mind evaluate the woman seated before him. She seemed to be middle-aged, a little ragged around the edges, perhaps slightly overweight with hair greying rapidly. Lymdyr zeroed in on the wrinkled skin that framed her tired, but still engaging eyes.

"Good evening, I meant to come over earlier, but sort of got hung up." An enormous, sulfurous burp erupted from his full stomach. "Excuse me!"

"So what can I do for you?" The nurse gave a polite smile and resumed filling out her daily charts. Lymdyr could tell by the slight irritation in her question that he needed to act quickly.

"Yes, yes. Sorry, I don't believe I caught your name."

"My name is Byrtymn, but everyone calls me Byrty." The nurse lifted her head to answer, then lowered it back down and continued writing.

"Wonderful, well Byrty, I have a rather daunting task that I need your help with." The nurse glanced up from her work. Lymdyr beamed back the most charming smile he could muster. "I need to get Mr. Phyrynk and Ryk Six Line together."

"Have that Ryk guy come up and pay him a visit. As you can see, Mr. Phrynk isn't going anywhere."

Her quick, unhelpful reply dampened Lymdyr's hopes. He stood listening to her pencil make scraping noises on the paper.

"I wish it was that easy. Ryk is pretty stubborn. I think a better option would be for us to take Mr. Phyrnk down to meet Ryk." The nurse stopped writing, tilted her head of wavy grey hair to the side, and stared up at him.

"I don't think that's much of an option. Did you say us?"

Lymdyr's beaming smile returned. "Yes! I would like to propose that you accompany Mr. Phrynk and myself down to Phyt Hill. All expenses will be paid by my company."

Byrty set her pencil down, leaned back in the chair, and crossed her arms. She lifted a hand up to stroke her chin.

"You're really serious about this meeting aren't you?"

The considerable amount to mynth Lymdyr had consumed earlier ignited his dramatic talents. He pulled in a deep breath, let it out with a sigh, and spoke in a voice befitting of an actor up on the stage.

"I am more than serious. Although I hate to admit it, I'm approaching desperation."

The nurse nodded and rocked gently in her chair. "So how many days are you anticipating needing to have Mr. Phrynk out and about?"

"Oh, it only takes about five hours by train to get to Phyt Hill, so there's one night. Meeting Ryk would take all of a day, there's two, and we could be back by night on the third day."

Byrty uncrossed her arms and swiveled her chair toward the hallway. She reached down to give her stockinged thigh an unlady like scratch.

"Boy, I don't know. Phrynk can be so hard to deal with. As you saw, there are some days he has no idea what's going on." She stared down the darkened hallway. Her pasty forehead was crisscrossed with worry lines.

Lymdyr decided to play his final card. "My company is prepared to pay you for your time away from work. I can't stress to you how important this project is."

At the sound of the word "pay", her face lit up. She turned and locked Lymdyr in a dead serious gaze. His eyes twinkled back.

"You know, I could really use a little time away from this place. Probably wouldn't be the worst thing in the world to get old Phrynk out for some fresh air, too. How soon were you planning on doing this?"

Lymdyr could hardly contain his excitement. His palms began to sweat. He slid his hands off the counter and wiped them on his dress pants.

"As soon as you can arrange to leave."

Byrty let go a little squeal and spun her chair around. She grabbed the white painted counter to stop her rotation.

"I'll need to get permission from his family, but that shouldn't be a problem. I'll just tell them that we are taking him out for a little afternoon trip." Her greenish brown eyes flashed mischievously. "Ooooh, this sounds like fun!"

"Believe me, it will be fun! My company doesn't do things halfway." Lymdyr leaned way over the counter to emphasize his point.

Byrty wrote down some contact information on a piece of paper and handed it over to him. After tucking it into his coat pocket, Lymdyr reached over the counter and shook her hand.

"Perfect. Mid-healer Byrty, I thank you for your assistance, and will contact you with the details of the trip."

"My pleasure Mr. Lymdyr. Oh, we'll probably need a good supply of pyryn to keep our sanity dealing with Mr. Phrynk. Will that be a problem?"

"Not a problem at all. Good night."

Lymdyr executed a little bow at the waist, spun on his heels, and charged out the door. Once back outside in the cool, quiet night, he triumphantly thrust a fist up into the air.

"Yes! Finally, something is going right!"

Chapter 31.

Three days later, Lymdyr woke early in anticipation of the trip. He tried to be quiet as he packed his big leather satchel, but still ended up disturbing his wife's sleep.

"Is it today you're leaving?" she asked groggily.

"Uh huh."

"And where are you going this time?"

"Back to Phyt Hill."

"Where is that?"

"You don't want to know."

"And who's all going?"

Lymdyr was beginning to become annoyed with the peppering of questions. The tone of his reply reflected it.

"It's just me, a styrn handler, Phrynk, and his mid-healer."

His wife gave a grunt and rolled over under the covers. She stuck her head of tangled black hair up over the edge of the blanket.

"So you're going to hang out with some pretty young mid-healer for a couple days?"

Lymdyr had his back turned toward his wife. She didn't see the smirking smile on his face. He wanted to say, "No, I wouldn't go near the mid-healer. It's the little Lymyr woman I'm going to klynk." Instead, he offered a more descriptive, but less volatile reply.

"The mid-healer is a middle-aged battle axe of a woman, don't worry." Lymdyr stuffed the last shirt into the satchel, buckled it with force, slung the heavy bag over his shoulder, and bent over to kiss her neck.

"I'd get up and cook you nymyr, but it's too dyth early," she grumbled.

"I can handle it. Say goodbye to the girls for me."

Twenty minutes later, Lymdyr jumped down from the hired buggy, and strode over to the railroad platform. High above him, the clouds were just changing color from peach to crimson. A smile broke across his face when he caught sight of the fancy, black lacquer executive car parked at the siding. Coupled behind it was a standard livestock car. Just as he was making his way across the gravel yard, the snort of several styrns behind him drew his attention. Lymdyr stopped and waited for the man holding the reins to approach.

The handler appeared to be approximately the same age as Lymdyr. He was dressed in a conservative tan mag skin outfit over which he wore a well-used corduroy work jacket. The handler walked up and gave a nod of his head.

"My name is Klyrk Twelve Line, and this is my wife Cyrny. You must be Lymdyr?"

"Correct."

"That the livestock car over there?"

"That would be it."

Lymdyr took a moment to size up the handler's wife. She was quite pretty. Dark, curly hair spilled out from under a very expensive black embroidered hat. The look she returned to him was nothing less that fierce. Klyrk patted the neck of the chocolate brown styrn he was holding.

"Guess I'll load 'em up, then."

Over by the platform, a black buggy pulled up. The cab door swung open, and Byrty leaned out into the hazy morning air.

"Mr. Lymdyr! Shall I have the driver pull up over....Oh! Is that the car over there?"

"Yes, have him pull up right next to it, and yes, that's the car."

Byrty gave a loud whoop, said something to the driver, and closed the door. The buggy bounced and rocked its way across the gravel yard. Lymdyr met them over by the executive car. He watched the wide-bottomed nurse ease her way down the metal step and extended a hand to help her with the final drop.

"Good morning. My, don't you look fetching today!" He took a moment to take in the details of her white leather fringed, mag girl outfit.

Byrty's middle-aged face lit up with joy. "You think so? I haven't worn this in years!"

"The red embroidered nymfyrs really add a lot. You know, I completely forgot to ask you if you know how to ride. Too many details."

"When I was young, I used to own styrns. I keep toying with the idea of getting another one. But to answer your question, yes, I can ride."

"Excellent, I assume Mr. Phyrnk is going to need some help getting out of the cab?"

"Most definitely." Byrty eased back up the steps and called out to the old man. "Okay Mr. Phrynk time to board the train!"

With some grunting and groaning, she and Lymdyr were able to get him down to the ground. When Phyrnk took the final step, the railroad man looked right into his vacant, fuzzy greenish-brown eyes.

"Good to see you again, Mr. Phrynk."

The old man scrutinized Lymdyr's face for recognition. His drooping lips moved silently.

"He's trying to remember who you are," Byrty whispered.

"Mr. Phrynk? My name is Lymdyr. I'm the one that talked to you about going and seeing Ryk." The railroad man's voice took on the tone of one speaking to a young child.

"Ryk?" the old man mumbled.

"Yes, we're going to see Ryk," Lymdyr replied enthusiastically.

A spark of happiness flash through the old man's eyes. Byrty and Lymdyr each held an arm while they walked him over to the car. Once Phrynk was inside, the nurse took a moment to survey the plush interior.

"This is really nice!"

"Yes it is, isn't it? Here let me show you your salon." Lymdyr led them down the corridor, the walls of which were decorated with red on black flocked wall paper. Custom made oil lamps were set at intervals along the way. He pulled the sliding door of the salon open to reveal dark wooden paneling with green leather upholstered seats along both sides.

"Make yourself at home."

After helping the two passengers in, he headed down toward the end of the car. The sound of glasses clinking grew louder as he approached the small kitchen. Lymdyr entered the cramped space and boomed out a greeting.

"Ryslyn old boy, how are you?"

The young, dark skinned steward spun around and shook Lymdyr's outstretched hand. "I'm just fine, Mr. Lymdyr. Haven't seen you in a while? What have you been up to?"

Lymdyr stared at the young man's broad nose and wide-set eyes. His fondness for the steward was obvious from the huge smile plastered across his face.

"Well, don't know if you've heard about the Dymran project, but I'm one of the leaders."

Ryslyn twisted his lips to the side in a contemplative manner. "You know, I can't say as I have."

Lymdyr let go a laugh. "I thought everybody would have by now! We're planning on launching some explorers out into space soon, and..."

"Oh that! Of course! I just didn't know what it was called." Both men grinned at each other. "So you're involved with that?"

"You betcha! We're going down to Phyt Hill to try and convince this championship roper to help us."

"Ah, I wondered what this was all about. Well, welcome aboard! As usual, anything I can get you, just ask."

"Thanks Ryslyn. Did the groceries I ordered get loaded?"

The steward turned and opened a set of wide cabinets at waist height. He stepped back to reveal their crammed contents. Lymdyr dropped to a squatting position and poked around the full cabinet. After a moment, Ryslyn bent down next to him.

"I do have a question though. If you were going to order all this stuff, why didn't you get the exec car with the full kitchen?"

Lymdyr pushed the cabinets closed and rose to his feet. "We're not going to be doing much cooking on board." Ryslyn sent a questioning look back at him. "I have a cook set up in Phyt hill. Basically, we're just going to sleep in the car."

"Ah, I see."

A loud train whistle blast reverberated through the walls, followed by a heavy thunk that shook the whole car.

"I think we're about ready to take off," Lymdyr commented just as the rear door to the kitchen popped open. Klyrk pulled himself into the small space and closed the door behind him.

"Livestock car is secured and ready." The handler slid his mag skin gloves off to extend a hand toward Ryslyn. After introductions were exchanged, the three men all gripped the counter while the train rolled forward. The glasses in the cupboard began to clink against each other with increasing frequency.

"I'm going to check on Phrynk," Lymdyr announced before turning to exit the kitchen. He had only taken two steps when a loud metallic bang echoed from the corridor. Both he and Ryslyn snapped to attention. The initial bang was followed by the repetitive clang of metal on metal.

"What the?" Lymdyr hustled down the corridor with the steward close behind. The rush of dusty air into the posh interior cleared up the mystery even before he reached the open exterior doorway. Lymdyr leaned out, grasped the swinging door, and pulled it shut.

"Be careful, Mr. Lymdyr!" the steward called out from behind.

"Klynking dyth it! I must have forgotten to close it after we struggled to get Phyrnk in." Both the men stood silently and examined the cracked window of the door.

"Oh, man. I am gonna catch some blyrt for this!" Ryslyn said in a hushed tone.

"Ah, don't worry about it. It's pretty minor damage."

"I know, but this car is my pride and joy."

Lymdyr looked up at the defeated face of the steward. "If this is the worst that happens today, we'll be fine! Come on, I'll introduce you to Byrty and Phyrnk."

The two of them worked their way along the rocking corridor. They stopped in front of the open salon.

"Did you figure out what that noise was?" Byrty asked. She smiled when Ryslyn moved into view. "Oh, hello! My name's Byrty."

Lymdyr laid a hand on the young man's uniformed arm. "This is our steward, Ryslyn. He's one of the nicest, most efficient workers we have. "

"Pleased to meet you ma'am. Would you like a drink?"

"You bet! Double pyryn please."

Both men turned their attention to Phyrnk. The old mag driver was gazing out the window. He sensed someone was watching him and slowly swung his head of stringy white hair around.

"Nice car ya got here. By the way, when is myrf?"

"Myrf will be ready in just a few minutes. We're having cold nyrynt soup and sliced mag sandwiches," the steward said in his official dignified tone.

"Sounds great. I'm starving," Phrynk replied. "It's nice to get out of the home."

While Ryslyn slipped back down the corridor, Byrty leaned over and patted the old mag driver's thin, bony leg. "We have quite an adventure planned for you, Mr. Phrynk. Are you up for it?"

His wrinkled, saggy face drew up in a grin. "What sort of adventure?"

Byrty looked up at Lymdyr with a "your turn now" expression. He stepped into the salon and took a seat next to the nurse.

"Well, Mr. Phrynk, we brought you out here because we need your help."

"Oh, what kind of help do you need?" he asked in a soft, somewhat childlike tone.

"We need you to help us convince Ryk to come into Tyrl, and train one of our people to do a very, very special roping job."

Phrynk's age spotted forehead drew up in deep lines. "What kind of a roping job do you need done?"

Lymdyr glanced over at the nurse. "Here goes," he whispered. "I'm one of the directors of the Dymran Project. Have you heard of it?" Phrynk shook his head. "It seems that several months ago, actually almost a year now, this miner accidentally discovered a way to listen to telemessages coming from some other world."

Phrynk's forehead wrinkled up again. "I see."

"We've been working on a way to send a group of brave explorers to this world, and in order to get them there, we need to rope a comet."

A spark of interest lit up the old man's fading greenish-brown eyes. He stared directly at Lymdyr. "A comet, as in the things what sweep through space?" The railroad man nodded. Phrynk let go a rattling laugh.

"Excuse me! I didn't mean to laugh at your idea, it's just that, wow. Never thought about roping a stryrk before! That sounds like one of our old mag driver songs." He crossed his leg, threaded his big knuckled fingers together around a knee, and leaned back. "So you need me to convince Ryk to leave the drive and come into Tyrl."

"That is correct," Lymdyr responded.

"Boy, asking a mag driver to leave the herd at this time of year is going to be tough." Phrynk chuckled, causing his small, round belly to bounce. "Bout the only thing that could get Ryk up and moving is a woman."

Chapter 32.

Four hours later, the train pulled into the desolate Phyt Hill station. After disgorging the few passengers that actually had a reason to get off there, the train backed the two special cars off at the siding, then chugged away. Ryslyn stood behind the broken window on the side door and looked out at the weather beaten buildings lined up along the main street.

"Whew, it's even uglier than I thought it would be."

"Yeah, nothing much to write home about," Lymdyr commented.

"Let's go see what's happening downtown!" Byrty shouted as she made her way down the corridor. She stopped next to Ryslyn and squinted out into the early evening light. "Geesh, not much of a town, is it?"

"Nope, this is it," Lymdyr replied. He shot a quick glance over at her slack jawed face.

"Is that a tavern over there?"

"I guess you could call it that."

"Let's go have a drink!"

Lymdyr scanned her faded, glassy green eyes. "You don't get out very much do you?"

She let go an alcohol-fumed cackle and swayed gently in place. "Are you kidding? Between covering for the klynk up staff I have that always calls in sick, and dealing with my ailing mother, no, I don't get out very much. This is like a vacation!"

Klyrk came walking out of his salon. He stretched both arms, then ran a hand through his short, brown hair. "Must have dozed off. Are we here?"

Lymdyr looked down the corridor at the wrangler's drowsy appearance and nodded.

"Excuse me boy, could you make me a pot of......"

"Hold on. Ryslyn is not your boy. He's an employee of Blue Circle Railroad. Please address him by his name," Lymdyr corrected.

Klyrk's wide, rugged face tucked up into a sneer. "Fine. Ryslyn, could you make me a pot of zyd?"

"Sure, Mr. Klyrk," the steward replied. He left his spot by the window and quietly walked back to the kitchen.

Byrty stepped forward and grasped the door handle. "Let's go see what's happening out there."

"How's Phrynk doing?" Lymdyr asked as she passed by him.

Byrty stopped just before descending the steps. "He fell asleep again."

"Is he out for the night?"

"Naw, he'll probably wake up in a while."

Lymdyr watched the nurse careen down the metal steps and make her way across the rutted street. He gave a little shake of his head before walking back toward the kitchen. Ryslyn was staring at wisps of steam rising up from the spout of the tea kettle when his boss entered the small kitchen.

"I'm going to head down and check in with the woman that is going to serve as our cook. You alright?"

Ryslyn turned his face away from the stove and looked directly at Lymdyr. His soulful, dark eyes betrayed a hint of sadness.

"Yeah, I'm alright." He shot a quick glance out toward the back door, then returned his gaze to the railroad man. "I really don't like that Klyrk fella. He seems a little smug."

A smile spread across Lymdyr's face. "I know what you mean. Just do your job and try to ignore him. I'll see you in a little while. Oh, Phrynk is asleep in his salon. Byrty went out to explore the town. She'll probably be back in a few minutes."

Lymdyr went back to his salon, pulled a wrinkled paper bag of candy and a pouch of pipe gynt from his satchel, then headed toward to the side door. He ran his hand along the cracked glass before opening it and stepping down.

Once on the ground, Lymdyr caught sight of Klyrk walking the animals around by the back of the livestock car. In order to avoid interacting with him, he walked directly across the unpaved street. The town was all but deserted. A few scraggly looking individuals hung out in front of the hardware store. Lymdyr nodded a hello as he walked by. They just stared at him with questioning expressions. He looked up and down both sides of the street for Byrty. She was nowhere to be seen.

He continued walking as fast as possible and soon passed the last of the collapsing sheds that formed the southern border of the town. The cool, dry air was filled with the pungent scent of desert plants. Lymdyr inhaled deeply through his nose to take in the exotic aromas.

Out of the gathering darkness, Gwydol's ramshackle dwelling came into view. The children were playing out in the front yard. Actually, they were screaming and throwing rocks at something near the edge of the yard. The two mangy fryns were braced on their front paws, barking furiously.

Lymdyr made it to within about twenty feet of the yard before his presence was detected. All three children stopped their activity and stood staring at him. The sudden cessation of their screams drew the attention of the fryns away from whatever they were barking at.

The powerfully built animals raised their domed heads and gave the air a good sniff. Already on alert from the children's screaming, the two tawny fyrns bolted toward the intruder. They barred their long, pointed teeth and charged low to the ground.

Jyk, the teenage son, recognized Lymdyr. As the fryns swooshed by him, he yelled out a command in his mother's language. Both animals skidded in the soft dirt. They looked back at him for further instructions. Jyk pointed toward the house and uttered another command. After giving the air around the visitor a thorough scenting, the animals lowered their heads and slunk off.

"Good afternoon," Lymdyr offered in a friendly tone as he approached the children.

"What're you doing here?" Jyk's question rang with adolescent defiance.

"I'm back here on business. Is your mother in the house?" He dug his hand into the bag, pulled out a fist full of candy, and held the wad of brightly colored objects out at waist level. "Here, I brought this for you."

All three of the children stared at his outstretched hand. Jyk took a step forward. The younger ones stood behind him lined up like timid fawns. After selecting two of the candies, Jyk muttered a low thank you. His sister daintily removed one from Lymdyr's palm and moved next to her older brother. The younger boy twisted up his mouth and stood trying to decide.

"I like these ones." Lymdyr pointed at the blue metallically wrapped candies. The sound of the front door creaking open drew everyone's attention.

"Chilren, come on in...." Gwydol stopped in mid-sentence. Her eyes zeroed in on the well-dressed man standing amid the rusted junk. "Didn't expect to see you around here so soon."

Lymdyr flashed a big, radiant grin. "Didn't you get the telemessages I sent?" She nodded her head. "Why didn't you reply?"

"What, you think I got dyrn to send telemessages at dyrm and a half a shot?" She cracked off a rapid fire laugh. Her gold front teeth flashed in the twilight. She looked down at the brightly colored objects in Lymdyr's hand. "You brung syps?"

Lymdyr dumped the remainder of the candy back into the bag, reached into his pocket, and pulled out the pouch of gynt.

"And I brought something for you." He held the thick, waxy paper pouch out and watched with a smile as she glided down off the porch and across the yard to accept it. Gwydol enclosed it in her small, rough fingers, and pressed it under her nose.

"Mmmmm, smells good."

They exchanged a brief, affectionate glance. Lymdyr handed the bag to her and motioned back toward town.

"I need to get back to check on the group. There are five of us, and a whole pile of food."

"You wanna have pyryst ta night?"

"Yeah."

"Okay, let me get de stove going."

Gwydol hustled back into the house while Lymdyr walked as quickly as possible back up the road. He arrived at the car in record time. With Ryslyn's help, food was packed into several wooden boxes. Lymdyr and the steward carried them out to where Klyrk was waiting with one of the styrns. The handler finished cinching up the last box, then turned toward Lymdyr.

"How we gonna get Mr. Phrynk down there?"

"Zym! I completely forgot about him!" The railroad man smacked his forehead in a display of humility. "Good thinking. Can you saddle up another of the styrns?"

"You don't think he can't walk that far?"

Lymdyr shook his head. Klyrk walked back to the line of animals tethered to the post, and returned with a slim, cream colored styrn. At that same moment, Phrynk stuck his head out of the salon window.

"What's going on out there?"

Lymdyr ran over to the side of the car. "Mr. Phrynk, we're going to go down to Gwydol's house for pyryst. It's kind of a long walk, so we're getting a styrn saddled up for you." He waited for the old mag driver to react, but all Phyrnk did was stare out into the twilight. His eyes moved across the rapidly darkening landscape, but didn't seem to be focusing on anything in particular. Lymdyr let out a sigh.

"Mr. Phrynk?" He called out the name again, this time a little louder. "Mr. Phrynk!"

The old man slowly lowered his head and looked down. "Yes, what is it you want?"

"Do you think you can ride a styrn?"

"Well, I don't know. It's been a very long time. I think I rode one in a parade not long ago. Why are you asking?"

Lymdyr ran a hand over his stubbly face. He directed his gaze over toward the bleak row of buildings in hopes of seeing the nurse.

Klyrk had finished saddling up the cream colored styrn and led it up along the side of the car. He stopped next to Lymdyr.

The animal extended it long, snake-like neck forward, and stuck its head up toward the open window. Phrynk stroked the coarse hair along its neck.

"Is he about ready to go?" Klyrk asked.

"I wish I knew where Byrty was." Lymdyr muttered. From the direction of the tavern, a wave of drunken laughter rolled out into the quiet night air.

"Ah! I should have known." He turned back toward the handler. "Are you okay with getting him in the saddle?"

"Sure, we take old folks for rides all the time. I'll just have him step out from the door of the car."

"Great, I'm going to get Byrty."

Lymdyr jogged off across the rutted road. The closer he got to the splintered wooden buildings, the louder the inebriated voices became. He pushed open the door and looked around. Over to the side of the dim, dingy room, two men sat hunched over their glass mugs of amber physt.

At the round table in the center of the room, Byrty, Jyrn the skeletal wagon driver, and his large, unkept wife sat. An empty pyryn bottle, and another that was three-quarters gone, kept them company.

Byrty picked up three pyramid shaped gaming pieces, shook them in her hand, then let them fall. Everyone around the table watched the pieces bounce across the wooden surface. It took them a moment to determine the outcome of the throw. Byrty slammed her hand on the table and let out a raucous laugh.

"Not again! I can't believe how bad my luck is tonight!" She rocked back in the chair, then suddenly caught sight of the railroad man.

"Lymdyr! Come and join us!" Byrty reached over and dragged the remaining empty chair away from the table. Lymdyr crunched across the sand covered floor and stood next to her. "These are my new friends. This is Myrnth, and her husband Jyrn. Sit down and have a drink!"

"I'd like to but, we're getting pyryst ready down at the cook's house. She lives right on the outskirts of town, probably, oh, a quarter mile west of here."

Byrty leaned heavily back in her chair. Her face was flushed and sweaty even though the air temperature in the stuffy room was on the cool side. "Whew! I could use some food. We're going to finish this game, then I'll meet you down there."

Lymdyr flashed a quick smile and turned to go.

"Oh! How's Phrynk doing?"

"Phrynk's fine," the railroad man replied over his shoulder.

Byrty let loose with another ear rending laugh. "Good! I'll see you in a little bit."

An hour later down at Gywdol's ramshackle house, the group was just finishing up dinner. Their host had begun clearing the table. Lymdyr got up out of his chair to assist. Once he and Gywdol were out of earshot in the kitchen, he leaned forward and whispered to her.

"I wish Klyrk would stop talking about the benefits of being a follower of Corian."

Gwydol set down the load of dishes she was carrying and smiled up at him. "Got dat right. Meesta Phyrnk didn't eat very much. You think he like my cookin?"

"Yeah, he did eat some of the tyf meat, and the other dish." Lymdyr set down the pile of dishes he was holding and followed her back into the dining room.

Klyrk gently laid his silverware onto a plate and was quiet for just a moment. After wiping his pouty lips, Phrynk leaned over the table in the direction of the children.

"Did you know that before this town was built, this whole area was under the control of a great Kuran chief?" The children shook their dark, diminutive heads. "His name was, uh. Oh, vryst! I can't remember what his name was, but I came through here on a drive years and years ago.

There were twelve of us, and we came riding down through that canyon east of town. There wasn't much pluge around here, and we had to get the mags a drink. As soon as we came out onto that flat area where the town is, we were met by a group of the Kuran warriors. They were not happy to see us on their land.

Before I could ride up to the head of our group, this cocky young driver jumped down off his styrn and walked up to try and get them to move out of the way. Well, that was a mistake. One of the warriors threw this animal bone scythe-like thing at him, and zip! His head fell clean off! Blood spurted everywhere!"

The children looked over at each other and grinned. Their wide, innocent eyes sparkled. While he and Gwydol collected the remaining dishes, Lymdyr sent a furtive glance toward the front door. Back in the kitchen, Gwydol set her load of dinner plates down, and laid her hand on his shoulder.

"What's wrong?"

"Huh? Oh, nothing."

"Nothing huh. You keepa lookin at the front door like you expecting something to come through it."

Lymdyr let go a tired laugh. "Yeah. I'm just wondering where the mid-healer is. She was supposed to meet us down here."

Gwydol wiped her hands on one of the threadbare towels and ventured a glance into the dining area. After making sure that neither Phrynk or Klyrk were watching, she gently grasped Lymdyr's hands, and hauled him over into the corner. Once fully out of view, she pulled his body tightly against hers. They gazed into each other's eyes for a moment.

"Thanks for bringing the syps and gynt. I was jus about out," she whispered. Her taut, dark cheeks pulled up into a huge smile. "You gonna come and see me tonight?"

He shook his head. "Maybe tomorrow. We've got to go down to talk to Ryk in the morning. I want to get an early start." He managed to get the last words out before a yawn consumed his face.

"You're tired. You should grab your people and go to bed."

"Yeah, it's been a long day." He leaned forward and kissed her. The smell and taste of pipe gynt combined with the physical pleasure of the kiss made him laugh.

"What so funny?" Gwydol asked after releasing him from her embrace.

"Oh nothing. We'll be back early in the morning."

Lymdyr walked back into the dining area and stood behind the old mag driver. "Mr. Phrynk, sorry to interrupt, but we need to get back to the car. We've got to get an early start tomorrow."

The children let go a collective "Aww." Klyrk rose up out of his chair.

"I was really enjoying the stories too, but you're right. We should turn in. It's been a long day."

They ushered the old mag drive out, got him propped back up on the styrn, and walked through the crystal desert darkness without speaking. Above them, the cloudless sky appeared as a swath of galaxies. The white smear of the comet hung motionless over the dark outline of hills to their right.

Right at the edge of town, they could see the glint of a fire reflecting off the shiny black side of the car. Ryslyn was squatting near a small campfire. He heard the thud of styrn paws and stood up.

"Ah, I was hoping that it was only you. Man, it's quite around here. 'Cept for the drunks over there." Rsylyn nodded in the direction of the tavern.

"Speaking of drunks. Have you seen Byrty?" Lymdyr asked. He walked up and held his hands over the fire.

"Ya know, I think she left with some round headed guy. Kind of big, walked real slow."

"That would probably be the bartender. Which way did they go?"

"Up around the back of the building. He had to help her up the stairs. She seemed like she was pretty hammered. Did you all have a nice pyryst?"

"Yes. Tomorrow morning, why don't you come down and eat nymyr with us. The car will be fine."

"Thanks." Ryslyn gazed off into the distance. "Sure is nice and peaceful here."

Out in the desert behind them, a nocturnal creature hooted loudly. Klyrk helped Phynk climb off the styrn and onto the small landing of the side door. The old mag driver looked down at the campfire.

"Well boys, we're riding clear to Smyra tomorrow, so better get a good night's sleep. Anybody seen my bed roll? I seem to have misplaced it."

"What's he talkin' about?" Ryslyn asked in a low voice.

"I think when he gets tired, his mind starts to let go. I better help him to bed." Lymdyr walked over and pulled himself up onto the narrow landing next to Phrynk. "I think your bed roll is in here. Follow me." He reached around, opened the cracked glass door, and entered the car. Phrynk shuffled in after him.

Hours later, Lymdyr rolled over for the hundredth time, trying to get comfortable. He lay on the upholstered bench in his salon listening to the lykrs chirp outside.

The sound of a pot being moved around in the kitchen persuaded him to rise. He pulled on his clothes and ambled down the corridor. Hazy light filtered through the window of Phrynk's salon. Ryslyn stood by the stove, attending to the tea kettle. He looked up with a start.

"Oh! You surprised me. I didn't think anyone was up yet. Good morning."

Lymdyr padded into the kitchen, rubbed his stubbly face, and leaned against the counter. "Good morning," he replied in a gravelly voice. His face had a slightly ashen look to it. Dark circles surrounded his usually, bright, animated eyes.

"You look tired. Not sleep well?"

Lymdyr shook his head. "That bench is just a little too narrow for me. How bout you?"

Ryslyn's face broke into a cheery grin. "I got a system worked out. I pull the cushions off the bench up by the front door and lay 'em out there in the pantry. It's nice and cozy."

"Maybe I'll try that too." Lymdyr gave his arms a stretch. "I suppose Byrty didn't show up."

"Nope."

"Dyth! Guess I'll have to go find her."

"The zyd'll be ready in just a second."

"Good. I'm going to wash up a little and put some clean clothes on."

"I'll bring you a cup."

A smile brightened up Lymdyr's haggard morning face. "Thanks." He patted Ryslyn's arm as he walked by. "It is nice to see you again. How is Plyny and the kids?"

"Fine. They're all doing just fine. I miss 'em when I go out on excursions like this, but a man's got to make a living somehow."

"That's the truth. I hardly even see my daughters these days."

Twenty minutes later, Lymdyr walked out into the dull morning light. There were no signs of life along the dilapidated main street. A short-legged animal with pointed ears and a striped tail ducked behind one of the buildings as he walked around the back of the tavern. Lymdyr ascended the rickety steps and stood on the uneven landing.

He pressed his ear against the weathered wooden door. From inside, the sound of a chair being moved across the floor drifted out. He stepped back and gave a gentle knock.

Heavy footsteps vibrated out to him. The door creaked open. In the diffuse morning light, the wide, puffy face of the bartender looked even more battered than usual. Their eyes met, and the door opened all the way.

"Suppose you're looking for her," the bartender said as he turned back toward the gynt infused interior. Lymdyr stuck his head in. A smile broke across his face. Byrty was sprawled out on her stomach, butt naked. A coarse blanket was balled up around her feet. One arm hung down off the couch and trailed onto the floor. Her pasty white face was turned toward the door.

"You could at least cover her up," Lymdyr said with a snicker.

"I tried, but she keeps tossing the blanket off." The bartender ambled back over to a small round table next to the wall and sat down. He took a drag from the rolled up gynt he had left burning on a plate.

"Want some zyd?"

Lymdyr shook his head. "No thanks. I need to get her up."

"Good luck. We was pretty late talkin'. I think she had a little too much fun last night."

"I'll bet she did." Lymdyr sent a quick glance over at the bartender's scarred, but now smiling face, then knelt down on the dusty floor. He laid a hand on the nurse's shoulder and gave it a gentle shake.

"Byrty! You need to get up. We're going to take Phrynk down to the river this morning."

She groaned and rolled up against the back of the couch. Her big floppy breasts hung down like two white deflated balloons, perfectly balanced by the pouch of her stomach.

"Byrty! Byrty! Come on! Time to get up." Lymdyr bent forward and shook her a little harder.

The acrid, sharp smell of pyryn rose up from her sleeping face. Byrty let go another rumbling groan and rolled back away from him.

"Doesn't look like she's getting up any time soon," the bartender commented.

"Well, I have things to do."

Lymdyr got to his feet and slipped out into the brisk morning air. After quietly closing the door behind him, he paused to take in the view. Far off to the northwest, the green swath of vegetation along the Hok stood out in stark contrast to the overall brownish-tan appearance of the rolling desert landscape. Long bands of mist floated along the valley cut by the river. Behind the gauzy layer, steep scrubby hills rose up. They were just beginning to catch the rising sun.

He cautiously descended the crooked staircase and made his way back to the car. Klyrk was leading four styrns over to the stone-lined well down the street, so Lymdyr adjusted his course to meet them.

"Good morning!" Klyrk said cheerily.

"Morning." Lymdyr replied in a decidedly un-cheery manner.

"Everything alright?"

"Not really. Byrty spent the night up there with the bartender." Lymdyr pointed back toward the row of buildings. "She's still dead drunk. You and I are going to have to take Phrynk down there by ourselves."

Klyrk lifted his gloved right hand and scratched the side of his cheek. "Well, that certainly complicates things."

"Yeah, is he up?"

"Not that I know of. I've been awake for about an hour. Didn't sleep worth a dyth last night. How about you?"

Lymdyr shook his head. "Me neither. I'm going to go get him up."

Chapter 33.

Phrynk was finally hauled out of bed, dressed, and brought down to Gwydol's house. The old mag driver ate so slowly that the trio didn't even get on the road till late morning. Small, winged creatures with metallic colored bodies buzzed in the warm air as they rode slowly down toward the river.

Lymdyr's stomach was wrapped up tightly into a ball. His wide forehead was creased with worry lines. The lack of sleep, absence of Byrty, and late start all combined to put him in a most foul mood. He was so absorbed in his own concern for the day that he completely missed Phrynk's entertaining commentary about his first trip to the area.

"We buried Pynyr back there somewhere, and the warriors escorted us right down this same road. Course back then, it was just a path between the scrub bushes......"

Klyrk rode right next to him, a grin etched across his wide, rugged face. He was enjoying listening to the old driver's stories immensely.

In an effort to speed up their journey, Lymdyr rode ahead of the other two travelers. For the fifth time since leaving Gwydol's house, he pulled back on the reins and slowed his styrn to allow them to catch up. When Phrynk was right next to him, Lymdyr leaned way over in the saddle.

"Excuse me, Mr. Phyrnk."

Upon hearing his name, the old driver broke off the commentary, and turned toward Lymdyr. "Yes?"

"Sorry to interrupt, but I just wanted to go over again what we'd like you to say to Ryk when we meet with him today."

"I know exactly what I'm going to say to him."

Phrynk straightened up in the saddle and gazed off down the road. His saggy, leathery face assumed a look of nobility. Klyrk let out a quick chuckle.

"Go ahead and finish your story Mr. Phrynk."

Lymdyr craned his neck back, shot an angry glance over at the handler, then returned his attention to the old driver.

"Actually, Mr. Phrynk, if you would, go ahead and tell me what you plan on saying to Ryk."

"Don't feel like talking about it."

Lymdyr's already stressed features took on a desperate appearance. His mouth became very dry. His sleep deprived hazel eyes blazed in the bright sunlight. He could feel his heart rate rise.

"Well, Mr. Phrynk, I really think that we should practice what you are going to say to him. That's the whole reason we brought you out here."

Phrynk swung his head around to meet Lymdyr's uneasy gaze. "I came out here to herd mags. Not sure what you're talking about. Fancy lookin' fella like you got no business being out here." He twisted his neck around to face Klyrk. "Ain't that right, Myrny."

Klyrk tried hard to stifle the laugh that was aching to burst out. He gave a fake cough to suppress it, then addressed the old mag driver in a matter-of-fact tone of voice.

"Now, Mr. Phrynk. We're not on a mag drive. That was a long time ago. We're here to have you convince Ryk to come back to Tyrl with us."

Rather than try and correct Klyrk's mostly accurate observation, Lymdyr decided to let it rest. The image of Byrty laying buck naked on the bartender's couch flashed through his addled mind. Anger welled up within him.

"Zym dyth it, sure would be nice to have her here! I'm docking her pay for that!" he muttered to himself. Lymdyr rode along stewing in his frustration. After a couple more minutes, his anxiety forced him to speak.

"Mr. Phrynk. I know you don't feel like practicing what you're going to say, but....."

"Alright! Don't chap your blyrt hole about it! Here's what I'm going to say. Ryk! Good to see you. How's the herd?" Phrynk looked over at Lymdyr's expectant face. "There. Happy?"

Klyrk couldn't prevent a choking laugh from spilling out. He bit his lip and turned toward Lymdyr. "Sorry."

The railroad man sent a scorching stare back at him, then returned his attention to Phyrnk. "Here is what we'd like you to say. Ryk, your expert roping services are needed back in Tyrl. We need you to train someone that is going to take part in a historic journey to the styrks. This will be one of the greatest accomplishments of your career." Lymdyr held his breath while waiting to see what Phyrnk's reaction would be.

"What a load of mag blyrt!" the old man replied with a snort. He gave the reins a little slap and continued on ahead.

Klyrk burst out in laughter. Tears squeezed out of his crow's feet lined eyes. They made little streaks through the fine dust already collecting on his cheeks.

"Sorry! I'm really sorry."

Lymdyr angled his styrn over toward the handler and was about to unload his anger on him when something caught his eye far down on the road ahead. Three dark objects appeared, bobbing in rhythm against the sandy, yellow ground. Klyrk saw them too. He slowed his styrn to a halt and stood up in the saddle for a better view.

"Looks like some riders. I'll go up and check on Phrynk."

Lymdyr held up his hand. "No, wait. He seems to be doing fine."

The old man was already about twenty yards ahead, riding along with his head hanging down slightly.

"I think this'll work well." Lymdyr gave his styrn a little jab in the ribs with his boot heels.

Klyrk nodded in agreement and slapped the reins gently. The two men trotted forward. They both stared fixedly at the old man riding smack in the middle of the road, and the three riders approaching.

As the riders grew near, Lymdyr recognized Ryk's dusky face. A glimmer of hope sprang up into his wrung out spirit. From down by the lowlands, a soft breeze that carried just a hint of the river's moisture blew across his overheated skin.

Ryk and his party rode right up next to the old man and pulled their styrns to a halt. Phrynk stopped also. No one spoke. Ryk stood up in the saddle and squinted in the blazing mid-day sun.

"Phrynk?"

The old man raised his head and looked over at the speaker. "Hello Ryk." A huge smile pulled up the sagging jowls of his face.

Ryk's eyes widened. He let go a laugh and shook his head in disbelief. "I can't believe it! What in Zym's name are you doing out here?"

Phrynk looked around at the scrubby desert vegetation, over at the rolling hills to the left, then stiffly turned his aged body around and pointed back at his escorts.

"I guess I'm with them."

Although still smiling, the old man's face now showed a trace of embarrassment. He sent a bewildered glance around in hopes of finding someone to offer more information.

Lymdyr and Klyrk came riding up behind him. The railroad man pulled his styrn up next to Phrynk, laid a hand on the old man's shoulder, and broke into a smile that could have melted icebergs.

"Ryk, men, good to see you." He paused momentarily to let the drama of the event sink in. "We brought Mr. Phrynk all the way out because he has something very important to talk to you about, Ryk. You boys heading into town?"

"Yeah. I got your telemessage. What exactly do you, I mean, does he want to talk about?" Ryk's voice was veiled with suspicion.

"If we can get him out of this cooking styrk, I think that would be a good idea. Mind if we head back down to camp?"

The three mag drivers conversed among themselves. Lymdyr watched their faces with the intensity of a fyrn stalking prey. He observed every twist of their mouth, every rise or lower of their eyes. The two other drivers both gave a nod, then continued on their way.

"Come on, let's go back to camp." Ryk swung his jet black styrn around.

Lymdyr's battered spirit soared to new heights. All his self doubt and uncertainty about the advisability of the mission evaporated into the hot, dry air. A newfound energy surged up within him.

Phyrnk poked the spotted styrn he was riding with the toe of his fancy red and white boots. The animal snorted and trotted up next to Ryk. Lymdyr reached over to punch Klyrk on the shoulder.

"See? I told you this would work out!"

The handler stared at the two friends riding off. "Ya, I guess maybe you were right."

When they reached the steep part of the trail, Ryk pulled his styrn to a halt. "Phyrnk, I'm gonna lead you down this hill. Okay?"

Beneath his wide brimmed hat, the old driver's greenish-brown eyes appeared to be glazing over. His down turned face was devoid of expression.

"Phrynk?" Ryk shot a worried glance over at Lymdyr.

"We need to get him out of the styrk. Go ahead and lead him down," the railroad man called out.

"Here we go. You might want to lean back a little when it starts getting steep." Ryk reached over and gently slid the reins out of Phrynk's limp grasp. He gave his styrn a little tap to the ribs and began jostling his way down the cut.

The other styrns dutifully followed Ryk along the dusty road. Their slow, uneven strides caused all the riders to sway back and forth in the saddle. Lymdyr patted the coarse, bristly neck of his styrn while it plodded along.

"Doing okay, Mr. Phrynk?" he called out as they entered the rutted switchback.

"This area used to be full of plygrs. You could hardly walk around a bush without spooking one. That's why the Kurans liked it so much. Oh, and look over there! Them rocks have still got the Kuran drawings on them. Amazing!"

Phrynk swung his portly frame around in the saddle and pointed at the red sandstone outcropping to his right. His styrn leaned left to compensate for the pitch of the cut. Lymdyr saw Phrynk's torso begin to swing over the side of the animal and spurred his styrn forward. He reached over to grab a fistful of the old man's leather vest just in time. Lymdyr had to brace himself in the saddle to haul him back.

"Easy there Mr. Phrynk! This is a pretty tricky spot. Better stay right in the middle of your styrn." Once the old man was again balanced, he let go.

"That was the toughest part. It evens out a little now." Ryk yelled over his shoulder.

They rounded the last switchback and Lymdyr let go a sigh of relief. The peppery smell of the salt bushes in the mid-day sun rose up and enveloped them. Ryk tossed the reins back up over the head of Phrynk's animal.

"Alright! That wasn't so bad. On to camp. Doing okay Phyrnk?"

"Yes, Ryk. I'm looking forward to getting out of this dyth styrk."

All three of the younger men chuckled. A few moments later, the group arrived at the tree shaded camp. Phyl, the scarred young helper, was re-arranging items in one of the wooden cargo boxes when Ryk came riding up.

"Hey, you're back sooner....." Phyl stopped in mid-sentence when the other three riders came into view. Ryk pulled his styrn over to the side and hopped down.

"Phyl, I think you know Mr. Lymdyr, and this here is........"

"My name's Klyrk," the handler offered with a tip of his hat.

"And this old timer here......Phyl, you know who this is?" The young helper shook his head. "This here is none other than Phrynk Nine Line his self!"

Phyl's jaw dropped. He looked over at Ryk's dusky, beaming face, then up to the old man.

"You aint' kiddin' are you?" His look of surprise blossomed into a huge grin. "Mr. Phrynk! I never in a zillion years figured you'd be coming down here to see us! Welcome. Here, let me help you down." He ran over, grabbed the reins, and held his hand up. Phrynk tried to swing a leg up over the back of his spotted animal, but failed.

"Fellas, I think I need a hand."

With considerable effort, the old man was safely deposited down onto the soft sand. He stood rather shakily. "I thank you much. Boy, is it nice to be back here at the Hok! Just look at the styrk glintin' off that pluge." Phyrnk pulled his wide, buff hat off and wiped the sweat off his head.

Lymdyr took a moment to scan the old man's serene face. Phrynk's eyes shone with happiness.

"It sure is pretty down here. I'd like to bring Cyrn down here. She'd love it," Klyrk commented while gazing wistfully up and down the tree shaded bank.

"So, I think I know why you're back." Ryk pulled the saddle off his styrn and stared hard into Lymdyr's dusty face.

The railroad man tried to maintain a businesslike appearance, but the joy of finally getting the old man down to the river was too much for him to hide. He broke into a fool of a grin.

"Yeah, not much point in my lying about that."

"Oh, hey! Mr. Phrynk! Let me help you." Phyl's exclamation took everyone by surprise. The young camp helper ran over to catch the old man before he could topple over.

"I think he needs a nap." Phyl led the old man over to a tent. He gently removed his hat, hung it on the tent pole, and guided Phrynk into the shady interior. "There, you just lay down, make yourself comfortable."

"I don't know what you were thinking, bringing that poor old guy down here, but it sure is good to see him." Ryk crossed his arms and looked over at the tent.

"These styrns need a drink. Okay if we just turn 'em loose?" Klyrk asked.

"Yeah, I need to take the mags out now that I'm here." Ryk turned and gave the handler a quick sizing up. "Ever run mags?"

A smile burst across Klyrk's wide, rugged face. "Why yes. Before I became a professional styrn wrangler, I run a few head. Need some help?"

Ryk suppressed the sarcastic sneer that was trying to form in response to Klyrk's less than humble response. "Sure, go ahead and pluge yours. Mr. Lymdyr, care to join us?"

"No, oh no, thanks. Think I better stay here with Phrynk. I'm the one responsible for him."

Ryk and the handler headed off down the path to the mag corral. Lymdyr and the young helper watched them leave.

"So Mr. Lymdyr, what brings you back down here?"

The railroad man pulled his sweat stained chocolate brown hat off and looked down into Phyl's goofy face. He tried hard to hide his disdain.

"Phyrnk has something he wants to ask Ryk. I figured it was the least I could do for the old guy." Lymdyr uncorked his ceramic water bottle and pounded half of it down.

"I see. You want some zyd? Heck, it's almost myrf time."

Phrynk slept solidly for three hours. During that time, Lymdyr grew tired of Phyl's simplistic conversation. He went off for a long walk and returned just as the sun had dropped mid-way down in the sky. Long, slanting shafts of gold hit the trees along the bank and sliced through the leafy shade. A constant layer of dust rose and fell in the alternating bands of light.

"Looks like Phrynk is awake," Lymdyr commented when he approached the smoky fire Phyl was tending.

The young camp helper laid down the wooden spoon he had been stirring an iron pot with and rose to his feet. On his way over to the tent, Phyl accidently knocked the spoon off its resting place. It flipped up and landed gracefully in the sand.

"Mr. Phyrnk! How ya doin? Did you have a good nap?"

334

The venerable old driver sat like Buddha under the bodi tree. His short, stout legs were splayed out from his sagging belly. His rounded shoulders heaved down by gravity.

"Ya, ya, ya, I'm okay. Help me up," he rasped.

"Let's put your boots on first." Phyl carefully slid the custom made red and white foot ware on the old man, then pulled him to his feet.

"Boy, I haven't ridden a styrn in years, and I can really feel it. What smells so good?" Phyrnk rubbed his back and took a long sniff of the late afternoon air.

"Are you hungry? I made some stew." Phyl led the old man over to the smoldering fire and eased him down onto a log.

The snort of a styrn coming from the direction of the corral announced Ryk and Klyrk's return. From his place by the fire, Lymdyr watched them amble along the narrow trail. Ryk was in the lead. It was obvious by the way he kept turning back toward the handler and nodding that Klyrk was expounding about some subject.

"Bet I know what he's going on about," the railroad man said with a smile.

Right at the edge of the trees, the two riders jumped down from their styrns, pulled the bridles and saddles off, and let the animals go. The styrns snorted at each other, then cantered off toward the river.

"So you see, Corians really have the ultimate plan. We live this life of service, and when we die, we get to live on our own planet," Klyrk concluded.

"Yep, sounds like quite the plan," Ryk replied. He shot a glance over at Lymdyr. His dark tan face pulled up in a grin. "Mr. Phrynk! How goes it?"

"Good, just woke up, and we're about to partake of some of this boy's cooking."

"Well, don't get all excited yet. You better taste it first."

The two burly fryns came plodding up the trail from the corral. Both animals lopped along with their long, pointed tongues hanging out. Once they had entered camp, the animals snapped to attention. Their relaxed, "end of a long day" posture soon shifted to upright and alert. A low, rumbling growl vibrated from the bigger of the two. It fluffed its slivery, blue mane out in a threatening manner.

Phyl had just picked the wooden spoon up off the sand. The growl from the male fyrn caused him to spin around.

"Uh oh!" Just as the bigger of the animals dug its paws into the sand and began to charge the visitors, Phyl stepped into its path and held up his hands. "Whoa, Persin! These is friends!"

His effort was just a tad too late. Sand flew up as the fryn galloped toward the group. An uneven streak of hackles rose up along its muscular back. The other fryn followed suit. Both of them made an arc around Ryk and Klyrk. The handler froze in place. Ryk continued coiling the rope in his hand and smiling with a touch of amusement.

The bigger fryn stopped right in front of Lymdyr. It braced itself with its front legs and barked ferociously. The smaller animal stopped next to the fire pit. It approached Phrynk in an aggressive manner, but seemed to recognize that he didn't present a threat. The hackles along its back dropped. Its triangular ears lowered. When the old man reached out his hand, the fryn gave a slight wag of its serpentine tail.

Phyl strode over had whacked the bigger animal hard at the base of its tail with the wooden spoon. "Persin! I said leave...." His words were suddenly cut off when the animal whipped around mouth open and ready to strike. Phyl let go a little yip of terror. The fryn blinked its big brown eyes twice, then cowered in shame. The young man pointed over toward the tree behind Phrynk.

"Go! Bad fryn!"

Once the animals had moved off, Phyl brushed most of the grit off the spoon with his finger, then finished cleaning it with his linen pant leg. He spooned some of the stew into a wooden bowl, knelt down, and handed it to Phrynk.

"Hope you like it. Sorry about the fyrns," he said with a smile.

"Thank you, young sir. It's okay, they was just doing their job."

Phyl's dirt streaked face lit up. He watched the old mag driver slowly dip into the bowl, blow on the steaming contents, then slide the brown mixture into his mouth.

"Not bad," Phrynk observed after chewing through his bite.

Phyl rose to his feet. "Who's next? I made a big batch."

Lymdyr stood motionless. His composure was quite rattled after the fryn's aggressive actions. Under his richly embroidered shirt, his stomach rumbled. He picked up one of the bowls and held it out.

"I'll take some of that." Once his bowl had been filled, he carried it over to where Phrynk was seated, and dropped down onto the sand. Lymdyr took a small taste. "Yep, not bad."

After working his way through half of the bowl, he leaned over and spoke to the old driver. "Mr. Phrynk. I think this would be a good time to ask Ryk about coming back to Tyrl to help us."

The old man continued to methodically transfer the bland, gloppy mixture from the bowl to his sagging mouth. He didn't respond to Lymdyr's words. A drip of the gravy-like stew rolled out of his dry lip. "Good stuff."

Lymdyr consumed his bowl with mechanical efficiency. He wasn't even aware of the taste. All his attention now was focused on getting Phrynk to make his pitch to Ryk. As the seconds ticked by, the railroad man's anxiety level began to rise.

Chapter 34.

The group ate in silence. The only sounds were the constant background rush of the river, and the occasion bellow of the mags in their corral downstream. Long shadows began to creep in around the edges of camp. The sun had just dropped below the highest peak to the south.

Lymdyr set his empty bowl down. He opened his mouth and was about to launch into a presentation when a loud, gutsy "Yahoo!" rang out from the main trail off to his left.

Everyone but Phrynk turned to see from whence the call came. Out of the steadily lengthening shadows, Byrty came trotting up on a red styrn. Her tough, but pleasant features shone with pride.

"Hey gents! Didn't know if I'd find you or not! I asked a fella in the store where you were camped. He said take the road down and follow it till ya hit the river. Looks like he was right!" She swung the lanky animal off into the sand and jumped down. "Did I miss pyryst?"

"No ma'am," Phyl said sheepishly. "There's still plenty here."

Byrty looked over at the ragged grey eyepatch and pronounced scar running down the young man's face. Her features assumed a look of motherly concern.

"Why, thank you. My name is Byrty, by the way." She began to tie the reins around a tree.

"No need to do that," Klyrk called out. "Just pull the bridle and saddle off, here let me help you." He set the mostly empty wooden bowl down and leaned forward, preparing to stand.

Byrty held up her hand. "Nope. Stay right there. I got it covered." She removed the tack from the animal, gave the flat part of its head at the base of the stubby horns a stroke, then watched it lope off toward the river.

"Mr. Phrynk! Did you miss me?" she commented on her way over to the fire.

The old mag driver sat staring in the general direction of the flickering flames. His big, swollen knuckled hands held the empty bowl between his splayed legs. Byrty squatted down next to him and laid a hand on his slumped shoulder.

"Hey! Phrynk old buddy! You in there?"

He slowly rotated his head of wispy white hair and gazed into her eyes. "Ya, I'm here."

She broke into huge smile, then looked over at Lymdyr. "Has he been drinking pluge today?"

Lymdyr gave a shrug and sent a questioning glance over at Klyrk. The handler shrugged back.

"Maybe a little bit," the railroad man answered.

Byrty rose to her feet and stood with hands on hips. "Well, he needs to drink a lot of pluge or he gets problems down here." She pointed toward her crotch.

Klyrk jumped to his feet, retrieved the ceramic water bottle from his saddlebag, and carried it over to Phrynk. While the old man drank, Byrty walked over to the fire, and looked down into the large skillet perched on the rocks of the fire ring.

"Mmmm, smells good. Got an extra bowl?"

Phyl dug another dark wooden receptacle out of the storage box along with a spoon and carried it back to her. He handed it over under the scrutiny of her gaze. The scruffy young man shifted his feet nervously as she examined his long purple scar.

"Thank you. Say, have you had a healer look at that injury?"

"No ma'am. There ain't but one in town, and he ain't that good. It's fine really, just about healed." Phyl tried to force a smile, but was only partially successful.

Byrty leaned over and set the bowl on a rock. She dusted her hands off, then turned back toward him. "Let's just take a little peek at it, okay?"

Phyl glanced around the group. He tucked his lips in tight. "Uh, it's really fine. I got to gather up the...."

Byryt reached out and laid a hand on his narrow shoulder. "There'll be plenty of time to clean up. You just sit right down, and let me take a look, okay? I'm a mid healer." She applied more than a small amount of pressure, forcing Phyl down to a sitting position on the log behind him. Byrty straightened back up and motioned toward Lymdyr to follow her.

When they reached the spot where she had dropped her pack, Byrty slid a bottle of clear liquid out, and held it high. "Thought we might need a little something to celebrate Phrynk's visit!" She lowered her arm and swung the bottle hard into the railroad man's stomach. Lymdyr let out a little oof. "Here, crack this one and pass it around."

After taking the bottle from her, he leaned forward and whispered under her tan colored hat. "After you finish with Phyl, I'm gonna need your help. I've been trying to get Phrynk to have his little talk with Ryk, but he's not tuned in right now. If you can get him to engage the objective of this whole whacky trip, I would be oh, so grateful." He added just a touch of sugar to his last words.

"Sure thing boss," she snapped before striding off across the sand.

Lymdyr eased the cork out the bottle with his very fancy gyr horn-handled knife and popped it open. "Life is short." He tilted it up and took a modest drink. The liquid burned all the way down his throat.

Klyrk sauntered over to the fire ring, and picked up the scorched, battered tea kettle. "I sure would like some zyd. You got any?"

From his seat nearby, Phyl stuttered out a reply. "Over th-th-there in that box with the lid open. It's in a round metal container."

Byrty returned to where Phyl was sitting and gently slid the putrid eye patch off. Her middle-aged face became serious and focused. "Klyrk, give me your pluge bottle."

The handler walked over to deliver it, then made his way back toward the supply boxes. Byrty pulled the edge of her plaid shirt out, poured some water on it, and began swabbing the wound on Phyl's face.

"Lymdyr! Where's that pyryn?" Her loud, commanding question snapped him to attention.

"Right here! Hang on." He jogged over and handed her the open bottle. She tossed back a good sized drink.

Lymdyr watched her deftly clean the wound. A lopsided grin appeared on his face. With the slanting, shadowy light of sunset illuminating Byrty's strong features, his addled mind conjured up an image of her dressed in a business suit, and sporting a short, masculine haircut.

Steam started to drift out of the kettle Klyrk had set on the fire. The handler dumped some loose zyd into a cup and held it aloft. "Anybody else want some?"

Phrynk slowly and ponderously hauled himself to his feet. Klyrk and Lymdyr both made involuntary movements in his direction. To everyone's surprise, he managed to stand.

"I believe I could use a cup." Phyrnk dusted off the seat of his pants and limped around to where Byrty was attending to her patient. He stopped and patted Phyl on the shoulder. "You're one lucky guy to have a pretty mid-healer help you out here."

Phrynk cracked a grandfatherly smile. He continued ambling over to where Klyrk stood holding two metal cups. The old mag driver took one from him and muttered a low thanks. Klyrk whispered something into his ear. Phrynk nodded, took a drink, then casually made his way around to where Ryk was standing. The old man stopped right next to him, gazed down at the fire, and hitched his crooked thumb in his belt.

"Surprised you're not helping yourself to that pyryn."

Ryk took a moment to respond. His face had a stillness and air of contemplation to it. "Don't really feel like drinkin."

"I guess you must be sick or something."

Phrynk's joke brought a polite laugh out of both men. A faint smile broke across Ryk's face. "Naw, feel fine. Just got a lot on my mind. Know what I mean?"

"I sure do. What say you and I go for a little walk?"

"Sure."

"Ow!" Phyl screeched from across the fire. "Zym! Feels like you're peeling the skin right off."

Byrty stopped dabbing the wound and sat back on her heels. "That's about the best I can do."

The young man rubbed the area along his scar. "Thank you ma'am. There's some stew left. Are you hungry?"

"Naw, once I start drinking, my appetite goes away."

Phyl picked the crusted pan up off the fire and called out over his shoulder. "Hey Ryk! Think I should save the rest of this for the boys?"

From his place by the river bank, Ryk stopped walking, and yelled out a quick answer. "No. I don't expect them back anytime soon. Flyr's been chasing that little Lymyr woman around lately. He's probably over there tryin' to sweet talk her. Who knows, maybe he'll even get lucky."

All of the group laughed at Ryk's comment except for Lymdyr. The possibility of Gwydol being romanced by the other mag driver made him supremely uncomfortable. He took another drink of the pyryn.

Ryk helped his old friend down the rutted path to the river. Once they broke out of the trees, the sky opened up above them. A band of high clouds streaked diagonally across the horizon creating the appearance of a giant watercolor painting. The leading edges shone bright crimson which bled into orange, slowly diffusing to purple.

At the end of the path, a wide, water smoothed boulder poked up from the bank. The river had hollowed out a comfortable semi-circular depression on the outside edge. Ryk eased his old friend down into it.

In front of the two men, the river slid by. It murmured, whooshed, and lapped happily. They both sat staring at the peaceful scene for several moments.

The setting would have been perfect save for the presence of the tiny, winged creatures floating about on the breeze. For an object no larger than a grain of sand, they could deliver a surprisingly noticeable bite.

"Sure is pretty here," Phrynk commented.

"Yep, sure is."

The old mag driver reached over and gave Ryk a pat on the knee. "Well, I suppose you know that I didn't come down here to jaw about the scenery?"

"Klyrk already told me what the purpose of you all coming down here was." Ryk broke into a grin which deepened the weathered lines around his eyes. He swatted away a small cloud of the biting creatures.

"So you know all about the, oh, what's the name of that project Lymdyr is head of?"

"Dymran," Ryk muttered with just a touch of contempt.

"That's right, Dymran. What do you think about that Lymdyr fella?"

"He's okay, I guess. Always seems to have some kind of big plan cookin'. He can be a little pushy."

Phrynk listened to Ryk's words and nodded. "Well, I don't know a whole lot about the project, but I do know that they are wanting to send some people up into space. Something about some kind of voices that they heard coming from out there? What do you think about that?"

Ryk let go a short laugh and rocked back onto the smooth surface of the boulder. "What do I think about that?" I think anybody that allows themselves to be shot up into space is crazy!" Both men sat grinning in the fading light. Ryk pulled his knees up against his big wide chest and let his chin rest on them. With difficulty, Phrynk raised the cup to take a drink.

"Yeah, I think it's kind of crazy, too. But ya know, people have done crazy things and had them turn out to be successful ventures for a long time. Think about Myrt First Line. If he hadn't tried to build the first steam engine, and had it blow up, where would we be now?

The way I see it, you have a chance to really make a name for yourself, and mag drivers all over Ulutrita if you help these people out. I mean, think about! When folks imagine mag drivers, what kind of image comes to mind? Dirty, rowdy, not well educated guys that come into town four times a year, and chase their daughters around, right?"

"Right."

"This is your chance to improve that. Ya gotta do it Ryk!" Phyrnk's raspy voice now took on a tone of urgency.

A thick cloud of the biting creatures blew up from the algae scented river. Both men swatted fiercely.

"I suppose you're right. I've never done nothing to help anybody else except me. I was thinkin' about getting leave from the company anyway. I met this cute little barmaid in Tyrl last year. We hit it off pretty good, and when I came into town for the roundup, vyrst if she didn't tell me she's pregnant with my baby."

Phyrnk stopped swatting long enough to reach over and give Ryk a hard slap on his muscular thigh. "Well, there you go! So that's another reason to go into Tyrl, and now you can make a name for yourself and have something for the kid to be proud of. Son, I'd love to sit here and jaw with you, but these nygnts ain't givin' us no peace!"

"Yep, let's head back." Ryk slid off the boulder and held out a hand. "Hopefully Phyl has a nice smoky fire going." He pulled Phyrnk gently to a standing position, then led the way back up the rutted trail. While he walked along, Ryk struggled with his desire to vocalize his love and respect for the old man, but just couldn't bring himself to do it.

Mid-way up the trail, Phyrnk stopped. His chest heaved in and out. "Dyth! This is steep." The two of them had to stop several times along the trail to let the old man rest.

Back at camp, Byrty and Phyl were bent over a small wooden box, examining its contents. Klyrk was sitting on a log drinking his zyd and staring into the smoldering fire. Lymdyr sat opposite him. He had been glancing down toward the river periodically. When the two mag drivers returned, he got to his feet.

"Ah, there they are." The anxious look on his face prompted Klyrk to speak.

"Relax, will ya. Ya been looking down there and fidgetin' since they left."

Lymdyr ran a hand over his spiky, short hair. "There's a lot riding on this little pleasure cruise, my friend. I envy you for just being responsible for the styrns." One of the tiny biting creatures landed on his neck. He smashed it instantly. "Zym! These nygynts are obnoxious!"

"Ya, I don't mind 'em all that much."

Ryk led the old mag driver back to the fire ring, one step at a time. Lymdyr wrung his hands while he watched their slow and ponderous approach. He searched both of their faces for any sign of how the discussion went. Phyrnk's face showed nothing but fatigue. His lower lip hung down as did his pouchy jaw.

"I believe I need to sit down," the old man said between gasps.

Byrty set down the bottle she was working on, walked over and looped her free hand around Phyrnk's arm. Ryk supported his other. They eased him down onto the log set on the north side of the fire ring. His whole body seemed to be pulled down by the power of gravity. The shoulders slumped. His big arthritic hands hung off his wrists.

"Boy, old timer! I think we've really tired you out this time," Klyrk called out from across the fire ring.

Phrynk gave a weak, embarrassed smile, but didn't answer.

"Ya know, I was thinking that seeing as how it's almost dark, maybe you all should just camp down here with us tonight," Phyl offered. His high pitched voice lifted with hopefulness.

Lymdyr's face contracted into a frown. Camping down at the river was the last thing on his mind. Before he could voice his opposition, Byrty spoke up.

"Why, that's very nice of you to offer, Phyl. I think we should probably get Mr. Phrynk back up to the car, though. I'm guessing that it gets kind of cold down here at night."

"It's not bad. We got extra blankets."

"I think Byrty is right. Mr. Phrynk looks like he has had it for the day. Klyrk, will you saddle up the styrns?" Lymdyr asked in a quiet, somber voice.

"Sure thing." The handler pulled off his leather glove, stuck two fingers into his mouth and let go an ear-splitting whistle.

Lymdyr shifted his gaze over to Ryk. The mag driver was staring down at his old friend, serenity and calmness still spread across his dusky features. Lymdyr took a deep breath. He couldn't wait any longer.

"So Ryk, have you made a decision on whether you want to come up and help us out?"

The mag driver slowly shifted his gaze from the old man over to Lymdyr. His difficult to read expression made the railroad man's heart rate began to rise. Ryk took a step forward and laid his hand on Phrynk's soft, mushy shoulder.

"Well Mr. Lymdyr, my old friend here thinks that this might be my big chance to make a name for us shiftless, no-good mag drivers, so I guess, yes, I have made a decision." The silence after his initial response grabbed everyone's attention. They all remained frozen in place waiting for him to finish. Ryk sent a quick glance down at Phrynk, then snapped his head back to address the group.

"I'm gonna do it."

Lymdyr released a massive whoosh of breath. His legs buckled slightly. Byrty let go a whoop that echoed off the bluff behind them. Phyrnk craned his neck around and looked up at Ryk with a kindly but exhausted smile.

"I knew you would," he whispered.

Chapter 35.

From the direction of the mag corral, loud snorts and the thud of wide pads announced the arrival of the styrns.

"Jyzr! Kym! Where you been?" Klyrk called out.

The burly chocolate brown styrn, and the more slightly built spotted animal trotted up next to him. They gave him a nuzzle with the flat part of their bristly heads. Both styrns were careful not to jab him with their short, blunt horns. After their show of affection had ceased, they cast a glance around at the group. Their big, long lashed eyes blinked with vacant, dumb animal happiness. They were ready to leave.

Phrynk held up his arm. "Think I'm going to need a little help, if you would."

Ryk reached down and pulled the old man to his feet. Phyrnk teetered unsteadily.

Byrty took another swig of the bottle she was holding, then made a clicking sound with her tongue. The red styrn had been cavorting around in the trees with Ryk's jet black animal. It responded to Byrty's audible command by slowly trotting over to her and bending its long serpentine neck down to nuzzle the rider.

"That's a good girl."

"Alright, let's all get mounted up while we still got a smidge of daylight left," Klyrk called out from where he stood. With Byrty's assistance, the styrns were saddled up and ready to go in record time. Ryk helped his old friend slowly make his way across the soft sand to the waiting mount.

Klyrk stood next to the spotted styrn. When the two men arrived, he let go of the reins and held out his hand. "Mr. Ryk, pleasure to meet you. Don't know if I'll be able to link up with you when you come to Tyrl, but if you have some free time, come on out to the Wyn Hill styrn ranch. I'd love for you to meet my wife."

Ryk shook his hand. "I have the feeling I'll be pretty busy, but thanks for the offer."

Byrty led her styrn over to where the three men were standing. She laid a hand on Phyrnk's shoulder and looked right into his slack jawed face.

"Mr. Phrynk, ready to ride home?"

The old mag driver's eyelids were mostly closed. Byrty's question caused them to lift slightly. "Where we goin?"

"Back home. It's time to leave."

Phrynk gave half a nod and stared over at the white pile of ash in the fire ring. Phyl came jogging up.

"Mr. Phrynk, it's been a pleasure to meet you." The old mag driver mumbled something not quite like a reply. Phyl titled his head back and whispered to the nurse.

"Are you sure he's alright?"

"I hope he's just tired."

"Okay Mr. Phrynk. Up we go!" Klyrk reached down and grabbed the old man's leg behind the knee. He waited till Ryk hopped up into the stirrup on the other side of the waiting animal, then both men hauled Phyrnk into the saddle. The spotted styrn underneath him snorted and stamped its long toed-feet into the sand, which caused Phrynk swung listlessly back and forth.

"He certainly don't look too steady," Klyrk commented just under his breath.

"No, he don't," Ryk agreed.

"Mr. Lymdyr! You and I are going to need to ride next to him on the way back," Klyrk shouted across the camp.

The railroad man was just finishing up securing the saddle on his tan colored styrn. Lymdyr's super-efficient mind was still agonizing about Ryk's mention of his fellow mag driver's fondness for Gwydol. Klyrk's instructions snapped him back to the task at hand.

"Huh? Oh, yeah. Sure."

Ryk strode around to where Lymdyr was standing and held out his hand. "Mr. Lymdyr, guess I'll be seeing you in a couple days."

"Yes, sir. The sooner you can come on in, the better." Lymdyr shook Ryk's hand, then reached into his vest, and pulled out a thick orange card. "Here, this pass'll get you in."

The mag driver scissored it between two fingers and held it up to his face. "Thanks. I'll need to contact the company to...."

"Already been done."

Ryk shifted his gaze from the card over to Lymdyr's shining hazel eyes. "Swell. After I arrange things with Kyrg and Flyr, they're not going to be too happy about me leaving, but.....I'll pack up my gear and head to the city."

He cast a wistful glance around at the now dark, peaceful surroundings. In the hills toward town, a pack of animals howled mournfully. "I sure will miss this place."

After several more goodbyes were exchanged, the visitors mounted up, and began maneuvering their styrns toward the trail. Ryk walked over to where Phrynk sat motionless in the saddle. He patted his friend on the thigh.

"Hey old timer! You ready to ride?"

Phrynk grasped the reins and looked down at him. "Not sure I'm ready for anything at this point." He gazed out at the dark tunnel of trees that outlined the exit trail, then back down toward Ryk. With a ponderous effort, the old man held his hand out.

Ryk reached up and gave it a bone crushing squeeze. "Awful nice to see you. When I get to Tyrl, I'll look you up." He moved forward and grabbed the bridle. "I'll walk ya as far as the road."

The group rode single file through the now quite dark tunnel of trees. Klyrk was in the lead, followed by Byrty, Lymdyr, and Phrynk bringing up the rear. With amazing dexterity, Ryk rolled a gynt cigarette with one hand. He stuck it between his lips, sparked the striker, and puffed away.

Lymdyr turned in the saddle several times as they plodded up out of the bottomland. In the blackness, he could just make out Phrynk's wide silhouette slumped forward, and the glowing cherry of Ryk's gynt.

Once they broke out of the trees, Lymdyr let go a sigh of relief. The twinkling stars gave off just enough light to bring out the details of their surroundings. He took a last look at the Kuran petroglyphs etched into the brown sandstone rocks along the road.

At the beginning of the switchbacks, Ryk ventured a glance up at Phyrnk's expressionless face. "Lymdyr! Hold up for a minute." He let go of the reins and jogged up next to where the railroad man waited.

"Boy, I don't know about the old fella. Doesn't seem like he's all with it at this point. You're gonna need to watch him really close."

Lymdyr rose up and shifted himself around in the saddle. He looked back at the motionless, piled up form of the old man.

"Mr. Phrynk? Hey!" He waved his arm in the air. The old man offered no indication of acknowledgment. Lymdyr turned back around and yelled up the line. "Klyrk! Come back down here. I think the old boy is asleep in the saddle."

The handler trotted back down the road, spun his styrn around, and pulled up next to Phynk. He reached over and poked the old man on the arm. There was no response.

"I do believe you're right. This is going to be an interesting ride back. Lymdyr, pull up on the other side."

The sound of rocks tumbling down through the dry scrubby vegetation above drew the group's attention. All of the styrns flexed their great round nostrils, sucking in whatever scent they could detect. After a couple minutes, two riders appeared out of the starlit darkness.

"Oh, it's just Flyr and Kyrg," Ryk said with a laugh. He waited till his partners stopped beside the stalled caravan, then poked his hat back, and looked up at them.

"Hey, Boys. How was town?"

"Same as usual," the dark haired one replied. He swung his head up and down the line. "You going with them?"

"Nope. Just walking them this far."

Kyrg nodded, then urged his styrn on down the trail. His light haired companion followed.

"Not real personable, are they?" Byrty piped up.

"No, not particularly. Well, guess I'll head back. See you all in a couple days." Ryk patted Phrynk on the leg and walked back to camp.

Lymdyr relaxed just a touch after seeing the riders pass. His chances of spending the night with Gwydol seemed much better now.

He and Klyrk positioned their mounts right beside Phyrnk's animal. The old man's slightly bowed legs bounced back and forth between the coarse, bristly flanks of the styrns as they plodded along. For the next twenty minutes, Lymdyr and Klyrk fought to keep him upright in the saddle. Byrty rode behind them singing obscene camp songs and swigging away at the bottle of pyryn.

While they were negotiating a curve in the road, Phyrnk slid toward the handler. Klyrk was riding just slightly ahead when he saw the old man begin to topple. Out of desperation, he leaned way over in the saddle and grabbed Phyrnk's vest with his left hand. Klyrk managed to keep the old man from falling over, but he let out a sharp yell in the process. Lymdyr directed his styrn right up next to Phyrnk. He pulled the old man back up to a more or less sitting position.

"You okay?"

Klyrk released his grip and rubbed his left shoulder. "Dyth! I think I tore a muscle! This shoulder has been gimpy for years."

Byrty rode up next to Klyrk, then reached out toward him. He recoiled and sent an angry, flashing look her way.

"Don't touch me!"

"Zym! I was just tryin' to help." Byrty pulled up beside Lymdyr. "What's his problem?" she asked in a not so quiet voice.

The railroad man sat in the darkness trying to control his feelings of frustration and futility. He was just about to comment on Byrty's question when out of his periphery, he saw Phrynk's slumped body topple off the styrn's backside. Lymdyr slapped the reins and maneuvered around just in time to place a hand against the old man's back.

"Whoa! That was close." Using only his legs, Lymdyr guided his styrn around, and pushed Phrynk upright.

Klyrk stopped rubbing his shoulder, then looked around at the uneven landscape. "This just ain't cutting it! He's getting more and more tired as we go. I'm thinking that we should probably just go off in the bushes, lay out our styrn blankets, and call it a night."

Lymdyr pondered the suggestion. The thought of sleeping on the ground with all sorts of things crawling around didn't appeal to him at all. He was looking forward to curling up next to Gwydol.

"You know, it's going to get pretty cold tonight. I don't think it'd be a good idea to have the old man sleep out. I'm sure Byrty would be fine with it. With all that pyryn flowing through her veins, she could sleep in a fyrf drift."

Klyrk let go a snorting laugh and turned to face Lymdyr. "Okay, but let's get this disaster over with as soon as we can. To be truthful, I'm pretty sick of dealing with her and the old man."

Lymdyr nodded. "Actually, I sick of all three of you klynkers!" He gave a slap of his reins and continued on.

Halfway back to town, Phrynk lost his ability to remain upright. The only way Lymdyr and the handler could keep him in the saddle was to take turns riding next to the old man and allow him to lean against them.

The styrns became agitated with having to walk so close to each other. Things finally came to a head when Klyrk's chocolate brown animal reached over and sunk his teeth into the neck of Phrynk's mount. In a panic, the spotted styrn jerked away, colliding with the one Lymdyr was riding. The quick motion sent Phyrnk sliding out of the saddle.

"Dyth royal Zym!" Klyrk roared. He caught the old man by the shoulders and strained to keep a grip. Klyrk's back was bent like a compressed spring. He had to jam his boots into the stirrups to keep from getting pulled over.

"Kick that klynking rag of a styrn back over here!"

Lymdyr managed to get his animal under control, then reached out with his boot and gave the spotted styrn a good hard shove on the flank. With amazing speed, the animal bent its flexible neck and tried to take a bite out of his leg. Lymdyr swung his linen pant leg out of the way just in time.

"Holy blyrt!"

The spotted animal barred its teeth and snapped the air as a warning. Klyrk managed to push the old man back up to an upright position. In the darkness, Lymdyr could see the pain etched on the handler's face. His sun burnished skin shone with sweat.

"Alright! That last move really hurt. Dyth it! I'm ready to lay the old fool out over there under those bushes!" Klyrk reached down and massaged the small of his back. He tried to arch his spine, but stopped halfway through the exercise.

"I didn't agree to any of this!"

"Listen, Gwydol's house is only about a mile and a half up the road...Oooops!" Lymdyr saw Phrynk's pile of laundry-like form begin to fall toward him and nudged his styrn closer. With both arms extended, he stopped the old man's fall, then pushed him upright.

"Like I said, Gwydol's house is just up the road. I'll make a compromise. Let's drop him off there instead of trying to get him back to the car. I really appreciate all......"

"Klynk appreciation! You hired me to get you down to see Ryk and back up to town, that's it! I'm gonna half to figure out what all this physical exertion is worth. I'm not a young man anymore you know!"

Klyrk and Lymdyr stared at each other in the darkness. Both their faces burned with the fatigue and frustration of the day. The handler rubbed his back again and sent a furtive glance up the empty road.

"It's really more like two and a half miles, but who gives a blyrt at this point!"

"So, we get him to the house?"

"Yeah, yeah, yeah. Let's go."

"If we both brace him, I think it'll be easier."

Lymdyr pulled his styrn right up next to the one Phrynk was riding. He reached out with his right arm and steadied the old man. Klyrk rode around to the other side and did the same. The heat from the tired, lathered animals rose up in a humid, powerful stinking cloud. Lymdyr could feel sweat roll down his leg.

Klyrk pulled his arm away and gave it a shake. "My Zym dyth arm is going numb. I swear! I'm gonna kill these stupid beasts and leave them for the blyzrs to eat."

Forty-five minutes later, the group arrived at Gwydol's junk strewn yard. Byrty continued on to the car. Lymdyr and Klyrk directed their styrns off into the deep dust beside the road.

From over by the house, the two mangy fyrns jumped up from their sleeping spots and charged. They barked furiously, domed heads lowered. The agitated styrns would have none of it. They lunged for the attacking animals. Lymdyr jumped down off his mount just before it bolted after one of the fyrns. The spotted styrn Phyrnk was riding did the same.

The old man pitched right off its rear end. Lymdyr raced over and caught his falling body. The railroad man staggered back, but managed to hang onto Phyrnk's torso. A poof of dust rose up when the old man's finely crafted red and white boots hit the ground.

Across the yard, Klyrk was trying to regain control of his panicked beast. The big brown styrn kept circling around one of the fryns. Every so often it would rear up, and swing its front paws out at the snarling, low slung animal.

Lymdyr managed to drag the old man up to the porch just as the creaking door opened a crack.

"Who out there?" a raspy voice called out from the interior.

"It's me!"

"Who me?"

"Lymdyr!" the railroad man's answer came out as more of a hoarse sort of grunt.

Gwydol opened the door and stepped out onto the sloping porch. In response to the mayhem surging out in the yard, she let go an ear splitting whistle.

"Nyn! Grotem be syszr!"

The two fyrns tucked their long tails between their legs and crawled back to the dusty holes where they slept. Klyrk's styrn stopped whirling. It stood wide eyed and panting. From their resting spots next to the house, the fyrns offered one last short growl. Gwydol looked down at Phrynk's motionless body.

"He dead?"

"No, just sound asleep."

Klyrk slid off his overheated beast and patted its neck. The animal stared out at the fyrns curled up in their dust pits. It let loose a low rumble.

"It's okay Jyzr."

The handler released his grip on the reins, and the styrn trotted over to stand with the other two in their place beside the road. Klyrk ambled up to the porch. Both fyrns growled and rose up as if to charge.

"Grotem be syszr!" Gwydol commanded in a loud whisper. The two ragged animals circled themselves back down into their shallow holes and grumbled quietly.

"You wanna bring him in?"

"Yeah." Lymdyr firmed up his grip under Phrynk's shoulders.

Klyrk stiffly bent down, grasped the red and white boots, and lifted. They carried the old man into the dimly lit living room.

"Let's put him on the couch," Klyrk suggested. He swung around the end of the scrap wood coffee table.

"No! Let's put him in the big chair over there," Lymdyr countered. He wanted to make sure the couch was available for adult activities.

Klyrk sent a questioning glance his way, then moved off toward the overstuffed chair. He was too tired to argue. After Phyrnk was deposited in the chair, Klyrk arched his aching back and gave it rub with his gloved hands.

"Oh man, I am going to be sore tomorrow."

Gwydol slipped between the two exhausted men, and bent over to examine Phrynk's expressionless, baggy face. She was dressed in a handmade shift that came down to mid-thigh. When she bent over, the shift slid up to just below her firm, round butt. Lymdyr stared at her bent-over form. He fought the urge to slip his hand up the inside of her thighs.

"He's really out, ain't he?" Gwydol straightened up and turned around to face the two men.

"I'm guessin' he'll be fine till we come back when its light." Klyrk continued to rub the small of his back.

"I'll stay here and keep watch of him," Lymdyr said in what his addled brain considered a matter-of-fact voice.

Klyrk raised his dusty eyebrows. "You want me to leave one of the styrns tied up so you can bring him up in the morning?"

"No! I'm sick of dealing with those stupid animals! Zym! I suppose there's no way he can walk back to the car. I'll deal with it tomorrow!"

Klyrk looked over at Gwydol, tipped his hat, and quietly slipped out the door. She and Lymdyr stood listening to him shout at the styrns.

After several moments, Lymdyr dragged himself over and dropped to the couch. A long sigh of exhaustion issued from his lips. Gwydol tiptoed over and slid next to him. He felt her small, rough hand slide across his thigh.

"You had a rough day?"

"You might say that."

She gave a little grunt of recognition. "Well, I had a big pyryst all ready. We wait, and wait, den I feed the chillrun. A couple of de drivers come in, and I feed dem too. They hang around for a long time. Dee light hair one, he keep looking over at me. I ask him. You still hungry? He just shake his head."

Lymdyr managed to work up the energy to smile. His worn out body was engaged in a fight between its need for rest, and the flickering flame of lust that refused to blow out.

"You hungry? Wan some food?"

He rolled his head back and forth across the worn fabric. "No, I would like something to drink."

"I make some nymfyr zyd. You want soma dat?"

"Yes please, a big glass."

Lymdyr closed his eyes. He heard the floorboards creak as she made her way out into the kitchen. Gwydol returned to the couch and wrapped his fingers around the glass. After pulling himself to an upright position, Lymdyr poured half the glass down his parched throat.

"Ah! That was marvelous."

Gwydol sat splay legged next to him. She let go a huge yawn. "It be morning soon. You wanna go to bed?"

Lymdyr finished the glass, set it down on the8 coffee table, and slid next to her. He kissed her neck then reached down and ran his hand provocatively up her thigh. She pulled her bare leg away.

"You really something, you know dat?" Lymdyr's level of passion dropped precipitously. He leaned against the back of the couch. Gwydol scooted over toward the side.

"Here you send me message, Gwydol, honey! I'm bringin' group out der, you gotta cook for us! Ha! You been down here for one meal. I see you for what, one hour? Now you come draggin' in, dirty, smelly, horny! I see you for another couple hours, den off you go! Yeah buddy, you are really something."

He sat frozen. The one event that he hoped would erase all the frustration and aggravation of the last couple days was becoming less of a possibility by the minute. Gwydol reached over, gave his dusty pant leg a hard slap, and let go a little, sarcastic yip of a laugh.

"Yes, you is..." When she noticed the vacant, demoralized look on his face, her attitude suddenly changed. "Oh, oh baby! I'm sorry! Dis not de time for me to go off on, is it?"

Gwydol slid back over and kissed him with force. They remained locked for several moments. Her tired, middle of the night woken up face softened as she pulled back and searched for signs of life on his haggard features.

"I wasn't even thinkin. I'm sorry baby." She lifted his hand to give his fingers a kiss, then stopped. "Uh, whyn't you go wash up a bit. You been riding those raggedy styrns all day."

"Yeah, I'm gonna get me some more of that zyd too."

Lymdyr pulled himself up off the couch and walked stiffly out into the kitchen. Phyrnk murmured something from his chair. Gwydol walked over and scrutinized his unconscious face. His eyes were firmly shut. Every once in a while, his lips would twitch. She heard Lymdyr walk back into the room and whispered to him over her shoulder.

"How long he been sleepin' like dis?"

After plunking back down on the couch, Lymdyr took a drink of the zyd, and began pulling his boots off. "Oh, I don't know. He was sort of awake when we started riding up. That was hours ago. I guess he didn't really fall asleep….Zym! I don't know. Three hours?" Lymdyr stripped his socks off, removed his shirt, and massaged his sore arms.

"What's your diagnosis Healer Gwydol?"

"I ain't no real healer. I jus don't like de way he's twitchin."

She laid her hands on the arms of the chair and bent forward to get a closer look. Gwydol was so absorbed in examining the old man's face, she didn't hear the clink of Lymdyr's pants as they hit the floor.

He rose up from the couch, walked up behind her, gently slid his now clean hands under the end of her short shift, and pulled her into his lap. She closed her eyes, let her head hang down slightly, and let out a soft moan. After giving him a playful little wiggle, she pushed off the arms of the chair which sent Lymdyr back a few steps. Gwydol slid away from him, reached down, and whisked the shift off her lithe, brown body.

"Der, now I make it easier for you." She moved forward, and they exchanged a smoldering kiss. The giggle that worked its way up Lymdyr's throat interrupted their encounter.

"Wha so funny?"

"I've never kissed a woman that tastes like gynt smoke before."

"I ain't even gonna say what you taste like!" she replied with a sassy grin. Her gold front teeth glowed in the dim light. Gwydol led him over to the couch and slid up onto the end of the battered piece of furniture. She braced herself against the arm, then rose up on her knees. Lymdyr climbed onto the sagging cushions and brought himself into her from behind.

"Kyrl! Get off her, she's your cousin!" Phrynk mumbled from across the room.

Both Lymdyr and Gwydol stopped and sent concerned glance over at him. The old man remained slumped against the back of the chair, eyes tightly shut. He began to chuckle in his sleep. "Ah, what a cute fyrn!"

Phrynk appeared totally unaware of the squeaking of the couch frame, and Gwydol's ecstatic gasps.

Chapter 36.

Three hours later, the patter of small feet and two hushed juvenile voices woke Lymdyr from his much needed sleep. He opened one eye and looked over the top of Gwydol's short, coarse hair. The girl and youngest boy stood at the end of the coffee table, staring in wonder. Lymdyr reached up and stroked Gwydol's hip. She groaned, then burrowed tighter against him.

"The kids are up," he whispered after planting a light kiss on her ear.

Her long lashed eyelids flickered, then shot open. Gwydol twisted her neck around and lifted herself off his chest. "Syrn, grab me night shirt."

"Where is? I don't see it," the young girl replied.

Gwydol cursed under her breath and looked around the dusty room. "Over der, at de man's feet."

The skinny young girl glided over, sent a questioning glance at Phrynk, then bent down and picked up the tan garment. She held it out to her mother.

"Momma, why you laying with……"

"Shhh! You'll wake de ol' man," Gwydol hissed. She tossed the night shirt up and slipped her arms into it. Phyrnk's wrinkled, baggy eyelids slowly drew open.

"Well, who do we have here?"

He pushed himself to an upright sitting position and gazed around the room. Both the children ran into the kitchen. Lymdyr bent over and grabbed his shirt from the floor. He wrapped it around his waist for modesty's sake and swung his legs over next to Gwydol's.

"Morning, Mr. Phrynk. How are you feeling?"

"Ya know, I'm a little sore. I think that styrn ride up the hill yesterday just about did me in."

Gwydol swiveled her head around toward Lymdyr. "You want some zyd?"

"Sure. That sounds great." He took the opportunity to give her a quick, soft kiss before she jumped to her feet.

"How bout you Missta Phrynk?"

"Yes, please."

The children helped Gwydol get a fire going in the stove, and a short while later, zyd was distributed to the guests. Gwydol slipped between the couch and coffee table, then settled next to Lymdyr. She snugged against up against him.

"So you gonna bring de group down fo nymyr?" Gwydol blew on the steaming liquid in her cup, and a took a sip.

"That's the plan..."

Lymdyr was going to say more, but the barking of fyrns outside, followed by a loud knock on the door interrupted him. Gwydol slid off the couch and swung the door open. Staggeringly bright sunlight flooded the room. Klyrk's wide frame blocked most of the searing golden rays as he entered. The handler pulled off his floppy hat and waved to Gwydol.

"Mornin' ma'am."

Gwydol pulled the edge of her short night shirt down and wrapped her arms across her chest.

"Mornin. Sorry I ain't dressed. We jus got...."

"No need to apologize ma'am. Is Lymdyr?...." Klyrk stepped forward and caught sight of the railroad man spread out comfortably across the battered couch. "Ah, you are up."

He continued his scan of the sparsely furnished room. "Phrynk lives!" Klyrk's boots creaked the floorboards as he walked over and knelt down next to the chair. "Well, you old bag of bones, you gave us quite a fight getting you up here yesterday. I fear you're styrn riding days are over."

"Over and long gone!" Phrynk replied. The two men shared a hearty morning laugh. Gwydol settled down next to Lymdyr. She squeezed her knees tight and pulled the edges of the shirt as far down over her lovely smooth thighs as it would go.

"You like some zyd Missta Klyrk?"

"No, no thanks. I've already had some. Been up for hours. The styrns are already loaded. Everybody's packed and ready to go, 'cept Bryty, still haven't seen her styrk shiny face yet."

Lymdyr let out a groan and set his zyd cup on the table. "What time is it anyway?"

Klyrk got to his feet and pulled a big scratched up pocket watch from his vest. He popped the case open, then tilted it toward the curtained window.

"Uh, nine eleven."

"Wow, we did sleep late."

"Yeah, like to catch the ten o'clock train if we could," Klyrk commented.

Lymdyr ran a hand over his very stubbly face and slapped his knee for effect. "Well, guess we better get up and get moving."

"No time for nymyr," Gwydol tossed out.

"Nope."

She looked over at Lymdyr, and her fine features dropped in sadness.

Phrynk held out his hand. "Help me up please." Klyrk yanked him up out of the chair and the old man teetered momentarily. "Gosh, I'm a little unsteady today."

"Today? You're about as unsteady as a klymr stalk in the wind all the time."

Phrynk staggered across the dusty floor, then stopped and turned toward Gwydol. "Thanks for everything, ma'am. I'd walk over and give you a hug goodbye, but I'm feeling a little shaky. Think I better get back to the car and lie down."

Gwydol rose to her feet, hustled around the end of the table, and opened her arms to embrace the old mag driver. The two of them remained locked in each other's arms for several moments. Phrynk rested his chin on her head and spoke in a soft whisper.

"You take care. Got some fine children. You're doing a good job of raising them."

Gwydol let him go and looked up into his eyes. "Thanks, it ain't easy, but I do the best I can." She rose on her tiptoes and kissed his leathery cheek.

"Wow, I ain't been kissed by a pretty girl in years. Now I'm feeling okay!"

Klyrk reached over and gently took Phrynk's arm. "Come on, you old bag, let's get you on for one last ride." He tipped his hat toward Gwydol on the way past. "Ma'am, sorry we didn't get to taste more of your fine cookin. Take care."

Gwydol grabbed the edges of her night shirt and curtsied. She watched Klyrk lead the old man out into the flashing yellow sunlight, then padded slowly back over to the couch. Lymdyr had just finished pulling on his boots, and was now working on buttoning his dusty, but finely tailored shirt. She plunked down next to him and laid her head on his shoulder.

"And now off you go."

He secured the last button and slid his arm around her. After massaging the cord like muscles running down her back, Lymdyr pulled her torso toward him and kissed her with force. She more or less responded in kind. He eased back and lifted her tiny chin with his hand.

The look of sorrow on her face tore at his heart. He took a moment to admire the narrow bridge and wide flare of her nose. His loving gaze dropped to the marvelous heart-shaped expanse of her lips.

"I can probably be back here in a couple months," he said quietly.

"Me husband supposed be back in two months."

"That'll be good. He can help take care of the kids, right?"

She shrugged. "Long as he don't take to fightin' and bustin' stuff up again."

Lymdyr grabbed her hand and got to his feet. She rose with him.

"I'd walk you up to de train, but I ain't dressed."

He rotated her around and pulled her strong, lithe body against him. They looked into each other's eyes. His were bright and smiling while hers appeared dark and filled with longing.

"I like it when you're not dressed." He reached around, slid his hands under her shift, and squeezed her muscular butt. The sound of footsteps creaking from the kitchen caused him to stop. The older son leaned against the door frame and shot a sleepy glance over at them.

"Oh, it's you. I thought maybe pa was home."

Gwydol broke away, walked over, and kissed the teenager's forehead. "Bout time you got up. Get dressed. I'll make nymyr while you go pluge de tynkers."

The boy flashed another disapproving glance, then disappeared beyond the wall. Lymdyr moved toward the door, opened it, and squinted into the glaring morning light. In the big thorn tree by the road, a flock of raucous long-tailed lykrs scolded and clattered at each other.

"Holy Zym, it's bright out there!" He stepped through the threshold, but then felt a tug on his arm pull him back. Gywdol stood staring at him.

"So dis is it, isn't it?"

"What do you mean?" Lymdyr's innocent tone of voice and feigned smile added to the irony of the situation.

"This last time I see you. Why a big important man like you wanna come back out to dis dusty nowhere, just to klynk me another time? I don't think so." She took a step back and crossed her arms tightly.

"Gwydo....." Lymdyr reached out and stroked her hand.

"Don't be passin' wood to me!" she snapped with a shake of her head.

"I'm not sure what you mean?"

"Don't lie about it."

"No, really. I kind of like it out here." He stopped caressing her and gazed around at the parched, brown landscape and the rusted junk littering the yard.

"Yeah? So you gonna bring your fancy wife out here? Ha! See you later."

Before he could formulate some kind of meaningful, considerate reply, she turned and dragged the door closed behind her. Lymdyr stood staring at the splintered, sun blistered surface. He half expected her to open it and rush into his arms one final time. Nothing happened.

Lymdyr adjusted his hat and stepped out of the narrow band of shade. He walked slowly back toward town.

"Well, Lymdyr old boy, you can really be a jerk sometimes. I do wish our goodbye hadn't been so painful. Oh well, I have things to do."

As he approached the car, the morning sun reflecting off the shiny black lacquer surface temporarily obliterated his vision. By raising his hand to block the glare, he could make out Byrty and Klyrk standing next to the car. They both stopped laughing and turned to watch him approach.

"Hey! Bout time you showed up. We're pretty much packed up and ready to go," Klyrk called out.

Lymdyr nodded and continued walking. He really didn't have anything further to say to him.

"You gotta try one! My sweetie baked us some Hylrisan sweet blynys." Byrty held up the pan of gooey, spiraled confections. Lymdyr looked down at the tray, reached in, and tore one loose.

"Thanks, I'm starving." He took a bite and stood staring at Byrty's pale features. After chewing through most of it, he paused to lick the frosting off his fingers. "So, everything's ready to go?"

"Eh, yep."

"How's Phrynk?"

Byrty shifted the pan around and gazed up at the open car window. "He's sleepin' right now. I'm a little worried about his left arm. He doesn't seem to have control of it."

Lymdyr let go a little grunt and headed toward the side door.

Hours later, the train pulled into Tyrl. Bokyl and Rymnyr had been waiting on the platform for forty-five minutes. Long purple shadows from the fading light of day washed over them.

They threaded their way through the crowd of passengers and stood next to the newly arrived train.

Inside the executive car, Lymdyr packed up his satchel, walked down the corridor, and stepped down into the cool, dry air. Bokyl and Rymnyr both scanned his wide, sun darkened face for signs of success or failure. The way his eyes twinkled, and lips quivered slightly brought a smile to Rymnyr's face.

"Well?" Bokyl rasped out.

Lymdyr set his satchel down and ran a hand over his half beard. "I need a shave."

"Out with it! What did he say?"

"He'll be here in a couple days."

Rymnyr squealed with joy, stepped forward, and smashed herself against him. "I knew it! I knew you'd come through. Thank Zym! Bokyl and I have been beside ourselves with anticipation."

The head regent stood in the gathering twilight, smiling from ear to ear. He reached out and shook Lymdyr's hand vigorously. "Well done."

While they continued to congratulate each other, Byrty appeared in the side doorway, and eased herself to the ground.

"Oh, I am so stiff and sore!"

Lymdyr and the two academics stepped aside to make room for her.

"Byrty, this is Head Regent Bokyl, and Professor Rymnyr."

"Hello," Bryty replied.

"She's Phrynk's mid-healer. How's the old boy doing?"

Byrty looked back up at the car, then over at Lymdyr. "Well, he's been sleeping since we left. I don't know how we're going to get him out of there. Suppose we can get Klyrk and a buggy driver to carry him out. I'm going to hail one. Nice to meet you." Byrty waved, then hobbled off toward the row of buggies lined up along the street.

"So there you have it. I need to go square up with Klyrk. Shall we meet tomorrow?"

"Absolutely. There is a lot we need to discuss now. Say, my office at three?" Bokyl suggested.

"Sounds good. If I have a conflict, I'll get a message out," Lymdyr replied. He turned and began walking back to the livestock car. Rymnyr reached out and grasped his arm.

"Mr. Lymdyr, thank you for taking the time and effort to do this. We seriously were this close to abandoning the whole project, and now, oooh! It gives me chills of excitement just thinking about it!"

Lymdyr looked into Rymnyr's flushed face. "My pleasure. See you tomorrow."

He flashed a tired smile and continued back to the livestock car. Klyrk and his wife had just started unloading the animals. She looked over and took a moment to scan his dusty, somewhat disheveled appearance.

"Hello Mr. Lymdyr. Everything go alright?" Her condescending tone made his uneasy stomach knot up. He fought the urge to say something really inappropriate.

"Yes, we had a couple snags as you would expect, but overall, we accomplished our mission. Wouldn't you say Klyrk?" The sarcasm in his question was all too obvious.

Klyrk finished coiling the rope he held, slid his arm through the loop, and stepped off the ramp. "Yeah Lymdyr, there were a few snags. Cyrn and I'll draw up a quote for the additional work."

Lymdyr nodded. At that point, he didn't really care. "Oh, one last thing. Byrty says Phrynk is still out. I need you to help one of the buggy drivers carry him....."

"Not a chance! I'm in such pain, I need to get to a healer as soon as possible." Just for emphasis, he rubbed the small of his back and grimaced. "Good night, Mr. Lymdyr."

While the two handlers led their styrns away, Byrty came huffing and puffing up next to him. "Aw, I was going to thank Klyrk for letting me ride his styrn. Oh, well."

"I thanked him for the both of us."

"I got a driver. How do you want to do this?"

Lymdyr stroked his scratchy chin. "Well, I guess Ryslyn and I are going to have to haul the old boy out."

With considerable effort, he and the steward managed to load Phrynk's unconscious body into a buggy. Byrty climbed down from the cab after getting the old man more or less arranged on the floor. She stood in front of Lymdyr, then reached out and grasped his hand.

"Thank you so much for inviting me to come. I can't tell you how meaningful an experience it was. I mean, (sniff), I think I just met the love of my life!" Before Lymdyr could comment, she stepped forward and gave him a massive hug. Her wide, soft body shook with sobs. Lymdyr felt the moisture from her tears soak into his collar. After a couple moments, she let go and wiped the remaining tears from the corners of her eyes.

"Sorry, I guess I just needed to let it all out. Thanks again."

"Thank you. We couldn't have done it without you," Lymdyr replied softly. He really wanted to admonish her for not staying sober, but instead reached into his wallet, pulled out a bill, and handed it to her. "Here, this should cover the buggy."

"You are such a nice man. Thank you again."

"My pleasure." Lymdyr patted her shoulder, then walked across the gravelly yard. The thought of having to face the upcoming interrogation his wife would subject him to concerning the trip filled him with dread.

Chapter 37.

At three o'clock the next day, the members of the Dymran Society began filing into Bokyl's sunlit office. Gyls was several minutes late, as usual. Out on the street in front of the Academy, Lymdyr shoved a bill into the buggy driver's hand and charged up the steps.

"I'm in fine shape today! Nothing like walking into the office late and getting grilled by executives first thing. I can't believe Bynhyld made me sleep on the couch."

By the time Lymdyr made it up to the second floor, sweat had soaked through his nice striped shirt. He plucked at the front of it several times to try and evaporate the moisture before sweeping into Bokyl's overly warm office.

A hearty round of applause greeted him. The clapping lasted an uncomfortably long time. Beaming, glistening, and smelling like a locker room into which someone had sprayed cologne, Lymdyr finally held up his hand to hush the group.

"Thank you, thank you. Whew! Sorry, I'm late. I had to rush over here from a meeting. I didn't have a chance to groom myself properly this morning, so, how shall I put it? Sorry that I stink."

Polite laughter circled around the room. Bokyl straightened up in his chair and rested his elbows on the desk. "We accept your apologies. Please have a seat. Should I open a window?"

Several of the meeting attendees nodded. Bokyl walked over to the window and pulled it open. The outside sounds of students talking in the courtyard, buggy styrns bawling, far off train whistles, and lykrs chirping in the thorn trees filled the room.

A shiver of relief ran over Lymdyr. The breeze rapidly dried his damp skin, in addition to carrying the worst of his aroma out into the hall. Bokyl returned to his desk and hunched forward to address the group.

"Alright, I've had a long day, and we have a lot to cover. First of all, our congratulations to Mr. Lymdyr for finally convincing Lyle...."

"Ryk," Lymdyr corrected.

"Ah yes, Ryk to come and train. That brings us to the main point."

"Head Regent, can we cover the other updates first? I suspect that if we get going on the engineer position, it will be difficult for us to move to anything else," Krynut suggested from his place halfway up the row of chairs.

"Yes, I do think that would be wise." Bokyl looked down at the sheet of paper lying in front of him. "So, who headed up the provision group?"

Rymnyr had stopped fanning herself and held up a folded piece of paper. "Mihyn and I met with the chair of the nutrition department. Basically, we asked her what kind of food she would take along if she were going on a long, long pluge voyage where re-supply would not be possible. She recommended taking along bags of Aldyn zylfr. I personally have never tried it, but she says it can be eaten raw or boiled. It makes excellent blyny, although we won't have a way to bake it."

Professor Grylt raised his long, slender hand. "I've eaten it. It takes some getting used to, but it will certainly keep you alive. For all practical purposes, it's all the Omo Kurans eat."

"Wonderful, and how many pounds of it per person are you estimating we will need?" Bokyl asked.

"The figure that the chairwoman gave us was half pound per day per person. She also recommended a variety of dried foods to complete the diet. So the gross weight per day per person came out to around three quarters of a pound per day per person."

"So just for rough figuring, five pounds per day for the whole crew. Let's say the voyage is a year long, that's eighteen hundred pounds of food!" Bokyl said with a snort.

Gyls shifted in his chair, coughed, then held his hand up. "If I may jump in. Krynut and I have been calculating how much luggage if you will, each person will be able to take. The figure we came up with was between, uh, thirty and fifty pounds. So with an additional two-hundred and fifty pounds of luggage, plus let's say sixteen hundred pounds of food, that's nineteen-hundred pounds total, minus pluge and the crew."

Low, fragmented discussions circled around the room. Bokyl waved his hand in the air.

"Quiet, quiet please. Yes, we are starting to approach a critical point weight wise." He turned his head toward Gyls. "And what did you calculate for the maximum weight that could be blasted out of the atmosphere?"

"Our rough estimate was a fully loaded craft of approximately twenty-one hundred pounds."

"Total."

"Yes, total," Gyls confirmed.

Bokyl settled back in his chair and surveyed the room with a decidedly skeptical look on his face. "It seems we are a little heavy."

"Krynut and I will run the revised figures through his calculation machine and see what we come up with."

"Thank you Mr. Gyls, so, we discussed food……" Bokyl scanned the list of items on the sheet, then raised his head. "I don't see Ymyl here. He was going to brief us on the comet's approach."

"I spoke with him earlier," Krynut added. "He says that it is moving as predicted, and that we should launch in six weeks to maximize our chance of intercepting it."

Professor Rymnyr reached over and squeezed Mihyn's soft, elegant hand. "You must be very excited!" she whispered. Rymnyr shot a quick glance over at the younger woman's expression. Nothing other than a certain extra seriousness in her deep brown eyes betrayed any trace of how she felt. Mihyn sensed that Rymnyr was looking at her and leaned in the older woman's direction.

"Yes, excited and terrified."

"Well, I guess that brings us to our discussion of the final roster for the crew," Bokyl announced with a touch of sarcasm. He set his palms down on the desk and looked around the room. His gaze fell on Mihyn.

"Regent, I notice that your husband is not here. Has he agreed to be part of the crew?"

"Handynr has been very busy with the current conflict in Bosyra. I have been advising him on the details of these meetings." All eyes in the room focused on her.

"Has he agreed to go?"

The decision of whether to level with the head regent about Handynr's hesitation at the offer gripped Mihyn's very core. Her small, delicate stomach jumped. She felt like throwing up.

"Yes, he has agreed."

"Good." Bokyl directed his attention back to Krynut. "Regent, I believe you are the unofficial leader of this voyage. Would you care to brief us on the engineer position?"

"At this point, we still have not determined exactly who will fill the engineer's position."

"Six weeks to go, and we still don't know who is going?" Bokyl asked with an air of incredulousness.

"Please allow me to finish what I was going to say." Krynut sent a brief, stern glance over at the head regent before continuing. "Several candidates have been proposed. Mr. Gyls is currently the most likely choice, although there is some concern about, um, ...he has been experiencing some health issues."

Gyls wheeled around in his chair and spoke directly to Bokyl. "It's just kyrsht allergies. The healer that I've been going to for years doesn't know what he's talking about. I'm seeing a new one, and he has given me some herbal medicine which is....."

A coughing fit interrupted his explanation. The inventor's lanky frame heaved uncontrollably for several moments. Once he was able to regain control, Gyls removed his thick black glasses and wiped the tears from his eyes.

"Whew! Other than dealing with these allergies, I'm fine."

"As I recall, there was some issue with headaches and nausea during the construction process, also."

"That was more than likely due to the adhesive we were using for the interior mounts."

The head regent focused his attention back to Krynut. "You mentioned other candidates?"

"We haven't formally presented the position to them, but there was talk of asking, uh, what's Kryzyck's nephew's name?"

"Blrsynt," Professor Myrvst replied.

"Ah, yes, thank you. Although I haven't personally spent much time with him, he...."

"The boy managed to impregnate my housekeeper. I don't think he's going to be going anywhere," Myrvst offered in a decidedly resigned tone of voice.

The professor's admonition sent a pall over the room. After several moments of uncomfortable silence, Bokyl spoke up.

"Are there other candidates?"

Krynut stroked his narrow, well-manicured goatee and leaned out from the row of chairs. He looked down at Lymdyr. The railroad man had been sitting and listening, basically just enjoying the lack of input required of him after his extremely busy day. He noticed several of the participants in his field of vision looking right at him.

"What? No, you're not suggesting that I be considered?"

"Well, Mr. Lymdyr. The effort you have put forth to facilitate this project is truly admirable. I would venture to say that you have invested as much time as any of us," Krynut said in a steady, calm voice.

Lymdyr straightened up in his chair and broke into a beaming smile. "Wow, honestly, I never have even considered being part of the crew. Ha! Will wonders never cease!"

"So, shall we assume that you are considering the offer?" Bokyl asked.

"Uh, I, um. I *will* consider it. There are so many things I would have to work out. When do you need a decision made?"

"Like, tomorrow."

"Excuse me for jumping in. I feel like I am quite capable of fulfilling my duties as crew engineer. I mean, as far as having knowledge of the craft. I built the dyth thing!" A desperate smile worked its way across Gyls' pale features. He searched the expressions of the other project members to try and determine their reaction. All he saw were blank, serious faces.

Bokyl cleared his throat. "Well, I've had a very long day. Is there anything else we need to cover?" Several heads shook in response to his question. "Good, Rymnyr, Krynut, will you stay for a moment. The rest of you may go. We'll reconvene when Ly....Zym! Why can't I remember that mag driver's name?"

"Ryk," Lymdyr answered just before rising up out of the chair.

"We'll reconvene after Ryk arrives. Thank you all for coming."

Bokyl watched his esteemed colleagues file out of the room. He paid extra attention to the desperate look on Gyls' face. The young man's narrow shoulders were slumped as he exited the room. Once the rest of the group had left, Bokyl motioned to the two remaining project members.

"Pull up a chair."

"I'd rather stand. I've been sitting all day," Krynut replied.

"I'll just sit on the edge of the desk." Rymnyr walked over and parked her fairly wide bottom on the upper corner. She crossed her legs, grasped her knees, and rocked back. "No real question about what you want to talk about."

Just the trace of a grin spread across Bokyl's face. "Oh, you think you have me second guessed?"

Rymnyr nodded her head. "Uh huh." She looked over at Krynut for confirmation. He took a step forward and placed his hands on the edge of the desk.

"So, you want to discuss the candidates?"

"How observant of you!" Bokyl leaned back and rubbed his small, tired eyes. "Zym! I wish this last decision was easier. I don't know about you, but I'm exhausted from dealing with this! How did I ever allow you two to drag me into such a hair brained endeavor?"

"Oh, you just wait. After this is done, and a new world is discovered, we'll all go down in history," Rymnyr tossed out with more than a hint of drama.

Bokyl let go a short laugh and shifted forward. His chair squeaked loudly under the strain. "Go down in history. Unless it all goes up in flames." He and Krynut smiled at each other.

"I don't think that's very funny," Rymnyr snapped.

"Okay, real quick. I'd like to hear your candid opinion about who would be the best choice for the engineer position. And please be quick, there is a tall glass of mynth calling my name from home."

Krynut extended his palm out as a sign for Rymnyr to go first. She released a long sigh before speaking.

"I would love to send Gyls up since he has worked so hard, but with only six weeks to go, I just don't see him being healthy enough. It doesn't look like he has been sleeping very well."

"I don't think there's much need to discuss it. I concur," Krynut added.

"So, is Lymdyr really a possibility?"

As soon as the question was posed, Gyls' thin frame appeared in the open doorway. All three people in the room jumped with surprise.

"I know it's wrong to eavesdrop, but I have to make my pitch!" He took two steps forward, head lowered.

From his place behind the desk, Bokyl glowered like some great angry pagan idol. One could almost visualize the flames of hell rising up around the edges of his robe.

"Mr. Gyls. This is not an open meeting." The head regent's stern rebuke carried more than a hint of annoyance.

"I know, I mean, yes, absolutely." The inventor stopped and wrung his hands together. "It's just that I didn't feel like I had a chance to support my position earlier, and wanted to…"

"You had an unquestionably adequate chance to defend your position." Bokyl waited a sizzling moment for a response. "Do I have to ask you to leave?"

Gyls looked up at the head regent with eyes pleading. He saw no trace of compassion in Bokyl's ever reddening face, so he directed his attention to Rymynr.

"Professor, you know how hard I've worked on this!"

Rymnyr shifted around to face the enraged head regent. The heat from his anger was now palatable in the room. In order to signal a pause in the tense situation, she held up a single finger. Once the professor was convinced that no one was going to explode, Rymnyr swung back around toward the inventor.

"Mr. Gyls. We would be happy to set up another meeting of the society to discuss this."

"Yes, ma'am."

"What kind of medication is this new healer giving you?"

The off topic question seemed to distract him from his desperate plea. Gyls' face relaxed and adopted a quizzical appearance. The stiffness in his upper body loosened. He pulled a folded up piece of paper from his pants pocket and clumsily opened it.

"Pargormic."

"Ah, that explains a lot. You do know that Pargormic is an addictive substance. It is great in suppressing coughs, but also easy to become dependent on." Rymnyr completed her statement by sending a kindly smile his way.

"No, I didn't know that." He hastily stuffed the paper back into his pocket. "I really should leave." Without further comment, he whisked out of the room.

Chapter 38.

Three days later, Ryk stepped off the train at the main Tyrl station. All his worldly belongings were packed into a pair of canvas satchels. He walked slowly across the platform, jostled by the passengers that were in a hurry. Ryk climbed up into the cab of the first buggy by the curb. He rode along with his arm and shoulder stuck out the open window. The buildings and homes rolled by without him really noticing them. His mind was elsewhere.

"Let's see. First stop'll be at that professor's house. Zym, I hope Syl is there! Then swing over to the Gyr Tavern. Lylyn never did respond to my letter, so she gets visited last."

He settled back slightly, rolled himself a gynt cigarette, lit it, and watched the smoke pull out into the open air. When the buggy turned onto the main boulevard, Ryk began to pay more attention to the surroundings. A slight uneasiness blossomed in his stomach.

"What if her boyfriend is there? Dyth! I didn't think of that. That could be awkward. Blyrt! Maybe I'll just have the driver roll by and take a look. What if she sees me look out the window? Hmmm."

Ryk was still wrestling with the plan when the buggy entered the tree-lined block where Myrvst lived. The driver stopped at the crossroad. He leaned down off the seat.

"Which way you want to go?"

"Go real slow by that grey stone house down there." Ryk stuck his arm all the way out the window and pointed toward Myrvst's dwelling. His heart began to beat fast.

The driver gave the styrns a slap of the reins, and the buggy rolled forward. Ryk slid against the far wall of the cab, then hunched down slightly so he could see out the window. His stomach tightened as they approached the house. The fingernails of his right hand dug painfully into the palm of his balled up fist.

"Slow down even more."

Ryk settled down at window level and watched the shutters on the outside of the house gradually creep into view. Through the front window, he could see the edge of the dining room and light coming in through the kitchen. In a flash, nothing but the thick hedge along the house was visible.

"Take me over to Jybyr." Ryk gave a little sigh of despair, then thumped back in the seat.

Bright and early the next day, he left Lylyn's humble upstairs apartment and headed to a bank just around the corner. Once inside, Ryk walked up to the telemessage operator.

"I'd like to send a reply." He held up a yellow sheet of paper.

The small, stooped operator slid the paper from Ryk's fingers and gave it a quick scan. "You want to send it to a Mr. Lymdyr?"

"Yes."

"And what would you like to say?"

"Tell him that I'm in town, and, uh, tell him to come find me."

Over at the railroad office, the second telemessage machine from the left rattled and hammered out the message. An operator dropped it in Lymdyr's box, and ten minutes later, his secretary came sweeping by.

Without stopping, Byrdyl reached in, grabbed the hand full of papers, and flipped through them as she walked. Her narrow, slightly slanted eyes grew large when she read Ryk's message. She quickened her step and swooped into the open door of his office.

Lymdyr was seated at his desk, writing a letter. He looked up and recognized the "I know something you don't know!" smirk on her face. "What?" His question rang with comic exaggeration.

"Here. You've been waiting for this." She walked forward and held out the sheet.

He rose up, took it from her, and read while sitting back down. "Oh, yeah!" Lymdyr spun his wheeled desk chair around, flapping the sheet above his head. He stopped his rotation, then returned his attention to Byrdyl.

"Well?" she asked, still smirking.

"Well? Well? Reply back and find out where he is."

Forty-five minutes later, the buggy Lymdyr had hired pulled up in front of the dingy, though not unfriendly, Gyr Tavern. He hopped down and paused to examine the dilapidated edifice before walking in.

Ryk and his obviously pregnant girlfriend were standing at the bar talking when the over-dressed railroad man entered. Lylyn caught sight of him and gave Ryk a poke to the ribs.

"Mr. Lymdyr! Good to see you!" Ryk swaggered across the dimly lit room, and the two men shook hands. A big, welcoming smile burst across his face.

"Good to see you too, Ryk."

"Lylyn, this is Mr. Lymdyr. He's the organizer of this whole crazy project."

Lylyn draped the rag she was dusting with over her arm and eased over to join them. A sweet smile brought some life to her otherwise, tired, working while pregnant face. "Nice to meet you."

The railroad man let his eyes drift over her pleasant features, paying special attention to her long, aquiline nose, and big sweep of wavy dark hair.

"I wouldn't say I'm the organizer of the Dymran project. Well, I guess maybe I am!" He let out a sharp bark of a laugh. Several of the patrons turned to see what all the commotion was about. "Well, ready to go meet the big wigs?"

"Yeah, I suppose. Bye, darling." Ryk leaned down and kissed Lylyn's forehead.

"Have fun boys," she responded before returning to her dusting.

The two of them climbed into the waiting buggy. Once they were rolling along, Lymdyr settled back in the seat.

"So, welcome back to Tyrl. The other members of the society are really anxious for you to start training whoever it is they designate as the engineer."

Ryk looked out the window. He let go a hmmpf of recognition. "Suppose we could swing by and pay Phyrnk a visit?" he asked without making eye contact.

"Don't really have time today."

"I sure would like to see the old boy. Maybe just a quick stop in and say hello?"

The old folk's home where Phrynk lived was across town from the Academy, so Lymdyr had to quickly offer an alternative to Ryk's request. He reached over and gave the mag driver a slap on the knee.

"I've got an idea! I'll get ahold of Byrty, tell her we're coming to visit Phrynk maybe, tomorrow? We can all go out and have some drinks afterward."

Ryk took a moment to ponder the suggestion. His sanguine face drew up in the beginning of a smile. "It'd be pretty hard for her to turn that down, wouldn't it?"

After twenty minutes of rolling along the side streets, they crossed onto the boulevard, and then pulled up in front of the Academy. Ryk stuck his head out the window to take in the view.

"Boy, it sure is a big building."

"Yep, full of big headed people. Come on." As soon as the buggy stopped, Lymdyr popped the door open and swung down to the curb. Side by side, he and Ryk ascended the marble steps. A pair of nice looking female students came gliding down beside them. Lymdyr flashed a smile and stared at their shapely figures.

"Definitely some gorgeous scenery around here!"

Ryk offered no reply. He was lost in thought. The two of them burst through the copper doors and into the noisy foyer. Lymdyr led the way up to the second floor.

A few moments later, they arrived at Bokyl's office. The head regent was signing a purchase order from one of the department heads when Lymdyr whisked into the room.

"Oh! Excuse us! We'll wait in the hall."

Bokyl looked up from his signing. "No, no, no need. I'm done." He handed the form to the professor standing next to him. Lymdyr waited for the man to leave, then strode up to the desk.

"Head Regent Bokyl. This is Ryk Six Line!"

The mag driver ambled over next to him and held out his hand. Bokyl rose up from his chair, reached out and received a mostly limp shake at best.

"Pull up a chair, gentlemen." Bokyl's perfectly round face glowed with pride. As soon as they were settled, he folded his fingers together and began to speak. "Ryk, I don't have to tell you how happy we are to finally have you here to assist with the project….."

While Bokyl droned on, Ryk's mind was wandering. The Head Regent's round face and wide body reminded him of a large amphibian. The opulent gold threaded, crimson and black robe he was wearing only served to increase Ryk's feelings of disdain.

Bokyl recognized the detached, slightly irritated look on the mag driver's face and stopped talking. He sent an urgent little glance Lymdyr's way. The railroad man just sat there grinning with satisfaction.

Rapid footsteps, and the sound of hushed conversation from the hall broke the tension in the room. After finishing the discussion with one of his students, Krynut came walking into the office. Both Lymdyr and Ryk got to their feet. Bokyl made the appropriate introductions, then watched the mag driver and newly arrived regent size each other up.

Krynut's sharp angular features, immaculately groomed goatee, and almond shaped eyes struck Ryk as humorous. He didn't bother to suppress the grin that formed on his face.

The regent was used to being evaluated by others. He took Ryk's reaction in stride. The only thing that stood out about the tall, well-built man standing inches away was the glimmer of mischief, or perhaps intelligence in the dark, deep set eyes. Krynut allowed himself to smile ever so briefly.

"Pleased to meet you. We've been waiting anxiously for your arrival."

"Why don't you two pull up a chair? Is Ymyl on his way up?" Bokyl asked.

"No, I think he's left for the day."

"I suggest we take Ryk out to the testing site. Might as well have him warm up," Lymdyr tossed out.

"Excellent idea! I apologize, Ryk. Your arrival is still such a surprise. We're usually not this disorganized." Bokyl's face flushed slightly from embarrassment.

"You know how to get there?" Krynut asked before heading toward the door.

"Yeah, it's at the foot of the north mountain, right?"

"Yes."

Lymdyr reached over and slapped Ryk on the shoulder. "Come on, let's rope us a fake comet!"

The two of them walked side by side down to one of the waiting buggies outside the Academy and climbed in. A solid ceiling of high clouds obscured the bright spring sun. It also gave the day a somewhat subdued aspect. Both men sat and watched the storefronts and neighborhoods roll by in silence.

After about ten minutes of riding, Ryk pulled his pouch of gynt and a package of papers out of his vest pocket. "Care for a gynt?"

"No thanks, I don't smoke."

Lymdyr watched him deftly roll a cigarette with one hand. Ryk lit the gynt, took a puff, then leaned back against the seat.

"So let me get this straight. We're heading out to a place where I'm going to train somebody to rope a comet?"

"That's the plan."

Ryk responded with a little huff of disbelief. "And at some point, that person is going to do that from some kind of kyrft out in space?"

Lymdyr crossed his legs and wrapped his fingers around the left knee. "I know, I know. It does seem a little impractical to me also, but I'm just coordinating this. Those folks at the Academy are the smart ones. I just work for the railroad!"

Ryk took another draw of the gynt and looked Lymdyr square in the eyes. "So you're not one of the smart ones, eh? Is that why you're wearing clothes that cost as much as the best styrn I ride? Yeah, you're not foolin' me bud."

It took Lymdyr a moment to recover from the shock of Ryk's strong words. He was about to offer a rebuttal when the buggy driver reached down and tapped on the door. Lymdyr rose up and stuck his head out the window.

"What's up?"

"We're just about to leave the paved road. It's gonna get pretty rough and dusty. You might want to close the window."

"Thanks." Lymdyr slid back down to the bench seat. "He says the rides gonna get a little rough and dusty."

Ryk nodded, and continued smoking. Sure enough, in the next instant, the two-wheel buggy pitched off the end of the pavement, tossing the men from one side to the other. After seventeen minutes of jostling, the driver pulled up to a flat area right at the base of a dry, rocky slope.

Lymdyr opened the door and jumped to the ground. Ryk eased down behind him. The railroad man patted his elegant brown suit a couple times to loosen the fine dust, then looked up at the buggy driver.

"Just hang out for a while, okay? I need to figure out some logistics."

The two men began walking up the only obvious path. On the hill above them, the practice scaffolding slowly came into view above the low, scrubby bushes. As they neared the site, the sound of excited young voices drifted their way.

The group of engineering students were sitting around on a big circle of rocks, taking a break. When the tall, frizzy-haired department head saw the two visitors approach, he got to his feet and met them just at the edge of the clearing.

"May I help you?"

"Hi there. My name is Lymdyr Nine Line. I'm part of the Dymran project, and this is Ryk Six Line. He's here to instruct you on expert roping techniques."

The department head's rough, bony, sideburned face lit up with surprise. "Oh! You're Ryk! Pleased to meet you." He extended his hand out, and Ryk shook it out of kindness.

"Ryk!"

Sylstyn jumped up from the rock she was sitting on and ran over to greet him. The department head stepped out of the way to allow her to enter Ryk's outstretched arms. He gave her a crushing hug, then loosened his grip, and bent down to kiss her gorgeous, full lips. Sylstyn turned her head at the last moment. His kiss landed right below her left eye. Both of them exploded with laughter.

"It appears that you two know each other!" the department head said with a big smile.

"Oh, yeah. We know each other, right Sly?"

"Yes, so Ryk, we were wondering when you'd show up."

"If I'd known you were gonna be here Sly baby, I'da come much sooner."

Slylstyn reached over and patted his wide torso. "Well, I'll tell ya. If there's one person that can show us how to lasso a comet, it's you!"

Ryk pulled her close and looked down into her lovely, smiling face. "Boy, is it good to see you! You're even prettier than last time I saw you." He took the opportunity to let his eyes drift up and down over her shapely form.

"Well, I'd like to stay and watch the fun, but I must return to work." Lymdyr interjected before shifting his attention over to the department head. "Sorry, I didn't catch your name."

"Oh, yes, sorry. Bynkr Two Line, head of mechanical engineering." The two men shook hands.

"Pleased to meet you Mr. Bynkr. So, would it be possible for Ryk to ride back into town with your group at the end of the day?"

"Yes, that would be fine."

"Wonderful, well, good luck all. Nice to meet you, and I'm sure we'll be in contact." Lymdyr flashed a smile of satisfaction and took a step back down the trail.

"Hey, Mr. Lymdyr! Don't forget to arrange that meeting with Phrynk. I sure do want to check in with the old boy. He's the only real reason I'm up here. Oh, and to see my best girl again!" Ryk gave Sylstyn another hard squeeze.

"Right, I'll set up the meeting today. Goodbye all." Lymdyr waved and strode off through the scrubby, pale green bushes.

Professor Bynk watched the railroad man gradually drop out of sight, then turned his attention to the group. "Well, I think our break is over. So shall we get to work?"

"No point in standing around! Let's see what ya got." Ryk and Sylstyn remained joined at the hip as they walked back to the circle.

Bynkr picked up his clipboard and called out to the waiting group. "Alright, everyone. Let's all head back up to the scaffolding." The students got to their feet and followed him up the well-used trail. Excited conversations rose and fell as the group made their way up the slope.

"So, you still seeing that farm boy?" Ryk whispered into Sylstyn's lustrous wave of pulled back dark brown hair.

She poked an elbow into his ribs. "He's not a farm boy. He works, or used to work, at a very successful mine, and yes, I'm still seeing him. Actually...." She caught herself and left the word hanging.

Ryk glanced down at her pensive expression. He waited for her to finish, but his attention now became focused on the tall practice scaffolding. "So who the Zym designed that thing?"

"Hey! We all worked really hard to come up a functional design for that." Sylstyn's rich, high voice was shaded with hurt pride.

"Sorry! I didn't mean to offend you. It's just that, well, I mean. This whole crazy idea of roping a klynking comet just strikes me as a colossal waste of time."

Sylstyn stared down at the stony ground for a moment. "I know. We're all really excited to be part of it, and I know the Academy has expended a ton of time and dyrn to make it happen, but I agree. It seems like such a long shot." They walked along without saying anything for a few moments.

"Hey! I've got a great idea. Why don't you convince farm boy to go up and be one of the brave explorers on this loony mission, and you and I can..."

"Ryk, stop! It's not going to work out."

He responded with a hmpf of disapproval. When they reached the base of the tower, Ryk craned his neck back to get a good look up at the platform. Bynkr walked over and stood next to him.

"Seems pretty high, doesn't it?"

"Yep."

"Ready to give it a try?"

"Suppose so."

"Alright, B crew! Grab the rope and head up the hill!" the professor yelled to the students below. Once he was sure they had heard him, he began climbing up the ladder.

Ryk reached over, grabbed Sylstyn's hand, and pulled her around to face him. "How bout a good luck kiss?" He bent down, puckered his lips, and moved toward her. She ducked to the side, but did plant a warm, wet kiss onto his cheek.

"There, good luck."

"That's my girl!"

Ryk ascended the final rungs up to the platform and took a moment to take in the view. Off to the south, the flat dusty expanse of Tyrl spread out until it hit the mountains behind to the west. Smoke from factories and trains rose up in the still afternoon air.

Bynkr cleared his throat to get Ryk's attention. The mag driver took one last look, then turned around.

"So Ryk, here's how this works. The ground crew will start swinging the ball, er, mock comet, down through that gully. We have this pole rigged up with eyelets that you can see the rope is running through, and it pivots, then....."

"Yeah, I can see how it works." Ryk took a few steps forward and grabbed the end of the pole from the professor. He gave it a couple practice swings left then right. With his other hand, he grasped the rope and pulled hard. "First of all, you need a stiffer rope. This is never gonna work."

He sent a most unkind little smirk over at Bynkr. Sylstyn's rejection of his attempt at reunion had put him in a foul mood. Ryk began to twirl the pole around on its pivot and pay out rope. He soon had a sixty-foot long section sweeping in a big circle above the gully. The two students up on the platform leaned over the rail and watched attentively. Every once in a while, they whispered to each other.

Ryk continued to rotate the pole in a clockwise direction. Right before it hit the 11 o'clock position, he slowed the rotation. This caused the rope to momentarily go slack, and as a consequence, the loop at the end opened.

"There, that's about as good as it's going to get. Need a stiffer rope." He looked over his shoulder at Bynkr. "You wanna have them get that thing swingin?"

"Huh? Oh, yeah, sure." The department head stepped to the back of the platform and gave a high arcing wave of his hand. On the ground below, the students began to pull the rope back, then let it slide through their gloved hands. While they chanted in rhythm, the pockmarked grey ball swung up to the head of gully and wobbled slightly before plunging down along the gash.

Ryk followed the swinging ball on its trajectory. His lips drew together, and all expression dropped from his face. Without taking his eyes off the object, he leaned his head back toward the students standing behind him.

"Alright boys, I'm gonna need you to pull the rope tight when I give the order, and also let the pole pull the slack back out as it swings. Think you can handle that?"

"You bet!" the sandy haired student yelled. The other, more quiet young man just nodded.

The chant of "Hoh...Oh...Oh!" from the ground crew grew louder as they pulled and released with more force. Ryk watched the grey ball rise up to its maximum height, pause suspended, then fall. He deftly swung the pole around, eased off at just the right moment, and readjusted his grip.

"Alright boys, we were really close on that last pass! When I say pull, pull 'er with all you've got! Bynkr, I might need you to coil up their slack. In case we miss, I don't want the rope to go zipping out and take one of these fine young gentlemen with it."

The professor jumped across the platform and stood beside his charges. "Isn't this great! Watching a true expert ply his craft. Almost makes me want to give up this academic life and become a driver!"

Ryk continued to watch the swinging target. Again, he leaned his head back slightly.

"I tell you what, roping is a Zym sight easier when you're sitting on a well-trained styrn. I'm not used to being in a stationary position like this. Ah! Here we go, ready.....Pull!"

He yanked back hard on the pole. It broke out of its circular arc and came slashing up beside the platform. A collective "aw!" of dejection resounded from behind him. Ryk stopped rotating the pole and shook out his gloved hand.

"Ooooh! We were so close! A little stiffer rope, and that would have been a winner. This is actually kinda fun, aint it? Kinda like a krydytr game," he called back to the students. Ryk leaned forward and gazed down at the ground crew poised along the steep brown mountainside. Still leaning over the rail, he craned his neck back toward Bynkr. "You ready to give it another go?"

"Give 'em the signal!"

Ryk made a big circle in the air with his arm. On the ground below, the students again began swinging the target.

"Alright, on this next pass, when I say pull, give that rope a one Zym of a pull, and don't stop till I say so. You dumb klynks ready?"

"Yes, sir," the student standing next to Bynkr answered.

Ryk hunched up his shoulders like a cat preparing to spring. His whole body swayed in rhythm with the target. "Okay, on the next pass! Get ready, one, two, three....Pull!"

When he heaved back hard on the pole, the rope whipped by him, leaving the vibration of its braided edges humming in the air. Ryk yanked the pole back sideways, then slammed the end of it down on the rail. A tremendous roar rose up from the ground crew. He took a moment to stare at the grey rubber ball dangling in front of the platform.

"There you go Mr. Department Head. Nothin' to it."

Chapter 39.

Back at his office, Lymdyr was feverishly compiling figures to see if he was going to make budget that month. His secretary appeared in the doorway. She grabbed the edge of the door frame and hung in at a sharp angle.

"How are the numbers coming?"

"Terrible. I may have to stay here and do some magic to make them work. The trip to Phyt Hill cost way more than I had anticipated."

"That's too bad. There's a woman named Byrtymn here to see you. She seems....."

"Byrty's here? Send her in!"

"Will do. You might want to open a window. It's a little stuffy in here." The secretary emphasized her suggestion by holding a brightly painted finger up to her nose.

Lymdyr had been glued to his desk for almost two hours. His nice mint green dress shirt was soaked with sweat. He jumped up from his chair, walked over, and cranked the window open.

The sound of the secretary and Byrty talking out in the hall brought a smile to his face. When he heard Byrty choke out a "thank you", then stifle a sob, the smile vanished. A creeping suspicion grew like a weed in the cracked pavement of his consciousness. He spun around just as the nurse entered the office.

"Byrty! Come on in!" Lymdyr walked around the edge of the desk and opened his arms wide. She hurried over, wiped her nose with a white handkerchief, and crashed into his embrace. Her head of wavy grey-brown hair bounced against his chest with each sob.

"Byrty? What's wrong?"

"Mr. Phrynk....He laid down for his nap a while ago, but he's not going to get up, ever!" Her sobs increased into a full on wail. Several people glanced into the office on their way past. Lymdyr made eye contact with them and shrugged.

"It's okay. It's okay. So Phrynk is gone?"

"Yes."

A whole spectrum of emotions bounced around inside his head as he stood holding the nurse's shaking frame. The shock of her startling news was quickly replaced by a deep, deep concern that perhaps he personally was responsible for Phryrnk's death. Lymdyr kicked notion aside and forced himself to be compassionate. He hugged her just a bit tighter.

"Byrty, I'm so sorry to hear that. I really liked the old boy."

Her sobbing began to slow. Byrty pulled back and gazed up at him with tear flooded eyes. "Oh me too! He was such a loveable old guy."

"So, did he seem like he was getting worse once we brought him back?"

Byrty wiped her nose again and looked at him questioningly. "You mean the paralysis of his left arm?"

"I guess. I just mean his health in general."

"Well, the paralysis did spread down to his left leg. I had to wheel him around the last couple days, but his attitude was wonderful. He couldn't stop talking about what a great time he had!"

"That's good." Lymdyr's legal anxiety lessened a couple notches. The smile returned to his face.

"Oh yeah, at meals, you couldn't shut him up! He would go on and on about how important this project was, and how Ryk was going to train the crew."

Lymdyr let his arms slide off Byrty's soft shoulders. He backed up and sat on the edge of the desk, cradling his chin with his left hand. "Boy, it sure is hard to believe he's gone. Have you notified his children?"

"No, my first impulse was to rush over here. I knew you would want to hear it firsthand."

"Thanks. Well, I still have his son's telemessage address. Do you want to help me put together a notice?"

"No, go ahead. You're much better at that kind of thing. I actually have to get back to work. Whew! I feel better now that we've talked about it. Don't forget to tell Ryk. He'll sure be broken up."

"I certainly will. You know he's in town now."

Byrty's tear-soaked face brightened. "Oh! I had no idea! Maybe we should get together and have a drink in Phrynk's honor."

Lymdyr slid off the desk to a standing position. "Zym, Byrty! That's a great idea! Well, thanks so much for rushing over here. We'll be in touch. Do you need us to call you a buggy?"

"Yes, if you would."

"Sure, just a moment."

Byrdyl had been watching the scene unfold from just outside the office. Lymdyr walked the nurse over to the doorway, then stopped right at the opening.

"Would you ring up a buggy for Byrty?"

"Sure thing." The secretary put her arm around Byrty and guided her out into the main room. Lymdyr watched them move off, then ducked back into his office.

"Got to find that release form first off!" He shot a quick glance up at the wall clock. "Hmm. Not really enough time to go out and tell Ryk today. I'll have to break away sometime tomorrow."

The next day just after lunch, Lymdyr rode out to the test site. He stepped out of the hired buggy, brushed no small amount of dust off his finely tailored pants, then called up to the driver. "Might as well relax. I could be here a while."

The mid-spring sun poured down as he walked up the trail. All around him, the dull green bushes released their sweet herb-petroleum scent into the air. He could hear Ryk shouting out orders from the top of the platform.

"You almost had it that time! Remember what I told you? As soon as the loop's heading directly toward it, give the pole a yank for all you're worth. What? Oh, let me see. Yeah, you've got a nice splinter jammed in there. Better go down and we'll pull it out."

Lymdyr shielded his eyes. He could see the silhouetted figures move to the edge of the platform.

"Ground crew! Take a break!" Ryk's powerful tenor voice echoed off the stony hills.

The railroad man watched the figures up on the platform descend the ladder and pick their way down the hillside. Professor Bynkr led the group over to where Lymdyr was waiting.

"Ah, Mr. Lymdyr! What brings you out here? Come to take your turn at lassoing the comet?"

"I might give it a try, just for fun. So how is the training going?"

"Well, Ryk seems to have it down. The students, eh, let's just say they are having a tough time getting the hang of it. Excuse me, I need to attend to a small medical issue."

Bynkr led the student with the splinter down to a big open wagon parked along the path. Several moments later, Ryk finished his conversation with the ground crew, and came sauntering down the trail.

"Lymdyr! What're you doin' out here?" The mag driver's face lit up in a smile.

"Just thought I'd come out and check up on you. How are things going?"

"To tell you the truth, not so good. We finally got some stiffer rope, but even though these are a great bunch of kids, not one of them is worth a Zym at roping. None of 'em. A couple of them have come close. How have you been?"

"I've been good. Hey, got time to go for a little walk. Just you and me?"

"I suppose." Ryk took a moment to take in the somber expression on Lymdyr's face. The mag driver's long, dark eyebrows twisted slightly. "What's up?"

Lymdyr took a quick scan of the area. He spied a faint trail heading off along the gully. "Come on, let's walk over here."

While they picked their way across the stony ground, he practiced the exact words that would break the news to Ryk.

When they were out of earshot of the group, Lymdyr began speaking in a low, thoughtful tone.

"Byrty came by to see me yesterday."

"Oh yeah? How's she getting along?"

"She was pretty broken up yesterday."

Ryk turned his head to face him. "What was she broken up about?" All the cheeriness drained out of his voice.

The railroad man drew in a quick breath. "I guess Phrynk died in his sleep yesterday." He couldn't force himself to look Ryk in the eye, and just remained focused on the bumpy, uneven path before them.

Ryk stopped walking. Lymdyr stopped also. He could sense the burning energy emanating from the mag driver. Fearing the worst, he slowly lifted his gaze toward Ryk.

The mag driver stood stock still. His face was frozen in disbelief, mouth set with tension. Ryk's dark, wide set eyes smoldered with intensity. His creased eyelids sagged at the edges.

"This happened just yesterday?" Lymdyr nodded. "Blyrt! I knew it. I klynking knew it! Something told me that first day I was back that I had to go see him. Dyth! Why didn't I listen!"

Ryk kicked the toe of his boot into the hard packed ground. A shower of dirt and rocks sprayed out into the bushes. He put his gloved hands on his hips and sucked in a shuddering breath.

"Well, that's not news I wanted to hear." The tremulous nature of Ryk's words left little doubt that he was fighting the urge to cry. He hung his head in sorrow. Lymdyr summoned all of his diplomatic skills to try and defuse the situation.

"She, uh, excuse me. I'm having a hard time talking. She said that he had been really happy since we got back, couldn't stop talking about the project, and how proud he was of you."

"Did he now?" Ryk's question was tinged with anger.

"I think we should still get together with her. It might help all of us deal with this."

Ryk lifted his chin and locked the railroad man in a piercing, agonized stare. "That's a nice thing to say. You and Byrty got to spend a whole three days with him. I've known him since I was really just a kid, just a stupid, stubborn kid."

"Byrty is really broken up. She's cared for him for....."

"Yeah, I bet she is!" Ryk snapped. He turned away from Lymdyr and wiped the moisture from his eyes. After looking off to the dusty outline of the city for a couple moments, he spoke in a quavering voice. "You got a buggy waiting?"

"Yes."

"Good. Let's get out of here."

"You want me to tell Bynkr?"

"I don't care." Ryk spun around and began walking straight through the bushes. He broke off handfuls of the dry, brittle branches and crushed them in his fists.

Lymdyr hiked back up toward the tower. The professor and a large group of the students watched him approach. "Everything alright?" Bynkr asked once the railroad man was within speaking range.

"Ryk's good friend and mentor Phrynk Nine Line died yesterday." A gush of compassion issued from the group. "He had wanted to stop and see him when he came into town three days ago, but there wasn't time. He's pretty upset about it. I'm going to take him back into town. I'm sure he'll be okay by tomorrow."

"Well, give him our condolences. We'll keep practicing."

"Yeah, I'll see you later."

Lymdyr gave a little wave, then spun on his heels and walked briskly back to the buggy. Ryk was already seated inside. Lymdyr jumped in, and they began rolling down the rutted track. Neither man said anything. Ryk just stared out the window. The pain he was feeling was all too evident by the creases running across his forehead. Lymdyr tried to think of something useful to say, but nothing came.

Once they reached the main road, the buggy driver slowed to a halt. "Where to?" he called from his seat.

Lymdyr looked over at Ryk's pained features. "You want to go have a drink?"

"Sure."

"You want to go over to that place where Lylyn works?"

"Last place I'd like to go."

For several desperate moments, Lymdyr wracked his brain to come up with a suitable destination. He rejected the option of a fancy drinking establishment or a rowdy Plugian bar.

Outside, the styrns harnessed to the buggy snorted in the dusty, late afternoon air. Suddenly, an idea came to him. Lymdyr stuck his head out the window. "To the mag yards!"

The buggy lurched forward. A wave of fatigue swept over him. Lymdyr settled back against the seat and let the weight of the day pull him downward.

"Man, I have lousy luck saying goodbye to people." Ryk offered in a low, steady voice.

"Yeah?"

"Yeah. I ran away from home when I was fourteen. My step dad was a real blyrthole. After I left, I didn't write any letters, nothing. After about six months, something told me to go back home. Well, Mom had died a week before I arrived. One klynkin' week! If I'd just come home earlier." He spit out the window and shook his head. "And now Phrynk's gone. Seems like I don't have much left."

Even though he was on the verge of nodding off, Lymdyr pulled himself upright on the seat. "All I can say is that according to Byrty, Phrynk was one happy old man. Couldn't stop talking about how you were going to help this project that was going to send people out to the stryrks. Oh, and I guess he really got a kick out of visiting the old camp down by the Hok."

Both the men spent the rest of the ride just staring out the windows. The desert landscape gradually gave way to rows of low buildings and houses. When they turned off the main boulevard, and entered the fairgrounds, Ryk stuck his head out the window. He pulled back in and sent a questioning glance over at Lymdyr.

"What're we doing down here?"

"I was having trouble thinking of a suitable place to go, so I thought this might work."

The slightest trace of a grin broke across Ryk's solemn face. "I'll say you were having trouble if all you could think of was this place."

The buggy wheeled around and pulled up in front of a non-descript, run down building\shack right next to the endless wooden rails of the stockyard. A sign on top was missing several letters, blown away by the wind long ago. It was supposed to read Water Hole. Without the missing letters, it read Hell Water.

Ryk opened the door of the buggy and jumped down. A breeze had kicked up. Wave after wave of brown dust from the empty yards pelted him as he stood waiting for Lymdyr. The railroad man eased himself out, pulled a couple bills out of his wallet, and handed it up to the driver.

"You want me to wait? This ain't a great place to try and hail a ride." The driver kept one hand on top of his tall, battered black hat to keep it from blowing away.

Lymdyr looked around at the deserted maze of wooden corrals. The dust storm that was brewing had just begun to blot out the early evening sunset. Above him, long bands of clouds reflected the fading orange light.

"Yeah, I guess so."

The desolation of the surroundings and his annoyance at the amount of money he was shelling for transportation further darkened his mood. He walked around the back of buggy and was hit full force by the wind.

"Zym! It's really blowing out here!"

"Sure is. Let's get out of the open."

Ryk pulled his wide brimmed hat down tight, tilted his head into the wind, and walked toward the low, non-descript building. Lymdyr held a hand up to keep the dust from peppering his face.

There were no windows on the front of the weathered structure. A collection of styrns were tied up to the rail outside, and a few wagons parked off to the side, but otherwise, an observer might not be able to guess that the building was a tavern. Just before reaching the big rough-hewn door, Ryk stopped and turned back toward his companion.

"You're sure you want to go in dressed like that?"

Lymdyr looked down at his finely tailored brown suit. "I don't see as I have much choice."

A gritty little smile drifted across Ryk's face while he tugged the door open. Both men ducked inside. The combination of thick gynt smoke and dim lighting obscured all details. Slowly, their eyes began to adjust. The only sources of light were two lamps set at the far ends of a shelf behind the bar.

Long benches and picnic table style furniture were the only adornments to the bare room. Several of the patrons took a moment to size up the new arrivals, then resumed whatever they were doing.

"Quite the place, huh?" Ryk commented.

"Yeah, a little on the bleak side."

"Come on, let's get a drink." Ryk led the way across the dusty floor and over to the long, well-worn bar. "You should see this place during the roundup. Boy, oh boy! It's packed with drivers. I've been in here when you literally didn't have room to move."

A tall, somewhat cadaverous man stood and stared at them from behind the bar. Ryk nodded a greeting to which the bartender did not react.

"Physt, please."

Slowly and ponderously, the man behind the bar slid a wooden mug from the pile next to him, popped the lid off a barrel sitting on the floor, dipped the mug in, then set the dripping receptacle down in front of Ryk. Lymdyr sent a quick glance over at the amber liquid spreading out on the dusty bar top.

"I'll have a pyryn." The bartender shook his head. "Physt, then."

A dripping mug was placed before Lymdyr. Both he and Ryk grasped the sticky handles and lifted their drinks.

"To Phrynk," Ryk offered in as celebratory voice as he could muster.

"To Phrynk."

They gently thudded the wooden mugs together, then drank. Droplets of the liquid dripped down and formed tracks on the soft brushed fabric of Lymdyr's suit. He tried to ignore the growing sense of revulsion for the place. Images of the classy bar at the Plynyr Hotel with its soft green leather booths, and cadre of beautiful, off-work dancers from the hall next door drifted through his mind.

The arrival of three, long antennaed creatures that came skittering across the bar dissipated his revelry. They stopped long enough to suck up some of the physt. Lymdyr raised his hand to smash them, but wasn't quick enough.

From one of the picnic tables in the middle of the room, a deep, ragged voice called out. "Hey, did one of you just say something about Phyrnk?"

Ryk swiveled around and gazed down at the rumpled character addressing him. "Yeah. What's it to ya?"

Another one of the patrons, a man with long stringy grey hair and a full beard to match, was about to take a drink at the table further down the row. He stopped raising the mug in mid-air upon hearing Ryk's sharp reply.

"Well, ain't you two a fine pair. What the Zym you doin' in here any how?"

Ryk rested his elbows on the bar and directed his attention to the grey haired individual. "Ya know what, bud? I been comin' to this dump since before I was legally able to. I think I first stumbled through that door when I was just about sixteen."

"You a mag driver?"

"Yep."

For the next ten minutes, Ryk and the long haired patron chatted about mag driving. Lymdyr stood next to the bar, trying not to touch any of the surfaces. His main objective now was to formulate a polite way of exiting. After a moment of silence, Ryk took another drink from his mug, and stared down at the wood plank floor.

"I still can't believe Phrynk is gone."

The skeletal barkeep stopped stacking boxes. "What'da mean Phyrnk's gone? Is he dead?"

"The tough old boy died in his sleep yesterday." Ryk held up the dripping mug. "To Phrynk, best mag driver there ever was."

"Well, dyth shoot. He used a come in here years and years ago. Tell you what, I'll top off all your drinks in memory of Phrynk."

One by one, the barkeep filled the mugs of all the patrons. Ryk held his high. "To my good friend Phrynk, may he ride through Myrnvar forever!"

"To Phrynk," the rest of the voices chimed in.

Lymdyr looked down to see several small brown chunks floating across the oily surface of the physt. After skillfully titling his mug just far enough to allow the now suspect liquid to touch his lips, he set the full container down on the center of the bar top.

"Well, gentlemen, I hate to say, but I must head on out." He glanced down at the dirt streaked, unfriendly faces glaring back up at him, then over at Ryk. "Again, I'm really sad about Phyrnk, also. He was a Zym of a great old guy. You want me to send the buggy back after I get dropped off?"

"No, I figure I can find my own way back." Ryk's tight skinned features had again become stern and emotionless.

"Alright, well, good night all." Lymdyr flashed a quick smile. He thought briefly about using the bathroom at the Hell Water, but opted to pee against the side of the building once he was back outside.

Chapter 40.

Three days later, Professor Bynkr walked down the hall toward Bokyl's office. He wrung his hands together as he approached the open door. The head reagent was sitting at his desk filling out evaluations when Bynkr gave the door a quick knock and entered.

"Good morning, Head Regent."

"Good morning. What can I do for you?"

Bynkr walked up to the desk and stood with his arms crossed. Bokyl studied his long, sideburned face. It wasn't hard to tell by the professor's dead serious expression that something was wrong.

"How's the training going?"

"Well, that's what I came up to discuss. Ryk hasn't showed up for the last two days."

"What? Why didn't you tell me yesterday?"

"It was late when we got back, and your door was closed."

"I was in here giving evaluations!" Bokyl pushed his chair back and folded his hands across his lap. "Great, just great. I suppose we should contact Lymdyr. Will nothing go smoothly for this project!"

"We *have* been continuing to practice," Bynkr offered with a touch of timidity.

"Thirty-five days to launch, and we still don't have an engineer that can successfully operate the propulsion system! Are you going back out to the test site?"

"Well, I thought I might try and get some word on whether Ryk was...."

Bokyl sprang up from his chair. "Get back out there, and I'll send Lymdyr an urgent telemessage."

Over at the railroad admin building, Lymdyr's secretary came swinging by her boss' wooden inbox, grabbed Bokyl's telemessage sheet, took a quick scan, then hurried over to his office. Through the closed door, Byrdyl could hear the familiar deep, scratchy voice of the regional vice president.

"Two things Lymdyr. Here is the invoice for the damage to the executive car. I don't have to tell you how disappointed we are by your carelessness. Now about this additional bill from the styrn handlers. Two thousand extra dymrs for, and I quote, excessive physical exertion required to safely transport Phrynk from the mag driver camp back to the car. We didn't okay the transportation of a feeble old man on styrn-back!"

On the other side of the closed door, Byrdyl re-read the short, urgent telemessage from Bokyl once, then twice. Summoning up all her courage, she gave the door a couple hard raps. Inside the office, conversation ceased. The door swung open to reveal Lymdyr's haggard face.

"Zym, Byrdyl! What is it?"

"I'm so sorry, Mr. Lymdyr, but this just arrived." She held out the yellow sheet.

Lymdyr snatched it from her hand. She watched his dry, red streaked eyes flash back and forth. Upon finishing the read, he tilted his head back.

"Why? Why today of all days?" Lymdyr let go a deep exasperated sigh, thought for a moment, then lowered his gaze back down to the secretary.

"Send Bokyl a reply. Tell him there is no klynking way I can break loose today. Maybe, early this evening, no! Don't say that! First thing tomorrow morning. Tell him I'll stop by in the morning. Got to go!"

A few minutes later, Lymdyr's short, direct reply reached the Academy's telemessage machine. The student operator tore the sheet off and immediately noticed the word "Urgent" printed at the top. He ran up the stairs and directly into Bokyl's office.

"A reply from Mr. Lymdyr." The student held out the sheet which Bokyl snatched from him.

"What? Is this really what he said?"

"I just pulled it off the machine."

Bokyl's round face drew down into a frown. "This won't work. Send another message." He grabbed a piece of paper and pencil off his desk and handed them to the student.

"Lymdyr, this is unacceptable. The success of this mission relies on getting Ryk back out there immediately. Please drop what you are doing, and proceed accordingly.....Got that?" The student repeated the terse message. "Alright, send that off, and let me know how he responds.

When Bokyl's telemessage arrived at the railroad office, the operator tore it off the machine, and hustled over to Byrdyl's desk. "Message from the Academy."

Without so much as a thank you, the secretary grabbed the sheet, power walked over to the office, and rapped sharply on the door. Lymdyr again swung the door open, and stuck his even more haggard, now sweating face out.

"Message for you." Byrdyl said quietly.

He snatched the paper from her, unfolded it, and gave a quick scan. "Zym! Not today!" Lymdyr glanced back at the two figures planted directly in front of his desk, then turned back toward Byrdyl.

"I am in such a bind today." He stepped back into the room without letting go of the door. "Gentlemen, can we take a five-minute break?"

"Five minutes! That's all," one of the executives called out.

Lymdyr nodded and slid out into the main room. He walked quickly and with purpose along the aisle.

"Tough day?" Byrdyl asked in a low, calm voice.

"You have no idea. What am I going to do?"

"Well, first of all, tell me what's going on."

"The head of the Academy is asking me to drop everything, run over to the Jybyr neighborhood, and find out why Ryk hasn't shown up for training the last two days. I have both Systrn and Ryft in my office grilling me about finances. I have every indication that they're going to be here all day. I'm so klynked."

"And you have to go talk to that Ryk fella today?"

"I don't see how, unless I go over tonight. Hopefully, those two won't want to go out to a lavish pyryst. Actually, they're so torqued about dyrn, there's not much chance of them wanting to spend a kryn."

At approximately six-thirty, Lymdyr staggered out of the mostly deserted admin building. He pushed the big, glass front doors open and looked up at the marvelous spring sky. A huge swath of high gauzy clouds extended from one end of the horizon to the other.

"What a day!" Lymdyr dragged himself over to the waiting buggy, climbed up in, and in a tired voice directed the driver to take him to the shabby, vice ridden neighborhood of Jybyr. He thudded lifelessly back against the seat.

"Bynhyld will be furious. I didn't even have time to send a messenger over to tell her I'll be late." He let go a little defeated laugh. "What's the point, anyway? She'll probably be leaving me soon." Lymdyr folded his fingers together and gazed out at the serene desert landscape.

Twenty-five minutes later, he stepped out onto the broken sidewalk in front of the Gyr tavern. Without hesitation, Lymdyr walked through the open door. Laughter and the smell of spilled physt greeted him. He ignored the stares from the mostly working class patrons and tuned out their snide comments.

Once he reached the bar, Lymdyr glanced along its length in hopes of sighting Ryk or the short, rounded form of his girlfriend. Much to his relief, Lylyn came wheeling around the big table to the left of the bar. She spotted him immediately, threaded her way around the standing drinkers, and sided up next to him.

"Out slumming?"

He stared longingly at the amber cascade of physt being pumped into the line of glasses behind the bar, then directed his attention to Lylyn. "You know it."

She took a moment to examine his fatigued, beaten down expression. "You alright? You look a little drained."

"Yeah, I'm fine. Nothing that a big old pull of physt can't fix." He did manage to send a tired smile her way.

"Well, you came to the right place."

Lylyn squeezed her noticeably pregnant self up to bar, waited till a full glass of the fermented grain beverage appeared, then jostled her way back to Lymdyr. He took the glass from her and pounded half of it down.

"Ah! I've been looking forward to that since noon."

"Bet you're wondering where Ryk is."

"How did you know!"

"Ole Ryk's been holed up in the apartment for two days now. He came home the other night in a first class funk, hasn't eaten nothing or changed his clothes. Just sitting in the dark, stewin."

Lymdyr took another drink and pondered her words. "Mind if I go up and talk to him?"

"No, not at all. You're gonna halfta talk real loud though." A smile spread across her pleasant, slightly filled out face.

"What'd you mean?"

"Well, I doubt whether he's going to let you in. You'll probably have to do all your talking through the door."

"Ah, I got it." Lymdyr drained his glass, and looked around at the raucous, partying crowd. "Might as well give it a try." He accidentally bumped into her swollen belly while reaching into his back pocket. "Oh. I'm sorry!"

"Don't worry. Happens all the time."

"You are certainly getting big. When is the baby due?"

"Just less than five weeks."

"Wow, that's going to be a big baby!"

"Yep, it's gonna be a big one. I gotta get back to work. The building is down the alley right next door, apartment two zero one. Good luck!"

"Thanks."

Lymdyr tucked a bill into her hand and headed back out into the street. Darkness had just fallen. From a doorway across the rutted street, two partially visible figures watched him make his way along the sidewalk. Above the fading noise of the bar, he could hear them whispering.

After sending a quick sideways glance over at the figures, Lymdyr ducked into the alley. A worn, splintered staircase rose up to his right. Just before climbing up the steps, he looked back to make sure no one was following him. There was no sign of the two figures.

He let go a sigh of relief and plodded up the stairs. Once Lymdyr reached the landing, he stopped and leaned against the wall. The drink had helped him to relax, but now the long, exhausting day was catching up with him. From somewhere down the row of doors, he heard angry shouts echoing.

Lymdyr pushed himself off the wall and walked up to apartment 201. He pressed his ear to the door, but heard nothing. A couple hard raps did produce a response.

"Who is it?" Ryk's tenor voice called out.

"Lymdyr. Open the door."

"Go away. I got nothing to say to you."

The railroad man cursed silently and leaned his forehead against the door. "Ryk, I just want to talk for a few minutes. I've had a Zym dyth of a day, and I need to get home."

"Talk away."

"I'd like to sit down."

"Go ahead and sit."

"This landing looks like people have been zynkng on it, smells like it too." Lymdyr smiled at his own humorous reply.

"Afraid you're going to dirty up your nice clothes?"

"Look, I know you're upset about losing Phrynk. All of us are. He was a really great old guy. People die sometimes."

Lymdyr bit his lip. He was way too tired to be negotiating anything. After rolling up his sleeves, he shifted around, leaned back against the door, and let his eyes close.

"Ryk, will you just open the door!"

"Like I said. I got nothing to say to you."

"People are depending on you out there at the site." Lymdyr's plea was followed by a moment of silence.

"I'm done trying to train them. There ain't no way it's going to work."

More shouting, and the crash of a plate against a wooden floor rang out from down the row of doors. A huge brown creature with long, stick-like legs scuttled over Lymdyr's fine leather shoe. He shook it off, then squashed it onto the slats of the landing.

"So there's nothing I can say to get you to go back out there?"

"Nope."

"Alright, see ya round."

Lymdyr waited for some kind of reply. When none materialized, he pushed off against the door and wearily descended the stairs. When he reached the now, dark street, Lymdyr stopped to take a quick scan of the surroundings.

On the opposite sidewalk, two couples staggered along. The women were singing a bawdy drinking song. Their ragged, off key singing added a welcome touch of levity to his somber mood. He rubbed his face several times to try and generate some vigor.

"Zym, I'm tired! Should have arranged a buggy. Where am I going to find one now? I really need to go home, but I sure hate to just leave this hanging. Maybe I should go talk to Byrty."

The image of the nurse's dimpled white buttocks rising up like two lumps of bread dough on the bartender's couch in Phyt Hill flashed through his mind. A smile broke across Lymdyr's face.

From down the street, the shouts and loud conversations of the tavern spilled out into the night. For lack of anything better to do, he walked toward the beacon of humanity in the otherwise deserted area.

A half dead black styrn tethered to a rickety wagon was parked out front of the tavern. A half dead driver in a frayed black suit sat motionless in the seat.

"Hey! I need a ride. You available?"

The old man's motionless form came to life. He lifted his head to speak. "Yeah."

"I need a ride over to Hyn Park."

The old man moved over in the seat and Lymdyr climbed up next to him. Neither man spoke as they rolled through the quiet streets. The railroad man sighed with relief when they passed the intersection leading out of the dilapidated neighborhood.

Fifteen minutes later, they pulled up in front of the dark, rolling lawn at the old folk's home. Lymdyr extracted several bills out of his wallet and held them out to the driver.

"Wait here."

With the sound of night creatures croaking happily in the pond nearby, he opened the gate and crunched his way up the walk. Light from a single lamp at the reception desk cast just enough illumination through the front window for him to thread his way onto the front porch. He glanced over at the line of empty rocking chairs, then stuck his face up next to the window. Through the gauzy curtain he could see a small figure seated at the desk.

Lymdyr stepped to his right and gently knocked on the front door. After several moments, the curtain at the window pulled aside, and a back lit face squinted out at him.

"May I help you?" a high-pitched voice inquired.

"I'm a friend of Byrty's. Sorry for showing up at this hour, but I'd really like to talk to her. Is she on duty tonight?"

"No, Byrty is on days this week."

Lymdyr fought the urge to slam his fist against the wood siding. After taking a deep breath to compose himself, he spoke in a calm, measured tone.

"I see. Would it be okay if I left her a note?"

There was a moment of hesitation before a reply was given. "Well, I suppose. She isn't in any kind of trouble, is she?"

"No, Myrnvar no!" Lymdyr let out a frustrated snort of a laugh. "I was a friend of Mr. Phrynk, and since his passing, I've wanted to contact her. It was such a shock."

"Yes, we were all very sad to have him pass. Hold on, let me get something to write with."

With the security chain still attached, a young nurse opened the door just wide enough to pass a pencil and paper to Lymdyr. He hurriedly scrawled out a message, then handed it back.

"Thanks, and good night."

Chapter 41.

After grabbing a quick four hours of sleep, Lymdyr arrived in time for work the next day. Byrdyl met him at the door.

"Good morning. You look terrible," she said as he entered the noisy main room.

"I feel terrible, thanks."

"Here, I made you a big cup of zyd. Also, the guy at the Academy has already sent you two messages."

Lymdyr took the steaming cup from her in one hand, the telemessage sheets in the other, and continued walking toward his office. Byrdyl hurried to keep up with him. He took a mouth searing drink and winced.

"Are the exec's here yet?"

Byrdyl nodded her head of brown, nicely coiffed hair. "They're in your office. They showed up about twenty minutes ago."

"Wonderful. What a way to start? Do I have any appointments today?"

"Just the Dymran meeting at four-thirty."

"Hmm. If I can get rid of these two flygrs, I might actually be able to make it. Oh! That's right!" Lymdyr stopped just before reaching his office.

"This is really important. I need you to send a messenger over to, dyth, what's the name of the old folk's home at Hyn Park? Something rest home. Anyway, I left a note for Byrty. I really, really need to get a reply from her. Let's see, what time is it?" He pulled his large, gold pocket watch out of his vest and popped it open. "Okay, it's quarter till. She should be there already....."

"Lymdyr! Is that you out there?" a commanding voice boomed from inside his office.

"Yeah, its me." He leaned toward the open door to respond.

"We've been here for almost an hour. Can we get started?"

Lymdyr bent forward and whispered. "She's already there. Have the messenger get a reply and bring it back here immediately."

Byrdyl nodded her head and whirled an about face. Lymdyr watched her curvy figure shift beneath her dress, tucked the yellow sheets under his arm, and charged into the office.

Across town, in the quiet, thorn tree-shaded neighborhood, Mihyn was busy cooking breakfast. Handynr was still asleep. Normally, the mundane activity would have absorbed all her attention, but this morning, she was distracted.

Every time she shuttled back and forth between the stove and kitchen table, Mihyn sent a gut wrenching glance down the hall. Handynr's leather work bag hung innocently on the closet door knob. Once the plates and silverware had been neatly put in their place, she succumbed to her curiosity and fear. Like a burglar creeping around the victim's house, Mihyn tip toed by the bedroom.

"Okay, he's definitely still asleep. Here goes."

Hands shaking with dread, she moved on toward the front door, and without making a sound, pulled the lip of the leather bag out so that its interior was illuminated. Sweat broke out on her graceful neck while she thumbed through the sheaths of papers.

"No letters. Whew!"

"Dear, what time is it?" Handynr called from the bedroom.

Mihyn jumped slightly. She hustled over to the doorway and stuck her head around the opening. "Time to get up. We both slept late."

Handynr rose up to a sitting position, yawned, stretched, and rubbed his stubbly chin. "Something's burning."

"Oh, blyrt!" Mihyn's smile of relief disappeared as the acrid smell of burning eggs reached her nostrils. She raced into the kitchen and yanked the scorched pan off the burner.

Handynr walked up next to her. He glanced down at the burnt breakfast. "Wow, you're usually so on top of things."

Mihyn let go a barely perceptible laugh. "Well, I have a lot on my mind today. Don't forget we have a Dymran meeting at four-thirty."

"Today?"

"Yes, today. This is a really important one."

"What time is it now? I have to be over at the regional office at nine."

Mihyn laid the pan into the sink, then craned her neck around toward the wall clock. "Almost eight."

"I don't know how I'm going to make it."

His wife handed him a steaming cup of zyd. "Go ahead and drink this while I toast some blynys."

Several minutes later, she set a plate of buttered rolls on the table. Handynr took a huge bite, chewed through it, then slumped back in his chair.

"I just can't seem to wake up today. I don't even know what time it was when I got home last night."

"It must have been late. I didn't even hear you come in." Mihyn stepped around behind him and slid her arms over his shoulders. Her husband leaned back to look up at her inverted face.

"What would I do without you?" Handynr watched a smile rise up on her pale features. He returned his gaze to the zyd cup in his hands.

"First thing I'll do when I get to the office is have Kym arrange for me to get from the hall over to the Academy this afternoon. So you honestly think this whole project is really going to come together?"

Mihyn stopped stroking his chest and reared back. "Yes, I think it's going to come together!" Her voice had just a touch of irritated incredulousness to it.

Handynr swirled his cup around. "I guess I've been so busy lately, I haven't really been keeping up with it. How long till they, I mean we, launch?"

She let go of him, glided around the table, and slid onto her chair. "You're not having second thoughts about going again, are you?"

"You know I can't lie to you. I've been having second, third, maybe even fourth thoughts about going." He let out a long sigh, leaned back in his chair, and stared up at the ceiling.

Mihyn felt herself tremble slightly. For the first time, her husband had actually vocalized his hesitation about being part of the crew. A sensation close to panic roared through her. She glanced up at the clock.

"Honey, I wish we had time to talk about this. Both you and I have places we need to be, quickly. If you have the slightest doubt about....."

Handynr snapped his head forward, reached over, and gave her hand a squeeze. "You know, I'm just a little tired from travelling. I'll certainly be at that meeting today." He leaned forward and planted a kiss on her soft cheek. "I better get moving."

10:30- Byrdyl came sweeping by the telemessage counter on her hourly rounds just as a uniformed courier entered the big, glass-paned front doors. The secretary altered her course to intercept. "Do you have something for Mr. Lymdyr?"

The courier thumbed through a pile of papers in her leather bag. "Yes, I do." She pulled out a yellow sheet which Byrdyl took from her.

"Thanks. He's been waiting for this."

The courier saluted, and headed back out the front doors, while Byrdyl sped off toward Lymdyr's office. She stopped in front of her boss' door and gave it a sharp, knuckle rap. After a moment, he opened the door just a crack. His eyes were fixed on the sheet in her hand.

"One moment gentlemen," he called out over his shoulder. Lymdyr eased into the open doorway. "What does it say?"

"Byrty says she gets off at three-thirty and would be glad to talk to Ryk."

"Dyth! That's going to be cutting it close. Send a reply and ask her if she can get off early. Bye!"

12:00- Byrdyl was addressing a pile of envelopes when she heard Lymdyr's loud voice. A moment later, he came striding up to her desk.

"How are things going today?" she asked while neatly stacking the pile.

Lymdyr shot a glance over at the two executives he had been meeting with as they exited through the front doors. "Better than yesterday. I think they're going to leave after myrf. Any word back from Byrty?"

Byrdyl shook her head. "The messenger said they could maybe get a reply back by two."

"Boy, making that four-thirty meeting with Ryk is not going to be easy. If the messenger shows up while we're at myrf, come and find me."

"Will do, sir."

Lymdyr flashed a quick smile and hustled to catch up with the executives.

1:30- Lymdyr and the two managers returned from lunch. Just before entering the building, the shorter of the two executives stopped and turned to face their underling.

"We need to head over to the office for a high level board meeting." He let the gravity and mystery of the announcement sink in for just a moment. "To summarize, we are very disappointed in the lack of judgement you exhibited during the trip to Phyt Hill. As a result, you may not use the exec car without written permission moving forward, and more importantly, no more expenditures of greater than one hundred dymrs without written permission. Any questions?" Lymdyr shook his head. "Very well, good day."

After shaking hands with his superiors, Lymdyr pushed the glass doors open, and drifted over to Byrdyl's desk. "Good, they're finally gone, and I still have a job! At least for now. No word from Byrty?"

"None."

"What to do? Should I wait and see what Byrty says, or just head over?" He drummed his fingers on the desktop. "I guess there's no point in rushing over if she can't get off early."

2:15- A tall, rail thin courier walked in through the front doors. Byrdyl saw him enter and got up from her desk. The courier smiled broadly as the curvy secretary approached.

"Hello, ma'am. Message for..."

"Mr. Lymdyr. I'll take it."

"Oh, alright." He swung his well-worn leather pouch around to the front, flipped through the stack once, then twice. "Hmmm, I know there's one in here."

Byrdyl glanced up at the wall clock. She tapped her foot. The courier dug around in the pouch and eventually found the sheet. "There you go."

"Thank you. We won't be sending a reply."

"Oh, thank you. Goodbye ma'am."

The secretary snatched the message from him and hurried over to Lymdyr's office. He was giving a play-by-play account of his meeting with the executives to the mailroom supervisor. Byrdyl walked right in. Lymdyr jumped up, reached over his desk, and took the sheet from her.

"Great! She did get off early." He looked up at the clock on the wall, then over at the jolly face of the mailroom supervisor. "Sorry, Hez, I'll finish the story later."

"No problem. I should probably get back to work anyway." The large, affable man whistled as he left the room.

"Quick Byrdyl, I'll need a buggy right away."

"Already got one waiting."

"Dyth, you are efficient!"

2:55-As soon as the buggy pulled up to the gate of the old folk's home, Lymdyr jumped out. Byrty was sitting in one of the rocking chairs, enjoying the afternoon breeze. She met him halfway up the walk.

"Afternoon! So we're off to talk to Ryk?"

"Yeah, I have a meeting at four-thirty that I really need to drag him to, so come on. We don't have a lot of time." The two walked side by side back down the gravelly path. "By the way, you look great."

"Thanks, I quit drinking after Phrynk's passing. I feel a lot better."

"Quit drinking, huh? That doesn't sound like much fun."

"Well, not completely quit. Just slowing down I guess."

Once they were seated in the cab across from each other and rolling along, Lymdyr bent forward and levelled his gaze at the nurse.

"Ryk's still pretty broken up about Phrynk's death. According to his girlfriend, he hasn't left the apartment since then. I need you to try and think of anything you can say that might motivate him. Did Phrynk say anything particularly inspiring in the days before he passed?"

Byrty had been looking out the window at the wide sweep of the park. Lymdyr's question caused her to shift in the seat.

"Well, he talked a lot about Ryk's role in the project, and how it will make people think differently about mag drivers."

"Good! Excellent! That's the kind of stuff I think we can use to get him back on track." Lymdyr rubbed his hands together.

3:15-The buggy pulled up on the street where Lylyn's apartment was located. As soon as the two of them climbed down from the cab, a horrible smell hit their senses.

"Ugh! Something must have died out here." Lymdyr held a hand up to his mouth.

Byrty just made an awful face and followed him down the broken sidewalk. "This is where he's staying?"

"Yeah, not the best neighborhood in town." The afternoon sun hit both of them full force as they hurried along. Lymdyr led the way up the creaking stairway. Byrty wiped a drop of sweat off her forehead halfway up.

"Boy! It's warm today."

"Yes it is."

They reached the landing and continued over to the door marked 201. Lymdyr knocked on it with enough force to be heard.

"Who is it?" Ryk's voice echoed from within.

"Lymdyr and Byrty."

"Hello, Ryk," the nurse cooed.

There was no answer. Lymdyr took a step forward. "We're here to try and convince you to come to the Dymran meeting this afternoon."

"Won't work."

Lymdyr made eye contact with the nurse. She recognized the exasperated, "See what I mean?" expression on his face and moved over next to him.

"Ryk, I know that you are still grieving for Phrynk. I am too. He was such....."

"Yeah, and if that fancy dressed blyrthole out there hadn't dragged him down there to the Hok, he'd still be around."

Lymdyr and the nurse again glanced at each other. She gave a knowing nod of her mostly grey haired head, then turned back toward the door.

"Listen Ryk, before Lymdyr decided to bring Phyrnk down to meet with you, the old boy was definitely on the way out. After he came back, he was the happiest I've ever seen him. He was so proud of you for agreeing to help out. He died a very happy man."

"I don't believe you! That slimy son of a hykr out there probably paid you to say that."

"How dare you! I loved Phrynk just as much as you did! I would never say anything like that if it wasn't true." Byrty stood in front of the door, staring a burning hole into it. Her pasty cheeks were now splashed with red blotches.

"Listen to me, you sorry excuse for a man! You promised Phrynk that you would come up here and help this project out. If you go back on your word, you are the lowest pond gyrk in Ulutrita. You need to open this door right now and come to the meeting!"

Lymdyr couldn't contain his glee. He had to force himself to breathe slowly and evenly to keep from busting out laughing. The sound of heavy boot falls sounded from inside the apartment. The door creaked open to reveal a tired and bleary eyed Ryk. He stood and stared at Byrty. Warm, musty air rushed out with him. Lymdyr recognized the same brown linen shirt Ryk had been wearing two nights before.

"Who's at the door?" Lylyn's disembodied voice called out.

"Nobody," Ryk replied over his shoulder.

The creak of wooden bed slats preceded Lylyn's emergence from the back room. She leaned against the door frame, holding a sheet wrapped around herself. "Is that Lymdyr and some woman?"

"Yeah."

"Don't you think about going out drinking with them! Remember, we got to spend dyrn on things for the baby, not...."

"I'm not going drinking with them! They want me to go to a meeting with them."

"Ha!" The laugh had a spiteful, distrusting snap to it. "How stupid do you think I am? You're going out drinking with them and leaving me here to go to work."

"Lylyn! Enough! I told you, there's a meeting they want me...."

"Don't yell at me! You've been here over a week, and haven't brought a kryn in." She advanced out of the doorway and was now standing next to the couch. Bags of loose skin drooped down under her eyes. Her thick black hair was nothing more than a lopsided pile atop her head.

"Excuse me, Lylyn, but he really....." Lymdyr attempted to jump in.

"You shut it mister!" She pointed a finger at him. "I know better than to believe anything you say."

"Come on, let's just go," Ryk muttered. He made a move out of the open doorway.

"Do you think you could change your shirt?" Byrty asked in a kindly voice.

Ryk looked down at the dubious yellow flecks dried in a flood pattern down his front. "Klynk!" He turned on his boots, unbuttoning the shirt as he walked.

"So what? You're just going to walk on out?" Lylyn snapped when he attempted to slide past.

"Don't mess with me!" Ryk pulled the drawer out of a cheap cardboard dresser, grabbed a new shirt, and headed back out of the bedroom.

"You bet I'll mess with you!" Lylyn reared back and punched him hard right below the sternum. Ryk wasn't expecting the blow. His eyes shot open. He let go a loud oof and doubled over.

"Dyth you, woman!" He put his hand square on her forehead and gave her a powerful shove. The back of her head thudded against the wall.

Lylyn let out a horrible scream. Ryk took the opportunity to step around her and make for the door. Upon reaching the landing, he stopped and looked down at Byrty.

"Better?"

His question caused the nurse to shift her attention from the very pregnant woman now leaning against the bedroom door jamb to his new shirt. "Much better. Maybe I should make sure she's......"

"You filthy lyin', half kygo fyrn!" Lylyn yelled once she regained her senses. Like some malevolent ghost bent on homicide, she came running across the living room. The sheet flapped behind her. Ryk stepped out into the landing, slammed the door, and held it shut.

"Go ahead and get a start. I'll hold her here for a while."

Lymdyr nodded and made his way to the stairs. Byrty remained where she was. A confused expression drew down her wrinkled, kindly face. At the head of the stairs, the railroad man stopped and turned around.

"Byrty! Come on!"

"Do you think she's alright? I mean she is pregnant, and she did hit that wall pretty hard."

"All I know is that she is now pregnant and angry. Come on!" Lymdyr turned and bounded down the stairs.

On the other side of the closed door, Lylyn pounded furiously. "Open this klynking door! Open it or I'll bust it down!"

Ryk held the door knob tight. He glanced over at Byrty. "For Zym sake! What're you waiting for?"

"I, I don't know." Byrty hesitated another second, then followed Lymdyr down the stairs.

"I hate you! I hate you! I hope this baby dies!" Lylyn's manic shouts gradually gave way to crying.

Ryk gently let go of the door knob and hustled down the stairs. He tucked the shirt in while walking down the alley.

Chapter 42.

After helping Byrty up into the cab, Lymdyr yelled at the driver before hopping in. "The Academy, please!"

Ryk was right behind him. He closed the door just as the buggy began to roll. Both of the other two occupants stared at his serene, but haggard countenance. Ryk looked back at their stunned faces.

"This has been building for a while. We never really did get along that great." He settled back and stared out the window.

Lymdyr slid the pocket watch out from his vest. He was dreading what he might see. With a flick of his finger, the lid popped open. The dial read 4:15. He closed it and gave a deep sigh.

"Byrty, we're going over to the Academy. Where do you want us to drop you off?"

The nurse sat staring blankly at Ryk. It took her a moment to respond to the question. "If you can drop me off halfway between the boulevard and Wystr street, I think a little walk in the fresh air would do me good."

Even though her request would take them miles out of their way, Lymdyr forced himself not to react. He stuck his head out the window again. "Can you detour over to Wystr?"

"Ya still wanna go ta the Academy?" the driver asked without taking his eyes off the road.

"Yes."

The trio was silent until the buggy slowed to a stop. Ryk continued to stare out the window. Byrty reached over and laid her hand on his knee.

"Good luck Ryk. I'll see you around."

Her voice caused him to break off his intent observation of the outside world. Ryk's face was stony and expressionless, but the outpouring of concern from the nurse's eyes softened him. He slid across the seat and gave her a hug. The two of them remained embraced for a few moments. Lymdyr opened the door, hopped down, and held out his hand.

"Thank you so much. You'll never know how much this means to me, and to the project," he offered in a hurried, shaking voice.

"My pleasure." Byrty glanced back up at the interior. "I just hope everything works out okay." Without saying another word, she walked off down the street.

"Now, to the Academy, and hurry if you can," Lymdyr commanded as he leaped back up into the cab.

The street in front of the Academy was a flurry of activity. Buggies were pulling up, loading up passengers and rolling off at regular intervals. Students were walking down the steps together, talking excitedly.

Gyls and his father had just parked their wagon against the curb when the buggy carrying Lymdyr and Ryk pulled up. The father lowered himself off the driver's seat, walked around past the two styrns hitched to the utility wagon, and helped his ailing son down.

Lymdyr had just swung down out of the buggy when he saw Gyls being helped up onto the curb. The folded up, convalescent look of the inventor sent a flash of concern through him. He ran over and gently grasped the young man's arm.

"Thank you," the father whispered. "Do you think you can help him up the stairs? I need to go park the wagon."

After giving a little nod of his head, Lymdyr led Gyls along the sidewalk. Ryk had climbed down out of the buggy and was admiring the massive gleaming white façade of the Academy. He ignored the rolling crunch of a vehicle approaching from behind. A familiar, high-pitched female voice coming from the same direction caused him to wheel around.

"Professor, come on! You're going to be late."

Sylstyn stood on the step of the wagon, trying to pull Myrvst to his feet. She was dressed in a simple off white shift that stopped at mid-thigh. The folds in the front of the shift masked her swelling belly. Her long, lustrous hair was tied back in a quick knot.

"I can get up by myself," Myrvst grumbled.

Ryk remained mesmerized as he watched her filled out body move beneath the thin fabric. Sylstyn got Myrvst to his feet, then happened to glance up the sidewalk.

"Ryk?"

"Hey, Syl baby. Am I glad to see you!"

Her radiant pink cheeks dropped into a quick scowl in reaction to his overly friendly greeting. She helped Myrvst ease himself down to the sidewalk.

"Go ahead and park, you know where to....Are you coming up?" the professor asked before making his way toward the steps.

"No! Do I look like I'm dressed for a meeting?" Sylstyn gave a huff of disgust. "I'll take the wagon back to the house. I still need to finish the floor."

Myrvst shrugged and began walking away. Ryk's eyes were glittering in the late afternoon light. He swaggered over to Sylstyn, arms open wide. She scowled again and held her arms rigid to prevent him from administering the crushing hug she knew he was going to deliver. Ryk ignored her non-receptive posture and embraced her anyway. His mid-section bounced against her hard belly. Sylstyn winced slightly.

"Yes, I'm pregnant. Don't worry, it's not yours."

Ryk's blissful expression changed to one of surprise. "Is it farmboy's?"

"Yes, its farm....Blrsynt's"

He let go of her, took a step back, and kicked the sidewalk. His dusky, weather beaten face was now a mask of disappointment. Before she could react, Ryk reached down and grabbed both her hands.

"Sly, honey. I really need to talk to you. We...."

"Ryk, stop! It's never going to work!"

Her words echoed in his brain. Ryk stared longingly into her deep green eyes. What he saw was a determined, powerful spirit. Gone was the dreamy, young woman's infatuation he was used to basking in. In a flash, he realized that their once close relationship was now over. Ryk lowered his gaze and stared blankly at her wide, white feet.

Sylstyn gave his hands a squeeze, then let go. "Look, you have Lylyn now."

A bitter, caustic sensation rose up in Ryk's throat. He lifted his head, but couldn't bring himself to look her squarely in the eyes.

"I better get up to that meeting." Ryk spun on his heels and ran up the steps. He focused on placing the toes of his boots firmly on the worn white steps. Her words echoed through his mind.

"It's never going to work."

He reached the landing, pushed the big copper doors open, and continued walking briskly across the now mostly deserted foyer. Halfway up the stairway, he passed Lymdyr boosting Gyl's bent over frame forward. The railroad man opened his mouth to speak, but Ryk whooshed by without stopping.

Several lively conversations spilled out into the hall as he approached the Bokyl's office. Ryk swung in without acknowledging anyone's presence and walked straight over to an empty chair at the end of the row where Professors Ymyl and Grylt were sitting. The force of his landing caused all conversation to cease. Professor Rymnyr and Mihyn froze in place. Bokyl's small, beady eyes were riveted on the new arrival.

"Ryk, welcome. We're all very glad to see you." There was a sense of hesitation and cautiousness to his greeting. The head regent could tell by the furrowed brow and serious set jaw that the mag driver was not in a good mood.

"I'm not sure if you know everyone here. This is...."

"I know 'em all."

Ryk's short, abrupt response caused Bokyl to pause. From down the line of chairs, Professor Ymyl leaned out to speak.

"I don't believe ve've met, my name is Professor Ymyl. I am the head of zee astronomy department."

The mag driver looked up at the professor's kindly face and offered a quick nod of acknowledgment.

Grylt swiveled in his chair to face Ryk. "And I'm Professor Grylt. I'm associate head of the two departments, biology and environmental science. Pleased to meet you!"

In response to Grylt's cheery introduction, Ryk just stared at the professor's thin, beaming face, and let go a little huff.

An explosive fit of coughing from the hallway drew the attention of everyone in the room. A moment later, Lymdyr and Gyls walked slowly through the door. Professor Rymnyr tapped Mihyn on the thigh. The two women exchanged a concerned glance. Lymdyr deposited the ailing inventor in the nearest chair and waved to all the participants before sitting down next to Ryk.

Bokyl waited for him to settle, then began speaking. "Krynut is on his way, but other than that, it looks like we're all here."

"Um, excuse me, my husband is running a little late, as usual." Mihyn offered in a decidedly apologetic tone.

The head regent sent an unkind smirk her way. "Well, we can't really wait any longer. We'll have to fill him in when he arrives. Ryk, can you update us on how the training at the test site is going?" All eyes swung over to the sullen mag driver.

"It's going fine."

Bokyl's face began to change from its usual swarthy pink to red. "Could you elaborate a little?"

Ryk pulled his hat off, leaned forward, and began running his rough fingers along the brim. "Once we got the right kind of rope out there, we was able to lasso the, whatever you wanna call it, the ball, just fine."

"By we, you mean the students?"

"Well no, me mostly."

Bokyl straightened up in his chair. "Which brings me to the biggest question, who is going to fill the final crew position?"

The discussion was interrupted by the sound of voices out in the hall. Laughter and congenial conversation drifted in above the echoing footsteps. Handynr, his secretary, and

Krynut entered the room. Kym stopped right at the door and stood smiling.

"Oh my! Look at all these prestigious people gathered here!" She sent a quick glance around room, finally zeroing in on Ryk. Kym gave a little toss of her languid, long brownish hair, and pursed her lips. "Well, I'm off." As Handynr swept past, she squeezed his arm. "Have a nice meeting."

The two men hustled over to the available seats. Handynr sat down next to his wife.

"You're late!" Mihyn whispered. She reached over and grasped his hand.

"I know. I got here as quickly as I could."

Krynut settled next to Lymdyr. "My apologies for being late. Head Regent, please continue."

Bokyl cast a reproachful glance at Krynut, then folded his fingers together. "As I was saying, our primary goal now is to determine who the last crew member will be. With just over a month to launch, it is of great concern to me."

Now that the attention had shifted away from him, Ryk drifted off into reflection. Sylstyn's honest but brutal rejection of his attempt at reunion rang out again inside his head.

"It's never going to work," echoed several times before he bit his lower lip to end it. His feelings of remorse for losing her gradually gave way to a bleak realization that maybe he was destined to marry a barmaid and spend his life chasing after dumb animals. Ryk didn't even hear the discussion taking place around him.

"Head Regent, before vee get into the heavy stuff, I have a letter I'd like to read." Professor Ymyl held up an official looking note on crisp white letterhead.

"Go ahead."

Ymyl adjusted his half glasses and held the sheet out in front of his face. "Dear Professor, yeah, I'll skip over zat. Here vee are, the Vyrbyn Optics company is pleased to announce zat a representative will be hand delivering the Fyr twenty-six telescope...."

"With all due respect Professor, we really need to concentrate on the most pressing issues. Thank very much for your efforts." Bokyl sent a quick nod toward the astronomer, then returned his attention to the group. "Any other updates before we start the main discussion?" Professor Rymnyr held up her hand. "Go ahead."

"Just a quick update. Grynk Garment company, the outfit that creates the wonderful regent robes, as in the one our head regent is wearing, has agreed to produce some for our crew." The room echoed with applause. Rymnyr waited for the clapping to cease, then continued.

"We'll need to have everyone go down for a fitting as soon as the last member is selected."

"Thank you Professor, anything else?" Bokyl waited for a moment, then directed his attention to Regent Krynut. "I believe it's all yours."

"It goes without saying that the time has come to determine who will be the final member of the expedition. As the unofficial person responsible for the crew selection, I would again like to offer the position to Mr. Lymdyr." Krynut leaned forward and directed his steely gaze down the row.

The railroad man sat pondering the current state of his employment, and life in general. The sudden silence of the room, and the sensation of being stared at, shook him out of his meditation.

"What? Excuse me, I was lost in thought." Lymdyr looked around at the collection of hopeful faces. "What did I miss?"

"You missed Regent Krynut's suggestion that you might be a good candidate for the engineer position," Bokyl calmly replied.

In response, Lymdyr let go a short, genuine laugh. "Oh, pardon me! I don't know where that came from. Please don't interpret that as an indication of me taking the regent's suggestion lightly. No, just the opposite. It certainly is a great honor to be considered, but I, seriously, why me?"

"You have been a solid part of this project from the very beginning. You're young, strong, intelligent...."

"I don't know about that!" Lymdyr's self-effacing reply drew some polite laughter from the otherwise serious group. "Honestly, I appreciate your confidence in me Regent, but I have to respectfully decline." He returned a congenial smile to the gallery of disappointed faces.

"There was some talk of asking the miner's nephew, why can't I ever remember his name!" Bokyl tossed out.

Professor Myrvst had been sitting quietly taking it all in. He stroked his tangled beard, then leaned forward to speak. "Yes, I did suggest Blrsynt, but....it turns out he and my housekeeper are expecting a child and may marry soon." A perceptible groan of despair floated around the room.

"Dyth, that's right. Well, that doesn't leave us many options, does it?" Bokyl concluded.

From his spot nearest the door, Gyls sat like a folded up lawn chair. He didn't have the strength nor will to argue. At the opposite end of the row, Ryk's endless loop of introspection was interrupted when he heard Blrsynt's name mentioned. His unwashed, dusky face burned with anguish. The fatalistic words of rejection from Sylstyn again echoed in his head. He couldn't stand it any longer.

"I'll do it."

Chapter 43.

All eyes swooped down to the end of the row where Ryk sat like some grim statue.

"You'll do what?" Myrvst asked in his tired, worn out voice.

"I'll be the final crew member."

A jolt of electricity shot through the room. The reactions of the stunned group were as varied as their diverse personalities. The two women leaned into each other, and both gasped with surprise. Rymnyr let out a little squeal of delight.

Krynut looked over at Handynr. His dark, intense stare conveyed the uncertainty he was feeling about the announcement. Handynr appeared to be somewhat dumbfounded by the announcement. He just shrugged his shoulders. Lymdyr reached over and slapped Ryk hard on the thigh.

"Outstanding! What an unexpected development!" The railroad man beamed with joy.

Professors Grylt and Ymyl began whispering between themselves. In his spot at the other end of the row, Gyls looked even more miserable that usual. He sat with arms wrapped tightly around his protruding ribs. Another strangling cough shook him.

Ryk sat staring blankly at the opposite wall. Four days of no food, and excess drink had already thrashed his stomach. The realization of what he had just agreed to sent red hot pitchforks into his gut. He tried to swallow, but his throat was paralyzed. Krynut shifted around and directed his razor sharp focus on the mag driver.

"We certainly take your offer very seriously Ryk and will need to discuss this among the project leaders." Krynut's stern, business-like voice cut through the murmured conversation of the room.

"Oh come on, Regent! Is there any doubt that Ryk is the best candidate?" Rymnyr blurted out.

Krynut stared at the professor's flushed and heavily painted face. Her head was tilted slightly off to the side in a show of indignancy. He ran a couple fingers down along his neatly trimmed goatee before answering.

"With all due respect Professor, my initial reaction is to agree with you, but I think due process encourages us to…"

"Klynk due process! We've just leaped over the last big hurdle and are now heading toward the finish line. Don't hamstring the project at this point!" Rymnyr's normally soft grey-green eyes flashed with intensity.

"She's right," Gyls chimed in. His voice was constricted by both fatigue and emotion. "Ryk has been the logical choice for a while. I can work with him to get up to speed on the details of the craft."

Bokyl remained silent and observant from his position behind the desk. He was struggling with the question of whether the Academy would even consider placing a project of such magnitude in the hands of a simple mag driver. The longer he pondered it, the stronger his feelings of inevitability grew. He let out a great sigh of relief.

"I must say, I agree with Professor Rymnyr. The time for discussion is long past. Let's call a vote to confirm Ryk as the new engineer for the expedition. All in favor signify by raising your hands."

All present raised their hand. Bokyl broke into a jack o'lantern smile, then looked over at Ryk.

"Vote is unanimous. Well, I commend your decision. You are about to become the most famous mag driver of all time. Are you ready for a grand adventure?"

With slow, determined movement, Ryk shifted his focus from the opposite wall over to the head regent. "Suppose so."

"Excellent. Well, unless there are further items to discuss, I adjourn the meeting."

Rymnyr let out a joyous squeal and threw her arms up in the air. "Oh, I just can't believe what a momentous day this is!"

Professor Grylt clapped his small hands together. "What a relief to finally have the last position filled!"

Ryk gazed around at the well-educated group that was now rising to their feet. His disdain for authority manifested itself in the little snarl that worked its way across his mouth. Without saying a word, he got up and marched toward the door. Just before he exited, Bokyl called out to him.

"Excuse me! Ryk? Will you be at the test site tomorrow?"

"Yep." The mag driver halted long enough to answer over his shoulder.

Just as Ryk slipped out into the hall, a harried looking young man appeared in the doorway. He knocked on the wooden frame and held up a hand full of yellow sheets.

"Pardon me. Is there a Mr. Lymdyr here?"

"Yes, I'm Lymdyr."

"Whew! I've gone to just about every office in this building. Glad I finally found the right one. Here, these are for you." The student walked over and held out several telemessage sheets.

Lymdyr's forehead rippled with furrows as he scanned the messages. "Hmm. This first one is from two this afternoon." He shifted his gaze from the page to the student's flushed face.

"Yeah, I know. I'm standing in for the regular operator. I just got trained yesterday. Um, they started to come pretty fast right after that first one, and, well, I kinda of wanted to wait till they stopped. Gee, I hope it isn't anything important!" The young man winced and scuffed his worn, brown shoes across the floor.

Lymdyr tried not to appear too annoyed. He glanced down at the sheets, then back up at the chagrined student.

"No, everything's fine. Thank you for delivering them." Once the student had exited the room, Lymdyr shook of his head and continued reading the correspondence.

"Message for Mr. Lymdyr Nine Line, head of Tyrl Operations Blue Line Railroad.

Need to speak with Lymdyr immediately! Am waiting at phynk for reply.

Sent- Bynhyld 2:09"

A knot began to grow in the railroad man's empty stomach. He flipped the first page over and focused on the next in the sheath.

"Reply from Byrdyl Second Line, executive office aide Blue Line Railroad

Mr. Lymdyr is out of office on important business. Will not be back today. Sent 2:40"

He flipped over to the next sheet.

"Reply from Bynhyld

I really need to contact him. Where is he? Sent 2:43"

"Reply from Byrdyl, executive office aide

He is at an important meeting at the Academy. Sent 2:56"

Lymdyr began to sweat. He flipped to the next sheet.

"Message for Academy.

My husband Lymdyr Nine Line is attending a meeting there. Please find him and have him contact me. I have been waiting at the phynk for an hour. Important that he is located.

Sent from Bynhlyd 3:07"

Lymdyr's fingers started to shake as he flipped the next page over.

"Reply from Academy

Need to know who he is meeting with. Sent 3:56"

"Forward of Reply- Bynhlyd - Message sent to Byrdyl, executive office aide Tyrl Operations

Who is Lymdyr meeting with? Sent 4:20"

"Message for Academy

Has Lymdyr been contacted?

Sent by Bynhyld. 4:56"

"Reply from Academy

No, still need to know who he is meeting with. Sent 5:05"

"Reply from Bynhlyd

I don't know who the klynk he is meeting with! Don't care! Tell him girls and I are moving out! Sent 5:05"

Lymdyr re-read the last sheet several times. His mouth became very dry. Professors Myrvst, Ymyl, and Grylt were standing together nearby. Myrvst recognized the shocked look on the railroad man's face. He walked over and laid a hand on Lymdyr's shoulder.

"Everything alright, old boy?"

"My wife was trying to get a hold of me and wasn't successful. I have a feeling some damage control is in order." Lymdyr tried to downplay the severity of the situation by forcing himself to smile. From across the room, Rymnyr's voice rang out above the other conversations.

"Excuse me! Excuse me! Before we all head home, a couple things. Don't forget that at five tomorrow, we are inviting the public to come and view the craft in the foyer downstairs. I expect all of you to be there, especially the crew."

The professor scanned the rapt audience to make sure they were all listening. With great dramatic pause, she directed her gaze over to Lymdyr.

"Secondly, I want to make sure we recognize Mr. Lymdyr's effort here. Without his dedication and tenacity in getting Ryk to come up to Tyrl, I doubt whether we could have filled the final position. To Lymdyr!"

The room was filled with loud applause. Bokyl waited till the clapping subsided, then turned to address the railroad man.

"Well said, Professor. Yes, thank you for your diligence. We were almost convinced that you were the best choice for the engineer position."

Lymdyr gave a little snort of a laugh and clutched the yellow telemessage sheets even tighter. "I appreciate your confidence in me."

Professor Rymnyr's beaming smile cooled when she noticed the deeps furrows folding across Lymdyr's forehead. She was just about to ask him if anything was wrong when Professor Myrvst spoke up.

"I still think that Blrsynt would have been the best candidate."

Rymnyr let go a long sigh. "Oh come now, he's going to be a father!"

"So is Ryk," Lymdyr added matter-of-factly.

"What!"

All eyes around the room shifted over to the railroad man. He stood motionless. A look of surprise had now replaced the somberness of his features.

"I assumed everyone was aware of that. He has a girlfriend that works over in Jybyr. She's due in a couple months. I'm sure he's made some kind of arrangement for the child's welfare."

"I can't believe he's going to leave just before the birth of his child!" Professor Rymnyr shook her head in disbelief.

Bokyl swept a pile of papers off his desk, strode over to the door, and placed his hand on the knob. "Well, regardless, he made his decision today. I say it's a done deal. Not to be rude, but I for one, am ready to go home."

The group filed out of the room and into the hall. Their excited voices echoed off the stone walls. Lymdyr brought up the rear of the contingent. All down the stairway, and across the high ceilinged foyer, he remained deep in thought.

"Oh, holy klynking Zym! Could things get any more complicated? What to do? Should I go drown my sorrows somewhere or go home and deal with it. She actually said they're moving out! I can't believe it!"

The next morning, Lymdyr arrived at work in an already foul mood after spending the night alone in the large, palatial house. He stepped out of the buggy onto the sidewalk and froze in his tracks. There beside the building was the black and red carriage of the two executives. He hadn't expected to deal with them again for at least a couple days. A deep, insidious feeling of dread took hold of him as he approached the building.

Once inside, Lymdyr was struck by the tense atmosphere of the main room. At that hour of the morning, the space was usually filled with loud, animated conversation. Today, the only sounds were the clacking of the telemessage machines.

Several people looked up at him, then averted their eyes. He glanced over at Byrdyl's desk. She was sitting with her hands covering her face. Her cheeks were wet with tears. She wiped her nose with a handkerchief and slowly rose up to greet him.

"Mr.,....Lymdyr.......the two gentlemen from......" Byrdyl's attempt to control her grief failed. She crashed into him and became a sobbing wreck. "I'm so sorry!"

He tightly wrapped his arms around her. The beautiful chestnut colored curls of her hair bounced with each spasm.

"Byrdyl, it's okay. Try and get a hold of yourself. I saw the carriage out there. I'm sure they're just following up."

The secretary dabbed the moisture away from her eyes and nose. She gave one last shudder, then stepped back.

"Whew! I think I'm okay now." Byrdyl brushed a couple strands of hair away from her forehead and straightened her tight fitting red and yellow striped dress. She forced herself to smile. "I must look a mess."

"You look fine. Are they in my office?"

"Yes."

"I'll go deal with them." Lymdyr patted her shoulder, then turned on his heels and walked with confidence across the room. The first things he saw when he banked through the open door were the bare walls where his pictures had hung and the boxes stacked on his desk. He came to a screeching halt just inside the door.

"Good morning," the shorter of the two execs said with mock friendliness.

"Morning."

"I suppose you're wondering why we're back," the taller executive added. He set the small trophy he was holding down onto the corner of the desk.

"Judging by the situation here, not much to guess about."

A smile momentarily lifted the taller man's hollow cheeks. He motioned toward a chair next to the desk. "Please sit."

"I'd rather stand."

"Suit yourself. Close the door."

Lymdyr turned to the side and grasped the door handle. Just before easing it shut, he looked out at the staff members clustered around Byrdyl's desk. They all stood with vacant, shocked expressions on their faces.

"Before you get all worked up, know that we are just moving you to a new assignment," the tall executive offered in a dry, lifeless voice.

Lymdyr gave a little nod of his head. The short, red haired executive put down the framed certificate he was holding.

"We're relocating you to a different office. It has come to our attention that during your largely unauthorized trip to Phyt Hill, you engaged in some behavior that reflects badly on someone in your position."

The statement hit Lymdyr like a well placed punch. Anger flared up deep within him and temporarily incinerated his feelings of the sadness. Questions about exactly what the executive was referring to, and who might have tipped them off, bounced back and forth inside his head. The executive's emotionless voice snapped him back to the present.

"Effective immediately, you will be assigned to the branch office in Pylgor. Your position there will be chief of mechanical operations."

"Holy Zym! Pylgor? That's the middle of nowhere!" Lymdyr sputtered. He struggled to maintain control.

"We realize that this will be an inconvenience to you and your family, but the decision comes down from above us. We will need your signature on this last invoice." The taller man slid a tri-folded piece of paper across the desk.

Lymdyr walked over and gently lifted it up. His eyes raced across the printed words. The invoice was from Klyrk's company for a total figure of twelve thousand dymyrs. Lymdyr lowered it from his face and stared at the tall man.

"This is absurd! What's he claiming all this for? The original quote was for fifteen hundred."

"It seems that he has hired a well know injury justice expert and is claiming that you had him carry that Zynck fellow, or whatever his name is...."

"Phrynk, his name was Phrynk. He's since deceased."

"Oh. That's unfortunate." The taller executive's face became even more hardened. "Anyway, he says that he injured his back carrying Phrynk up from the river. I haven't seen the actual transcript of the claim. It's in legal being evaluated."

Chapter 44.

Out at the test site, one of the engineering students was waiting for his turn to swing the practice nucleus when he happened to look down at the road from town. The presence of a small dust cloud caught his eye.

"Hey! Is that a buggy coming up the valley?"

Several of the other idle students shielded their eyes from the sun to confirm his observation. Vryny dropped her hand from her forehead and gave Sylstyn a punch on the arm.

"It dyth sure is! Hey Syl! Maybe your mag driver boyfriend has decided to show up." Her sarcastic words were cut off by the hard shove Sylstyn administered. "Hey! What the klynk was that for?"

Sylstyn turned her face away from her classmate and walked off into the scrubby brush. The other students standing around watched in silence. When Ryk's tall figure appeared coming up the trail, one of the students ran to the base of the tower and yelled up toward the platform.

"Professor! A buggy just pulled up, and it looks like Ryk is back!"

Over the top of the upper rail, Bynkr's long, sideburned face appeared. He looked in the direction that the student was pointing.

"Well, I'll be! Yeah, that's him alright."

The professor rapidly descended the ladder just as Ryk was coming up the hill. A cheer rose up from the group of students down below. It took Bynkr a moment to work his way through the celebrating mob.

"Boy, oh boy! Are we glad to see you! Bokyl says that you are now part of the crew?"

Ryk was enjoying the adoration being heaped on. He poked the edge of his wide brimmed hat back and took a quick scan of the smiling faces all around.

"Yeah, chalk up another crazy decision by yours truly. Maybe the craziest yet."

Another cheer and round of applause echoed in the still afternoon air. Once the noise died down, Bynkr motioned toward the tower.

"Ready to do some roping? After you."

The two men walked side by side up the hill. Ryk leaned toward the professor. "I didn't see Sylstyn here."

Bynkr craned his neck around while walking. "No, she's here. Hmmm, maybe she's taking a break."

Ryk pulled a sealed envelope out from the inner pocket of his vest and held it out. "Well, in case I don't have a chance to talk to her. This is for her."

The professor took the envelope from him, gave a little lift of his eyebrows, then tucked it into the clipboard he was holding.

Later that day, the Academy foyer was abuzz with activity. Most of the Dymran Project members plus a host of dignitaries and press corp had arrived for the craft unveiling. After the obligatory speeches by the city elders and Academy staff, Professor Rymnyr got up from her chair, walked over to the sheet-covered craft, and took up a place next to the nose.

"Thank you all for those important words. It is now my great pleasure to ask the crew of this amazing voyage to come up and join me here. Regent Krynut, will you help me with the unveiling?"

Rymnyr couldn't suppress the happiness that shown from her middle-aged face as the crew members assembled in front of the craft. Krynut walked around behind it and stopped next to the back end. On the count of three, he and Rymnyr whisked the sheet off. The foyer was filled with exclamations of surprise, and whispered comments.

"Wow, so that's the actual craft!"

"My, it's certainly does look sturdy."

"What wonderful workmanship!"

The professor waited till some of the noise had died down, then again turned to address the crowd.

"Thank you all for coming to help celebrate this grand adventure! We invite you to come up and have a look inside. Please form a line to my right. Feel free to ask questions to the crew as you move past. Regent Krynut, will you open the hatch?"

Immediately, the crowd moved forward and obediently queued next to her. Several people in the crowd reached out to touch the dull, grey metal surface.

For the next three hours, the interested citizens filed by the craft. At its longest, the line stretched out the front door, zigzagged down the steps, and meandered up the street in front of the Academy.

Ryk and Krynut were positioned just forward of the hatch. The mag driver looked out at the long line of expectant faces, then leaned over toward the crew chief.

"Don't know about you, but I'm about done answering questions."

Krynut gave a little smirk of a smile. "Good thing you're not a professor. I'm used to it."

"While we're here, I do have a couple things I'd like to talk about."

"By all means."

"So the plan is for us to get blasted up in space and swing a big rope around a comet. Granted I'm no styrk watcher, or whatever you call them...."

"Astronomer."

"Yeah, I'm no astronomer, but from what I see looking up, that comet just looks like some long, wispy thing."

"What you're referring to is the tail. The nucleus is more than likely a big ball of frozen pluge. What you see up in the sky is pluge vapor being spewed out as it melts." A kindly smile broke across Krynut's face. Ryk took a moment to ponder the last bit of information.

"So you want me to try and lasso a fifteen-foot wide ball of frozen pluge?"

The question caused Krynut to chuckle softly. "I apologize for not briefing you. No, we think the nucleus is perhaps, three to four miles in diameter."

"Well, that makes a bit of a difference!" A grin lifted the edges of Ryk's weather beaten face. Both men stopped their discussion to answer a question, then resumed their conversation once the visitor had moved on.

"Can we maybe get a bigger target out at the test site then? Again, I ain't an astronomer, but seems like something out there in space is going to move different than a ball hangin' on a rope."

"Hmmm, good point. Are you thinking that a floating target might be better?"

"Yeah, like a big old balloon of some kind."

On the other side of the hatch, Handynr, Mihyn and Professor Grylt stood next to each other. After another group of visitors passed by, Grylt leaned over and whispered into the regent's ear.

"I've been smiling so much, my face hurts."

"Stop smiling then," Mihyn offered in a quiet voice.

"Good suggestion." The professor let his deeply lined face relax for a moment.

Down the line of visitors, a thick bodied man with grey frizzy hair, and a grey frizzy beard bent forward and waved a hand at the group.

"Kybark! You made it!" Grylt called out once he noticed the man standing in line.

"Yes indeed. I rushed across town, braved the smelly, boisterous crowd, and have presented myself as such."

Grylt clasped his hands together and smiled broadly. When Kybark reached the spot where the three crew members were standing, the professor put his arm around Mihyn's shoulder.

"Fellow crew members, I'd like to introduce my roommate, Kybark. Kybark, this is Regent Handynr, and his wife Regent Mihyn."

The newcomer's face pulled up into a sneer of a smile. He softly grasped Handynr's outstretched hand, and let his eyes drift up and down the regent's lanky figure.

"Charmed to meet you."

Handynr's eyebrows arched at the overly affectionate greeting. Kybark let go of his hand, then bowed at the waist. He gave Mihyn a passing glance. Professor Grylt stepped to the side and extended his arm toward the open hatch.

"Behold the interior of the craft!"

Kybark leaned in, knocking the woman ahead of him over slightly. "Excuse me," he said half-heartedly. The woman scooted ahead, then glared back at him. Kybark adjusted his round wire rimmed glasses before taking a long look at the interior.

"So this is the artificial womb that you voyagers are going to be either birthed out of onto a new land, or become entombed in thousands of miles from Ulutrita. Yes, I can see this hull bobbing on the endless sea of space, your bleached, desiccated bones rattling around the interior." His pitted face drew up in a most sinister smile.

"Oh, please! Can you for once put your cynical, twisted sense of reality away?" Grylt whined.

Kybark withdrew his head from the hatch and stared the professor down. "I'll drop my bitingly sarcastic view of the world, when you stop chasing around it, measuring fryn testicles and examining piles of blryt."

Several of those within earshot snickered at Kybark's caustic reply. While his roommate exited the line, Grylt whispered to the crew members next to him.

"Please do excuse him. He's a poet, and more used to writing down whatever comes spilling out of his head than conversing with distinguished people."

The next day, Sylstyn walked past the engineering office just as Professor Bynkr stepped out into hall.

"Sly! Hold up a minute! I have something for you."

She waited while he ducked back into the office. Bynkr came hustling back out into the hall and held out the letter Ryk had given him. Sylstyn cautiously took it from him.

"What's this?"

"Uh, the other day when Ryk came out to the testing site, he, uh gave me this and said it was for you." The flashing, furious look she sent his way blew the smile off Bynkr's face. "I'll see you later."

Sylstyn watched the professor rapidly walk toward the stairs. She fingered the letter several times before tearing it open.

"I wish he would just leave me alone." Her young heart beat heavily while she read the sloppily written words. "Oh for Zym's sake Ryk! What a freak you are!" Sylstyn waded the letter into a ball and stuffed it into one of the wall mounted waste cans.

Later that afternoon, Blrsynt was just thumbing through a pile of mail when Sylstyn returned home. She gave him a kiss on the cheek and tossed her backpack onto a kitchen chair.

"Anything interesting?"

He held up an elegantly embossed envelope. "Just this."

After tearing it open with her finger, she pulled out an invitation to the "Grand Departure Party" at Rymnyr's mansion. Sylstyn's youthful face lit up with joy, then darkened over like the summer sky when a sudden rainstorm appears. She walked into the living room and plunked down in a chair. Blrsynt waited for several moments before following her in.

"So?"

"Here," Sylstyn answered morosely. She held up the gilt stationary. Blrsynt snagged it from her and read it while standing next to her.

"Wow, this looks great, don't you think?"

"Yeah, just great."

Blrsynt looked down at her unhappy, dead serious expression. He sat on the arm of the chair and ran his fingers through her dark, lustrous hair.

"So, what's wrong? Usually, you'd be overjoyed to receive an invitation like this."

"Usually." Sylstyn leaned back and stared up at the ceiling. "If I didn't know that Ryk would be there, I would be overjoyed."

"Ah, I see. Well, there's going to be lots of people there I bet. We'll just have to avoid him."

"I suppose you're right. It's going to be tough for me to be at such a big fancy party and not be able to drink."

Blrsynt gave a humph of acknowledgment. "True, but think of all the great food Professor Rymnyr is going to have laid out. I mean, come on! I have a feeling she is going to go all out on this one."

Sylstyn reached up and intertwined her fingers in his. "You're right. I'm just being weird."

Chapter 45.

On the day of the party, the guests began to arrive around four-thirty. Several large metal braziers on the lawn wafted the smell of roasting meat out over the main gate. A stiff wind had kicked up. The carefully constructed garlands swung wildly from the poles they were strung on. White and pink flower petals rained down.

Professor Rymnyr and Kryzyck shuttled between the long food tables, making sure everything was in order. She was resplendent in a long gown with alternating panels of gold thread and gauzy white fabric. He had purchased a snappy, black suit for the occasion.

Guests continued to file in, and soon, the patio was alive with laughter and pleasant conversation. A quartet of string musicians had set up over in the corner. Their furtive efforts could barely be heard above the din.

Out at the main gate, Blrsynt pulled the buggy up next to the elegantly dressed gate keeper. Professor Myrvst held out the invitation which the man accepted from him. The gate keeper scanned the paper, then gave a quick bow, and motioned for them to move forward.

"Look at all the buggies lined up!" Blrsynt observed.

"Yes, looks like it is going to be quite the affair." Myrvst reached over and gave Sylstyn a pat on the arm. "Feeling okay, dear?"

She had been staring down at the floor of the cab. The professor's question caused her to raise her head.

"I'm fine."

The group followed the metallic gold streamers strung through the trees to the rear of the stately brick mansion. By this time, the crowd had spilled off the patio, and out onto the lawn.

Sylstyn's eyes darted around the crowd. Her lips were drawn tight. Blrsynt slid his arm around her.

"Why are you so nervous?"

"I just know Ryk is going to be here, and…..Oh no! There he is over there!"

Like a frightened child, she squeezed in between the two men. Blrsynt tried not to laugh.

"Come on, let's go say hello and get it over with."

"I'll meet you over by the food," Myrvst commented before splitting off from the couple.

The two young people walked over to where Ryk and his now very pregnant girlfriend were standing beneath one of the lantern-festooned thorn trees. Ryk was wearing a very smart brown and tan suit. Lylyn had borrowed a deep crimson gown that fell off her shoulders and piled up on top of her enormous belly. Blrsynt led the way up to the tree.

"Hello Ryk."

The mag driver looked the young man right straight in the eyes. "Hello, I'd like to introduce my girlfriend. Lylyn, this is Bylyry…."

"Uh, actually my name is Blrsynt."

Ryk's face drew up in a rather sheepish grin. "Dyth! I just can't seem to pronounce your name right, can I?" He reached over and smacked the young man hard on the arm. "Good to see ya, and Sly, how are you doing?"

"I'm fine." Sylstyn ventured a look up into Ryk's face, then averted her eyes.

"Looks like you're gonna have a baby too!" Lylyn cawed. Sylstyn forced herself to smile. Lylyn tipped her glass up, finished it, and pulled Ryk across the lawn. "Well, nice meetin' ya, gotta get another drink."

At that same time, Handynr and Mihyn came walking around the side of the mansion. Professor Myrvst caught sight of the couple and strolled over to greet them.

"Regents, you both look very stylish tonight."

"Thank you. Have you seen Professor Rymnyr?" Mihyn asked.

"No, we just got here, also. I was just heading over to the refreshments." Myrvst walked beside the two regents as they approached the noisy crowd.

Just behind the trio, Krynut and Princess Janela moved arm in arm. She was dressed head to toe in several layers of mint green, gauzy fabric. The bottomless black spheres of her eyes were outlined with brilliant blue shadow and an intricate accent of gold dust. As she glided past, more than one guest stopped to take in her exotic appearance. When they arrived at the edge of the crowd, Krynut stopped and whispered into Janela's ear.

"See that couple up ahead? The tall handsome one is Regent Handynr, and that's his wife, Regent Mihyn next to him. They are also part of the crew."

"So a man and wife will be part of the crew?"

"Yes."

"At least they won't be lonely. Do you think you will get lonely?"

Krynut took a moment to carefully construct his answer. "As crew chief, I'll probably be too busy to get lonely, at first." He gave her hand an affectionate squeeze.

Professor Grylt and his roommate arrived and followed the line of guests making their way across the yard. The professor looked down at the disheveled appearance of his companion.

"The least you could have done is dressed up. This is a big deal!"

Kybark let go a snort of revulsion. "A big deal. Just a bunch of wealthy people patting themselves on the back. I see no reason to dress up for that!"

When they rounded the southeast corner of the building, Grylt stopped and clapped his hands over his mouth. "Oh, my! Just look at all these people!"

"Come on, let's go get something to drink."

A peal of raucous laughter from behind caused both men to turn around. On the gravel drive in front of the mansion, a large Baroque carriage pulled by four styrns was parked. The double doors to it had just been flung open, and four nicely dressed men tumbled out.

"Oh, here comes Mytry and the boys," Professor Grylt said with a grin.

"Who?"

"See the one with the violet suit? That's Mytyr Seven Line. His family started the Hynmn clothing store."

"How wonderful." Kybark's comment was laced with sarcasm. He and Grylt watched the quartet zig zag toward them.

"Professor! So good to see you!" The rail thin man in the violet velvet suit opened his arms and gave Grylt a hug. The professor reciprocated, then took a step back.

"My, what a fetching outfit!"

Mytry gently grasped the bottom of the open jacket and spun in a half turn. "You don't think it's a little too gaudy?"

"Oh, Zym no! It's lovely! Kybark, I believe you know all of these gentlemen?"

"Yes, I know them all," the sullen poet muttered. He sent an unfriendly glance around at the smiling faces.

Grylt and his friends continued along the side of the mansion and joined the large crowd. When they arrived, a roar of welcome filled the air.

Head Regent Bokyl and his wife were standing at the edge of the crowd. The only one of the carriage riders that was not dressed in a flamboyant manner walked up to the couple. Bokyl broke into a sweeping grin and shook the man's hand with force.

"Senator Kylr, nice to see you. You know my wife, Gyrty. I have to ask you, what are you doing hanging out with this notorious bunch?"

The short statured senator let go a laugh. "Well, Nym is away visiting her mother, so I thought I'd link up with Mytry and his friends. They really are a very lively lot."

The two men shared a knowing smile. "Yes, but....."

"But what? Look at them! They're extremely successful members of Tyrl society. Besides, they were great supporters of my campaign last year. You should join us for a night out sometime. They'd add some excitement to your dull life."

"Thanks, I don't need that kind of excitement," Bokyl replied in a dead serious voice.

Ryk and Lylyn stood under a big thorn tree watching the ever growing crowd. She let go a giggle as Mytyr and his group swept by. "Ain't that a fancy bunch!"

After taking a drink, Ryk leaned against the rough bark of the tree. "Yep, lots of fancy people here. Only reason I came is I'm gonna be sealed inside that can soon with some of them. Zym, I hate crowds! Oh look, there's Krynut. Come on! I want you to meet the crew chief." Ryk literally dragged his girlfriend across the stubbly lawn.

"Hey! Slow down! I'm spillin' my drink."

Krynut noticed the pair moving toward them. He spoke to Janela out of the corner of his mouth. "Here comes another member of the crew."

Ryk came walking up and gave the regent a quick nod. "Krynut, I'd like you to meet my girlfriend Lylyn....and I guess I don't know your girl's name."

Being referred to as the crew chief's "girl" had a noticeable effect on Janela. Her sweet smile shifted to an expression of shock and indignation. Krynut worked hard to suppress the little smirk trying to form on his otherwise stoic features. He laid his hand gently on the small of her back.

"Ryk, this is Janela."

"Pleased to meet you, " she offered in a soft, musical voice.

By that time in the evening, Lylyn was about half drunk. She swayed gently in place. "I think we should sit down." Her watery brown eyes drifted up and down Janela's exquisitely attired figure. "My, but you're pretty, and.....different!"

For an uncomfortable moment, none of the four knew what to say. Janela shot a quick desperate, look up at Krynut. The smile faded off Ryk's face.

"I better find a place for us to sit. Lylyn's been on her feet most of the day. Nice meeting you." He whisked her off toward a row of metal chairs out on the lawn.

"Stop pushing me! I'm gonna trip and fall, then you'll be sorry!"

Over by the food table, a large group of Academy personnel, dignitaries, and project members had gathered. They were engaged in a lively discussion. Head Regent Bokyl held up his glass.

"A toast to the completion of one of the last steps toward launch!"

The group all raised their glasses in unison.

"And what just got completed?" Senator Kyl asked.

"We just filled the last of the crew positions. By the way, is Gyls here?"

Krynut took a quick scan of the patio. "You know, I don't recall seeing him. We owe him so much for all the hard work he did. It's too bad that Lymdyr couldn't make it, also. From what I hear, he got reassigned to a new position somewhere. He really was instrumental in getting Ryk to come to Tyrl.

I can't express what a great relief it was to have Ryk volunteer to be part of the crew. It's one less thing to think about. I've been thinking about a lot of things, lately such as what I'll miss about Ulutrita. Like this." He paused to sip the fine, yellow liquid in his glass.

Professor Rymnyr stood behind him. "But think of all the marvelous new things you'll encounter. Most likely a whole new world!" she added with just a touch of drunkenness.

"Yeah, Mihyn and I are still getting arrangements made for our departure," Handynr commented from his seat at the table. "I have to say, it still doesn't seem real to me. It's like some wild idea that you cook up, then wisely abandon. Only with this, we're not abandoning it!"

He let go a laugh, but it lacked sincerity. The somber expression that now manifested itself on his long, handsome face left little doubt about the sense of remorse he was experiencing. Mihyn slid her hand under his arm and gave it a squeeze.

"Oh, come on! You and the regent both sound like you wish you weren't going."

"My dear, it's perfectly normal for travelers to have doubts about a journey beforehand. Especially one of this magnitude," Rynmyr added. She tottered ever so slightly in place.

"So what's the next step for the project?" the senator tossed out.

"Tomorrow night, we're going to have the crew enter the craft, close the hatch, and spend an entire day and night inside. Sort of a trial run just to make sure no one has any, uh, space issues."

"I think that is an excellent idea!" Professor Ymyl pipped up. "Might as vell see how everyone adjusts to zee close quarters."

Kybark had been pacing around the perimeter of the patio. The loud conversation of the group standing by the table attracted his attention. Without saying a word, he walked up and stood beside Professor Grylt.

"I don't think it would be a bad idea to practice cooking either," the biology professor added.

"Ha! Doubtful that you'll ever be able to duplicate the conditions you're going to encounter up there!" Kybark raised his index finger and pointed toward the star filled sky. All eyes in the circle pivoted toward his puffy, thickly bearded face.

"And vat sort of conditions are you referring to?" Professor Ymyl asked.

A smile exposed Kybark's big, yellow teeth. "Let me illustrate." He walked over to the table and examined the pile of mostly worked over food. A large bowl of small purple fruit sat toward the back of the table. He leaned over, grabbed it, and returned to the group.

"So, here on Ulutrita, the force of the air keeps these pynfrs from flying out of the bowl, correct?" Ymyl nodded his head in agreement. "Once you leave the atmosphere, there will be nothing to hold them. The easiest way to represent this is to think of what would happen if I jumped off a cliff while holding this. As soon as I began to fall, I'd lose the push of the air." Kybark gripped the edges of the bowl and gave it quick thrust upwards. The small purple fruit sailed up off the glazed surface.

"More than likely, once you leave the atmosphere, anything that isn't tied down inside the craft is going to float around like these pynrs."

"Ah, you've been reading zee work of Wyntyrn," Ymyl commented.

"Kybark fancies himself a physicist as well as being a poet!" Grylt tossed out.

Several of the circle laughed quietly at the professor's enthusiastic observation.

"Laugh all you want. I say if you don't make arrangements to distribute the food and pluge in a contained manner, you are going to have a klynking mess inside! Come, Grylt! We're going for a walk."

Kybark grabbed the professor firmly by the arm and dragged him off the patio.

"What are you doing? Let go of me!"

"That pompous bunch of tight blyrted snobs! How dare they laugh at me," Kybark grumbled once they had left the crowd.

Grylt shook off his grasp, and stood staring at his roommate's angry, pockmarked face. "What are you talking about? They weren't laughing at you?"

"Oh no? Just because I'm not one of your elite educated circle...."

"Oh, come off it! Let's go look at the lykrs."

Grylt led the way around the side of the house. The servants had just placed the evening food into the huge wire enclosure of the aviary. Happy chirps, and the fluttering of brilliantly colored feathers filled the space.

"Filthy primitive creatures! Look at them blyrting all over everything. Next, they'll be klynking each other in plain view!" Kybark said with a snarl.

Grylt watched the activity with a beatific smile. "No, you're wrong! They are simple that is true, but they have complex social interactions just like us."

"Oh yeah? Well how bout if I throw you to the ground, and klynk you right here to show them how primitive we are?" Kybark stepped behind his roommate and grabbed him firmly by the arms.

"Let go of me!"

"Ha, you think that by signing onto that voyage you can rid yourself of me? Don't be so sure. I still have two weeks to torment you!"

"I said let go of me!"

Kybark thrust his groin up against Grylt, then gave him a hard push. The professor stumbled, but managed to catch himself. He whirled around to confront his roommate.

"You're a monster!"

"Yes, I am."

Back at the patio, the circle of academics was still engaged in lively conversation.

"Did the poet know what he was talking about?" Bokyl asked.

Ymly stroked his narrow chin. "A very vell respected physicist in Rybort has proposed zee theory of airless motion. I haven't really decided whether I believe it or not."

Mytry and Rymnyr's head chef came swinging out of the double doors to the house. They spied the circle of serious looking individuals and sauntered over.

"Oooh, this is a high-powered group!" the chef gushed.

Senator Kylr glanced over in the direction Grylt and the poet had gone, then looked over at the new arrivals. "You two follow me, please." He turned back to the group. "Gentlemen, if you'll excuse us." Kryl got to his feet and walked purposefully around the side of the large brick structure.

"What's the hurry? Slow down," Mytry called out from behind.

The senator rounded the corner first. Grylt was standing with his head hung down. Kybark remained in an upright, aggressive position nearby. Kryl stopped right next to the professor.

"Everything alright?"

"Yes, (sniff), everything's fine," Grylt choked out.

"Everything doesn't look fine to me." The senator sent a stern, piercing glance over at Kybark.

Mytry and the chef came strolling around the corner of the building. "Professor! What's wrong?" The chef hurried over and put his arm around Grylt. Tears burst out of the professor's down turned eyes.

"This is a personal matter. It is of no concern to any of you!" Kybark snarled.

"Oh yes it is! Come Grylt! You're going with us." The chef led the sobbing professor back toward the patio.

"Go ahead! Leave with your elitist, closed minded friends!"

Kybark was left standing by himself. Grylt and the three other men approached the table where most of the Dymran group were sitting. After wiping the moisture off his face, the professor drew in a shuddering breath, and bent down to plant a kiss on Rymnyr's painted cheek.

"Thank you so much for organizing this wonderful party."

"Everything okay?" she whispered.

Grylt nodded his smooth, bald head. Krynut waited till their exchange was over, then addressed the group in a steady, authoritative tone.

"See you all at five tomorrow afternoon. Might as well bring a dyrft to read, or something to do."

Handynr let out a small, creaking groan. "Oh boy, sealed up in the foyer. Sounds delightful!" Mihyn reached over and playfully swatted his arm.

Chapter 46.

Just before five o'clock the next day, the crew began to assemble in the foyer. The high ceilinged room was still echoing with the footsteps and conversation of staff and students leaving for the day. Long shafts of sunlight poured in through the copper doors. Regent Krynut and Professor Grylt were the first to arrive. They both entered the foyer from the east stairwell.

"Good afternoon Professor. Ready for our night and day in the craft?"

"Yes, I suppose so." Grylt held up a sheath of papers. "I'm going to go through graduate student projects. Might as well get something useful done."

Mihyn and her husband came pushing their way through the sun warmed front doors. The four crew members converged on the cylindrical craft at approximately the same time.

"Good afternoon, Regent, Professor," Mihyn said with a smile.

"Good afternoon, Regents!" Grylt answered. "Ready for our trial run night?"

"Oh yes." She accepted the hug he offered.

Handynr laid a hand on the smooth, dull grey metal exterior, and stuck his head into the open hatch. "Looks nice and cozy."

Krynut ran his fingers over the rear stabilizer fin. "Cozy and superbly constructed."

Mihyn sided up to her husband and leaned into the open hatch. "I still can't believe what a marvelous job the design department at the railroad did with the detailing. In many ways, this is really a work of art."

She took a moment to examine the ornate floral designs and animal motifs that had been carefully worked onto even the most utilitarian aspects of the interior.

Door handles, hinges, corner brackets, almost every visible metal surface had been transformed into twisting vines, flowers in bloom, flapping lykrs, and a host of other natural forms.

The creaking of wheels approaching drew her back out of the hatch. Krynut turned to greet the two students pulling a cart across the foyer floor. "Ah, here comes the food."

The two young people parked the cart next to the opening. The student nearest the craft, a tall black haired youth, flashed a quick smile at the crew. "Where do you want this stuff?"

"I'll climb in and you can just hand it to me," Krynut replied.

"I'll join you." Handynr followed him in.

While the staff off loaded the goods, Grylt reached up and ran his hand along the shiny bronze length of the telescope. It protruded up out of the top of the craft two-thirds of the way back toward the rear.

"I still can't believe that Mynr Optics donated an A forty-six for this project! I mean, the Academy has only one of these. It's a shame we aren't going to spend the night outside. I could stryrk gaze."

"Yes, I thought about hauling it out onto the lawn," Krynut replied from inside. He hefted a burlap bag from the staff, stowed it in the space at the rear of the craft, dusted his hands off, then returned to the opening.

"My thoughts were that since it's supposed to be quite warm tomorrow, we will probably be more comfortable with the relatively stable temperature in here. Especially being sealed up."

"So, when we're up there, how are we going to heat and cool?" Mihyn asked. She pointed up toward the domed ceiling.

Krynut grasped the two water jugs being held out, then set them down next to the wall before answering.

"Once we enter the tail of the comet, pluge vapor will get sucked into the collectors up front. The flow runs through the spiral tubing next to the cockpit. Some of the liquid gets shunted to a storage tank, some of the vapor turns the generator. Current from the generator will break the pluge down into hydrogen and oxygen. The oxygen goes into one storage tank, the hydrogen into another."

He rose to a standing position and pointed down the passageway. "In the rear compartment, there's a jet coming out of the wall. You can see it when you climb in. We can burn the hydrogen for heat and cooking."

Mihyn stuck her head into the opening to follow his movements. "I see. And what about cooling?"

"According to Ymyl and his group, the flow of pluge vapor over the craft should be sufficient to keep us cool. His assumption is that we will probably need to heat more than cool."

"My word! I hope all these assumptions are correct," Grylt added.

When the students had finished off-loading the goods, they stood gazing into the hatch. Handynr leaned against the side of the opening and looked out at their beaming young faces.

"You two want to come in and take a look?"

"Could we?" the pony tailed young woman standing outside asked.

Handynr sent a quick inquisitor glance over at Krynut. The regent gave a shrug and moved to the side. "I don't see why not. Come aboard."

The young woman let go a giggle and stepped over the lip of the hatch. Her companion waited till she was in, then joined her.

"Wow, this is really elaborate! Who did all this amazing metal work?" the young woman gushed.

"Blue Line Railroad has an entire department of craftsmen from Pydia. They kind of went wild with the artistic touches," Handynr commented.

The two young people milled around the opening, examining all the brightly polished details. The young man pointed to the handle of the nearest crew cabin.

"May I?"

"Sure," Krynut replied.

With exaggerated care, the student swung the door open and stood aside to let the light from the foyer illuminate the space. "Wow, it looks just like a fancy kyrft cabin!"

"Go ahead and go in," Handnyr said from his place by the opening.

The young woman gently pushed her companion forward. He opened the door fully and stepped in. They both gave the narrow cabin a good looking over. The young woman plunked down on the bed.

"I could sleep in here! It's nice and cozy."

"I hope you realize that you all are the envy of many people here in Tyrl. What am I saying! The envy of all Ulutrita! The first people to venture into space. What a great honor," the young man added. His companion took another quick look around the small cabin, then got to her feet. A somewhat embarrassed smile spread across her face.

"I have a, kind of funny question," she asked in a quiet voice.

"Sure, what's your question?" Krynut asked.

"Where's the bathroom?"

Her innocent inquiry brought a laugh out of the young man standing next to her. "Oh for Zym's sake, Gyny! Is that all you can think of to ask?"

"Well, I'm just curious."

"No, that's a good question. Come this way."

Krynut walked back toward the rear of the craft and waited for the two young people to follow. When they both entered the roughly eight-foot by twelve-foot rectangular area, he reached over and parted the deep purple velvet curtain that hung across the back end of the space.

Behind it, a wooden seat set at an angle stuck out from the rear wall. Both the young people took a moment to look over the wide footrest below, and brass handles for griping that were secured to the wall on either side.

"One more question?" she asked timidly.

"Go ahead."

"How does the, you know, stuff, get removed?"

"See that brass lever over on the left? When it's depressed, it also opens a companion brass cover at the end of the waste pipe. It exits at the bottom of the stern."

The young man sent another quick glance around at the rear compartment. "Well, again, thank you so much for giving us the tour. It's really exciting to actually be able to stand in here!"

"Yes, thanks you very much." His fellow student reached up and brushed a tear out of her big, dark eyes. "Oh, excuse me. It's just that we're so proud of your courage and dedication to this. Come on, we better go."

The two students quickly exited the craft and wheeled their empty wagon across the now vacated foyer. A banging sound from the big front doors quickly drowned out the sound of their footsteps. Handynr stuck his head out of the open hatch and squinted at the face pressed against the glass.

"Bout time Ryk showed up."

Mihyn walked over to the sun flooded doorway, gave the handle a push, and let the mag driver in.

"Sorry I'm late. I had some, uh, things to do."

She flashed a quick smile, then closed the door. They walked side by side back to the craft.

"Evening, everyone," Ryk said with a note of cheeriness. "So we're ready to go?"

"Pretty much," Handynr replied from just inside the opening.

Krynut stepped over the hatch lip and stood next to Ryk.

"Sorry I'm late," the mag driver offered in a quiet voice.

"That's fine. Just don't be late for the real launch." The crew chief's comment brought a round of polite laughter from the group. He glanced around at the bottom of the craft. "Did they drop off a bucket by chance?"

"Oh yes, I put it over here." Professor Grylt bent down and picked up the object in question.

Krynut slid the bucket under the four-inch diameter waste pipe jutting out of the rear hull. "There we go. Well, shall we climb in?"

"After you Regent!" Grylt held out his thin, bony hand. One by one, the crew eased their way over the lip of the hatch. Once they were all inside, Krynut pulled down on the long bar running across the inside of the hatch and closed it with a click. The only source of illumination was the shaft of light shining in through the chevron shaped window above the cockpit.

"Going to be kinda of dark in here, don't you think?" Ryk commented.

"Yes, when we're under way, the generator that Myrvst so generously donated will power these four bulbs we have." Krynut pointed to one of the large, hand blow light bulbs screwed into its porcelain fixture next to the cockpit.

"So, what do we do for light tonight?"

"Since this is a trial run, I brought candles. Unless you want to crank the generator by hand."

"Candles're fine."

Krynut opened a box of thick white candles and distributed one to each crew member. Once they were lit, the interior glowed with warm, flickering light.

"Sorry to be asking so many questions, but, ain't it gonna get kind of stuffy in here?" Ryk asked.

"It probably will. I have the collectors disconnected, so we should get some fresh air, but yes, it will get kind of stuffy in here. That's why I decided not to move it outside. My guess is tomorrow afternoon we would have been really uncomfortable in the midday heat."

Ryk nodded his head and took a step down the passageway. "So which cabin belongs to who?"

"Mine is this one closest to the cockpit. Yours is next to it. Mihyn and Handynr are here, and Professor Grylt is closest to his beloved telescope."

Grylt clapped his hands together. "Wonderful! That's right where I want to be."

"So, let's all take a look at our cabins. Is anyone hungry?" Krynut asked. Shaking heads all around provided an answer to his question. "Alright, we might as well get comfortable and enjoy the evening."

The crew all followed Krynut's suggestion. Ryk sat in his small, compact cabin, and looked around at the finely crafted interior. His gaze fell on the empty bookshelf, down onto the built in desk, then around to the bed under him. He held the candle up and swung his boots up over the frame. The bed was just long enough to accommodate his lanky body.

In the cabin next door, he could hear Mihyn and her husband chatting about something. Ryk let out a sigh and stared up at the wood slatted ceiling. His eyes focused on a small wooden door set into the sidewall up near the ceiling. He glanced over at the wall he shared with Krynut. An identical wooden door was mounted there. Ryk made a fist and thumped on the wall.

"Krynut! What's that little door up by the ceiling for?"

"Open it and you'll see."

Ryk lifted himself up and gave the brass handle affixed to the small door a good hard tug. "I'm tryin', but it won't pull open."

"Try sliding it to the side."

With minimal effort, Ryk was able slide to the door into its recessed space. "Ah, that's got it."

There was a rustling from the other side of the wall, followed by a muffled thump.

"I have mine open. The designers thought it would be a good idea to install these so heat and air flow into the cabins when the doors are shut." Krynut's voice spilled out through the opening.

"That makes sense."

The crew chief stood up on the edge of his bed and peered through the opening. "So what do you think? Feel like you can live in here for a year or two?"

Ryk responded with a snorting laugh. "A year or two, huh? Guess I hadn't really thought about how long we'd be up there."

Krynut watched Ryk's dark eyes flit around under the shadow of his wide brimmed hat. "You seem a little shocked by my question."

Before replying, the mag driver looked down at the flickering candle flame, then back up at Krynut. "So much has happened so quickly in the last couple weeks that this whole trip hasn't seemed real. You know what I mean? You gotta understand. For most of my life, I've lived outdoors. At fourteen, I ran away from home and camped out all by myself. Spending a year or two in a confined space like this is going to take some getting used to."

"I understand. None of us are really accustomed to living in a space quite this small." The two men remained silent for several moments. Krynut flashed a quick smile at Ryk, then lowered himself off the bed.

"Well, this seems like a good time to do a walkthrough to familiarize ourselves with the craft. Let's get everyone together up front."

Once the crew had assembled in the space between the cockpit and front edge of the cabins, Krynut climbed over the back of the left hand pilot seat, and knelt facing them.

"So obviously, this is the cockpit. On the floor behind me are foot pedals that control the right to left movement. On either side of the seats, those metal cranks control the vertical movement." He transferred the candle to his left hand and extended his arm out to illuminate the space over by the hull.

"Back here are the gauges and control levers for the pluge, air, and hydrogen tanks. Handynr, I'd like you to be in charge of monitoring the pressure on these. When any of them get near capacity, a turn of the brass lever will take off the pressure."

Handynr left his wife's side and eased between the back of the seats and the front wall of the forward cabin. He took a quick scan of the maze of tubing and gauges, then turned back around. "Doesn't seem too difficult. A question, what happens if the tubing gets clogged?"

"Excellent question!" Krynut scooted as far over toward the hull as possible. He stretched across the back of the seat and laid a hand on the tubing below the bottom gauge.

"There's a wrench tucked back here. In the event that something gets clogged, we shut off the flow, undo the seal, then ream it out with that long stiff wire just above your head." Krynut waited for further questions, then slid back over toward the center of the cockpit. He reached up and grasped the thick brass handle that was mounted into the ceiling.

"Ryk, this is going to be your area. We don't have the spar attached, but when we do, you'll be able to swing the rope around by using this."

"Kinda like out at the test site."

"Exactly, so now, let's all go back to the common area."

Krynut led the way into the rear compartment and took up a position in the corner. Once the crew had spread out around him, he reached up and stroked the shiny surface of the telescope.

"I expect that Professor Grylt will be camped out here most of the voyage. Keep in mind that this area will be full of supplies, but our goal is also to try and retain enough space for us to meet here. And next, if you'll pull that curtain back Handynr, is the bathroom facility." The regent complied with the request and slid the elegant velvet curtain along on its large brass rings.

"Pretty basic. You have the lever on the left that allows the waste to flow out the egress tube. While we're in here tonight, I suggest we run some pluge down to remove everything."

Krynut shifted his gaze from the toilet over to where Grylt was standing. "Professor, if you'll move to the side, you all will see the pluge spigot, and next to it our gas burner."

"Regent?" Grylt pipped up.

"Yes."

"I believe I'd like a cup of zyd. Do you mind if I test out the burner?"

"No, not at all. I think that the cupboard just above your head has some pans in it."

The professor rose up on his tiptoes and extracted a small saucepan from the cupboard. "Would anyone else like some?"

Both Handynr and Mihyn nodded their heads. Krynut waited till Grylt filled the pan and got the burner going before moving off toward the passageway.

"Well, that concludes the walk through. I think I'll go get the dyrft I was planning to read."

The group spent a pleasant evening telling stories and drinking a bottle of myth Grylt brought with him. At around eleven, they all turned in.

Chapter 47.

Ryk was the first to wake. He fumbled around trying to find the candle in the absolute pitch darkness of his cabin, then gave up and opened the door. Dawn was just breaking. A diffuse grey light filled the foyer. Some of it managed to filter in through the chevron-shaped window above the cockpit. He pulled his boots on, slipped his hat over his tightly curled hair, and walked out into the passageway.

Everything in the interior was a soft charcoal color, save for the shiny brass fittings. Trying to make as little noise as possible, he tip-toed toward the rear compartment. Grylt snored rhythmically in his cabin at the end of the row.

Ryk lit the burner and set the pan over the yellow flame. He instinctively reached into his vest pocket to pull out his gynt pouch, then stopped.

"Oh klynk! I probably shouldn't fire up a gyntette in here." His face twisted in a scowl. "Okay Ryk old buddy, we got us a dilemma. I can deal with going a year or two without a drink of physt, probably be good for me, but no gynt? Whew, that's gonna to be tough."

The bubbling, sizzling sound of the pan distracted Ryk from his discourse. He shut the stopcock off, dumped a handful of zyd leaves into the frothing water, and leaned against the side of the hull.

"I gotta have a smoke."

While the zyd steeped away, Ryk pulled out his gynt pouch, a paper from the roll, and deftly formed a perfectly cylindrical cigarette. He considered opening the hatch to blow the smoke out, but decided against it. His gaze fell on the toilet. Ryk shot a quick glance back down the passageway, then stuck the cigarette in his mouth, and stepped up on the footrest. Again, his weather beaten features contorted into a frown.

"I'll be dythed if I gonna sit like a lady and zynk!"

He lifted the lid, took one more quick glance over his shoulder, and relieved himself. Ryk pushed down on the brass lever and listened to the sound of liquid flowing down metal. When the sound gradually tapered off, he lit the cigarette hanging out of his mouth, inhaled deeply, and blew a lung full of smoke into the bowl.

Much to his dismay, it came rising right back out into his face. He let the lid drop back down. The remainder of the smoke drifted up around the wooden seat. With both hands, he fanned the air to try and dispel the smoke.

"Klynk! That didn't work very well."

After one more unsuccessful attempt to blow the smoke out the waste tube, Ryk pinched the cherry off the gynt and tucked the stub into his pocket. Grumbling to himself, he pulled a metal cup out of the cupboard, poured some of the steaming zyd in, and sat down hard on the nearest chair.

From down the passageway, he heard a clunk, then the creaking of a door opening. Seconds later, Krynut's nightshirt clad form appeared at the end of the passageway.

"Oh, you're up. I smell smoke."

"Yeah, sorry bout that. I'm used to having a smoke first thing when I get up, and thought I'd see if I could blow the smoke out the zynk tube." The best Ryk could do was offer an apologetic smile.

Krynut rubbed his face and stared back at him blankly. "Well, uh, don't, I mean….What time is it?" He finished his question with a yawn.

Ryk pulled a beaten up pocket watch out of his vest. He tilted it toward the passageway and angled it several times till the dial was visible.

"Five twenty."

"Ah, not too early."

Low voices and the thud of feet on wood drifted in from behind Krynut. Mihyn came stumbling down the passageway. Her eyes were barely open. Her light brown hair was nothing more than a haphazard pile that spilled down onto her neck.

"I smell smoke. What's going on?"

Krynut rubbed his face again. "Ryk was experimenting with ways to smoke a gyntette without filling the craft with smoke. He wasn't totally successful."

Mihyn stood at the entrance to the rear compartment, trying to absorb the information just presented. She nodded, then turned her attention to Ryk.

"Well, as long as we're not on fire, I'm going back to bed. Is that zyd?"

Ryk held up his cup. "Yep, nice and strong."

"Oooh. That's hard to resist. Can I have some?"

"Why sure. Hold on." He rose up from his chair, extracted another cup from the stash, filled it from the pan, and walked over to her. A warm, relaxed smile spread across Ryk's face as he handed it over.

Mihyn took it from him, and stuck her narrow, elegant nose over the steaming vapors. "Mmmn, smells good. Thanks." She turned around and shuffled back down the passageway.

"Okay, guess I might as well have some, too." Krynut passed by Ryk and got his own cup. After filling it, he eased down in the chair nearest the telescope.

"How'd you sleep last night?"

Ryk took another drink and returned to his chair. "Oh, I slept alright. I'm used to spending all day working hard, so when I'm jest sitting around like I did yesterday, my body don't really get that tired."

A few moments later, the married couple entered the rear compartment. Handynr was still wearing his linen pajamas. Mihyn's hair was pulled back in a loose knot. She had a thin robe wrapped around her nicely proportioned body. Handynr eased down into the chair next to Krynut. His wife curled up in the empty chair next to him. The group sat and sipped their zyd in silence.

Ryk got up and strode down the passageway. He jammed his head up next to the chevron-shaped window. Through the thick glass, he could see the outline of the copper doors. A fuzzy yellow light illuminated the quiet foyer. He returned to his chair.

"Yep, it's definitely getting light outside. Only what, ten more hours to go?"

Krynut smiled. "That sounds about right."

A moment later, Grylt came walking into the rear space. He was rubbing the side of his bulbous forehead. "Good morning! Looks like I'm the last one up."

"Would you like some zyd?" Mihyn asked from her comfortable position leaning against her husband's chest.

"Yes, please." Grylt slipped past the married couple and sat down in the chair beside the telescope. "Well, here we all are, sitting cozy in our new living room." The professor's face broke into a wide grin as he gazed around at his fellow crew members.

"You sure wake up happy," Mihyn commented.

"Oh, in general, I'm a pretty happy person." He tilted his head back and sniffed the air. "Something's burning."

Ryk had just set the pan back down on the burner. "Oh, that would be me. I thought I'd see if I could get away with smoking a gyntette in here. Didn't work too well."

"Yes, I would say that my only comment about the accommodations is, the ventilation seems a little ineffective."

The group was silent for a moment. The hissing of the jet was the only sound. Handynr pulled his arm out from behind his wife's neck.

"Sorry dear. My arm was falling asleep. So, I guess we can spend most of the day reading or something?"

"I brought some samsyrs to grade," Krynut replied.

Grylt let loose a short little cackle. "As did I. I was going to bring my Sydtr board. Have any of you ever played it?" All heads in the circle shook in response. "No? Oh, it's a marvelous game. Each player gets ten tiles, and you have to move around the board based on mathematical combinations. Such fun."

"Could be tough playing it if all the tiles are floating around," Ryk commented.

"Floating around?"

"I believe Ryk is referencing Kybark's theory about the lack of air and how it might affect the craft during the voyage," Krynut added.

At the sound of his roommate's name, the professor's thin, bony face became shaded. He wrung his hands together.

"Well, he was in quite a mood the other night. I don't really know what's gotten into him lately, but you have to consider what he says carefully. He has a tendency to expound on things of which he may not be completely knowledgeable."

Ryk got up from his chair and opened the cabinet just above the burner. "I don't know about the rest of you, but I'm hungry. Shall we see about fixing some nymfyr?"

"Yes, I believe I could eat something," Grylt replied. "Isn't there supposed to be a sack of kymr somewhere?"

"Yes, there's a bag of it, and some oil down in that compartment by the floor," Krynut added.

Ryk squatted down, set his cup next to his foot, and opened the small rectangular door. He poked around for a moment, then reached in, pulled out a cloth bag, and handed it over to Grylt. The professor brought it up to his hooked nose.

"Ah, this reminds me of my last trip to Snouwda. The Kurans there rely heavily on kymr for their diet. That and the meat of a small hymr is really all they eat."

"Are you serious? That sounds like a pretty dull diet," Ryk commented. He looked over at the professor while he pulled a bottle of amber oil and a jar of honey out of the compartment.

"Yes, I suppose it's a matter of what you are used to."

Ryk rose from his squatting position and held the two vessels up. "Anyone feel like cooking?" He glanced around at his fellow crew members, but eventually focused his attention on Mihyn.

"Oh, no! Just cause I'm the only woman in this group doesn't......"

"Jest calm down. I do plenty of cookin' out at camp. I was just asking."

Mihyn's look of indignance immediately changed to one of amusement. She leaned over and elbowed her husband playfully in the ribs. "Mag driver cooking. This should be good."

Ryk prepared a stack of pancakes which the crew managed to finish off. He and Mihyn cleaned up as best they could. Once the dishes had been stashed back into the cabinets, Handynr moved off toward the passageway.

"Well, looks like you two have it covered. I brought some correspondence to read, so guess I'll get to it."

"Yes, I have some research projects to review. Oh, excuse me!" Grylt let go an oily burp just before following Handynr out of the rear compartment.

The rest of the day passed pleasantly. The crew alternated between reading, napping, and sitting around conversing. Just after two in the afternoon, Mihyn woke from a short nap. She lay on the bunk, examining the finely coffered ceiling. Handynr was seated at the desk with his back to her.

Mihyn rose up to a sitting position which caused the rail of the bunk to creak. Her husband quickly stuffed the mauve piece of paper he was reading into the middle of the thick sheath of reports in his other hand.

"You startled me!" Handynr shifted around on the simple wooden chair and looked over at his wife.

Mihyn's large brown eyes flitted between her husband's guilty expression and the corner of the mauve letter not quite hidden in the sheath of reports. She eased herself off the bunk, stood next to him, and slid the letter out of the sheath of papers. Her anger began to build like a small fire fanned by hurricane force winds as she read the words.

"Dearest Handynr, I know you asked me to stop writing these letters, but my love for you is so strong that........"

Mihyn held the letter out and leaned against the back wall. She let herself hit the wood paneling with enough force to generate an audible thump. "You want to tell me what this is?"

Handynr's lips began to quiver. He lowered his gaze to the floor. Several supremely uncomfortable seconds ticked by before he spoke.

"I, uh, have been planning to talk to you about this." The involuntary laugh that escaped from his mouth provided the final ignition to Mihyn's anger.

"You were planning on talking to me about what?"

"Please! Lower your voice." Handynr's expression suddenly twisted into a mask of pain.

His wife tilted forward and placed both hands on the desktop. Their faces were now only inches apart.

"You think this is a surprise to me? I've known about these letters for months. You burned a stack of them in the backyard."

All his considerable diplomatic skill couldn't prevent the look of shock and exposure from sweeping across Handynr's countenance. He reached over and pushed the door closed.

In his cabin nearest the cockpit, Krynut stopped writing his evaluation on a test paper in mid-sentence at the sound of the couple's angry voices. Ryk and the professor were sharing interesting stories in the rear compartment when Mihyn's shout echoed out to them. Both men froze in place and stared at each other.

Back in their cabin, Handynr managed to regain a fraction of his composure. He took a deep breath, then looked directly into his wife's blazing eyes.

"Darling....."

"Don't call me darling!" Mihyn's furious whisper cut through the interior of the cabin like a buzz saw.

"We need to talk about this, but please, can we do it later?" As soon as the words left his tongue, Handynr realized how ridiculous the suggestion had been. He held up his hand in a futile attempt to signal a halt, but it was too late.

"What a cowardly fygr thing to say! You want to talk about it later? Why put it off?"

Before he could stop her, Mihyn pushed off against the back wall, yanked open the door, and stomped off toward the rear compartment. Ryk and the professor sat motionless when she entered the space.

Mihyn stopped in mid-stride, shot a quick glance at their blank, questioning expressions, then spun around and hurried up toward the cockpit. Krynut watched her sweep past his open cabin. She swung down onto the left side cockpit seat with enough force to cause a bolt to squeak.

For thirty agonizing seconds, not a sound was generated. The two men in the rear compartment tried to communicate non-verbally. Ryk held his big, rough hands up and shrugged. Grylt shrugged back. He got up from his chair and stuck his head around the edge of the crew cabin.

Krynut eased out into the passageway. He slipped into the married couples' cabin and closed the door behind him. Handynr stood next to the bunk, head hung down in shame. The mauve letter laying on the desk caught Krynut's eye. He took a couple steps forward and bent over to examine it.

After releasing a pitiful sigh, Handynr swept the letter off the desk. "Here, go ahead and read it. No secret now."

Krynut's eyes shot back and forth over the beautifully executed script of the gushing love letter. He folded the paper up and handed it back. "So, how long has this been going on?"

Handynr leaned back against the desk, threaded his fingers around his crossed leg, and stared up at nothing. "I guess it all started shortly after Kym started working for me. One day she wore this very revealing dress, and....Dyth it! What a blyrthole I am!" He bent forward and covered his face with both hands.

After quietly exiting the cabin, Krynut walked into the rear compartment and sat down in the corner chair. For several seconds, the three men just exchanged looks of concern.

"I take it there has been some kinda issue with them?" Ryk asked in a whisper.

Krynut nodded, then beckoned for Grylt to draw close. "It seems that Handynr and his secretary have been carrying on a, uh, relationship, and Mihyn just found out."

The professor let go a tiny gasp. He held a hand up to his mouth. "Oh dear, dear, dear. Are you going to go talk to her?"

Krynut shook his head. "Not right now. The hurt is probably way too fresh for her to be able to..."

"What're you whispering about?" Mihyn stood at the entrance to the rear compartment. All eyes were fixed on her tear streaked face. With powerful, determined steps, she made a beeline for the far corner of the compartment, and settled against the paneled wall.

"Never mind. I know what you're whispering about." She let go a deep, anguished groan, and looked up at the ceiling. "I just can't believe my worst fears are actually true. Why, oh why didn't confront him?"

The last hour and a half of their experimental day in the craft dragged by torturously. Both Krynut and the professor buried themselves in the work they had brought. Handynr remained by himself in the cabin. Ryk tidied up as best he could while Mihyn hung in her corner like a malevolent ghost. At four fifty, Krynut packed up the papers he had brought in, and walked out into the passageway.

"Ten more minutes to go," Ryk announced after taking a look at his watch. He slid it back into his vest pocket and joined the crew chief in his place next to the hatch. Ryk held up the stub of a gynt cigarette. "I know exactly what I'm going to do the minute we leave."

Grylt exited his cabin and joined the other two crew members. On her way toward the hatch, Mihyn sent a scathing glance into the open door to her cabin.

Through the hull, the sounds of the big copper doors opening followed by excited voices reverberated. Ryk jammed his head against the side of the window.

"Somebody just came in."

"That sounds like Rymnyr," Mihyn commented.

"I see three people, make that four people. Oh, yeah that's Professor Rymnyr. I just caught a glimpse of her hair. I think your girl is out there Krynut, and that's probably Kryzyck."

A high, youthful female laugh bounced off the walls of the foyer. Ryk looked around at his crew members for signs of recognition. The echoing footsteps and laughter grew louder. There was a sharp rap on the metal hull, followed the appearance of a hand waving above the window.

"Hello voyagers! How was your night and day?" Rymnyr's voice echoed through the hull.

"Just fine. We're coming out in how many minutes?" Mihyn asked.

"I think we can call it a day." Krynut stepped forward and turned the crank on the sealing mechanism. After several rotations, there was a loud click. He pushed the hatch up to reveal the smiling faces of Professor Rymnyr, Kryzyck, Janela, and Kym.

"You all look well! We brought some chinz along to celebrate." Rymnyr held up two thick green bottles. "May we come in?"

"Certainly." Krynut stepped to the side and held out his hand. The professor passed one of the bottles over to Kryzyck, grasped the regent's hand, and swung her thick leg over the lip.

"Thank you. My, it's stuffy in here." Rymnyr waved a hand in front of her face.

"Yes, we noticed that the ventilation is pretty nonexistent," Krynut commented as he offered his hand to Janela.

Mihyn took a step forward and gave Rymnyr a kiss on the cheek. "So good to see you," she whispered.

Rymnyr looked into the regent's deep brown eyes. The pain and anguish were all too evident. "So, were you comfortable last night?"

Mihyn nodded a reply. Janela stepped over the lip and hugged the crew chief. Kryzyck eased himself in behind her.

"Isn't someone going to help me in?" Kym called out before ducking down under the hatch cover.

Kryzyck reached out to grasp Kym's hand. The secretary hiked up the hem of her dark red dress and stepped over the lip. "Ooooh, this is so exciting to actual stand in the craft!" Her exuberance helped to lighten the somber atmosphere.

"Well, I'm gonna duck out for a smoke. Go ahead and crack the chinz. I'll be right back." Ryk gave Kym a tiny tip of his hat before slipping out under the hatch.

The secretary wandered down the passageway and stopped by the open door of the middle cabin. Handynr was just making his way out.

"Hello-o-o!" Kym's musical greeting caused him to stop in his tracks. She stood blocking the doorway. "Looks like this is the marri....Oh!"

Kym and Handynr were only six inches apart when she noticed the dead seriousness expression on his face. Her beaming grin faded instantly.

"Is, is, something wrong?" In a flash, Kym zeroed in on the mauve letter laid out flat on the desk. "Oh, Zym!"

"She knows," Handynr delivered with bone chilling honesty as he gently moved her out of the way.

Just behind the cockpit, Janela stood next to Krynut with her willowy arm wrapped around his waist. "Did you miss me?"

"Yes, of course."

She let go a deep sigh. "I cannot honestly believe that in twenty-one short days, you will blast off, and I'll never see you again."

Her last words were obscured by the flood of emotion. She held a hand in front of her mouth. After wiping tears out of her dark, luminous eyes, she sniffed several times, and fought to regain composure.

"I'm sorry, I don't mean to let my grief darken the celebration. Open the chinz!"

Krynut pulled her close and kissed the top of her head. The arrival of the somber and joyless Handynr sent a hush over the group. Rymnyr scrutinized his pained, wane features when he passed by her. In one quick move, he stooped down, and hopped over the lip of the hatch.

Ryk stood beside the nose of the craft, luxuriously smoking his gynt. He watched Handynr rise up from under the hatch. The two men shared a quick, unfriendly glance. Ryk ground out his gynt and was about to climb back into the craft when Kym's head of long brown hair appeared in the opening.

"Excuse me." Her voice was choked off with emotion.

After waiting till the secretary exited, Ryk ducked back into the craft. Kryzyck seemed to be the only one not paralyzed by the drama unfolding. He popped the bottle open while Rymnyr passed crystal flutes all around. After everyone's glass was filled, she addressed the group in a loud, proud voice.

"A toast to the brave voyagers as the beginning of their great journey approaches! Life is short!"

"Life is short!" the group echoed.

Rymnyr waved a hand in front of her face once more. "I don't mean to sound rude, but the stuffiness is starting to get to me. Could we move back out into the foyer?"

"Certainly." Krynut eased out over the lip of the hatch and helped both his girlfriend and Rymnyr exit. The professor stood next to the hull while the rest of the group filed out.

"Whew! Much better. I'm really not fond of closed in spaces. Don't forget, tomorrow at ten, fitting for the flight robes at Gyrnk Fabrics."

Against the far wall of the foyer, Handynr and his secretary were engaged in an intense conversation. The rest of the party tried to be discreet by not staring for more than a second at the distraught couple. After sending another quick look their way, Rymnyr laid a hand on Grylt's shoulder.

"Professor, be a dear and assemble your belongings. Kryzyck and I have an engagement tonight, and you're coming with us."

"Oh, how nice! I'll be back in a minute." Grylt slipped back under the open hatch.

Ryk finished off his glass and offered it to Kryzyck. "Much obliged. Well, I'm heading out also." The mag driver tipped his hat, then strode off toward the front doors.

Rymnyr eased next to Krynut and cupped a hand around his ear. "What the klynk is going on?"

"I'll have to tell you later. Let's just say that a relationship issue erupted earlier." Krynut sent a quick little flash of concern her way before walking toward the rear of the craft.

Rymnyr looked over at the old miner to see if he had some clue to the mystery. He just shrugged. All the while, Mihyn stood motionless. Her attention was completely absorbed by the activity next to the wall. Kryzyck tapped her on the arm.

"Regent, can we give you a ride some…"

"No! I mean, no, but thanks. The buggy stand should still be open. I can find a ride home."

Rymnyr's face melted into a wash of compassion. She stepped forward and gave Mihyn a crushing hug. Before letting go, she spoke directly into her mass of auburn hair. "Let's talk about this soon."

At the back of the craft, Krynut bent over and examined the contents of the bucket. He wrinkled up his narrow, straight nose. After emptying it down in the basement sink, he returned to the foyer. All was quiet when Krynut entered the high domed, white marble space.

"Everyone must have left. And there's the craft. So in twenty-one days, I'm really going to climb in that thing, and get blasted off the surface of this planet. Am I crazy?" He drew in a breath and walked over to it.

"Janela?"

"I'm in here." Her reply was barely audible from the inside of the craft.

Krynut bent down, stepped over the lip, then made his way down the passageway. Janela was sitting in one of the chairs against the far wall. She was leaning forward, head slightly lowered. Her long brown fingers were intertwined in her lap. When he entered the space, she looked up at him.

"So this is where you are and your friends are going to live. Well, I hope you all are happy together." Her voice was brittle and strained.

Krynut turned back toward the hatch. "Come on, let's go."

Janela got to her feet and walked up next to him. "I still don't understand why you have to be the one to go! Why was I ever so foolish to become involved with you?" She leveled a flashing, diamond hard stare right at him.

"Janela, we've been through this before."

"How can you be so cold and unfeeling? Don't you have any feelings?"

Krynut stood at the end of the passageway like a statue. His sleep deprived mind searched for an honest answer to her question. "Yes, I have feelings. I'm also a very determined man. With only three weeks left before launch, there are so many things to think about. I guess it's just the way I am."

Chapter 48.

The following morning, the crew and Professor Rymnyr gathered at the prestigious Grynk clothing store for the final fitting of the specially made robes. Mihyn and Handynr arrived separately and stood as far apart as possible.

Two reporters for the local newspaper were on hand. While one of them set up the bulky, primitive camera, the other interviewed the crew. After scrawling down their answers to the fairly generic questions he asked, the sandy haired reporter stuck the end of his pencil into the corner of his mouth. He sent a mischievous glance around at the crew.

"So, I assume that you all have heard the theory that the voices are coming from what is being referred to as, the Cloud?" Several of the crew nodded. "Very well, and can you confirm the speculation that your ultimate destination is indeed, the Cloud?"

Again, his question was met with more tentative nods. Irritation, and just a hint of anger began to send color into Krynut's cheeks. Rymnyr stole a quick look over at him, then stepped toward the low platform set against the back wall.

"Excuse me, thank you for your interest, but I believe we need to get started on the....."

"No, wait. Let him finish." Krynut's voice was darkened with suspicion.

The reporter grinned over at the crew chief and resumed his inquires. "Thank you Regent. I'll cut to the quick. Have you also heard that there are some who believe that this, Cloud is actually the Door of Zym mentioned in the writings by Collria?"

"Yes, I have heard that." Krynut responded in a steel edged tone.

"The passage by Collria predicts that someone will enter the Door, and that will trigger the end of all things. Are you...."

"No, we are not concerned about that. By the way, where did you get your information about the Cloud?"

The intensity of Krynut's stare sent a visible shudder through the reporter. He shuffled his feet back and forth several times before daring to face the crew chief's blazing countenance.

"I, uh, never reveal my sources. Thanks you for allowing me to ask." He gave a little bow and whisked over to stand next to his fellow reporter.

Krynut motioned toward the designer of the robes. The very business-like small woman was standing on the platform next to the rack of garments. She looked up at the wall clock over the top of her pointy, wire-framed glasses, then turned toward Rymnyr.

"It's ten o'clock. Is everyone here?"

The professor glanced around at the small crowd packed into the workroom. She took a quick head count. "Yes, they are all here."

"Mihyn?" the designer called out.

The regent walked up onto the platform and stood beside the rack of finely tailored garments. After flashing a quick smile, the designer pulled a stunning, sky blue, gold threaded robe accented by a swirling black pattern off the rack.

"Arms out please, dear."

Mihyn stood still while the dazzling garment was slid over her outstretched arms. The designer carefully pulled the cuffs up to Mihyn's wrists, then stepped back and examined the fit.

"Can I lower my arms?" Mihyn asked with a touch of distress.

"Just a second dear." The designer walked around behind and smoothed the folds off the regent's shoulders. "Yes, that will do. You may lower your arms."

Mihyn gave a whoosh of relief. "My, this fabric is heavy!"

Sporadic laughter drifted up from the assembled crowd.

"Well, it should be. Each robe has two pounds of gold thread woven into it."

"That seems like a lot."

"That's what the Academy asked for, and that's what we delivered. Chin up." The designer proceeded to slip the fastening loops over the yellow metal buttons, starting at the top.

"Can I lower my chin?"

"Of course dear."

Once she completed securing the buttons, the designer stepped back, tucked the clipboard under her armpit, and brought her hands together in applause. The crowd surrounding the low stage responded likewise. Mihyn began undoing the buttons. The designer reached over and grasped her gently by the arm.

"No dear. Hang on. We want to get a picture with all of you in your robes. It'll just take a couple minutes. You can go stand over with the other crew members."

Mihyn hiked up the bottom of the robe and carefully stepped down off the platform.

"Grylt," the designer called out after examining her clipboard. While the professor made his way up to the platform, she pulled a brilliant jade green robe off the rack. Grylt jumped up onto the platform and stood next her. "Arms out please."

The professor complied with the request and gazed wide eyed at the shimmering material. "Oh, it's just marvelous! Green is my favorite color."

"And you're a biologist right?"

"Actually, I'm the head of the natural science department, but yes, biology is one of my specialties."

"Well, this one took extra time embroidering all these fancy lykr and nymfyr motifs." The designer yanked on the left sleeve, then passed along behind his back. She stopped to whisper in his pointy ear.

"If you ask me, this is the crowning achievement of our effort. I hope you like it."

Grylt let go a little squeak of delight and reached up to brush a tear away. "Oh, excuse me! My emotions have been running kind of high lately. Thank you. Thank you so much. I just love it!"

"You can lower your arms. So glad you're happy with it." The designer smoothed out the shoulders, then quickly fastened the buttons. Her amazingly dexterous fingers flew down the front of the robe. When she stepped away, several in the crowd gasped at the artistic mastery of the fabric.

"Go ahead and turn around. Let them see the design on the back."

Grylt's face glowed with pride. He slowly rotated. When he had turned a full one-hundred eighty degrees, the designer laid her hand on his shoulder to halt him.

"Notice the sweeping pyfg pattern. This took our best needle worker three solid days to complete." Applause erupted from the crowd. The designer bowed at the waist. "You can go back down now."

"Thank you again!" Grylt leaned forward and planted a kiss on her cheek, then hurried off the platform to where Mihyn was standing.

Handynr was called up and fitted with his elegant red and black checkered robe. Regent Krynut's garment was another big hit. It was created with an amazing celestial pattern of deep blue with gold and silver threads interlaced throughout. Ryk was the last crew member called up. He sauntered over and stood next to the designer.

"Yours we had a hard time deciding on the pattern for. I hope you like it." The designer let out a low groan after pulling his large, brown, red, and gold robe off the rack. "This one and Krynut's are the heaviest. Arms up."

She slid the garment over Ryk's thickly muscled arms and smoothed out the folds. "Good thing we made these extra wide. You're built a little different than the others." The designer pulled the lapels together, pushed Ryk's outstretched arms down, and buttoned him up.

"Go ahead and turn around. Might as well show this one off too." When his back was exposed to the audience, she ran her hand up and down the sides of the fabric.

"You'll notice the styrn motif. It's repeated on the sleeves and wraps around both flanks. Since Ryk is the expert roper of the group, we also trimmed the cuffs, collar, and hem with braided gold strands." She spun him back around and patted the richly textured robe another couple times. "I hope you're as strong as you look. This is the heaviest one."

"Can I get down now?"

"Nope. Need to get a picture of the whole group. Relax, you're famous now."

When the picture of the crew was finally snapped, Ryk's expression reflected the anger and irritation swirling within him. Immediately after the camera clicked, Professor Rymnyr came bouncing up to the stage.

"Oh, this is a wonderful, historic moment!" She paused to fan herself with a gilt-edged letter she held clutched in her hand. "So much is happening in the next two days. It makes my head spin around! Remember, Fyn day at seven thirty, our presence is requested at the Collrian Society monthly meeting." Her eyes glittered under the long, accentuated lashes. She dropped her voice to a whisper.

"I have a very strong suspicion that they are going to bestow some great honor on all of you!"

"Do we have to wear our robes?" Ryk tossed out.

"Of course! I would encourage you to wear them everywhere for the next twenty days. People need to recognize what a fantastic journey all of you are about to embark on."

Grylt raised his hand. "Can we bring a guest to the Collrian meeting?"

"Yes, each of you may bring one additional person. Alright everyone! See you on Fyn day. Please don't be late!"

Five days later, buggies began rolling along the deserted storefronts where the Collrian Society met. Mihyn leaned out the window, scanned the cracked windows and fading wooden signs, then yelled up at the driver.

"This doesn't look like the place. I'm not sure this map is correct!"

From up in his seat, the driver answered. "Don't know what to tell ya. I've never…Oh, hang on. I think there's other buggies coming down this way."

They rounded a corner, and a line of black styrn carriages parked along the broken curb came into view. From these, a steady stream of toga clad men, some alone, some accompanied by women, filed out.

The buggy Mihyn was riding in came to a stop at the near end of the line. She opened the door, brushed the hem of her robe aside, and eased down to the curb.

A pair of toga clad men came walking up behind her. "Absolutely stunning robe! We are honored to have you here tonight," one of the members called out.

"Thank you. I wasn't sure this was the right neighborhood. I had imagined something more, uh, impressive?"

The other toga wearer rasped out a laugh. "Yes, secrecy is a big part of the Collrian pledge. Have you ever attended one of our functions?" Mihyn shook her head. "Ah, well you are in for a treat. Tonight is a very big event. Just follow us."

When they reached the door of the dilapidated store front, both men lifted a hand to display their massive silver rings. The door keeper took a quick scan of Mihyn's invitation, then allowed the group to enter.

Mihyn glanced at the dust covered shelves and counter while they walked to the back of the room. She had to hike up the hem of her gorgeous blue robe in order to negotiate the rickety stairway.

As they neared the landing, laughter and excited voices drifted down toward them. They stepped into the large waiting area and were absorbed into the noisy, bustling crowd. The serving staff held their trays high as they fought to work their way from the kitchen into the main hall. Head Regent Bokyl was positioned over by the big double doors.

"Regent! Over here!" He gave a wave of his hand as Mihyn appeared at the edge of the crowd. While she made her way over to him, Bokyl leaned over and whispered to his wife.

"I don't see Handynr. Not a good sign."

When Mihyn arrived, the head regent's wife Gyrty reached out and grasped her hand. "Oh my dear! You look absolutely stunning in that robe." She ran her fingers along the finely embroidered sleeve.

Bokyl took a moment to evaluate Mihyn's striking blue, gold, and black patterned garment. "I concur. You look just magnificent."

"Are the others here?" Mihyn asked.

"I believe several of them are. Rymnyr hasn't arrived yet. Go on in. We have seats reserved for you right up next to the podium." Bokyl stepped aside and let her squeeze past.

Mihyn shot a quick glance at the guards standing rigidly at attention on either side of the doorway to the main room. Their ornate glinting headdresses and long ornamental spears shone in the flickering lamp light. When she stepped across the threshold, Mihyn let go a small cough. A haze of gynt smoke already hung in swirling clouds around the perimeter of the rectangular room.

"This is going to be tough. I hate gynt smoke!"

She spotted Krynut standing against the far wall, and carefully worked her way around the groups of mostly men conversing loudly, drinking, and puffing on thick brown cigars. Krynut broke off his conversation as she approached.

"Good evening, I think these are our places." He motioned over toward the long table behind her. "Handynr's not with you, I take it?"

Mihyn drew in as deep a breath of the smoky air as she could manage. "No, I believe he is planning on showing up, though."

Krynut was going to ask about the condition of their relationship, but changed his mind. While she moved off to find a seat, he returned to his previous conversation.

At each place along the table, stiff white cards had been set upon which the names of the crew were rendered in marvelous sweeping script. Mihyn leaned forward and located hers midway down from the podium.

Back in the rickety stairway, Ryk, Grylt, and Handynr were just approaching the landing. The mag driver's face was pulled down in a scowl. "Don't know about you two, but all I want to do is get this over with and take this stupid, heavy robe off."

"Oh, I'm sorry to hear that! Personally, I can hardly contain myself. This is an honor, I for one, never expected to receive," Grylt gushed.

Handynr just smirked in the dim light. The noise of the crowded hall grew louder as they ascended the stairs. Ryk stepped out onto the jam packed landing and stood with his mouth partially open. "Whoa!"

Bokyl recognized the mag driver's brown, wide-brimmed hat above the milling crowd, and waved his hand several times before catching Ryk's attention. The three crew members threaded their way across the landing. At regular intervals, they had to stop to receive slaps on the shoulder and offers of congratulations. Eventually, the trio made it to Bokyl's position by the open door.

"Welcome Ryk, Professor, Regent. I think all of you have met my wife Gyrty," the head regent offered. All three crew members nodded a greeting to Bokyl's wife. "Well, go right on in. We're seated on the right side next to the podium."

After the new arrivals worked their way into the crowded, noisy room, Gyrty leaned over toward her husband.

"The mag driver looks great in that robe. Think you could get him to take that beaten up hat off?"

Mihyn sat at her designated place setting with empty chairs on her left and right. "Zym, I feel like the lonely teenager at a second level school dance. I sure hope Rymy shows up soon. I need some female support."

She reached over and fidgeted with the elegantly scripted place card. The sudden roar of voices from over by the hall door caused her to shift around in her seat. Mihyn's sense of isolation disappeared when she caught sight of Ryk towering above the crowd. Just as she was starting to relax, her gaze fell on Handynr making his way across the room.

Ryk spotted Krynut carrying on a discussion with some of his colleagues and led the other two crew members over toward him. The crew chief excused himself from the conversation upon their arrival.

"Good evening, welcome to the Collrian Society," Krynut offered while guiding them over to their designated table. A sense of relief washed over him when he realized that Handynr had not brought his secretary along.

"Quite the fancy place here." Ryk took a quick scan of the room. The scowl on his face had long since been replaced by a big, toothy grin.

"Yes, this is where the elite of Tyrl society meets." Krynut sent a sideways glance over at Handynr. He too was gazing out at the crowded, energized space around them. The regent's handsome face was a picture of smugness. "Your seats are right next to the podium. I need to finish up my discussion, then I'll join you."

Professor Grylt stood trembling slightly. "Thank you, Regent. Oh, I can hardly contain my excitement!"

Krynut flashed a quick smile, then returned to the circle of academics. Grylt watched him re-enter the group.

"I think that's Professor Symyr over there."

He hustled over to join the circle. Handynr also recognized several of the academics and followed close behind. Ryk remained where he was for several seconds, then walked over to the table. When he passed behind Mihyn, she reached up and snagged his brown and red sleeve.

"Hello Ryk."

"Hello Regent."

"Lylyn didn't come with you?"

"Naw, she had to work today, plus she's been feeling kind of wore out."

A harried waitress distributed several shining silver goblets of mynth to the academic circle, then edged her way over to the two seated crew members. After brushing a sweat plastered strand of dark hair away from her forehead, she rested her hands on the back of their chairs.

"Welcome. I'm guessing that this is your first time here?"

Ryk leaned back and sent a charming smile up at her pretty, but rough looking face. "Yeah, first time."

"Well, like something to drink?"

"Sure, how bought a glass of physt?"

The waitress gave a little twist of her bright red lips. "That's about the one thing we don't have here. Got lots of excellent mynth."

"Not much of a mynth drinker. How 'bout pyryn?"

"Let me go see what we got. And you ma'am?"

"Just some pluge please."

When the waitress turned to leave, Ryk reached out and laid his hand on her bare arm. "Hey, can I get one of those gynts?"

"Absolutely, Love." After giving a little flip of her wavy black hair, she slipped back through the crowd.

Chapter 49.

Out in the crowded landing, Bokyl scanned the slowly decreasing number of new arrivals. "I sure hope Rymnyr gets here. It's almost time to start.

"I'm sure she will," Gyrty responded. She reached over and grasped his hand.

At that very moment, Rynmyr was struggling to make it up the stairway. The hem of her elegant gold trimmed robe didn't seem to want to stay in place. Four times on the ascent, it slipped under the toe of her expensive, authentic Styrynt sandals, sending her plunging forward. The last time, right near the top, she went down on her hands and knees. Kryzyck bent over and pulled up back to her feet.

"It's alright dear. We're almost there."

"I know we're almost there, but look at me! I'm a wreck! I'm covered in sweat. My hands are filthy from catching myself on this should-be-condemned excuse for a stairway!"

Kryzyck brushed off the front of her toga, pulled his handkerchief out, and mopped her glistening face. "You look lovely."

"Thanks, but I don't feel lovely. I'm a mess! Oh well, here goes."

Rymnyr patted the dust off her hands, hiked up the hem of her garment, and with steady, slow steps, ascended the last five feet of stairs. She put on her best radiant smile and stepped onto the landing. Her arrival was met with a loud burst of applause.

"Thank Zym she's finally here." Bokyl gently grasped his wife by the arm and led her into the main hall.

Rymnyr shook hands all around, still maintaining her forced smile. "Pardon my hands. I really need to go clean up." She turned toward Kryzyck. "I'll meet you inside."

The professor hurried through the crowd that now had begun to move toward the big double doors. Myrls, the lead waitress, was just heading into the main room when she spotted her making a straight shot for one of the restrooms. The waitress altered her course accordingly. Rymnyr plowed through the door and over to the sink.

"Oh, Zym!" she exclaimed upon gazing at her disheveled appearance in the mirror. While Rymnyr began washing the dirt off her hands, Myrls butted the door open and came waltzing in. After setting the tray she was carrying down, the waitress sided up next to her.

"Hi, doll!" she whispered in a luxurious bedroom voice.

"Hello. Excuse me, but I have to hurry up and make myself presentable," the professor replied without lookup up.

"I heard you were coming again," Myrls purred. She ran the tip of her tongue around Rymnyr's ear lobe.

The professor reacted by pulling her head away and staring angrily into the waitress' leering face. Myrls reached up and attempted to slip her hand into the fold of Rymnyr's open front toga, but the effort was knocked away.

"Uh, what are doing?"

"Oh come on, don't be a tease. I've been dreaming about seeing you again ever since the last time you were here." Myrls blew a kiss and picked up her tray. "Can't wait till the fun starts later!" She whisked out of the room, swaying with extra bounce.

Rymnyr blotted her face as dry as possible, re-assembled her piled up hairdo, and took one last look in the mirror. "Well, dear. This is as good as we can do."

Back in the main hall, the waitress had just returned to the crew table. She set an old, peeling-label bottle down next to Ryk, and bent forward so he could hear her above the din of conversation.

"I found this in the back. Is it okay?"

Ryk picked up the vintage bottle, pulled the cork out, and gave it a sniff. The powerful, aromatic fumes hit his nose with a jolt. He recoiled in response, accidently compressing the waitress' ample breasts with the back of his head.

"Oh, sorry!" Ryk swung around and their eyes met.

"No problem at all." The waitress looked down at his handsome, dusky face and flashed an inviting smile.

A wave of desire roared up within him. He smiled back. "Yeah, I think this will do."

Up on the stage, Bokyl got to his feet, and waved his hands in the smoky, noisy air.

"Members of the Tyrl Collrian Society. Please take your seats! The last of our guests of honor has just arrived, and we will commence with tonight's most historic program."

The group of academics that Krynut and several of the crew had joined offered some quick final comments, then moved off to their seats. Handynr and Grylt sat down at exactly the same time. The regent cupped his hand and spoke directly spoke into Grylt's ear.

"Is that obnoxious roommate of yours here? I don't see his frizzy hair anywhere."

"No. He thinks this whole Styrynt-themed organization is silly. Just between you and me, I'm glad he didn't come. He probably would have made some kind of outrageous scene. I'm already nervous enough without him here." The professor held his shaking hand out as proof.

Handynr nodded briefly, sucked in a deep breath, and shifted in his chair to face the inevitable. His wife sat with her head slightly lowered.

"Good evening."

"Good evening."

"How have you been?"

"Fine, and you?"

"Fine."

The married couple's totally emotionless exchange was interrupted by the waitress' return. "You gentlemen want anything to drink before the program starts?"

While Grylt placed his order, Handynr was busy examining the waitress' short, low cut tunic. After ordering a glass of mynth, he watched her sway back toward the kitchen.

Mihyn bit her lip. Part of her really didn't care how he behaved, and another part still cared about his sense of etiquette.

"You don't need to stare at her."

His wife's seething comment brought Handynr's attention back to the table. "Oh, I wasn't staring! I was just looking at the fairly authentic Styrynt servant's outfit she was wearing. I've seen pottery from that era with renderings of costumes that look almost exactly like that. Are you okay?"

"Yes, I'm fine." A flash of embarrassment swept over Mihyn. She took a deep drink of water. "I just don't like all this noise and smoke."

Rymnyr entered the main hall, spotted Kryzyck's backflip of white, wavy hair, and hustled over to where he was sitting. Myrls sashayed up behind the professor and gave her a little bump of the rump. She set a big, jewel encrusted goblet down on the table.

"Just for you, sweets."

Rymnyr leaned back and looked up into her grinning, middle-aged face. "Thank you."

Myrls winked in an obvious manner and turned toward Kryzyck. "And who might this be?"

"This is my uh, companion, Kryzyck Fourth Line," Rymnyr answered after taking a drink.

The waitress made a little twisting motion with her lips. "Huh, well hope he's ready for some fun later. What can I get ya?"

"A small glass of the mynth would be fine," Kryzyck said graciously.

"A small glass huh? Okay."

Over in the far corner of the room, Kryzyck noticed that a tall, black haired individual was staring in their direction. The man repeatedly said something to his neighbor, then looked back with a big smile on his face.

"Rymnyr dear, that guy seated over in the corner table keeps staring over at you. Do you know him?"

The professor set the goblet down and sent a quick glance across the room. When the dark haired man saw her look his way, he pulled a bottle of dark amber liquid out of a sack on the floor, and held it high. Rymnyr smiled politely.

"I think that's Stymyts the industrialist. I have no idea why he's looking over here."

From his place up on the stage, Bokyl waited till everyone was seated, then motioned for all to rise. The entire room got to their feet. "We will now recite the Collrian pledge." All present focused their attention on the large gilt statue in the front corner of the room. When the oath was completed, Bokyl again addressed the audience in his deep, booming voice.

"You may be seated. We have a lot to cover tonight, so we'll dispense with the usual financial reports, and get right into it. I will turn over the program to Gymryn." Two chairs down from where Bokyl was seated, a lanky older man with a long, hooked nose, got to his feet.

"As special award coordinator for our chapter, it is my great pleasure to announce that the society has voted to recognize the brave crew of the upcoming comet voyage with the highest award we have. Would the crew please take a place up here behind me."

Krynut rose up out of his chair, waited for the crew to stand, then led them around the end of the stage, and up the stairs. Once they were all assembled, the speaker opened a long, rectangular blue flocked box, reached in, and lifted one of the satin ribbons out.

"This is the Order of Plynth Award! It was originally presented to the Styrynt warriors that bravely fought and succeeded in the liberation of Plynth. It is now used to recognize individuals that put forth exceptional efforts in modern day struggles. The Tyrl chapter would like to present these awards to the crew of the upcoming voyage that will expand the boundaries of Ulutritan exploration far beyond that which we have known before."

A thunderous applause, followed by the scraping of chair legs on the floor, and rustling of toga material filled the room. When the standing ovation began to die down, the presenter carried the first ribbon over to Regent Krynut, slipped it over his head, and gave him a firm handshake.

One by one, he moved down the line. When the presenter reached Ryk, he sent a little questioning glance up at the mag driver's brown, well-worn hat, then leaned forward. "Could you remove your hat? I don't think the ribbon with fit over it!"

Ryk slid the hat off and bent down. With the last ribbon in place, the presenter turned and held his long, bony arms wide.

"Please congratulate the new recipients of the Plynth Award!"

More applause and cheering echoed around the wood paneled walls. When the noise level began to subside, the crew walked back to their seats. From the back of the room, the industrialist raised the magnum of amber liquid.

"I propose a toast of Mintexia to honor our brave voyagers!"

The presenter looked over at Bokyl for confirmation. In response, the head regent gave a shrug of his wide, humped shoulders. He turned his attention to the wait staff standing on the left side of the podium.

"Some small glasses please."

An assortment of fluted crystal glasses were filled and placed in front of each attendee. When the last one had been delivered, the industrialist raised his glass, and spoke in a loud, clear voice.

"A toast to the voyagers. Safe journey, and Zym's speed. Life is short!"

"Safe journey, Zym's speed. Life is short!" the room echoed.

Glasses were lifted and emptied all around the tables. The industrialist stared over at Rymnyr with a wicked grin on his face after emptying his glass.

Kryzyck took a small sip. "Why does that guy keep looking over here?"

Rymnyr tossed her drink back and leaned next to him. "I have no idea. Zym, I hate the taste of this stuff!"

Laughter and pleasant, low conversation rolled around the room. Bokyl waited till it appeared the toasting was done, then got to his feet. "I have another great award to present. Professor Rymnyr, would you please come up to the stage."

Bokyl's round jack o'lantern face beamed with pride. He watched the professor carefully walk up the wooden steps and take her place next to him.

"Most if not all of you know our dear professor. She has served as head of the linguistics department for over fifteen years and has been active in many important organizations here in Tyrl. Just recently, she played an instrumental role in convincing the Academy to support the voyage that these brave men and woman are about to undertake.

After much discussion amongst the chapter, and the international board, it is my extreme honor to announce that Professor Rymnyr Third Line will be the first woman inducted into the Order of Collria."

His announcement was met by a variety of responses. There were gasps, exclamations of joy, and more than a few grumbles.

Rymnyr herself appeared to be in shock. She stared over at Bokyl with wide, heavily painted eyes. Her mouth was open, but no words came out. The head regent waited a moment to see if she was going to vocalize her feelings, then turned toward the presenter.

"The scroll and ring, please."

From a box under the table, the official produced a roll of parchment tied with a purple ribbon, and a small, blue jewelry box. He solemnly walked over, gave a bow, and offered them to Bokyl. The head regent returned the bow and took the box from him.

"Please read the proclamation."

With practiced ceremony, the presenter lifted a shiny gold helmet from its place on the table, slid it over his bald head, untied the ribbon, and unrolled the scroll at arm's length.

"To all present on this nine hundred thirty-fifth day of the seven hundredth year, I present to you Professor Rymnyr Third Line, the first woman ever to be inducted into the Honorary, Eternal, and Auspicious Order of Collria!"

Cheers, whistles, and applause followed the proclamation. Bokyl reached out, gently grasped her left hand, and slid a massive silver ring over her finger. She stared without blinking at the lustrous purple-blue stone shining up from the ring. Her lower lip began to quiver. Bokyl let go of her hand.

"If you want to cry, it's alright," he said in a low voice.

She looked up at him and exploded with emotion. Tears flooded her painted cheeks. Her whole body shook with the outpouring. Rymnyr opened her arms, stepped forward, and hugged Bokyl with force. She managed to reach up and wipe some of the tears out of her saturated eyes. "Thank you, thank you, thank you. This is all so overwhelming!"

Bokyl stroked her damp back. When she appeared to have regained her composure, he turned to face the audience. "How about another round of applause for our newest member!"

The crowd responded enthusiastically. Rymnyr waved several times, then walked back down to her seat. Bokyl shook hands with the presenter. He waited till the man returned to seat, then spoke to the audience.

"Well, after all that excitement, we have some regular business to take care of."

While the officials carried out the remainder of their meeting, Ryk sat working his way through the bottle of vintage pyryn. Grylt leaned over toward him.

"I think that was a great gesture. Rymnyr has been so instrumental in this whole operation."

Ryk nodded. The pretty, dark haired waitress came swishing up behind him. She rested her elbows on the table and bent down beside his face. "Quite the big deal tonight, don't you think?"

He looked over at her fine, straight nose and long lashes. "I guess. Like I said, this is the first, and probably last time I've ever been here."

"Notice how you and I are by far the youngest ones in here?"

"Yeah, some of members aren't a lot older than I am," Ryk commented after glancing around at the predominately senior attendees.

The waitress let her fingers sweep across his arm as she straightened back up. "If you're not doing anything after the meeting, maybe we could go out."

Ryk leaned back to make eye contact. "Suppose we could."

Across the room, Rymnyr was showing Kryzyck the scroll. Stymyts, the tall, gruff voiced industrialist came walking up behind them.

"Professor Rymnyr! Let me personally congratulate you on your induction. It takes a certain number of sponsors to even get nominated, and as a member of the candidate review board..." The industrialist paused and lowered his voice. "I can tell you that your nomination breezed through. It had a little help, if you catch my drift!" He stared down at her with a leering grin.

"Why thank you, Mr. Stymyts," she managed to reply. Lines of worry had begun to form on her forehead.

After a moment of uneasy silence, he set the magnum of Mintexia on the table. "When these boring business items are taken care of, then the real fun starts!" He took his eyes off her for a moment and looked down at Kryzyck. "And who is this?"

Rymnyr took a deep breath to dispel her growing sense of annoyance. "This is my companion, Mr. Kryzyck."

Stymyts' big, angular face drew up in a combination smile and sneer. He gave Kryzyck a nod. "Well, neither of you are drinking enough. Here, let me pour you some...."

"Thank you, Mr. Stymyts, but we have a very busy couple of days coming up, so we're taking it kind of easy." The coldness of her response, and the way her eyes glared back at him successfully conveyed her message. He let go a little snort of indignation, grasped the neck of the bottle, and stalked back to his seat.

"That concludes the business items on the agenda, and the meeting is officially adjourned. As usual, feel free to socialize, and don't forget to congratulate our honorees before you leave," Bokyl announced from the stage.

The level of conversation erupted upon completion of his statement. Gynts were relit, more mynth poured, and the atmosphere turned from official to festive. A steady stream of well wishers passed by both Rymnyr and the crew.

Chapter 50.

Professor Ymyl worked his way along the space behind the long tables. He skirted around the group talking to Mihyn and her husband, then stopped beside Krynut. "Regent, eef I might take a moment of your time."

Krynut looked into the wrinkled, leathery face of the professor. "Absolutely, go ahead."

The astronomer wedged himself into the spot between Krynut and Professor Grylt. He began speaking in a low, serious voice. "Of course, my congratulations on your much deserved commendation."

"That's not why you came over," Krynut responded.

"No eets not." Ymyl took a drink of the goblet he was holding. His heavy lidded green eyes narrowed with concern. "Two of my assistants have been monitoring zee comet from up on Mount Zygr. I got a telemessage from one of them, a young man I half a great deal of hope for. He said zat there appears to be a lot of debris trailing off behind zee comet, possibly smaller asteroids caught een its wake." Ymyl dropped his voice to a whisper.

"When zee comet sweeps around Ulutrita, he is concerned zat there may be a rash of meteor strikes, particularly zee day of zee launch."

Grylt gave a little gasp. "Oh dear. Should we postpone the launch?"

"No, Zym no! The timing for your interception should be just perfect. If you launch on zat Dyns day right around eleven, and make it into orbit by one, you vill be on a textdyrft intercept course. Of course zat's based on our calculations of speed, air drag, etc." Ymyl continued to stare into Krynut's eyes for just a moment longer than seemed necessary.

"Thank you, Professor. Is there, uh, something else you wanted to say?" Krynut asked.

The astronomy professor hesitated again, then finally spoke. "Yes, zee anomaly we refer to as zee Cloud, seems to be growing larger all the time. Phylr says zat they are now quite certain zat it ees also the source of the transmissions we are picking up. I don't really know vat that means for your voyage, but I do find it interesting, and a little...."

Both Grylt and Krynut stood motionless, taking in his observations. Rather than complete the sentence, Ymyl laid a hand on Krynut's shoulder. "I'll keep you up to date on zee asteroid situation, but just thought you'd like to know."

Ryk stood a few seats down from his crew members. A long line of well wishers snaked by offering congratulations. He shook hands and made small talk without a break. During the mundane conversations, he let his attention drift off to the waitress picking up empty glasses and clearing the vacant spots at the long tables. She looked up from her work several times to meet his gaze.

Across the room, Professor Rymnyr yawned deeply. "Oh excuse me! I think the anticipation of this event, and all the excitement has taken it out of me."

"Yeah, anytime you're ready to leave," Kryzcyk commented.

She reached over and gave his hand a squeeze. "Thank you for coming with me."

Kryzyck's tanned, weathered face pulled up into a smile. "Glad I was able to be here."

They joined the stream of attendees making their way toward the exit. A line had formed right at the entrance to the landing. Bokyl and his wife were at the end of the line. When Professor Rymnyr and Kryzyck took a spot right behind them, the head regent turned to face her.

"I just wanted to congratulate you again."

Rymnyr wrapped her arms around him and planted a quick kiss on his ruddy, pockmarked cheek. "I have a quick question," she whispered directly into his ear. "Last time I was here, did I behave myself?"

Bokyl eased her torso back a little and stared into her mascara streaked grey-green eyes. "Trust me, you don't want to know. Let me just say that you and several other people had lots of fun in the back room." The head regent finished his answer by flashing a devilish grin.

"Oh, dear!" Rymnyr let him go and took a step back. "That explains a lot."

Gyrty reached over and grasped the professor's hand. "Thank you for breaking into this all male society." The two women high-fived each other.

Above the conversations of those waiting to leave, the sound of loud, thumping footsteps echoed up from the stairwell. The two spear-carrying door men burst up from the stairs.

"Where's security chief Hydyr?" the darker skinned door man asked.

Bokyl and his wife stepped out of the way to let the large, muscular individual pass into the hall. At the head of the stairs, the other door man stood with his long wooden spear held across his chest. Bokyl walked over and stopped next to him.

"Pardon me, is there some kind of problem?"

"Sorry sir, there's a, uh, disturbance down on the street."

"What sort of disturbance?"

"It seems that Lycrk and some of his followers were tipped off that the Dymran crew was going to be here. Highly irregular and in strict violation...."

"I see."

The crowd behind Bokyl parted to let Stymyts and another bull of a man through. Both of them carried thick wooden clubs in their hands. When he reached the stairway, Stymyts held up his arms to signal a request for the keyed up crowd to silence.

"Sssssh! Quiet please. Thank you. Seems that Lycrk and his followers are downstairs causing a ruckuss. As a result, we're going to ask you all to exit through the back of the building. If you all will head into the kitchen in a calm, orderly manner, the staff will direct you to the back stairway. Be aware that the law enforcers have been called, so nothing to panic about." With that, he turned toward the burly head of security. "Ready to go bust some heads?"

Krynut had been listening from the door to the main room. He stepped out of the way and stood next to Phylr while the crowd noisily began to file past.

"Did he say that the enforcers had been called?"

A huge grin spread across the Phylr Communications president's face. "Why yes he did! We just installed one of the first non-administrative televoice devices here just last week. They can talk by wire directly to the local enforcer office."

While the attendees made their way toward the back exit, Stymyts and the head of security wasted no time hustling down the front stairway. A crowd of about twenty people, some carrying burning torches, were lined up in the street. Lycrk stood in the middle of the group.

"My followers! The Collria members should be coming down any minute. This is our chance to finally see who in our community are part of this secretive and elitist group. My sources tell me that they are actively supporting the misguided search for the source of the demonic voices, and that the voices are coming from something out in space called the Cloud which might very well be the Door of Zym!" Shouts of anger and supportive cheers rose up around him. "Look! Here come the first ones now!"

Stymyts and the security head eased their way out of the front door and stood side by side. The industrialist tightened his grip on the wooden club in his hand.

"Alright! Time for you all to go home! You have no reason to be threatening this organization."

Lycrk let out a cynical, deep laugh. He spun around to address his followers. "Did you hear that? We're being asked to go home! Are we going to leave?" To accentuate his question, the leader cupped a hand around his ear.

"No!" was the resounding answer. The crowd slowly began to close in around the toga clad industrialist and burly security head.

"Okay Hydyr, looks like things are going to get interesting." Stymyts swaggered up to the edge of the curb. "Folks, I'm not going to ask you again. Get the Myrnvar out of here before we...."

His proclamation was interrupted by the impact of a large, rotten vegetable that came sailing out of the darkness and washed its foul contents across his cheek.

"Son of a fygr!" The industrialist reacted by running headlong into the crowd, swinging his club at will. From down the street, a chorus of shrill enforcers' whistles cut through the darkness.

On the other side of the building, the distinguished Collria crowd was carefully picking their way down rusty, external metal staircase.

"What a truly horrible end to a great night. Dyth it! I just about fell again!" Rymnyr called out over her shoulder. Kryzyck reached forward to steady her.

"Yes dear, it is unfortunate."

Behind them, Mihyn and her husband cautiously descended. Halfway down the staircase, the line of people suddenly came to a halt. Handynr took the opportunity to lean forward and whisper into his wife's pile of auburn hair.

"I need to come by and pick up some things."

Mihyn slowly craned her neck around and stared up at his somber, handsome face. "Fine with me."

"Unless you think I should just come back." The hopefulness in his voice failed to generate any sympathy on her part. Mihyn just let go a huff of disdain, then turned away from him.

A line of buggies had already formed in the narrow alley at the bottom of the metal stairway. While they were waiting to load, Kryzyck happened to look up into the night sky. A bright yellow streak appeared from the east and swept overhead. He slid his arm around Rymnyr's shoulder.

"Dear, look up for a moment."

The professor lifted her head just in time to see a flashing green meteor sail by. All around them, the waiting crowd oohed and aahed over the display.

Three days later, Mihyn was sitting at her desk filling out a lesson plan, when she heard footsteps approaching, followed by the sound of a something being dropped into the mail collector on the outside of the door. She got up from her desk and retrieved the thick telemessage envelope from the mail collector. After tearing the envelope open, Mihyn read the message while walking back to her desk.

"Message from Handynr Third Line, premier representative of the nation of Plyrm sent 10:38

Will be coming by tonight after 5 to retrieve some things. If this does not work for you, please respond."

Shortly after five that afternoon, Mihyn heard Kym's voice and chortling laugh grow louder from out in front of the house. She put down the book she was reading and made an extra effort to calm herself.

"Okay, breathe. Holy Zym, I feel like I'm going to have a heart attack." A knock on the door brought up out of her chair.

"It's unlocked!"

Handynr and his secretary came walking into the house. Midway down the hall, Kym let go of his hand, and approached Mihyn.

"What a nice, tidy little place. Oh, hello Mrs. Third Line, I mean, Mihyn."

"Hello Kym."

The two women stood fixed in each other's gaze for just a second.

"Would you like some zyd?" Mihyn offered in a tepid tone of voice.

"No, thank you." Handynr ran a hand over his short, brown hair, and continued on into the kitchen. After sending a quick wistful scan of the room, he leaned against the counter and crossed his arms.

"Where to begin."

"Kym, would you be so kind as to go out into the backyard? I'd like to speak to Handynr alone," Mihyn asked while moving around the kitchen table to face her husband.

"Sure!" The secretary sent a "hope everything goes well" smile at Handynr before ducking out the back door.

There was just a moment of charged silence as he watched the younger woman exit the house. Handynr let go a sigh and slowly turned his attention to Mihyn.

"So, how are you doing?"

"Fine, how are you?"

A shallow little laugh escaped from his lips before he answered. "Happy. I've really been happy the last week."

"That's nice. What has made you so happy?"

The blazing stare from his wife stripped away any composure Handynr had managed to maintain. He looked away. Mihyn counted the seconds waiting for a reply. She finally lost patience.

"Look, let's just get this...."

"I know, I know." Handynr rubbed his face with both hands and bent his neck back to examine the ceiling. With slow, measured movements, he lowered his head back down.

"I needed something new, and I found it with Kym." Handynr's hazel eyes flitted over to take a gauge of his wife's reaction. "I guess what I'm saying is, things have been really weighing on me lately. Do you know what I mean?"

"No, I don't know what you mean."

The severity of Mihyn's answer made his chin quiver. "Okay, that probably wasn't a good way to present it." He took several moments to compose his next statement.

Mihyn watched his lower lip slide in and out between his teeth. "While you search for words, let me fill you in. I'm glad you're happy. I really am. I guess I had no clue that you were unhappy." Her emotions started to swell. Images of their eighteen-year marriage began to parade across her psyche. She shook them away.

"Yes, I haven't been very good at communicating my real feelings to you lately. The trip to Bosyra, and narrow escape Kym and I made, really brought us close together."

"It doesn't matter to you that she is what, ten years younger?"

Handynr winced at the question. "I guess that's part of it. I really enjoy her energy and vitality."

"So our relationship is over?"

The last question seemed to jolt him. A half smile, half look of panic swept across his face. "Wait! That's not what I'm saying! Maybe I just need some time to figure things out."

Blood started to flow into Mihyn's cheeks. She could feel heat radiating off her face as the anger built.

"Well, time is not something we have a lot of right now. It seems that in your newfound happiness, you've forgotten that we are part of the Dymran project, and in eleven days...."

"I'm not going."

Mihyn's large brown eyes threatened to jump out of her head. She bent forward and began to visibly shake. "Oh, for Zym's sake, Handynr. Are you serious?"

He gave a quick little nod of his head, then forced himself to face his wife's glowering mask of fury. "You know that I've had some serious reservations about going. I'm just not ready to drop everything and head into space. I need time. I mean, come on. Even you've mentioned how crazy that whole concept is. I feel like a huge weight has been lifted off me since I've made the decision."

It took every ounce of strength Mihyn possessed to not burst out crying. Slowly and in incremental steps, she forced her level of panic down enough to speak. Her voice came out in trembling, unsure tones.

"If you're really sure about that......we need to let the rest of the crew know." The emotions were too strong for her to continue. Tears began to flow into her eyes.

"I'm sure. Please don't cry."

Mihyn wiped the first wave of moisture away. "I need to blow my nose." She slipped around the corner and let the floodgates open. With both hands on the bathroom sink, she hung her head and released. Warm tears spattered on the ceramic surface.

The back door creaked open, then banged shut. Muted voices from the back yard ebbed and flowed through the walls of the house. Just as Kym passed by the bathroom window on her way back out to the street, her voice rang out.

"I love you!"

The back door again creaked open followed by Handynr's rhythmic footsteps. He stopped in the open doorway.

"You're right. I need to take a couple days to really think this out. Please don't contact the rest of the crew till I confirm. I'm sorry."

Chapter 51.

At that same time, Lymdyr stepped off the train in the had-seen-better-days mining town of Pylgor. He shouldered his over-stuffed leather travel bag and stopped to access the surroundings.

"Oh, my Zym! It's even more depressing than last time I was here!" Lymdyr looked over at the mountains of uniform, brown mine tailings that rose up on the left and right. No trees, no plants of any kind obscured the drab, lifeless mounds.

A few passengers made their way past him. They walked with heads lowered in silence. He pulled the letter with his new address written on it out of his leather duster and let go a hopeless brief chuckle.

"Home, sweet, home. Wonder what kind of blyrt hole my new place is. Guess I'll go over to the maintenance shed and introduce myself."

Lymdyr stuffed the letter back in his pocket, and walked across the tracks to the falling apart, sheet metal building. Not a sole was visible in the general area. He opened the office door and stepped in. Several file cabinets and a desk scattered with papers and stained ceramic cups were the only objects in the room.

"Klynk! I wonder if anybody's even here."

He continued on into the main workroom. The only source of illumination was the panel of skylights that ran along the spine of the high ceilinged shop. Just as he was about to return to the office, he heard the sound of coughing, and deep, coarse laughter from the far side of the building.

A side door swung open, and two individuals entered. The language they were speaking was not familiar to him. Lymdyr stood glaring at the two shabbily dressed individuals.

After a moment, the smaller of the two spotted him and grabbed the sleeve of his comrade. The smaller man muttered several words, then ducked back out into the dull, late afternoon light. Lymdyr and the new arrival stood staring at each other. The husky, grease covered individual slowly made his way across the room. He gave a quick scan of Lymdyr's immaculate leather duster, then spoke in a deep, rumbling voice.

"Kin I help you?"

"Maybe. Do you work here?"

The man nodded and flashed a cold-blooded smile which revealed a row of gynt stained teeth. Lymdyr fought the sense of revulsion that swelled up within him. He normally would have offered a hand, but there was no way he was going to shake the man's greasy paw.

"My name is Lymdyr Nine Line. I'm the new maintenance chief."

The man gave a huff of disgust. "Call me Byrno."

"Where's the head engineer?" The question was delivered with no trace of nicety.

Byrno let go laugh. "He walked out two weeks ago."

"So it's just you?"

"Just me."

"Who was that other guy that came in with you?" Lymdyr tossed away any congeniality. It was all business now.

Byrno's crooked little smile vanished. His big, curling eyebrows narrowed into what looked like a line of barbed wire. "That's my cousin. He helps me out here since the engineer is gone."

Lymdyr searched the cold, staring grey eyes for any sign of deceit. His stomach began to grumble.

"Well, I'm going to have to clear that with the head office. Anyway, I just arrived, and need to get settled. I need a buggy to take me into town, so I'm going back over to the station, but tomorrow...."

"Don't bother."

"Don't bother what?"

"Don't bother looking for a buggy. None here anymore."

"So how do people get around?"

Byrno leaned against a dust covered lathe and crossed his arms. "They either get a styrn or walk. As you might have noticed, Pylgor is not doing well these days."

Lymdyr fought the urge to scream at the smirking man before him. "Guess, I'll walk. See you tomorrow." He spun around and opened the door to the office.

"Hey, don't you want the key to your house?"

"Yeah, I guess I need the keys. Sorry, it's been a long day."

Byrno walked past his new boss, pulled a massive gold alloy key ring out of a drawer in the desk, and unceremoniously tossed it cross the room. Lymdyr caught it mid-air, then hustled out into the yard. After shouldering his overstuffed bag, he began the joyless walk toward town. He had to pull his spotless black felt hat tight to prevent the chilly wind from stealing it.

"Oh my dear Zym! These people look like refugees! This is like a war zone without the war."

Grim faces watched him make his way along the uneven wooden boardwalk. One solitary store in a unbroken line of abandoned buildings seemed to be the social hub. The laughter and loud, unfamiliar language being spoken by the group crowded around the front door ceased as he strode by on the opposite side of the street. Lymdyr shot a quick glance at the now silent individuals.

"Ha! They probably think I'm some kind of law enforcer! I should probably ask them where the house is, but at this point, I'd rather not interact with anyone."

For the next half hour, he wandered up and down the shabby neighborhood perched on the hillside. Just as darkness was settling, he found a street sign laying in the weeds that matched his address. Lymdyr stood on the dirt road and assessed his new home.

"Wow, I had no idea that it was going to look like this. Man, talk about a change in surroundings. This place makes the garage back in Tyrl look posh. Oh, now I've really depressed myself."

Images of his palatial home and family members swept over him. Lymdyr hurried up the steps, unlocked the mostly bare wood door, held his breath, and walked in.

In the rapidly fading light, he took a moment to examine the small, sparse living room, complete with ancient furniture. After lighting one of the oil lamps on the end table, he carried it like a cave explorer through his new home.

"One bedroom, no surprise there. Tiny little kitchen. Metal laundry tub. Closets. Wait! There's no bathroom?" Lymdyr retraced his steps, then squinted out through the wavy glass pane of the back door. "Oh for Myrnvar's sake, an outhouse!" That was the final straw. He walked into the living room and thudded down on the faded couch. A puff of dust rose up in the yellow lamplight.

"This is for sure my worst nightmare."

The next morning down in Tyrl, Rymnyr swung into the linguistics office, and headed straight to Mihyn's door. Much to her surprise, there was a note pinned to the surface. Rymnyr squinted as she read it.

"Mihyn sent word in that she is sick today," the office secretary called out from behind.

"She's never sick, most unusual."

After her last class, Rymnyr rode in a hired buggy over to the regent's prim, tidy house. She walked up to the door, knocked several times, but there was no answer.

"Mihyn darling! It's me Rymy. Are you alright?"

She waited several moments, then stuck her ear next to the door. Hearing nothing, Rymnyr stepped off the porch and peered in each of the windows along the side of the house. Through the kitchen window, she caught sight of Mihyn sitting on the couch. Her beautiful auburn hair was a tangled mess, her pale, severe features blank. The professor continued around to the back door, opened it, and walked in.

"Mihyn dear! Are you ill?"

There was no response from her friend. Rymnyr quietly moved over to the couch and eased down. She reached out and grasped Mihyn's hand.

"I know you are very upset about things. I apologize for not coming over sooner, but I've been completely absorbed in getting the food supplies together. Just yesterday...."

"He's not going." Mihyn offered in a barely audible voice.

"I know he's gone. You and I need to put together a plan to bring him to his senses. First thing, we get you to a beauty..."

Mihyn turned and fixed the professor in a throat grabbing stare. "He's not going!"

Rymnyr's soothing, conciliatory mood vanished. "He's not going where?"

"Handynr has backed out of the project." Mihyn delivered the words, then stared out the window. The professor let out a gasp.

"Oh dear, dear, dear. I was afraid of that. I don't suppose he's told Bokyl or any other of the crew?"

"I don't think so." Mihyn rose up off the couch, walked over to the kitchen table, and lifted Handynr's gorgeous red and brown robe off one of the chairs.

"He and his secretary did stop by yesterday. He dropped this off, and a pile of legal papers I have to sign."

Meanwhile up in Pylgor, Lymdyr was trying his best to immerse himself in work as a distraction from the misery he was experiencing. On day three, he got around to going through the box of invoices that sat next to the office desk. Hunched over the pile of slips from the Tygrt Tool Company, a feeling of serious dread began to build within him.

"Okay, something is very wrong here. We've purchased nine of the same size twenty bolt wrenches every month. This doesn't make sense."

Lymdyr rubbed his eyes and pushed back away from the desk. He happened to glance out the smudged front window of the office. Byrno's cousin was walking across the front of the building. A sagging black cloth hung off his shoulder. With each step, it swung out then banged against his back.

"Hmmm, maybe that's his myrf bucket?" Lymdyr leaned back in the chair and folded his hands behind his head. "I do remember seeing him arrive this morning. Did he have that bag with him?" In a flash, the reality of what was going on hit him. "Oh holy Zym! I'm slipping. Of course!"

Lymdyr jumped to his feet, swept up a hand full of the invoices, and entered the workroom. Over in the corner, the ancient steam generator huffed and chugged away. Byrno was bent over a grinding wheel in the center of the room. Bright yellow sparks shot off of the piece of metal he was working on. Lymdyr moved around the various pieces of machinery until he was standing next to him.

Byrno stomped on the foot switch to stop the grinder. The big leather belt that powered the device from above flapped to a halt. He pulled the wet, brown cigarette out of his mouth, and rose up from his bent over position.

"Yes?"

"Got any idea why we keep ordering the same tool every month?" Feeling very proud of himself, Lymdyr didn't try to mask the point of his question. His old pride and self-assurance began to return.

Byrno snatched one of the sheets from him, took a quick look at it, then slowly lifted his gaze to make eye contact with his boss. Before speaking, he adjusted his grip on the razor sharp blade he was sharpening, and jammed it into the wooden rail below the grinding wheel.

"So, you want to know why we order these?"

Lymdyr stared directly into the man's steely grey eyes. The fury that blazed back took his breath away. Byrno carelessly ran a finger up along the edge of the blade.

"Look Mister fancy guy. You not in the big city anymore, right? You think you can come up here and make all kind of changes. Ha!"

Slowly and carefully, Byrno rolled up the sleeve of his shirt to reveal a crude, bluish-green snake tattoo winding up his forearm. A chill ran through Lymdyr. In an instant, he recognized the tattoo as the insignia of the Krushian gang. Byrno sent a vicious sneer toward his new boss and stomped on the pedal to re-start the grinder.

Lymdyr left work early that day. To say he was depressed would have been a gross understatement. The overcast sky, cold wind blowing off the pile of mine tailings, it all weighed heavily on him. He walked along, not even aware of his surroundings.

"Well, Lymdyr, you've really done it this time. You knew you were pushing your luck, you knew it." For emphasis, he kicked a rusted can on the dirt path in front of him.

"What to do, what to do? I suppose I could contact the head office and have them send security up here. Hmmm, the message would probably get intercepted."

His meditation was interrupted when he turned up a side street. There in front of him, a large green, twisting snake gang sign was painted the side of an abandoned house. Lymdyr stopped momentarily to examine it, then continued on. From behind several of the curtained house windows he passed, unfriendly faces peered out.

Lymdyr dragged himself up the steps of his house, pulled out the key, then stopped. Tucked into the crease of the door jamb was a dark tan, very official looking letter. Even before he opened it, he could tell by the red lettering that it was something of importance. Lymdyr entered the house, closed the door behind him, and tore it open.

"The law office, 1st ward city of Tyrl, here by issues an order of no contact between Lymdyr Nine Line, and his soon to be ex-wife Bynhyld, and daughters......" His hazel eyes flew across the line of legaleeze and zeroed in on the offense. "Due to offensive immoral actions incurred in the town of Phyt Hill as witnessed by..."

He crumpled the page and threw it across the room. Rage and sadness fought a battle within him. After plunking down on the couch, he pounded down half the contents of the klymr bottle sitting on the crude coffee table. The alcohol temporarily blunted the pain, but only for twenty minutes. A great, unyielding fatigue dropped upon him. He managed to pull himself upright and stagger into the back room.

A thick roll of rope lay in the corner, and next to it, a three-legged stool. Lymdyr looked up at the blistered, rotten ceiling slats, then shifted his attention to the six-inch thick beam running the length of the room.

"I'm finished." He slowly made his way back into the living room, scrawled out a goodbye note on the back of the summons, and killed off the bottle. "Zym dyth Klyrk! What a hypocritical hyrk he is. Him and that dyth bitch of a wife!"

He returned to the back room, and with quick, violent jerking motions, tied a hangman's noose into the rope. Using the end of a broom handle, he bashed away at the rotten ceiling boards till he had cleared a space above the beam. Again using the broom handle, he poked a length of the rope through the space. It came swinging down on the other side of the beam. Lymdyr cinched a knot tight up near the ceiling, then stood staring at the bristly rope.

"Do I really want to do this?" Tears began to form in his eyes. Images of his two daughters playing as small children ran through his anguished mind. "At least they'll be well taken care of. I should have been more careful. I should have known better."

Lymdyr watched his hands position the stool beneath the noose. It was as if they belonged to someone else. After stepping up onto it, he felt his fingers open the noose, slip it over his head, and tighten it. Lymdyr took a last deep, regretful breath, closed his eyes, lifted his right leg, and gave the stool a powerful kick.

A loud sickening crack, followed by a savage pain to the base of his neck were the last sensations he experienced before all went black.

Chapter 52.

Like the dawn breaking through a heavy fog, fuzzy images began to materialize before his eyes. What appeared to be a large wooden throne of some kind with two flickering torches on either side, slowly took shape out of the blackness. Something heaped up lay across the seat of the throne. While his vision slowly cleared, the heap revealed itself to be a dark figure, and it began to move.

"Holy klynk! It's Gwydol, and she's buck naked! I must in Myrnvar. This is so weird. Everything is slanted to the right. I must be laying on my side."

Lymdyr tried to reach out, but had no sensation in his body. Out of desperation, he forced himself to speak. "Gwydol!"

The small dark figure seated on the throne jumped slightly at the sound of her name. "Who's that? Who said that?"

"Gwydol! It's me Lymdyr." He attempted to wave, but nothing moved.

She leaned forward and peered into the darkness. "Limedar? You out there?" Gwydol shifted around in the throne and pulled one of the torches from its bracket. The sight of her lithe brown body moving in the flickering light sent a wave of hope through him.

"Yes! I'm here."

Gwydol held the torch high, then let out a cackle. "Mercy, mercy, it is you! Oh man, you got yourself in a fix now, didn't you?'

"I'm not sure quite what is going on, but it's good to see you."

She moved her head back and forth to get a better look at him. "Good to see you, too. Tell you what, you ain't got much time, so listen up."

"What? What do you mean? I'm dead! I got all the time in the world."

Another sharp crack of a laugh escaped from her lips. One of her gold teeth glinted in the torchlight, as did the large gold wrist guard she was wearing.

"No, no, you ain't dead. Not sure how you got here, but I gotta tell you this before you go. You got an amazing opportunity, take it! Bye, bye, Love! See you in a while." She blew him a kiss, and all became black again.

Lymdyr blinked several times. Ever so slowly, the details of the back room came into view. Judging by the orientation of the surroundings, it appeared that he was laying on the floor.

A small furry creature with long whiskers nosed its way toward his face, sniffed the air, then scampered away. Its movement caused him to reflexively kick his foot back. It struck something heavy.

"Great holy Zym! My neck and back of my head hurt like crazy. I'm not dead though. What the klynk happened?"

Lymdyr loosened the knot around his neck and rose to a sitting position. The roof beam lay across the floor in back of him. The end nearest the wall was jagged and splintered.

"Oh for klynk sake! This house is too dilapidated to even carry out a suicide." He ran a hand along the back of his head. His fingers hit the damp knob where the beam had whacked him. Lymdyr slipped the rope over his head and crawled on all fours out to the couch. He managed to pull himself up, then promptly fell asleep.

The next morning in Tyrl, Rymnyr walked up the sidewalk to Mihyn's house. Before she could even knock, the front door swung open. Mihyn slammed it shut and swept by her. A huge smile erupted on Rymnyr's face.

"Feeling better today?"

"Yes, come on. I have a lot to do at the office, then later, we need to drop the bomb on Bokyl. You didn't tell him yet, did you?"

Rymnyr had to hustle to keep up with her. "Oh no. I'm leaving that honor to you. He's going to blow a gasket, you realize."

"Absolutely."

At that same time, the early train out of Pylgor was just picking up speed. Lymdyr sat and watched the barren, mine ravaged shell of the town race by. He settled back in the seat. The pressure of the leather against his damaged skull made him wince.

"As soon as I get into town, I'm going to march up those marble steps and talk to Bokyl. I need to get an update on the project. Zym I feel great! My head hurts, but I haven't felt this alive since I was a kid."

In the linguistics office on the second floor of the Academy, the wall clock three. Mihyn's hands were shaking when she returned the exam papers to their folder. She left her office and stopped in front of the secretary's desk.

"Where's Professor Rymnyr?"

"Ah, let me check. It looks like she went to run an errand about an hour ago."

Mihyn offered a quick thank you, then strolled out into the hall. She took extra time making her way to Bokyl's office in hopes that Rymnyr would show up on time.

Over at the train station, Lymdyr gazed out at the familiar buildings of Tyrl through the windows of the newly arrived train. The feeling that he had just been rescued from the brink of disaster flooded him with joy. He tapped his foot impatiently while waiting for the other passengers to disembark.

After being dropped off at the Academy, Lymdyr walked as fast as possible along the sidewalk. The door to a buggy parked along the curb opened, and Rymnyr climbed down just in front of him.

"Professor! Hey Professor!"

Rymnyr wheeled around at the sound of the urgent voice. Her mouth dropped open. "Why Mr. Lymdyr, what a surprise. I thought you had been sent away."

He took a moment to wipe the sweat off his face using the cuff of his striped shirt. Salty moisture was rolling down into the rope burn around his neck.

"Yes, yes, I just escaped from Pylgor. Zym, it's great to be back in Tyrl! How are you? Sorry I'm talking so fast, but, uh, is Bokyl in today?"

A look of confusion spread cross Rymnyr's face. His sudden appearance had rattled her a bit. She stared hard at the railroad man's jubilant expression, then down at the rough, red abrasions visible above his collar.

"Well, I'm fine, busy...um, regarding Bokyl, Mihyn and I have a meeting with him, like...oh, Myrnvar! Probably, right now."

The two of them followed the stream of people up the sun splashed marble steps. Lymdyr sent furtive side-eye glances over at the professor while they ascended. Her less than enthusiastic response to his presence had him a bit concerned. Once they entered the cool, but noisy foyer, he managed to calm himself enough to speak in a more professional tone of voice.

"So, I assume the project is moving forward as scheduled?"

Rymnyr let go a little huff of displeasure before answering. "Oh, I wouldn't say that, but yes, we are theoretically still on track."

The two of them made their way up the steps to the second floor in silence. As soon as they turned the corner at the top of the stairs, Mihyn came running toward them.

"Rymy, thank goodness you showed up. I've been waiting outside the office...." The regent stopped in mid-sentence when she realized who was accompanying her friend. "Oh, Mr. Lymdyr, what are you doing here?"

The coldness of her question blew right past him. He just smiled and continued walking. "I am, or was part of this project, you recall. I'd like to get a status on things, and the professor says you and she have a meeting with the head regent. Is it okay if I sit in?"

Mihyn bit her lip. The absolutely last thing she wanted to do was discuss the details of her broken marriage in his presence. The trio swept into the head regent's office before Lymdyr's question was answered.

Bokyl was seated at his desk talking with a department head. He glanced up at the clock, drummed the pencil he was holding on the desk, then held up his hand.

"Professor Lydyr, we'll have to finish this discussion later. I have an appointment with the Dymran group, or at least part of them, it appears."

The tall, black haired department head flashed a "good luck" smirk to the trio as he exited. Bokyl watched the three individuals pull chairs up around his desk. Once they were settled, he focused his attention on the railroad man.

"Mr. Lymdyr, I'm surprised to see you. We had heard you were exiled to some Zym forsaken place up in the Zymgr mountains."

Lymdyr couldn't help but laugh in response to the comment. "Head Regent, yes, I was exiled, but have made my triumphant return. I ......" Out of the corner of his eye, he could see that both the women were glaring at him. "I believe the regent and professor have something they would like to say?"

After shifting nervously in her chair, Rymnyr smoothed the folds of her dress, then titled her greying head toward Mihyn. "You want to tell him, or should I?"

Mihyn remained in her rigid position. "Head Regent, my husband, er, Handynr has withdrawn from the project."

"What!" Bokyl thumped the desk hard with both hands. Rymnyr had anticipated the concussion, but the other two flinched. The head regent reared back in his chair like a harpooned whale. Slowly, he hunched forward. His deep set eyes burned everything in sight.

"This is most disturbing, most disturbing. The whole town knows about the indiscretion with his secretary. My condolences, Regent." The sting of his words caused Mihyn to look away. Bokyl threaded his fingers together and aimed the artillery stare at the professor. "Well, Rymnyr, what now?"

The middle-aged professor's chin began to quiver. She opened her mouth to speak, but hesitated. Mihyn reached over and grasped her hand in a show of support. After another second or two, Rymnyr was able to vocalize.

"Head Regent, this development is so new that the project team hasn't had a chance to discuss it. To my knowledge, you are the only one who is aware of this."

Lymdyr sat stock still. His eyes bulged out. The news of Handynr's withdrawal sent his mind into a frenzy of activity. Rymnyr's circumspect voice returned his focus to the discussion.

"This indeed is a critical development, for the project and for the regent. Handynr's abrupt actions seem to have thrown...."

The sound of rapid footsteps preceded Krynut's arrival. At maximum walking speed, he turned the corner into the office, then slid to a halt just behind the row of chairs.

An expression of deep concern froze his narrow, olive skinned face. His eyes flitted between all three of those seated. When his attention worked its way around to Bokyl, the head regent motioned toward the empty chairs against the wall.

"Go ahead and take a seat."

"Thanks, but I'd rather stand. I've been sitting all day. I just received a telemessage from Handynr. He's withdrawing from the project."

Mihyn leaned back hard in her chair and stared up at the ceiling. "He wasn't supposed to contact anyone."

"Well, I guess that makes it final. Regent, we were just discussing that situation," Professor Rymnyr added.

Krynut stroked his carefully clipped goatee. "I see. This puts us in an extremely tenuous position."

Before he could stop himself, Lymdyr raised a hand. "Excuse me, but I've had a bit of an epiphany lately." A humble little chuckle of disbelief escaped from his lips. "Something very profound happened to me yesterday, something I don't quite understand. Sorry, I know I'm not making much sense." He drew in a chest expanding breath. "I'd like to volunteer to take Handynr's place."

His offer elicited a variety of responses. The crew chief's bright green eyes enlarged into two perfectly round spheres. Mihyn let out a gasp of distress. Rymnyr just sat stunned. Bokyl's bushy eyebrows ticked up and down like some hay-wired machinery. He sent questioning glances at both women. Rymnyr returned a desperate, pleading non-verbal reply before speaking.

"Mr. Lymdyr, will you please step out into the hall for a moment? I believe the Head Regent, Mihyn, Krynut, and I may need to confer on this. Please be assured that your offer is being taken very seriously. It's just that, I mean, we, uh...."

Lymdyr patted her on the shoulder as he rose up out of the chair. "Professor, I understand." The railroad man very calmly walked out of the office and stopped a sufficient distance down the hall.

As soon as Lymdyr exited the room, Bokyl scooted up against the desk and glowered at the professor. "Are you mad? Why wouldn't you consider him? He works for the klynking railroad, he knows machines, he's an executive! Krynut, help me out here."

"Let the professor say her piece," Krynut countered in a dead serious voice.

Rymnyr let go an exaggerated sigh. With measured determination, she rotated in her chair to face Mihyn. "Regent, if I'm not mistaken, I believe you may have an opinion on the matter?"

The sudden, agonizing decision Mihyn was facing tore Rymnyr apart. She knew how devastated her friend was by the apparent dissolution of her marriage, and now the regent had to either agree to be sealed up in a metal can with someone she really didn't care much for, or in all probability, derail the project once and for all. Tears began to form in the professor's heavily mascaraed eyes.

Bokyl sat watching his colleague slowly being swept away by her emotions. "Excuse me, maybe I'm just a daft old man, but will one of you please tell me what the Myrnvar is going on?"

Mihyn lifted her pale, expressionless face. "Certainly, Head Regent. Nothing is going on. I support Mr. Lymdyr's offer."

Professor Rymnyr groaned loudly enough to be heard out in the hall. She raised a hand to her open mouth. "Mihyn dear, are you sure?"

Rymnyr continued to stare over at Mihyn's stony, serious expression for several seconds before shifting her attention back to the astonished head regent. "Alright! Alright! I'm going to say it. Lymdyr is the last man on Ulutrita I'd want to be cooped up with. There, I said it."

Much to the surprise of the two women, Bokyl began to laugh. It started out with a couple little hiccups, then broke into a full, body shaking guffaw. The laughter gradually trailed off. He wiped tears away from his eyes, then settled back in the chair.

"Oh, this is too rich, too rich! There are some things we men will never, ever understand. Krynut, do you have a clue what is going on here?"

"Head Regent, I believe I do. Please go get Mr. Lymdyr."

Bokyl sent a slanted, questioning glance over at the regent, then rose up and hustled out of the room.

Out in the hall, Lymdyr was leaning against the cool stone wall. He quite clearly heard the groan from Rymnyr and the head regent's booming laugh.

"What does *that* mean? Maybe I acted too quickly. Maybe I should just run out of here and go visit Gwydol! Klynk! My duster and bag are still in there. Oh well, I can buy new ones."

Just as he turned to leave, Bokyl's large shape appeared in the hall. "You're leaving?"

"I, uh, well, yes, that was...should I?"

Bokyl waddled over and delivered a slap to the railroad man's shoulder. It was so powerful that it sent Lymdyr sliding into the wall. "Dyth! I'm sorry. I didn't mean to injure you. Get back in there before they change their minds."

While the two men made their way back to the office, Rymnyr reached over and grasped Mihyn's hands. "We don't have to do this. There have to be other options. We can find someone else. If I had to climb into that kyrft with....." The sound of footsteps nearing the hall door stopped her urgent confessional. The professor leaned forward and whispered. "It's not too late."

Mihyn's narrow elegant jaw was set with determination. She squeezed both of the professor's hands and looked her right in the eye. "Yes, Rymy it is too late. He's the logical choice." Still gripping the professor's hands, Mihyn shifted her attention to Krynut. "Regent, do you agree?"

Once Lymdyr and Bokyl had again settled in their chairs, Krynut drew in a deep, fatalistic breath, and lowered his rifle sight gaze to the head regent.

"I believe the question here is whether our new candidate is deemed compatible with the present crew." He let the words sink in, then perceiving no urgent reaction, directed his attention over to Mihyn. "Regent, since your, uh husband is the one that is being replaced, I think your opinion is the critical issue here."

For several tense moments, she and Krynut remained locked in a death grip stare. Mihyn was fully aware that the responsibility of the success or failure of the project now rested on her shoulders. For just a second, she allowed herself to weigh the alternatives.

Her sense of duty slowly began to erode any opposition to the decision she had to make. Mihyn shifted in her chair and looked over at the railroad man's somber profile. "Mr. Lymdyr are you really prepared to commit on the spot like this?"

While the others were engaged in their serious conversation, Lymdyr had been assessing the turmoil in his own life. Upon hearing his name, he swung around to answer. Even though Mihyn's face was drained of all emotion, her beauty and inner strength struck his heart strings. He forced the sense of exhilaration that was roaring up inside down to a manageable level before speaking.

"Regents, Professor, Head Regent, I officially accept the offer to be part of the crew."

Chapter 53.

Bokyl clapped his hands together with thunderous force. He knocked pen holders, papers, and file folders over as he stretched his considerable bulk across the desk to shake Lymdyr's hand. "Well done! You've saved the project."

Mihyn and the professor just watched in silence. Krynut allowed a small, triumphant smile to work itself across his face. Once the elation of the moment passed, Rymnyr stood up and lightly touched the railroad man on the shoulder.

"Congratulations, there is a lot for us to pull together in the next five days. I suggest you get your plans in order, also. One of the things we'll need to do is get you down to Grynk Fabrics. Handynr turned in his robe, and we'll need to get it re-fitted. Can you meet me there, say at, ten tomorrow?"

Lymdyr nodded his reply. The professor waited for Mihyn to get up from her chair, then the two of them left the room. Once they were out in the hall, Rymnyr sent a sarcastic little smile over at her friend.

"Well, you've really done it now, deary. I wouldn't have gone for it. You're a braver woman than I am."

Mihyn walked along beside her, head bent down.

Back in the office, Bokyl fell back into his chair. "I must say, this whole affair is like nothing I've ever been involved with and will never be foolish enough to engage in again!"

Lymdyr's head was spinning with thoughts. After several moments, he regained enough composure to speak. "I, uh, guess I need to let some people know. Would it be okay if I used the telemessage service downstairs?"

"By all means, just tell them the Head...."

Krynut held up his hand. "Why don't we let Mr. Lymdyr use the new televoice system. My guess is the parties he's wanting to reach are also connected."

Bokyl again slammed his palms down on the desk, this time with less force. "You're dyth right! I keep forgetting we even have that now. Yes, of course. Regent, will you show him where the device is?"

Lymdyr picked up his belongings and followed Krynut out into the hall. Halfway to the stairs, the regent began speaking in a low, serious tone. "Congratulations."

"Thanks, I think. So much has changed in my life lately. It seemed like the thing to do."

"So do you understand why the professor had a, how shall I say this, less than enthusiastic response to your selection?"

Lymdyr's brain was so busy processing the stream of emotions pouring into it that he was really only partially engaged in the question. "I think I do. My take is that she was worried that Mihyn would not be happy that her husband was not going."

"That's part of it." When they reached the noisy foyer, Krynut led the way down to the basement. He waited till they were in the quiet of the lower level to continue speaking.

"I'm going to be blunt with you. You were, maybe are, it's not for me to say, a well-respected member of this community. You also have a reputation as a womanizer."

The last sentence stung like a hornet. Lymdyr felt his cheeks flush. "So *that's* what they were hesitant about."

Krynut opened the un-marked door, reached around the frame, and flipped a T-shaped switch on the wall. A large glass bulb overhead crackled to life.

"Wow, all the modern conveniences," Lymdyr exclaimed while looking up at the light source.

"All of them." Krynut walked over to the solitary desk and pulled the chair back. "Have a seat." When Lymdyr had settled into the chair, the regent leaned over the desk, and lifted the metal handset of the primitive telephone.

"Hold this end up to your ear and speak into this end. I'll demonstrate. Were you going to contact someone at the railroad office?" Lymdyr nodded. "And you were stationed at the regional maintenance office?"

Another nod answered the question. Krynut straightened up, held the handset against his head, and pushed the cradle on the side of the phone box. "Please connect me to the Blue Line regional maintenance office."

"Checking for a connect. Connect available, hold please," a fuzzy voice rattled out of the handset. It was followed by a series of electronic blips. After a moment of crackling static, another voice became audible.

"Blue Line, Admin Byrdyl speaking."

Lymdyr's heart thumped hard in his chest. "May I?" He reached up and took the handset from Krynut.

"Just lock the door when you're done," the regent whispered before ducking into the hall.

"Byrdyl, this is Lymdyr." There was a moment of silence on the line.

"Mr. Lymdyr? Oh my goodness! Are you calling from Pylgor?"

The smooth, lilting sound of his secretary's voice made him swoon. He fought to contain his joy. "Byrdyl, it's so nice to hear your voice. No, I'm not in Pylgor. I walked out."

"Oh!" The secretary's voice jumped in volume, then became hushed. "Listen, there are people all around in the office. I'd love to meet up with you. Where are you?"

"I'm at the Academy. What time do you get off?"

"In forty minutes, you want me to come by and pick you up?"

"That would be superb."

After placing the hand set back in the cradle, Lymdyr got up and wandered out onto the street. For a full hour, he just stood lost in meditation. The sun hitting his face, and steady stream of people walking by helped to calm his frazzled nerves.

Eventually a buggy pulled up, the door swung open, and there was Byrdyl's smiling face. He picked up his bag and duster, ran over, and jumped up into the cab.

"Where to?" the driver called from the seat.

Lymdyr stuck his head out the window and yelled the name of his favorite restaurant. Before he even pulled back in completely, Byrdyl slid her arms around him. A feeling of warmth and happiness rained down as he hugged her with dangerous abandon.

They remained in the embrace for blocks. He incrementally released his grip and took a moment to drink in her beauty. She desperately searched every inch of his features for clues to his condition. Before either of them was even aware of their location, the buggy pulled to a halt. Hand in hand, the two of them exited the buggy and entered the posh restaurant.

"A booth in the back please," Lymdyr requested. They followed the waitress through the field of tables and were deposited in a dark corner. After staring into each other's eyes for several moments, he cleared his throat and began speaking.

"So much has happened in the last couple weeks. I...where the klynk do I start?"

"Calm yourself. We have time."

"Pylgor was a nightmare. A Zym awful nightmare." Lymdyr lowered his head. A portion of the euphoria flooding over him evaporated. He again brought his gaze up to her maddeningly beautiful features. "There was an opening on the Dymran crew, and I took it."

Before his eyes, her expression changed from dreamy, near infatuation to disbelief and shock. "Let me get this straight. You abandoned your position with Blue Line, and now you're going off on that crazy journey?"

After staring at his blank, humbled features for a moment, Byrdyl pulled her hands away from his, and thumped against the back of the booth. She let go a little yip of a laugh. "Well, you really know how to make a scene, don't you?"

Her grinding, powerful condemnation brought Lymdyr back to reality. All the romantic lykrs circling around inside his head flew away, and the soft music playing dissolved into dissonance. It was back to business now.

"Perhaps I am a bit overly dramatic. Look, I need your help."

"Anything."

"Good, you probably already know this, but Bynhyld has a no contact order filed."

"Yes, I did hear that. We were also told that if you showed up at the office, we were to contact security."

"What? Why would they do that?" Lymdyr ran a hand over his unshaven face.

"What happened to your neck?"

"You don't want to know. Listen, I need to get word to my girls. We launch in five days. I have to talk to them."

"That's not going to be easy."

"I can use the televoice at the Academy. Do you think we can get them on a set somewhere?"

"Possibly. You're just dyth lucky that we got one installed, and that I answered." Byrdyl was silent for a moment. She averted her eyes and absently toyed with the cloth napkin on the table in front of her. Lymdyr watched her actions without breathing.

"What?"

"Excuse me?"

"Come on Byrdyl. I've seen that look before. There's something you want to say, out with it."

She twirled a long strand of her hair that happened to fall longingly against her ear. "You realize that you're in a pile of trouble."

"How much trouble?"

"Heaps."

At that moment, a waitress appeared. "Can I get you anything?"

After a moment of reflection, Lymdyr looked over at his companion for signs of approval. She shrugged. "A couple double flymrs please."

"Make those triples," the secretary chimed in. "You're gonna need it." Once waitress had left, Byrdyl threaded her immaculately manicured fingers together. "So, you know Glyny, the lady in billing?"

"Sort of."

"Well, she knows Bynhyld from the office parties. She's also a Corian, and is friends with Klynk, or whatever that styrn handler's name is, and his little jyz bomb of a wife."

Lymdyr let out a snorting laugh. "Klyrk, his name is Klyrk."

"Yeah, well, you must have really zynked him off there in Phyt Hill." There was another heavily weighted pause. She leaned as far across the table as possible. "Did you really sleep with a Lymyr woman out there?"

Her question smacked him hard. Lymdyr let go a whoosh of breath. Shame and regret flooded over him. The most fleeting image of Gwydol's mahogany body, muscular and lit by torch light flashed through his mind.

"I'll take that as a yes." Byrdyl's cynical little smirk of disapproval drove his self esteem further down.

The waitress returned with two tall triangular glasses full of a greenish liquid with a bright yellow slice of fruit floating in it. Lymdyr raised his glass, clinked Byrdyl's, and took a long drink.

"Ah, that's good. So getting back to my predicament. I need to meet with my girls and tell them about the situation."

Byrdyl downed a healthy sized portion of her drink. A shudder ran through her narrow frame. "Whoa! That is strong! Yeah, I've been thinking about that. Here's my plan. Glyny likes you, so I think I can convince her to play along with telling Bynhyld that the girls need to come into the office and sign some kind of form. We'll make up some mag blyrt legal term. If we work it correctly, maybe I can pick them up, and say, we meet here."

The alcohol, combined with Byrdyl's sense of loyalty, helped to buoy Lymdyr's attitude. He tossed back the rest of the drink. "Another?"

"No. I'll be lucky to finish this. What time is it?" She pulled a small pocket watch out of her purse and flipped it open. "Dyth! Drynny has a home game tonight, so I gotta run. Here you finish this."

"Take one more drink." Lymdyr held up a hand in protest.

Byrdyl gulped down another good size swallow. Both of them slid out of the booth at the same time. The secretary embraced Lymdyr in a crushing hug. While they were still embraced, she spoke into his chest.

"Men are such funny creatures. Drynny is really just a big, simple guy. He plays ball, he comes home, he goes out on road trips. You're way more complicated."

"Yep, I have a knack for complicating things. Thank you so much for your help. Keep me in the loop." He bent down and planted a kiss on her forehead.

"You're welcome. Give me a couple days to get this set up, then call me at the office." She slipped away from his grasp, and speed walked out of the restaurant.

The next morning, Lymdyr met Professor Rymnyr at the fabric store, and got measurements taken for the re-fitting of Handynr's robe.

"Thank you. Where are you headed now?" she asked once they were back out onto the sidewalk.

Lymdyr looked up at the late spring sun already blazing up in the sky. "I have a couple things to do today. I need to make a call at the Academy."

"Good, we'll ride over together. I need to talk to you about something."

The two of them climbed into a waiting buggy. Once they were underway, Rymnyr scooted over in the seat so that she was directly across from him. "So, I'm sure you saw how pained Mihyn was by your acceptance of the crew position."

"I was."

"You've been out of town, so you probably haven't heard all the gyrky details about Handynr's fling with his secretary."

A wide grin formed on Lymdyr's otherwise serious face. "No, I haven't."

"Not much to say about it, other than Mihyn is understandably upset about it. And, how shall I say this? I'll just be blunt, okay? She is not at all pleased with the thought of being sealed up with you, a mag driver, Krynut, and well, the fact that Grylt is a mono probably won't be an issue."

"Why, I didn't know that!" Lymdyr replied with comic exaggeration.

"Anyway, my point is, you and Ryk will need to make sure you give her all the distance she needs. Understand?"

"Yes, ma'am."

The buggy arrived at the Academy, and the two of them chatted while ascending the steps.

"Has the weight of your decision sunk in yet?" Rymnyr asked once they reached the front doors. Lymdyr peeled off his tan suit coat before answering.

"Oh, my life has sort of turned upside down lately, so no. I expect to wake up the morning of the launch and get fully hit by the impact of it all." He held the big copper door open and followed her into the foyer. Rymnyr got a key to the televoice room from the front desk, then held it out to him.

"Here you go. Please don't get the impression that I don't appreciate you saving our tymyr at the last minute. I really am truly grateful for your sacrifice. I think Krynut wants to brief you early next week, so you might want to check in with him."

"I'll do that. Thanks for your vote of confidence. I was beginning to wonder."

Lymdyr snatched the key from her and hurried down to the basement. He had to wait almost twenty minutes till the phone was available. Once the room was empty, he plunked down, repeated the steps Krynut had shown him, and waited till the line was connected.

"Blue Line, Byrdyl speaking."

"Good morning, almost afternoon. Lymdyr here." The staticky pause caused deep furrows to form on his forehead. "I said....."

"I heard what you said. Someone just walked by that doesn't need to hear of our plan. Okay, good thing you called. The girls are coming by on their own around two. I'm going to have a buggy waiting to take them to the restaurant. Hopefully, they don't raise a fuss."

Lymdyr thrust his free fist up in the air. "Byrdyl! You are the best. Thank Glyny for me, please."

"I will. One more thing......" There was another second or two of staticky silence. "Glyny knows that you're in town, but no one else does. I suggest you keep a low profile. Word has it that a summons is waiting. Bynhyld already sent a messenger out to Pylgor, but of course, you weren't there. I had to lie to her about your whereabouts. I hate to lie!"

"So do I."

Her sharp, echoing laugh made his ear drum bounce. "Oh, that is hilarious! Well, got to hang up. Best of luck."

Chapter 54.

At two in the afternoon, Lymdyr procured a booth in the back of the restaurant and waited. Every time the front door opened, he jumped up from his seat to see who had entered. Finally, at almost two thirty, the silhouettes of his twin daughters appeared against the bright light coming in through the doors. Lymdyr's whole body began to quiver.

"Calm! We have to remain calm."

The two young women were escorted by the waitress to the back area. When the more solidly built, sandy haired daughter caught sight of her father, she ran over, embraced him, and swung him around in circles.

"Daddy, oh Daddy! My Zym it's good to see you!"

While being spun around, Lymdyr managed to catch intermittent glimpses of the slender, dark haired twin. She stared at him with a scrutinizing intensity.

Lymdyr eased his other daughter to a stop and planted a kiss on her cheek. "Pryn, so wonderful to see you. Let me give Dyn a hug." He released the light haired daughter, and with some formality approached her twin.

"Hello Father." The non-affectionate tone of his daughter's voice let Lymdyr know he was in for a battle. He leaned forward and kissed her high cheek boned face.

"Hello Dyn. Let's grab a seat." His daughters piled into one side of the booth. Lymdyr took just a moment to gaze lovingly at them. "First of all, how are you both doing?"

"Fine. Does mother know you're back?" the light haired twin asked. Before Lymdyr could answer, the dark twin shot out a curt response.

"Of course she doesn't. I for one don't appreciate you and your secretary planning this underhanded meeting. We need to all sit down with Bynhyld. She has several things to say to you. I think we should send a messenger over to the house."

When Dyny made a move toward the end of the bench, Lymdyr reached over and gently grasped her arm. She whipped her head around and stared at him with ferocity and defiance.

"Let go of me!"

"Oh, Dyn! Come on. Daddy just wants to talk to us. We'll have time to meet with Mom later. You're always so dyth serious. Daddy, it's so nice to see you!"

Lymdyr released his grip, then eased back down. His anxiety was melted by the big, sunny smile on Pryn's face. The other twin sat sulking.

"You two! Pryn, you are so much more like my side of the family. Heck, you even look just like your Aunt Ryty. Anyway, big news." The totality of what he was about to level on his offspring made Lymdyr's throat constrict. Pryn's jubilant expression dissolved off her face. The other twin raised her smoldering dark eyes to meet his.

"I've made a life changing decision in the last couple days. I'm going to be part of the Dymran crew."

Both the young women froze in place. Pryn's mouth was open in an expression of confusion. The dark twin drummed her painted nails on the tabletop. "What exactly does that mean?"

Lymdyr leaned toward them and grasped each of their hands. "My darlings, what that means is that in five short days, myself and four other brave souls will be climbing into a specially built craft, and blasting off...."

"What?" The shock and pain in Pryn's voice wrung every drop of emotion from him. Her big greenish brown eyes sagged in grief.

Dyny tossed her head back and let go a groan. "Father, you've really lost you mind. Haven't you?"

"Daddy, you....can't be serious. What's going to happen to us? I'm going off to advanced school in three months, you're going to miss......"

Before his eyes, the light haired twin collapsed. She folded her arms on the tabletop and buried her head in them. Dyny just sat, shaking her head, and occasionally rolling her eyes in disbelief.

"Okay Father. That's all I need to hear. I'm going to break the news to Bynhyld. Unless you're man enough to!"

"Wait for me!" Pryn wiped her broad, dripping nose on her sleeve and followed Dyny out of the booth. "Daddy! How could you?"

With stiff, robotic movements, Lymdyr eased out of the booth, and allowed the sobbing twin to hug him. "Can we meet again, before the launch?" he managed to choke out while Pryn cried in his arms.

Dyny just let go a snort, then stomped off toward the door. The light-haired twin managed to pull herself together. "Yes, of course. Don't worry. I'll keep Dyn under control. I love you Daddy!"

The warmth and power of Pryn's kiss on his cheek sent a glimmer of hope into Lymdyr. He watched her disappear out the front door.

A half hour later, Lymdyr walked into the Gyr tavern. Small, winged creatures buzzed in and out of the open door. Even for a Spyrday, there was a large crowd. He stopped to let his eyes adjust to the dim interior. Ryk's deep booming laugh shot through the noise of the room.

Despite the smoky haze, Lymdyr caught sight of the Ryk's battered brown felt hat, and worked his way past the patrons till he was right next to him. The mag driver took a long pull of his physt mug, then turned to see who was standing beside him.

"Lymdyr! What the klynk are you doin' here? Didn't think I'd see you before we blasted off. Hey Lylyn! Lymdyr's here!"

Ryk's tremendously pregnant girlfriend delivered the drinks she was carrying and hurried over to her boyfriend's side. After snuggling up against him, she sent a friendly but confused look over at the railroad man.

"Hello Mr. Lymdyr."

"Hello Lylyn."

"So, what brings you out here? Ryk told me you got shuttled off to some blyrt hole in...."

Lymdyr let loose an abrupt blast of a laugh. "Yeah, that didn't work out. Say, do you suppose I could get a mug of that physt. I have some pretty big news to relay, but I'm thirsty as Myrnvar."

While they waited for Lylyn to fetch a glass, the two men stood fidgeting. "So Ryk, how are things?"

The mag driver swirled the amber liquid in his mug. "Oh, things is going okay. Getting ready to blast off." He made a rocket noise and shot his index finger up into the smoky air. Lylyn returned with the physt which Lymdyr immediately pounded down half of.

"Ah that's great! Alright, brace yourselves."

Lylyn looked up at Ryk's cocked eyebrow expression, giggled, and pulled herself even closer.

"Handynr has backed out of the project, and I've taken his place."

Ryk's face lost all trace of emotion. After a couple seconds, he seemed to overcome the initial shock. "Did I hear you right? Handynr's out, and you're taking his place?"

"You heard correctly."

Ryk reared back and let go a mag driver hoot. His girlfriend reached out to tug at Lymdyr's finely tailored sleeve.

"Mr. Lymdyr! That's great news. Ryk's always said how easy it is for him to talk to you and not them high educated folks. Whoeee! You boys are going to have a some kinda adventure, that's all I gotta say."

At that same time, in the train station across town, Mihyn stood next to one of the big stone pillars on the platform. People wandered back and forth without her even noticing them. Exactly every eight minutes, she looked at the massive clock on the wall of the depot behind her. The sun dropped down beneath the lip of the metal platform roof, plunging the area into hot, white light.

"Zym, now I have to wait in the heat. Oh well, I'd rather be here than at home. I almost wish none of my family was coming. I honestly don't feel like feeding them, cleaning up after them, having to answer their questions. *Mihyn darling, I'm so surprised! You and Handynr seemed so happy!*" She looked out at the dusty rail yard and felt a pang of guilt way down deep. "I do want to see them, though."

She was hot, sweaty, and worn out by the time her parents and one of her lifelong friends arrived. Mihyn put on her best "glad to see you" face and pressed into the crowd waiting for the passengers to disembark. After a few moments, her father stepped out of the car and pulled his oversized carpet bag down to the platform.

"Mihyn! Hello!"

She gave him a hug while other passengers jostled by them. After letting go, her father motioned up toward the car.

"The train was packed, as you can see. Mom and Glyndy should be coming down shortly." His wrinkled, kindly face softened as he took a moment to evaluate his daughter's appearance. "You look well. A little tired maybe. How are you feeling?"

"I'm doing fine, Father."

"Well, again, so sorry to hear about you and Handynr. I always had a sneaking suspicion.....Oh, here comes Mother."

A moment later, an older, grey version of Mihyn stepped down and spread her arms wide. Behind her, a young woman with highly styled brown hair and surprisingly wide shoulders waited on the steps. Once mother and daughter had disconnected, the woman stepped forward and gave Mihyn a bone crushing hug.

"Oh my. I think I'm going to cry!"

Mihyn managed to wriggle out of the woman's powerful grip. "So glad you could come, Glyndy. It's been way too long. Come on, I need to get out of the styrk."

The next morning, both Krynut and Grylt arrived at the Academy within seconds of each other.

"Good morning Regent. I assume you're here to pack up your office also?" the biology professor asked as they walked together across the foyer.

"Yes indeed. By the way, I have an important update on the project. It seems that Regent Handynr has backed out."

"Oh dear!" Grylt continued to walk forward, his mostly bald head lowered.

"The good news is Mr. Lymdyr has agreed to take his place."

The professor stopped at the foot of the stairs and laid his hand on Krynut's arm. "Mr. Lymdyr? I thought he was shuttled off to....."

"We all did. He arrived back in town yesterday, and....I know it's all rather confusing, but he has agreed to go."

"I see."

Throughout the morning, Grylt and one of his assistants loaded items into a large leather satchel.

"Now remember professor, you can only take forty pounds of gear."

"Forty pounds! What a joke! I could easily take nothing but dyrfts, but that wouldn't be practical." He opened a cabinet, grabbed some tools, and held them out. "Here, put these in."

One floor below, Krynut was also selecting things to take on the voyage. He stood staring at his desk.

"Seven years. I've been in this office for seven years. Time certainly goes by fast. Am I making the worst mistake of my life? Am I throwing a superb opportunity away on some impractical, dangerous venture?"

His musing was interrupted by the sound of squeaking cart wheels out in the hall. Two students with shop aprons still tied around their waists wheeled the wooden cart into the room. Their cheery, hopeful faces erased his gloom quite effectively.

"Regent, we just finished making the modifications. I think you're going to be pleased," the taller, red haired student said with glee. "Rytry had a great idea just as we were putting in the metal bars."

"It was your idea!" the student with his back to Krynut protested. A smile pulled up the edges of his full black beard.

"Anyway, thank you both. Let's see what you have."

The students wheeled the cart next to the desk, then carefully lifted the smaller scale calculating device to an upright position. Krynut bent down and let his eyes drift over the newly modified apparatus.

"Let me just say how grateful I am that you two decided to make the last minute modifications. If we hadn't taken into account the lack of air pressure in space, this device could quite possibly have been useless up there. Show me how it works."

The taller student rubbed his hands together and eased down next to Krynut. "We set it up so that you can use it either as is, or in zero air pressure. Up in the craft, you're going need to pull up these stops to activate the bars, just like you would do by placing a ball in the cup. What that does is allow these gauges at the bottom of the metal bars to move as the bar vibrates. You'll need to keep track of the movement and add it all up. Here, we'll demonstrate." He picked up a shiny metal horn from the bottom of the cart. "Rytry, think up some kind of calculation we want to make."

"I have one," Krynut tossed out. He opened a book lying at the edge of his desk and began flipping the stops open across wooden rack on the upper face of the device. After double checking the figure in the book, and the position of the bar stops, he straightened up to a standing position. "You want me to play, or you got it under control?"

"I've been practicing." The student took a deep breath, pointed the bell of the horn at the rack of dull grey metal bars, then blew out a familiar folk melody. He repeated the phrase four times before the bars reached enough frequency to begin moving the gauges. On the fifth repeat, his cheeks began to redden.

The other student watched the gauges rise, and when the needles had stabilized, he turned toward Krynut. "Regent, go ahead and write down the figures." As soon as Krynut finished copying down them down, the dark haired, bearded young man held up his hand. "You can stop playing now, Phyr."

Krynut tallied the increments of the ruler-like gauges, ran a quick calculation, then flipped the book to the back section where the answers to the sample problems were. His face became intense and drawn as he compared his numbers with the figure in the book.

"Outstanding! We calculated the answer to two places farther than the dyrft."

The taller student let out a loud whoop of joy. He reached over, and punched his dark haired companion on the arm, then looked over at Krynut. "Regent?"

"Yes?"

"If Rytry and I can get our hands on some scraps of that metal, would you mind if we build a smaller one of these?" The student's question was loaded with humility and anticipation.

"Certainly, you men have done a fine job on this. By all means, make one for yourself."

Over near the center of town, Lymdyr had just conducted his daily walk from the hotel where he was staying to the bank nearby. Byrdyl was forwarding all important telemessages there, and one had been waiting since late the day before. He read it on his way back to the hotel.

"Message from Byrdyl, Exec Admin Blue Line Railroad-

Lymdyr, do you know why someone would leave a massive, dead hyrk painted blue out on the front sidewalk of the building? Whoever it was also drew a picture of a blue hyrk on the side of the building. By the way, management sent a review board up to Pylgor based on the letter you gave me. Guess what? They fired that guy for stealing tools. Also, Bynhyld knows you're part of the crew, and is looking for you."

Lymdyr's stomach did a small flip. He stopped outside the glass front door of the hotel and took a quick scan of the buggies rolling back and forth in the bright morning sun.

"Dyth! That is not good news. I'm going to have to lay low if both Bynhyld and maybe the Krushians are looking for me. How am I going to meet with the girls? Zym dyth it! Byrdyl's gonna have to help me get word to them."

Chapter 55.

The crew spent the next two days hurriedly making last minute preparations. On the eve of their launch, the bon voyage celebrations started. Ryk's kicked off first. At 4:50, he grudgingly slipped on his heavy brown and red robe and stood in front of the mirror.

"Holy Zym! I look like some kind of mag driver school teacher!"

He made his way down the outside stairway and around the corner to the tavern as quickly as possible. Several pedestrians and people in wagons stared at the marvelously decorated robe. Ryk pulled his hat down even farther than usual.

The sounds of laughter, clinking glasses and loud conversation spilled out of the open door as he got closer. Without breaking his stride, Ryk swept into the dark interior. A huge, raucous cheer arose. He was besieged by well-wishers.

"Ryk! Good to see you!"

"Hey that is one fancy robe!"

"Here's the hero of the voyage right here!"

One of the women next to him raised up on her tiptoes and gave him a kiss on the cheek. "For good luck!" The crowd roared their approval.

"Klynking Zym! Don't everybody stand around. Get the man a drink!" a voice from near the bar called out.

A massive ceramic tankard was thrust into Ryk's hand. Yellow, foamy physt sloshed over the side, coating several of the merrymakers' shoes. No one seemed to care. Ryk raised it high and chugged down a considerable amount.

"Ah! Been waiting for that all day!"

Lylyn worked her way through the crowd and stood next to him. "My but you look good!" After sliding her arm around his waist, she turned to address the crowd. "Don't you all think he looks great in this?" She pinched the open lapel of the finely crafted garment for emphasis. A deafening response shook the walls.

In the park next to the old folk's home where Byrty worked, Lymdyr sat on one of the benches. For the tenth time, he glanced down at this pocket watch, then around at the mostly deserted landscape. A soft breeze rattled the spiky needles of the evergreen trees around him.

"Where are they? They were supposed to be here twenty minutes ago." Anxiety and worry brought a row of wrinkles to his forehead.

"Hey Daddy!"

The sound of Pryn's high, musical voice coming from behind him caused Lymdyr to swivel around. He jumped up and ran the short distance over to greet the twins. After a quick hug, they all took a seat on the bench.

"Did you guys follow my instructions?"

Dyny rolled her dark eyes before answering. "Yes, Father. We're not little kids you know! We took a buggy to the Green Pyfg café, waited inside to make sure no one was following us, then walked over here. Are you really that worried about Bynhyld hiring someone to follow us? Why don't you just man up and face her?"

"Dyn! For Zym's sake! Daddy is blasting off into space tomorrow! Can't you lighten up just a little?" Satisfied that she had made her point, Pryn snuggled up against her father.

Lymdyr let go a harried, exhausted little chuckle, and pulled both of his daughters close. "You two! How different you are."

For a few moments, the three of them just sat and watched the lykrs flit about in the evergreen trees. Pryn finally slid to the side and extracted a wrapped package from her small backpack. "Here, we got you a going away present."

After pulling himself up to an upright position, Lymdyr carefully tore the tissue paper wrapping off, opened the stiff cardboard container, and gently pulled the metal daguerreotype plate out. He tilted it to get a better view. The image portrayed both daughters dressed in long formal dresses, standing sideways, holding hands, and smiling at the camera.

"Oh my goodness! This is wonderful." He took another quick look at the plate, then kissed both of them on the cheek.

"We figured you'd want something small to take along," Dyny offered in her usual deadpan voice.

"It's just wonderful. Thank you so much!"

Lymdyr lovingly gazed over at his daughter's faces. Try as he might to remain present, his mind kept jumping back to the list of things that still needed to be done. Most immediately, he had promised to pick Byrty up and take her to Ryk's going away party. Lymdyr let out a long sigh.

Pryn reared back and stared at him. "What? I know that sound."

Both the twins now locked their focus on him. A flash of embarrassed heat swept over Lymdyr. "I, uh, have an appointment....."

"Oh for Zym's sake Father, you are always in a hurry, aren't you?" Dyny pulled her arm out from behind him, smacked both knees for emphasis, and rose up off the bench. "Come on Pryn, time to go."

"Wait!" Lymdyr applied force to the twin's shoulders, halting their attempt to leave. "Okay, normally I would throw a big old bash to celebrate something like this."

He struggled for several uncomfortable moments with how to explain his predicament to the young women. Finally, he just levelled with them. "I've gotten myself in a bit of trouble with the railroad, and with...the Krushians."

"The Krushians?" The twins exclaimed in unison.

"Yeah, they had a little side business going up in Pylgor, and I busted them." He paused to let the words sink in. "That's why I've been laying low. Just be extra careful for the next day, alright?"

Pryn leaned over and planted a warm kiss on his cheek. "Yes, we'll be careful. See you tomorrow."

Dyny also gave him a quick smooch, then stood up and led the way across the grassy lawn. After watching the lithe forms of his daughters slowly disappear from view, Lymdyr got up from the bench, and walked over to the nursing home. His normally animated face was now set with seriousness.

"Boy, do I need a drink."

He opened the front door, stepped in, and was immediately met by Byrty and her bartender boyfriend.

"Mr. Lymdyr! Just on time!" the nurse opened her arms and gave him a powerful hug. "How are you?"

"Uh, good, I'm good."

"You remember Hyryl, right?"

"Yes, of course." Lymdyr shook the bartender's hand and made a sincere attempt to smile.

"Well, no point in standing here, let's go party!" Byrty led them down the walk, and into the waiting buggy.

On the ride over to the Jybyr neighborhood, Lymdyr was content to let Byrty yack away. The meeting with his daughters had left him in a contemplative mood. He did answer the few questions she posed to him, but other than that remained silent.

It wasn't until they stepped out onto the sidewalk in front of the Gyr tavern that his ebullient spirit began to return. The roar of the crowd inside hit them as soon as exited the buggy.

"It sounds like the party has already started," Byrty observed.

She grabbed her boyfriend's hand and entered the noisy, smoky bar with Lymdyr right behind. The three of them threaded their way up to where Ryk was holding court.

Lylyn spotted them when they finally slid past several of the patrons. "Mr. Lymdyr! Welcome. Hey Ryk, look who's here!"

"Byrty! Good to see you!" the mag driver spread his arms wide, and the nurse all but disappeared inside the open robe. She pressed her head against his chest, held it there for a moment, then stepped back.

"Byrty, you look great." Ryk's face shone with happiness. "And, I forgot your friend's name."

"Ryk, this is Hyryl."

The burly, scarred ex-boxer leaned forward and the two men exchanged a bone crushing shake. Ryk took another gulp from his oversized tankard. "You all need a drink?"

"I haven't had a drink since we came back from our trip with Phyrnk, but seeing as how tonight's this big celebration, I guess I better catch up!" Byrty replied.

"As I recall, pyryn is your favorite. Lylyn honey, will you get us four shots?"

"Sure Ryk, whatever you want." The uncomfortably pregnant waitress waddled back through the crowd. Byrty watched her laboriously pick her way into the wall of bodies next to the bar.

"So how's she dealing with the fact that you're going to be leaving tomorrow?"

Ryk wiped a line of foam off his upper lip. "Ya know, Lylyn's not really the emotional type. She kinda keeps everything bottled up inside. She's alright I guess." He held up both arms and turned in a circle to address the crowd.

"Hey everybody. I wanta thank you all for coming out, and also, they's someone else here what needs to be recognized. My good friend, and now, fellow crew member, Mr. Lymdyr, uh…"

"Nine Line," the railroad man whispered.

"Yeah, Lymdyr Nine Line is here. Just a couple days ago, one a the crew backed out, and Lymdyr has taken his place."

The room erupted with cheers and waving of hats. Lylyn returned with a tray weighted down with a row of shot glasses and several physt mugs. The celebrating group all grabbed a shot glass, clinked them, then tossed back the fiery liquid. Byrty made a sour face and shook her head several times.

"Whew! I haven't felt that burn for a month now!"

They all handed the shot glasses back to Lylyn. Ryk eyed the red and white satin ribbon hanging around his girlfriend's neck.

He reached out and gently grabbed her by the wrist as she turned to go.

"Hold up. Byrty, look at this fancy award that the Collorians gave to all of us the other night. Dyth, I forget what it's called, but it has something to do with bravery and service."

Byrty and her boyfriend took a step closer to Lylyn and examined the award. "It's very nice. How come you're not wearing it?"

"Ah, I gived it to Lylyn, and when the baby is born, he or she can have it."

"I still can't believe that tomorrow, you're going to be blasting off forever!" A flood of tears filled Lylyn's dark brown eyes. While she was busy wiping them away, Ryk leaned over and pulled her close. His action only served to increase her level of emotion. She stood blubbering in his arms.

Ryk gazed around at those close by. He smiled out of compassion and a touch of embarrassment. Byrty pulled a handkerchief out and blotted his girlfriend's cheeks.

Lylyn drew in a deep, shuddering breath. "Thank you. Oh, I'm sorry! I guess all this celebrating just got to me. Byrty, do you need another?"

"Yes, please!"

Across town, a decent sized group of family, friends and coworkers had assembled for Mihyn's going away party. A table of food was set out in the backyard. Guests mingled, ate, drank, and continually offered their congratulations and wishes for good luck.

Her long-time friend shuttled back and forth between the kitchen and food table. A huge pot of stew sat on the stove, which she dutifully stirred. Late in the afternoon, Mihyn came in through the back door and walked over to her.

"Glyndy, why don't you let me take care of the food for a while? You need to relax and have some fun, too."

The tall, statuesque woman brushed a strand of hair off her glistening forehead and looked over at Mihyn. "Nonsense. This is your big night. I'm happy to take care of things. I still can't believe that tomorrow you'll be taking off." Her lower lip began to quiver. She quickly turned away and stirred with a fury.

"Okay, but if you need any help, just let us know." Mihyn reached over and gave her friend's shoulder a gentle stroke.

"Yes, I will. Thank you."

Mihyn walked back to the rear door and leaned against the frame. Watching her cousin's children playing catch over by the back fence helped to ease the deep anxiety she was experiencing. Her mind temporarily drifted away from the upcoming journey. She took a moment to enjoy the bright pink blossoms on the thorn trees. The weeds springing up in the flower bed elicited a brief feeling of things left undone.

Her moment of reflection was interrupted by the touch of a hand on her back. Mihyn turned to see her father standing nearby. A smile graced his wrinkled, kindly face. He took a step forward and slid his arm around her waist.

"Are you doing alright? You look kind of sad."

Mihyn rested her head on his shoulder. "Well, Dad, I'd be lying if I said I wasn't a little sad about leaving all of you and all of this." She made a little sweep of her arm toward the backyard. "But no, I'm really not sad. Just a little apprehensive."

For several moments, father and daughter just stood enjoying the intimacy of each other. The older man finally spoke in a voice just above a whisper.

"You know, if someone had suggested that my only daughter would be heading off into space to chase a comet a year ago, I'd have said they were crazy."

His comment brought a smile to Mihyn's worry lined face. He gently cradled her narrow chin between his thumb and index finger. "You look tired. Have you been sleeping okay?"

Mihyn shook her head. "No, not really. You know I always was a little nervous. Having the family here does make me feel more at ease."

The front door creaked open, and in walked Handynr and his secretary. Mihyn felt a jolt of irritation as she watched the couple approach. Her father's smile transformed into a much more serious, disapproving expression. He whispered into his daughter's ear just before ducking out into the yard.

"The nerve of that man."

Handynr entered the kitchen holding a massive floral display of brilliant red flowers. "Here, I know these are your favorites. I hope you don't mind us coming over. I really wanted to say goodbye one way or another."

"Thank you, they're beautiful." Mihyn accepted the flowers and managed to force a smile onto her face. "No, I'm glad you came." She directed her gaze over to Kym. The secretary stood next to, and slightly behind Handynr. "Welcome Kym. This is my good friend, Glyndy. We went to advanced school together."

Mihyn's friend stopped stirring the stew, walked over and extended a hand. "Please to meet you. Handynr, good to see you again."

The secretary let go of Glyndy's hand, gave her long, languid brown hair a toss, then took a quick scan of the kitchen. "I just love the way this house is set up. So simple, so efficient."

In response to Kym's exuberant proclamation, Glyndy rolled her eyes. "Would you mind helping me carry these blynys out to the back table?"

"Sure!"

Once the secretary and visiting friend had slipped out the back door, Mihyn turned toward her more or less ex-husband. "So you really wanted to come over and say goodbye?"

"Yes. I know that you're probably pretty angry with me right now, but if we had more time to work this out, it….." Handynr realized how futile his words were, and let the statement trail off.

"Well, I appreciate you at least coming by. I really do." Mihyn could feel the great, yawning chasm between them widen. His blank, helpless look of defeat didn't improve things. "I suppose you two will move in here after the launch."

"Yes, what do you want me to do with your things?"

"Glyndy has offered to take some of it, but get rid of the rest." Mihyn waited till one of their guests who had just entered the kitchen passed by before continuing. She took a step closer to him.

"And don't under any circumstance let Kym touch any of my things after I'm gone, agreed?"

"Agreed."

"One last thing. Will you please wait till we are up in space before you two klynk in our bed?"

The sheepish nod, and infinitesimally small smirk from Handynr was all the assurance Mihyn needed. "Thanks." With that, she spun around, and exited the house.

Chapter 56.

In the small apartment near the Academy, Krynut, his brother and mother were sitting around talking. The regent's narrow, pointy features were drawn up tensely. He leaned back in the chair and rubbed his palms together.

"I feel bad about taking off, and not spending the evening with you, but....."

"I know dear, it's alright. We know how important it is for you to honor Janela's family tradition. It's too bad she's taking it so hard," his mother replied in a smooth, soothing tone.

"We'll be with you tomorrow morning." His brother forced a smile and looked over at Krynut's darkened visage.

The regent patted the arms of the chair with both hands, then jumped to his feet. "You're right. It's not like we didn't get a chance to spend the afternoon together. It's just that I have so much going through my head. I don't feel like I'm really in control of myself today."

"It's a big job being the head of the crew," his mother responded while stiffly rising to her feet. The other son rose up also.

"It sure is. We don't have to tell you how proud we are. Father would have been proud too."

Krynut walked over and hugged his brother for all he was worth. They remained embraced for a moment. After letting go, he stepped across the floor rug to where his tiny, frail mother was standing. He gave her a kiss on the cheek and a light hug. Tears glistened in her eyes.

"Say hi to Janela and her parents for us."

"I will."

Krynut waved to them both, then slipped out the door. All the way over to Janela's parents' house, he sat in the buggy and stewed. Deep lines furrowed across his forehead.

"I'm not looking forward to this at all. I never did get along that well with them, and now, whew, if I can just make it through this last pyryst, that's one thing I can stop worrying about."

When the buggy finally pulled up in front of the modest house, Krynut drew in a deep breath, and stepped out into the pleasant evening air. Small night creatures were chirping in the thorn trees. Their monotonous rhythm helped to calm his frayed nerves.

He struggled to contain the rising level of anxiety while walking up toward the house. After taking a moment to slow his rapid breathing, Krynut reached out and knocked once on the front door. It swung open immediately. Janela appeared in the opening, her smooth, dark face drawn down in sadness.

"Come in," she offered in a voice just above a whisper.

"You look lovely tonight." It took all his determination to force out the compliment. Her grim expression made him want to turn and run. Instead, he lowered his head and walked in.

"Thank you." She closed the door, and the whoosh of air blew the hem of her gorgeous indigo dress back. Krynut glanced briefly at her perfectly shaped ankle before the fabric folded back over it.

Janela grasped both his hands. "I know you have a hard time dealing with Mumer and Pumer, but it means a lot to them for you to make this gesture."

She rose up on her slippered toes and gave him a ceremonial kiss. The faintest spark of passion rose smoldered in Krynut, then extinguished. She led him across the darkened living room and into the dining area. A simple round table covered with an exquisitely crocheted white cloth almost filled the small room. The only sounds were pots banging around, and the unusual sing-song cadence of her parents conversing in their native language.

"Mumer, Pumer, hyng duneer Regent Krynut!"

Janela's parents came shuffling out of the steamy kitchen. Her father was almost as tall as Krynut. He was quite thin, with tight dark skin stretched over his exaggerated facial bones. A shocking white beard trimmed his protruding jaw line. The mother was just over five feet tall. Her large expressive eyes were set above the arrow straight line of her nose. One could easily tell that in her younger days, she must have been considered a beauty.

The father walked forward and offered a formal bow. His crisp, drab green suit made a crinkling sound as he bent. Krynut returned the bow. The mother glided over and held out both hands. Krynut grasped them and looked down into her delicate features. Her coal black eyes searched back and forth across his face.

"Dihay hi," she offered in greeting.

"Dihay hi."

"Please, sit." Janela motioned toward the far side of the table. Once their daughter and guest were seated, the parents returned to the kitchen.

Janela reached under the table and grasped Krynut's hand. "Relax," she whispered.

"I wish I could."

"Oh, hang on."

She let go of his hand, rose up from her chair, and swept into the kitchen. Another rapid fire exchange of the native language drifted out to him. Janela came back into the small, bright room carrying a bottle of mynth and two glasses. She set one in front of him, and the other at her place.

"Would you like some?"

"Yes."

Janela poured some of the dark purple liquid into the glasses. After sitting back down, she raised her glass in a toast.

"To your great voyage."

Krynut picked up his glass up, gave hers a clink, and took a sip. The parents entered the room carrying a collection of steaming copper dishes. An aroma of spices and savory sauces filled the room.

"Oh, that smells wonderful," he remarked.

"This is a very special dish. Momrah has been cooking all day," the father said with pride.

Bowls were dished out all around. For the first six minutes of the meal, the only sounds were little groans of pleasure from Krynut, and the scraping of spoons against ceramic. The father finished chewing through a mouthful, wiped his lips, then eased back in his chair.

"Is it too hot for you?"

Krynut shook his head and. "No, not at all, well maybe just a little."

The father's jet black cheeks folded into a smile. "So, who is taking over at the Academy for you?"

"One of my longtime colleagues, a woman that I have enormous respect for will be stepping in."

"She's a bitch!" Janela snapped.

"Janelet! No language like that at the table please," the father replied. His white, bristly eyebrows narrowed with disapproval.

Janela finished her bowl and slammed down the rest of her mynth. She reached over, refilled her glass, then held the bottle up. "More?"

Krynut waved her off. "No thank you. I have so much to do tomorrow. I want to make sure I'm in top form."

"Well, you might as well drink up. No one here is going to finish it."

The crew chief polished off a second bowl. He tried to think of something pleasant to talk about, but was not successful. His super-efficient mind was too busy running down the list of tasks for launch morning.

"Well, would you like some zyd or something?" The father's somewhat annoyed question snapped Krynut out of his meditation.

He ventured a quick glance around and realized that everyone had finished. Janela and her mother were both staring down at the table. The father sat upright and rigid. His small knob of a chin was lifted ever so slightly. Krynut reached over and laid his hand on top of Janela's.

"You know, I really should head home. Tomorrow is going to be...." He let go a weak, futile laugh. "A big day to say the least." Krynut returned his focus to the diminutive, defiant man seated across the table. "Are you coming down to watch the launch?"

"No."

The father's simple, cutting reply hit him like a punch to the gut. Krynut felt his temperature rise. He blotted several beads of sweat off his forehead and upper lip.

"Thank you so much for the meal." After giving Janela's hand a gentle squeeze, he leaned toward her. "How do I say the meal was delicious in Mygr?"

Without moving anything but her beautiful plum colored lips, she uttered the correct phrase. Krynut shifted his attention over to the mother, and repeated the words as best he could.

The older woman's face lit up. She nodded twice and locked him in her gaze. Krynut spent a couple fleeting moments looking deep into her dark eyes. What he saw was an expression of understanding, and not a small measure of regret for what could have been.

His emotions surged to a level he was barely able to contain. The finality of the moment crashed down on him. He knew that this was his last chance to offer these people some words of conciliation.

Krynut slowly turned his attention to the father. He tightened his grip on Janela's small hand to the point of it being painful. She squeezed back. "I wish things had worked out between Janela and I. It was very difficult for me to make the decision to go on this voyage."

"Well, we all must make decisions and live with them, don't we?"

The bluntness of the father's reply cut through all of them. His lower lip, chin, and white fringe of a beard began to quiver. He bounded up from the table, and reached his long, skinny arm across toward Krynut. The crew chief was still somewhat in shock from the father's stark words. He slowly rose, maintaining his grip on Janela's hand.

A trace of tears filled the older man's red streaked eyes as they shook hands. Janela's mother got up from her place, walked silently around the table, and stopped next to Krynut.

When the two men finally released their grip, the mother reached over and gently grasped Krynut's free hand. She muttered a quick prayer three times, bowing in between each utterance. After planting a quick dry kiss on the back of his hand, she let go, and padded over to stand next to her husband.

Krynut pulled Janela to her feet. She rose like an anchor being pulled up from the sea bottom.

"Good luck and may Zym watch over you!" the father shouted. His voice cracked with emotion.

"Thank you." Krynut sent a final conciliatory glance over at the parents, then hauled the limp shell of Janela out of the room. "Will you walk me out to the curb?" he whispered.

She just nodded her down-turned head. Krynut led the way across the living room, and out into the inky black night. The clicking of the night creatures filled the air. His wet skin sighed with relief as a dry, cool breeze swept across it.

Janela stumbled halfway down the walkway. Krynut paused to look over at her. Shining streams of tears glinted in the starlight as they trailed down both of her cheeks. A moment later, she and Krynut reached the street. He pulled her around to face him.

"Will you come to the launch tomorrow?"

"Yes, of course. I will wear black though." She took a moment to examine his pained expression. "I will wear black for one year. If you do not return in that time, it's over."

Krynut hugged her with fury and anguish, cradling her head of lustrous, thick black hair against his chest. Slowly, ever so slowly, he rocked her side to side. Eventually, Krynut relaxed his hold. She pulled back, rose up on her tiptoes, gave him a short, peck of a kiss, then whooshed out of his grasp. He stood and watched her sweep along the path.

"So delicate and beautiful, like some dark, tortured spirit floating away. No, the way her long, gauzy dress billows out, she's more like a lovely lykr flying from captivity."

At the doorstep, Janela stopped, turned back around, and sent one final scorching glance his way. In a flash, she yanked the door open and slipped inside.

The sound of the door slamming shook Krynut back to the present. He turned and walked with long, powerful strides away from the painful scene. On his way to the buggy stop, he passed a line of storefronts. The only sign of life was a small tavern plunked right in the middle of the block. Light poured out from its open door, as did the sound of laughter and friendly voices.

"I'd sure like to go in and knock back a couple drinks to kill this gloom. Right! What would I say? Hey, guess what? I'm blasting into the unknown tomorrow, so I thought I'd get drunk and forget about it!" Krynut rubbed his hands along both cheeks, and continued walking.

Up in the foothills of the mountain just outside the northern city limits of Tyrl, Grylt's going away party was still in full swing. He and his male friends were lounging in the carefully landscaped garden pavilion behind the house. Specially made celestial lamps of silver paper hung from the thorn trees around the wooden structure and along the paths.

Kybark sat off by himself on one of the grey stone benches. He was furiously composing poems. The only break he took was to urinate in the bushes, and down glasses of the chinz.

From the direction of the house, three servants walked single file along the gravel path. Each one held a platter of sumptuous food.

Grylt watched them approach the pavilion. He let out a groan. "Oh, Zym Mytry! Not more food! I can't even look at another bite."

His friend wiped the grease off his mouth and settled back in his finely wrought garden chair. "Dear professor, we've got to fatten you up for your long voyage. If all you are going to be eating for the next couple months is that awful, bland grain from the way down in Zylfr, you'll waste away to nothing!"

The comment drew a laugh from all those seated at the big round table. Grylt gazed out at the lush collection of plants growing in carefully tended planters around the pavilion.

"You know Mytry, it's still hard for me to believe that in ten hours, I'll be climbing in that craft and leaving Ulutrita, probably forever." The professor's eyes began to fill with tears.

His friend reached over and patted Grylt's arm. "It's hard for us to fathom that, also. There's still time to back out, you know."

"No, I'm committed. When they first offered the position to me, my heart leaped inside my chest. To explore some strange new world, with Zym knows what kind of unique flora and fauna, is truly a once in a lifetime experience. No, I'm going. As a matter of fact, I should probably drag Mr. Grumpy Pants off his bench, and head home."

A collective groan of displeasure rose up for the group. The gentleman seated next to Grylt gave his long, waxed moustache a twist.

"I suppose you're right. My bakery is providing all the food for the mayor's post launch celebration tomorrow. I told the head pastry chef that I'd show up early to give him a hand with the blynys."

Grylt reached over and placed his hand on the man's shoulder. "I'm sure your spread for the mayor will be something to behold." He patted the shoulder, then stood up. "Kybark! I think we should head home."

The curmudgeonly poet looked up from his writing, picked up his glass, drained it, then tossed it into the bushes. Mytry winced at the sound of breaking glass.

"I honestly don't know what you see in that foul mouthed, nasty person," he commented in a not so quiet voice. "I can tell you this, once you leave, he will never be invited up here again!" The host motioned for all the seated guests to rise. He held up a perfectly manicured finger.

"Professor, if you will pause for just a moment. I shall return." The host strode out of the pavilion and disappeared down the main path to the house. Moments later, a brass gong sounded from the direction of the house. The deep, sonorous vibration grew louder, and from up the main path, a procession of servants carrying an ornately decorated sedan chair appeared through the overhanging foliage.

"Oh, my!" Grylt gasped and lifted his hands up to cover his open mouth.

The procession snaked around the pavilion in a whirl of brightly colored silk and glinting brass with Mytry at the head. Once the entire entourage had entered the circular opening, the host stepped up on the wooden deck, bowed deeply, and extended his arm toward the awaiting sedan chair.

"When I did my time with the defense service in Hotem, it was their custom to honor guests by carting them around in one of these. I had this built especially for you. Bid your friends farewell, and then we will follow you out to your buggy."

Mytry's thin, razor sharp features glowed with pride. Grylt moved around the table, hugging and kissing all those gathered. He wiped a tear away and embraced his host last of all. "Thank you my friend. I couldn't ask for a more fitting send off."

After looking down at Grylt's small, compact face, Mytry turned and called out into the darkness. "Kybark, would you like to ride along?"

"I'll walk."

Chapter 57.

The next morning, Krynut was the first of the crew to wake up. Faint light filtered in through his bedroom window. Lykrs sang their monotonous songs outside. He rolled over and flipped open the black enamel pocket watch on the nightstand.

"Whew! Glad I didn't oversleep." The crew chief eased back and stared up at the ceiling. "Calm. Think calm."

He breathed deeply in, then out. The pounding in his chest gradually slowed. From the kitchen, he heard the ping of a metal pan, and the door of the oven squeak open. Krynut slid out of bed, pulled his pants on, and walked out to investigate. He stuck his head around the doorway.

"How many times have I woken up to see Mom bent over in her quilted morning coat like that? A hundred, a thousand, ten thousand times? Same fuzzy morning light, same silver hair tied back in a tight bun. Same knobby, small hands working to get the stryker to light. She is certainly aging well. A little more stooped and bent over. Not bad for a woman who had to raise and provide for two sons all by herself."

He made a little coughing noise. His mother stopped flicking the wheel on the stryker and turned with a start.

"Oh, it's you! I didn't hear you come in." A warm smile lit up her wrinkled but still soft face. Krynut walked over and wrapped his arm around her. She snuggled up against his chest.

"So, are you ready for your big day?"

"I suppose."

"Thought I'd get some zyd ready."

"Good idea."

"How did you sleep?"

"Oh, not great. I have a lot on my mind."

"I'm sure you do." She released a small sigh and rocked him gently back and forth. "Ever since you were a boy, I knew that someday, you would do something great. I just knew it. You were always so serious, so determined."

She gave him another quick squeeze, then eased back far enough to grasp both his hands. "And this is it, isn't it?"

His lips twisted to the side. "This is what?"

"This is it. This is what you were destined to do."

"Yes, I think it is."

She squeezed his fingers tightly. "And you'll do a fine job. I just know you will."

Across town, Ryk, Byrty, and Hyryl were the sole survivors of the night's festivities. Hyryl had just slid down in his chair and was now snoring softly. Byrty let go a cackle after looking over at his battered face.

"Oh boy! Time for bed." She pushed her empty glass away, then pitched her head in Ryk's general direction.

"It's getting light outside," he commented in a quiet, somewhat defeated tone of voice.

Byrty squinted toward the long rectangular window high up on the front wall. "So it is. What time do you have to be, wherever you have to be?"

"Parade starts at nine. They're coming by to pick me and my grip up at eight thirty." Ryk sat statue-like. His big, thick fingers were tightly wound around the pyryn glass. He stared straight ahead.

"What time is it now?"

Ryk leaned over and looked at the clock ticking away behind the bar. "Five thirty."

"Well, I guess we can grab a couple hours of sleep before the big deal." Byrty gave Hyryl's thick muscular shoulder a shake. "Wake up! It's time to go to bed." She let loose a sharp stab of a laugh. "Wake up and go to bed. Ha!"

The battered ex-boxer grumbled some unintelligible words before pulling his hulking frame upright. He shook his head and blinked several times. Byrty tugged on his hand.

"Come on. Let's go grab a couple hours of sleep, then go see the parade."

"Parade? What parade? What are you talking about?"

"Ryk says there's a parade at nine before they take off. Come on. I'm tired." Byrty unsteadily rose up to a standing position. Her eyes briefly rolled back into her head. Ryk jumped up and caught her before she toppled over.

"Whoa! I shouldn't have gotten up so fast."

Hyryl tucked his arm behind her and began moving toward the door. "See you in a couple hours," he called out over his shoulder. As the couple made their precarious way out the door, Byrty sang another of her bawdy camp songs.

A fleeting smile fought its way onto Ryk's stoic face. He took one last glance around at the dingy, physt-soaked room. In several of the booths, revelers were slumped over the tables, or laid out with their feet hanging off the end of the cushions. Ryk tipped his hat and walked out into the hazy sunrise.

Mihyn was the first one up at her house. Just before daylight, she hopped out of bed, stepped over some sleeping relatives on the living room floor, and made her way into the kitchen. She looked around at the remnants of sandwiches and fruit trays spread across the counters.

"Normally I'd be anxious about cleaning this up, but not today. I don't really give a blyrt what kind of shape the house is in." A small measure of satisfaction entered Mihyn's groggy mind.

The sound of soft, measured footsteps echoed from the hall. Glyndy yawned and walked into the kitchen rubbing her long, slender arms. "Good morning. I thought you would probably be up early." She walked over and kissed her friend on the cheek.

Mihyn slid her arm across Glyndy's shoulder. "Good morning to you. It's so nice having you're here. I should probably get nymry going."

"No way. Last night, your mother said she was going to do that."

"She's not awake yet."

Across town in his second floor hotel room, Lymdyr's eyes shot open. The faint light of morning was just bright enough for him to see his fancy silver pocket watch on the nightstand. He reached over, popped it open, and let go a sigh of relief. "Thank goodness I didn't oversleep." He returned the watch to its place, rolled over, and looked at the brown hills south of town which were now just a dark smear behind the gauzy curtains.

"Sure wish I had made it out to Phyt Hill. Well, Gwydol, hope you are okay. Dyth! Lymdyr, you haven't done a very good job of tying up the loose ends." He stroked the still tender lesions on his throat. "Tying knots, loose ends."

The dark irony of the words brought a smile to his face. With one quick move, he kicked the covers off and jumped to his feet.

In the modest apartment just west of the Academy, Grylt rolled up out of bed, and glanced down at his sleeping roommate. Kybark's big woolly head was the only part of his anatomy visible. As soon as the professor's feet hit the floor, the animals in his private menagerie began calling for food.

"Alright! Alright!" I'm coming!"

He pulled on his beaten up robe and wandered into the back room. The feathered lykrs hopped up and down in their cages. The small furry byngyrs hugged each other and chirped happily. Grylt grabbed a bag of seeds off the table in the corner. He scooped a handful out, undid the cage door, and dropped it into the food tray.

"Later today, some nice people are coming over, and you are all going to have new homes. I want you to behave yourselves, and remember……"

Grylt choked up. Tears flooded his eyes. His compact frame shook with sobs.

"Oh for Zym's sake!" Kybark's gruff voice called out from the behind. Grylt spun around, and stared at the poet's sleep roughened, doughy face.

"Here, I got you a going away present." Kybark held out a thick, tissue paper wrapped rectangular object.

The professor wiped the moisture off his face and walked over toward his roommate. Without saying a word, he took the present, tore off the wrapping, and began flipping through the book. "Why these are magnificent! Whoever did you get to do these?"

"A painter friend of mine. I used the money I got from the last poems I sold."

Grylt nodded. He paused to examine the fine ink and watercolor painting of his favorite lykr. "Thank you so much." The professor closed the book, walked over, and kissed his roommate. "This is the perfect thing to take with me. Oh Zym! What time is it?"

"Seven thirty."

"Whew, I was afraid time had gotten away from me. I was thinking, should we go down and have nymyr at the Pylnor?"

"Excellent idea. I didn't feel like cooking anyway."

"You never do. Let me get my bag packed, and we'll head down."

Several blocks away, Krynut had just finished placing the last of his things into a leather satchel. His brother and mother stood in the doorway to the kitchen watching him whirl around the room. He stopped for a minute, stroked his pointy goatee, then continued fastening the snaps.

"Got everything?" his brother asked.

The crew chief slung both pieces of luggage over his shoulders, then took a last look around. Krynut's gaze swept over the bookcase, curio cabinet, and finally to his waiting family members. "I believe so. Don't forget, take whatever you want before you leave. The rest goes up for sale."

"I don't need anything," his mother replied.

"So, when you get to the launch site, make sure to go up to the steps beside the platform. I should be up there already, but

I want to make sure you are right up front. Okay, I'll see you later."

Krynut gave a quick wave, then ducked out the door. He ran down the steps and out onto the sidewalk. "The Academy please," he called up to the driver of the nearest buggy. After tossing his satchels into the cab, Krynut pulled himself up, and eased the door shut. He calmly gazed out the window while the familiar stores and business rolled by.

When they arrived at the Academy, Krynut stuck his head out the window. "Pull up next to that wagon."

As planned, a wagon with two buff colored styrns was waiting in front of the big marble steps. When the buggy rolled to a stop, the man sitting on the driver's seat of the wagon looked over and smiled.

"Good morning. I was wondering when you'd get here."

"Good morning. Just follow us. We're going to pick up the rest of the crew." Krynut gave the side of the cab a little bang with his open hand. "Next stop is the corner of Syms and Hyrkvyn."

Grylt and Kybark were still seated at their place by the window of the restaurant when the nondescript buggy followed by the wagon rolled by.

"Oh! I bet that's Regent Krynut!" The professor jumped up from the table, grabbed his suitcase, and ran out the front door. The two vehicles had stopped in the middle of the block. Grylt waved his arm as he ran. "Regent! Regent! I'm coming!"

Krynut jumped down to the curb and walked back to the wagon. The professor came running up, slightly out of breath.

"Kybark and I were just having nymyr. Am I the first one you're picking up?"

"You are the first."

Grylt heaved his big brown leather suitcase up on the edge of the wagon rail. "Can you help me drop it down? There are some delicate items in there."

Once the suitcase was loaded, the two men climbed into the buggy. As it started to roll forward, Grylt stuck his head out the window, and brought a hand up to his mouth.

"Did you forget something?" Krynut asked.

The professor scanned the busy sidewalk scene as it slowly diminished from view. He pulled his head back into the cab.

"I was in such a hurry to catch you that I forgot to remind Kybark to get to the launch site early. Oh well, he can take care of himself."

Their next stop was Mihyn's small bungalow. Children were running back and forth on the front lawn when the buggy and wagon pulled up. Krynut opened the door and stepped down onto the stubbly grass. Two of the children came running up and stood staring at him.

"Are you going to blast into space with Aunty Mihyn today?" an adorable little girl with blond hoop braids asked.

Krynut looked down at her small, expectant face. "Yes, I'm the crew chief."

"Wow!" was all the boy standing next to his sister could say.

An older woman opened the front door, squinted out at the waiting vehicles, then yelled over her shoulder. "Mihyn! They're here!"

The front door burst open. Mihyn was just pulling on her gorgeous sky blue and black robe. Half a piece of bread was jammed into her mouth. She succeeded in shoving her arms through the sleeves, and removed the bread so she could speak. "Sorry, I'm running just a tad late."

"That's okay. We're doing fine time wise," Krynut replied in a calm voice.

"Okay, come on in." Mihyn took a quick bite of the bread and opened the door for him. The interior of the small house was alive with activity. It seemed every room was humming with excited conversation. Mihyn walked up to the older woman standing just inside the doorway.

"Regent, this is my mother, Shyrl. Mother, this is Regent Krynut. He's the crew chief."

"I'm very pleased to meet you. What a brave group you are. We're so proud of Mihyn." The older woman held out her hand.

Krynut gave it a quick shake. "Certainly easy to see where Regent Mihyn gets her beauty."

The worry lines on the older woman's face vanished. "Why, thank you."

From inside the house, the sound of hurried goodbyes, laughter, and occasional crying echoed out onto the lawn. Mihyn walked out through the front door carrying a large leather satchel. A contingent of relatives followed close behind. She gave her father, mother, and friend Glyndy a quick hug, then followed Krynut down the sidewalk.

With a groan, Mihyn swung the satchel up into the bed of the wagon. After waving to the crowd lined up in front of the house, she climbed up into the buggy cab.

"Goodbye! See you in a little while!" Her family called out as the vehicles rolled away.

Mihyn plunked down in the seat, and let out a great, long sigh. Grylt sat watching her. An impish smile broke across his face. "Good morning, Regent. My, what a gang of family you have!"

"Yes, I do." Mihyn remained sprawled across the seat while the buggy jostled along.

Over on the sidewalk in the Jybyr neighborhood, Ryk stood smoking a gynt cigarette, his third of the morning. A battered canvas grip bag sat at his feet. The effects of last night's party were beginning to take their toll. His stomach was starting to fill with churning acid. His mouth had suddenly lost all traces of moisture.

"Really should be going to sleep. Oh well, time to mag driver up."

"Ryk! Ryk! Why didn't you wake me up!" Lylyn's shrill voice cut through the still morning air. She speed-waddled down the rickety outside stairway. Her huge belly bobbed up and down. Twice it threatened to throw her off balance. Ryk used up some of his waning energy to turn and watch.

"Slow down! I ain't going nowhere yet! If you fall, it'll bung everything up."

"How could you! Did you plan on just heading down there and not waking me up?"

"Doll, I thought I'd be a nice guy and let you sleep."

Once she made it to the ground, Lylyn braced her sagging belly with both hands and hustled over to where he was standing. The oversized linen shirt she was wearing hung off her mid-section like a curtain. Her wavy, dark hair was nothing more than a tangled mess.

"Ryk, I swear, sometimes, you just don't use that head of yours. Look at me! I'm a Zym awful mess! You should'a waked me up so I can git ready."

He took a quick look at her disheveled self and dropped the butt of the gynt onto the broken sidewalk. "Yep, you are a mess."

Lylyn made a fist and smacked him hard on the shoulder. At that moment, the crew buggy and gear wagon came wheeling around the corner.

"Here's my ride." Ryk leaned over and kissed her cheek.

"What?"

He pointed to the approaching vehicles. "There's my ride. See you at the launch."

Lylyn looked down the street and blinked several times in the dull yellow morning light. The buggy pulled up just past where they were standing. Ryk hefted his beaten up grip bag and dropped it into the back of the wagon. Krynut leaned out of the open buggy doorway.

"Oh, good morning." He took a minute to assess Lylyn's ragged condition, then directed his attention toward Ryk. "Ready to go?"

"Yep." He wrapped his arm around Lylyn, gave her a squeeze and another kiss.

"I can't believe you let them see me like this. By the way, you smell like a physt brewery," she whispered.

"No time to clean up. Gotta go."

Ryk sauntered over and two-hopped up onto the steps of the buggy. The cab rocked to the side as he climbed in.

"Morning everybody." He pulled his big brown, red, and black robe off his shoulder, sat down next to Professor Grylt, and laid the finely crafted garment across his lap.

Mihyn stuck her head out the window once they began moving. "Isn't your girlfriend going to the parade?"

Ryk looked over at her and offered a slightly embarrassed smile. "Well, she's not going lookin' like that."

"You might want to put the robe on. The reporters are going to be waiting for us at the Academy," Krynut added.

"Do I hafta?"

"Yes."

"Excuse me professor," Ryk muttered. He stripped off his tattered canvas jacket, tucked it beside the cab wall, and unfurled the massive, thick robe. He had to stand in the moving buggy to get his arm into the stiff fabric. Ryk braced himself against the wall of the cab as the buggy lurched around a corner.

"Ryk, you look positively regal in that robe." Grylt commented after ducking under the mag driver's outstretched arm.

"Thanks professor. I feel stupid wearing it." Ryk finished pulling on the ornate robe, then sat down with a thud. The brim of his wide, dusty brown hat folded against the buggy wall. "Looks like Lymdyr is the last one to be picked up."

Krynut had just finished yelling an address up to the buggy driver. He eased back down from the open window and gave Ryk a quick scan from head to foot.

"Yes. Did you have a good going away party?"

Ryk's shiny, unshaven face broke into a smile. "It was swell. Lymdyr made it most of the night. Hope he's feeling better than I do."

Out in front of the hotel, the railroad man nervously tapped his shoe on the sidewalk. A loud, sulfurous burp exited his mouth. Try as he might, Lymdyr was unable to force his impulsive, alert mind to focus.

"Do I have everything? Did I sign all the samsyrs? Is there anything I forgot? Zym's beard! Shut up, will you?"

He tried to shake the annoying voice out of his head, but all that served to do was send him into a thankfully short bout of dizziness.

"Okay, let's not do that again. Where the Myrnvar are they? Did they forget me?" As a distraction, he gazed over at a pair of garbage collectors dumping the metal cans into the back of their wagon.

"I wonder if those guys have any idea what is going to happen today. When they go home to their families in their little blyrt hole houses, we're going to be climbing into that craft and blasting off."

While Lymdyr was watching the two men work, one of them dusted off his hands and happened to look across the street. The garbage collector muttered something to his coworker, who also shifted his attention over to Lymdyr. The slightly shorter garbage collector gave a nod of his head and took off at a run. For just a brief moment, the remaining worker made eye contact with the railroad man, flashed a quick, sinister smile, then climbed up onto the wagon.

"Hmmm, wonder what that was all about?"

The snort of the styrns approaching drew Lymdyr's attention away from the situation. A huge wave of pride washed over him when he saw the elegantly robed crew chief jump down to the curb.

"Regent, sorry. I forgot about the robe!" Lymdyr quickly opened his big travel bag, pulled the red and black checked robe out, and stuffed his leather duster inside. He swung the strap of the travel bag over his shoulder and hurried down the sidewalk.

"Here, let me help you. You can put the robe on once we get rolling." Krynut tossed the bag into the back of the wagon and followed his crew member over to the buggy.

Lymdyr bounded up into the cab and plunked down next to Ryk. The two men shook hands. Both of their faces beamed with happiness. Ryk released his grip and poked the brim of his hat back up.

"You doin' alright this morning?"

"Moderately alright. Glad I went home when I did. Did you get any sleep?"

Ryk gave a proud shake of his head before answering. "Nope. My last night on Ulutrita, not a chance."

The door to the buggy slammed shut, and Krynut slid onto the seat. "Let's put your robe on."

While they rolled along, Lymdyr shifted around to extend his arms while Mihyn and the crew chief helped him pull the red and black checked garment on.

"I assume they had to make some alterations." Grylt reached over to smooth out some wrinkles.

Lymdyr pulled the lapels together and held his arms up high. "How do I look?"

"All in all, you look marvelous," the professor replied.

Chapter 58.

Several minutes later, the crew pulled up in front of the Academy. A huge crowd had gathered at the foot of the blazing white steps. Out in the street, a line of buggies and carriages all decorated with flowers and colored streamers stretched for blocks. Krynut opened the buggy door, then turned back to the group.

"Wait here, I going to go out and find Bokyl. He's the grandmaster I believe." After threading his way through the noisy crowd, the crew chief located Professor Ymyl standing with a group of academics. The professor flashed a huge grin as Krynut approached.

"Good morning Regent! Ready for your big day?"

Krynut reached out and shook his offered hand. "I suppose so. Have you seen Bokyl?"

"Oh yes, he's already waiting way up there at zee head of the line. I think you and zee crew vere supposed to have been here a half hour ago. Just a warning, he ees in a state this morning."

"Thanks." Krynut fought his way back to the buggy, pulled himself up onto the step, and stuck his head into the open cab. "I guess we need to walk up to the head of the line."

While the crew made their way along the sidewalk, a round of applause rippled through the crowd. Shouts of congratulations and a few playful slaps to the back greeted them as they moved forward.

"I had no idea it was going to be this big of a parade," Mihyn commented. She attempted to walk next to Grylt, but the crush of spectators and participants preparing to line up forced them to walk single file.

Halfway up to the front of the line, the crew passed a group of women dressed in sparkling outfits that were designed to look like the colors of the Tyrl flag. They were all seated on styrns that also were decorated in orange, green, and black.

"Hey! It's the Nytyn Riders!" Ryk stood on his tiptoes and pointed. He reached over and punched Grylt lightly on the arm. The professor swung his head around to see what Ryk was pointing at.

"What?"

"The Nyntyn Riders. They open up the Phynk Roundup each year. I know all them girls." Ryk cupped his hands around his mouth and shouted above the din of the crowd. "Hey! Lyr! Shynty!"

One of the riders near the perimeter of the group heard her name and began searching through the sea of heads. She scanned left, then right.

"Shynty! Over here!" Ryk lifted his arm and gave a sweeping wave.

When she finally located him, Shynty's mouth dropped open. Her bright red lips formed a perfect circle of surprise. "Ryk! Oh my Zym!" Her sparkling orange, green, and black mag driver's hat glinted in the sunlight as she turned toward the rider next to her. "Wynt! Here, take these. I gotta go say hi to Ryk!"

The rider next to her grabbed the leather reins while Shynty hopped down onto the street. In a whirl of sparkling color, she plunged into the crowd, and with some force, pushed and dodged her way over to Ryk. He opened his arms and administered a crushing hug. They separated, allowing her to get a good look at his robe.

"My oh my, don't you look fancy! Ryk! I'm so glad I had a chance to say goodbye." She rose up on the toes of her boots and planted a warm, sloppy kiss onto his lips.

"Ah, Shynty doll, I'm sure gonna miss you."

"Me too, Ryk. Well, gotta go. Good luck!" After giving him another peck of a kiss, she turned and dove back into the crowd.

Ryk took just a moment to watch her lovely figure disappear into the mass of bodies lining the street. He let go a long, satisfied sigh and continued along the packed sidewalk.

Krynut was making his way over to the huge open carriage at the head of the line when Bokyl caught sight of him. The head regent thumped the upholstered leather seat next to him with force. "There they are! For Zym's sake, I thought we were going to have to start without them!"

His wife reached over and patted the sleeve of his fine, gold thread enhanced robe. "See, I told you they'd be here. Now maybe you can stop worrying!"

Krynut arrived at the waiting carriage and pulled himself up onto the step. "Sorry Head Regent, it took us longer to get here than I expected. The others...."

"You're dyth right it did! The parade was supposed to start five minutes ago. Get in here and sit down! Where are the others?"

The crew chief slipped around in back of Bokyl and his wife. "Good morning Gyrty."

"Good morning, Regent. Don't listen to him! These things always start late."

Mihyn, Lymdyr, and Professor Grylt worked their way out of the crowd and approached the carriage. One by one, they climbed up and filled in the seats behind Bokyl. Krynut looked back over his shoulder once the last of them had taken a seat.

"Where's Ryk?"

"He stopped to say goodbye to one of the fancy dressed riders. That's the last time I saw him," Grylt replied.

Krynut rose up out of the seat and scanned the enormous crowd. "He should be easy to spot with that wide hat. Hmm, I don't see him."

"Well, if he doesn't show up soon, we'll have to start without him!" Bokyl snorted.

"Oh, will you stop! We can't start without him," his wife countered.

"Ah. There he is!" Krynut pointed to the unmistakable dusty brown hat bobbing their way. A minute later, Ryk bounded up into the carriage.

"Looks like I'm the last one!"

Bokyl reached forward and tapped the carriage driver on the shoulder. "You may proceed."

The driver nodded his tri-cornered hat, and gave the reins a slap, as did his companion on the seat next to him. The eight styrns harnessed in front of them shook their gear once, then began moving forward. Their long, knobby legs lifted and dropped in precise rhythm.

Mihyn gripped the side of the carriage and scanned the vast sea of color and faces. "Oh! Isn't this great? I haven't been in a parade since I was a little girl."

The crowd lining the street roared their approval as the fancy gilt carriage rolled by. Each member of the crew waved at the passersby. A third of the way behind them, the intermediate level school band thumped on drums, and blasted out a tune on their long, spiraling horns. When the parade reached the intersection of the main boulevard, the drivers of the carriage both pulled back on the reins.

"Why are they stopping?" Mihyn asked to no one in particular.

"Just wait, you'll see." Bokyl answered over his shoulder.

Above the murmur of happy voices from the parade participants behind them, the sound of boots stomping, and voices chanting in rhythm gradually rose from barely audible to definitive. From one of the side streets, the glint of polished silver helmets flashed.

"Oh look! It's the Land Force's Color Guard," Mihyn shouted.

"What a sight!" Grylt sat transfixed. He scooted around in his seat to address Krynut. "Regent, you were in the Land Forces, weren't you?"

"Yes, I made it all the way to Mid-commander Fran rank."

In perfect step, two columns of soldiers in uniform entered the main boulevard. They all shouldered either long metal pikes or the primitive concussion rifles. Their short brown capes flapped with each step. Brown shorts with tan leggings comprised the remainder of the uniform.

"Here come the sylb stickers!" Ryk yelled.

Grylt turned and glanced over at him with a questioning expression. "Sylb stickers?"

"Yeah. See the long pointy spikes sticking up from their helmets? Out in the field, they use them to roast sylbs on."

"Oh, come on. That can't be true," Lymdyr commented.

"No, it really is! When we get close, look at some of the spikes. The ones that have that bluish black tarnish have actually been heated. I really think they should do away with those old fashioned uniforms. I think they look kinda silly."

"I think they look very elegant," Mihyn replied in a voice of mock disdain.

"So do I dear," Gyrty added. She turned around and sent a big approving smile in Mihyn's direction.

The soldiers fell in ahead of the carriage and spread out in formation. Once they were in position, the drivers gave the reins a slap, and the parade moved on.

"Where exactly is the launch site?" Ryk asked.

"The roundup grounds. We figured if anything happened, it would probably be the safest location," Krynut answered.

Ryk sat back down against the burgundy leather seat and nodded in recognition. "What could happen?"

"Well, with one hundred sixty pounds of packed kykpowder loaded, a lot could happen."

The parade wound down the boulevard, out toward the western edge of town, past the empty stockyards, and into the roundup grounds. A large stage had been erected in the field just behind the arena.

On a wide platform behind the stage, the craft sat. The dull grey metal glowed in the bright sunlight. Steam engines huffed and puffed in preparation for the filling of the ascent balloons. In the bleachers set up at the back of the stage, the friends, relatives, and colleagues of the crew were already taking their seats.

Upon entering the actual roundup grounds, the parade dispersed. The carriage rolled up next to the stage. All the occupants got to their feet once it stopped.

Mihyn and Grylt stood next to each other, waiting to disembark. Both of them stared in the direction of the stage. The professor's gaze settled on the long, cylindrical craft.

"There she is," he said in a wistful, low voice.

"Yes, and there's Mother." Mihyn raised her hand and waved at the row of her family seated in the bleachers. "Oooh, I'm getting goosebumps!"

"Me, too. My hands are starting to sweat." Grylt rubbed his palms together.

Krynut just stood upright and took in the spectacle. His stoic expression effectively hid the enormous sense of pride rushing through him. Lymdyr reached over and gave Ryk a playful punch on the shoulder.

"What a crowd, eh old boy?"

"Yeah, quite the show."

The mag driver jumped to the ground and walked over to the steps leading up to the stage. The two uniformed guards standing side by side bowed, then parted to let the group ascend. Mihyn hiked up the hem of her blue and black robe, lowered her head, and carefully made her way up. She gave a slight gasp upon reaching the top.

The air around the open stage was charged with excitement. Everywhere she looked there was nothing but smiling, jubilant faces. Grylt arrived at the stage and gently grasped her arm.

"A little overwhelming, isn't it?"

"You can say that again."

When Lymdyr was far enough up the stairs to see the full bleachers, he scanned the crowd for the familiar faces of his family. A feeling of desperate sentimentality that grew greater by the second threatened to engulf him. On the third pass, he caught sight of his wife and daughters near the top of the bleachers. He let go the breath he'd been holding and continued up the stairs.

Once they were all up on the stage, the crew walked together over to the empty chairs beside the podium. Mihyn had to force herself to breathe normally. She took a seat next to Grylt and gazed out at the massive crowd assembled in the dirt field. The sea of heads seemed to extend as far as the eye could see.

From his position at the raised podium in the center of the stage, the mayor of Tyrl tapped the big, egg-shaped microphone. The dull thud, thud of his action reverberated out across the roundup grounds.

"Can you hear me?" The crowd roared out in affirmation. "Good. People of Tyrl, visiting dignitaries, friends and relatives of the crew, welcome!"

The thunder of applause and cheers swelled like an earthquake. After it died down, a smile broke across his ruddy, jowled face. "We are gathered here to witness one of the greatest achievements in Ulutitran history." Another titanic roar rose up from the crowd.

"In a few short minutes, these brave voyagers will climb into their kyrft, and sweep up toward Myrnvar to explore a place that few of us have even dreamed about. At this time, I would like to recognize a few individuals that made this whole adventure possible." The mayor lifted up a sheet of paper and adjusted his glasses.

"First of all, Head Regent Bokyl." A travelling wave of applause swept through the warm morning air. "Without the head regent's unflagging determination to see this project to completion, it may very well have died along the way. Next is Professor Rymnyr." Another blast of clapping hands resounded off the wooden stage. "Her vision and faith in this project also were instrumental in making it happen."

While the mayor droned on, a messenger on a red and white spotted styrn came charging in from the main road. The people on the southern end of the crowd parted to let her through. Blond pigtails flying, and face powdered with dust, the messenger pulled up beside the stage. She jumped down out of the saddle, tied the styrn to a post, and ran up to the uniformed guards standing at the foot of the stairs. A heated discussion ensued. Their exchange was so loud and emotion filled that the mayor broke off his speech.

"Excuse me," he said to the audience, then walked over to the edge of the stage. After a few moments of discussion, the messenger was allowed to ascend the stairs. She held up a yellow telemessage sheet and watched as the mayor read it.

His face became still and solemn. After thanking her, he slowly walked back to the podium. His balding head was lowered, lips tucked in. He appeared to be deep in thought.

"Fellow citizens of Tyrl, and honored guests. I have just received some rather serious news." The crowd reacted to this ominous opening statement with gasps, and low mutterings. "I have just been informed that the great city of Pyra, one of my favorites, has just experienced a direct hit by an asteroid of what this sender of this message describes as significant size. Fires have broken out all over the city, the pluge system has been destroyed, and loss of life seems great. The sender ends with a request to send Zym's prayers their way."

Emotion surged through the crowd. Some wept, others looked over at their neighbors in shock.

"I feel that this latest tragic event is even more reason for us to celebrate this great, courageous adventure that we are about to witness. Ulutrita has experienced many, many, of these cataclysmic asteroid strikes, three that I can think of in my lifetime. Perhaps with the advent of his new wave of exploration, we can better understand the forces that generate them, and one day, send some of our people out to colonize other worlds."

A subdued round of applause greeted the mayor's comments. He folded the yellow sheet up and tucked it in his jacket pocket. "A terrible tragedy," he mused out loud. The mayor drew in a deep breath, stared down at the podium, then lifted his face back up to the crowd.

"At this time, I would like to introduce to you all the brave crew that will be taking off here shortly." One by one, he acknowledged the members of the group. The crowd clapped and hooted enthusiastically after each introduction. When the mayor finally made it to Ryk, the crowd response was especially loud. Lymdyr leaned over and poked the mag driver on the shoulder.

"Wow, didn't know you had so many friends out there, did you?"

"Nope. Guess all of them are here." Ryk commented in a somewhat shaky voice. His head had begun to pound. The roaring, clapping crowd noise just made it worse.

Once the jubilant response had died down, the mayor stepped to the side and motioned back toward the bleachers. "Thank you all for your support. Now I'd like to invite the crew to spend the next thirty minutes saying their goodbyes to their friends and families while the technicians prepare the kyrft for launch. If the crowd could all move to the fence along the road, and assemble behind it, that would be appreciated."

With a great murmuring of voices and thudding of feet on the dusty ground, the crowd complied with the mayor's request. The crew dispersed from their line and moved up into the stands.

Chapter 59.

Lymdyr flew past his fellow crew members. On his way up the bleachers, several local officials called out to him. He replied with an out of breath, "Thanks" and sped by.

When Lymdyr reached the row where his wife was sitting, he offered a quick hello, then sidestepped over toward the twins. The expectant, heart breaking expression on Pryn's face tore at every fiber of his being. A sudden tug on his robe stopped him. He craned his neck around and looked down into Bynhyld's flaming, dark eyes. On the row above, a tall, official looking gentleman stood up.

"Say your peace to the girls, then you, Hymr, and I need to talk." Bynhlyd let go of his robe and eased back on the bench, lips pouted out in triumph. She crossed her gorgeous, black shear stockinged legs once he had slipped past.

Lymdyr yanked his robe closed and dove into Pryn's embrace. She hugged him for several moments before giving any indication that she was going to let go. With the side of his face smashed against her solid shoulder, he at least could smile and offer a few words to Dyny.

The bleary appearance of her smoky, dark eyes left little doubt that she had been crying. With some effort, he freed his left arm and grasped her folded hands. She responded by scooting over next to him. The daughters and their father remained locked together in one great heap.

"I'll never forgive you for this, but I love you. You know that," Dyny whispered into his ear.

Lymdyr nodded and squeezed her hand extra tight. After several more seconds, Pryn eased off her grip. She wiped the tears away and drew in a shuddering breath. "We both love you and will miss you. Do you think there's any chance you'll come back?"

The childlike aspect of her question wrung an extra couple drops of sorrow from him. "Honey, I don't think so. Listen, I want you both to carry on with your lives, do good things, get married, have lots of beautiful children, and try to remember me in kind ways."

After getting one last massive double hug, Lymdyr stood back up and sidestepped away from the twins. The tall, official looking gentleman on the row above was waiting for him.

Below the front of the stage, Kybark and a thin, bespectacled man were attempting to ascend the stairs. The poet was engaged in a heated discussion with one of the guards. "I'll tell you one more time. I'm Professor Grylt's lover. I would like to say goodbye to him."

The guard made a most unpleasant face, looked the shabbily dressed poet up and down, then crossed his arms. "You gotta do better than that to convince me."

"Come on Kybark, it's obvious that this person is not going to honor your request," the poet's companion commented. He turned to go.

"No, wait. I'm not giving up that easily." Kybark reached around and grabbed him by the arm. The poet then turned his head of shaggy, unkept black hair back toward the guard. "Now see here. Grylt and I have been together for almost two years."

"Look bud, I don't you who you are, but I'm not buying your story." The guard let his arms drop and tucked his hands into his pants pockets.

"Alright, you leave me no choice." Kybark walked around to the area just below the center of the stage and unfolded a sheath of papers. He cleared his throat, then began speaking in as loud a voice as his barrel chest could produce.

"On this day marked with surprise, so the styrk will also rise. Upon these voyagers, tall and straight, oh that their courage and dedication be great. For as the styrk will set for sure, so is the pain they must surely endure. Who knows what horrible death they may see. Sailing through the blackness of eternity!"

The guard frowned and took a step toward the poet. "You see here! Who the klynk do you think you are blabbering this gibberish about pain and death when these people are going to risk everything?"

Kybark looked over at the guard and broke into a maniacal smile. He again began reading in a loud, projected voice. "Will the styrks that burn out beyond our reach, bleach their bones as on a desert beach, or will they be crushed into one small ball, when onto the rocky surface of an alien world they fall?"

"Gimme that!" The guard reached out and snatched the papers from Kybark's grubby fingers.

"You styrn's ass!" Kybark leaped forward, crashing his huge, bulbous stomach into the guard. Both of them went tumbling into the dust. Kybark's companion let out a gasp, and stood with his long, slender fingers covering his face.

The guards from the other side of the stage heard the commotion and came running. Up onstage, several people heard the shouts and grunts of the combatants and stepped over to the edge.

"What's going on down there?" the mayor yelled.

After the two guards from the opposite side pulled Kybark and their comrade away from each other, the combatants stood breathing hard. Showers of fine tan dust drifted off each of them. Kybark raised his dirt covered head.

"Get Grylt!"

The mayor scowled at the pitiful sight below him, then turned and walked off toward the stands. He passed by Mihyn's group of relatives on his way up the bleachers.

Grylt and his influential friends were still hugging each other and saying their goodbyes. The mayor waited till the professor let go of his banker friend, then reached up and tapped him on the shoulder.

"Sorry to interrupt, but there's a dumpy looking, shaggy haired man below the stage asking about you."

Grylt's jubilant expression suddenly darkened. "Oh my, that sounds like Kybark."

"Leave him. He's not worth worrying about," the banker commented.

Grylt lifted the hem of his magnificent green floral themed robe, whisked down the stairs and over to the edge of the stage. He took a moment to scrutinize the five silent and uncomfortably tense figures standing in the dust.

"Kybark! What is going on?"

"Ah, there you are! Well, I want to introduce you to my new lover." Kybark turned back toward the thin, slightly effeminate man standing behind him. "Pylgyst, this is the esteemed Professor Grylt. The drawings you did were of the stinking, defecating, noisy animals he had imprisoned in the apartment."

"You're a sick, unhealthy, tortured man. Goodbye." Grylt shifted his attention out to the artist. "I would suggest you get as far away from this monster as you can."

"Well, in a few short minutes, you are certainly going to accomplish that!" Kybark shouted.

Grylt shook his head and walked slowly back to the bleachers. Krynut had just bid his family goodbye and was making his way over to the craft. He waited at the bottom of the stairs when he noticed the professor approaching.

"Everything alright?"

Grylt looked up at the crew chief. His greenish-brown eyes were weighted with sadness. He glanced back toward the edge of the stage, shook his head once more, then returned his gaze to Krynut.

"Yes, everything is fine. There are certainly some things I will miss about this place, and some I will not." He forced himself to smile.

"Shall we go?"

"Indeed." Grylt let go a sigh, then walked beside Krynut toward the back of the stage. Professor Myrvst, Sylstyn, and Blrsynt followed them over to the craft.

Up in the bleachers, Mihyn was methodically working her way around to offer final goodbyes to all her family. Two rows above them, Handynr and Kym watched the tearful exchanges.

"I'm so glad I made the decision not to go." He reached over and squeezed Kym's hand. Out of the corner of his eye, Handynr shot a quick glance over at her profile. Kym was staring down at Mihyn. The expression on the secretary's roundish face was veiled and somewhat pensive.

"Are you okay? You have that faraway kind of look."

Kym gave a little sniff and ran a finger along the edge of her eye. "Wow, all of a sudden I feel like I'm responsible for breaking you two up. It makes me want to cry." She hung her head and did just that.

When Mihyn reached the end of the row, she looked at her husband. In response to her fiery gaze, Handynr instinctively slid an arm around the sobbing secretary. Mihyn drew in a deep breath for courage and ascended the last couple steps.

Kym managed to regain some control of herself by the time Mihyn reached their level. She slowly lifted her tear-streaked face. "I feel so terrible! It's all my fault that you two aren't going to spend the rest of your lives together. I wish all of this had never happened." Kym burst out into tears again and covered her face with both hands.

Despite her own grindingly raw emotional state, Mihyn was able to maintain enough composure to speak without breaking down. "Handynr, I wish you the best. Too bad we didn't have a chance to bring some closure to this. I need to get down to the kyrft, goodbye." Her somber, emotionless words hit him like a punch to the face.

"I, I guess I've been avoiding thinking about this moment. Zym Mihyn! I'm sorry. Things just happened too fast!" He rushed past Kym and hugged his wife. After several seconds of being entwined, he whispered in her ear. "It's not easy for me to say goodbye, my darling."

Mihyn pried herself away from his grasp and took a step back. "It's not easy for me either, but goodbye." Without even taking a final look at him, she spun around and hurried down the stairs.

Three sections over, Ryk sat with his arm wrapped around Lylyn. "Well, doll, guess I better stroll on down."

"Ryk, don't go! I need you. What am I gonna do with this baby?" She tightened her grip on him for emphasis.

"Oh come on, hon. We been through this a hundred thousand, zillion times. I left all the dyrn I had in...."

"It ain't the dyrn. How'm I gonna raise a kid all by myself?"

"Look, if things get rough. I gave you the address of the lady that used to live next to us when I was a kid, remember? She's a real sweetheart, and I'm sure she could help. Anyway, I gotta go, they're startin' to load up."

Ryk pulled Lylyn to her feet and bent to down to give her a kiss. In the middle of the smooch, she burst into tears.

"Ryk, don't go! I need you."

Lylyn allowed him to slide from her grip, then sat back down with a thud. All the women nearby had stopped what they were doing to watch the pitiful farewell. Professor Rymnyr and Bokyl's wife Gryty were seated on the row below. Both of them climbed up over the bench and sat next to Ryk's sobbing girlfriend.

From her position over by the craft, Sylstyn watched the mag driver leisurely make his way down the bleachers. She reached over and squeezed Blrsynt's hand. "Don't ever just up and leave me like that, okay?" she whispered.

"Don't worry. I'd never do that."

Ryk dropped off the bleachers and was about to light a gynt cigarette when he caught sight of Sylstyn. He hurried over to her and opened his arms wide. She gave Blrsynt's hand another squeeze, let go, and rushed over to embrace him.

Ryk stroked her long, lustrous dark brown hair, and swayed her back and forth. With the gynt sticking out of his mouth, he spoke softly into Sylstyn's dense mass of hair.

"Boy, Syl baby, you are the one person that I'm glad came here. Honestly, I could give a blyrt about the rest of them."

"Don't say that. Your girlfriend is up there crying her eyes out."

"She'll get over it."

Sylstyn backed away just far enough to look him in the eyes. "Ryk, you can certainly be a heartless son of fyrn. You know that?"

"Yep. Always have been, always will be. Well, see ya Syl baby. Take care. Oh, and thanks for the present."

"You're welcome." She flashed a wicked little smirk, rose up on her tiptoes, and kissed his dust flecked cheek. The two of them walked over to where Blrsynt and Professor Myrvst were standing. The professor held out his hand.

"Well Ryk, good luck, and thanks again for volunteering to be part of this. I still wish that Blyr....." Myrvst caught himself. His wrinkled face broke into a small, embarrassed smile.

"Thanks professor. See ya round." Ryk let go of Myrvst's hand and turned his attention to the young couple. He and Blrsynt exchanged a firm handshake.

"Blrsynt old boy, you take of Sly, deal?"

"Deal."

Ryk nodded to both the young people, tipped his hat, then strode over to the craft. On his way over, he lit the gynt in his mouth. One of the technicians preparing the craft stopped what he was doing and stepped in front of him.

"That probably wouldn't be a good idea. We're going to start loading the cylinders of kykpowder. If you wanna smoke, why don't you walk back over by the bleachers."

Krynut and Professor Grylt were standing beside the open hatch of the craft. The crew chief bent over and peered down the passageway. "Boy, it's even more crowded in there than I had imagined."

Back in the rear compartment, Gyls and two of the technicians were scrambling back and forth making sure all the supplies were secured. "Okay, that box of dried nyrynt looks like it's going to slide out. Come on! We really need to finish. Whoa! Just about banged my head on the rafter again. Zym! I'm sweating up a storm."

The inventor let go a peal of giddy laughter. Professor Grylt eased down next to Krynut. "Gyls certainly seems to be excited."

Krynut didn't answer at first. He continued to observe Gyls' frantic movements for a moment, then stroked his goatee. "Yes, he certainly does."

Gyls passed by the open hatch, humming to himself. Krynut leaned in just a bit farther. "If you don't mind me asking, you seem to be in an exceptionally good mood."

After tucking the clipboard he was holding under his arm, Gyls sat on the edge of the hatch. "Yes! I'm in a great mood. I have a new healer now, and he has prescribed me this amazing new medication." He flashed a wide grin out to the crew members.

"I don't mean to be nosey, but what medication might that be?" Grylt asked timidly.

"Absolutely! It's call Donrax. Well, got a couple more things to do before I turn her over to you." Gyls leapt up and hurried back toward the rear space.

"Hmm. Donrax is relatively new. In moderate doses, it seems to be fairly safe. I believe it does cause insomnia," Grylt commented.

The droning of the steam pumps behind the platform suddenly became louder. The chug, chug, puff rhythm of the pistons increased in frequency.

From her place up in the bleachers, Professor Rymnyr stroked Lylyn's back a final time, then got to her feet. "Sounds like they are going to start filling the balloons."

She and Kryzyck carefully picked their way down to the stage. When they reached the bottom of the stairs, the professor paused. Above the noise of the steam pumps, the sound of voices chanting in the distance drifted her way. "Do you hear that?"

Kryzyck had also stopped. "Hear what? From blasting ore for years, my hearing is pretty well shot."

"I'm going to investigate. I'll meet you back by the craft." Rymnyr hustled over to the podium and stood next to Bokyl.

"Do you hear that noise?"

"You mean the chanting?" the head regent answered while still gazing out over the crowd.

"Uh huh. Seems to be coming from......Over there."

Rymnyr pointed toward the mass of people jammed up against the far stockyard fence. Many of them had turned around and were staring out onto the street. The afternoon breeze suddenly kicked up. Dust swirled off the roundup grounds and peppered those on the stage. "I smell smoke."

"What do you think is going on?" Bokyl shielded his eyes with his hand and squinted out toward the commotion behind the crowd.

"Not sure. There appears to be some kind of group making their way down the street. There! Smell that?"

The head regent lifted his short, straight nose up into the air. He gave several confirmatory sniffs. "Someone out there is burning zygt pitch."

On the back side of the stage, Krynut walked over and stood next to Professor Bynkr. The head of the engineering department was watching the big, off-white rubber balloons being filled.

"Professor, how goes everything?"

"Oh, all things considered, we're right on schedule. This wind that has kicked up is really batting the balloons around. We do have extras if one gets popped, but it would be unfortunate to have to fill another one."

Krynut nodded and shifted his attention to the four-styrn team wagon out in the middle of the field. Behind the two men sitting on the front seat, a sturdy, enclosed wooden structure rose up.

"What's that wagon doing out there?"

"Ah, that's the munitions squad. Commander Hygr is the stern-faced one in uniform."

"I see. I'm going to go talk to Bokyl." Krynut made his way over to where the head regent and Rymnyr were standing. Both of them were watching the activity behind the crowd. "So, what seems to be going on back there?"

Without taking his eyes off the group advancing toward the roundup grounds, Bokyl spoke out of the corner of his mouth. "Still not really sure. All I can see is a bunch of people marching down the street carrying what looks like an assortment of tools, and a few have lit torches. They're just about to come around the end of the fence."

The three academics watched the chanting group pass through the gate leading onto the roundup grounds. At the head of the group, a short, bald figure dressed in a red and gold robe walked along with his arms outstretched.

"Oh dear, oh dear. I had a feeling it was him." Worry lines crisscrossed Bokyl's ruddy face.

"Who?" Rymnyr asked.

"Lycrk. Remember the second time the miner demonstrated his telesound device in the assembly hall? Oh, maybe you weren't there. Lycrk and some of his fanatics were there, and they claimed the voices were those of demons. As I recall, they chased Myrvst and his group out of the building. And then the Collria meeting. Well, it looks like they've shown up today."

A wave of uneasiness swept over Krynut. He took a quick look at the line of marchers now snaking toward the stage, then hurried over to the craft and ducked under the open hatch.

Professor Grylt was standing against the rear wall, listening intently to the inventor. Krynut stopped right next to the ever growing pile of supplies. "Wow, you weren't kidding about needing to pack things in here."

From behind the low wall of boxes laid out in the center of the compartment, Gyls rose up from his squatting position. "Ah, Regent. Good timing. I was just explaining to the professor how the battery powered telesound device works. Listen to the sound clarity we can achieve with the added power."

He gave the volume knob a turn, and a crackling, hissing sound filled the area. Gyls rotated the tuning dial until the hiss was replaced by a distinctly British voice that came rumbling out of the wall mounted horn.

"Very nice," Krynut commented.

The inventor wiped a profuse amount of sweat off his forehead, cranked the volume down, and disconnected the wires from the battery. "I was also explaining to the professor that it's really important that while you are aloft, no sparks or flames of any kind be generated. The tubes of kykpowder that are going to be loaded are really, really, volatile. I even have a special liquid ignitor built for extra safety. Now where did I put it?"

He jumped up from his seat and began scrambling around the crowded interior. Shouts from outside drew the attention of both Krynut and Grylt.

"I wonder what's going on?" the professor asked.

"We better find out."

The two men worked their way down the short corridor and out onto the platform. Krynut headed back over to where Professor Bynkr was standing. Out in the field behind the stage, three men were trying desperately to keep the balloons from bashing into each other.

"How much longer till they're filled?"

The professor chewed on his lip for a moment before answering. "I'm thinking about another ten minutes. Time to load the powder."

Krynut nodded in acknowledgment, then hurried to the front of the stage. By that time, a sizeable crowd of spectators had gathered. He pushed his way right up next to Bokyl.

On the flat, dusty ground below them, a line of people dressed in white flowing robes spread out the entire length of the stage. Smack in the middle of the line, Lycrk, the religious firebrand, stood with his arms crossed.

"No deal! The craft and this launching structure need to be destroyed!"

Krynut's already uneasy stomach jumped. He glanced over at Bokyl. The head regent's bulldog like jaw was set in tension. Snaking purple veins rose up from his temples.

"Lycrk, I appreciate your dedication to the pursuit of Zym life, but really, there is nothing evil about this project," Bokyl's baritone voice was squeezed with exasperation.

The short, bald man standing below him spread his arms wide, and turned first to the right, then to the left. "Do you hear that? Now, they are mocking us!"

Angry shouts rose up all up and down the line. An array of axes, sledgehammers, and burning torches were raised up in the air. Krynut leaned over next to the head regent's overheated face. "This is not looking good. We're about ready to start loading the powder. Those torches have to be put out."

"I know. I don't seem to be getting anywhere with him. The best I can do is stall."

The abrupt cessation of noise from the steam pumps brought a temporary feeling of stillness to the tense atmosphere.

"Do what you can," Krynut whispered. He squeezed Bokyl's thick trunk of an arm, then returned to the craft. The crew was standing outside the hatch. Ryk stood off to the side quietly puffing on his gynt. All eyes were on Krynut as he approached.

Gyls stuck his sweat plastered head out of the open hatch. "I found it! Here's the liquid switch." He held out a small, oblong fabric-covered object. "This is going to be attached to the powder fuse. When you reach thirty thousand feet, crush this glass ampule in here, and toss the fuse out into the air."

"Toss it out into the air? How're we gonna do that?" Ryk asked between puffs.

"It'll be tucked up the inside of the waste pipe. Come in and I'll show you. Hey! Put that gynt out! They're going to start loading the powder."

Ryk took one last huge draw, dropped the burning object to the deck, and ground it out.

Chapter 60.

From the stairs at the back of the stage, the clomping of heavy boots and knock of a wooden cane announced the arrival of the munitions officer. He was of medium build, with a wide forehead and stern, scarred face. A faded Land Forces issue cap sat snuggly over his head. He heaved himself up the final step, then gave the crew a good looking over.

"We ready up here?" he asked in a gruff, weary voice.

"It seems that we are," Krynut responded.

"I smell smoke."

"I just crushed a gynt out. Come on Chief, Gyls wants to show us something," Ryk offered before ducking under the open hatch.

With a stiff, jerky motion, the munitions officer twisted his neck around and yelled down the stairs. "Alright men, start bringing them up!"

He limped his way over to the craft and watched his workers carefully haul the eight-inch thick, five-foot long tubes of powder up the steps, and slide them into the metal brackets screwed into the shell. While his men worked away, he leaned on his heavy black cane.

Angry shouts echoed from the front of the stage. The munitions officer straightened up and turned in the direction of the sound. "What's going on over there?"

"There's a group of individuals that are opposed to the project," Krynut replied.

"I see. By the way, Munitions Field Officer Hygyr at your service." The officer extended a hand toward Krynut.

"Fran Krynut, crew chief." The two men shook hands. Another series of loud shouts echoed from the front of the stage.

"I better go take a look." Hygr clumped his way across the stage and stood next to Bokyl. "So what's all the fuss about?"

"These are Lycrk's followers. They claim that the voices the telesound device picks up are demons, and that by blasting up into the sky, we're going to open up the Door of Zym for them to come and invade Ulutritra."

"You're kidding me!"

"I assure you, these people are dead serious."

Hygr let go a snort and moved a step closer to the edge of the stage. He leaned on his black knobby cane. "You people down there! Put those torches out! We got over a hundred pounds of kykpowder up here. The last thing we need is sparks flying back there."

Angry responses drifted up from below. Lycrk looked up at the munitions officer. "A hundred pounds of kykpowder? That ought to be just enough to blow up that cursed vessel, and this stage. Come believers! This is our chance!" With his red and gold robe trailing off behind him, Lycrk made a run toward the nearest stairway.

Hygr gave a humpf of surprise and looked back at Bokyl. "I didn't think they'd do that."

"Me neither."

Inside the craft, Gyls stood next to the crew cabins, checking items off the list on his clipboard. Krynut and Ryk waited just behind the cockpit.

"Oh! I almost forgot! Quick, follow me."

Gyls opened the door to the double cabin and ducked in. Krynut and Ryk followed him. The inventor climbed up onto the edge of the bed. He reached up and placed his hand on a lever attached to an apparatus screwed into the ceiling. A thick spring was mounted just to the left of the lever. In the center of the apparatus, a fat square of folded fabric was affixed.

"This is your parachute. When you re-enter the atmosphere, wherever you are, someone is going to have to climb up here and unlock this lever. When you do that, this spring will pop the little door open, and out goes the chute. Pretty straightforward."

"Powder canisters are loaded. You are ready to go," one of the munitions technicians called out from under the open hatch. "Oh and by the way, you might want to come out and see what's happening over by the podium."

Krynut spun around, slipped by Ryk, and hopped over the lip of the hatch. He could see Hygr and Bokyl standing at the head of the stairs. The munitions officer was swinging his black cane up in the air.

"Time to load," Krynut announced to the gathered crew.

Professor Rymnyr hugged Mihyn and planted a kiss on her cheek. "Oh my dear, I am so going to miss you." Tears began to stream down the sides of her face.

"I'll miss you too."

Professor Grylt opened his arms wide. Rymnyr took a step forward and the two of them wrapped up in a tight embrace. "Goodbye madame. Wish us luck."

She gave him a kiss on the cheek, then reached over and laid her hand on the Krynut's shoulder. "Regent, good luck."

The crew chief tore his gaze away from the desperate situation unfolding across the stage and looked into her eyes. "What? Oh sorry, I was a little distracted. Yes, thank you."

Up in the bleachers, Lymdyr, his wife, and her lawyer stood in a circle. "Sign it!" Bynhyld shouted. Her dark, smoldering features blazed with anger. She held out a clipboard.

Lymdyr knocked it away from his face and started down the stairs. "Sorry, I'm not giving you guardianship over the girls' portion of my railroad settlement. Now, if you'll excuse me, I have someplace to go!"

Bynhyld shot a desperate glance over at her lawyer, then let out a shriek. "You're just going to let him walk away?"

"Ma'am, we can't make him sign the form."

"Goodbye Daddy! We love you!" Pryn yelled as her father made his way down the bleachers.

"We'll miss you, and will always love you," Dyny chimed in.

Lymdyr stopped to give the twins a final wave goodbye, then resumed his descent. Off to his right, the angry voices of

Lycrk's followers grew louder with each step. He ventured a quick glance over at the white robed mob.

Just behind them, Lymdyr noticed four dark haired men standing in a line. Even from his position up on the bleachers, he was able to make out the bluish snake tattoo on one of their arms.

"Oh, holy klynking Zym! Not them! What are they doing here?"

In his place several rows above Lymdyr, Handynr laid a hand on Kym's arm. She was no longer crying, but just stood with her head hanging down.

"I'll be right back." He slipped by his secretary and started down the steps.

"Where are you going?" she called out with a touch of panic.

"I need to say goodbye to Mihyn!"

Handynr came charging down toward the stage. His narrow shoulder clipped Lymdyr as he swept past. The railroad man cursed under his breath and continued his own rapid descent.

Every couple steps, Lymdyr switched his gaze over to the four men out in the field. When he was halfway down, one of them recognized him, and pointed. Another of the dark haired men lifted the long, canvas covered object he was holding, and patted it with his hand.

That was all the warning Lymdyr needed. He began leaping down the steps two rows at a time. Slightly out of breath, he arrived at the open hatch of the craft to find Handynr kneeling down with his head under the lip.

"Mihyn! I need to see you one last time!"

Lymdyr had pretty much reached the end of his patience at that point. "Do you mind? I suggest you give it up, pal." He grabbed Handynr's shoulder, moved him to the side, and entered the craft.

After waiting for Lymdyr to pass by, Mihyn squatted down under the open hatch. "What do you want? We're going to take off in a few minutes."

Handynr leaned even farther in. "I made a huge mistake! I should be in there with you! Things have just happened too fast." He reached out toward the arm Mihyn was supporting herself with. She jumped back away from him.

"Don't touch me!"

"Regent, please step away. We're getting ready to launch." Professor Bynkr stood behind Handynr. After delivering the warning, he dropped down next to him and stuck most of his torso over the edge of the hatch.

"Krynut, we're just about ready to launch. On my command, the men out in the field will release the balloons, and I'll supervise the paying out of the tether rope, all three miles of it."

The crew chief had been observing the exchange between Mihyn and her husband from down the passageway. After listening to Bynkr's update, he rushed over to shake the professor's outstretched hand.

"Good luck, my friend." Bynkr broke into a gleaming smile.

"Thanks." Krynut let go of the professor, then directed his attention toward Handynr. "You need to back away, now!"

The regent grudgingly withdrew from the opening and took a couple steps back. His narrow face was a picture of loss and defeat.

Once the hatch was clear, Krynut wheeled around and rubbed his hands together. "Alright, let's go. Everybody prepare for launch." He immediately caught sight of Gyls standing in the corridor. The inventor was still ticking items off his list. "Mr. Gyls, I need you to exit. We are just about to launch."

"Oh, alright. I just have a couple more...."

"I don't think you understand. We are going to...."

A great angry roar from the edge of the stage caused Krynut to stop in mid-sentence. He stuck his head under the hatch just in time to see Hygr swinging his cane wildly at a clot of people forcing their way onto the stage.

"Mr. Gyls, now!"

"Yeah, sure." The inventor walked by him, took a last quick look around the interior, and stepped over the lip of the hatch. He knelt outside with his hands resting on the rim. "Well, I guess this is it. Hope she performs exactly like we designed her." Gyls let go a little sigh, then disappeared from view.

"Release the ballons!" Professor Bynkr shouted to the technicians standing out in the field.

Inside the craft, Krynut began cranking down the hatch mechanism. "Everyone hang on. We're heading up."

Ryk tightened his grip on the back of the cockpit seat. "Aw, I thought we could leave 'er open for a little bit. Be a great view as we rise."

Krynut stopped cranking. "Well, I don't see why not." He turned toward the rear of the craft. "We're going to leave the hatch open for a while. Brace yourselves, it might be a little bumpy." Just as the words left his mouth, the craft lurched sideways, slid off the end of the stage and up into the air.

Professor Bynkr let loose a shout of joy and craned his neck back to watch the dull grey object swing toward the sky. "Oh, I better mind that the rope!" A euphoric laugh escaped from his lips while he ran across the stage. After bounding down the back stairs and across the field, the professor stopped next to the enormous pile of reinforced rope paying out behind the craft.

From his place near the top of the front stairway, Lycrk watched the four huge off-white ballons rise up behind the stage. His mouth dropped open. "No! Oh, no! They've taken off!" He let go a frightening roar and charged up the last couple steps.

Hygr stood blocking the stairs. He had turned to watch the launch, but the religious zealot's inhuman roar brought his focus back around. As Lycrk rushed up at him, the officer lifted his cane, and brought it down with terrific force over the crown of the zealot's bald head. Lycrk's arms fell to his side, and he collapsed backward onto the line of his followers.

"You can't do that!" an enraged woman just down the stairway screamed.

"Oh yeah! Well, I just did," Hygr yelled back.

"Get them!" Two of the followers held Lycrk's unconscious body while the rest of them rushed up the steps. The munitions officer was knocked over by the onslaught. Bokyl managed to step out of the way as the angry mob stormed across the stage.

At that same moment, a loud bang reverberated behind the bleachers. The sound caused many of those watching the launch to quickly shift their attention back down to the field.

Up in the craft, the sharp ping of metal against the outer skin rang out. "What the Myrnvar was that?" Ryk shouted. The crew all looked around at each other for answers.

Professor Rymnyr and Kryzyck had been hugging each other and dancing with happiness on the launch platform when the gunshot brought a sudden end to their celebration. Before they could react, the thudding footsteps and agitated voices of Lycrk's stirred up followers approaching made both of them stiffen to attention. Rymnyr let go of the miner's arms and turned to face the white robed mob.

"This doesn't look good." She bent over and picked up the magnum of chinz that was waiting to be opened. Rynmyr gripped the neck of the heavy green bottle as if it were a baseball bat.

In the bleachers beside them, panicked observers were yelling to the massive crowd lined up along the fence and pointing to the group of four Krushians huddled in the middle of the field. Mihyn's father cupped his hands and shouted at the top of his lungs.

"Somebody! Run out there and stop them! They're reloading!"

Like a raging torrent, a stream of individuals took off at a full run toward the assailants. Over at the back of the stage, Kryzyck cast nervous glances around at the growing chaos. He took several steps toward the rear stairway.

"Dear, I think we should probably try and make a quick exit. Things are getting a little touchy."

"No way! I haven't spent the last year pushing and prodding this along to see this bunch of whackos try and ruin it!"

Rymnyr planted her feet firmly onto the decking and prepared for the assault. Kryzyck stood off to the side, plotting possible escape routes.

A massive tree trunk of a man came jogging up toward her. The wooden slats of the platform bowed under his weight. His white robe was barely large enough to cover his ridiculously wide shoulders. The hem ended right at knee level.

"Sorry ma'am, but you're gonna have to let me pass!" His deep voice rumbled like distant thunder.

"What was that? I didn't catch what you just said." Rynmyr turned her head sideways so that her ear was pointed at him. She tightened her grip on the neck of the bottle.

The man leaned forward and repeated his request. Just as he spoke the word "have", Rymnyr spun on the heels of her high, lace-up boots. She let her weight carry the force of the blow. The thick green end of the bottle smacked the man right above the temple with a loud clunk. In a motion similar to a tree being felled, he wavered a bit, then toppled over. Rymnyr lost her balance and spun like a top, eventually sprawling out on the platform.

"Give me a hand please!" she hissed.

Kryzyck snapped out of his state of shock and pulled her to her feet just as the rest of the mob arrived. When they saw their fallen comrade laid out in front of them, the white robed group came to an abrupt stop. Their attention shifted from his motionless form to the defiant woman standing before them. Rymnyr raised the bottle back up, poised for a strike.

"Who's next?"

With Lycrk, and now their muscle man out of commission, the mob began to slink back. In the field behind the bleachers, a brawl between the group of four Krushian gang members and a contingent of spectators raged.

Chapter 61.

Most of the crew were kneeling by the open hatch, enjoying the view as the craft gained altitude. Lymdyr sat wedged in the doorway of the far forward cabin. He knew exactly what had made the pinging noise and was quite concerned about a second shot being fired.

Mihyn and Grylt were squeezed into the space between the hull and the left side cockpit seat. The wind gusting into the craft tossed her light brown hair in several directions.

"What a view! Look, there's a train coming into the station down there."

"I never thought I'd ever get to see Tyrl like this," the professor added.

Ryk held himself along the other side of the hatch. After looking out at the brown landscape for several minutes, he re-directed his attention to the crawl space behind the cockpit.

"Hey Krynut! Think I could smoke a quick gynt before we have to close the …."

"Absolutely not! If you so much as touch that stryker, you'll put us all in great danger." The crew chief cursed to himself and continued watching the altimeter.

"Oh this is just marvelous! We're starting to enter the clouds," Mihyn observed.

A shudder ran through Ryk's big, wide frame. "Notice how it suddenly got cold."

"We just passed three thousand feet," Krynut chimed in.

While the rest of the crew were enjoying the view, Lymdyr stared blankly out the open hatch. Thoughts were ricocheting and colliding inside his head. "So this is it. Goodbye Tyrl. What am I saying? Goodbye Ulutrita. Did I forget anything? Zym, I need a drink!"

A moment later, the craft was completely submerged in a bank of thick, white clouds. The air pouring in became quite cold and damp.

"I think we should close the hatch," Ryk commented after pulling his robe tight.

"Go ahead. We just passed five thousand feet."

Ryk pulled the hatch closed and spun the large sun-motif brass crank till the mechanism locked with a resounding click.

"Now, let me see about opening the vents." Krynut began running his hands over the collection of metal release valves spread out amongst the tubing till he found the correct one. He gave it a turn which sent cold, bracing air whooshing out from the ornate floral design grates positioned along the floorboards.

"Oooh, can you turn it down just a bit?" Mihyn wrapped her arms tight and moved away from the vent at her feet. Krynut backed the valve down a quarter turn.

"How's that?"

"Perfect. One thing I'll say about these robes, they sure are warm."

Now that the hatch was closed, several of the crew members dispersed to various places in the craft. Ryk slipped behind the left side pilot seat and began examining the controls. Mihyn walked over to where Lymdyr was sitting, and gently laid a hand on his shoulder.

"Everything alright? You look a little stressed."

The railroad man forced a smile, then got to his feet. "I guess I'm just a little overwhelmed by all this. I mean, here we are. A month ago, I had no idea I'd be taking Handynr's place." He let go a laugh, the tone of which contained little humor.

Grylt was still seated beside the closed hatch. He slid both arms around his knees and pulled them tight. "I know what you're saying. My life has been so planned out and scheduled. Now, all that has changed."

"Ten thousand feet," Krynut called out.

Lymdyr worked his way around the edge of the crew cabin and stood next to him. "How high before we have to turn the air tank on?"

"If we're lucky, right before we ignite the rockets."

Ryk continued surveying the interior of the cockpit. "They sure did a good job of designing these controls," he commented to no one in particular. "Foot pedals for the rear fins, hand cranks for the front. Oh, and this here little jobber." He reached up and grasped the spar controller set into the ceiling.

"I'd hold off playing with that till we lose the balloons. I'd hate for that to puncture one, or tangle the lines," Krynut warned. "Eighteen thousand feet."

Down on the launch platform, a tense standoff had developed. At the same time some of the crowd had rushed toward the Krushians, another large contingent had poured up onto the stage. They stood in a silent, surly line blocking off the front stairs.

Lycrk's mob was huddled in a group next to the bleachers, murmuring nervously amongst themselves. Many of the family and friends of the crew had dropped down to seal off the rear stairway.

Professor Bynkr remained at his post out in the field, making sure the three-mile long rope didn't snag. Kryzyck, Professor Rymnyr, Myrvst, Blrsynt, and Sylstyn stepped over the fallen muscle man, down the stairs, and out across the dry grass to join him. Sylstyn shot a quick glance over at the angry group surrounding the Krushians on the far side of the bleachers.

"What exactly happened over there?"

Myrvst adjusted his wire frame glasses before answering. "It's obvious that whoever those people are, they wanted to prevent the launch."

When the group reached the spot where Bynkr stood, he momentarily took his eyes off the rapidly paying out tether. "What a crazy day! First Lycrk and his loonies show up, then somebody takes a shot at the craft!"

"Seems like they're gaining altitude just fine," Kryzyck commented. He looked down at the now, small coil of reinforced rope. Several moments later, the lariat end swooped up and away into the high, gauzy clouds.

"Oh! That means they're just about to ignite the rocket!" Rymnyr exclaimed. All heads tilted back and scanned the sky for any sign of the craft. Blrsynt and Sylstyn moved close together and intertwined their arms.

"I sure hope everything goes okay," she whispered.

"Me too."

Up in the craft, Krynut left the crawl space, and stood behind the cockpit seats. "Alright, let's go over what's going to need to happen for the rocket ignition. Everyone has to be strapped into a chair once they go off. Ryk, you and I will be up front. Professor, I want you to be the one to break the ampule."

"Okay, and where exactly is it?"

"Come here. Actually, let's all go back." Krynut made his way down the passageway with the crew following in single file. He stopped next to the vertical toilet and grasped the piece of fuse hanging under the lid. At the end of the thick, powder sprinkled fuse, an oblong, silk covered object was affixed.

"There's a glass ampule in here. At my command, give it a good hard snap with your fingers, open the chute, and let it slide out."

"Sounds pretty easy." Grylt moved over next to the wall to get a better look at the ampule.

"At that point, you have three seconds to get back to your chair before the fuse ignites."

"What happens if it doesn't light?"

"Well, if it doesn't light, we have a problem. Let's just hope it does." Krynut looked around at the faces of his fellow voyagers. "I can see that you all are a bit concerned. I'm very confident we won't have any problems."

"Boy, I'm starting to feel a little lightheaded," Mihyn commented. She reached over and steadied herself on the pile of supplies stacked and secured in the center of the compartment.

"It's probably the altitude. Ryk, let's go back up front. The rest of you get ready." The two of them returned to the cockpit. Krynut slid into the crawl space and brought his narrow pointy features up next to the altimeter. "Twenty-two thousand feet. Not much farther to go."

"Twenty-two thousand feet!" Ryk echoed back down the passageway.

"And at what altitude do we light the fuse?" Lymdyr shouted in response.

Krynut took a couple steps back toward the hatch and leaned out around the edge of the crew cabins. "Thirty thousand."

Just before returning to the crawl space, he sent a quick glance over at Ryk. The mag driver was propped against the back of the cockpit seats, a wide grin spread across his latte colored face.

"You doing alright?"

"Yeah, I think the altitude is starting to get to me. I feel a little giddy. Maybe it's just the excitement of the voyage. How high are we now?"

"Twenty-eight thousand."

"Twenty-eight thousand! Grylt! You ready?" Ryk called out. He rubbed his hands together in anticipation.

"Yes."

"Lymdyr, Regent. You strapped in?"

Both the crew members yelled back a response. Krynut nodded to Ryk and took another look at the altimeter. "Alright, I'm shutting the vents and turning on the air." His thin, smooth fingers were shaking slightly as he pulled the vent lever shut and opened the air valve. "Let's get strapped in."

Krynut eased himself in between the hull and the edge of the right side seat while Ryk spun around and moved in the opposite direction.

"Shall I give him a three count?"

"Be my guest," Krynut replied without looking up. He was busy tightening his security strap.

"Grylt? You ready?" Ryk shouted down the passageway.

"Ready!"

"On the count of three. One, two, three!" Ryk plunked down hard in his seat. Just before securing the safety strap, he stopped and yelled over his shoulder.

"You okay back there?"

"I can't seem to get the glass to break! I don't have very strong fingers."

Ryk whipped his head to the side and met Krynut's slightly panicked gaze. The two men stared at each other for an instant.

"Go!"

Ryk jumped up, stumbled as he ducked around the seat, then ran down the corridor. Grylt stood with the ampule in his fingers, a pitiful expression spread across his features. Ryk the seized white, fabric covered object from him.

"Open the zynk chute!"

The professor yanked on the metal lever. Ryk stooped down, dug his shoulder under the toilet seat, and pushed upwards. A blast of chill, frozen air whooshed up out of the tube. Ryk squeezed the ampule hard. It broke with a loud crack. He held it for just a moment, then tossed into the toilet.

"Yow! That baby is hot!"

A line of white smoke drifted up just before the fuse slid out the waste hole. Grylt let the lever spring back to the closed position. He stood staring at the lid. Ryk reached over and slapped him on the shoulder.

"That's got it. Better strap in! The ride's about to begin!" Ryk ran back up to the cockpit, slid into his seat, and hurriedly cinched the security strap. He ventured a quick look over at Krynut. The crew chief's narrow face was set with tension. His eyes blazed with a mixture of fear and excitement.

"Did you get it lit?"

Ryk nodded. "Relax, chief. You're sweating."

Krynut reached up and swiped his prominent forehead. "So I am." A weak smile worked its way onto his face. He looked up at the chevron shaped window above them.

"I can see the edge of one of the balloons against the blue sky. "Should be any….."

His words were cut short by the loud report of the first rocket. The force of the blast shook the entire craft. Mihyn sent a terrified glance over at Lymdyr.

"Are you nervous?" he yelled above the roar of the rocket.

"Yes, I've been praying for….." The last of the rockets ignited with a deafening boom. Mihyn's scream added to the colossal level of noise. The crew was thrown back hard against their seats. All five lost consciousness.

Back on the ground, a collective ooooh rose up from the spectators when the first bright flash shone high above them. It was followed by a huge echoing boom. Loud whistles and cheers swept over the area as the thin yellow streak tore out of sight. Tears poured out of Rymnyr's heavily painted eyes. She and Kryzyck hugged each other with fury.

"Oh, I do hope they're alright!" she said between sniffs.

"I'm sure they are, Dear."

About the Author

MC Schulman has always had an abundance of creative energy. Finding ways to express this energy gives meaning to his life. In the past, he has directed his energy towards music, wood sculpting, and writing, with writing now being his main focus. MC has always been drawn to epic stories and mythology due to his adventurous spirit. Some of his favorite authors include Hemingway, Joyce, Steinbeck, Bradbury, Le Guin, Vonnegut, Pynchon, Robbins, Atwood, Murakami, Franzen, and DeLillo. His love of music and keen interest in history inspired his work "On the Wings of Music." He used to contribute regularly to the online entertainment blog *Skagit Art Music*. Recently, MC hosted a writer's group in his small town, with regular attendees including a poet, a passionate essayist, an adventure writer who sailed solo around the world, a memoir author, and a screenplay writer. MC grew up in the Midwest but now lives in the Pacific Northwest. In his leisure time, he enjoys supporting live music, exploring the mountains, woods, and coastlines, as well as spending time with his family.

Visit him at mcshulman.com